PENGUIN
ARKANA

THE WESTERN WAY OMNIBUS

Caitlín Matthews is the author of twenty books, including *Sophia, Goddess of Wisdom* and *The Celtic Book of the Dead*. She teaches on many aspects of Celtic traditions, leading experiential courses on shamanism, ritual and spirituality. She has a shamanic counselling practice in Oxford.

John Matthews has written and edited thirty-five books, including *Gawain, Knight of the Goddess* and *Choirs of the God*. He is best known for his authorship and teaching in the field of Arthurian and Grail studies. He lectures worldwide on the Celtic and Arthurian tradition.

The Matthewses have collaborated on many other books, including *The Arthurian Tarot* and *The Faery Tale Reader*. They are past presiders of the Order of Bards, Ovates and Druids, and are active in promoting a wider appreciation of the ancestral wisdom of North West Europe.

D1082391

The Western Way Omnibus

VOLUME 1: THE NATIVE TRADITION

VOLUME 2: THE HERMETIC TRADITION

Caitlín and John Matthews

ARKANA
PENGUIN BOOKS

ARKANA

Published by the Penguin Group
Penguin Books Ltd, 27 Wrights Lane, London W8 5TZ, England
Penguin Books USA Inc., 375 Hudson Street, New York, New York 10014, USA
Penguin Books Australia Ltd, Ringwood, Victoria, Australia
Penguin Books Canada Ltd, 10 Alcorn Avenue, Toronto, Ontario, Canada M4V 3B2
Penguin Books (NZ) Ltd, 182–190 Wairau Road, Auckland 10, New Zealand

Penguin Books Ltd, Registered Offices: Harmondsworth, Middlesex, England

Volume 1: *The Native Tradition* first published 1985
Volume 2: *The Hermetic Tradition* first published 1986
This omnibus edition first published 1994
3 5 7 9 10 8 6 4 2

Copyright © Caitlín Matthews and John K. B. Matthews, 1985, 1986
All rights reserved

The moral right of the authors of the preface has been asserted

Printed in England by Clays Ltd, St Ives plc

Except in the United States of America, this book is sold subject
to the condition that it shall not, by way of trade or otherwise, be lent,
re-sold, hired out, or otherwise circulated without the publisher's
prior consent in any form of binding or cover other than that in
which it is published and without a similar condition including this
condition being imposed on the subsequent purchaser

Contents

VOLUME 2: *THE HERMETIC TRADITION*

Authors' Preface
to the New Edition of
The Western Way

This book was written as an overview of the Western Mystery Traditions at a time when the full spectrum of the indwelling spirit had begun to refract its ancient glory. That light has not dimmed but rather spread its rays abroad to rekindle personal spiritual practice, illuminating the places which nurture our roots and helping all to find effective ways to manifest their revelation in the world.

After the first publication of both volumes, the original series editor of this book, Eileen Campbell, asked us to write a third volume to complete the story of the Western Way's development. We agreed to do so, but only if delivery was acceptable in three incarnations' time, since there were still so many spiritual movements that had not reached their full flowering.

Since this book was written there have been subtle changes in the way we view the world. There is greater awareness of our environmental responsibility, of the necessity for appropriate spiritual nourishment. But, wherever we turn, a collective soul-loss threatens our world. A sense of disorientation is abroad, deriving from a rejection of the creative, mystical and spiritual dimensions which have always sustained humankind. A literal-mindedness which ignores the mystical dimensions of life pervades our culture, fostering a narrow and fearful spirit that turns to fundamentalist 'certainties' for support. In this corridor of creative repression and growing fundamentalism, it seems even more essential to reaffirm our spiritual belonging and practice, to find the connections between our own story and that of this planet. This is how traditions are upgraded by each subsequent generation: by a consideration of how ancient wisdom can be applied most effectively for our time.

It is so that the Mysteries enter a phase of chaotic readjustment which challenges all we have held as fixed and immovable. At such times the necessity for spiritual re-education and supportive community becomes more urgent. Many idealists envision the skilful weaving together of generations, social structures and ancient wisdom, yet this cannot come about until outworn patterns of racism, consumerism, poverty and war are overcome. We are still far from universal social justice because the spiritual principles which underlie the Mysteries are not being applied by governments. Nevertheless each individual who maintains his or her spiritual practice with impartial compassion widens the way to this possibility.

The two traditions which we have written about in these pages are complementary. Their wisdom is now receiving widespread recognition in quite unexpected ways. The enduring power of the native traditions, the ancient earth wisdom of indigenous peoples, is at last being acknowledged as an essential guide to living wisely upon the planet. Similarly the alchemical map of the hermetic traditions is being traced in theories of chaos physics and the newer science of complexity, showing us that the antique formulas of spiritual progress do indeed reflect the subtle and creative connections of the universe. The wisdom of the Western Traditions is being restated and borne forward by many energetic vehicles. Any container of the tradition *becomes* the tradition, in due course; only time will tell which vehicles are most effective.

In the meantime the seeker must be vigilant to steer a course around spiritual materialism, to avoid poorly trained teachers promising immediate results for cash, and be wary of the rootless trend of 'mystical tourism' which pervades training courses. The Western Way cannot be walked in the course of an afternoon's workshop. The Mysteries call initiates of many kinds to their service in every age and the dues are always paid in the coin of total commitment. To be worthy of our hire, we must work with integrity.*

To keep our practice supple and effective, we need simple rituals which link the Inner and Outer life in respect and honour, as well as training programmes which encourage a better integration of esoteric principles in practical ways and a lively imagination, while maintaining regular meditative and contemplative periods and a compassionate heart for all living beings.

*An updated list of groups and organizations offering responsible training in the interrelated branches of the Western Mysteries can be found on pp. xi–xii.

The Mysteries cannot die, be diminished or be way while there are people keeping the sacred path open. The Western Way has been walked by the ancestors, as well as by those now living; it will be trodden by children yet to come – whose ancestors *we* will be. Our task is still to keep the pathway clear by walking it with honour and enable the mystical rose to bloom once more upon the tree of tradition.

Caitlín and John Matthews
Oxford, July 1993

Contact Addresses

The following groups and organizations offer training courses. For more details, please write sending a large, self-addressed, stamped envelope (if within country of addressee) or two international reply-paid coupons (for those overseas).

NATIVE TRADITIONS

Foundation for Shamanic Studies, Box 673, Belden Station, Norwalk, CT 06852, USA. Founded by Michael Harner. Training in core (non-cultural) shamanic techniques worldwide.

Green Circle, BCM-SCL Quest, London WC1N 3XX, England. Founded by Marian Green. Networking association, with local groups in Britain, for those seeking companionship and training in natural magic and pagan traditions.

Order of Bards, Ovates & Druids, PO Box 1333, Lewes, E. Sussex BN7 3ZG, England. Founded by Philip Carr-Gomm. Druidic order rooted in the Celtic Mysteries, offering experiential training and correspondence course in druidry.

Scandinavian Centre for Shamanic Studies, Artillerivej 63/140, DK-2300 Copenhagen S, Denmark. Courses in Europe led by Jonathan Horwitz and Annette Horst in core (non-cultural) and Scandinavian shamanic techniques.

Sulis Music, BCM 3721, London WC1N 3XX, England. Training courses and tapes by leading British practitioners, including R. J. Stewart, Gareth Knight, Caitlín and John Matthews, etc.

Walkers between the Worlds, BCM Hallowquest, London WC1N 3XX, England. Experiential courses in Celtic and British Shamanism led by Caitlín and John Matthews.

HERMETIC, GNOSTIC AND MYSTICAL TRADITIONS

Builders of the Adytum, 5010-05 No. Figueroa St, Los Angeles, CA 90042, USA. Offers correspondence courses on qabalah, alchemy, tarot, etc.

Creation Spirituality, Holy Names College, 3500 Mountain Boulevard, Oakland, CA 94619, USA. Offers courses and certification programmes in Creation Spirituality, based in mystical Christianity and ancient wisdom traditions. British contact: *Creation Spirituality*, St James's Church, 197 Piccadilly, London W1V 9LF, England. Other individual CS groups meet worldwide; ask for local details.

Fellowship of Isis, Clonegal Castle, Enniscorthy, Co. Wexford, Ireland. International non-sectarian association for all who venerate the Goddess. Training courses and ordination in mysteries of the Goddess are offered by groups worldwide.

Servants of the Light, PO Box 215, St Helier, Jersey, Channel Islands, UK. Mystery school, offering correspondence course and training events based on Qabalah and Western Mysteries.

Society of the Inner Light, 38 Steele's Rd, London NW3 4RG, England. Mystery school founded by Dion Fortune, offering correspondence course on Qabalah.

Way of Kabbalah, Flat 2, 31/33 Priory Park Rd, London NW6 7UP, England. Courses and training by Z'ev Ben Shimon Halevi (Warren Kenton) in practical kabbalah.

Caitlín and John Matthews issue a quarterly newsletter giving information about their upcoming courses, tapes and books. For details, send an SAE, within Britain, or two international reply-paid coupons to BCM Hallowquest, London WC1N 3XX, England.

VOLUME 1

The Native Tradition

TO DOLORES ASHCROFT-NOWICKI

And to all who believe in the possibility of
bringing things back from Faery-Land

The mythic truth is the whole truth.
P.L. Travers in a radio broadcast

Acknowledgments

We would like to thank all those who helped make this a better book ... though of course any mistakes are our own responsibility. Special thanks go to Basil and Roma Wilby, Bob Stewart, Marian Green, Naomi Humphrey, Jerry Ozaniec, Vivienne Jones, Dick Swettenham, Tony Willis, and all the rest of the Company of Hawkwood; also to Geoffrey Ashe, Delenath and all at Chanctonbury, and all those who helped test-drive the practical exercises.

Foreword

Here is a book that answers a great need of our times. And it answers it very well.

That need is for a rational and informed description of how to apprehend the forces that form the structure of the 'inner worlds': those hidden forces that underpin and mould the outer world that we know through our physical senses. For a realization of the need to come to terms with these other dimensions of reality is fast coming upon Western man.

Those who have not yet understood this need are at times dismayed by what they see as a 'flight from reason'. However, this 'flight' ought to be realized for what it is. It is not a mindless rout of the irresponsible but the winging pinions of an informed intuition no longer content with intellectual preoccupation with surface appearances.

Others decry what they choose to call 'dabbling in the occult', which they consider either idly foolish or perversely misguided. Whilst we too would not wish to encourage the occult dilettante, those of us who have spent more years in this research than we care to remember feel, with all due humility, that we have gained in wisdom and human fulfilment rather than lost.

There is no shortage among us of able, responsible citizens – even if those less well informed may sometimes gasp incredulously when confronted with our view of truth. We who know, know it to be no facile escapism, but a hard and testing, though infinitely rewarding struggle towards truth: truth about what we ourselves are; our place in the universe; and our duties before God and the rest of the creation.

Stock political, scientific and religious answers to these questions leave many people unsatisfied today. Seeking within for the deeper issues may be one way out of a nuclear or ecological crisis – although ultimately it is more profound even than that! Crises pass – or come to pass. Man's relationship to eternity lasts for ever.

John and Caitlín Matthews bring to the subject not only erudition, balance and commonsense, but also a wide practical experience. In some areas of that experience I have shared and so I confidently recommend anyone to put themselves in the guiding hands of the writers of this book. They will not be led astray.

Furthermore, the authors have a breadth of knowledge and wisdom that puts many more strident occult pundits to shame. They are as much at home in the angelic heights of Christian mysticism as with the 'lordly ones' in the depths of the hollow hills. And this is a living experience, not mere book knowledge. Although as readers will soon gather, their literary resources are profound.

This is an instruction book for the present and the future. The old time occult groups with their body of doctrine and rigid esoteric structure are fast becoming a thing of the past. Their good has been done. Their weighty volumes of doctrine remain as monuments and milestones along the way.

They may still help us now. But the esoteric students of the present and the future will be ones who take what they can find, in eclectic freedom, for the immediate purpose in hand. Their training will be no less rigorous for being more open and unstructured, their working groups no less powerful despite their relatively transitory, even *ad hoc*, nature.

To use a familiar, if somewhat over-used phrase, this is the approach to occult training in the New or the Aquarian Age.

John and Caitlín's *Western Way* will provide an Ariadne's thread to help a new generation of seekers find their way through the labyrinth. And go some way to enlighten less adventurous souls as to what the maze we call this world is all about.

Gareth Knight

INTRODUCTION
The inward spiral

[Our task is to be] the Secretaries, the interpreters and pre-servers of the memorials of our ancestors.

William Stukeley

Mankind, more than is realized, is an expression of the part of the earth upon which he subsists. A rose of the West should not aspire to bloom like a lotus of the East.

Gareth Knight: *The Rose Cross and the Goddess*

THREADING THE MAZE

In 1968 a book appeared called *The Western Mystery Tradition* (105). Its subject matter was the bedrock of primitive myth upon which most systems of Western magic are based. Its author, Christine Hartley, was a member of one of the leading esoteric schools of the time, and she was thus uniquely placed to comment on the magical tradition from within. Surprisingly, her book was almost the first since the Renaissance that attempted to deal with the Western Mysteries separately from those of the East, and with particular emphasis on the primitive material. There have been, and there still are, numerous publications on Qabala, Tarot, Astrology, and any number of other disciplines; but there has still been no serious attempt to follow Christine Hartley's lead. While her book is still valuable for its insights and perceptions, it leaves many questions unanswered. It does not, for example, attempt to relate the more ancient, native mystery traditions with those of the later, so-called Hermetic schools. Yet the one could scarcely have existed without the other, and an important relationship still exists between them. It is in part to fill this gap that the present work has been written, as well as to disprove the old adage that you cannot bring anything back from the world of Faery. There is indeed much to be brought back, much that can be of value to us now, in our perennial quest for a transcendent reality. Above all, it is our intention to present a conceptual rather than a chronological view of the Western Mysteries: one that will serve as a practical guide to that vast realm, where, though we may go visiting, we remain largely strangers in a strange land.

But first it is necessary to define some of the terms used throughout this work, and which, for various reasons, may be unfamiliar.

The first is the term 'Western Way' itself. By this we are referring to a body of esoteric teaching and knowledge which constitutes a system of magical technique and belief dating from the beginning of time – the 'Foretime' in which our ancestors first began to explore the inner realms of existence. And it is a 'Western' way to distinguish it clearly from the Eastern and Oriental systems which have found so strong a foothold in the West in recent years, but which are really less applicable than our own native traditions.

We have chosen to use this term rather than the more usual 'Western Mystery Tradition' for two reasons. Firstly, because the disciplines normally included under that heading – Qabala, Alchemy, Gnosticism, the Occult Sciences – do not constitute the whole story; and secondly, because it is very much a path we shall be following: one which has been walked by many others before us, and which will be walked by many more to come. None the less, the term still stands as a most useful frame of reference when it comes to definitions: 'Western' rather than Eastern; 'Mystery' because hidden, an esoteric knowledge; 'Tradition' because it consists of material handed down orally or received from the group soul of the planet or the racial consciousness of the tribe.

With these few definitions in mind we can begin.

Imagine, then, that you are about to embark on a journey to an immeasurably distant and strange country. Whom do you take with you for companion and guide? If you are wise you will choose someone who knows the way and is familiar with the terrain. In the same way, if you choose to explore your own *inner* landscape, peopled from your cultural background and tradition, you should seek to know all that you can about those you may meet along the way, what they will say to you, what symbols they will show. You need to know the words that will open certain doors, and how to address those who guard them. You will need maps.

The inner spiral   The outer spiral

Figure 1   The Maze

One such map is the symbolic diagram known as the maze, and though you will meet with many other recurring images throughout the book – the tree, the circle and the cross, to name only three – it is one of the most important. The maze as a symbol of the path of initiation is found at many mystery sites throughout the world. It is a living glyph of the Western Way, through which all must pass in pursuit of their destiny within the framework of the Mysteries.

Taken together, the two volumes which make up this work constitute a completed maze pattern. That is to say, a journey *inward*, to the centre; and a journey *outward*, to the periphery. Volume one, which deals with the Native Tradition, from its origin in the Foretime to its present day manifestations in Neo-Paganism, is the inward spiral. Volume two, which concerns itself with the Hermetic Tradition – so called after its supposed founder Hermes Trismegistus – from its beginnings in Classical Antiquity to its current renaissance in the work of contemporary magical schools, is the outward spiral.

Together these two paths form the *prima materia* of the Western Way: the Native Tradition, more intuitive, earth conscious, Goddess-oriented; and the Hermetic Tradition, with its emphasis on the pursuit of knowledge, oneness with the godhead, superconsciousness. Together they balance each other out: the one probing deeper into the first mysteries of human awareness; the other seeking to utilize this inner understanding in a clearer, expositive way. Here the traveller learns to use what was taught on the inner journey – carrying it back into the light of day. By definition the journey outward cannot lead back to the same place.

The Hermetic Way is grounded in the perennial philosophy; the Native Tradition in the Otherworld. God or Deity is seen in terms of elemental forces by the Native Traditionalists; while in the Hermetic Schools perception shifts from 'God out there' to God within the self. The evolution of consciousness is encompassed by both traditions. Just as the Hermetic cannot exist without the foundations of the Native, neither can the Native progress without the projection of the Hermetic. They are the root and branches of the tree of the Western Way.

Christine Hartley pointed out, in her pioneering study, that 'the original working of the Mysteries looked first backwards, and then forwards, and upon their basic teaching we may found the traditions and mysteries of our Western schools' (105). The two-way journey, into and out of the maze, is a continual spiral of discovery: we go inward to come out again, and when our thread is wound out fully we must return inwards to take stock, to garner our findings and rest. This is the pattern we must follow, if we desire to learn.

WESTERN FOLK-WEAVE

While most people consider the 'real' Western Mystery Tradition to reside in the Hermetic Tradition, others are coming to see it in the context of its foundations. Those who look to the major civilizations of the Middle East and Mediterranean for insight into the Mysteries fail to see the past about them. A tradition, like a prophet, is without honour in its own country. Other grass is greener and more succulent, and so it will ever appear. We have drawn many examples from the British tradition, not only as representative of the Western Way, but also because we have drawn from our own experience, ancestral memory and traditional heritage. What we have done here can be done just as well for other traditions and cultures. The Native Tradition of the West is approachable by all who have a Western consciousness and cultural identity.

Ultimately, East and West are unimportant, but each has its place. The Western Way has been so neglected, mostly since the onset of organized religion, that the individual quest has tended to be lost sight of. The saviours and prophetic figureheads have all had their purpose, but it has been above all to stimulate that interior search. 'Seek you first the Kingdom of Heaven – which lies within you' (21). To go beyond organized forms of religion we must first pick up the pieces of our development, the cross-currents, the influences and causes, before we can go onwards to the time when mystery traditions will be neither Eastern or Western.

How, then, do we define West in Western Mystery Tradition? Geographically, from the Middle East westwards. Culturally, the margin is less easy to define. None of us are really natives of anywhere any longer. Even those families who lived in, say, Scotland for generations, were originally Norse, Pictish, Gaelic invading stock, with perhaps a few drops of 'native' blood. There are no pure blood-lines, no incontrovertible evidence for an apostolic succession in folk tradition. What happened once in the British Isles has now happened in the USA and elsewhere. Ethnic minorities have 'invaded' America in successive waves – English, French, Spanish, German, Scandinavian, Italian, to mention only a few. Latterly the cultural margin has been extended by Jews of all lands, Greeks, Russians, Japanese, Asian and African peoples.

This hotchpotch of racial types tends to keep up its various native traditions in its new homeland, for a few generations at least. Traditions were once upheld for longer periods, but now the influence of the media is tending to break down all separatist barriers. Whatever the prognostication it is doubtful whether humanity of the future will be possessed of one skin colouration, one cosmo-culture and one language: differences matter and home is still best. But the twentieth century has uprooted many people who are 'exiled' from their homes as refugees or immigrants in a strange land which no longer knows its own cultural identity.

The authors hold no brief for racism or extreme nationalism of any kind, merely wishing to point out that humanity consists of territorial animals who want their own plot of land and their own customs. For those who cannot achieve that much, their cultural being is deeply important. The folk-traditions and religious practices are made more precious because they are the one possession which cannot be taken away – they can be practised under the most rigorous tyranny, as we know from the Jewish experience of the Holocaust, from Christians in Russia, or indeed all religions under the present regime in Albania. Yet even in Communist and non-religious states, the folk-soul is never jettisoned, since even here it is understood how deep is the appeal to the people.

Hitler's reversion to Teutonic mythology during the rise to popularity of the National Socialist Party has been pointed out as a salutary reminder of what damage the folk-soul can wreak, when let loose or harnessed to one manic individual's vision. But while it is true that following the native tradition too closely can result in reversion to type, and that beneath the veneer of civilization, religion and sophistication, the folk-soul is still strong, this is not a negative factor in our make-up. It can be powerfully on our side in times of crisis and war; it can serve to anchor us if we are confused or unhappy, and give us a sense of belonging in the face of exile or loss.

Folk traditions and religious beliefs as well as cultural values are sometimes imposed upon one people by another, as in the case of European Americans upon American Indians, Dutch settlers upon black South Africans, British immigrants upon Australian aborigines – but the subsequent culture has dug itself a pit thereby into which it must fall in the course of time. The adverse karma and resulting social confusion will be still to reap.

Yet it is out of the supposed separateness of Occident and Orient that a transcendent unity emerges. In esoteric circles there are no real opposites – only different ways of approaching the same goal. The West is a place of manifestation: the East a place of beginnings. Just as the sun tracks from East to West across the heavens, so does esotericism reflect this movement. In the East religious devotions are practised at the day's beginning – bathing in Mother Ganga; hymns to the sun; morning pujas performed in answer to generations of belief. In the West the devotional practices come at the day's end with vespers, evensong, the greeting of the Sabbath. Although religions of both East and West perform their devotions throughout the whole of the day and night, these are significant aspects of esoteric manifestation.

In no way should we spurn or undervalue the Eastern achievement, nor decry the practice of Eastern techniques by Westerners. The East has opened to us the possibilities of the Western Way, giving precise terminology to concepts no longer expressible in European languages – avatar, dakini, karma, nirvana, sakti, mandala, yantra, mantra – all have become established words in esoteric practice. Eastern religious and esoteric techniques are as relevant as any practiced in the West, although Eastern concepts and understandings are sometimes difficult to comprehend until a mature spiritual level has been achieved. Culture and heredity give insight into certain metaphors and conceptualizations, so that a Parisian may have a perfect sympathy with Taoism because of incarnational links, and likewise a Sikh experience strong bonds with Catholicism. The fact remains that birth into a certain place, time, and family demands an answering response – a life-lesson to be accomplished in this incarnation. After this is met and accepted, it is again possible to pursue these incarnational links.

The West remains very much anchored in earth, in material expression of itself; while the East seems impoverished materially, hiding its interior riches. This is changing as Westernization strikes to the heart of even remote lands. The necessary transfusion must be allowed to take place: interior and exterior progress to be exchanged. But careful, responsibile transplanters are needed.

Our intention in making a study of the Native Tradition in the West is to seek the roots of our consciousness, to track our development in accordance with the needs of humankind. This is after all where our genetic impulse has been coded, from where our hereditary memory first springs. To go beyond our roots is the intention of this book, not to remain among them.

The mystery traditions – Western and Eastern – are concerned with keeping open the door between the worlds, of letting through and mediating energies from inner to outer worlds, of co-operating with the Otherworld reality of which our world is a yet unrealized resonance. The spiritual purpose of life is easily lost sight of, but more and more people are dissatisfied with the quality of a totally materialist-oriented life and are searching with a good deal of determination to find that purpose for themselves. This individual search has not always been a matter of choice – it was once only to be found within the at once liberating and limiting area of organized religion. This is changing. By the often unthinking use of terms like 'Aquarian consciousness' and 'New Age enlightenment' many people are rejecting the old for the new and untried cults of the day – many of which turn out to be organized on the same materialistic lines the escapees thought they had left behind.

In finding the right way for them, individuals are driven back on their own resources, with which they must discover their needs and expectations, as well as their potential. No system or search for spiritual purpose is valid without self-criticism or self-knowledge. A formal expression, such as joining a religious group, is not always necessary, although it can give guidelines to follow.

A more interesting phenomenon is the way in which large numbers of people are seeking their roots in the earliest and oldest forms of belief. Circles and standing stones exert a growing fascination, shamanistic ways and other cultures are a draw, the re-emergence of the Goddess as a clear religious archetype all point to a rediscovery of ancient, traditional knowledge. While this is connected in a larger way with the pursuit of the perennial philosophy, it is also indicative of the self and its roots in the native traditions.

We need to communicate with our folk-soul if only to dismiss the spurious uses to which it can be put. We have our belonging – in our tribe, our nation, our people, and this is how it should be. But we are also citizens of the world, of the new Aquarian Age. It is possible to foster national pride yet to reject racialism; to balance our love of the past with our responsibility for the future. We must ask ourselves if we want to belong to the earth on which we walk, or be cut off forever from our roots, bereft of a sense of belonging.

If, as we claim, the Western Way has its roots in the earliest times, do we have any assurance of uninterrupted descent from those times to our own? Certainly, if we are looking for some kind of apostolic succession, we are going to be disappointed. There may exist families whose life-style has altered little over hundreds of years, who have retained their intimacy with nature and have handed down a collection of wise lore and belief, but they are surely rare (see chapter 5). Nowadays people are not bound to their place of birth, but move wherever work and circumstances take them; adherence to the faith of one's parents is rare, and where the religious instinct persists, it will as likely lead to some baseless cult as to one of the great Eastern philosophies. So how can we share knowledge to which we have never had physical access? Given that continuity of tradition is to some extent severed, how, for instance, can we learn why certain ancient stone circles were erected and what rites were performed there?

Some methods of recalling this type of information are presented within this book, though there are many others. The Age of Reason has established itself so firmly in the Western imagination that such techniques may well be frowned upon; we hope to show, however, that besides the cult of the Noble Savage and the worship of scientific Enlightenment, we have another heritage. The tales and traditions of our homeland are also ours, to be immediately seized and loved; for we have other gifts than reason at our disposal. The creative imagination, so often repressed, needs to be unleashed before it can be trained. We are all capable of foresight, hindsight and insight if we take the trouble to find out about such things. And while it is perhaps too easy to play the visiting archeologist in our own past – to fashion romantic fiction into historical fact – the knowledge of head and heart need not be at variance if we balance our instinctive awareness with rational judgement and cool assessment.

However, though the threading of the maze may become a symbolic journey from A to B – whatever the digressions – the Western Mystery Tradition cannot be dealt with chronologically, any more than it can be dealt with in a frame of pure rationality. Insights come in many guises and at many different levels of time and experience. One may learn as much about the inner reality of Atlantis from Dion Fortune (79) or Helena Blavatsky (23) as from Plato (20). All three *experienced* what they describe at a deeper level than most, yet their approach was individually different.

Esoteric knowledge generally, subjected to empirical scholarship, may reveal things unrecognized by those who set them down. But there is no hard and fast method of telling true from false in these areas – unless it be through the individual's response to the *symbolic* reality expressed by images and signs of the Mysteries, behind which can be discerned the essential truth.

In the past, this has all too often been made the excuse for speculation without even the most basic foundation. Perhaps inevitably so. Speculation is certainly no stranger to these pages – it could not be given the nature of the subject – but all that we have to say about the Western Mystery Tradition has been submitted to the test of personal experience. We have tried all the exercises, followed the pathworkings, done the meditations and worked with the techniques – mostly over a long period and with the help of others. To them, as to our other supporters, both outer and inner, we owe a debt of gratitude. But even more do we owe a debt to those who have walked the Western Way before us, who have left signposts along the road for us to follow. By working with these vital images it is possible to trace the pattern of the maze, inward and then outward again towards the future.

It requires patience to retrieve lost material by these means, but the knowledge that the way has been walked by others before us is comforting: they have left the path clearer for us, and their knowledge is currently available for our guidance. Such knowledge lives on in the oral traditions of song and story, of which we retain a surprising amount thanks to the exertions of nineteenth century folklorists, who rescued much material due for cultural demolition in the nick of time.

The other source of lost material is the folk-soul, the group soul of each nation which exists in the blood as well as the memory, and forms a collective wellspring of imagery and belief. Whenever a legend lives on or a tradition survives, there lie the clues we must seek. The fragmentary nature of such clues renders them frustratingly elusive; but truth will surface from deeper levels not appreciable by normal consciousness, and can be encouraged to do so by various techniques, such as those provided here.

It may be argued that the stimulation of early belief patterns in this way is unhealthy and even dangerous, yet we would do well to remember that civilized though we account ourselves, there has been more savage destruction in this century than the world has ever seen. We are all aware of the impulse for destruction within our society, but is this not because we have ignored the knowledge of the mysteries by which our ancestors lived? They once lived in harmony with the universe as they saw and understood it; it would seem that now that we know so much more we have lost the way of that harmonious relationship. Our responsibility is surely, therefore, to relearn techniques for holistic living – ways which extend to the spirit as well as the body – not by relegating consciousness back several millennia, but by integrating our newly rediscovered knowledge into twentieth century life.

Some very pertinent words by the anthropologist Bronislav Malinowski on the subject of magic and myth are worth quoting here. Myth, he maintained,

> is not a dead product of past ages. It is a living force, constantly surrounding magic by new testimonies. Magic moves in the glory of past tradition, but it also creates its atmosphere in ever-nascent myth. As there is the body of legends already fixed, standardized, and constituting the folk-lore of the tribe, so there is always a stream of narratives linked to those of the mythological time. Magic is the bridge between the golden age of primaeval craft and the wonder working power of today. Hence the formulas are full of mythological allusions, which, when uttered, unchain the powers of the past and cast them into the present (156).

THE RITUAL STANCE

It is this 'bridge', of which Malinowsky writes, that we have set ourselves to re-establish by walking the Western Way. Hence our insistence on the importance of the beginnings of esotericism, which are too easily avoided or neglected by many as childish or primitive.

It is true that an incestuous, insular and murky spirit can pervade any study of primitive levels of awareness, but this is not our intention. The clear and primal energy of the Foretime is alive within the timelessly active present of the Otherworld – which is reached by many means. The New Age has seen many come to grief through reaching for 'higher things', through a forced assumption of unrealized spirituality and idealistic mysticism. The techniques of any art – occult or otherwise – are hard-won and painfully maintained, as any dancer, singer, or performer will attest; the way of the shaman, magician and mystic no less so. Any work on the inner levels must be sustained by effort, based on hard graft, informed by spiritual dedication and aimed towards a balanced good. Fervent would-be mystics arrive all too often at *un*balanced good which causes unaccountable suffering to both themselves and others. What is needed are the skills of the technician, combined with an inspired intention. This is the ritual stance of the initiate, who is able to travel within both the past and the present and know them for the same despite all their initial differences.

We are really starting afresh, therefore, in an effort to show the way back to our roots – so long neglected except by a minority, often misunderstood or misrepresented, but still very much a living force. Thus in chapters 1–3 we have dealt with the beginnings of the Western Mystery Tradition, those first stirrings of the religious impulse which led our ancestors to focus their attention on the elements: the earth beneath their feet, the sky above them, the stones and trees and rivers which were, to them, living beings capable of independent action and thought, and with whom they shared the inheritance of the earth their Mother. From there, in chapter 4, we have taken the journey to the Otherworld, that vast paradigm of our own consciousness which extends as limitlessly as the realm of the imagination – in other words as far as forever – and which contains everything else in its timeless and placeless grasp. Those who have travelled the road to *and* from that place have formed their own world within the borders of our own. They are the Secret People, who build and maintain the inner realm in the heart of every land (279), who stand at the centre of the maze, looking backward and forward. With them we follow the movement from tribal to individual consciousness. In the movement outward we must look for a consciousness that will contain both, a mingling of Native and Hermetic traditions.

Here we can offer only definitions: some widely accepted, others less so. Who, for instance, can say what they mean when they talk of inner plane entities, or of the Inner Plane itself? We can define these things, but can we reach at the reality behind them? Nothing is so fixed that it remains unchanging, or unchangeable. Those who set out to experience these things personally may well return with new definitions which are just as acceptable as any that are currently held.

If this seems confusing, or suggests that there is no certainty in these things, one must look behind them, at the reality from which they stem, a reality with which most have lost contact in this age, but which nevertheless exists as it has always done, as a foundation upon which to build. We may talk of God or Goddess, Mother Earth or Father Sky, or we may use the abstract terms of science and call it Creation; but whatever we do we cannot ignore it for long. It is the fundamental reality behind everything we do and are and feel.

Accusations of parochialism aimed at followers of the Western Way fail to recognize this, and that the images dealt with under the headings of myth or magic, Foretime, or Otherworld, are transcendental. They belong to no culture, tribe, or nation, but are part of a universal wisdom. They happen to be the Western projections of something which is really world wide.

In popular imagination, notably within overtly occult circles, the Western Mystery Tradition carries connotations of conservative 'traditional' magic – that of the qabalist and the ritual magician rather than the shaman or the priest. It is connected with heavily nationalistic mythology, with philosophical and complex mysteries. Too often it is associated with learned and complacent esoteric knowledge: a kind of middle-aged, middle-class freemasonry for undecided Christians and dissenting Jews. Such an image avoids the challenge of many New Age developments which are emanating from a new generation of seekers eager to walk the Western Way, and it neglects the accomplishment and dedicated survival of many home-grown movements: witchcraft – the native shamanism of Europe – the village healer and folk-singer. Revivals of interest in the Native Heritage arise and fade, but the real tradition is passed on.

These movements may appear to many as the dregs of a dying religion or folklore; but the same comment could be levelled at what passes for mainstream Western Mystery Tradition. The time for dynamic reappraisal has come. The Native Tradition formed the basis of the Hermetic Tradition. Now the Hermetic Tradition, in its late nineteenth century guise, is foundering, needing to be replaced and remodelled in the light of New Age realization. We now know everything: the world has been catalogued, exposed, explored. There is nothing more to seek – except within: the mystery of ourselves and our inner levels. As a civilized people we have lost any sense of a real inner perspective: the mythologies of revealed religion have been made virtually irrelevant by contemporary restatement. Once reduced to the lowest common factor they fail to excite or inform the average seeker after spiritual nourishment. The trained shaman, magician, mystic is an anomaly in the modern world. Maps of the inner world are as rare as maps of Treasure Island. We have lost our inner currency on the way to civilization and industrial progress. The teachers are now few and the seekers many. How shall they be fed? We give our children stones instead of bread when we force them from childhood to adulthood without the salvific story, the ritual response, the inner dimension which transforms the mundane world with its touch. The world is crying for a better, brighter thing: but it will not be found among materialism and spiritual bathos.

We know better than to scrap all the old ways of spiritual survival, however. Now, as never before, the world is engaged in a great rediscovery of its spiritual heritage, and though few are aware of their part in this process, more are learning. Tracing our links with the distant past can be difficult, like trying to discover our matrilineal forebears – an exacting task requiring intuitive and sensitive research. In the West, a child takes its father's name; the mother's lineage being soon forgotten. We all know well enough about our patrilineal, exoteric self; but of our matrilineal, esoteric self we remain largely innocent.

The Western Way holds many of the secrets of our kinship with the earth. As we will hope to show in chapter 2, it guards the knowledge of who we *really* are, and can confer the keys of our true heritage.

But do not be misled into thinking that this is yet another system to grant you quick riches or cosmic knowledge. The way is often long and hard, requiring great discipline and dedication. There are few short cuts. We are dealing with questions of personal identity and relationship with a tradition as old or older than recorded time. We are dealing, ultimately, with our place in the cosmos. What will be found within these pages is a journey – long and sometimes strange – leading inward to the centre of the maze of being, and out again. As to what point is finally reached, that will depend on the individual – what he or she brings to the work, and on his or her intentions. We have only the stuff of our own common clay to work with. For the rest, the forces and energies of the traditions themselves will be found to give both a sense of direction and a rate of travel.

There is no executive board or central authority governing the Western Way. No church, no pope, no king of the witches. Instead there are disparate movements and groups, some of whom would not associate very happily together, but in whom can be discerned the seal of the Western Way. This seal is also a recognition made between individuals following the same path. That imprint may be overlaid by pride and bigotry, hidden by fear and uncertainty, but it is always apparent – a common kinship which binds the Western Mystery Tradition into a loose family unit.

At no time does the Western Way advocate a retreat from the real world. Western esotericism has always integrated spiritual and material worlds into one unit: the way of the sadhu, sannyasin and monk has always been a specialist one. We ourselves have not set out to convert anyone to anything. What we have written may reveal your path, or show the path you have already been walking in a clearer light. There are now so many people who have dropped out of or never belonged to a tradition that certain understandings once common can no longer be taken for granted.

We have no wish to set up neo-pagans against any revealed religion. The dawning of the new Age of Aquarius sees many people searching for 'whatsoever things are good and perfect' (Rom. 12:2) wherever they find them. Systematization is not an Aquarian consideration: closed spiritual disciplines and incestuous esoteric groupwork are now being discarded in favour of individual, personal commitment and public meditation. Much confusion arises from solitary work however, and commitment does not have much drive when enthusiasm flags. The realization that all religions and spiritual systems have their confluence in common purpose is a strength. We hope that those already following a defined path will increase their awareness of and commitment to it, considering how far they are meeting its demands and how they are best suited to cope with its challenges. We hope that those who are struggling to clarify their path will find it, perhaps not as a result of reading this book but in reaction to it. We ask the reader to use whatever is personally useful, to individualize the material in whatever way is practicable – while respecting the specific instructions which preface certain exercises.

The product of this inner journey is the recovery of our own traditional wisdom, often revealed by symbols during dreams or insights received through meditation. The guardianship of the Western Mysteries has been, until recently, in the hands of esoteric orders and their followers; increasingly things have changed and will change still more drastically. The esoteric schools have done their work well, seeding the knowledge of the Mysteries throughout the world; but the time is approaching for the symbols and systems to be regenerated by an influx of new yet ancient material, arising from within the group-soul and hereditary memory of ordinary people.

The work of recovery has already begun on many levels and within many disciplines. We are not all equipped to become mystics, magicians, healers, or wise women; yet by virtue of our blood and by our location within the West, we are inheritors of the Western Way. While there will always be special mediators, the new way is to take up a personal responsibility for our inner path. If you have the courage to try some of the techniques and exercises to be found within this book, you will find yourself able to contact and work with the Western Mystery Tradition.

The guardianship passes on, as it ever has, to the next generation: but with a difference. The emphasis now will be on individual work, either at ancient sites or within the home — always seeking a closer affinity with the tradition which taught us once before and will teach us again, if we give it the chance.

In effect, you, the readers of this book, are the new guardians. It is your generation which holds the threads of the great tapestry which makes up the Western Way. It is for you to continue the weaving, spun out of countless separate threads, which together make up the wondrous pattern of our tradition.

PLEASE READ THIS SECTION BEFORE ATTEMPTING ANY OF THE EXERCISES

NOTES ON THE EXERCISES IN THIS BOOK

Each of the techniques in this book carries its own instructions, but a few general remarks here may help clarify matters for the inexperienced practitioner. We believe that the Western Way is a living path, not a theoretical concept, and that you, the reader, have a right to experience it for yourself. As with a good cookery book, every exercise has been tested and tried. The provenance of the techniques varies: our own work within the Western Way has provided us with the basis of them, and we have drawn liberally on oral tradition, written lore and received material for the substance. We have tried not to be sectarian in our choice of material – the Western Way is diverse, combining Pagan, Christian and Qabalist with priest, witch and magician, as well as including other gentle souls who range the whole gamut of the New Age groups. The exercises have been designed for the lone reader with little or no experience, but each is adaptable for use in groups and can be 'stepped-up' judiciously for those who know the ropes. Some exercises cannot be done without prior reference to others, but otherwise there has been no attempt at grading. If they are taken in the order of appearance, a logical progression through the mysteries will emerge.

All the exercises, unless otherwise stated, should be performed seated comfortably in an upright chair and in circumstances free from interruption: put your phone on the hook or warn your family that you are not disturbable for an hour. Some of the outside exercises, especially at sacred sites, are likely to be fraught with interruption: while it is difficult to tune into a sacred earth-centre in the midst of the tourist season, it is still possible, given a modicum of common sense and a great deal of concentration. It is assumed that the reader will be aware of the importance of quiet, rhythmic breathing and of bodily relaxation when performing the exercises. Without these two essentials, so often stressed but so seldom applied, the results of your performance will be negligible.

The meditations within this book can be worked in two ways.

Either you can read through the instructions and memorize them or you can record them on tape and perform them while listening. Pathworkings, as meditations are often called these days, stem from the Qabalistic method of working upon the paths of the Tree of Life – they should not be confused with the kind of guided imagery techniques often used by the psychological schools. If you decide to record the meditations remember to leave sufficient pauses in between the text where you may need to visualize or think about the material. The technique of pathworking is easily learned: it is like listening to a story, only you are the protagonist. Instead of seeing yourself as on a television screen, *be there* with all the clarity of your visual powers; you should be looking out of your own eyes at the scenes before you, not seeing yourself doing something – which indicates that you are not in alignment with the pathworking.

Immediately after meditating, and indeed after each exercise, write down your impressions. Like dreams, they will escape otherwise. Having a record of your work is a useful check for the future when you may wish to branch out into other areas of exploration. Meditation is a means for you to explore your inner world which borders the Otherworld (see chapter 4). The reality you meet in the Otherworld is consistent within its own boundaries and if you follow its code you will be safe: follow the way set down, respect the guardians, and be alert for landmarks. Pathworking is not a form of Dungeons and Dragons fantasy-gaming, so keep a serious approach as well as your sense of humour. If you take a wrong step, if you meet with something you didn't expect, or are reminded of some terrible past event in your life which is painful to contemplate, don't panic; all this is grist to your mill. Meditation tends to throw up aspects of the personality which have not been integrated fully, but the theme of the mysteries is 'know yourself'. Learn not to run away but to face up to your propensities; start bearing responsibility for your personal development and your spiritual growth will go forward steadily.

Your experiences will be uniquely different from anyone else's so that, while it is sometimes helpful to compare notes with fellow travellers on the Western Way, it can be confusing and detrimental to your progress to attempt to speak about your findings to someone who is not involved in similar work. This is not said to foster secrecy or inspire suspicion among your friends, but because everyone must experience *for themselves* the realizations implicit on the path. However much you love other human beings, you cannot attain enlightenment on their behalf: they must find their own way, make their own metaphor and do their own realizing. We each aim to potentize our individual capabilities and to perceive more clearly our relationship with the spiritual evolution of our planet, not with the object of self-aggrandizement, but in order to gain control over our bodily, psychic and spiritual vehicles, enabling them to be effective instruments in the work of planetary service. This pattern of service underlies the work of the Western Way and should be borne in mind by those who have any qualms about working on themselves in a seemingly selfish manner. Any measure of control which you gain over yourself has a positive effect on the world around you. World powers may seem to run our lives, but in effect, we each have a contribution to make towards self-governance.

It is useful in meditation to have some kind of opening and closing device, to demarcate your areas of operation. These devices are used to avoid confusion between physical and physic levels and to establish both mental adjustment and right intention. We have offered some suggestions below, but if you don't care for them, then write and use your own – they will be far more efficacious than devices written by others and employed without thought. Like the Celts who, in the presence of strangers, swore oaths by 'the gods of my tribe', feel free to do the same, according to preference.

To start a meditation, imagine yourself dressed as a pilgrim about to pass between the worlds. Say the following:

> I stand at the door with staff and pack,
> May God [or the Gods] protect me there and back.

To take protection upon yourself is not necessarily to expect devils and dangers, but to show that you undertake your inner journey with intention – and that is probably the most important requirement of all. You can substitute the name of your spiritual protector and incorporate your personal or clan totem (see exercise 1) in the following chant:

From light to light,
From this world to the Otherworld,
Through the thresholds,
In the name of [protector], I come bearing the [symbol or totem].

To return from meditation, you can repeat your entry chant with the intention of going back, or modify the second chant to read:

> From the Otherworld to my world,

strongly imagining your personal symbol as you do so. Many people employ the simple device of opening and closing a pair of imaginary doors or curtains.

Consciously close off any esoteric work you do from the rest of your life: this is common sense psychic hygiene which is often neglected. If you have ever tried to get a good night's sleep after doing your accounts or after having a flaming row with a friend, you will know what we mean. A quick sealing-off gesture made with intention takes only a few seconds and is preferable to leaving your psyche running like a car engine.

None of the exercises in this book are actively harmful if you follow the instructions carefully and use your common sense. Any technique which develops little-used abilities can be initially disorienting, so expect a certain upheaval of consciousness in the first few weeks. Do you remember your first day at school or at work — how tired you felt and how disinclined to repeat the experience? Well, these exercises may be like that. Likewise, any technique can be abused by those individuals who account themselves experts on everything (read Franny's experience of the Orthodox Jesus Prayer in *Franny and Zooey* by J.D. Salinger, 222). Generally speaking, take one exercise at a time, until you understand how each works. After all, no one would attempt to learn Greek, how to drive, or master the cello in one week. The Western Way will wait, so be patient with yourself and take time to master each technique. There are no instant, slot-machine results here, and no 'right' answers. You alone possess the key to them for, without your participation, the techniques are worthless.

We are not here concerned with promoting or producing psychic phenomena. No doubt parapsychologists and psychic dabblers find much to instruct and entertain them in spoon-bending and matchbox levitating, but the producer of gratuitous psychic phenomena is an embarrassment to family and friends, as well as to him or herself — one who has need of help, not encouragement. Just as sufferers from epilepsy need medical assistance to cope with their disability, so the genuine psychic or sensitive needs to understand the nature and problems of psychic gifts. The follower of the Western Way need not be concerned with becoming psychic so much, as aware of his or her own potentiality as an opener of ways, a walker between the worlds of spirit and matter, an inheritor and wielder of traditional wisdom within the human scheme of existence, an enlightener of dark places within the human consciousness.

As you become more deeply involved in inner work so will you begin to sensitize your being to the workings of both inner and outer worlds: life-lessons will be thrown up more frequently as you participate in the earth's own subtle changes and disturbances. This may be disturbing at first, but gradually you will learn to cope with the kind of inner pressure which sometimes builds up. Minor headaches are to be expected from time to time in this work. At the onset of any physical problems, however minor, check that you are sealing-off properly and 'earth' yourself in with a good hot meal after meditating. If you are ill, depressed or otherwise under the weather, leave the techniques alone until you feel better. They are intended for practical application to your everyday life and if that is under pressure and your circumstances emotionally fraught, then they are a burden you can do without. Beware also of using the Otherworld, your inner landscape, as an escape from life's traumas. If you are pushing yourself on all levels, outer and inner, your physical vehicle can become very depleted in vitality, resulting in an etheric body which is paper-thin and offering little protection. The only cure is regular rest, relaxation and a complete break from inner work. Read harmless novels rather than improving literature; watch television or do the gardening, but don't step up the inner work.

Do not attempt these exercises if you use drugs whether for kicks or medicinally. Hallucinogens may seem to offer a quick route to nirvana but they more often result in a short-circuit rather than a short-cut. Whatever your path, the truth is the same: you can only get there under your own steam. Rocket-engines won't help you and the pressure can be crushing. If you have a condition for which medicinal drugs are prescribed, then you should not be attempting inner work while that condition prevails. Imbalances in the body are the result of inner disturbances in your being and while drugs correct the imbalances to some extent, they often do not penetrate to the root cause.

Walking the Western Way in isolation can be a lonely business at times; nevertheless, there is a genuine companionship among practitioners of the way which transcends time and space. The landmarks on the path, the guardians whom you encounter on the way have been recognized and experienced by others before you, as they will be again by those who come after you. The authors wish you a happy and enjoyable journey into your heritage. They would be interested to hear from anyone who has any unusual or interesting experiences resultant from using these techniques over a long period. A stamped, addressed envelope sent via the publishers of this book will contact them.

At the end of the book is a discography which may help provide suitable music to accompany the exercises, where this is appropriate. Music is the greatest opener to the mysteries, though we are now so desensitized to its effect through hearing muzak wherever we go, it may take some adjusting to its full potential.

CHAPTER 1
The old religion

The cult-man stands alone in Pellam's land . . .
he can fetch things new and old . . .
the things come down from heaven together
with the kept memorials.

David Jones: *Anathemata*

In the old days when we were a strong and happy people all our
power came to us from the sacred hoop of the nation, and so
long as the hoop was unbroken, the people flourished. The
flowering tree was the living centre of the hoop and the circle of
the four quarters nourished it.

John G. Neihardt: *Black Elk Speaks*

RITE AND FORETIME

'Once upon a time, there was no time, and it was then that . . .' is the
traditional opening of a tale told by a Breton storyteller, immediately
placing his audience into another realm of existence. It is into this
'once upon a time' that we must go to find the first traces of the
Western Way, for to start our story within recorded history would be
to leave out the most important of beginnings. It is in this 'no time'
that we find the Otherworld – a dimension where the gods live yet in
the inner landscape of our spiritual home. The Otherworld is the
Western equivalent of the Australian aborigines' Dreamtime. It is
not a memory of the past, nor a remnant of some Golden Age, but a
living present where past and future meet and mingle.

The scope of this first volume is contained within the world and
work of the shaman and the shamanka, his female counterpart.
They, together with their lineal descendants, are the Native Traditionalists who work within a known and familiar pattern which has

evolved from earliest levels of tribal consciousness. The current upsurge of interest and revival of the Old Religion has tended to focus the events and beliefs of the Foretime in a spotlight of reverential awe: revivalists of the Native Tradition tend to imitate shamanic rites and primitive beliefs slavishly as though the intervening centuries were as nothing. When and where these practices are relevant to modern life, the experience of the Old Religion and of the shaman are totally valid: the essential seed-ideas and ancient knowledge of the Foretime onward are available to us via the Otherworld journey (see chapter 4 and exercise 8) where the archetypal wisdom is stored. But that there should be no error, we must consider that life in the Foretime was hard, and religion was not a leisure activity to be luxuriously indulged in. Religion was a fundamental way of living life. Magic, as we understand it, did not exist: the whole of life was magical, in one sense. Yet there was nothing within creation which was truly supernatural. These seemingly contradictory statements are resultant upon any attempt to enter the Foretime – wherein life was infused with the numinous nature of the gods – from the standpoint of today – wherein everything is explicable from a scientific premise.

Before we make that attempt we must understand where we are in relation to consciousness, for the Western Way is very much the path of consciousness and its evolution. Symbolic truth is as true now as it was in the Foretime, yet the means of that truth – often conveyed by image, story or music – changes as the consciousness of humanity evolves. According to the prevailing consciousness at any one historical cross-section of linear time, so will different levels of symbolic truth be revealed. The development and evolution of human consciousness is the motivating factor in the Western Way; it is the impulse which sets seekers upon the path, from shaman to scientist, determined to find the unifying factors of physical or outer life with spiritual or inner life. The capacity to understand and equate these factors is dependent upon the level of consciousness brought to bear upon this search.

The first steps upon the way are taken within the Native Tradition where tribal or collective consciousness prevails: out of the tribe emerges the shaman who experiments with individual consciousness – the next step – by means of identifying with the numinous quality of creation as personified by the gods, by synthesizing this experience and transmitting it in an appropriate form to the tribe. The necessary next step to individual consciousness is one which cannot be taken simultaneously by all: this evolution takes many generations and is partially achieved by the presence and work of the shaman and a growing body of initiates who have already begun to make the transition within the tribe. The Native Tradition of any country takes its people on the long journey from tribal to individual consciousness, just as its Hermetic or esoteric Tradition attempts to lead people from individual to cosmic consciousness, in which evolved humanity will perceive its collective responsibility (Figure 2).

Native tradition   Hermetic tradition

Tribal consciousness   Individual consciousness   Cosmic consciousness

Figure 2

The task of religions, both old and new, has been to inculcate this evolutionary process through the means at its disposal. The varying success of this movement can be gauged by a quick mental reconnoitre through one's own life experience to date. In the Foretime this search was begun by means of contact with the mineral kingdom and with the earth's vital energies, which led on to an understanding and personification of these energies with god-forms. While the Native Tradition works from the immediate and familiar forces of the earth towards an evolved understanding of a cosmic plan or single, centralized Deity, it is the way of the Hermetic Tradition to perceive the cosmic and hierarchical forces which motivate the universe and identify their operation within elemental and imagined god-forms, as we shall see in volume 2.

Currently, the Western World is still struggling to throw off the last vestiges of tribal consciousness which have not yet worked themselves out. The revival of the Old Religion under the form of the neo-pagan movement and renewed interest in the Native Traditions of many lands are resonances of this struggle: it is one wherein the best of the ancient ancestral wisdom is retrieved and the unregenerate forms discarded as inappropriate. We shall be looking closer at this phenomenon in chapter 5 and assessing the development of the Native Tradition since the Foretime. But before we can follow the way of the earth and of the gods, before we take ship for the

Otherworld, we must enter the world of the Foretime – the 'once upon a time' of our ancestors.

> There is an Everliving in which past, present and future are one, and when we brood upon the past it may be that our intensity brings us to live in that which we brooded upon. It is not only in vision that we revisit the past; our hearts may sink into it and know what others have known,

wrote the nineteenth century poet and mystic, 'A.E.' (218). To 'know what others have known' is never easy and when we make excursions into the prehistory of the Foretime we need atavistic sensitivity in order to see with the eyes of our ancestors and perceive with their consciousness. Imagine a time when feeling and sensation were a means of perception, when people shared a common consciousness, communicating in subliminal ways, sensitive to changes of weather – as animals are – aware of the seasonal round, and so deeply connected to the land that there could be no distancing from it. These were the Firstborn – we do not speak of Neanderthal, Mesolithic or Homo Erectus, for these are but convenient labels to hang on old bones. All cultures have had their Foretime – indeed, some primitive peoples are still living through theirs – and what is written here may stand for many of them in times when land-masses, which we know today as continents, were connected and when national divisions were undifferentiated.

The first intimations of deity were subtly blended of many understandings: of the earth energies whose currents crystallized into natural features of hill, stream and tree; and of the ever-present power of the ancestors before the ancestors. It was a nameless, sensitive evolution at first, little more than a realization of the signature which made stone other than wood, and both again different from flesh or bone. The slow immobility of stone, the quick, liquid gushing of water, took on individual characteristics and qualities. Fire, air, earth and water were the elder brethren of humankind, energies to be recognized and greeted with respect, the elementals of life which endowed the earth with power or *wakanda*, as the Sioux Indians called the great mystery of the earth-spirits.

The Foretime was the time for naming and recognition. True naming only comes after true knowing of a thing. While the English language no longer differentiates nouns by gender, many languages distinguish between the maleness or femaleness of things. Before developed concepts of deity, the earth was already understood as female – the Mother, the bringer-forth, the provider: the sky too was discerned as male – the Father, the rainer, the thunderer, the shiner. The verbal name and the mental image combined to formulate the seeds which would grow into the gods. The ability to bestow names, together with the art of visualization, distinguished the shaman from the tribe. The first stirrings of imagination are perceptible in the ability to 'have a picture' in one's head. William Golding's *The Inheritors* (89) gives an insight into the consciousness of the Foretime and the way in which perceptions are tentatively shared.

Place was of the utmost importance. The sense of belonging to the land can be clearly understood in the statement of a modern Australian aboriginal woman of the Pitjantjara tribe who said that the moles, warts or skin discolorations on her body were the same as marks left by her ancestors upon a particular rock at her birthplace (169). Although we still acknowledge the place of our birth to be important, still experience the *frisson* of power at a sacred site, or even yearn towards some remote place which we feel is our spiritual home, we can seldom know with any intimacy the network of influences which are set up when one site is continuously occupied over many generations. The natural features of that place take on characteristics friendly to their inhabitants, coalescing into spiritual forces – the *genius loci*, or spirit of the place. The ancient numen of the place can still be encountered at ancient wells, hills and woods today; although few people still make a wish, or tie a prayer rag from a branch, the *genius loci* remains.

The tribe was a unit, an extended family: its common aim was self-maintenance and survival. To be part of the tribe was to be one of the family: to be cast out of it was almost certain death. To be part of the tribe's customs, laws and privileges was to participate in the group-soul of tribal consciousness. This tribal consciousness was built up over many generations until a group-soul began to operate, comprising a common symbolism and understanding which was upheld by domestic custom and transmitted through traditions of ritual behaviour. Ritual is a method of formalizing and therefore of remembering things, a way of codifying the functions of humanity within a spiritual sphere of reference, so that the deeds and responsibilities of tribal ancestors are transmissable to the tribe. Tribal consciousness is usually concentrated in the here and now, concerned with the body's magnetic relationship with the earth; tribal rites reflected this obsession in the cult of the severed head, the bones of the ancestors and the blood of sacrifice poured out upon the stones

(33). The recurrent rhythms of life and death were the tribal reality, and these are the bases from which stem those ancient historical or religious promptings which still sway our opinions today. The early encodings of tribal ritual are with us yet, sometimes enshrining irrational and aberrant beliefs, at other times giving us access to the group-soul of our people and their potent wisdom. Because these rituals are based in earth it might be easy to deride their efficacy for our own time but we must remember that 'The heavy matter through which we move is not the antithesis of cosmic consciousness but its densest and most inert expression' (216). The first stirrings of consciousness often appear crude and barbaric but, *within the context of their times*, they are valid signs of a people attempting to relate to the hidden realities behind appearances; they are the foundations of religion.

For the time of which we are speaking the word 'religion' is a misnomer; yet some explanation of the term 'Old Religion' is necessary. It is a term normally used in totally diverse contexts, applied by members of opposing camps about their own antecedents: by the Catholic Church about itself after the Reformation in countries where Catholicism was outlawed, in order to differentiate it from Protestantism, and also by present-day witches about their own ancestral beliefs. We shall be discussing both of these factors in due course, but in the context of this book the 'Old Religion' applies to the earliest form of native belief. It covers the vast period from the Foretime right up to and including the beliefs of the Celts, who welded their own practices onto the older native patterns.

Such is the welter and variety inherent in the Old Religion that we cannot trace every single factor in its make-up. In its earliest form it was not a religion, as we understand it, at all; more a way of living with intention than a formal expression of worship. Some notion of this can be grasped by looking to the traditional sayings and prayers from the islands and Highlands of Scotland collected by Alexander Carmichael in the *Carmina Gadelica* (42). No aspect of life is too humble to be excluded from its own special saying and blessing: from the smooring or subduing of the fire for the night and the blessing of seed-corn for sowing, to the invocation against the evil eye and the charm for travellers.

> May the man of this clothing never be wounded,
> May he never be scathed,

sings the woman who weaves the cloth on her loom, aware ever of the vital interdependence of the animate with the inanimate. The *Carmina Gadelica* was collected in the late nineteenth century, but it gives a clear impression of how too, household gear and weapons participate in their users' lives. Each everyday activity has its particular blessing which cannot be omitted without danger; ongoing work is exhorted with rhymes and songs to help its continuance; and the protection of saints, angels and fairies is still sought. Places of accidental or violent death have their memorials not in stone but in songs of lamentation and sad remembrance. Of the dead themselves, there is little mention because the realms of the living and the dead overlap: the gateway is always open to the world of the ancestors.

We have shown how the first formulations of deity arose from recognition of the *genius loci*: this was the first germination of the god-idea. The second germination stemmed from the cult of the ancestors. The dead were both inhumed and cremated in the Foretime. The preparation for entombment was carried out with the same care and exactitude as though the dead person was to be rehoused. Food and personal equipment were placed in the grave as though death were but another form of living: which was exactly how it was understood. The ancestors were the go-betweens in the Otherworld which was itself a continuation of this world. The ancestors were those who had gone before. In life they had helped establish the fundamental shape of tribal existence by being links in the chain of tradition, by transmitting the tribal wisdom. Reverence for the ancestors is by no means extinct today. The great festivals of the dead are still celebrated in South America where candles are placed over ancestral graves, as in other parts of the world where it is usual to tell news of one's family to the deceased (34). The deeds of the ancestors were related in the Foretime and transmitted to the next generation, often growing in stature until the distant ancestor resembled a god. Sometimes these retellings show how the behaviour of the ancestors helped to codify tribal laws and precedents. The Irish *Book of Invasions*, which chronicles the history of successive invasions, sets many such precedents: the *first* adultery, the *first* fire to be kindled, the *first* fair to be assembled – these are all activities in which the ancestors participated in the tribe's distant past, memories encapsulated and sung (136). In these early tales the ancestors seldom figure in stories of happy family life, but in violent dissertations of chaotic relationships and bloody slaughters. Similarly in the Welsh *Triads*, bardic mnemonics in which the ancestors and their deeds are celebrated in triplicities, we read of the three famous shoemakers, the three amazons of Britain, and the three unfortunate assassinations (268). Here are the yardsticks and comparisons of the tribe by which they shared in the mythical exploits of the dead-who-did-not-die.

While everyone had ancestors to contact and aid them, it required a specialized member of the tribe to interpret the realities of the Otherworld. It is in the person of the shaman, the priest, the walker-between-the-worlds that we find the third germination of the god-idea and a beginning of formal religious practice.

WALKERS-BETWEEN-THE-WORLDS

While every one of us is an 'earth-walker' only certain people can perform the shamanic function: these are the psychics, the sensitives, the mystics and dreamers. In our society we exclude such people from the circle of community life out of fear or ignorance: for us, they have no useful purpose. Yet a tribe without a shaman was a tribe without a spiritual representative.

The shamans were the first guardians of the Western Way, the first keepers of tradition. Although the word 'shaman' belongs properly to Siberia, it is more applicable within the Old Religion than witch, magician, or priest, for the shaman or shamanka fulfilled many roles: lore-keeper, healer, prophet, diviner, ceremonialist as well as ambassador to and interpreter of the gods. A shaman was born, not made. But only a shaman could train or guide another. The candidate-shaman would meet the ancestors or the tribal totem for the first time in the vision-quest, an interior journey in which an otherworldly protector or teacher would be encountered. This initiation was undertaken in an isolated place where the candidate would stay, often near death from the ordeals of fasting or self-mutilation by blood-letting, to make the first encounter with Other-world realities. If successful, the initiate would return to the tribe and be inaugurated into the shamanic function by the elders (134).

The shaman was literally a walker-between-the-worlds, one whose attunement to both tribal consciousness and the gods was so fine that he or she could slip between the hidden parallels of life and death, between this world and the Otherworld; the shaman affected the quality of the group-soul on levels not immediately appreciable to normal consciousness. We can instance those mystics of many religions, the Christian St John of the Cross, the Jewish Nahman of

Bratislav and the Islamic Rumi – who by their silent witness and intimate contact with the inner forces of their faiths, carried the religious group-soul forward by intensive meditation upon the images and symbols inherent in their religions in such a way as to make them strongly evocative for others. The shaman's role was even more crucial because his or her personal revelation shaped the tribal consciousness, formulated and named the gods.

> This special and sacred awareness of the universe is codified in song and chant, poetry and tale, carving and painting . . . it gives structure and coherence to the unfathomable and intangible. By 'making' that which is the unknown, the shaman attains some degree of control over the awesome forces of the *mysterium* (100).

It was upon the shaman's revelation and visualization that the Old Religion was built and from which, ultimately, subsequent god-forms and spiritual practices are derived.

While tribal members had only a vague notion of the threshold dividing the worlds, the shaman could not only divine, through observation of wood, stone and elemental forces, but was also supremely sensitive to the will of the ancestors, the first gods. The first stories of the gods arose from a weaving of the relationships between one inner-world energy with another.

The shaman was also the guardian of the tribe's luck or totemistic symbol, similarly bound up with the ancestors. Certain Highland clan-chiefs today retain their clan's luck: the Macleods possess the Fairy Flag – an Otherworldly banner with the power of protecting the clan from peril (171). The form of the tribal totem varied: if the tribe took its dependence from an animal, an animal skin or horn might be worn by the shaman in great ceremonies. Or it might take the form of stone or implement to be wielded as an emblem of office by either shaman or tribal ruler. The stories attached to the tribe's luck were bound up with the first beginnings of the tribe itself, and these can often be traced within the genealogies of certain families. In the Foretime, the shaman was responsible for the esoteric ordering of the tribe, the tribal ruler with its exoteric governance. Sometimes the function of shaman and ruler were combined in one person or family, which led to a close identification of that family with Other-worldly entities or with the gods.

Kings were descended in legend from gods: the peace-kings of Sweden from Freya, the Saxons from Woden (136) and the Emperors of Japan from the sun-goddess, Amaterasu; while others might be descended from animals, like the Macfies who are descended from a seal-woman, or the French Lusignan line, whose later descendants became kings of Jerusalem during the Crusades, from Melusine, a water-goddess or mermaid (70). In some senses the shaman was also an early form of herald, bearing the arms or symbols of his tribe on their behalf. 'Arms represent people or groups of people as though they themselves were present. The presence of a coat of arms acts as a substitute for the person, *even after his death*' (171 italics ours). Since we are all intimately related through a handful of common ancestors we each, by virtue of our blood-link, have some share in a tribal symbol. Although we may not be eligible to bear arms, certain symbols or mascot-images crop up everywhere and are particular to us. The animal 'familiar' of the witch is of this category, as is the teddy-bear or tribal symbol is given on p. 42. Such clan-totems are still power- which belong to us, and a technique for establishing such a shamanic or tribal symbol is given on p. 000. Such clan-totems are still power- ful keys when walking the Western Way, being releasers of memory.

The shaman was not just the spiritual representative or herald of the tribe, but also its memory. The shaman's journeying between the worlds gave him or her a familiarity with two realities. It is with this interior reality that we have lost contact. Most of us have lost the facility of entering into the Otherworld, but it is still the province of poets, priests and initiates both in the Western Way and in other areas. The process of *analepsis* or the remembrance and recovery of 'forgotten' knowledge is skilfully discussed by Robert Graves in chapter 19 of *The White Goddess* (92). Analepsis is a technique everywhere used by poets, historians and mediums, as well as others: that it is little written about is not surprising. It is an inheritance available to all who stand in the line of succession from our shamanic ancestors, as we shall hope to show. Two examples will serve to show how it functions. In this century one James Fraser, a cartwright in Beauly, told of a recurring dream in which he witnessed the Battle of Blar-na-Leine in such detail that the hearer was in no doubt as to the accuracy of his account. The battle in question had occurred in 1544 when nearly all the Frasers were killed fighting the Clanranald: James Fraser told of his dream just after the Second World War. His description of contemporary dress, equipment and methods of fight- ing could only be checked by recourse to obscure sources unavailable to the dreamer (171). If one of James Fraser's ancestors had survived that battle, could this be some form of hereditary memory?

Many theories have been put forward to explain this phenomenon, such as Jung's theory of the collective unconscious (123), reincarnational memory (107), or access to the ancestors (238). Each of these theories is using an idiosyncratic metaphor for a single understanding. If we understand the Otherworld as a reality which is always available because continuously happening, not subject to linear time, we begin to see how analepsis may be one of the keys into the Western Dreamtime. A technique for developing far-memory is given on p. 44. A second example of analepsis concerns Alfred Watkins, the developer of the ley-line theory, who spoke of an experience he had in which he was beset by a 'flood of ancestral memory' when he 'saw' ley-lines for the first time, etched upon the countryside (281). Such sudden memory-recall is deeply gratifying because an ancient facet of our tradition can be retrieved by those means to enlighten our own age. Whatever metaphor we employ to speak about analepsis – whether it be 'communications from beyond the grave' or 'from out of space' rather than the ancestors or the Otherworld – we each possess the means to use it for ourselves.

Nothing is ever truly lost, and this is the joy of the Western Way: that recurrent themes crop up in a seemingly isolated way in individuals and, when synthesized, form a body of knowledge which has lain forgotten for centuries. The shaman ensured that such knowledge was not left to chance: each tribal member's initiation into adulthood was a lesser version of the shaman's own Vision-quest – an introduction to the symbols and totems of the tribe – where the candidate would be left alone and fasting in order to bring back a vision or, as we would say, a visualization, by means of an unconditioned response. Initiation into arcane knowledge is now the protectorate of the Examining Boards of universities who still incarcerate their candidates for a certain period of time in which the required response is sought, though this method is itself a shadow of an older form of lengthy training and memory testing. For these methods of enabling the initiate to remember lost knowledge was the preserve of the shaman's successors – the Druids.

First of all dismiss from your mind the image of bearded, white-robed druids, sickles in hand, trooping off to a druidic conference. So has popular imagination been conditioned by the druid-revivalists of the last few centuries. That the true image is in keeping with the Foretime shamans we can well see if we look at the Irish *Book of Invasions* (136). Here we read how one chief druid, Mide, kindled the first fire upon the hill of Uisnech at which the 'indigenous druids'

complained bitterly, because he was usurping their function. Mide
then had them brought together and had their tongues cut out,
buried the tongues on Uisnech and then sat upon them: a suitable
parable demonstrating the power struggle between the old and new
shaman, and how the old ones' powers and knowledge were appro-
priated by the new.

The druids did not just arrive fully fledged with the Celtic
invasions then, but shared the function and position of the old
shamans. As links in the chain of succession, the druids were the
strongest guardians of the Western Way. Yet even in the Classical
accounts of druidism they do not constitute a priesthood as we
understand it today. The accounts of Strabo, Caesar and Tacitus (37,
255) give us a slanted view of a society which was at odds with
Rome, but none of these witnesses are concerned with the religious
character of a priesthood so much as with the political threat posed
by druidic powers of council. Parallels have been pointed between
the class structure of Classical India and that of the Celts (20). Druids
and kings were brahmins, aristocrats of Celtic society, following the
usual association between the ruling and priestly clans. A druid
ranked above a king, and was attached to the court as both shaman
and learned divine, being adviser, teacher and prophet in one.

The Romans sought to extirpate druidism yet, ever mindful of a
land's *genius loci* and its gods, they retained the native god-forms for
their own use and encouraged the overt similarities between native
and Roman deities – just as, five centuries later, Pope Gregory the
Great was to advise missionaries to convert old sites to Christian
worship in accordance with the locally established *genius loci* and its
interpenetrating geodetic axes (216 and see Chapter 2). The power
of the aristocratic shaman may have been crushed or temporarily
diverted during the Roman occupation, but Rome did not succeed in
suppressing the group-soul of the people, nor did it quell their
systems of law-giving – as established by the druids. Nor did Rome
ever penetrate to or conquer Ireland: here druidism remained intact
as the ancient literature shows us.

In one tale, Mog Ruith, a West Munster druid, dons a bulls hide
and the *enchennach*, or bird-dress, and soars above the heads of the
opposing army to bring back details of their troop's disposition –
clearly an early example of astral flight. His dress is the standard
shamanic one for such activities. The King of Ulster's druid, Fingen,
looks at people's illnesses and injuries and gives them remedies
(160). In the *Táin bó Cuailnge* (256) the royal woman Nes asks

Cathbad, a passing druid, 'What action is auspicious for this hour?'
'It is good for getting a king on a queen', he prophesies. Seeing no
other male handy, she takes him to bed with her on the spot. Here we
have mention of shaman, healer and prophet. Besides these, the
druids exercised the functions of judge, administrator and philosopher. While Continental druidism may have developed differently,
we begin to see that the role of shaman is subject to specialization
within druidism. No 'colleges of druidism' emerge from the
evidence. Although children were sent to the druid to be fostered by
his wife and raised with his children to be taught his craft, the
household would have resembled a later Culdee foundation more
than a high-powered assembly of druids.

We are told that Ireland liked Christianity so well that it converted
quietly and without fuss. Conversely, Christianity adapted itself
so well to the druidic elements that they were accepted without
question. As the missionaries of Ireland set out to convert Scotland,
Wales and Northern England, druidism was further reinforced
under the sign of the new faith, giving Celtic Christianity its own
distinct flavour: that of Native Tradition Christianity. At the coming
of Christianity in Ireland many of the specifically non-religious
druidic functions devolved upon the poets. Poet is the correct term –
a bard was a much less noble person, having only half the worth
under law of a poet.

Instead of an all-purpose shaman then, there came to be a number
of specializing experts: the *brehon*, or judge: the *seanchai*, or
professional storyteller, historian and genealogist; and the poet
or *file*, who had the equivalent of a small library in his head.
The degrees of knowledge were marked by the equivalent to our
degrees of batchelor, master and doctor in modern universities. Each
of these learned men and women shared the shamanic function of
walker-between-the-worlds, being concerned with the passing on of
traditional knowledge and deep learning; but of them all the poet
retained both the shamanic and druidic ability best (121).

Throughout the corpus of Celtic literature we come across poems
which boast the impossible. The Irish Amairgen says,

> I am a sunbeam
> I am a skilful sailor
> I am a cruel boar
> I am a lake in the valley (160).

Likewise, Taliesin, the Welsh poet-priest, says:

I have borne the banner before Alexander . . .
I was at the place of the crucifixion of the merciful Son of God . . .
I have been in the firmament with Mary Magdalene . . .
I shall be until the day of doom on the face of the earth (146).

In these boasts we see the seeds of analeptic memory at work, remembrances of other lives, times and places, as well as an intimate acquaintance with the nature of the Otherworld. These boasts indicate knowledge gained in initiatory rites: the seed-ideas and essences of knowledge hidden within esoteric poetic utterance. These poems are often intense compressions of symbolic concepts which enter the understanding of the hearer with the penetration of an invisible arrow into its target.

The poetic training was long and arduous, lasting at least twelve years during which time the candidate was expected to memorize the history of the race, the genealogies of kings, secret languages, the complexities of metre and prosody as well as the laws and customs of the people. A poem is never made up, it is extracted from the Otherworld by the inner journey there; it is the result of personal experience – of being one with the nature of a bird or fish, of sharing the revelation of a hero or god. The poet's initiation, like that of the shaman, is indeed a journey through the maze where the mysteries met upon the way are codified and assimilated into the initiate. Like Taliesin, whose words are quoted above, the Irish Tuan mac Cairell (160) experiences successive transformations into a deer, boar, eagle and then a salmon when he is eaten by the wife of King Cairell and reborn of her. Tuan is the sole survivor of the invasion of Partholon and is able to chronicle the events of passing generations for the benefit of later ages. By both reincarnation and memory, Tuan survives. And, though we are merely 'earth-walkers', with training we may yet succeed to the heritage stored up for us by the walkers-between-the-worlds.

Druids and poets were polymaths as great as any living during the Renaissance. Indeed, their reputations are greater considering that they memorized their learning without reference to either books or writing. Our modern aids – the tape recorder, video and notebook – are useful, but they have left us with lazy brains. Yet it is still possible to hone our senses and mental faculties, if not to razor-sharp druid standard, at least to a greater awareness of the Western Way and its treasures. The use of the creative imagination and the cultivation of analeptic recall can put us in touch with the mysteries which are our heritage. Though the role of shaman, druid and priest are scarcely recognizable in our society, the need for guardians of the mysteries is still with us. Now more than ever when the links are tenuous, do we need to become walkers-between-the-worlds, ourselves finding the way over the threshold and reinterpreting the mysteries we find there. Though there are no longer shamans or elders to initiate us into these mysteries today, we have given one very old method on p. 128, which will give you access to the Otherworld and your own vision-quest.

MYSTERIES AND INITIATION

Mysteries are gateways, thresholds between this world and the Other, the meeting place of gods and people. As symbolic verities they appear removed from the mundane world, difficult for the uninitiated to approach: from the viewpoint of the Otherworld, mysteries are a language in which spiritual concepts can be communicated and stored. Just as the Christian Eucharist uses the mundane elements of bread and wine to express the presence of Christ, so did the Foretime share and experience the Otherworld realities by means of mundane signs and by ritual enactments of the incommunicable mystery. An oak-tree was a tree, but also the indwelling god of the forest, a totem of the Green Man. When the tribal ruler dressed himself in oak-leaves he became the living embodiment of the god himself (272).

The word 'mystery' comes from the Greek *myein*, to keep silent. The overtones of secrecy and elitism attached to mysteries have alienated many who approach the Western Way for the first time, but, just as a family excludes outsiders from the intimate family circle however hospitable it may be to strangers, so does the group-soul require its own mysteries and their guardians. Entering the mysteries is to participate in the nature of the gods.

> The Altaic shaman describes his or her adventures through the ecstatic and theatric action of trance. He or she physically performs the journey while undertaking it on the spiritual plane. The interior state is revealed, made known, and then ultimately exorcized through performance. The venerated images of the awakened psyche are communicated as living symbols in the process of inner spiritual transformation (100).

These mysteries cannot be arbitrarily open to all, if only for the sake of individual safety: they must be guarded and communicated with caution. Even for those born into the tribe, initiation into the mysteries was an earned privilege not an automatic right: one won by suffering, sacrifice and ordeal. But the real secret about the mysteries is that *they cannot be communicated by one being to another*: the mystery-guardian can only give guidelines and keys to knowledge, not the actual knowledge itself, which is revealed to the initiate *by personal experience and revelatory realisation*. The impact of participating in the mysteries has been largely discounted today by those who now appreciate them intellectually and are virtually symbolically illiterate, but to one who stood revealed to the personified energies of the gods and naked to the group-soul of the ancestors, the experience was terrifyingly unforgettable and deeply nourishing.

As the mysteries formalized so did a structured priesthood emerge to guard and dispense the keys to their teaching. We shall be speaking further about the development and work of the mystery schools in volume 2. The survival of the native shaman and shamanka will be dealt with in chapter 5 of this volume. The ritual means of the mysteries tended to fall into a three-fold pattern: personal, seasonal and tribal.

The personal rituals were concerned with rites of passage: with birth, life and death. The three stages of life were connected closely to the Otherworld, and each was marked by a ritual of initiation to indicate the transition from one state to the next, as the subject died to the old and was born to the new. Just as the new-born has to find its way in the coils of the worldly labyrinth, so does the newly-deceased have to find its way through the unremembered mazes of the Otherworld. In our own society we have no formalized rites of passage to ease the young into life and the old out of it into the wider world of the inner spaces.

Initiation does not necessarily confer great powers or show how knowledge is to be used: it is merely the implantation of a seed which life's experiences will help germinate, depending on the resources of the initiate. It stimulates the latent potential of the candidate, enabling him or her to share in the patterns of life at deeper levels than that of surface awareness. Because a new-born child had but recently come from the Otherworld its grip on this world's reality was weak: it might be stolen away or return there again. Hence it was protected by salt and iron – two substances inimical to the Other-world (see chapter 4). Rituals were performed on the baby's behalf: a tree might be planted to link the life of the child with that of the earth (164). Charms were recited over the child and talismans tied about its neck. The shaman might prophesy the child's life-pattern and bind some *geasa* or prohibition upon it, forbidding it to kill or eat certain totemistic animals.

This pattern was reinforced by initiation at puberty – a time when everyone stands on the threshold of the worlds and is sensitive to the Otherworld energies – when the childhood personality was set aside in order to make way for the new responsible member of the tribe. In many parts of the world today where tribal consciousness is analogous to the Foretime, the women still ritually weep in token of their children's 'death' as the young candidates are led away to suffer the ordeal which will make them adult: they are kept in seclusion, subject to many prohibitions, they are told the ancestral lore, and suffer circumcision or the painful marking of the flesh with ritual tattoos and scars, preparatory to their appearance at the ceremony in which they will re-enact the mysteries of the gods (34). In a ceremony parallel to, if not as testing as, the shaman's vision quest, the initiate was often left among the tombs of the ancestors, in caves or chambered tombs which signified the descent to the Underworld. It was a daring step across the threshold of the worlds: a dangerous journey, the return from which was greeted with joy, signifying as it did the emergence of a new adult tribal member.

Although the keys to the mysteries are given to the initiate of the Western Way, each must still find the way in darkness by the light of personal intuition. To enter the chambered passages and caves of ancient initiation scenes today can still be a revelation: to grope in the labyrinthine darkness and find the finger holds and ledges once grasped by earlier initiates of the Western Way. But suffering and pain are only one feature: at the heart-chamber of the maze-mystery is freedom and mastery over the elements of life.

The pattern was shattered at death: the body was left to dis-integrate in the air before burial, or it was burned and the ashes placed in an urn. The deceased's gear was sometimes smashed to indicate that it was, henceforth, relegated to Otherworld use (33). Chants were sung to help the spirit's transition to the ancestral realm. Death was but a threshold between the worlds and was not feared as it is today.

The seasonal rituals were concerned with the cultivation of the land and the interdependence of animals and people with the elements. Modern farming methods, the importing of foreign food and the deep freeze have severed us from our dependence upon seasonal changes for our daily bread – though this is still a determining factor between plenty and starvation in the Third World. The fertilization of the soil, winter sowing, lambing, spring sowing, cultivation and harvest followed each other in a constant round of activity in which the whole tribe shared. The lunar and agricultural calendar can still be discerned in the later Celtic Fire-Festivals of Samhain, Imbolc, Bealtaine and Lunasadh, celebrated on the eves of 1 November, 1 February, 1 May and 1 August respectively. These were the times when the Otherworld was felt to be particularly close. We have given suggestions on p. 47 in which these festivals are revealed as the hidden doorways through which we can still pass. They are still recognizable to most of us as All Souls, the Purification of the Virgin, May Day and Lammas – days when traditionally either priest or people still celebrate the mysteries. The solar calendrical days are retained by universities and lawcourts as times of sittings and circuits – an inheritance from druidic practice: the equinoxes, 21 March (Lady Day) and 21 September (Michaelmas), as well as the solstices, 21 June (Midsummer) and 21 December (Midwinter) were important in the Foretime, as research among standing-stones, circles and earth-works shows us (29).

Of all the rituals from the Foretime, those relating to the seasons are most approachable, combining as they do both high mystery and tribal enjoyment (94). They are still a good excuse to stagger, as a modern folksong has it,

> from the Old Half Moon to the Rising Sun,
> with our pint-pots in our hands (298).

Something of the communal celebration and joy of life can be captured if we participate in the surviving seasonal rituals enacted today; though often overlaid with later obscurity, they stir deep-seated memories offering us access to the Foretime.

The tribal rituals involved the whole clan in great ceremonial assemblies; the secular side of these gatherings was celebrated with games, music and dancing but, whether they were held to enact the god-stories or to inaugurate a new leader, they served to reinforce the group-soul. Something of this feeling of communal cohesion can be seen in modern Highland Clan gatherings in Scotland. Dame Flora MacLeod of MacLeod has spoken of the bond of affection and obligation which she and her clan owe to each other which 'in all the airts of the world is indeed a living tie that neither mountains nor a waste of seas can divide . . . the spiritual link of clanship embraces them all' (171). And however blasé we may be about our own national cohesion, the coronation of a monarch is still an event surrounded by numinous awe, bridging the ages with its pageantry, the exhibition of heraldic totems, the exchange of promises, and the rituals which marry the sovereign to the land – in the case of the English monarch, with the Wedding Ring of England – a potent and ancient ritual (16). The inauguration of a president, although a diminished form of the royal ritual, shares the status of a great tribal event: in some parts of the world the rivalry and competition for the honour is analogous to that of the Foretime when rival chieftains fought each other in deeds of arms for the privilege of becoming tribal leader.

In the modern coronation rite many early ritual practices are enshrined, but this marriage to the land is the most fundamentally important. The tribe had its being from the earth which bore it; the king, as chief representative of the tribe, had therefore to have a closer link with the earth energies. We have said how the first formulations of deity began; in many parts of the West the *genius loci* became personified as the Sovereignty of the land, seen as a royal queen of great bounty who either symbolically, or in the person of the shamanka, was married to the king. She was the mother of the people, and the king was her consort-steward. He administered the land in her gift and by her right (149).

But while the king aged, Sovereignty did not; if his vigour did not equal hers, the king was replaced, often undergoing voluntary death to become an ancestral guardian (248). Here the kingly and priestly roles overlapped. The union with the land was ruptured if the king was maimed or blemished – a feature which we find of importance within the Grail Legends, as noted in essay six of *At the Table of the Grail* (162). A wounded king meant a wasted land: the obligation upon the king to be sacrificed was very great. In terms of the Western Way this spiritual concept is important today: only by the close meshing of people, shaman and ruler with the earth can it achieve its fulfilment and the people themselves be made whole (see exercise 5, p. 70).

The place of the king-making was often an ancestral place. The kings of Argyll were inaugurated by stepping onto the royal footprint graven into the rock at the hill of Dunadd: literally stepping in the footstep of the ancestors. The stealing of the Stone of Scone – the ancestral inauguration stone of the Kings of Scotland, and said by some to be the ancient Irish Lia Fail – by Edward I in 1296 was an attempt to purloin the sovereignty of Scotland. Its illicit return from Westminster Abbey's Coronation Chair in 1951 to Scotland was greeted with shrieks of fury south of the border and cries of glee in the north: a people does not give up its native heritage very quickly, but the sacred stone was returned in time for the inauguration of Queen Elizabeth II, the lineal successor to the Scottish kingship (16).

Loyalty to the racial archetypes and ancestral patterns is still very deeply seated within us. The domestic propitiations, the seasonal rituals, the ancestors and their power remain. These are the roots of the Old Religion, of which a few leaves from the traditional family tree can still be seen today. By themselves they are powerful, but without the inspiriting of their history they are nothing.

It is to the racial symbols of our Native Tradition, its archetypes and myths, that we must look as living scions of that tree, and beyond them to the god-forms. The surest way to approach them is through the sacred sites and temples of the old earth magic.

EXERCISES

EXERCISE 1   FINDING YOUR CLAN TOTEM

In the Western Way it is usual for the practitioner to adopt some motto, device or secret name. Just as candidates for confirmation or the monastic life still take another name – be it of saint or ancestor – so do initiates take a new name for their wayfaring. Names are easy to find. Symbols can be acquired. But the clan totem is a symbol of your belonging to the family: those who have followed the Western Way before you. As the number of people alive in the world only thirty generations back is theoretically exceeded by the number of ancestors we each have, counting our two parents, four grandparents, eight great-grandparents, etc., to a total of 1,073,741,904, we are therefore intimately related one to the other and share a common set of ancestors (62). These ancestral families had their unique clan totem or symbol which, by right of blood, we share. Your family may already be privileged to bear arms of its own, in which case you have a ready-made heraldic totem. But most of us cannot trace our genealogies with any certitude; we have no knowledge of what this totem might be.

This method bypasses rational knowledge, using sleep as a way of learning things which are not consciously knowable. The ancients used incubation or temple-sleep to help cure sickness of mind and body, as well as helping the client to solve a deep-rooted problem (197). Sleep transports us to the Otherworld very speedily and it is here that we shall find what we seek.

Lie down on the floor with a cushion for your head if you attempt this technique during the day or you don't want to stay asleep too long. Otherwise you can go to bed as normal at night. Curl up on your right side and repeat the entry chant (see Notes on Techniques p. 16) over and over in your head. Feel yourself getting heavier and heavier until you experience the pleasant sensation of slowly sinking through the floor or bed. Visualize yourself sinking gently through the layers until you reach the earth and carry on down. You are descending the trunk of your family tree, inside its bole, like Alice down the rabbit-hole. Sink as far as you are able until you reach the bottom of the trunk. Don't be frightened of going too far; you land gently at the bottom, stand up and pass through the trunk in which a door is clearly seen.

At this point you may already have fallen asleep, but don't worry; practice makes perfect. On the trunk at your eye-level is the totem or symbol you are looking for. (You may have been aware of seeing other symbols as you fell down the tunnel of the tree's inside, but these are not the ones you are looking for.) Your family tree towers above you, its branches disappearing into the far distance of the heavens: it is green in leaf and the trunk is a living thing, full of the vital sap which it draws from the green earth about it. Don't walk about exploring, though. Look carefully at the symbol on the tree and make the strong intention of bringing it back in your remembrance.

If you are doing this during the day, now is the time to return, by the way you came. Few people can achieve this kind of light sleep-consciousness, however. Most of us will find that we wake in our beds the next morning with little or no remembrance at all. Don't be deterred, keep practising. As with a dream, you may find that the day's activities will 'break' your remembrance free of its fetters. The symbol can remain a long time in the psyche until it is recognized, but you will begin to notice the continuous recurrence of a theme or image which will push itself forward into your notice. Don't dismiss the trivial or the bizarre – you may not yet have sorted out the finer points – for the brain often stores things in a kind of symbolic shorthand. If you keep getting a kettle, say, then a kettle it probably is: perhaps a cauldron translated into modern imagery. The cauldron would make a good clan symbol as it cooked the tribe's food and it is still called a kettle in some parts of England today – as in 'a kettle of fish' – a pot which hangs over the fire. It is the ancestor of the Grail symbol itself – a host of imagery lies hidden here. Likewise you may suddenly realize that the neighbourhood dogs have started to take a friendly interest in you and congregate when you appear in the street – could it be that a dog is your clan symbol?

You may be fearful in this first exercise of deceiving yourself and making things up. At first it is difficult to tell when you are 'seeing' an image and when you are consciously 'pushing' it to be there. Only experience will teach you the difference and, when you come to work with the symbols which have arisen, you will know if this is so because the symbol should have that same pulsing vitality as the trunk of the tree had: if it feels lifeless in your hands, then try this

technique again with more discernment. Check back on the tree itself
to see if this is right.

How will you use the symbol when you have it? On your journeys
to the Otherworld it is your call-sign, your passport and recognition
symbol which has been brought from the very root of the Western
tree of tradition. It can guide you back if you get confused, and has
power to grant you certain 'clearances' when you meet difficulties.
You can use it visually as a meditational device in itself by painting,
drawing or embroidering it and thus making it yours by recreating it
in this world. The clan totem is your symbol of belonging and when
you work under its aegis you are directly in touch with your
ancestors who have walked the Western Way before you.

Keep it secret and keep it safe: others have their own devices which
belong to them. If someone has the same token as yourself, this may
indicate a deep link between you. We belong to the human race as
well as to our clan, so don't let the symbol divide you from your
human fellowship with those on whose behalf you tread these paths:
for if you cannot apply what you learn in these pages to your own
condition, the path you walk is a dead end.

EXERCISE 2   ANALEPTIC MEMORY

The first time you perform this exercise, enter your family tree as in
exercise one, only, instead of stepping out where the trunk meets the
ground, carry on down the tree through its mighty roots and emerge,
underground, among the roots of the tree. A clear pathway is before
you: follow it until it opens up into an underground cavern where a
large lake is found. On the left-hand side is a wellspring and beside it
a whitened, rotted tree-stump. You do not wish to drink of these
waters which flow away from the lake into the ground, for these are
the waters of forgetfulness. On the right-hand side of the lake is
another wellspring which feeds the lake. Behind this wellspring,
which is the well of memory, stand the Guardians. As you meditate,
these Guardians will formulate themselves in your imagination; they
are different for everyone. You have come here in order to retrieve
the memory of something you have either lost or which has not been
accessible to you in this life; perhaps for many centuries this knowledge has not been available. Whatever you seek to know and
remember, be sure you have properly formulated it beforehand, for
when you face the Guardians they will require a clear request or

mental image from you. If your request is one of idle curiosity you may be denied: but worse still, you may be permitted to remember or know. You will forever afterwards have responsibility for that knowledge.

Approach the well of memory. You will not be given to drink unless you speak the following password:

> I am a child of Earth and of the Otherworld,
> But my race is of Heaven alone.
> I thirst for the living waters.
> In the name of the three worlds,
> Give me to drink of the well of memory.

The Guardians will dip a crystal cup into the waters of the well where they spring from the rock and give it you to drink. Although it is only spring water you are drinking its coldness and clarity sparkle in your veins like iced wine . . .

At this point you have a choice. You can remain seated in meditation, quietly absorbing the draught through your being and examining the thoughts and images which rise in connection with your request. Or you can go to sleep, as you did in the first exercise, allowing the images to arise in your dreams. Either way is effective. At first you may get no clear results from either method but, as we have already said, these exercises often work in circuitous ways. There may be no flash of revelationary awareness so much as a quiet rising intuition which pushes at the back of your thoughts waiting to be perceived.

What happens when you get results? Knowledge which remains theoretical is no use to anyone. Analeptic memory of arcane and abstruse matters is likewise worthless if it goes no further than mere possession of facts. Don't keep drinking from the well of memory retrieving further information which will lie unused or you might as well have drunk from the well of forgetfulness. Whatever you have been given you have been made guardian of and therefore you are responsible for its keeping and dissemination. Some memories will be personal while others may be teachings applicable to many. Continue to meditate on the uses of these memories and their actual usefulness in everyday life. Rather than bothering experts with your astounding findings about how our ancestors lived or what reincarnations you may have had, do researches of your own, following up what little evidence there may be. If you use this exercise as a means of past-life retrieval be ready for the results which can sometimes have a shocking effect as the full flood of memory releases all kinds of pain and emotional trauma. Memory can be excessively painful, but it can also be used as a positive means for identifying current life problems. Avoidance of certain life-lessons which recur is a refusal to grow. We may not drink of the waters of forgetfulness while we are in manifestation: these waters are for the dead who die to Middle Earth and are reborn into the Otherworld – they need to forget the world of physical reality in order to progress in their new world. We should not forget that when we are born of our physical mother we also 'die' to the Otherworld: when we die physically we are being born into the Otherworld.

This is not an exercise which ought to be repeated often. If you get no results after about two weeks, leave it alone for a few months before trying again. Analeptic recall is not easy for some people. More importantly, do not use the period your body needs for rest and sleep as a springboard for psychic experience or experimentation every night. Your sleep patterns will become disturbed if they are being constantly interrupted by a pre-programmed exercise. If you are already interested in the Western Way it is likely that your training has already begun under the aegis of sleep: you will be aware of places which you visit often in dreams, or certain sorts of instruction which are imparted. The fact that little or no remembrance of this teaching rises to the surface of consciousness is not important. The exercises in this book are not graded in any way but some may stimulate remembrance and others will give shape and purpose to vague longings which are seldom pursued, because they remain unrecognized at the subconscious level.

It is not necessary to take this journey right from the beginning when once you know your way about. Simply visualize the lake before you and the two wells and take it from there. Those who know their Classics may well recognize this landscape as part of the mystery instruction given to Orphic initiates: we have adapted it hardly at all, for it is part of the native underworld tradition in another guise. The well of knowledge appears again in the Celtic Otherworld tradition, sometimes as a well, sometimes as a cauldron or Grail. But the underground waters of this exercise are the same waters which our ancestors drank, bubbling up from the roots of the earth.

EXERCISE 3   THE FESTIVALS AS HIDDEN DOORWAYS

The native seasonal festivals are popularly seen as excuses for nothing more than indulgence in quaint folk-custom and rural junketing, but the exoteric celebrations hide the fact that they can be approached on a deeper level. It is not within the scope of this book to give exhaustive lists of such festivals, but the following suggestions can be applied to any festival in whatever part of the world you live.

First of all choose your festival and meditate on its inner meaning: is it primarily religious (Christmas, or Pesach, for instance); agricultural (Lammas); solar (the equinoxes and solstices); from primal folk-tradition (Pace-Egging) or historical commemoration (Oak-apple day — commemorating Charles II's hiding in an oak-tree — or Thanksgiving)? Obviously, the historical and commemorative festivals will not have the powerful spiritual force of the others listed, but these can be used to gain helpful insights into the national consciousness. Some celebrations have been given saints as protectors, replacing the old god-forms, such as the patronage of St Brigit at Candlemas; but though the forms change, the inner protective energy remains the same (94).

If you have no religious or folk festivals because you follow no particular tradition or because you have made your home in another land, you might do worse than adopt the yearly round of the Celtic calendar which is now celebrated among English-speaking groups throughout the world. Although a festival may be assigned to a particular date, calendrical shift and seasonal inclemency should be taken into account when deciding the right time to celebrate. In inner terms, the right time is more important than the right date. Those living in the Southern hemisphere are already well aware of this.

Choose your festival then, finding out all you can about its origins. Celebrate it exoterically with the kind of rejoicing suitable — with the fruits of harvest or by rising early to greet the midsummer sun — meet with friends, being all the time aware that you are capable of mediating the spiritual energy of this festival to those present as well as to others in your community. This is not by verbal teaching but by deep meditation on the forces involved, by example and inner attention. At the approach to the festival begin to plan and research. At the same time, meditate each day, being aware of the approaching festival, visualizing it as an inner impulse which is striving to be born. Consider the quality of the festival — joyful, reflective, life-giving or one of gathering-in. Consider your own life in relation to these qualities, freely using the gifts of each festival for your self-development.

In this manner the festivals can indeed become hidden doorways in your life – allowing the influx of inner vitality, fostering sensitivity to the important psychic tides which energize the world. This is the way festivals were always intended to work, but exoteric practice has tended to obscure this purpose. You can make of this exercise what you will – it looks undramatic on paper, but it is applicable to any tradition. Its full effect will be experienced by those who work hardest on it. Festivals are times of rejoicing, yet their origin designates them as holidays, literally, holy-days; not excuses for self-indulgence, but times set aside for physical recreation and spiritual uplifting.

This exercise can also be used in conjunction with other techniques outlined in this book. The festivals are the times when the way to the Otherworld stands open. They are celebrations out of time, subtle demarcations which cut doorways in linear time. They have been hidden for too long. You will learn which times are best for contacting certain forces, for Otherworld visiting, for making a retreat. Everyone makes their own doorways, but while some entrances shift, the festivals themselves remain embedded in our national, religious and folk year ready to be opened by those who know how.

CHAPTER 2
The magic earth

Stand ye in the ways, and see,
and ask for the old paths,
where is the good way,
and walk therein.

Jeremiah: 6:16

Human life was enriched by means of a force activated through
the correct geographical relationship of sacred centres.

John Michell: *New View Over Atlantis*

SACRED SPACE

The earth is alive, and because of it there is nowhere that has not been
a holy place for someone, for some people. Our proper relationship
with the environment is one of complete harmoniousness, though we
seldom if ever attain it. This is for a number of reasons: we do not
always know *how* to relate to our surroundings; we are too often
selfish: we neglect the qualities of life for a quantative appraisal. But
none of this need be so. Our ancestors, the Firstborn, knew better,
were skilled in husbanding the power and life-force of the earth.
They knew themselves the children of a great mother, a mother
whose body they trod upon daily, who nourished and fed and
sheltered them as a mother should. With this understanding came a
sense of the earth's energies flowing in their own bloodstream; and
this gave them a feeling of oneness with the rest of creation, a belief in
a vital force which linked all matter in a great rhythm of becoming.

So far in this book we have looked at the first springs of the
religious impulse, the reactions of the Firstborn to the world in which
they found themselves. In this chapter we shall deal with the earth as
something to which we can respond at a personal level. But it is

essential first to understand the nature of the rapport which our ancestors possessed with the great store-house of energy beneath our feet, and why we should be required, as followers of the Western Way, to re-establish that rapport for ourselves.

The land on which we walk is really a great book, in which the history of our race is recorded, layer upon layer, age upon age. Archeology, the scientific investigation of this book, can tell us a great deal about the past and the kind of people who lived there; but there are other ways of reading the book of the land which can open to us the secrets of our ancestors – how they worshipped and where, and perhaps more importantly, who.

To do so we have to reconstruct, within our own minds and with our own imagination, the landscape of the Foretime: filled with strange and frightening things, with a power that could as easily create or destroy – but every part of it uniquely holy.

> The image of the earth as mother, producing from her womb not only crops, cattle, men and women, stones, minerals, and forests, but also the knowledge to make all these fruitful and useful, may be considered the dominant symbol in the holy places (3).

It was from this that there grew the idea of the *temenos*, the sacred place where the life-force of the earth's energies was focused, and where those properly trained in the mysteries could, for a time, become one with that vital essence.

This understanding was open to all through the agency of the shamanic priests, whose task it became to guard the collective interior heritage of the tribe. And, to ensure that the holy places could never be desecrated, become forgotten or lost to view, they decreed that the sites should be marked out in such a way that they would always be clearly defined, even though the knowledge of their use died out – as has often been the case.

Certain places, where the life-blood of the planet ran closer to the surface than elsewhere, were already distinguished – at first by no more than lines scratched in the earth, or a few scattered stones placed to indicate the sacred boundaries. But some time in the megalithic period of history they began to be marked out by more permanent signs: stone monoliths, carved and decorated with patterns that, to the initiated, conveyed their sacred function.

Because from the start the circle was a natural shape – evolving from the threshing floor or the site of ritual dancing – the stones were set out in a circular formation, within the boundaries of which the ground was sacred, set apart from the rest of the earth. Here the people could worship the elemental forces of the living earth, which were to become their gods.

At some time during this period – more than 3000 years ago – when the first stone circles were constructed, their builders discovered that through an exact orientation of different kinds of stone, shaped and cut to a particular design and varying in size and volume, the primal currents of energy within the earth could be tapped, amplified and directed, with equal effect as through trance or vision quest, and that the resulting energy could be drawn upon both individually and collectively. How this realization came about we shall probably never know but, from this moment the stone circles were no longer simply places of worship; they were storehouses of vast and unique energies, which were to fuel the religious and magical activities of mankind for thousands of years, and may indeed still do so today.

Of course, this did not come about overnight. A lengthy period of experimentation followed the initial discovery. Various shapes were tried out, though always the circle was returned to, circles of trees as well as stones being found to be effective in focusing the magic of the earth. 'Sophisticated engineers erected Avebury, the three Stonehenges, the 20,000 barrows and smaller stone circles signalling to a sky thick with gods. Salisbury Plain was . . . embossed with temples, palaces, sprayed with avenues and roads' (273). We can see just how long it took to evolve some kind of fixed pattern from the examples of larger sites such as Stonehenge, where archeological investigation has found evidence of an almost continuous state of growth, extending over a huge span of time, as knowledge of the earth mysteries increased.

The addition of a bank and ditch around the perimeter of the circles helped to seal off the energies within, and the observation and measure of the changing heavens became part of the discipline of the priesthood who worked with the mysteries of the earth.

Great importance was attached to star-lore, as a visible and measurable correlative to daily life. The moon's connection with tides, and with the human cycle of fertility, was recognized, and the passage of the fructifying sun across the sky, with the mystery of its night-time journey, during which it was said to visit the Underworld, was allotted great attention. Sophisticated techniques for measuring and recording the mysteries of the heavens and the way in which they related to those of the earth gradually evolved into an exact science (29).

The laws governing the lay-out and siting of such holy places and the shaping of the landscape around them is properly called Geomancy, and was once a world-wide discipline. In recent years a great deal of research has been done in this area by writers such as John Michell, Nigel Pennick, Paul Devereux and Paul Screeton, who between them, and with the aid of a legion of known and unknown helpers, have begun to map out the sacred geometry of these islands (168, 195, 66, 227). Many acknowledge an inspirational quality in their work and have described the feelings they experience when walking some ancient trackway between one sacred site and another, as enlightened. They have become subtly aware of links between the holy places, and have been able to plot them with map and compasses in such a way as to allow others to follow their lead, thus extending our knowledge of the sites into an increasingly detailed pattern.

Only recently, with the work of scientists like Alexander Thom (261) and Iuen Mackie (153) has it been possible to see just how accurate these ancient systems of alignment really are. Indeed, many have refused to accept such findings at all. Yet it is now possible to show that there once existed a system of sites linked by countrywide paths of energy. From this it is only a small step to believing in a global network, spanning the world in a vast energy grid which connected sites as far apart as Scotland and Australia. Perhaps most extraordinary of all, this seems to have happened more or less independently – and yet one finds the same kind of siting, the same carving of patterns and symbols at sites in America, China, Egypt, Norway and the British Isles (216). It is as though a dream was being shared on a world-wide level, a single impulse rising simultaneously in the consciousness of temple builders in the farthest corners of the globe.

Alfred Watkins, the nineteenth century antiquary who 'rediscovered' the system by which the sacred centres in this country were connected – dubbing them 'ley lines' – spoke of an almost visionary experience in which he saw the landscape revealed in a new light: the hills and tumuli, stone circles and megaliths, connected by shining paths, golden veins standing out amid the green and brown of the land (281). Such visionary glimpses, strongly akin to the analeptic thinking of the Foretime, are all a part of the earth mysteries, and often come unbidden to transform the world about us. By following the shining paths which cross and recross our land, ancient sites long lost to view are being recovered, and we are at last beginning to perceive the overall plan with which our ancestors sought to interpret and later encode the mysteries of the world which surrounded them.

Equally important are the great barrows, the circular and oblong mounds of earth which covered the bones of the sacred ancestors, or which later became caves of initiation and enlightenment where the seeker found entry only after long and arduous tests (238). Carved within, on the stones used to support the weight of the earth, are spiraling patterns and shapes of the maze and its kindred forms – meant to be read and understood by those who penetrated the mysteries – or perhaps by the dead who were laid there. More than 2000 have been excavated in Britain alone, and many more are known to exist. They too are part of the all-embracing pattern, the magical diagram of the life-force, the bloodstream of the earth.

> No wanderer in enchanted barrow-land, among those forsaken shrines of dead heroes mightier in their dissolution than in the springtime of their lives, can doubt that such piles of sacred earth were raised of a proud and set purpose to dominate the scenes they do. Our barrows were reared where they could contemplate the world *without and beneath them* and, like the deified lords resting within them, lived in a mid-world between earth and heaven. Seen along the skyline, they are indeed the stepping-stones of the Gods (161, our italics).

Nor are these death-houses, or the stone avenues built on alignments of sun, moon and stars, the only such stepping stones. Even greater arrangements of terrestrial geography are believed to exist.

At Glastonbury in Somerset recent research has detected the presence of a vast terrestrial maze coiling about the Tor which has, together with the land about it, been called 'this holiest earth' (7, 211). Others, notably the Elizabethan magus John Dee (65) and latterly Katherine Maltwood (159) in the 1930s, have detected the outlines of a vast zodiac laid out in the landscape around Glastonbury. Whether this is actually present, or a memory of older mysteries, remains a vexed question. There are now some half-dozen projected zodiacs under investigation, and more will doubtless be uncovered in the future (290). The second exercise at the end of this chapter is designed to offer an exploratory voyage which can be adapted to fit other sites of similar provenance; it also asserts the importance of the Arthurian impulse, which can be seen as the latest example of the rising of earth energy, combined with the racial myths of the country.

In recent years the techniques of dowsing have been extended and refined to include the measurement of energy fields emanating both from individual stones at the sacred sites, and larger groupings. Varying degrees of measurable magnetic force have been detected – at times so strong as to be outside the scale of ordinary instrumentation. The precise nature and cause of this energy has yet to be established, but it has been noticed that many of the stones possess a circulatory current, and that this changes its polarity from male to female and back again during the time between one new moon and the next (110).

In this connection the ithyphallic nature of certain stones becomes important; for though the earth was generally seen as female and the sky as male, these attributes subtly reversed themselves at times, so that the exchange of life-forces could take place.

In these links between sky and earth there seems to lie a mysterious extension of human birth-patterns. As the stars were believed to influence those under whose aegis they were born, so perhaps the *place* of one's birth and the phase of the moon were of equal – perhaps greater – import. Suppose that, as in many primitive cultures, women sought out certain ancient sites when it came time to give birth (182)? They would, in essence, be tuning in to the very energies of creation. Such children's abilities would be blessed as offspring of the mother, and may well have been revered as future shamans. Certainly the image of the maze, when applied here, is again apposite. What else is the womb but a maze, to which the umbilical cord is an Ariadne's thread leading out into new life?

In this perhaps we have the origin of folk-tales connecting certain of the sacred sites with fertility rituals. Not that such rites did not in all probability take place there; but that they may have been symbolic of a far greater exchange than that between men and women – in fact between the elements themselves. Thus the maypole, a comparatively recent manifestation in the history of mystery celebrations, can be seen as a symbolic linking of earth and heaven, binding those who dance around it – holding ribbons coloured red and green for earth, blue and yellow for sky – into the pattern of birth, life and death which lay at the heart of the maze of earth mysteries.

Theories such as the ley-line system, or the terrestrial zodiacs, are frequently dismissed as pure fantasy by the sceptically minded, and many are indeed based on 'received' evidence, which cannot be subjected to normal methods of proof. But it is not necessary to subscribe to any such ideas in order to feel the mystery and power of the ancient sites. Whether one sees them as accidental formations of the landscape or freakish mementos of forgotten religion, or as part of a universal pattern of belief, worship and western magical practice, one cannot, unless one is deliberately insensitive, ignore the often profound effect they can have on the individual psyche.

The sheer size of the overall plan indicates something of the ability of our forebears to interpret natural forces, and of the importance they attached to them. All we would ask of the prospective followers of the Western Way, is that they should keep an open mind and heart, and when visiting the sites, try to feel for themselves the flow of energy. This magical force, which springs from deep within the earth, can affect us very powerfully if we let it. It can open doors to the past, as well as demonstrating that these energies are still present, giving life and vitality to all things, and a wisdom to interpret the mystery of the land itself and its relationship to ourselves.

THE PATHS OF THE DRAGON

One particular symbol became associated with the earth mysteries: the Dragon, or winged serpent. The reasons are not hard to see. In the Foretime the snake represented life, death and renewal. It lived in the ground, which made it sacred to the Mother, and it shed its skin, emerging renewed. Creation myths in which the World Snake gave birth to the egg of generation, warming and hatching it as actual reptiles were seen to do, were widespread, and we shall meet with this symbol again, not least in the Gnostic and Orphic mysteries to be dealt with in volume 2 of the present work.

At the heart of the myth of the dying and rising god lay this same belief in the magical power of the serpent. Like it, the god went into the earth (or below the horizon) and came forth renewed. This is the basis of most, if not all, initiation rituals, which enact the 'death' of the uninformed spirit, and its rebirth in a new, wiser form. Thus in the mysteries of Osiris, the god was represented by a vessel filled with Nile water, often with a coiled snake carved upon it. As the Jungian Marie-Louise von Franz remarks: 'This snake is the numen who guards the tomb and protects the transformations of the God.

Psychologically it symbolizes the deepest levels of the collective unconsciousness, where the transformation of the god-image occurs' (277). This is basic to all ideas of initiation, in which we reach the profoundest depths of the human psyche. To plunge this deeply into the fabric of our universal awareness is to sharpen the senses to a degree almost beyond expression. Here changes occur which alter the very construction of the soul. The world grows thin, allowing the voyager to see beyond the patterns of normal understanding. In this state visions are real, and the earth sends her dreams to lodge in our minds like arrows. Our blood sings with the energy of the Dragon, and we are truly changed.

The numen who guards the transformation of the god has its parallels in the outer world: it was common to find temples of the Classical period and earlier guarded by pet snakes, fed on milk by the priests and priestesses, and encouraged to take up residence in or near the sacred precinct.

The Dome of the Serpents at Rouffignac in France may well represent the earliest illustration of the magical power of the serpent to be found anywhere. Dating from many thousands of years before the more famous Lascaux murals, (probably around 7000 BC) a multitude of coiling forms covers the roof of a cave cut deep into the ancient rock. One recent investigator has suggested they were set there as a form of protection against the unknown; but a far more likely hypothesis is that they are simply a visual glyph of the energy which courses through the body of the earth like a snake within its nest (282). Even archeologists, generally wary of committing themselves, have suggested that certain of these earliest cave paintings may represent water cults – suggesting the flow of earth energy so often linked with actual underground springs and rivers.

Among the Warramunga tribesmen of Australia the serpent is a sign of manhood which they wear painted on back and breast. A part of their sacred ceremonies consists of crawling to the back of a hollow scooped out of the earth beneath a huge rock, from which position alone it is possible to view the painted picture of the sacred snake, Yarapi, painted on the underside of the stone (174). This is clearly reminiscent of the carved spiral and maze forms found inside tombs and mounds in the Celtic world, where only the dead (or those temporarily suspended by an initiatory drink) could see and understand their significance.

That the snake was also sacred to the Moon Goddess is well known, and is preserved today in the astronomical terminology for the points at which the terrestrial and lunar orbits coincide. The ascending node, where the moon's orbit passes first through that of the earth, is called the Dragon's Head, and the descending node, where the two intersect again, the Dragon's Tail. The line drawn between the two is called the Dragon line, and the time between the passage of the moon through the same lunar node is termed the Dragon's month. If this were not remarkable enough in itself, the symbols used to represent these intersections are very closely similar to the decorative patterns worn by the Warramungas (Figure 3).

Warramunga		Astronomical		Ascending
Tribal		signs of		
Signs		Lunar nodes		Decending

Figure 3

As Joseph Henderson points out in *The Wisdom of the Serpent,* having remarked upon the universality of the snake as a symbol of renewal:

> This lies essentially in mankind's having projected into this . . . creature his own secret wish to obtain from the earth a know-ledge he cannot find in waking daylight consciousness alone. This is the knowledge of death and rebirth forever withheld except at those times where some transcendental principle, emerging from the depth, makes it available to consciousness (108).

Just such a transcendental principle was the Dragon energy, which emerged from the depth to illuminate and transform mankind's relationship with the earth.

So far we have looked chiefly at the terrestial power of the Dragon as it is seen to reflect the energy of the earth. But just as its shining coils linked the sacred sites into a network of vitalizing force, so in the heavens it was seen to perform a similar function. The Dragon was identified with the constellation Draco, whose chief star, Draconis, was once the Pole Star of the ancient West. Around this the heavens revolved, protected by the coils of the Dragon, prompting the Italian astronomer, Sabbathai Donolo (c. AD 940) to write: 'When God created the two lights [sun and moon], the five stars [the planets] and the twelve signs [the Zodiac] he also created the fiery dragon, that it might connect them together, moving about like a weaver with his shuttle' (18).

In Australia, where the Aboriginal culture still contains much that parallels the Foretime, the vital force which animates the land is still recognized; it travels roads laid down by the Gods themselves, in the Dream Time. These ways are cast in a mirror image of the star-paths and are recorded in a visual glyph known as a *tjuringa,* a small stone carved in patterns of lines and circles which encode the paths of the earth-force. They can be used for orienteering, and enable their wielders to travel great distances across the trackless Australian bushland (168).

More than one researcher has noticed the similarity between the marks found on these *tjuringas* and those found at megalithic sites: in particular the curious cup-and-ring markings discovered at a large number of sacred places but never satisfactorily explained (99). It becomes clear, however, that such marks are far more than ordinary maps. They represent not merely geographical formations, but are also guides to the Otherworld; a shaman, wishing to make contact with the hidden vitality of the land, contemplates the *tjuringa,* using it as a gateway to the inner realm.

Everywhere around them our ancestors saw signs of the forces which guided and inspired them. Here was a hill which gave access to the Otherworld; there a stream where the gods of Summer and Winter fought for the hand of the Spring Maiden. But there were other, more potent, signs.

It is still quite common to come across curiously striated hills, roughly conical in shape but with flattened tops, and to find in connection with them an accompanying folk-tale of the Great Worm which, meeting its fate at the hands of a local Hero or Saint, squeezed the hill in its coils, imprinting the land with the shape of its agony.

Here is embodied the story of a great change which overtook the Dragon power and its relationship with mankind. It may seem a long way from the Dragon priests to the heroes remembered chiefly as *slayers* of the dragon; yet they are closely related to the pattern of change and decay which overcame the Native Mysteries. Dragon-priest to Dragon-slayer is but a small step when seen in the light of the Christian adoption of ancient sites to build their churches.

Where the ancient priests stood as interpreters and purveyors of earth energy, the new religion brought condemnation of the old ways. Dragon energy and its related symbolism became outlawed, and was later identified with the Edenic Serpent, a creature to be spurned beneath the heel of its slayers – usually St Michael or St George, whose role is recorded in the dedications of churches to them at places once associated with Dragon power.

But the importance of the old serpent mounds remains. On the one hand they indicate the presence of Dragon energy, which may be invoked by the action of climbing them – though this is best not done without some prior intention. But their main importance is their relationship to the maze.

We have encountered this image several times now. We shall do so again. Nor should we be surprised to find that in connection with the mysteries of the earth it is of considerable importance. The serpent, as we have seen, is a symbol of the magic power of the earth; its sinuous form is a subtly changing, *living* maze, closely associated with initiatory experience. In the mythology of the Hopi Indians of Arizona, these elements come together even more closely.

For the Hopi the symbol of the maze is that of the Mother, and represents a passage through different levels of understanding (280). It points the way, through symbolic truth, to actual experience – the way of the serpent being synonymous with the way of the earth, and both represented by the initiation of the maze.

Hills possessing a serpentine shape, such as Glastonbury Tor or the Herefordshire Beacon, or indeed the great mound of Silbury Hill which lies adjacent to one of the most important temples of serpent power in Britain – at Avebury – are all associated with earth mysteries. Geoffrey Ashe has recently suggested that the Tor was intended as a ritual site, which, when walked in procession, gave admittance to an interior world (7). Silbury, for all attempts to explain it, remains an enigma unless seen as a spiral dragon-hill.

The importance of the serpent in the Foretime can be seen in the shapes adopted by their temple builders, who laid out many of the great stone edifices to conform to the pattern of the earth-force. Thus at Avebury, whose serpentine form was first recognized in the eighteenth century, the circle is crossed by a serpent-like avenue, while at Carnac in Brittany, the name of which is derived from 'Cairn-Hac', Hill of the Serpent, the coiling shape assumed by the many hundreds of stone avenues is both an image of the serpent and the maze.

But perhaps the most sensational image of this kind is found in the United States, at Adams County, Ohio. It takes the form of a vast serpentine earthwork, over 1,254 feet in length, arranged in seven coils ending in a triple-coiled tail. In its jaws it holds an egg, symbol of creation, and it combines to express both maze and spiral in a single form. Built by the earliest inhabitants of the American continent, it is one of the clearest representations of the Native Tradition in the USA. Coupled with the Hopi symbol already discussed, it makes a clear statement of the universality of the cult (232).

The oldest way of raising the power of the serpent was the Maze dance – performed as a path to enlightenment and a joining with the gods. Traces of these ritual dance-floors have been found as far apart as Germany, Greece, Australia, and Britain, where relics of several hundred labyrinths can still be detected (230). To enter the maze is to try the passage of death; to emerge is to be reborn – patterns which still bear meaning for us today. In this, as in the carved spirals of the tomb builders, the serpentine coils through which the initiate moved or danced towards his birth were representative of both the womb and of the seed which passed through it – from both came new life, the energy of creation carried through the earth by the power of the Dragon/Serpent.

This was the function also of the barrow mounds discussed earlier in this chapter. Maes Howe in the Orkneys, La Houge Bie in the Channel Isles, Brugh na Boyne in Ireland, West Kennet in Wiltshire – all were to some extent images of the earth-womb. Here, just as the initiate would lie in drugged sleep to take the vision quest and return with word of the ancestors, so the bones of the dead were laid in foetal pose to await rebirth. Painted red to signify the life-force, the blood of the tribe, they were a reminder of the way back into the earth which all must one day take.

The final period in which Dragon power was actively worked with and recognized was marked by a steady decline which all but obscured knowledge of the lines of force and the true use of the ancient sites it vivified. After the Foretime, when the shamanic priests focused the energy felt by all, a change took place. Gradually, the priesthood came to stand between the people and their gods, becoming increasingly the guardians of a secret knowledge intended only for the few. By the advent of Christianity there were few who remembered the old ways well enough to offer opposition. Those who did were either killed or held up as objects of ridicule by the followers of the new way. It was a pattern which would be often repeated throughout the ages, and is still prevalent in our own time.

But though obscured for ages, the mystery of Dragon power and the sites of its tenure remained largely untouched by the passage of years. They awaited their recovery, and in time it came, in the shape of Alfred Watkins and the ley-line enthusiasts – many working in ignorance of the real significance of what they had stumbled upon – and in a few Hermetically trained magicians of our own time, who have begun to see the Dragon energy as a source too long neglected.

Though it is no longer possible to see the pattern whole and entire as it once was, there still exist enough fragments of knowledge which, combined with the evidence of the sites themselves, can enable us to restore the picture. Reports by such eighteenth century antiquaries as John Aubrey (11) and William Stukeley (251) who saw many of the sites virtually intact (and incidentally praised their 'classical' design) give evidence of their original form. Other evidence is hidden in folk-lore (185) where the Dragon appears regularly as a creature of fearsome character and fiery breath – and as a guardian of immense treasure: a half-conscious harking-back to the treasure of life and energy once found beneath its sign.

None of this can substitute for a personal visit to one of the ancient sites. They are still largely neglected; speculation about their purpose has obscured the fact that they are there to be used, and that within them lies a source of contact with the Native Wisdom Tradition which constitutes the backbone of the Western Way.

THE WISDOM OF THE EARTH

We have spoken of the first magics, the passionate awareness of the living being upon which we walk, and of the way her worshippers discovered this and the energies which flowed through it. The symbol of the Dragon represented those energies until it fell into disrepute. But no matter how we see the energies of the earth we have to learn to exercise responsibility for what has been held in trust for us for thousands of years. The wisdom of the earth is ours for the seeking; but we have to be careful how we go about the search. Nowadays we have grown away from the earth and out of step with her rhythms. Where once we acknowledged her influence on our lives, cared for and garnered her riches, we now rape and destroy, greedily snatching all she has to offer by way of food and mineral resources, leaving her barren and ruined, her once fair face furrowed by our roads and pocked with our houses and factories. The earth is now considered by many as a dead object whose resources we can strip at will.

This has been the story since the advent of civilization. We have taken what we wanted and given back increasingly less; we have lost touch with an ages-old understanding, a relationship with the environment which was once one of sharing, and where the division of spoils never exceeded the necessary; where we gave back to the earth, in a full and complete understanding of the act, our most precious commodity – the body – to feed and nourish her.

Even the recent ecological trend has recognized this. When the scientists Lovelock and Epton developed their theory of the globe as a living entity (216), they named her Gaia at the suggestion of the novelist William Golding; thus echoing her classical and pre-classical worshippers and answering to an instinct which predates ecological science by many thousands of years. As Theodore Roszak, commenting on this, noted: 'There clings to the image something of an older and once universal natural philosophy that quite spontaneously experienced the earth as a divine being animated by its own moods and intentions – the primordial Mother Earth' (216). It is this 'universal philosophy' which lies behind the stone circles and Dragon paths, the Serpent power and the initiation-dreams of the mound builders. Within the earth lay all secrets: the way to the Otherworld and the Ancestors. But more than this the earth was a dwelling place for personified energies, the first Shapers of the world, who laboured long over its perfection, and came in time to be bound beneath it.

The classical myths of the Titans are the clearest representation of this, and if studied they can offer us a profound message about the way we treat the earth and what may happen if we fail to restore the original state of balance which once existed between ourselves and our environment. The clue lies in the use of the word 'titanic' – originally meaning 'lord', but now more often applied to the most awesome energies of the earth: the force of the volcano, the whirling wind, the hunger of the ocean.

The Titans were the children of Gaia and Uranus, Earth-Mother and Sky-Father, and they sided with their mother against the cruelty of Uranus, who had banished their elder brothers to the underworld of Tartarus. Choosing Cronos for their leader, they laid siege to their father and Cronos castrated him with a flint sickle. The blood from his wounds fathered the Erinnys, the Furies, who are bound to avenge crimes of family bloodshed. On Uranus's death, Cronos assumed his father's power (91, 129).

These are the first, the primal ones, whose deeds are immeasurably savage, whose stature is huge. The next generation of gods were no less so. Cronos married his sister Rhea – another Earth-Mother. But Uranus and Gaia had prophesied that Cronos would be dethroned by one of his children, and so every child born to him by Rhea, he devoured. But Rhea secretly bore another child, Zeus, and hid him away, substituting a stone for her child in the cradle, which Cronos duly swallowed. Zeus returned as cup-bearer to his father when he was grown up, and gave Cronos a poisoned drink which acted as an emetic. Rhea's children were disgorged and restored whole to her. Cronos in turn was banished – some say to the British Isles, where he sleeps still. Zeus and his siblings formed the Olympian pantheon and the Titans were chained beneath the earth.

While these legends tell us much about the power struggle which took place between succeeding Greek races, the archetypes have their resonance with our own times. Nothing has changed in one sense: we are still the children of Gaia and her energies are still ours to command – to be freed, loosed or harnessed, according to our needs. As is all too obvious we are not in control of them, and the Titanic energies which spilled over into violence in the myth threaten to do so again today.

The forces of nature have always been rightly feared and human-kind's relationship to them has always been a changing one. In one sense it has always been a struggle to combat and protect ourselves from them. Fear of giants and monsters, perpetuated by these early Greek models, recurs again and again in the mythologies of other lands. It was this which resulted in the change of the Dragon into the Serpent of the Judeo-Christian Fall: the Beast of the Apocalypse, overcome by the Woman Clothed By the Sun in Revelations chapter 12 (21). Yet the Titanic nature of the Dragon is well attested. In the Babylonian myth of Tiamat and Marduk, Tiamat is a gigantic sea-dragon, and her children are also Titans. She is conquered and her body riven apart to form the matter of the cosmos – her liquids become rivers, her breath the air, her bones the rocks. Once again the story is of Titanic forces, imprisoned through the creation of life, and the Tiamat story in part explains the fear of the Symbolic Feminine in her primal, Titanic closeness to the elements (71).

Today the Titanic forces have made their latest manifestation in the shape of the nuclear threat. Gaia's children rise again and one above all dominates the scene – Uranus. The first-born personified the earth's energies as gods, and confined the Titans within the earth while the Olympians were assumed into heaven as constellations. The Titans gave their names to minerals and elements, one of which is currently to the forefront of consciousness: uranium, the major component from which the world's most destructive weapons are made.

Uranium has not, of course, always been used for nuclear technology; nor is it evil in itself. Left in the earth it is a positive source of energy, as are the Titans themselves. They are Gaia's children, the personifications of her energies, without which all would be barren. But this is reversed when they are brought out, or when uranium is exposed under the light of the Olympian heavens. Again we seem to hear an echo of the ancient myth which poses the gods of heaven against those of earth.

We have not had much respect for mineral life in this century. If we treated the minerals we mine from the earth as living entities, we would at last be showing responsibility towards the forces we seek to master. As followers of the Western Way we have a unique opportunity to work with the Titanic energies, and to channel their power through the earth, by the activation of the ancient sites.

We are the people of the earth, the guardians of her energies, the custodians of her wisdom. As the nuclear question becomes a key issue for all manner of people, we begin to reach an understanding that all energy – Titanic or human – has its own flow which can be misapplied or used appropriately – and that we are its wielders.

Stories of the Titanic forces of the earth have not remained static. They grew and changed with time. Ultimately all stories of giants derive from memories of a projected Golden Age where Titanic energy was seen as beneficial rather than as destructive.

But, as with all perfect states, the edges were blurred with time. Memories of the Titans were replaced by those of quarrelsome and all-too-human gods and goddesses. Finally they too were reduced to the Faery-Folk, the dwellers-under the-hill. Paradise, the Realm of the Shining Ones, became the Otherworld, and the people of the Golden Age became its inhabitants.

However, the Titanic archetypes have left their images on the landscape itself. The vast shapes incised on the plains of Nazca, or the great chalk hill figures of Southern Britain, are testimonies to the way in which the first-born saw the originators of our race: the Gods before the gods (45). Echoes of Atlantis, of a time when evil, sickness and death were virtually banished, remain at the deepest levels of our consciousness. From Plato to Tolkien the archetype of the Golden Age continues to fascinate, and behind it lies an awareness of the old earth magic in its earliest form.

But the natural forces which vitalized the earth became something to exploit rather than something to work with, and as a result, the ancient ancestral levels of experience sank deeper into memory, becoming harder to reach except by long and often perilous paths. Yet inwardly the ancient chthonic powers remain unchanged, gradually rising again from immeasurable depths, until in our own time they have begun to return to the surface again. The Old Gods may thus be said to walk abroad again; but it must be said that they do not always take a palatable form. The example of Uranus is apposite here: the current misuse of uranium has caused it to assume monstrous proportions.

Properly understood and recognized, it is still not too late to redeem the misuse to which Titanic energies have been put; many are once again being tapped into and worked with creatively. But we have to get to know them thoroughly, to recover them from beneath the layers of unconscious thought to which they have long been consigned.

Nor does this imply a back to nature mentality: we are everywhere the unknowing possessors of a lost landscape of circle and stone, trackway and mound. If we are once again to be in tune with the Titanic energies which still vivify them – though in changed form – we must visit them, get up early and find them in the dawn or even earlier, when the silence is complete and the Titanic beings close at hand. It matters not where or even how we approach the earth, save only that we do so in the spirit of love and caring and with a just degree of respect. Awesome strengths lie just beneath our feet, not to be used for idle curiosity. Remember that you tread on sacred ground and that you have already taken the first step towards a relationship with the mystery beneath, and that here you may invoke the old powers of the Western Way, sleeping lightly under the surface of the earth. Cernunnos, the Horned God, or Wayland, Smith of the Gods, or even earlier, more primaeval forms, may rise to greet you from the green hill sides.

The task we set ourselves is one of spiritual ecology, the seeking of our own personal contact with the spirit of the earth, whether we find this in the image of the Dragon, through walking the maze, or in following the outlines of a stone circle. There are many hundreds of sacred sites in our homelands; many are ruinous or totally destroyed; others still active. They await your visit, for in the right frame of mind you can awaken their slumbering energies. To vitalize a single centre of the energy grid is to send out ripples to every part of the land. And then you may indeed find that you 'stand in a place that is holy ground and . . . breathe the intoxicating exhalations as did the sibyls of old' (218). But whether these things happen or not, one thing is certain: you will never be quite the same again. And neither will the land.

MAGIC EARTH EXERCISE NOTES

As we have said, the best way to experience at first hand the power of the earth energies is to visit one of the sites. Try to approach the old places along one of the sacred ways. Many are described in the writings of Watkins, Michell, Devereux, Screeton or Pepper (281, 168, 66, 227, 197). Others await your own discovery. They may be either stone circle, chambered tomb or serpent mounds – but the question still remains of what to do when you arrive. There are many possibilities, given the right circumstances, which you may discover for yourselves; two are offered here as a way into the world of the earth mysteries.

The first exercise is for use in relation to one of the old tracks, and may be applied to any ancient pathway which still retains the serpent energy. It comes from the great assemblage of native myth and lore known as the *Mabinogion,* and concerns the figure of Sarn Elen, or Elen of the Roads who is, according to Sir John Rhys (213), a goddess of sunset and dawn who watches over the ancient ways by night. To invoke her, and to walk one of these ways from dusk to dawn, is to open up the inner landscape of your country to your waking eye. The pathworking which follows is part of her story, and use of it is to invoke the most ancient laws of dream and mystery. So use it with care and in a proper frame of mind, remembering that these are not merely images or archetypes to be juggled with at our will – but the most potent energies which underlie all our life and being. Treat them with respect and they will respond. Enter their presence in a spirit of disrespect or levity and do not expect to experience anything.

The second exercise is intended primarily to give a deeper understanding of the nature of the terrestrial zodiacs. Although it is based upon what is known of the example to be found at Glastonbury, it can, with only a little adaptation, be applied to other such sites. Thus the serpent mounds of the Americas would be suitable, as would Mont Saint Michel in Brittany. It is not necessary to have visited any of these sites – though of course to have done so would be useful. Careful study of a photograph or painting of the place before attempting the meditation would be just as satisfactory – the essence of the realization being in *what* happens rather than in *where* it happens.

EXERCISE 4   THE SHIMMERING WAY

As you relax with eyes closed, gradually let your surroundings fade. You find that you are standing at the top of a hill: not a high one, but one which nonetheless permits you to see for a considerable distance across the countryside that surrounds you. Facing West you see before you a faint but well-trodden path leading down from the hill and out across the flat lands at its foot. On every side stretches a chequered pattern of fields, and as you look down at them they move and whisper, stirred by a warm breeze from the South, looking for all the world like a many-coloured sea. But through the midst of them all the path leads away and away into the distance, vanishing at last into a haze of mist which might hide higher ground.

Starting down from the hill you begin following the path. Insects hum round you and there is a sound of distant birds, but otherwise the world seems as silent and still as though it had only recently woken from a long sleep.

For a long while you walk onward, always following the faint track. Gradually the sun begins to descend in a fiery glow, and dusk advances towards darkness. As the daylight fades you become aware that the path is rising again, and that it is faintly glimmering with a light of its own.

Still you follow it, climbing steadily all the while now, until you find yourself at the beginning of a range of hills leading towards a soaring bulk of mountainous country. The moon has risen now, and floods the scene with silvery light. Though you wonder that you do not feel tired, you press on, climbing higher through the cool night air, scented with night-time flowers and a sense of growing and burgeoning life.

At length, after climbing for some time, you round a shoulder of the mountains, and see before you the entrance to a narrow valley, filled with moonlight and shadows. As you pause for a moment you see that at the head of the valley on a wide shelf of rock at the foot of more mountains, stands a great circle of ancient, weathered stones, wreathed in coils of white mist. The path you have been following leads straight to the circle. Hurrying now, you press onward, for this is your destination.

Arriving at the circle you find that the stones are far greater than you had realized. They tower over you, casting long shadows on the ground. But there is no sense of threat about them. You are welcome here, and press forward without fear.

Inside, at the centre of the circle, is a great monolith, lying lengthwise on the earth. Seated upon this, as though in a natural chair, is the slender figure of a woman. Her hair is long and glinting, and her gown is of rich red stuff edged with gold. Over it she wears a rich blue cloak, fastened at the left shoulder with a round brooch of intricate workmanship. Her face is of such beauty that you know she cannot be of mortal stock, and you bow low before her in awe and wonderment.

For several moments you kneel thus before the golden Lady, until at last you hear words that seem to form themselves within your mind.

'What seek you here?'

You must answer truthfully and without hesitation:

'I seek Sarn Elen. I seek a key to the Shimmering Way.'

'Sarn Elen you have found. Why seek you the Shimmering Way?'

'That I may come to learn the mystery of the land.'

'Then you are well come.'

Silently the Lady, whom you now know to be Sarn Elen, rises from the stone and beckons you to follow. As you do so you notice that both the central stone and all the rest of the circle are intricately carved with spirals and lines, like huge maps. Try to remember something of what you see, for you may need them later.

You follow the Lady to the Western edge of the circle, and find that you are standing as though in a gateway. Before you the ground falls rapidly away towards a great plain that stretches to the horizon. Criss-crossing it are many faintly glowing lines, interspersed at certain points with spirals of light. You realize that the designs on the stones of the circle are related directly to them, and that what you are seeing is a network of ancient trackways connecting other circles and standing stones across the whole country and beyond.

As you watch, the Lady raises her arms and at her command the lines of light burn brighter until you can hardly bear to look at them. You feel the energy coursing through the land to your feet and then rising through your own body until it reaches the crown of your head and flows over you. You feel yourself bathed in light, and though you dare not look directly at the Lady you know that she shines forth like a great beacon-star into the night.

Slowly the light begins to fade, until it is once more only a faint glimmer in the moon-washed land. Turning away you find that Elen of the Roads is no longer at your side, nor indeed anywhere in the circle, and that the sky is beginning to be flushed with the first rose-hue of dawn. As you stand amid the circle of great stones, the scene slowly fades, and you find yourself once again seated where you began the journey. Let yourself return slowly to normal consciousness, but remember that now the Shimmering Ways are open to you to visit at any time, and that when you next walk one of the ancient ways you will be aware of the energy and life which is a part of them, and is now a part of you.

EXERCISE 5   THE TERRESTRIAL ZODIAC

You are standing at the top of a rise looking towards the shape of a great Hill. It is night, but there is a full moon and you have no difficulty in seeing what follows. The Hill is surrounded by water upon which small, light craft ply to and fro in the moonlight. Mist rises from the earth on all sides, so that you seem to be standing on an island in more senses than one. You can see people moving about on the side of the Hill nearest you. They are dressed in long robes and carry torches that flare and smoke in the damp air, adding to the miasmic quality of the scene. At the top of the Hill is a great trilithon of ancient stones, and as you look, a brilliant glow begins to shine out from within them. It grows brighter and brighter until the whole scene is bathed in light and a great ball of fire rises from the Hill and climbs heavenward, where it hovers, casting a brilliant glow over everything. From it rays of light shine forth, falling on the tops of hills on every side, some close to, some far off. Answering gleams of light come from these hills, and you become aware that a great host of people is gathering on all sides, though you cannot see them. Your eyes are again drawn to the Hill, and there you see a great figure which you know to be the King climbing the last stretch of the hillside, bearing across his outstretched arms a great sword in a sheath of red and gold.

At the summit, just beyond the edge of the trilithon, stands a figure clad in shimmering robes. This is the Lady, and though she seems no taller than the King, she is somehow larger than life, invested with titanic stature and majesty. At her shoulder stands a great white horse, its coat gleaming in the light, its eyes flashing as it tosses its head. The King advances and exchanges a symbolic greeting with the Lady of the Hill. He then mounts the great steed and raises the sword, still sheathed, above his head. From the darkness that seems impenetrable around the stones, twelve figures appear, each with a sign of the Zodiac painted on their brows. Each one bears a symbol, some of which you may be able to see, and others not. These are the Twelve Treasures of the Year, linked with the inner life of the Land, and the figures are their guardians. They form a circle, raising their symbols towards the Lady and the King. Then they turn until they are facing outwards and begin to move. Faster and faster they move, until they form a bright ring of light. The King and the Lady always remain still at the centre, the axle of the turning wheel. Soon the light grows too bright for you to see the figures clearly any longer. They become a whirling wheel of light, which now rises from the Hill and ascends towards the glowing light which still hovers overhead. The two meet and become one, burning even brighter for a moment before beginning to fade, dispersing outward to the stars. Slowly the scene returns to normal. The Hilltop is deserted and only the light of the moon shines serenely over all. Awake slowly to your own place again, but try to remember as much of what you may have realized as possible.

You have the opportunity to work with one figure of the Zodiac every month, as the wheel of the year turns. See the wheel surrounding your land and people, and mediate the energies of the requisite sign outwards. In times of national crisis, focus upon the King and Lady of the Hill as the axial balance of the wheel, for they are the symbolic guardians of the land.

CHAPTER 3
Meeting the gods

An innate knowledge of the Gods is coexistant with our very essence.

Iamblichus: *De Mysterii.*

All the gods are one god; and all the goddesses are one goddess, and there is one initiator.

Dion Fortune: *Aspects of Occultism.*

NATIVE MYTHS AND GOD-FORMS

Every country has its native myth cycles: they are what makes the inner reality of the land. Thus it is very important for us to be familiar with the mythology of our own place, and to understand where it fits in the overall myth-patterns of the West. Anthropologists like Ken Wilber (287) or John Layard (135) can help us here; as can mythographers like Joseph Campbell (39) and Robert Graves (92). But we need to go further than any of these if we are to achieve the kind of intimate knowledge required. In a book of this scope it is obviously not possible to deal with more than a selection of the archetypes and scenarios which make up the native mythos. We have chosen to deal primarily with Celtic myths, since these are generally more accessible than, say, Nordic or Teutonic cycles. In keeping to one mythology, and that one with which we are familiar and have worked with ourselves, we can more easily show a complete set of archetypes in use.

This is not to say that others are less valid. To a native of the Germanic world the Siegfried myths incorporated into the *Nibelungenlied* (187) would be more appropriate than the Ulster cycle or the Arthurian mythos. The same is true of the Finnish Kalevala (125), the French Charlemagne cycle (50) or the Spanish epic of the Cid

(55). In the Americas there are the earth magics of the Hopi Indians (280), or the grim mythology of the Aztec and Toltec cultures (138). Each of these is the native myth of the country concerned. All are part of the Western Mystery Tradition, and many have lent aspects of themselves to our own more familiar magical territory. This is because all myths were once the same myths: the quest for fire, the naming of the gods, the rites of passage, and the discovery of agriculture and animal husbandry, as well as the process which metamhorphosed the *genius loci* into anthropomorphic forms. Only the immense stretch of time has confused and darkened the lines of the mythic universe, combining deities of sun and moon, earth and stars, dividing those of corn and wine, lightning and rain; mingling and intermingling form with form, until it takes a considerable effort of mind to separate them into their original shapes and descriptions.

It is no easy thing to see the outlines of the early Celtic deities. Written records are scarce. Caesar, to whose account we owe most of our contemporary information, is less reliable than he might be (37). Yet, if we cannot read about the ancient gods we can be aware of them in other ways. If we are to learn to work with the major Western archetypes, this is what we must do. And we can only do so by learning to recognize and work with the individual qualities of our native god-forms.

Once, every tree, stone and spring had a tutelary spirit which those who approached it could seek out, with which they could establish contact. In a larger sense the whole country had a national identity embodied in the spirit of place, or as it would nowadays be termed, the racial archetype. The wrinkled faces of ancient stones were the faces of the gods, and the voices of brook and stream the voices of their identity. We have largely forgotten the names of these person-ifications – though they may still be detected in the old names of those places where our ancestors once worshipped. The greater forces, those whose characteristics went beyond the merely local, were neglected also, but not forgotten. They lived on in changing form, through the stories and poems which grew up around them, enshrining something of their mystery and worship as their outer forms grew blurred with time and neglect.

These were the Gods, and their children were the figures of fairy-tale and hero-story: like the Bear-God, Artos, whose cult was once widespread in Britain, but who became absorbed into the cycle of stories centring around the figure of national hero – Arthur of Britain. Or like Arianrhod, once a moon-goddess, but who in the

Mabinogion (146) becomes a semi-human character, the only vestige of her original role remaining in her name which means 'Silver-Wheel'.

So the forms changed, and the old names were either forgotten or grew new meanings and identities. But they never went away; their worship continued in isolated areas, long after the coming of new ways and beliefs. Sometimes here, at last, they died out, or became absorbed by new deities. Or else they dwindled to become the dwellers in the Hollow Hills, the Faery-Folk, of whom so much has been written and so little understood. Folk memory enshrined their names and natures, but seldom their functions. They grew old and weary and perhaps in time they went away. But others adapted, retreating into the deep places of the earth or passing into timeless sleep that took no thought of the strange antics of human beings.

Until at length, people began to seek out these ancient denizens of the inner world, to acknowledge their once proud heritage as rulers of earth and sky. The medieval witch-cults recognized the mystery of the natural elements and began to worship as their ancestors had done. They were following the natural cycle of decay and rebirth of which we have spoken already: the law that says that nothing is ever wasted, that causes seemingly forgotten beliefs and powers to spring up again with renewed vigour, and to find new followers among the disaffected and the wise.

Those who go forth on the Western Way are just such people: to them, the old gods and goddesses are not dead, they are potent forces in archetypal guise. If we are to follow the native mysteries, we must be able to recognize the faces of the gods. Study the very selective gazetter which follows: these archetypes should become part of your daily meditation and practice. This is the first step towards a deeper appreciation of the gods behind gods, the archetypal energies of which we spoke in chapter 2. However, it is important to realize that what is worshipped in the outer world as deity may, in the inner realm, become a personalized energy to be worked with directly.

This is one of the most profound mysteries of the Western Way. It shows how we may re-establish a harmonic with the inner reality represented by the children of the earth. Our ancestors knew this well, and enshrined it in their religious beliefs and practices. To our ancestors, the earth's first children were the Gods, and *their* children the heroes who came after. In the blurring which occurs in the immense distance of time separating us from them, it is often hard to tell where god or goddess ends and hero or heroine begins. Thus the figure of Bran, in the Welsh pantheon, is clearly a god, and Gawain, in the Arthur cycle, just as clearly a hero, but one who happens to assume the sun-mantle of midsummer godhead. But who, or what, is Merlin? No god perhaps, but certainly a great tutelary guardian of the inner realm. There are many answers to these questions, and no one may know them all. The Gods have many garments and each is a name. We can make no attempt here to separate them into ranks of mortal and immortal. The answers to such questions are just as likely to be provided by those who work with these archetypes as by the authors of books. No matter what your own background may be or what country you may hail from, you will recognize the type of the Gods – Thunderer, Shiner, Watcher over the Land. The lord or the lady of the moon is known in all lands, as are the gods of river and tree and stone.

Much is written about the gods, especially those of the Norse and Greek worlds – but few writers ever go beyond the delineation of type and character: whether Bacchus was a typical wine-god or Poseidon purely a god of the sea. Yet these were no mere abstractions to those who worshipped them. We seem to forget that the people of the ancient world were also possessed of faith, that they believed in the absolute power of their gods. One has only to read Iamblichus (115) or Plutarch (203), or Apuleius (5) to see the truth of this. They had a system of belief, a theology, quite as complex and meaningful as any held today. The Gods permeated everything. As the Neoplatonist, Iamblichus (AD 250–325), says:

> The power of the Gods is not partibly comprehended by any place or partible human body . . . but is wholly everywhere present within the natures that are capable of receiving it. . . . Moreover, existing itself prior to all things, by its own separate nature, it becomes sufficient to fill all things, so far as each is able to partake of it (115).

It is doubly important for us to realize this today, for it is telling us to tread carefully. We are not wholly empty vessels waiting to be filled up by a sudden inrush of god or earth energy. Iamblichus is clear about this: the power is sufficient to fill all things, *so far as each is able to partake of it*. These are not mere empty abstractions with which we are dealing. Remember also, that while the god-forms of the Native Tradition can still be utilized in as valid a way as the Messianic figures of revealed religion, they need first to be regenerated. One of the problems of working with ancient archetypes in esoteric work is the quality of the material which is communicated by means of analeptic memory. The nature of the pagan contacts often reflects earlier and more primitive concerns. The material and contacts are valid in themselves but need to be synthesized into modern consciousness by a mediating of love, wisdom and power.

Those who find the worship of orthodox religion difficult are unlikely to find work with ancient god-forms any more congenial. The truth of the matter is that *the god-form is the representative of an abstract energy*, which the esotericist, rather than worshipping, mediates to Middle Earth. God and initiate are co-creators, each reflecting the worlds in which they live (see chapter 4). By identification and subsequent affiliation with the god, the initiate works with certain energies which are themselves transformative. By close attention and sensitivity to the energies represented by the god-form, the initiate is drawn into intimate contact with and awareness of that archetypal energy. This is what is meant when we speak of someone 'being contacted'. It forms the basis of religion when it is informed by cosmic understanding rather than naive superstition. In this way, it is possible to work with pagan god-forms (relating as they are to energies now represented by later archetypes), as long as their energies are fully synthesized into modern consciousness.

If once we accept this we are able to understand the full significance and efficacy of the signs which are the faces of the Gods. Iamblichus calls these *synthamata*, inexplicable images, and accords them an individual power to work within the framework of creation. 'We do not' he says,

> perform these things through intellectual perception; since if this were the case, the intellectual energy . . . would be imparted by us . . . [instead] when we do not energize intellectually, the *synthamata* themselves perform by themselves their proper work, and the ineffable power of the Gods itself knows by itself, its own images (115).

This is to restate that the realities we recognize *outwardly* have their own *inner* correlatives, whether we call them Gods or archetypes, and that to work with them is to relate to them, in partnership of the divine work.

THE FACES OF THE GODS

Arianrhod. Goddess of moon and stars. Her legend appears in the *Mabinogion,* in the story of Math, Son of Mathonwy. Like Ceridwen (q.v.), with whom she has much in common, Arianrhod is an enchantress and initiator. She is a hard, stern mistress of destiny, setting heavy *geasa* (prohibitions) upon the candidate. Taliesin (q.v.) says that he spent three periods in the prison of Arianrhod, referring to the ever-spinning castle of the Celtic Otherworld, of which she is mistress, and to his initiation there. Caer Arianrhod is both the castle of Death and of Rebirth, and in Welsh stands for the Corona Borealis – the Crown of the North – suggesting a link between Arianrhod and the Greek Ariadne, who received a crown from Dionysus which became known as the Corona in subsequent myths. As she is so firmly rooted in the Otherworld, Arianrhod has no associated places, though she is most definitely a stellar contact.

REFERENCES *Mabinogion* (146), Gruffydd (96), Ross (215).

Arthur. Son of Uther Pendragon, King of Britain, and Igraine, an Atlantean princess brought hither by Merlin (q.v.). Taken by the enchanter at birth to be brought up in secret and trained in the arts of kingship, war and magic, Arthur subsequently achieved the mystery of the Sword in the Stone, by this proving his right to rule. He founded the Round Table of knights dedicated to bringing order in the world – their work reflected in inner as well as outer realms. He married Guinevere, who represented the matriarchal mystery schools of Britain, and who through her love for Lancelot brought about the downfall of Arthur's kingdom. He passed to Avalon, one of the many names for the Otherworld, after a final battle, in which he slew and was wounded by his son Mordred, there to be healed of his wounds by Morgan le Fay (q.v.). By some seen to be waiting for the time when he will be needed, he sleeps beneath hollow hills as far apart as Alderley Edge in Cheshire and Mount Etna in Italy. No single place of contact can be singled out, though there are numerous sites which bear his name. Really the tutelary spirit of the British Isles, he may be encountered at almost any site if the heart and will of the seeker are truly bent upon discovering him.

REFERENCES Malory (157), *Geoffrey of Monmouth* (85), *Mabinogion* (146), *The Welsh Triads* (268), Loomis (144), Morris (172), Ashe (8), Knight (132).

Bran the Blessed. Titanic God of the Celts. So vast was he that when once his followers desired to cross the ocean he waded across towing their ships behind him. A god of earth and mountain, his story is long and complex and can be found in the *Mabinogion*; but the deepest mystery associated with him concerns his 'death' at which he commanded that his head be struck from his body and carried thereafter by his followers. It continued to communicate with them for some time, and led them at last to a mysterious island (sometimes identified as Bardsey, off the South Wales coast) where the 'Company of the Noble Head' found lodging and were fed and entertained by Bran's head in a state of timeless joy. Finally one of the company opened a forbidden door which looked West and in this way they were reminded of their mortality and of the passing of time. Thereafter a few of the company, of whom Taliesin (q.v.) was one, carried the miraculous head to the White Mount (now called Tower Hill, in London) and buried it there. It was believed that while it remained undisturbed no enemy could ever conquer the land, but Arthur (q.v.) dug it up in the belief that no one but he should protect the country of Britain, and thereafter it was lost. There are many aspects of the story and character of Bran which make him a prototype Grail contact – his links with the fate of the land being the most obvious. He is also a type of the Cronos figure (q.v.) whose influence may still be felt at certain places. Dinas Bran, in Wales, has strong associations with him; though like Arthur his presence is diffuse and may be felt at many sites throughout the country.

REFERENCES *Mabinogion* (146), Ross (215), MacCana (148), Newstead (186).

Brigit/Brigantia. Irish Brigit, daughter of the Dagda of the Tuatha de Danaan (q.v.), is the goddess of poets, healing and smithcraft. She is sometimes called a triple goddess. She is remarkable in that her cult has passed down to the present with hardly any change. St Brigit of Kildare (AD 525) incorporated in her legend much of pagan Brigit's corpus. The Christian shrine at Kildare was maintained by twenty nuns – the twenty-first being Brigit herself; a sacred fire was kept burning in the middle of a sanctuary which was forbidden to men. It was extinguished at the Reformation, but the cult of St Brigit is still strong. She is a secondary patron of Ireland, but her Christian influence is somewhat softened in Scotland where she is concerned with the ills of women and the care of cattle. Her feast-day is

1 February, and invocations to her pagan as well as Christian aspect are best made at that time. In Britain she is associated with the figure of Brigantia, the local goddess of the Brigantes, a Celtic tribe of Northern England. A statue of Brigantia was found at Birrens where she bears the emblems of Victory and Minerva in Romano-British guise. Her places are (for St Brigit) the shrine at Kildare, Co. Kildare, and (for Brigantia) the whole of the West Riding, which has strong natural associations with her.

REFERENCES Ross (215), Rees (210), Carmichael (42), *Oxford Dictionary of Saints* (191).

Cailleach Beare or **Bheur, Carlin**. Cailleach means 'hag'; in polite Gaelic it is still used to refer to an old wife, or grandmother. The Cailleach is one of the great titans of the British isles: references to her remain in folklore, rarely in textual sources. The Cailleach Beare, or Hag of Beare, is the primeval goddess of South-West Ireland and, like her Scottish equivalent, the Cailleach Bheur, leaps across mountain ranges which are formed from stones dropped from her apron. Like Ceridwen (q.v.) she pursues her son – although the story is sometimes reversed so that she is the quarry, and the two follow a half-yearly chase, in which Summer and Winter compete for mastery. Like the Middle-Eastern goddess Tiamat, the Cailleach has many associations with water-dragon stories. Although she appears as a withered hag, she has the ability to show herself as a young maiden: the folk-rituals which accompany the feast of St Brigit (q.v.) hint that this transformation is accomplished at the transition from Winter to Spring. In Scottish lowland folklore the Cailleach becomes the Gyre Carlin, sometimes also called Nicnevin, or Daughter of the Bones, not unlike the Indian Kali in effect, from which it may be divined that she is scarcely the most comfortable of archetypes to work with. Places associated with the Cailleach are too numerous to be listed, but are often found in place names like the numerous mountains called Sliabh na Cailleach in Ireland and Scotland. The old rocks of the Beare Peninsula, Co. Cork and the glacial outcrops of North-West Scotland remember her and are her places.

REFERENCES MacKenzie (152), Ross (215).

Ceridwen. Goddess of Corn and of inspiration, she is described in *The Welsh Triads* as one of the three most beautiful women of the Island of Britain. She is the supreme initiator, the mistress of the

Mysteries. She possesses the Cauldron of Rebirth, the earliest proto-type of the Grail. In it she brewed an initiatory drink which Taliesin (q.v.) accidentally tasted, receiving all knowledge thereby. She is a shape-shifter, appearing in many guises to the candidate for initi-ation. As a guardian of wisdom, she can assume some frightening shapes, such as that of the Sow goddess, but her purpose was to inculcate responsibility for knowledge and its uses. Echoes of her personality are to be found both in Morgan le Fay (q.v.) and with the Celtic Battle Goddess known as the Morrigan. Her roots are deep in the earth of which she is mother, and is thus best encountered at earth mounds or the generally more ancient sacred sites. She is especially associated with Llyn Tegid, Bala, in Wales, and with Glastonbury in Somerset.

REFERENCES *Mabinogion* (146), Spence (240), Graves (92), Ashe (7).

Cernunnos/Herne. God of green and growing things; huntsman, spirit of earth and birth and masculinity. He is most often pictured as seated cross-legged and with antlers sprouting from his brow, as on the Gundestrup Cauldron (149). Sometimes seen as consort to Ceridwen (q.v.), with whom he is tutelary deity of many modern witch covens. As Herne the Hunter he is depicted leading the Wild Hunt, a pack of white hounds with red ears, rather in the manner of Gwynn-ap-Nudd (q.v.) or Arawn (q.v.). He is still to be seen at certain times of the year in Windsor Park, though the tree generally referred to as 'Herne's Oak' is not the best place to seek him. Indeed he is best not sought at all, as he will certainly come of his own accord once he has scented activity in his neighbourhood. A powerful and primitive contact, who opens the eyes to the deepest levels of nature.

REFERENCES: Spence (237), Ross (215), Markale (160), Petry (198), Mottram (173).

Cronos. Oldest and first of the primitive gods. Really belonging to Classical myth, his nearest comparable Celtic figure is Bran (q.v.), but Cronos is significant particularly for his association with Britain. He was reported by Diodorus Siculus (67) to have been bound in eternal and unchanging bondage, deep within the earth of the British Isles (see chapter 2). Thus he becomes the oldest of the many 'sleep-ing' god archetypes, of which Arthur (q.v.) and Bran both partake. As a tutelary spirit he is extremely powerful and should only be approached with caution. It is his destiny to wake in some future age, and since he is said to have ushered out the last great golden age of humanity's past, his eventual waking may well be the signal for a return to the ways and beliefs of that time. He is a god of earth and time, and only in the timelessness of cave or earth-mound can his presence be felt.

REFERENCES: Ashe (8), Graves (91), Powys (205).

Gawain/Cuchulainn. Heroic figures who share many aspects of the solar deities while retaining their own individuality. Both are noted for fiery temper, red hair, and for the waxing and waning of their strength throughout the day. Cuchulainn, also called the Hound of Ulster, is the more primitive figure in Irish myth, though one may catch glimpses of an earlier Gawain in the *Triads*, where he is called Gwalchmai: the Hawk of May. He becomes successively Christian-ized as his character develops, until in the great medieval poem *Sir Gawain and the Green Knight* he has become an exemplar of the Christian virtues set against the evil magic of Morgan le Fay (q.v.) and the Green Knight, a far older and darker figure akin to Cernunnos (q.v.). Gawain displays only dim echoes of the 'battle madness' of Cuchulainn, who goes through physical transformation during a fight. As solar beings, both have a freshness and strength which make them excellent companions on the way, and which is easily felt in the open air under a hot midsummer sky. To some, Gawain represents the ancient Hibernian mysteries, reaching back into Pictish times, and his association with the Orkney Islands suggests an Otherworld connection, since the Orkneys were regarded as a gateway to the Shining Lands. Cuchulainn can be said to be present in Ulster especially.

REFERENCES: *Sir Gawain & the Green Knight* (233), Malory (157), *The Welsh Triads* (268), O'Rahilly (190), *Tain* (256), Sutcliff (254), Steiner (247).

Gwynn ap Nudd/Arawn/Nuada/Nodens. Gwynn is the lord of Annwn, the Underworld, and the King of Faery. He is mentioned in the *Mabinogion* (q.v.) as a companion of Arthur (q.v.) and is responsible for the carrying off of Creiddylad, the daughter of the god Llyr. He must fight to possess her every first of May, challenging Gwythyr, son of Griedawl, in a contest which is a trial of Summer and Winter. This tale is a parallel to that of Pwyll and Arawn in the first branch of the *Mabinogion*. Arawn is also Lord of Annwn, the hunter with a pack of white, red-eared hounds – the Hell-Hounds or Gabriel hounds who are also said to hunt with Herne (q.v.). Pwyll also has to fight for his bride Rhiannon (q.v.) in a yearly contest. In the Welsh poem, the *Preiddeu Annwn* – the Spoils of Annwn – Arthur voyages to Gwynn's kingdom to bring back the magical treasures of the Island of Britain (q.v.) including the Cauldron watched over by nine maidens – an early prototype of the Grail. In the medieval *Life of St Collen* there is a meeting between the Saint and Gwynn: St Collen enters Gwynn's palace by descending into Glastonbury Tor from the top, where Gwynn's evil influence is supposed to have been banished by the application of Holy water.

Geoffrey Ashe (8) equates Gwynn ap Nudd with the Romano-British god Nodens, himself a variant of the Irish Nuada. Nodens was seen as a hunter, a woodland guardian, and a guide of souls. His temple, excavated at Lydney, has facilities for incubation – where pilgrims might come to sleep so that the god might give them messages through dreams.

Nuada Airgetlam (Silver Arm) was King of the Tuatha de Danaan (q.v.) and was so called because he lost an arm in battle. As Irish kings – and indeed most ancient kings – were unfitted to reign if maimed or blemished in any way, he resigned his kingship and was given a silver, fully-working arm by the god of healing. When this was later replaced by one of flesh, he resumed his kingship.

These related gods all have special powers of guardianship and responsibility for the land. As underworld gods, Gwynn ap Nudd and Arawn are in distinct polarization to the gods of light, but they still have a definite place in the scheme of things, and may be seen as the guardians of the winter half of the year with their Persephone-like consorts. They are patrons of the underside of things, of the psyche's harrowing, and may conduct the voyager into the deepest of inner realms. Places associated with them are Lydney, Gloucester-shire (for Nodens); Glastonbury, Somerset and Neath, Glamorgan (for Gwynn); Arbeth, Pembroke (for Arawn).

REFERENCES: Ross (215), Ashe (8), *Mabinogion* (146), Rees (210), Spence (239), Markale (160).

Helen of the Roads. Goddess of trackways and ancient roads. Known sometimes as Elen she features in the 'Dream of Maxcen Wledig' in the *Mabinogion*, where she rules over the country of dreams. Known also as the goddess of evening and morning, she performs the role of guide and instructor to those seeking the old serpent ways to the sites of arcane knowledge (see chapter 2). Perhaps one of the oldest native deities, she assumed Roman influence, and was identified with St Helen of Colchester, the Mother of Constantine the Great. One of the great old trackways in Wales is known as Sarn Helen, Helen's Road, and to follow this on foot is an excellent way to establish contact with this particular archetype. How she may assist in opening the gates to the old sites can be seen from the exercise given at the end of chapter 2.

REFERENCES: *Mabinogion* (146), Chant (48), Spence (239), Ashe (8).

Mabon/Maponus. Very little textual evidence remains for Mabon, who must take his place as the *puer aeternus* of the Celtic pantheons. He is always referred to as Mabon, son of Modron – Youth, son of Mother – and his incarceration is told of in the *Mabinogion* (q.v.) in the story of Kilhwch and Olwen. He is the primal child who was in existence at the beginning of things, and throughout the story is sought for with this question: 'Say, knowest thou aught of Mabon, Son of Modron, who was taken from his mother when three nights old?' Birds and animals give testimony of him and clues as to where he may be found, but this question is repeated over and over with sad, liturgical inquiry. The mysteries of the lost child are closely related to the Mother, the Matrona or Modron – the Goddess of earlier times – and though no personal names come down to us, the impact of Mabon and his mother is still strong. Maponus, or Divine Son, is a Northern Romano-British variant, often associated in inscriptions with Apollo. Gloucestershire is the place associated with Mabon, and Lochmaben and Lochmaben stones, Dumfries, with Maponus. Many inscriptions to him are to be found along the Scottish borders.

REFERENCES: Ross (215), *Mabinogion* (146), Gruffydd (96), Ashe (7).

Manannan/Manawyddan. He is the master of the seas, the pilot of souls who seek the way to the Blessed Isles; but his interest does not rest only in things marine. Although he is not originally mentioned as one of the Tuatha de Dannan (q.v.), in later texts he is incorporated into them. His title is Mac Lir – of the sea – and he finds his Welsh equivalent in Manawyddan, who in the *Mabinogion* helps lift an enchantment laid on the land and is one of the Children of Don (q.v.). Both Welsh and Gaelic figures are shape-changers, visiting this world in the guise of travellers and craftsmen. Manannan's horse or his glass boat will bear the seeker to the Otherworld. He also has a host of treasures which are kept in the Crane-Bag, itself a receptacle of wisdom. His places are the Isle of Man; Emain Abhlach or Emain of the Apple-Trees which is identified as the Isle of Arran in the Firth of Clyde; and any place of enchantment which has its resonance with the Otherworld. His symbol is the three-spoked wheel or Triskel, which may be seen in the symbol of the Isle of Man.

REFERENCES: *Mabinogion* (146), Rees (200), Ross (215), Graves (92).

Math vab Mathonwy. Archetypal god of wizardry and transformation. Although he has some of the characteristics of Merlin, he is a much older figure whose brand of magic is at times both savage and unrelenting. He acts very much according to his own laws and as such is more a god-figure than a wizard. He excels in the ability to transform both himself and others into the shapes of animal or bird. In the *Mabinogion* he is responsible for the fashioning of a bride made from flowers for the god Llew (q.v.). He is guide to many mysteries and seems indeed to represent a stage of wisdom both older and deeper than most of his fellows.

REFERENCES: *Mabinogion* (146), Markale (160), Spence (240), Graves (92), Garner (84), Gruffydd (96).

Merlin. Not a god, but one of the most important figures in the Western tradition. He spans both pagan and Christian mysteries, is the prime mover behind the age of Arthur (q.v.) and stands at the heart of the Grail story. To make contact with him is to place oneself squarely at the centre of both the ancient 'Druidic' mysteries (see chapter 1) and the high Christian magic of the Hermetic way (see volume 2). Like Taliesin (q.v.) he is a contact who opens many doors: those to Atlantis, the Otherworld, the country of the Grail and the Druid way of which he is a part. There are many places where his influence may be felt (Merlin's Cave at Tintagel in Cornwall or the whole area of Marlborough in Wiltshire), but nowhere as strongly as at the hill-top site known as Dinas Emrys in Wales. Emrys is the name by which Merlin is known in certain parts of the country, and the hill is the supposed site of his first great adventure in which he revealed the meaning of the red and white dragon which lay beneath the earth, and from where he made his first great series of prophecies (you may read the whole story and the text of the prophecies in *Geoffrey of Monmouth's History of the Kings of Britain*, 85). A lord of seashore and cavedark, Merlin is a link between many diverse forces. When sought he can be elusive, but he is prone to seek out the seeker at the most unexpected moments.

REFERENCES: *Geoffrey of Monmouth* (85), Spence (240), Markale (160), Jarman (117).

Morgan le Fay/Nimuë/Lady of the Lake. In many ways one of the most important figures of the Western tradition. As 'Morgan le Fay' she appears as a force of chaos and evil in the Arthurian cycle (q.v.) though, bewilderingly enough, she is also depicted as caring for Arthur (q.v.) when he receives his wound at the last battle of Camlan. Also present at this scene, where a dark boat appears to carry Arthur to Avalon, is Nimuë who is both another aspect of Morgan and also the beguiler of Merlin (q.v.). Together with the mysterious figure known as The Lady of the Lake, they form a triplicity which dates back to the character of the Morrigan in Irish and Welsh myth, where she is known as a battle goddess. Their roles, throughout the Arthurian mythos, are those of helper and hinderer. Thus the Lady of the Lake fosters Lancelot and provides Arthur with his magical sword Excalibur; while Morgan le Fay frequently opposes both Merlin and Arthur with her dark magic. Nimuë serves as a lure and is eventually the downfall of Merlin, but before this is a trusted confidante at the Arthurian court. Behind all these figures is a far older, darker and more mysterious figure – a mother goddess of both fearsome and gentle aspect, a teacher and guide, and a ruthless slayer and render of hopes in one. As a contact she brings with her both these aspects, and requires careful handling. She may be found on open hillsides, in thorn-trees and by the banks of rivers, dressed in a dark cloak and hood and sometimes keening for the souls of dead heroes; or as a bird, usually a raven, keeping watch from high trees or outcrops of rock.

REFERENCES: Graves (92), Spence (240), Markale (160), Malory (157), Rhys (212), Ross (215), *Vita Merlini* (276), Knight (132).

Rhiannon. Her story is to be found in the *Mabinogion* (q.v.), in the story of *Pwyll, Prince of Dyfed*. She is deeply linked with the mysteries of Mabon and Modron (q.v.) for she also loses a child, suffers a heavy punishment and regains her former glory. She is without doubt the Welsh Persephone. Her name has been taken to signify 'Great Queen' and her cult is connected with that of the Gaulish Mare-Goddess Epona, which may itself derive from early worship of the Greek Black Demeter. Rhiannon is also the mistress of otherworldly birds whose song brings forgetfulness and perhaps visions to the listener. Her places are Arberth, Pembroke, whose mound was an entrance to Annwn; and any underground place and sites sacred to the mare, such as White Horse Hill, Uffington, Berkshire.

REFERENCES: *Mabinogion* (146), Ross (215), Gruffydd (96), Graves (92).

Taliesin. Chief Bard of the Islands of Britain, one of the 'Company of the Noble Head' (see Bran) and a magician second only to Merlin in stature. The mystery of his birth, outlined in the *Mabinogion* (q.v.) is one of transmogrification through bird and animal forms, and hides an initiation ritual at one time current in many parts of the world, in which the initiate drank a specially prepared draught which caused him to see visions and pass through differing states of consciousness. From this originate many of the surviving poems of Taliesin, to be found in *The Black Book of Carmarthen* (81), which in riddling form describe a journey through all of history. In part unravelled by Robert Graves in *The White Goddess*, much work yet remains to be done on them. Taliesin has the power to conduct the individual who establishes rapport with him through many dimensions of place and time, and through the elements themselves. He is the companion of all who tread the difficult, solitary 'narrow way' of understanding through the highest elemental contacts.

REFERENCES: *Mabinogion* (146), Nash (178), Skene (81), Markale (160), Spence (239).

Tuatha de Danaan/Children of Donn. Names given respectively to the pantheons of Irish and Welsh deities of the early Celtic period. Native gods did not normally follow the classical model of a linked family, but generally fell into separate and individual cults of local provenance. We must assume that the family of Donn or Danu were the hereditary gods of an invading people. In the Irish *Book of Invasions*, the Tuatha de Danaan are the fifth body of invaders and are themselves subjugated by the Milesians, bringing historical chronology to the Christianization of Ireland. This shape is by no means as clear in the Welsh stories. Although traces of the Tuatha are appreciable within the Children of Donn, they are by no means identical in character or story content. This is perhaps explicable if we look at the known colonization of Western Wales, particularly at the Pembroke coast of ancient Dyfed; reminders of this time remain in the shape of forty ogham stones still standing in Wales today. Danu, Anu or Donn is a shadowy matriarch whose origins are unknown to us; she has been equated with the Indian goddess Dánu, mother of Vrtra in the *Rig Veda* (214). However we see her, she is a titanic figure, comparable to the Greek Rhea who also founded a line of gods.

The character of Danu or Donn's children is defined by their mastery of the arts, skills of many kinds, magic and fighting. They have no skills in agriculture and this function is relegated to the vanquished lesser gods. Danu is the mother of the gods; Dagda – the Good God – also called Ruad Rofessa – Lord of Great Knowledge – is the god of magic. His daughter Brigit (q.v.) is patroness of poets, smiths and women. Diancecht is god of healing. Nuadu (q.v.) is king of the Tuatha. Lugh, called *Sabd il Danach* or Prince of Many Skills, is the Tuatha's champion who finally defeats the older gods. Manaanan (q.v.), although older than the Tuatha, becomes one of their number and bestows many immortal gifts upon them. Both he and Lugh survived strongest in folk-memory after the Tuatha had been driven to the Hollow Hills when the Milesians vanquished them: they appear as otherworldly helpers to kings and heroes, Manannan in particular having an interest in the fosterage and care of unprotected children and women. Goibniu (q.v.) is the god of smiths. Ogma, surnamed Grian-ainech or Sun-Faced, is the god of poetry and writing; the invention of the magical language known as Ogham is ascribed to him.

The Welsh Children of Donn are particularly distinguished for their magical skills. They appear within the *Mabinogion* in the story of *Math, son of Mathonwy*, where their influence upon events turns the world upside down. Gwydion (q.v.), described as a son of Donn and nephew to King Math, is the arch-mover and magician. With his brother, Gilfaethwy, he starts an intrigue which kills Pryderi, Rhiannon's son (q.v.). This may well indicate the supression of an older family of gods, as Rhiannon's origins are of the Underworld and therefore closer to the beginning of things. Gwydion's sister Arianrhod (q.v.) gives birth to two sons, Dylan, son of Wave, whose nature is one with the sea, and Llew Llaw Gyffes, Lleu or the Skilful Hand, the equivalent of Lugh Lamhfada, Lugh of the Long Arm, in the Tuatha. Arianrhod puts upon him an insuperable *geasa*, or prohibition, that he shall not marry a human of mortal stock. As a result Gwydion and Math make a woman out of flowers, Blodeuwedd, Flower Face, for Lleu. But she betrays him, and Lleu, who cannot be killed outright, transforms himself into the shape of an eagle. Blodeuwedd is herself turned into an owl as punishment for her betrayal, while Lleu is returned to mortal shape. Owls are to this day called by her name in parts of Wales.

A convention of early Christian Ireland had members of the Tuatha appear to monks or hermits to relate their deeds and get baptism so that they could pass out of the Hollow Hills into the Christian heaven, showing how strong the hold of these archetypes was even after their reign was supposedly over. Those who walk the inner realms of the Western Way are likely to meet with any or all of them, and may find them both helpful or hindering according to their natures. They are, so far as this may be understood esoterically, our native Titans.

REFERENCES: Rees (210), Ross (215), de Jubainville (64), MacCana (149), Garner (84), *Mabinogion* (146).

Wayland/Govannon/Goibnui. Three types of the one figure: the Smith of the Gods. An immensely strong deep-rooted contact, he is said to offer to shoe your horse if you have the right payment to offer; and he may also open the door to the underworld where he is a King in his own right. Wayland's Smithy in Berkshire has the strongest associations with him. He is interesting in that he is almost the only Saxon deity who has remained active, assuming the roles of both earlier Welsh and Irish gods. This is an indication of the special position accorded to smiths, who were the first Makers and knew the mystery of iron – the origin of the folk-belief that witches and fairy-folk cannot cross a threshold protected by 'cold iron'. Wayland shares many affinities with the ancient Green King, the Man of the Woods, who leads always to the deeper levels of lore. He is also said to have made many magical weapons, including, in all probability, Arthur's sword Excalibur.

REFERENCES: Branston (28), Hayles (106), Graves (92).

Most of the beings discussed above have a place in the great mythological cycles of the West: the cycles of Arthur, of Fionn, the Ulster Cycle, and the Four Branches of the *Mabinogion*. Each of these requires considerable study and really deserve whole books in themselves. All that we can do here is indicate, however partially, their essential qualities, which include some of the most profound mysteries of the Western Way. Knowledge of these cycles is essential for anyone wishing to follow that way: its characters and stories are all gateways to other realms which the present-day neophyte should be able to wander in and out of at will. Some tried and tested methods whereby this can be achieved will be found later on in this chapter, but before that we append a brief discussion of the individual cycles and their inner meanings.

The Arthur Cycle. The most familiar to most people of the four cycles to be discussed, due to its enduring fascination for all ages and kinds of men. The stories of King Arthur and his Knights of the Round Table are really a loosely-knit body of myth, legend and hero tale drawn from Celtic, French and Germanic background, elaborated and re-elaborated by countless authors down the ages. From the height of the myth's popularity in the Middle Ages we have the image of a band of mail-clad knights, lead by a mighty king, advised by the wise seer Merlin, going in search of love and battle on the one hand, and of the Holy Grail on the other. They stand for many of the noblest aspirations of human endeavour, the need to create harmony out of chaos, to preserve what is most worthy, to aspire to the highest possible ideals. Thus the cycle as a whole probably contains the widest possible spectrum of human love, folly, desire and attainment. Arthur is the noblest of men and stands for the very stuff of the land – indeed he *is* the land and is thus depicted as sleeping in caves beneath it until called upon to return and succour the human race. Guinevere, rash and human in her impetuous love of Lancelot, yet stands for an older, feminine mystery (see Knight, 132), as do many of the figures of the cycle, some already mentioned, such as Morgan, Nimuë, Lunet, Lionors, Dindrain and Isolt. Their counterparts, the great knights: Galahad, Gawain, Perceval, Lamorack, Gareth – their names, like their deeds, are legion – each stand to some degree in relation to the Western mysteries. As companions on the way they can be powerful guardians, guides and exemplars, endlessly fascinated by the modern world as by their own. They have become invested with timelessness by the unending interest lavished upon them; and they respond well to direct contact in meditation or dream. Once contacted, you may find that a single knight or lady will attach him or herself to you, acting as an escort throughout your daily life, both magical and mundane.

Because the basis of the mythos is Celtic, Germanic and even Atlantean, working with the Arthurian cycle can be particularly rewarding, leading as it may to one or more of the inner realities of these cultures. For those who become concerned with the mystery of the Grail, knowledge of the Arthurian stories is essential. The adventures of the Grail seekers and the intimate understanding of the esoteric Grail kingdom possessed by many of the romances are without equal as a guide to these often bewildering places. The mystery at the heart of the Grail is service, and each of the knights who achieved that mystery possesses the ability to help and instruct us in our path to the place where the Wounded King awaits our coming as eagerly as he has for time beyond measure.

Arthurian source-books abound, and there are several good histories and bibliographies to help the seeker into the dense woodland of Arthurian Britain. A select list will be found at the back of this book. Nor should fictional retellings be ignored: many contain great insights from which we can learn, and are included for this reason. A more detailed consideration of the role of modern storytellers will follow later in this chapter.

The Four Branches of the Mabinogion and related stories, known collectively as the *Mabinogion* (146) – 'Mabinog' translates as 'youth-tales' – really consist of two separate though related kinds of material. The Four Branches themselves, *Pwyll Prince of Dyfed, Branwen Daughter of Llyr, Manawyddan Son of Lyr* and *Math Son of Mathonwy*, form a loosely knit cycle of tales, written down in the ninth century but incorporating material from much earlier times. They are the earliest 'complete' myths of Britain – though they were garbled and rewritten by Christian monkish scribes who made such changes as are hard to reconcile with original material. None the less, they are a rewarding source from which to quarry the stuff of the mysteries; for nowhere else will you find such complete delineations of the native god-forms.

The remainder of the tales grouped under the heading of 'Mabinogi' are more disparate, consisting of several Arthurian stories, generally believed by modern scholars – Loomis (144), Brown (31), Bromwich (268) – to be copies of Mediaeval French poems by Chretien de Troyes (though this is by no means necessarily true), as well as a very primitive Arthurian tale *Kilhwch and Olwen*, which contains some of the earliest material extant of the whole cycle; and two primary mythic stories: *The Dream of Maxcen Wledig* (see chapter 2) and *The Dream of Rhonawby*, both of which contain material of a significantly early kind. The collection is completed by the story of *Lludd and Llevellys*, which relates to the dragon myths and to Merlin; and the very important *Hanes Taliesin*, omitted from more recent editions of the texts because of its 'difficult' and fragmentary nature. It can, however, be found in the original edition by Lady Charlotte Guest (146) and should certainly be read for its magical and initiatory content.

Unlike the Arthurian cycle, the overall bias of the *Mabinogion* is towards the heroic rather than the chivalric. Despite a thin overlay of later material, it is here that will be found the earliest and most primary matter of the native Celtic mythos. In one of the three Arthurian stories *Peredur son of Evrawc*, is to be found the most primitive form of the Grail legend; in another, *The Lady of the Fountain*, the atmosphere is very much more magical than in Chretien de Troyes' elegant French version (54). In *Geraint Son of Erbin*, the third of the pieces, the same holds good. However the material came to be transmitted, it is manifestly older than the medieval versions from which it is assumed to depend.

Finally in this context mention must be made of the loose body of gnomic material known as the *Triads* (268). These are a form of mnemonic used by the old story-tellers and bards to preserve the principal themes of their extensive repertoire. Thus the 'Three Disastrous Revealings', or the 'Three Golden-Torqued Bards of Britain', would immediately recall the stories associated with them – sometimes a brief, shorthand version was appended, and as many of the stories have perished, they offer tantalizing glimpses of a world of which we know all too little. Indeed one of the best exercises we know of for becoming familiar with the native god-forms is to take one of the Triads and use it as a theme for meditation. You may be surprised at the amount that can be 'recovered' in this way, and at the insights it can throw up in your daily life.

The Fionn Cycle is similar, though lighter in tone, to the Ulster Cycle (q.v.). Fionn MacCumhal is the captain of King Cormac MacAirt's band of *fiana* or heroes. They roam the countryside of Southern Ireland, and much of the cycle is taken up with their adventures. Admission to the band is restricted to those who can achieve all kinds of physical feats, such as when the candidate has to run through a forest and not displace a hair on his head or a branch of a tree, or to be able to draw a thorn from his foot while running but without slackening his pace. The candidate was expected to be accomplished in the arts of poetry as well as fighting. The parallels with Robin Hood (q.v.) and his band are not hard to draw. As in the Ulster cycle (q.v.), the story is brought to a tragic close because of a woman: Grainne, the intended wife of Fionn, runs away with his best friend, Diarmuid, to Scotland, where they live an idyllic if temporary life in the wilds. The close links with both the Arthurian stories and that of Kilhwch and Olwen (*Mabinogion*, q.v.) are particularly clear, as are those with the Tristan and Isolt legends. Fionn himself is an initiate after the Manner of Taliesin (q.v.), having touched the Salmon of Knowledge while cooking it for his poet-master. This gives him immunity from his enemies (poets enjoyed exemption from attack) as well as access to the Otherworld, with which he is still connected in folk-tradition. Oisin, Fionn's son, is made to survive right up until the Christian era, when he meets St Patrick and relates to him the deeds of the Fiana. Like all the more primitive myths discussed here, the heroes of the Fionn cycle make fine companions in the investigation of the native magical sites and areas of the country.

REFERENCES: Rees (210), MacCana (149), Sutcliff (253).

The Ulster Cycle. As the Fiana are to the South, so are the heroes of his cycle to the North. Indeed the warlike character of Ulster, still apparent today, has its roots within the Ulster cycle of related stories. Here, we are still connected to the high days of the Tuatha de Danaan (q.v.); but if the Tuatha represent the Golden Age, then the heroic tradition of Ulster represents the Silver Age. High deeds, honour, heroic codes of behaviour put us much in mind of the Trojan Wars as described by Homer. In the Ulster cycle people are placed under severe *geasa* or are subject to ill-wished enchantment which restricts their actions to such a degree there can only be a tragic outcome. Ulaidh, ancient Ulster, was ruled by Conchobar mac Nessa, whose court was at Emain Mhacha, near the present day city of Armagh. In his court are the champions and heroes who together form the Red Branch Knights: Conall Cernach, Fergus mac Roich and, most famous of all, Cuchulainn, whose exploits form almost a cycle in themselves (q.v.). The fate of Ulster is tied up with tribal feuding, particularly with the rival court of Queen Maebh of Connacht. The most famous tale is that of the *Tain Bo Cuailnge*, the Cattle Raid of Cooley, after which Cuchulainn is killed by the magic of the Morrighan – the primal Cailleach (q.v.) whose malice stems from the time before even the Tuatha de Danaan reigned (q.v.). Related stories in the cycle are *Deirdre and the Sons of Uisnech*, which has its parallels with the *Pursuit of Diarmuid and Grainne* from the Fionn cycle (q.v.), in which the beauty of Deirdre and the honourable and impossible *geasa* imposed on those about her form the basis for the subsequent tragedy of Ulster. *Bricriu's Feast* and *Mac Da Tho's Pig* are humorous interludes in which the heroes have otherworldly adventures and very real humiliations. The former story has the first instance of the Beheading Game, which later appears in the medieval *Sir Gawain and the Green Knight* (233) attached to another Cuchulainn-type hero. The Ulster cycle as a whole remains one of dark vengeance and proud honour, and is perhaps the most difficult to work with in the present time.

REFERENCES: MacCana (149), Rees (210), *Tain* (256), Sutcliff (254).

Robin Hood. Probably better known to cinema audiences than to students of the esoteric, Robin Hood or Wood is none the less an important figure in the Western mysteries. Originally a spirit of the woodlands of Britain, he is a supremely English character. His beginnings are lost in the mists of time, and have become overlaid with a doubtful historical figure known variously as Robin of Huntingdon or Robin of Locksley. A series of ballads dating from the twelfth and thirteenth centuries outline the adventures of the great outlaw of Sherwood Forest: a small cycle of tales involving such picturesque characters as Little John, Will Scarlet, Alan à Dale, and Friar Tuck; many with older and darker selves become little more than dim memories by this time. Robin is very much a man of the people, an equalizer whose image still reappears in contemporary figures such as the solitary masked avenger of injustice. As a contacted archetype he opens the mystery of woodland and shadowy overgrown glades. He is deep and quick and eager to lead those who follow him upon new and surprising paths. With Maid Marian as his consort he rules over the woodlands of Britain like a Faery King.

REFERENCES: Holt (112), Child (53), Vansittart (272).

MODERN MYTHOGRAPHERS AND STORY-TELLERS

The Native Tradition possesses no authorized book, no Holy Scripture which succeeding generations may quote from, refer to and use as an index to living. Instead there are the primal myths, archetypal situations and themes strung together on a loose framework and exemplified by characters in the guise of Gods and Goddesses, angels and demons, heroes and lovers. Texts such as the Bible, the Koran, the Popol Vhu (204) or the Vedas, once they are formalized, remain virtually unchanged: they are there to be referred to at any given moment in time. Myths, however, continue to grow and change. They are open to endless reinterpretation. James Joyce can make us see Ulysses anew by setting him down in modern Dublin. The seemingly endless repetition of Greek or Arthurian myths from the Middle Ages onward further proves the point. The themes contained therein are endless and timeless and reach the most profound depths of human experience – the same which gave them birth. These are the roots of story, the preserve of myth and archetype, whether of the legendary birth of a hero or an individual response to the crisis in Northern Ireland. The art of the story-teller is to reach the deepest possible level, and all true practitioners of the art can be recognized in this way. By doing so they both preserve and add to the layers of meaning which each successive generation finds in the bedrock of the original story.

As we saw in the first chapter, the shaman/priest was the first myth-maker – and the first story-teller. Drawing on their immediate experience of the Otherworld and its archetypes, and of their own inner reality, they gave birth to the first myths. Thereafter the stories and events relating to these myths became the core of religion, of the mysteries and the tribe's place in the scheme of things.

But, as with any story that is told more than once, the myths acquired accretions and additions, as more and more people embroidered them into complex retellings. While myth remained the province of the shaman/priest, and was thus considered sacred, the story was for everyone. Later this was to change, as the subject matter became debased into legend and fairy story and finally into nursery entertainment. But no one doubted the power of the word. Ray Bradbury's famous Science Fiction novel, *Farenheit 451* (26), tells of a future time when books are forbidden as subversive elements in society: they stimulate the emotions and give an entirely different view of the world from that accepted by the administration.

In Bradbury's story various people take upon themselves the task of learning and remembering a whole book, word for word, so that the story will not be lost. They each become a 'living' book. This state of affairs seems far-fetched perhaps, yet this is exactly what the ancient story-tellers did – learned a story by heart, which could often last for several weeks in the telling, and thereafter gave the story at important tribal events. This tradition remained until recently in Ireland and the West of Scotland, when the demand for such long stories ceased with the advent of radio and television. A particularly sad fate for the story-teller became the lack of an audience:

> There came a time when it was but rarely that he had an opportunity himself of practising his art in public. So, lest he should lose command over the tales he loved, he used to repeat them aloud . . . using the gesticulations and the emphasis, and all the other tricks of narration, as if he were once again the centre of fireside story-telling . . . On returning from market, as he walked slowly up the hills behind his old grey mare, he could be heard declaiming his tales to the back of the cart (210).

This almost extinct tradition stemmed from the highly organized repertoire of the professional poet, whose duty is was to learn up to a hundred and fifty stories in the course of training. These stories were classified into categories which were considered suitable for recitation at certain events. Classifications such as destructions, cattle-raids, abductions, conceptions, visions, voyages, invasions, and so on. As each story was considered to carry the element which particularized it, and which communicated itself to the hearer, the story was usually told at an event in keeping with the tale related. Thus the *Wooing of Emer by Cuchulainn* would be recited at a wedding or betrothal. The traditional blessing, curse or abjuration often went with its telling and this element seeped into medieval literature, where the reader was warned against altering a word of the story or shortening it, and where a blessing is included to 'one who hears these words and keeps them'.

The words of the story are therefore words of power which the unskilled must beware of tampering with. Hence the opening of many stories with the formula 'This story is a true story and I had it from X who had it from Y. Whoever doesn't believe me had better go from this company than hear the story unbelieving.' The power of the word to this degree has remained with scriptures and sacred writings of all people. Even today among unsophisticated Muslims a strip of paper with a surah from the Koran is considered more effective as a healing agent when bound about a wound than a piece of sticking plaster. The Guru Granth Sahib, the sacred book of the Sikhs, is treated as a living being and consulted accordingly; while Hindus still go to a priest in time of trouble to have some verses of the sacred writings read over them.

We accord stories little of this respect. The word 'fiction' when applied to stories has become a term of scorn. If it is fiction, then it is not factually true, goes the argument. Yet the lives of many are held in thrall today by the power of the soap-opera – itself an immensely long story which lasts many nights in the telling. When a character in a soap-opera is about to marry or is killed, the audience feels delight or pain in proportion to the amount of identification shared with that character.

The story certainly still has power when it is heard, read or enacted. It is character-forming, as the hearers subtly alter their own life-style to accord with that of the hero or heroine of the piece. The story is nurturing, feeding our hours of leisure now as once it blotted out the reality of the long, cold, dark nights of winter, when the story-teller was a welcome guest, treated like royalty and given the best the household could supply, or when the old ones with long memories were called upon to tell again the stories of long ago:

> One of the ancient wise ones of the tribe comes to take his place. Around his neck hangs the string of bear's teeth, numbering the tales he knows. He may carry his own drum or an apprentice may carry it, one who is learning the tribal tales and the act of telling them. The drum sets the rhythm for the chanting; it marks the pauses; it beats gloriously for the ending (224).

The literary or 'high' telling has always been a major part of story-telling: the poetic lamentations of Deirdrui in Alba, the intricate descriptions of Helen of Troy in Homer, the *entrelacement* techniques of the Medieval romancers, or the multifaceted narrative of Lawrence Durrell's *Alexandria Quartet* (72) all share this style of storytelling. Likewise, there is room for the family saga: from the *Nibelungenleid* (187) to the *Forsyte Saga*, they possess the same attraction. So too with the adventure story, whether of the Voyage of Bran or the latest journey of Tim Severin (229). Tales of war from the *Tain Bo Cualigne* (256) to the Battle for the Falklands, both stories of reeving of one kind or another, show that the themes return incessantly to the classical definitions of story.

Truly there is only a handful of stories and all are variations of THE STORY. The folk-tale, from 'Get up and Bar the Door' to the latest television situation comedy has a permanent appeal, dealing as it does with the common experiences of life; awkward situations always appear funnier to the hearer than to the subject, and the story-teller has to make his audience laugh as well as cry.

The power of the story may well be discounted among the ranks of the wise and powerful, but its staying power will outlast their rule. They may try to bend it to the uses of propaganda, but the result is not of long duration. Governments that behave as in *Farenheit 451*, banning and censoring the publication and dissemination of books, discover that the story has its way of escaping, as we see from the experience of samizdat-underground literature – passed from hand to hand in rough photocopied format, or more subversively circulated orally to be chuckled over at street corners.

Stories never die; they change. The new folk-legends, such as that of the Phantom Hitch-Hiker or the UFO kidnap, are a well-established phenomenon now – later versions of the mysterious guest. Likewise the poltergeist-haunted council-house is only the latest haunted-house story. So, whilst we must not fear too greatly for the demise of the story, we must beware of the passing from memory of those orally-transmitted tales which are our heritage. They are easily overlooked or undervalued in an age which writes everything down or stores it on computer-disc, and as a result suffers from a poor memory. But if a time should come when many are unable to read, then Ray Bradbury's vision might well become reality, and the classic novels and stories of our literature the subjects of a new oral tradition.

A much greater fear is the loss of the miraculous dimension from the literature of the future. If some cultural commentators were to have their way this would have happened long ago. They have already succeeded in banishing much that was of great value to the seeker to the realm of the children's story or the nursery tale. There is at present an apparently endless demand for pulp-fantasy and the various genres of Science Fiction. But these are pilloried by the establishment and those who write or read them are accused of 'escapism', of burying their heads in the sand and refusing to acknowledge the 'real' world. Yet, as we have seen repeatedly, the kind of reality – perhaps of super-reality – offered by the endlessly unfolding dimension of the Otherworld, by far transcends anything to be gained from watching a dozen episodes of the average soap-opera. The Otherworld, of which the great traditions – both Native and Hermetic – are a major expression, possesses a timeless and dimensionless reality, in which the archetypes of the kind investigated by Jung (123), Rank (208) and their like, range freely and have their being. Modern mythographers such as 'A.E.' (219), W.B. Yeats (291), George Macdonald (150), J.R.R. Tolkien (263) and C.S. Lewis (142), have all written from a deep understanding of this archetypal reality – hence the phenomenon of their popularity. Individuals react violently towards such literature, loving or hating it according to their awareness of the reality upon which it draws.

Beneath this is a very fundamental problem. 'Mankind cannot bear too much reality' said Eliot (73), while both Lewis (141) and Tolkien (264) have written warnings of the way in which our very humanity is undermined by those who insist that to believe in anything that cannot be seen, felt, or heard is both childish and demeaning. This is not the place to argue the point fully, but it should be said that those who bury themselves in the daily round of one-dimensional reality – whether in their living or their artistic appreciation – who cannot bear the reality of their inner lives, are least fitted to follow the way of the Western Mysteries – though paradoxically they stand in the greatest need to do so. As one of the best writers of contemporary fantasy literature, Richard Monaco, commented in a note to a recent book (170):

> Some of us confuse fantasy with escape from reality. . . . Escape? But to where? Into your own mind and images, in the end. And you'll have to deal with the facts and fears, agonies, frustrations and hopes . . . the quest that leads towards inner freedom and an intensity that brings more joy and real passion than you'll ever find in any literature of daydreams.

He might have added that it is this confusion between escape and escapist that lies at the root of much that is amiss with our present society. In entering the inner realms we are not running away or hiding from the outer world, but rather seeking to deepen and enrich our awareness of a multi-dimensional universe. Fantasy opens our lives. It is a laboratory where the alchemical possibilities are tested and tasted first. It is the magical waking of our lives. This is the quest of which Richard Monaco speaks: the search for the reality behind the Gods and inner archetypes of the Otherworld. Whether you come to them through the myths of Greece or the adventures of the American folk-hero Coyote, through the legends of Arthur or the strange wild myths of the Celts; or become attuned through the modern myth-based techniques of Psychosynthesis (10) or the dream workshops of Progoff (206), Whitmont (285) or Spiegleman (242), you will find yourself led inevitably to the realm of the Otherworld and the figures of the gods who rule it and their servants. There are as many entrances as there are stars in the heavens – indeed some of those stars are themselves entrances – some of which we will be discussing in the next chapter. The way of Story is one entrance only, but an immeasurably valuable one: for through it you may make your first encounter with the landscape and characters to be met with again and again on your quest. Someday you may even encounter the Lords of Story themselves, to whom tradition gives the origin and shaping of all stories, myths and tales, told in the light of the campfire or found in the pages of an ancient book or some new myth-oriented saga of sword and sorcery. It is they who control the destiny of the creative artist, constantly shifting and redefining the perimeters of the archetypal worlds. They are guardians of experience and the shapers of beginnings and endings. To meet them is to encounter fear and joy in almost the same breath and in equal measure: not unlike the feeling when one takes the first step beyond the boundaries of the 'real' world into that endless and timeless place where all adventures and quests begin and end, but where paradoxically there are no final beginnings or endings at all, only a timeless flux in which all shapes and forms have their origin, and where the mysteries of creation itself are kept. As the Irish mystic and visionary 'A.E.' wrote, of the moment 'When inner and outer first mingle' as 'the bridal night of the soul and body':

A germ is dropped from which inevitably evolves the character and the psyche. It is a seed as truly as if it were dropped into earth or womb. Only what is born from it is a spirit thing, and it grows up and takes its abode in the body with its other inhabitants, earth-born or heaven-born (218).

These are things still far from the start of the quest. Perhaps you have known them already without recognition; perhaps you never will. But you may be sure that the search will be endlessly challenging, and that though you grow weary in its pursuit, you will never really want to give it up, once you have begun.

EXERCISES

EXERCISE 6   MEETING THE GODS

In this exercise you are going to attempt to establish a rapport with an Otherworld character. Begin with a figure for whom you feel sympathy. It need not be one of those listed in the gazetteer. It can, for example, just as easily be a saint as a god or hero; but whoever you choose you should begin by reading as much about him or her as possible. Become familiar with his story and, if you can, any sites especially associated with him. (Where possible, indications of this have been given in the gazetteer.) If there are no sites, try to think what kind of place you would expect to find him at: by a river or lake, on mountain or hillside, in woodland or on cliffs overlooking the sea. But always remember that he or she can be anywhere – in your own front room as well as in a wild and desolate place in the open. (Your Otherworld character may be male or female; when we use the male pronoun it is for clarity only.)

Begin to use your imagination to visualize how your chosen character would look: how he would be dressed, what colour hair or eyes he might have and so on. Gradually build up a picture in your mind – draw it if that helps – but take your time: these things do not come easily and you have all the time in the world at your disposal.

When you feel that you have a good visual image that can be called to mind at a moment's notice without effort, go to the site you have previously selected. It may be necessary to go there quite often to begin with, until you get the feel of it. Preferably it should be deserted, apart from any friend you may take with you; but if this is not possible (as for example at one of the major sites which are seldom deserted, even early or late in the day), do not worry. All you have to do is sit, or stand, quite casually, and bring to mind the character you have been building up over the past weeks. Do not be surprised, or disappointed, if nothing happens at first: these things take time. You may, if you wish, make up a chant containing the name of the character you have chosen, repeating it silently or aloud as circumstances permit. Or you might read over some familiar passage, or a poem you have written or enjoyed which is to do with the subject in question.

After a time you should begin to get 'flashes' of insight about the character in question, who may even begin to 'speak' to you. But, if you have taken your time building up the image in your mind, this will seem quite natural. Because there is always an exchange between inner and outer worlds, some of what you have put into your visualization will have been supplied from the inner reality, and this will make the image all the more vital. You should find that after a time you build up a consistent rapport with your chosen subject, and that he will begin to guide you further into the realm of which you are a part. This can be one of the most rewarding experiences open to us today, and is in fact an exact correlative of the way in which our ancestors worshipped. In this way, you are establishing a bridge or gateway between the worlds which will ever after be open to you.

However, a word of warning. Many energies are being unleashed in this way which have been unrepresented for centuries: earth energy, Native Wisdom links, and ancestral potencies which bring with them remembrances that can be helpful to our present time (see chapter 2). While it is perfectly allowable to make contact with the vital energies, there is always the danger that unregenerate forms may emerge also. These have to be allowed to depart, and should not be held onto for the sake of native traditional old times. Many of those old times were not good times, despite memories of the lost Age of Gold. Life was too near the survival point for highly evolved energies to manifest. Those energies and their representative god-forms which can still operate have been listed in this chapter: no element of pagan worship need necessarily be applied to them. Mediating their energies is, however, of prime importance. Those who visit ancient sites often remark that the stones are lonely, or that the earth is hungry – subjectively perceiving the kind of rites performed there once. It is one thing to awaken a site and another to close it down again. Our suggestions are concerned with awakening, purging if necessary, and operating these centres effectively for the good of all comers.

First contact with an ancient site may be frightening or at least very powerful. Whatever your religion, whatever the energy you are used to mediating, invoke its protective influence if you feel threatened or that something is out of balance. It often happens that after initial contact and awakening a huge rush of primeval energy is released. You should concentrate on this dispersing harmlessly into the atmosphere as a vapour. The ancient sadness of some sites is due to loneliness or isolation of an important energy and this will be willing to co-operate with the initiate who is able to mediate it objectively. This mediation will often be felt in small, insignificant ways throughout the months which follow your visit, and it should be carefully meditated upon to sift for its real usefulness for this time-scale.

Finally, always remember to dismiss your contact after you have spent however long you desire in his or her company. This can be easily done by some formula of your own devising. But never leave the impression of your chosen figure behind, as this can be disturbing to other sensitive visitors, and may make the continuation of the rapport you have begun to establish difficult.

Any impression that you have picked up a compulsive or obsessive contact should be swiftly acted upon. If you are experienced you should be able to patiently sift the contact and control its impatience to get working. The less experienced should ritually sever the contact and return it to the earth – it is possible that a more experienced person will be able to synthesize this energy at another time.

To sever such an obsessive contact, take a cleansing bath of salt water, make contact with the god-form or energy which you are used to working with and ask for assistance; request the troublesome contact to leave you, firmly and compassionately, remaining emotionally objective. With a small glass jar or cup-shaped stone before you, imagine your breath to be a circle of light which surrounds you: when you breathe in, your circle of surrounding light is flooded with blue; when you breathe out imagine the contact and any other negative energy leaving your system, beyond the pale of your blue circle of light. See it enter the container before you: a circuit of ten breaths should be quite sufficient. Carefully take the container outside and bury it in the earth where it will be neutralized.

With these precautions in mind you may pursue a rewarding relationship which will teach you a great deal and help you in your quest for further knowledge of the Western Mysteries. But remember that the gods, as we have tried to show, are also formalized 'pictures' of archetypal energies. To contact them also means to contact the energy they represent; a reality beyond the outer god-form. This also has to be worked with and assimilated before a full understanding of the gods is reached. When once you have made a direct contact with one of the rulers of sea, sky, or earth, these elements, which surround us but which are often seen as separate from our daily existence, will never again seem other than an essential part of experience. To know them is to be initiated, in a way both ineffably simple and hugely complex, into the mysteries of life itself.

CHAPTER 4
Voyages to the Otherworld

Facilis descensus Averno;
Noctes atque dies patet atri janua Ditis;
Sed revocare gradum, superasque evadere ad auras,
Hoc opus, hic labor est.

Aeneid vi, 126

Smooth the descent and easy is the way
(The Gates of Hell stand open night and day);
But to return and view the cheerful skies,
In this the task and mighty labour lies.

trans. Dryden.

How beautiful they are,
The lordly ones
Who dwell in the hills,
In the hollow hills.

From libretto of 'The Immortal Hour' by Rutland Boughton,
text by Fiona McLeod (William Sharp)

THE ANCESTRAL PARADISE

We have spoken about the Otherworld throughout this book, but
what do we really mean by this? Our perceptions readily inform us
about the physical reality of our world, but they are less capable of
telling us much about other realities, especially metaphysical ones.
This is a facility we have lost or neglected since the Foretime.
Shamans, mystics and visionaries have always had access to the
Otherworld, just as unsophisticated, 'primitive' people have been
aware of the Dreaming. The truths of the Western Way do not lie in

the self-evident reality of this world, although those truths are exercised in Middle Earth, as we can term the physical plane of existence; the wisdom of the West lies deeper than surface reality, in the Inner or Otherworld, which has its correspondence in inner states of consciousness. The Otherworld is a reality, but each generation has found its own metaphor to describe its existence: ancestral place of the dead, earthly paradise, heaven, happy hunting ground, hell, the land of faery, the astral plane, heightened consciousness and the collective unconscious – all these terms are applicable to describe the Otherworldly reality which has been perceived in many cultures as a place, condition or after-life abode. Because exposure to metaphysical concepts leads to a sense of unrelated confusion we would like to make a broad distinction between the kinds of reality as we will be viewing them.

There is now such a multiplicity of jargon connected with psychological states and cosmological conceptualization relating to different spiritual schools of thought, that we have avoided the usual terminology for the sake of simplicity. We would wish to distinguish three states or worlds: the world of here and now, or physical reality, which we term Middle Earth; the metaphysical world, or psychic (astral) reality, called the Otherworld; and the Spiritual Realm which is the abode of imageless Deity. These are crude distinctions which do not take into account the overlapping and interdependent nature of humanity, the ancestors, angels and gods, but let them stand first of all as representatives of a many-layered understanding.

In the Foretime, Otherworldly concepts were bounded by the realm of the ancestors, the Underworld. This chapter is headed by the famous warning of the Cumaean Sybil to Aeneas as he attempts to journey into Hades to consult with his dead father: the descent is easy, but the return not so (116). Shamans trained long years to make this very journey to the ancestors, a journey that was fraught with danger and from which they must return with ancestral advice for the benefit of the tribe. The dangerous encounters were so real that the shaman's drum, like the Aborigines' tjuringas mentioned in chapter 2, often depicted an Underworld map, charting the landmarks, showing both helpful and unhelpful spirits and, importantly, the way of return, often indicated by a personal symbol. The Underworld was understood to have an entry which bordered Middle Earth; often this was a cave-mouth, or a semi-dormant volcanic fissure such as Aeneas descends into at Lake Avernus, the birdless entrance to the classical hell. As the bones of the dead were buried in the ground it was natural to assume that they took up residence under it, in the Underworld. Most native cultures have an Underworld tradition of their own: Norse mythology, which is closest to northern shamanic practice, has Niffheim; Classical, Canaanite and Sumerian mythologies shared the view of a miserable, dreary Hades, full of twittering ghosts; while the Welsh Underworld, Annwn, was a chthonic, powerful place full of mighty ancestors. The idea of the Underworld as a place of judgment for an evil life was foreign to the Foretime; it was merely the place to which all the dead went, unless the infringement of some tribal law condemned the deceased to wander as a lonely ghost, outlawed from the tribe even beyond death.

The powerful and effective interaction of the Underworld with Middle Earth has been persuasively argued by the writer and musician Bob Stewart in his book, *The Initiation of the Underworld* (248). He has explored the British Underworld tradition by means of shamanic entry-meditation over the course of many years and has shared his experience on a tape, entitled *The Underworld Journey* (312). The immediacy and power of this primal experience puts one in touch with the ancestors in a manner which cannot have been equalled since the Foretime. The Underworld is the basis and foundation of the Otherworld reality: it is the deepest stratum of native consciousness where we meet with the most uncompromising inhabitants. Stewart prefers not to call them 'archetypes', because that implies a set of psychological personae, implying unreality. Like the Gods (see chapter 3), the Otherworld and its inhabitants are real *in their own worlds, in their own right,* they are not the result of imaginative or mental states; for although, as we shall see, their forms often vary between cultures, there is a close correspondence in the ways in which they are perceived.

Otherworldly cosmology is not easy to grapple with. It is dependent upon the manner of its perception. We rely on travellers' tales, those reports of the shamans' journeying: we remember that 'people listened to the poets and heard the versions of those who were thought to have penetrated the veil' (116). One factor emerges from listening to these tales: Otherworldly travel was at the heart of many mythologies.

To take Underworld descents, for example: these formed a genre of their own in Classical Greece, the *katabaseis* (116), but accounts of such descents are present in every tradition. We have already spoken about Aeneas' descent for information, but visiting the

Underworld is for a deeper reason than mere curiosity. Ishtar, the Babylonian goddess, like her earlier prototype, the Sumerian Inanna, descends to the Underworld to release her beloved from the realms of the dead where she undergoes a ritual stripping and death herself. Ishtar's experience is like that of Norse Odin who hangs nine days and nights on the ash-tree, Yggdrasil, as an offering to himself:

> Myself given to myself
> On that tree
> Whose roots
> No one knows . . .
> Into the depths I peered,
> I grasped the runes,
> Screaming I grasped them,
> And then fell back

This is the experience of the shaman and is at the heart of the mysteries: a costly self-discovery which brings knowledge and power by means of initiation in the Otherworld. The World-Tree, Yggdrasil, has its roots in each of the three levels we have spoken about: in Middle Earth, in Hell, and in Asgard, the place of the gods (60) Odin learns eighteen runes in all, giving him knowledge from each of the three levels, but especially from the realm of the dead. The central tree is the axis about which the Otherworld, in all its appearances, is set out. The tree appears, in different guises, in many of the exercises in this book and is a vital image for both Native and Hermetic Traditions (59). It is the tree of life, death and rebirth; it is the shaman's pole or ladder (100) and the qabalist's ladder of light (93); for Christians, the Tree of Knowledge in Eden and the Tree of the Cross are of one wood.

Parallels between Odin, Ishtar and Christ are easy to point to: each suffers death and transformation upon a tree, gaining knowledge of the dead or release of the dead by this means. The Underworld visitant's passport is desire for another's good: love kills death. Gilgamesh and Orpheus both journey to the Otherworld to release their friend or wife, respectively. Quetzacoatl returns from the Underworld with the bones of previous generations in order to create a new race, at great cost to himself (138, 40). Christ harrows Hell in apocryphal tradition (4), which is consistent with native Underworld traditions throughout the Western world. The toll of Underworld visiting is high, as old Vainamoinen, the Finnish hero, found. He visited the dead in order to learn charms which would magically finish the boat he was building. He says nothing about his visit but warns:

> Do not, future people,
> Do not, former people, set out to get charms from Death's Domain
> ... many have gone there,
> not many come back ...
> from the eternal cottage of the Abode of the Dead (126).

What can be achieved in Middle Earth must be done by ordinary means first: curiosity is no passport to the Underworld.

The gods and heroes who visit the Underworld to redeem the dead are frequently written off as fore-runners of the later saviours of revealed religion, but it is important to remember that each of these figures embodies tribal responsibility at every level of history and consciousness, fulfilling a task, outside of time, which is vital for every people, in every age. The place of the ancestors is not seen in a fearful light. For the Jews, to die was to be gathered to Abraham's bosom: this expression found its native level in the Christian era when to die was to go to Arthur's bosom. Sleep and death are but the first impingings of Otherwordly travel; but they are exploratory journeys and, unlike those of the trained shaman, undertaken without control. The ancestral abode of the Underworld serves as the basis for further exploration, but it should not be utilized as an excuse to contact the recently deceased, as in spiritualism; rather it should serve as an opportunity to contact the vast reservoir of collective ancestral wisdom. The Underworld is powerful and potentially helpful to anyone upon the Western Way, if it is approached in this spirit.

It is easy to think of the Underworld as 'down', but we must never forget that directional participles are inapplicable to Otherworld realities: we merely employ them with regard to metaphysical planes in order to give us some relation to the Otherworld. This confusion over the Otherworld's positioning appears in many cultures. Hy Brasil, Avalon, the Hollow Hills, the Blessed Isles, Summerland, Faeryland are all conceived of in these relative terms – they are distant, but not so distant that it would be impossible to travel thence (8, 175). In the Foretime, heavenly and paradisal places were not conceived of as somewhere in the sky; they were firmly situated in the earthly sphere, in the place beyond the sunset, ever-westward, where the light is always that of twilight. The Celtic Otherworld tradition is particularly rich from internal evidence of mythological

texts and folk-story, but it is significant that the Greeks referred to
the British Isles as Hyperborea – the Land Beyond the North Wind –
where the Titans still lived, the place to which they had been exiled.
The Greek poet, Pindar, spoke of these islands in connection with the
initiate's journey:

> All who have endured three times
> In a sojourn in either world,
> To keep their souls utterly clean of wrong,
> Go by God's road to the Tower of Kronos,
> Where the Airs, daughters of Ocean,
> Blow round the Island of the Blest (200).

Plutarch's description of the Fortunate Islands:

> Rain seldom falls there . . . they generally have soft breezes
> . . . the air is always pleasant and salubrious (165)

was enshrined forever by Tennyson in his *Idylls of the King*, where he
puts these words into Arthur's mouth:

> I am going a long way . . .
> To the island-valley of Avilion;
> Where falls not hail, or rain, or any snow,
> Nor ever wind blows loudly (259).

It is a place to which not only the dead go, but where heroic mortals
live still in the fullness of their powers; it is the place of traditional
learning and wisdom, where springs the well of inspiration. While
none of the Celtic Otherworlds has an exact geographical location,
they are thought of as somewhere in the Atlantic. But neither this nor
the strong Atlantean tradition which has exercised its fascination
since the time of Plato need imply a physical island which fell in some
historical era, but can point rather to Otherworldly remembrances
which have slipped from psychic into earthly realms (77, 132).
Atlantis, like Eden, was a place of inspirational knowledge which
was kept *in potentia*. The Fall of Man is concerned far more with
banishment from or cessation of communion with the Otherworld,
than it is with the consequences of sinfulness. This realization has
been the impetus for interior exploration in every time and place,
among every people; a realization of an essential birthright which it
is possible to contact. For, alongside official pronouncements about
heaven and hell, there have ever flourished the Everliving Realms
which have been preserved within the native tradition. The official

way to heaven is often cold and legalistic, but the Native Tradition has ever preferred its own familiar ancestral places and ways.

Paradise is not synonymous with heaven, however. It has its roots in the Persian *paerodaeza,* meaning park or enclosed garden. But paradise is an apposite synonym of the Otherworld – an intermediate state between incarnation and bliss. The enclosed garden and island-paradise are therefore primal states, interior realities where every vital component of life is in potentiality. It still has its first wildness, yet it has its own grace and rules of governance. There is no human trickery or deception here – nor will such debased coins serve in our transactions with the Otherworld. It is a waiting place, a place of learning and nourishment. The happy Otherworld is an earthly paradise in many legends, a place where feasting and love continue harmoniously. The Celtic Otherworld tradition is distinguished by the fact that it has no Hell, nothing parallel to the classical Hades with its grey emptiness. Although the Underworld is present in good measure – represented by the Hollow Hills and the Faery Realms – the Celtic Otherworld retains its ambience of joy. It is aptly described as the Fortunate Island, the Honeyed Plain of Bliss, the Apple Island and the Summercountry: all set somewhere West of the sunset in the mighty ocean.

Otherworld travel to these islands was such a noticeable feature of Celtic life that the poets coined a special genre of stories about them, called *imrama,* or voyages. The most famous of these was the *Voyage of Bran, son of Febal, to the Land of the Living* (165), which describes the travels of Bran and his companions, their arrival at an Otherwordly island and their sojourn in the Land of Women. It tells how, after a short time, one of their number becomes homesick, and they prepare to go home. As they reach the shore they are hailed and asked to identify themselves:

> 'I am Bran the son of Febal', saith he. However the other saith;
> 'We do not know such a one, though the Voyage of Bran is in
> our ancient stories' (165).

The man who leaps ashore becomes as dust, leaving Bran and his companions to sail away. As in Keat's *La Belle Dame Sans Merci,* the traveller who seeks to return from Faery wakes from too long a sleep 'on the cold hill's side'. We will be speaking more about Otherworldly travellers, and this time-discrepancy.

Why did the voyaging stop? The Otherworld did not go away, though conceptions of it narrowed or accommodated themselves to

Christian cosmological patterns; we can say that the Otherworld went literally underground, sometimes fusing with the ancestral Underworld, sometimes withdrawing itself, as it did in Scotland and Ireland, into the Hollow Hills, where the Otherworld and its inhabitants carried on interacting on the level of the folk-soul, but never quite disappearing from consciousness. The voyaging, the walking-between-the-worlds continued, but secretly and in fear of persecution or ridicule. The energies which had once been worshipped in the Foretime, and which had engodded streams and hills, put on ragged clothing as disguise, while in the Otherworld they were revealed as they really were – the Shining Ones whose power was still respected, whose help was still sought by those who knew them. The Otherworld might shrink to the appearance of a grassy mound, and its inhabitants to rustic elementals, but the reality of Faeryland was more virile than anything envisaged by those who looked hopefully for diminutive fairies at the bottom of their garden (130).

When the Gods speak of themselves, a different picture emerges:

> We are from the beginning of creation
> Without old age, without consummation of earth,

says Manannan mac Lir, the Otherworldly king in the *Voyage of Bran* (165). He speaks about the inhabitants of the Land of the Living: it is to these Shining Ones that we turn next.

THE SHINING ONES

I have always made a distinction between pictures seen in the memory of nature and visions of actual beings now existing in the inner world. We can make the same distinction in our world: I may close my eyes and see you as a vivid picture in memory, or I may look at you with my physical eyes and see your actual image. In seeing these beings of which I speak, the physical eyes may be open or closed: mystical beings in their own world and nature are never seen with the physical eyes (283).

So speaks an anonymous Irish seer, interviewed in the early part of this century by Evans-Wentz for his book, *Fairy-Faith in Celtic Countries*. He perfectly describes the method by which Otherworld beings are perceived. Although there is a definite interaction and communion between Middle Earth, the Otherworld and the Spiritual Realms, the five physical senses are not employed: rather a state of inner vision is required. However, this should not imply that Otherworldly beings, the Shining Ones, are unreal. As the seer says, they belong 'in their own world and nature'. But what are they? There have been many theories; they are alternatively conceived of as a folk-memory of a small native people, a remembrance of a mighty priesthood, remnants of forgotten gods, immortal heroes, or the ancestors. As we have already seen, the ancestors play a great part in Underworld theology, and, like the gods, they are a force to be reckoned with. More recent psychological theory, particularly Jung's theory of the Collective Unconscious, has suggested that the Shining Ones are nothing more than archetypes – collective, formalized energies which inhabit our psyches. There is some truth in all these theories because it is normal and natural for every people to find their own metaphor for a condition that is understandably difficult to express in human terms. We leave it to the reader to find the most acceptable method for understanding's sake, as long as each remembers that archetypes may inhabit the Otherworld as well as the psyche, that the Shining Ones are real in their own world and not the inventions of a disturbed mind. While it is currently acceptable to speak about the possibility of life on other planets, life on other levels is dismissed as nonsense.

We have suggested in chapter 1 how deity is formalized: a gradual image-building which grows in power and effect in relation to the visualization of the group-soul. Similarly, in our discussion of the god-forms of the Native Tradition, we saw the importance of the latent power of the elements which crystallized into the *synthemata* of the gods. Deity or pure spirit has no form and for it to have any communication with humankind it must assume an acceptable form or symbol. There is no way any of us can escape the language of symbolism which lies, sometimes deeply hidden, within our cultural and genetic memory. In the Foretime the world was visited and guarded by homely and familiar spirits whose manifestations came in numerous forms and varying gradations of intensity. The Otherworld beings range from the psychic equivalent of animals – the elementals – right up to highly evolved spirits whom we know as gods, with many variations in between which we might call angels or tutelary spirits. Some native Otherworld traditions have lost access to the full range of the Shining Ones through a shifting religious focus: elementals are usually the first to suffer. It is a truism to state that the gods of an outgoing religion become the devils of the incoming one, but it should not be forgotten. The potent god of the hunt or of the Underworld was associated latterly with God's opponent, the Devil, although the magnificent antlers of Cernunnos were derived from a totally different symbolic basis than those of the Devil. Horns, once synonymous with power, became associated with evil (58). The female spirits of wells and springs, conceived of originally as beautiful women, became dragons, water serpents and sirens. The guardians of the wood became malevolent ogres, just as the potent earth forces as personified by the dragon became debased. Whenever people neglect their dependence upon nature, this inversion of symbolism occurs. The elementals go wild and cannot be persuaded to give help.

Mechanised instruments of slaughter and harvest now complete the picture and typify the degradation of the Shepherd of Flocks and John Barleycorn: it is no wonder that field and forest are haunted by neglected elementals, and that wanderers are prey to ghosts which cannot find their ancestral abode. But there are more evolved beings within the Otherworld. We have spoken at length upon the gods and the many forms that they take. Some have made more successful translations to the modern world than others because their aspects and symbolisms remain vital to our world. The gods, as well as elementals, are dependent upon humankind, but after a different manner. Whereas elementals misbehave and run wild, the energies which have been formalized under the appellation of gods withdraw themselves for a time. It is impossible to say whether or not these energies return to the source of Deity ready to come again under different guises, or how long they remain in abeyance awaiting the restimulation of human attention. We believe that they are available, on tap, to those who familiarize themselves with their 'call-sign', their symbolism. The true gods are those Lordly Ones on a higher arc of evolution within the Otherworld; the opportunity to meet them is now rare and the encounter often frightening. Like Platonic forms, these are the primal forces personified: vast storehouses of a particular kind of energy. Exposure to the gods has left many mad or deranged, which is why contacting the primal forces is best left to the priest or shaman, or through the medium of earth-contact and carefully programmed meditation as we have suggested in chapter 3. It is also important to contact only the regenerate forms appropriate to modern consciousness, rather than the unregenerate forms used in the Foretime. This is where the Otherworld journey can help us: here the *essential energy* of the god-forms is available and contactable.

The gods may not choose to manifest themselves and should not be commanded in the same way as elementals who are our younger kindred. Similarly their energies should not be allowed to overwhelm you. When travelling in the Otherworld it will be noticed that there are no blurred edges to reality there. The inhabitants are, if anything, realler than in Middle Earth. To a weak personality the gods may appear as distillations of everything known and experienced, a primal pattern to which they must submit. Or there may be a superimposition of one reality upon another so that the traveller is bemused as was St Peter on the occasion of the Transfiguration (St Matthew 17: 1–13). He, a human being, had been taken up Mount Tabor by Christ, an incarnate god, and both were visited by Elijah and Moses, two Otherworldly entities: no wonder he was all for setting up camp for the four of them! Levels of consciousness, or different world realities, can be confusing. As we have already said, the uncharted realms of the Otherworld demand a good guide or inside contact, and this is the prerequisite for Otherworld travelling.

There are as many means of perceiving the Otherworld as there are guises of its inhabitants: these depend upon the Native Tradition of a people. We cannot hope to cover the full variety any more than we can present a complete map of Otherworldly travel, although we want to help you contact your own tradition. Every potential traveller needs a guide, and these are available and contactable. Call them angels, spirits, guardians or daimons, we each have access to a personal guardian. Suggestions on how to contact yours appear in exercise 7, Contacting the Guardian.

We do not all aspire to become shamans, magicians or mystics – for most of us the duty is to fulfil our vocation within the boundaries of a job, home and family. But something of a collective responsibility is being felt more generally – call it a pressure from the Otherworld to an inner evolution. The way to inner, spiritual growth is greatly desired and though many methods are available, not all are suitable or practical. A personal grounding in Other or Inner world living is the most precious experience which can promote spiritual growth within its own limits or serve as a basis for a more collective religious adherence or spiritual evolution. The inner guardian is the initiator for each of us. It need not be Mother Bunches in her rags or Black Elk in his rain-cloud suit, but someone familiar to whom we have never given a face; an inner voice or secret companion may be the link for you. The ancient teachers may be dust, but our voyages need not be rudderless. The inner guardian is our true North, the keeper of the charts, and the way shower. He or she is one who has already trodden the paths we are walking for the first time. Just as the shaman in the Foretime made Otherworld visits to his totem-spirit or ancestor for teaching and guidance, so can we draw upon the wisdom of the guardian. The seemingly modern notion that after death and a suitable number of incarnations humankind progresses to the angelic condition to become teachers in the psychic world can be found in many traditions of some antiquity.

'Poets say truly that when a good man dies he has honour and a mighty portion among the dead, and becomes a daemon, which is a name given to him signifying wisdom' (201, 'Cratylus'). The word *daemon* means 'he who apportions' (116): the guardian who allots experience to each of us. But does this imply that Otherworldly inhabitants have already plotted our course – that we are not free agents? Each individual has a destiny to fulfil, a task, a spiritual purpose which is nothing to do with hoarding up pious devotions but about bringing through, by individual effort, that work of creation which is still to be achieved. The Otherworld borders on the Spiritual Realm from which emanates the blueprint of creation: the guardians, like the angelic hierarchies we shall be meeting in volume 2 of the *Western Way*, are those who promote our creative potential, feeding us with the life-experience each of us needs to be an effective human being. This still leaves us free to co-operate with our potential or to avoid it. There is no fixity of destiny, we are free to make our own way.

The guardian acts as an ambassador of the Otherworld; his or her task is the Otherworldly equivalent of the shaman's – to explore Middle Earth and consult with individuals in this world. In volume 2 we shall meet this interpenetration of worlds again.

Contact with the Otherworld changes one's life forever. Once a pattern of communication has been established the inner life is vastly enriched and this, correspondingly, has repercussions on Middle Earth, and the outer life. But before we go on to discuss how we can travel, let us look at some Otherworldly visitants and the methods others have used to travel there.

Many have used a special symbol or token as a passport: Aeneas plucks the Golden Bough which he has to present to Proserpine in the Underworld; similarly, Bran, son of Febal, has a Silver Branch of an apple-tree. These are obviously both scions of the axial tree of life around which the Otherworld rays out. In Irish poetic tradition the gold or silver branch was actually an item of shamanic regalia borne before a poet of high status, signifying his connection with Otherworld wisdom and teaching. The silver branch of Rhiannon brought sleep and respite from Middle Earth, making mortals forget how long they had been in the Otherworld. Very often music is a factor in Otherworld transactions. The Faery Folk often teach faery music to musicians who sit patiently near their dwellings in the hollow hills. This aspect is particularly strong in British faery lore where Otherworldly tunes presage the arrival of the faery host: mysterious music is often heard near the haunts of these potent Otherworld beings who bear no relationship to Victorian fairies.

Music and dancing are often linked. In the Algonquin story of Algon the hunter, the hero finds a circular pathway on the prairie, worn as though by many feet, although no footprints can be found outside this area. Hiding himself in the long grass he hears music which becomes louder and he sees descend from the sky a host of star-maidens in an osier chariot. They alight and dance, and he captures one to be his bride (241). The Otherworld parallels between America and Britain are readily apparent as we see also from the story of another Algonquin brave whose wife dies. Like Orpheus, he determines to find her. An old man tells him, 'To reach the Island of the Blessed, you must cross yonder gulf you see in the distance' (241). He finds himself in a glass canoe and his wife in another: they row towards a wooded isle set in the middle of the water like an emerald set in silver. This glass boat features also in Celtic Otherworld travel.

True Thomas, or Thomas of Erceldoune is a border ballad which tells of how Thomas the Rhymer met with the Queen of Elfland who conducts him thence, pointing out the landmarks. He is so apt an apprentice that

> He has gotten a coat of the elven cloth,
> And a pair of shoes of velvet green,
> And 'til seven years were past and gone
> True Thomas on earth was never seen (53).

He is not the only Scot to have vanished. Michael Scot, the twelfth century scholar, also vanished after a life of seemingly fabulous length and achievement. His posthumous reputation as a magician was so widespread he entered the folk-imagination as a type of Merlin. A seventeenth century clergyman, Robert Kirk, who documented the experience of seers and faerylore of the Scottish Gaelic-speaking people, never returned from an expedition to Faeryland; although his gravestone is exhibited at Aberfoyle, there is nothing under it (130). These were, of course, Master-Men – those who had contacts with Otherworldly beings and who were seasoned travellers in other realities. They were the inheritors of the shamanic tradition, long after the Foretime was over. People are nowadays kept alive for years on life-support systems, or are refrigerated against the coming of more sophisticated technology, so who are we to say that these men have disappeared? Years in Middle Earth are but days in the Otherworld – perhaps their visits are not yet over or, like Elijah and Enoch, they have not tasted death but have passed on to the role of Otherworldly helpers.

Visitants from the Otherworld have also been reported in Middle Earth. The legend of the Green Children tells of how two children with green skin were found wandering in the vicinity of a cave during the reign of King Stephen: they would eat nothing but green, vegetable food. The boy died but the girl learned to eat ordinary food and so lived. She said that the land of their origin was a place where the sun never shone but where the light was that of twilight or sunset (30).

More often, the Otherworldly visitant is taken as a lover. The ghostly or demon lover is a theme which runs throughout world folklore. The dybbuk of Jewish legend, the medieval incubus and succubus, the seal-woman of Scottish and Scandinavian story all testify to close communication between the worlds. The Otherworldly lover and the earthly partner must observe certain prohibitions if the relationship is to work: the true appearance of the Otherworldly being must never be revealed, the earthly lover must never speak unkindly or demand that the other eat of or dress in the sacred totem animal. To mix physical plane sexuality with astral plane polarity, to confuse the worlds or to fall in love with a shadow is disastrous (see chapter 5). The misplaced fantasy of Otherworldly origin causes trouble in human living, so a clear understanding of the levels is necessary. We will be seeing later on in volume 2 how the partnership of Otherworld and Middle Earth beings acts as a positive device of visualization and power. Let us now examine the ways in which we can travel. The Otherworld level is rising into consciousness once more: it will prove a vital link between tribal and cosmic consciousness, enabling the necessary evolution to come about and facilitating the speedy release of unregenerate forms from the Native Consciousness. Learning to become a traveller in these realms will connect our spiritual and heriditary yearnings, as well as helping us to cope more effectively with the experiences of Middle Earth.

PASSPORTS TO INNER REALMS

The Otherworld reality stands at the centre of the Western Way. Its appearances may shift, the traditions merge, yet the way stands open for you to join those who have conversed with the dead, had the knowledge and conversation of their holy guardian angel, or been given the means to spiritual wisdom. This can be done through meditation and we urge you to find your own metaphor for the Otherworld, and to explore your own inscape. Because of each person's unique background and ancestry there will be as many approaches and entrances to the Otherworld as there are individuals: you already possess your key or symbol (see exercise 1), and the Two Trees entry-meditation (exercise 8) will lead you further into a landscape which is your own, where you can work on getting to know your guide (see exercise 7). Your journey will be both unique and at the same time similar to that of others. Comparing notes may not be helpful as every person enters at their own level. There can be no 'right way' to travel. Lone individuals take their own risks as well as having their own adventures, while others may prefer a package holiday under the auspices of a mystery school which supplies maps and ready-made guides for the cautious.

Why travel at all? This is hard to justify to the pragmatic and self-determining realist who acknowledges no world beyond Middle Earth and no other evidence than those of his five senses. The feeling of self-delusion can be very strong. Guides and gods may turn up in confusingly modern guises. The right amount of control is sometimes hard to establish at first, but aim for a waking state of consciousness, with controlled breath and breathing. With practice you will enter the Otherworld and meet with your guide and others. You will discover your destiny, your guiding theme, your inner impulse to act creatively, which you can then experience and fulfil within Middle Earth and your everyday existence. The images and encounters will be elusive as dreams at first, but you will learn to record and remember. The concentration required to make and hold contact can be wearing at first, you may even go to sleep. But because your experience of the Otherworld fades between sessions it does not mean that the Otherworld is a shadow, any more than familiar but long-absent friends are shadows without reality.

There will be days when Otherworld travel is easy. At other times it will seem that the two-way swing door is jammed and will only open outwards onto this side of things. The doors do shift, of that there is no doubt, but you will always find them. As the children in C.S. Lewis's *The Lion, the Witch and the Wardrobe* are told:

> I don't think it will be any good trying to go back through the wardrobe door . . . you won't get into Narnia again by that route . . . don't go trying the same route twice. Indeed, don't try to get there at all. It'll happen when you're not looking for it . . . and don't mention it to anyone else, unless you find that they've had adventures of the same sort themselves (142).

Some times are more suitable than others, but when you have mapped out the approach, you do not need to go through the whole customs procedure again. While Otherworld travel has been described by us in terms of meditation, it can equally well happen during sleep, in day-dream, initiation, vision, astral travel, during loss of consciousness and near-death states. Two famous examples of this latter experience occur in *The Vision of Aridaeus* (163) and the 'Vision of Er' (201, *The Republic*), when experiences of the Classical Otherworld, both Hades and Elysium, are described by one who is thought dead and afterwards revives to tell of this. Modern examples of this kind of recollection are manifold (107). The many-textured mantle of consciousness can be both waterproof and workaday, or become an invisible cloak, depending on our needs.

Contacting our native Otherworld is not to neglect our own world, but to sensitize the whole being to its requirements, seeing the earth as a living entity whose interdependence is as much upon the Otherworld as ours is in Otherworld beings, the Shining Ones. The scale of evolution is vaster than we ever realized, as the new science is beginning to discover: as mystics, shamans and philosophers have been telling us for ages.

To co-operate with the Otherworld fully we need first to look at ourselves. The maxim, 'Know Thyself', stands squarely in the front of each individual bent on walking the Western Way. This injunction is essential: it is a task which will never be finished. If we fail to clear ourselves and attempt a deep exploration of the Otherworld we will inevitably meet with our own worst qualities personified. If we are capable of recognizing and working with our own worst traits we may explore the deeper hinterlands of the inner worlds. We cannot be glamoured if we know ourselves, but we will begin to appreciate how we fit into the scheme of things, and how the Otherworld can help us to achieve our destiny. But human nature being what it is, no sooner have we cleared our psychic attics of the lumber stored there than we start accumulating more. The Augean stables will perhaps never be entirely clear, but we can at least try to keep them to manageable proportions. Some suggestions for self-clarification can be found on p. 151.

The primal importance of Otherworld travel is to go and to return. There have been many who have been lost in the mazes of the Otherworld, who wander beglamoured, no longer in touch with themselves but led by the will-o-the-wisp. The glamour of spiritual and psychic work leads many astray (15). Unless we are well-earthed in the physical plane, unless we first of all make our commitment to the path of the hearth-fire and organize our lives to a satisfactory standard before approaching esoteric paths, we have a tendency to drift off. This is why many esoteric schools insist on the attainment of a mature age before accepting candidates. Unless the individual character has first developed in Middle Earth to be an effective human channel of communication, the Otherworld traveller is apt to be weak and easily swayed by everything he or she meets. It is as important to make a stand against anything which seems contrary to one's own integrity in the Otherworld as it is in Middle Earth. The Otherworld is peopled by archetypes whose energy is distilled to great strength. The help of the inner guide and the use of one's own common sense will guard against coming totally under the control of one of the Shining Ones for, while we should never forget that we can help achieve the Otherworld's purposes for spiritual evolution, we must never lose sight of our earthly responsibilities. The touch of the Shining Ones is sometimes inhuman because their purpose does not take into account the individual: their collective energy is towards a common end, a cosmic purpose. Any Otherworldly attempt to influence your life-direction in a sweeping and off-hand manner should be met with firmness and integrity. Refer to your personal guardian and to your highest spiritual resources.

If we look at examples of Otherworldly travel we will see that, if certain rules are observed, the traveller will meet with no harm. Those who fall into Faeryland by mistake are saved by their possession of salt or iron – the elements of earthly life which are not the common coinage of the Otherworld. Boasting of their offspring's talents or beauty – gifts of the Otherworld – causes incautious women to lose their children to the faeries who leave in their place a loathly changeling as a lesson. Attempts to avoid hard work are met with more hard work on the Otherworldly side of things by the elder sisters who wish to share their younger sister's good fortune when she returns home from Mother Holle's house covered with gold (95). Pride, curiosity, improvidence, ingratitude and dishonesty disqualify the traveller; whereas obeying the rules, observing common-sense precautions, behaving with humility and straightforward courtesy enables the traveller to journey far. Most often the impediments to safe travelling lie with the traveller. Aragorn's advice to Boromir who distrusts the idea of going to the paradisal realm of Lothlorien in *Lord of the Rings* is sound. When Boromir complains that 'few come out who once go in; and of that few none have escaped unscathed', Aragorn replies, 'Say not unscathed, but if you say unchanged, then maybe you speak the truth. Only evil need fear it, or those who bring some evil with them' (263).

Human faults are amplified in inner work and can create obstacles. As with the hero of a folk-tale, we have to face a series of dreary tasks which reflect our unprepared and untrained nature, tasks which must be accomplished before the hand of the princess can be achieved. But any achievements we make are not to be reserved for our own use. This is revealed nicely if we contrast the example of Galahad, the later Grail hero who, after his achievement of the Grail, is assumed to a spiritual state at the city of Sarras and dies to the world for ever, with Peredur or Perceval, the earlier Grail hero, who after his achievement returns to the world, becomes a Master of Grail tradition, one who teaches others. To travel *and to return* with the gifts of the Otherworld is our destiny (162).

The idea of the Otherworld providing mortals with gifts, the Faery-Godmother who bestows blessings and creative propensities upon the newborn child – these are valid concepts which provide us with further clues to the Otherworld's ability to recharge Middle Earth with vital and redeeming energy. We are each gifted with the ability or aptitude to do certain things. Some of us perfect these abilities, becoming the creative artists who fructify the folk-soul of the people, others never work with their aptitudes so that they become stale and unmanageable. Our lives are only effective in so far as we bring through energies from the Otherworld and earth them by creative effort in this world. In each generation artists make this mystical journey into themselves and return charged with new life and purpose: this is how Otherwordly teaching is disseminated – not by overt teaching methods, but through song and story, play and film. These innocuous methods of transmission have a sweeping influence on all levels of consciousness. It is therefore imperative that that transmission is in the hands of those who know what they are doing.

The seedbearers within each generation receive the impulse and transmit their art by every means of creativity known to them: so the torch passes from hand to hand. The vocation of the artist is truly a holy one: those who fulfil that vocation with humble awareness of the debt they owe to the Otherworld are the true artists of our generation, not the self-vaunting, self-seeking egoists whose art merely reflects themselves. But for all of us the Otherworld call remains to be fulfilled. The sudden insights which arise without our bidding, the overwhelming urge to create some new thing out of our abilities, the sense of fulfilled destiny resultant from these urgings – these are clear signs of our allegiance to the common work.

> For the gods have hidden and keep hidden
> What could be men's livelihood (109)

and it our duty to find out for ourselves what we can best do in Middle Earth.

PARADISE LOST AND REGAINED

Without access to the Otherworld, Middle Earth becomes a sad, dead place. Today in the West our common perception of it is repressed to a level dictated by both Classical and Christian fundamental concepts – demons, ghosts, evil spirits and witches are the sole inhabitants of the modern Otherworld – one whose joyless, souless face can be seen almost any night as represented on videos of Satanic manifestation and alien interference. This is not the true Otherworld but Shadowland, a mere mirage of an inner reality whose gentle, healing power is deflected, represented by images of violence and sickening horror. The way between the worlds has never entirely closed, but obstructions have been put in front of it and many no longer believe it exists. Those for whom heaven is a Victorian myth and Hell an ever-present reality are cut off from the guiding mythology of the Otherworld. Without trust in the Spiritual Realms, the Otherworld and the Underworld, we become a prey for threadbare doctrines, of despair: and their increasing hold on the world spreads still, counselling doubt and destruction. When we stop praying for the dead, for those in purgatory, for those in the ancestral places, we begin to fear ghosts and unhoused spirits (32). When we cease listening to the voice of our inner guide, we hear the temptations of our worst side. When we cease to fulfil our spiritual aspirations, God becomes Devil.

Into this vacuum of doubt and uncertainty many new Otherworld scenarios have sprung which have been grasped despairingly, hopefully, longingly. God as an astronaut and interstellar, supervisory visitants seem to be new metaphors of the Otherworld for the modern age. Others grasp at psychological discoveries which seem to parallel shamanic experience but which often remain theoretical in their application to life. Some, grown weary of the bland Otherworlds proclaimed by Church, Synagogue and Mosque, look East to find more satisfying paradigms. But though the native Otherworld tradition looks dead, it is far from defunct. It informs each of the new Otherworld concepts still, from the same source.

Those who look to alien intelligences to help our world overcome its mistakes and save them from the tentacles of technological disaster, may find the old Shining Ones returning. If travel to the Otherworld is now confined, in popular imagination, to space-travel – the new *imrama* – may the paradisal islands not relocate in the stars as we look outwards rather than inwards for help? We may consider the constellations as the star-gates of the Otherworld, which mediate its archetypal forces, and which also have their mundane correlatives upon the earth itself (see exercise 5). It is possible that the purgative experience of psychoanalysis may put damaged psyches in touch with their own inscapes again where they may converse with Otherworldly archetypes. There is no doubt that Eastern techniques, themselves derived from valid spiritual disciplines, can stimulate our own Native Otherworld Traditions, although these need to be recast into the appropriate Western metaphor.

Otherworldly realms and their inhabitants can translate to other countries and cultures, by means of spiritual heritage and blood-lineage. Celtic immigrants brought their faery folk, the People of Peace, with them to America and Australia, although each of these countries have their own native Otherworlds in Red Indian and Aborigine cultures. It takes a long time for the Otherworld to establish itself, as John Crowley says about America in his novel about the Otherworld, *Little, Big*:

We as a people are too young to have cultivated stories like those told of Arthur, and perhaps too self-satisfied to have felt the need of any. Certainly none are told of the so-called fathers of our country; the idea that one of those gentlemen is not dead but asleep, say, in the Ozarks or the Rockies is funny but not anywhere held. Only the despised ghost-dancing Red Man has a history and a memory long enough to supply such a hero (61).

But the rediscovery, begun in the last century, of our folk heritage and its Otherworld tradition continues. The movement known as the Celtic Twilight produced at one end a never-never land woven of unrealistic yearnings, and at the other a broad and informed picture of the Otherworld whose proponents included the great poet, W.B. Yeats, and the mystic, 'A.E.' (George Russell). Their genius and vision inflamed the whole Celtic world and is still the basis for many fantasy novels whose authors glimpse, through them, the gleams of paradise. In other countries folklorists collected the last remnants of native traditions before the last story-teller forgot his craft. Antiquarians and poets began to realize the importance of their heritage: in all too short a time the living links with the past would be dead. We must not imagine that professionals and experts on folklore will record all this for us. The Otherworld traditions of many living cultures are in danger. In the last century and well into this, many Red Indian tribes lost their own links, were hounded into extinction or second-class citizenship. The vital impulse of these traditions has, fortunately, been preserved or revived, but in the face of unprecedented opposition and systematic rooting out of cultural identity. The move is on in Australia, motivated by the Aborigines themselves, to transmit their life-style and their access to the Dreaming to those members of their people who have no place in the white man's ecology. And everywhere the guardianship of native earth-sites and holy places is taught, along with transmission of the Otherworld tradition. This is heartening, but we cannot afford to be complacent about our own traditions.

An understanding of the Otherworld is essential within the context of the Western Way, or, indeed, any spiritual tradition. It is the basis from which all mystical writings grow. The Otherworld focuses the spiritual experience of seers, prophets, shamans and visionaries, who in turn inspire followers. Without a vision the people perish, yet there is never any shortage of a spiritual vision. The rediscovery within each generation of Otherworld reality has been the impetus of spiritual life. Spiritual wisdom does have a common source, even if its Otherworldly apparatus is perceived and interpreted in so many diverse ways, according to cultural requirements.

Our part in this transmission of tradition is vital. We travel to the inner home, to which we are silently called, and from which we journey out again into our ordinary lives, bringing with us that which we have experienced. It cannot be spoken about in words, but it can be communicated by gesture and attitudes which are apparent to others on deeper levels than any of us realize. Without the influence of the Otherworld, the Western Way would be a dead-end, its travellers merely armchair esotericists. The Otherworld call is heard by many who have no means to come to it consciously, although they visit it in dreams, day-dreams and visions. They read about it and yearn for it: 'Jerusalem, my happy home, when will I come to thee?' It is the longing of the heart to have a permanent home, an interior place which is bright and unfading in its delight. The longing for an earthly paradise has led many to explore the unknown Middle Earth, to stake a claim in holy places, just as Muslims, Jews and Christians have all claimed Jerusalem as their own. But the earthly paradise cannot be secured by armies; it is an exploration which leads in a totally different direction (162) And at its finding a different kind of homage is rendered. We are apprenticed to the Otherworld, just as the Shining Ones themselves are but journeymen to the Spiritual Realms which lie beyond.

The native Otherworld tradition is generally overlooked as a means of spiritual realization, but we present it side by side with the ways of revealed religion and hermetic esotericism which we will examine in volume 2. As Dante explored his three worlds of Purgatory, Hell and Heaven with his guide, Virgil, so with our guide we can pass through the seemingly complex time-scales of the Otherworld, meeting ancestors, archetypes, gods, angels, faeries, people dead and those yet to be incarnated. We can exclaim, with the seventeenth century English mystic, Traherne:

> A stranger here
> Strange Things doth meet, Strange Glories See;
> Strange Treasuries lodg'd in this fair World appear,
> Strange all, and New to me,
> But that they mine should be, who nothing was,
> That Strangest is of all, yet brought to pass (265).

The path to inner enlightenment and the journey outwards to actualize the realization is a long, painful one, fraught with many failures. But the journey is worthwhile. It is the only journey.

Take ship for your blessed islands, go there, learn wonders and mysteries. Voyage, but *come back*.

EXERCISES

EXERCISE 7   CONTACTING THE GUARDIAN

The beings you meet in the Two Trees meditation (exercise 8) are guardians, but they are also general guides who post you onwards to the next experience; they do not assume any responsibility for you. The personal inner guardian is perhaps closer than you think, although many are not in touch with theirs. We all have one, call it daimon, inner companion, guardian angel or guide: the guardian's role is not to keep you from experience but to initiate you into experience which will stretch you. Each guardian acts on behalf of his or her own guide – an inner teacher of great spiritual wisdom who has his or her being in the spiritual realms, but who can sometimes be encountered in the Otherworld. The collective wisdom of these teachers can be contacted within the Two Trees meditation, as well as within other spiritual disciplines. This interlinking chain of responsibility is seldom taught in the West: angels, like faeries, have become optional within the spiritual ecology. And although it is still common to appoint godparents to a new-born child, creating a spiritual kinship and mutual obligation, the function of an inner guardian is now almost entirely lost sight of.

The golden age of childhood gives us our first introduction to the guardian when a secret companion is formulated, visualized as active within times of quiet play. This image retreats at adolescence to be replaced by what the Jungian school call the anima or animus: the female and male psychic counterparts of man and woman respectively. Not everyone is aware of these inner influences which formulate themselves within the imagination according to cultural and experiential colouring. Everyone finds his or her particular metaphor, symbolism and imaginative clothing for the guardian, although they might not refer to it by that name. Others are aware of an unformulated inner voice or conscience, or of a watcher. If you have experienced any of these within your life you are already in touch with your guardian. But if you have not?

Sit in meditation. See before you a full-length mirror in a frame. Approach it. Its surface does not reflect you because it is opaque like milky opal. Within the mirror someone is sealed away from your vision. Breath upon the surface; see your breath as a flow of rainbow sparks of light. This is life-giving breath. Slowly see the frosted surface melt away under your breath. The figure of someone comes clear in the mirror. It may be male or female, old or young, but it is never an animal or non-human entitity, nor is it someone known to you in life. If the figure is still indistinct, concentrate upon your breath and the rainbow sparks of light. You are not giving life to your guardian so much as giving life to yourself. Your guide has always waited at this door to greet you and now you create the opportunity of your own volition. The surface of the mirror is now clear as day; the frame is as a doorway.

Greet your guardian and ask his or her name. In all your dealings with the guardian you must always speak first: your guardian will not speak to you unless you first make contact. This is important to remember so that you will not become dependent on or deluded by the appearances of the psychic world. If you cannot catch the guardian's name, establish a mutual recognition sign which you can exchange on future meetings – a small hand gesture will do. This will immediately establish the being as your own guide and not some stray contact in future meditation.

Now that the door is open between the worlds, you can meet and talk to your companion-guardian whenever you want. You may wish to do this privately in your room by speaking aloud, or by conversing on paper. Otherwise contact can be established by visualization and inner listening. Find your own level and be patient. As with all relationships, friendship and understanding will grow together in time.

Your guardian can be a sounding board, adviser and guide, not just of help in the Otherworld but in Middle Earth also. Good rapport with the daimon or muse is still considered valuable among creative people whose livelihood depends on inspiration, technique and concentrated effort: the friendship of the guardian enables them to fulfil their destinies by interpreting Otherworld concepts into crafts, arts, performances and music. One does not have to be a creative artist in order to live creatively at every level.

If you have a tendency to follow wonders or be dependent upon stronger personalities in your everyday life, beware. Do not act on everything your guardian tells you but reflect whether this advice is right for you at this time. Test the guardian's advice against your highest principles, submitting it, if necessary, to the source of your spiritual focus. Don't totally surrender yourself to the guardian, but try to be responsible for your own actions and thoughts. Don't worship your guardian like a god; he or she can be seen as an older brother or sister, a companion with a little more experience than yourself.

This contact is intimately personal and can take many forms. We can only broadly hint at the variety of relationship to be had, but it will be found that further contacts will come as a result of practising it. Both inner and outer life are enriched and fructified by contact with the inner guardian. Flexibility of personality results together with a new self-awareness which will promote confidence and humility in good measure.

EXERCISE 8   THE TWO TREES MEDITATION

This meditation is not just another guided imagery game but an initiatory entry to the Otherworld, the inner world whose reality runs parallel to our world, but which can be entered at any time because it is timeless. This ritual entry has been orally transmitted from teacher to pupil over many generations in the native tradition of Britain: it has been guarded as a hidden treasure and never before been written down. Because of its importance and because the Native Tradition is coming into the forefront of consciousness once again, the authors have felt that the time has come to give it out. Within it you will meet certain images and characters; they will teach you and show you certain aspects of yourself. Those who don't work at it will get nothing from it: as an initiatory method it is safe-guarded. Those who work with it and benefit from its practice are the ones for whom it is intended: for in the work of oral transmission, the living spark of the teaching must seed in the heart of the hearer.

Like an unfinished story, this meditation stands as a challenge to all who have felt the vital impulse of the inner levels in their blood. There is no end to this inner exploration, no correct way, no right order of events: each finds the journey tailored to his or her needs. The landscapes, the events and characters appear different according to the individual's perceptions, yet common images recur in assorted experiences which the authors have collated. This is not an easy journey to take because you go alone here. As this oral device was intended for use within a teacher-pupil relationship, with at least a minimal amount of supervision, certain things should be borne in mind: if you can get no further than the beginning or you get stuck or encounter recurrent images, stop. The time is not right for you either to start or continue your inner charting. It may arise later. Some may find that they do not do the meditation – it does them. This can be disconcerting, but manageable if you keep a sensible balance in your life. If it is not possible to retire for the kind of retreat outlined on p. 154, to complete the journey, then strenuously block any images which try to intrude on your daily life, following the guidelines set down in the basic instructions to the exercises on p. 16. This exercise, like much in esoteric exploration, can become obsessive but you will find that once the initial 'blockbuster' effect has manifested, the meditation continues at a more even rate.

In many ways, the Two Trees meditation is a compendium of the other exercises in this book. Some seekers have emerged from this experience alternately shattered and enlightened. Its effect is deep, so do not approach it facetiously. Those you meet beyond the two trees take many forms: recognizable religious leaders, animals, interior companions and guides, as well as what appear to be misleading characters who set obstacles in your road. These should be firmly faced and challenged if they threaten your integrity. However, they can have a salutary effect on those who have been avoiding personal issues and who seek to hold on to cherished and mistaken precepts.

Over a period of time the images and teachings will integrate themselves into your lives, becoming part of your 'interior furnishing'. It is good to keep a written record of your journeying for future reference. When attempting to compare notes with a friend or group who are working this meditation, remember that results will be variable and that no qualitative judgments can be made on one's progress here. Even the teacher is not in a position to judge or comment, except to help and advise in the event of difficulty. The authors are willing to help in this regard if such difficulties are met with: any communications should be addressed to us c/o Routledge & Kegan Paul.

The Two Trees

You are standing at the top of a low hill. Below you is a shallow valley at the centre of which lies a lake. Beside it are two trees – silver birches – which are reflected upside-down in the water. Walk down from the hill and around the margin of the lake until you pass between the two trees. As you do so focus your attention on the sky well above the horizon. There you will see either the sun or the moon: is it day or night? When you have established which, lower your gaze and see a figure approaching. It may be male or female, veiled or unveiled. This is your guide. Follow the instructions he or she gives to you. Your guide may accompany you or appoint a companion, or you may be sent on alone. Remember that no actual harm can come to you. Follow the way laid down for you and seek the goal to which you will be led.

You may return from your journey at any point that you choose. You will probably find that you slip in and out of the landscape of the journey at unexpected moments, and that after a lapse of several weeks or months you may find yourself taking up the journey again. Sometimes it may seem to continue even though you are not conscious of it, so that you may re-enter the landscape at a different point but in full awareness of what has passed, like remembering a dream. It should be understood that this inner journey may take years, possibly a lifetime and that, once begun, it will continue to reappear in your life. You need not start the journey from the beginning each time but simply follow its course.

CHAPTER 5
The Secret Commonwealth

For you took what's before me and what's behind me;
You took east and west when you wouldn't mind me.
Sun and moon from my sky you've taken,
And God as well, or I'm much mistaken.

'Donal Og', traditional Irish folk song

There are nine and sixty ways of constructing tribal lays,
And – every – single – one – of – them – is – right!

Rudyard Kipling: 'In the Neolithic Age'

NATIVE WISDOM

The Foretime is no more. While that historical era is over, its native wisdom survives, intact within the Otherworld, but fragmentedly within folk tradition and esoteric revival. Revival presents its own problems, often representing the values of the Foretime in the rosy glow of a Golden Age rather than in the light of the Secret Commonwealth which it represents. Robert Kirk (130, and see chapter 4) used this title to describe the land and manner of living of the Faerykind. The wisdom of the Native Tradition, from the Foretime up until the present, is literally our common-wealth, the treasury upon which we can draw for spiritual nourishment. Into its storehouses go every aspect of tradition, both pagan and Christian, old and new: its coinage is freshly minted anew every time one aspect of it is validly exchanged in Middle Earth. Only when the treasury is viewed as some kind of museum do its coins turn to leaves, like faery-gold. Revivalists who seek to employ traditions 'authentically' have to gang warily if those traditions are not to petrify under their touch.

Tradition is never static, endlessly reproducing itself to the last detail; it must change, adapting itself in different circumstances.

The transmission of the native wisdom is a miracle, although the symbiosis of its values is often overlooked by revivalists who either carefully invent 'ancient' tradition or who overstate fragments of it, constellating their meagre method around its dimly flickering beacon. We have shown how the traditions of the Foretime have returned: how the god-forms re-emerge, how the earth's energies have been recontacted and how the Otherworld is the key to native wisdom. Tracing the course of the Old Religion is less easy. Its path has been cross-tracked and overlaid with confusion; without the confirmative resonance of the Otherworld, theories of transmission choke each other like weeds. Any consideration of traditional transmission must be necessarily short, so within this chapter, we will attempt to show how this has been effected by the tribal unit as represented by shaman, ruler and people.

The modern pagan revival movement, known within its own circles as *the Craft*, is interesting in that it claims descent from the Old Religion of the Foretime. It disclaims any correspondence with what is popularly known as witchcraft, which is seen to derive from evidence extracted under torture in medieval and Jacobean times, and from the excesses of public imagination. Revivalist witches who proclaim their uninterrupted lineage from the Foretime are often embarrassed to explain how their tradition has survived untainted by accusations of cursing, child-sacrifice, orgies and devil-worship. If there seems to be an unexplainable hiatus between the Foretime's Old Religion and the modern Craft, it is because the links are either invisible or plainly were never there. Yet if there is any successor to the shaman then the most likely candidate is the revivalist witch.

While the legend of 'old families' keeping alive a dying tradition has been much embroidered by those commentators seeking rationalization for their claims, there were and still survive certain families where the Old Religion was transmitted in some form. One famous East Anglian witch, George Pickingill (1816–1909), who was consulted by Masons and Rosicrucians from Europe and America, traced his descent from Julia of Brandon, a witch who died in 1071 (271). His hereditary tradition descends through the nine covens which he founded over the course of sixty years, and so may be said to be operative today. Instances of hereditary succession are too fragmentary for any case to be made, however. Just how did the native shaman become a witch?

As druid succeeded shaman, so priest succeeded druid. Spiritual leadership is always exercised by the mystically percipient who are drawn towards the priestly role; yet the priesthood became increasingly involved in ecclesiastical administration and theological intellectualism. Thus, the spiritual needs of those enmeshed in tribal consciousness were neglected. Despite the intermittent sniping of the Church, paganism and Christianity rubbed along: priest, people and ruler often exercising their dual membership of old and new religions in much the same manner as modern Japanese still avouch themselves both Shinto *and* Buddhist. By this time the shaman had either become a priest of the new religion or continued to function in the old one, albeit secretly.

At the Renaissance a new wind began to blow. The Reformation of the Protestant churches was an attempt to restate the Native Tradition in Christian as well as national terms. It is at this point that the major persecutions of Old Religionists, now called witches, began. Medieval Catholicism had strong links with the Native Tradition. Pope Gregory the Great had encouraged the siting of churches on pagan centres of worship and the continuation of pagan festivals in Christian guise. The Mother and Father of the Foretime, the Lord and Lady of the Old Religion whose aspects and avatars were the gods and goddesses of paganism, were present in the forms of Our Lord and Our Lady – Jesus and Mary. Under Protestantism and its offspring, Puritanism, the reverence to the Virgin was banned and the celebration of native festivals outlawed. Those whose dual allegiance was unthinking found themselves forced to take sides. The Protestant restatement of the Native Tradition did not include pagan revival; it sought to purge the native character of the pollution of both pagan and Catholic influence.

The Old Religion as a Foretime survival was forced into extinction: but before it died it showed its ugly side. Revivalists like to think of the 'burning times', as they are known in Craft circles, as a parallel to the persecution of the early Christians: small, fervent bands of dedicated pagans striving to keep the old ways alive, meeting secretly at night for fear of spies, and virtuously going about their daily business, ill-wishing no one. The reality was often far more human. To have one's spirituality derided, to lose one's livelihood, to see one's family suffer did not inspire feelings of goodwill: those with the power to heal and hurt often chose to hurt in vengeance and retribution. There were few on either side of the fence, whether Christian or pagan, who maintained the highest principles of their faith in practice. The notion of the Devil as God's opponent had been propounded from pulpits both Catholic and

Protestant. Under threat of persecution by their oppressor, some did turn for active support from the Devil: if God allied himself to the persecutors, let them join the opponent of God.

The basic compatibility of pagan and Christian was overturned in a hysterical purge. Christianity, shamed by its pagan beginnings and its urges from the tribal consciousness, eradicated offending members. Yet the fascination with the earlier levels of religion remained voyeuristically embedded within the hearts of Christian persecutors. It has been observed, that, at this time, 'treatises on witchcraft came near to being a pornographic genre' (278). The spectacle of two sets of shamans fighting each other is not a pleasant one. The tragedy of two religions turning sour might have been avoided, but the age was not noted for its tolerance. Yet all was not dark.

In his introduction to Carlo Ginzburg's *The Night Battles*, a study of pagan survival within the context of agrarian cults, E.J. Hobsbawm remarks of this sixteenth century Italian phenomenon:

> here we have not Margaret Murray's subterranean old religion hostile to Christianity but ritual practices which had long established a symbiosis with the dominant religion – the *benandanti* (literally, 'those who go well') originally regarded themselves as champions of Christ against the devil – but which are forced into opposition . . . by Church policy (87).

These *benandanti*, ordinary country folk, went forth at night to do battle with those who threatened the crops. Doubtless some families retained this ancient guardianship, while isolated individuals with quicker wits than those of their contemporaries bore witness to the old ways. But the impetus of the Old Religion was broken and its shamans dead. There survived certain wise-women and cunning-men, like George Pickingill, at the tribal level of belief, whose role was nearest to the shamanic one; apart from them, the story-tellers, poets, musicians and craftspeople retained the ancient themes and skills, although usually in ways superficially unrelated to that of religion.

But just as ancient sites were discovered by gentlemen arche-ologists and the old mythologies aired by bored divines, so the Old Religion was investigated. We owe a debt of gratitude to the commentators, collectors and amanuenses who recorded what would otherwise have been lost; as Pausanius recorded ancient Greek customs and religious sites before the coming of Christianity

(192), so did Stukely and Aubrey record the British landscape before industrialization (251, 11). Cecil Sharp and Sabine Baring-Gould (193) collected folk songs, stories and dances before radio and television came to replace them. But we should ever be aware that a visit from the anthropologist is often a visit from the undertaker as traditional customs become self-aware.

A number of theories about the survival of the Old Religion as witchcraft began to fertilize and stimulate the native consciousness from the beginning of this century onwards. Charles G. Leland, an American folklorist and himself a descendant of John Leland the Royal Antiquary in 1553, uncovered evidence about Italian witchcraft and published his findings in *Aradia: the Gospel of the Witches* (137). The anthropologist, Margaret Murray, wrote two books: *The Witch Cult in Western Europe* (1921) and *The God of the Witches* (1933). While Leland's findings were an isolated instance of survival from a first-hand informant – a witch called Maddalena – and only concerned with Italian practices, Murray's books attempted to take witchcraft seriously as a survival of the Old Religion. There were no witches to come forward and gainsay their findings. Persecution had resulted in an understandably deep-dyed secrecy, and the laws against witchcraft were still on the statute books in England. It was not until 1951 when the Witchcraft Act of 1736, under which those 'pretending to be witches' were liable to imprisonment, was repealed that other kinds of evidence began to turn up (270). The spearhead of the new evidence was Gerald B. Gardner, an amateur archeologist and anthropologist who had formed links with a coven in the New Forest in Southern England; he was subsequently initiated into the group and, after the repeal of the Witchcraft Act, he began to publish books about the Old Religion from within. *Witchcraft Today* and *The Meaning of Witchcraft* exploded the old misconceptions surrounding witches and propounded a cult of shaman-like practitioners of the Old Religion who kept the old festivals, worshipped the old gods and who worked only beneficent magic.

Gardner's claims have perturbed both those inside and outside neo-paganism. Doreen Valiente, who knew and worked with him, has this to say: 'the rituals he had received were in fact fragmentary . . . and to link them together into a coherent whole . . . he had supplied words which seemed to him . . . to strike the right chords in one's mind' (270). It would indeed be astonishing if anything like a coherent text had survived through oral transmission of old rituals. The Old Religion, never a codified whole even in the Foretime, was fragmented and obscured. The tradition which Gardner contacted in the New Forest was different from those pagan survivals in other parts of the British Isles or in Europe. Whatever the leaders of other covens might say, Gardner's ideas sparked the dry tinder of a seemingly dead tradition into a great conflagration. Individuals who had fallen out of orthodox religion were attracted to join Gardner's covens and soon a great mushrooming of neo-paganism occurred. The Craft of the Wise, so called from the etymology which derives 'witchcraft' from the Saxon word 'wicce' or wise, grew at a phenomenal rate. Growing covens soon exceeded their autonomous units of thirteen, and sent off daughter covens. The Craft soon crossed the Atlantic where the boom was even bigger.

Gardner was not alone in his attempt to spread the Old Religion; other individuals, some with inflated egos, were soon claiming witch grandmothers and special powers. Neo-paganism had become cultist. Margot Adler discusses this phenomenon in the United States in her book *Drawing Down the Moon*. All the ingredients of the Foretime's Old Religion are present within the Craft: the worship of the old gods, celebration of agrarian and calendrical festivals, the joint priesthood of men and women, but why was this revival necessary?

The popular response to neo-paganism has been overwhelmingly large even in an age which turns to new religious cults to fill the gaps of orthodox faiths. It is likely that the push towards a reintegration of the Native Tradition is being experienced. In the thirty years since Gardner began his revival in all good faith, a significant pattern is emerging. While there are still those adherents who play at witches with a pathetically unadult enthusiasm, with plastic flowers in their hair, their middle-aged spreads ashake and their feet planted firmly in a never-never land of pagan peace, there are others who are remembering the old ways by analeptic means and who are practising them seriously as modern-day shamans. They may be unashamedly revival, yet their effect is directly influencing the New Age to appreciate some native wisdom.

Whilst revival Craft will always attract the childish adult, the fervent (usually male) servant of the Goddess and the power-seeking High Priestess, as well as the sexually immature and the religiously undecided, it is a force to be reckoned with when it is truly in touch with its native potency. Yet here also lies the danger of revival. What was common custom in the Foretime – blood-sacrifice, ritual mating, etc. – does not obtain today. And while the Craft as a whole does not subscribe to these practices, those for whom these memories ring strong can be easily seduced from their spiritual evolution into inappropriate atavism. The esoteric dictum of evil being misplaced energy holds good here. What is correct in the Foretime is not correct now. Contact with unregenerate forces demands great personal integrity. Those who have a taste for the nasty or the naughty do not need to join the Craft to get their kicks, but those who 'bring their evil with them' do it no good service. If the Native Wisdom is contacted via the Otherworld, then the dangers are minimal, yet the question still needs to be answered, 'does this revival tradition work now in the twentieth century?' If the answer is no, then it is a form of play-acting, not a road to spiritual development.

What has been written here about the Craft applies equally to other neo-pagan groups. In so far as they are genuine attempts to contact the Native Tradition and bring it forward into the New Age, they are doing the work of the aeon. In so far as they are living in an ideal past, they are a waste of effort. These hard words apply to anyone who is walking back down the inner spiral of the Western Way for holidays in the past with no intention of returning. If the Craft seems to lack the integrity of, say, the Christian church, where are the modern mystical interpreters of the Christian tradition? Although neo-paganism works from the grass-roots up, at least it is sending out some scouts to explore the possibilities of its own tradition.

But while 'modern neo-mystics . . . have been drawn by . . . a rebirth of interest in mythology and especially British mythology; by the ill-defined belief in a New Age . . . by a rejection of Christianity which is not the old atheism or humanism, but a search for an alternative spirituality, often with magical and occultish aspects' (7), they cannot altogether ignore the mystical cohesion of Christianity which has preserved aspects of the Native Wisdom quite as successfully as the Craft has done, as well as imparting its own wisdom as a spiritual path. Geoffrey Ashe has written that 'The Strong Magic is creative as well as demoralizing' (7). If the 'strong magic' is able to operate instead as 'miracle', then the old and new religions need never be a stumbling-block to each other as they have been in the past. The renewal of the Secret Commonwealth happens by many means and its mediators may not necessarily be those occupying the shamanic or priestly role any longer. Ultimately it does not matter who mediates this renewal, as long as factionism can be avoided. The past is 'neither pagan nor Christian, it belongs to no nation and no class, it is universal' (202).

THE SECRET PEOPLE

They have given us into the hand of the new unhappy lords,
Lords without anger and honour, who dare not carry their swords.
They fight by shuffling paper; they have bright dead alien eyes;
They look at our labour and laughter as a tired man looks at flies.
And the load of their loveless pity is worse than the ancient wrongs,
Their doors are shut in the evening; and they know no songs (52).

That quotation from G.K. Chesterton's poem 'The Secret People'
might well stand with that of the Irish folk song 'Donal Og' which
heads this chapter as an indictment of the people of the Native
Tradition, wherever they may be. Those who have followed us this
far will perhaps have glimpsed the reasons why we think the Native
Tradition is as important as the Hermetic in the formation of the
Western Way. Those secure in their religious fastnesses, who have
fixed and reassuring views on all aspects of life, can afford to be smug
about the secret people from whom sun and moon, East and West,
and any approachable concept of God have been riven.

To speak of the secret people in this regard is not to be patronizing
about the 'lower-class' or peasant stock, because each of us is one of
the secret people exiled from our tribe. The Western Way's Native
Tradition has never gone in for autocratic priestly leadership: the
spiritual well-being of the tribe has been exercised collectively by
priest, people and ruler – the priest/shaman being the expert in
spiritual matters. We have seen how the shaman survived as either
priest or witch, just as the shamanka had the dual option of nun or
wise-woman. The tribal rulers survived as feudal barons or else
perished in the internecine squabbles for tribal leadership. 'Families
of priests and noblemen, blessed with family trees as old as the
Creation, were obliterated' (202) with such vigour that one is tempted
to consider Margaret Murray's theory concerning the sacrificial
divine victim which was demanded every seven years for the good of
the land (176). Theories of Divine Kingship were upheld most
strongly by the Stuart Kings – notably insisted upon by that same
James I who had written a denouncement of witchcraft, the
Daemonologie (Edinburgh 1597). After the demise of the Stuart
cause and the institution of constitutional monarchy, the sense of
tribal leadership was diminished. The cohesion of the tribe was
broken and the secret people were leaderless or in the hands of those
who cared only for their physical well-being – those 'new unhappy

lords' who were so out of touch with the urgency of the Native Tradition that 'they knew no songs'.

The secret people may have been like lost sheep, yet they were not fools. They knew that the high-sounding names of God, the alien rituals and political theorizing were not for them – that there was a homelier and easier way than this. Yet, equally, they often let themselves be duped by a lazy dependence on tribal consciousness and were manipulated to fight in foreign wars, to go hungry and landless – anything save find the salvific story, the essential spiritual destiny which was rightfully theirs. Rather than seek for the Secret Commonwealth they sank back into the fleshpots and superstitions of exoteric religion, clinging fondly to the worn-down and vitiated customs of their ancestors.

After the Foretime had receded to a faint memory and under successive invaders, the secret people continued, adapting themselves as minimally as possible to the new ways. Yet there rose from within their ranks certain individuals – not esotericists or those whose names spring to mind with regard to the Hermetic tradition – but continuators, connection-men and women, marginal shamans whose names we shall never know. These hidden shepherds acted as seed-bearers on the marginal thresholds of experience: they had no part in political exhortation, nor did they employ their charisma to become popular figure-heads. They were the poets, story-tellers, folk-singers, visionaries, craftspeople and synthesizers of the inner vision whose hidden duty was to transmute the Native wisdom into something more immediately usable. If we mention the names of a handful of these continuators but briefly, it is not in disrespect of their wisdom and insight.

The Native mystics are represented by Mother Julian of Norwich (c.1342–1420) whose insight into the nature of Deity was expressed in both masculine and feminine imagery, and whose concern was for her 'even-Christians' and the immediacy of love's action within humanity (122). While across the Atlantic, the non-conformist vision of Mother Ann Lee (1736–84) founded the Shakers who employed an ecstatic tradition of dance and song as a means of worship (286).

The Native visionary poets William Blake (1757–1827) and George Russell, or 'A.E.' (1867–1935) are both in the tradition of Kirk's Master-Men, walkers-between-the-worlds whose visitations were recorded in their poetry and other writings (22, 218). While the Native nature mystics and poets, Coleridge, Wordsworth and

Shelley, are better known; Walt Whitman (1819–92) and Richard Jefferies (1848–87) both explored the pantheistic response with cosmic insight (284, 118).

As embodiments of a dead culture we have the testimonies of Black Elk (1863–?) who spoke of the Lakota Indians of his tribe and their demise under white culture (180), and Peig Sayers (1873–1958), an illiterate Irishwoman who had no English, yet who was a fund of traditional stories (180).

We spoke earlier about the skill of poet and bard: the degeneration and revival of the native poetic tradition is amply dealt with in Robert Graves's *The White Goddess*. Long after the great Celtic poets had sunk to the level of horny-handed itinerants plying their songs and stories through an impoverished land, the ancient traditional tales and ritual scenarios were remembered and sung by nameless folk-singers on both sides of the Atlantic (175, 193).

The shamanic skills of healing fell to the village witch whose practice of folk-medicine is now being revived in a world impatient of orthodox healing methods. Stripped of the old healing chants, techniques of balancing the subtle psychic body and its energy fields are dismissed as witch-doctoring – they are, but still effective for all that.

The crafts-tradition of creating an object and fixing it in Middle Earth by means of wood, clay and iron is a paradigm of the esotericist's art. Eric Gill (1882–1940), the sculptor, reminds us that 'art' originally meant 'skill' and that the artist 'is the person who actually has the skill to make things . . . to bring into physical existence the things which abide in the mind' (86). Through the craftsperson many religious and mystical truths are transmitted from one generation to the next, without need for concealment, because they are 'self-evident truths' and open mysteries. The analogy of craft-work has been absorbed by both the Craft, as a neo-pagan movement, as well as by Freemasonry, as a Hermetic revival. The strength of the crafts-guilds enabled the traditions to be transmitted in a unified way which was appreciable to all at many levels. Yet more often the continuators were inspired individuals who were the leaven in each generation, engaged in the cyclic action of restating and rediscovering the truth of the Native Tradition. Their very namelessness is unimportant – we have mentioned only a scattering of these marginal shamans whose work has informed our own century – for it is said:

Every cycle has its prophets – as guiding stars; and they are the burning candles of the Lord to light the spiritual temple on earth, for the time being. When they have done their work, they will pass away; but the candlesticks will remain, and other lights will be placed in them (286).

THE MOTHER-COUNTRY

Yet in some eras the light burned less brightly when the continuators were less skilled or their influence absent. Although the secret people never ceased to be psychically sensitive, without training or some kind of shamanic supervision their efforts often failed to result in anything more than a low-level psychism which runs after signs and portents rather than concerning itself with the spiritual well-being of the world. The Otherworld communicated its messages still, yet these were cast into the immediate language and symbolism of everyday life. There was no shortage of communication between the worlds, just a shortage of experienced decoders. The prevailing popular interest in what might be called 'low-level' occultism – a surface fascination with astrology and divination – might lead one to speculate whether indeed occultism was not the pornography of religion. Yet, as H.P. Blavatsky has commented:

occultism is not magic, though magic is one of its tools. Occultism is not the acquirement of powers, whether psychic or intellectual, though both are its servants. Neither is occultism the pursuit of happiness, as men understand the word; for the first step is sacrifice, the second, renunciation (24).

We shall be discussing the split between religion and magic in volume 2, yet 'tampering with the occult' is regarded as dangerous by the conventionally religious who quite happily digest miracles, propitiatory prayer to the saints, the existence of guardian angels and the sanctity of church precincts. It is worth juxtaposing this list with the beliefs current among esotericists of many kinds: the use of magic, mediation of god-energies, the protection of the circle-guardians, and the sanctity of ancient temples both of stone and earth. Spiritual bigotry results from fear of the unknown and the threat to one's own comfortable ride to heaven. However, spiritual progress is full of such challenges and threats – without them there is no progress.

Yet the negative examples of occultism are always being stressed by those who seldom or never examine the short-comings of their own tradition. Two pictures emerge. The Native Tradition is exemplified by the Witch, stirring her cauldron, cursing all and sundry: a woman of evil intent whose sexuality is of a disturbing kind, unless she is portrayed as an ugly hag. Significantly, she is a *woman*. The Hermetic Tradition fares no better, being portrayed by the Black Magician, safe within his circle, wrapped in his emblematic cloak and hat, invoking demons and commanding elemental power: significantly again, he is a *man* of malicious intent whose devious brain threatens the well-being of the world. These fearsome projections are frequently trotted out of the esoteric cupboard by those who are ignorant of the complementary opposites of these pictures. While it would be a gross simplification to identify the Native Tradition with the feminine, and the Hermetic with the masculine, there is a symbolic truth to be uncovered here. The witch is more often the wise-woman or sibyl, personifying the integrated wisdom of the earth, mediating natural magic and prophetic insight; just as the black magician is more often the alchemist who transmutes the perennial wisdom into a way of spiritual evolution. This identification cannot be pressed too far since it fails to take in the subtler level at which gender ceases to have any importance. Yet the fact that the negative images of the Western Way constellate around the feminine and masculine in this manner should remind us of the fact that the older 'feminine' mysteries of the Native Tradition have suffered from neglect just as the 'masculine-oriented' mysteries of the Hermetic Tradition have been over-stated and become rigid.

We spoke in the introduction of the fact that we are aware of our patrilineal heritage – our exoteric side – but that we have neglected our matrilineal side – the esoteric side of ourselves. The Native Tradition is very much the mother-tradition in which we are born and to which we fail to succeed. The secret matronym of our mother-country has been withheld from us and to discover it we must go on a long journey of self-discovery.

How each of us interrelate with our secret mother-country, our esoteric selves, is a measured reflection of how we respond to the Mother herself – the Goddess, whose re-evaluation within the twentieth century is an attempt to trace the first inward spiral of our spiritual journey. The re-evaluation of early modes of worship has produced at one and the same time some of the most profound and the silliest concepts in popular consciousness. The primal understandings of the Foretime were uncomplicated compared with those facing any revival of Goddess worship today. The same problems of reversion to primitive modes of behaviour apply again, as a variety of groups are spawned, all concerned with re-establishing the Golden Age of Matriarchy when the Mother ruled and women were treated right. The Craft has had its feminist variants in the shape of Dianic Craft – covens for women only (1). The radical wedge of feminism has split old understandings of sexuality, gender and their application to the archetypes of Deity with greater or lesser skill (63, 244).

Within the field of esotericism and spirituality – and indeed throughout this book – there can be no differentiation of intent between the men and women who walk the inner path. On the inner levels there are no such political problems as those now facing us on the outer levels of life. Certainly, work on the inner levels is experienced differently by men and women as Dion Fortune implies in her enlightening essay, 'The Worship of Isis' (78):

> Isis is the All-woman, and all women are Isis. Osiris is the All-man, and all males are Osiris. Isis is all that is negative, receptive, and latent. Osiris is all that is dynamic and potent. That which is latent in the outer is potent in the inner; and that which is potent in the outer is latent in the inner. . . . This is the law of alternating polarity, which is known to the wise.

Women are potent upon the inner levels, acting as sibyls, seers, bringers of spiritual fertility – yet artists of both sexes operate upon this principle also. Men are potent on the outer levels, acting as directors and synthesizers, reflecting inner inspiration and earthing it – yet researchers of both sexes also actualize inner confirmations of their theories in this manner. There are no hard and fast rules, yet this circuit of polarity is a fact of inner working. While we can say, generally speaking, that women tend inwards on the spiral path and men tend outwards, once the principle of polarity is understood these directions can be accommodated in reverse: thus women can operate as directors of inner work, while men may act as mediums for the inner levels.

Confusion is rife on the levels of meaning surrounding sexuality, polarity, and the gender assigned to Deity. Male and femaleness are the symbolic masks worn by Deity for our comfort and understanding. Although the female mask has not been exhibited in the West for many centuries, it remains a valid working form for those who are willing and able to mediate the energies of the Mother. Although there were women-only and men-only cults – those of Bona Dea (13) and Mithras (274), for example – and while there will always be male and female-oriented mysteries, the present concern is not with exclusivism. The archetypes of God and Goddess are common and powerfully effective energies, flowing from the Spiritual Realms, which are for all people – not limited in application to man or woman only. We should beware of projecting our repressions and longings upon the divine archetypes, nor should we confine their operation within the limits of historicity.

Sexuality merely determines our gender function as human beings who have the potential to physically reproduce themselves. It is frequently misapplied and confused with *polarity*. The sexual circuit is made between a man and a woman. The polarity circuit is made between outer and inner levels – or between the Otherworld and Middle Earth. When 'horizontal' and 'vertical' circuits are crossed, the result is confusion of intent, and its effect can be traced throughout the history of the esoteric world where sordid little episodes cloud the clarity of inner working. If there ever was a form of Western Tantra, its principles have been mainly lost sight of.

These definitions need to be borne in mind when discussing those hackneyed designations: patriarchal and matriarchal religion. Where feminism has successfully campaigned for women's elevation from subservient or slave status to the level of a human being who has equal rights, it has done the work of education. If its occasional stridency grates upon the ear, it should be considered that sexual equality is far from established in many areas of the world, both West and East. Where feminism has claimed exclusive rights over spiritual areas it is as guilty of spiritual appropriation as the so-called patriarchal religions.

Yet there should be no cause for concern: women have held the guardianship of the mother-country, acting as the repositories of religion during the dark times. But it is important that their instinctive knowledge should be disseminated freely now and not held in stasis where it is liable to decay unused. If patriarchal trends have kept the wisdom of the mother-country of the Native Tradition in check, then the compassion of the Divine Feminine should be applied as an antidote not as a blindfold. The automatic rejection by women of anything masculine – whether it be symbolic or actual, god or man – is childish in the extreme.

Both sexes have a lot to teach each other. While each may retain their own mysteries, it is vital that skilful initiators, both male and female, emerge soon before the Western Way is lost in a welter of misinformation about its own traditions both Native and Hermetic. The neo-pagan movement has opened the way for both sexes to re-experience the Mother in a practical sense. But perhaps more importantly, the essential symbolic verities of the Divine Feminine have been intelligently presented for the first time in this century – mostly by female psychologists. The work of Esther Harding (102), Sylvia Perera (196) and Helen Luke (145) has gone a long way to educate the twentieth century consciousness. Before the century is out the response to discussion about the Goddess will not be 'which goddess?' – a question unthinkable if applied to God – but an acceptance and understanding unparelleled since the Foretime when the earth herself was first called mother.

REDEEMING THE TIME

A great renaissance of neo-paganism and shamanistic techniques is abroad. Modern consciousness has latched onto something old and primeval. For many it is an escape from the present; for others it is a welcome alternative to the watered-down versions of orthodox religious practice remembered from their youth. This neo-pagan upsurge has brought with it an understanding of our belonging to the earth, a discovery of the Mother-country and of the native wisdom of the Secret Commonwealth; but it has another dangerous side – one which would apply ancient principles to modern consciousness with no regard to the passing of time and circumstance. Thus those who walk the Western Way through its Native Tradition should bear in mind that:

> the mind of the student must be clearly focused in objective consciousness. *Development on top of an atavism* is the cause of most of the difficulties that occur in [esoteric] training (236, italics ours).

As we have tried to point out throughout this book; the Native Tradition's soil is fertile for present research and future growth, but it does need to be well-turned first. Those who seek to use its images and its ancient wisdom undiluted with common sense will come to grief.

The regeneration of old forms through modern consciousness is of prime importance. The coincidence of ancient resonances with present understanding should alert us to the fact that the inward path of the maze has been threaded as far as it can go. The work of manifestation and return as inspired by the cosmic rhythm, belief and acceptance of reincarnation, the growing concern with the planet's survival are all currently symptoms of the Aquarian Age consciousness – or of its crankiness, depending on your standpoint. Certainly the paradigm-shift (74) whereby one set of concepts is exchanged for another, proven over periods which are not appreciable within the context of one lifetime, is occurring before our very eyes. The actual shift of ideas may seem chaotic from a subjective viewpoint; indeed, as old forms break down and are replaced by others, the transition seems disordered. It is safer to cling to the forms we know, easier to subsist within a framework which is predictable, but the imposition of a new set of values is really more like moving house – we decide what we will pack and what we discard. It is then a question of seeing where our old possessions, our ancient knowledge, will sit most harmoniously with the new within our house.

The image of movement, change and exile is implicit within the Western Way, often expressing itself in *actual* movement. The image and the actuality are superimposed on each other as the inward impulse to seek Otherworld realities are expressed by means of physical journeying. The Heavenly Jerusalem cannot be established in any place but the heart: to seek a location for it on earth and then people it with all-too-human people is to build the Profane Jerusalem. Yet the Western Way has grown up among peoples who sought for new lands during the great migrations of the Foretime. Those invaders who migrated West across Europe, those whom we call the Celts, reached the utmost West in the British Isles: they in their turn were invaded. Their brash entrance into these islands can be contrasted with their sad leaving of them. During the Irish potato famine and the Scottish Clearances during the eighteenth and nineteenth centuries, boat-loads of disconsolate people, their spirit broken and bereft of their adopted soil, mourned and lost heart when they sighted their new homeland on the Eastern seaboard of America:

Thig iad ugainn, carach, seolta,	They come to us, deceitful, cunning,
Gus ar mealladh far ar n-eolas;	In order to entice us from our homes;
Molaidh iad dhuinn Manitoba,	They praise Manitoba to us,
Durthaich fhuar gun ghual, gun mhoine.	A cold country without coal, without peat (231).

In time they made new lives, preserving their native tradition and weaving its threads into the new weave of America. Likewise, those who were transported to Australia were to form the nucleus of a new civilization in the Southern Hemisphere. Both sets of emigrants were partially responsible for the disruption of then existing native traditions in America and Australia. This is but one example of the pattern of migration and invasion underlying the development of the Western world. It is being currently re-enacted again in our own time as waves of migrant workers and refugees arrive in search of work or a new home. Those who object strongly to this movement conveniently forget the karmic debt of Western colonialism. Racial bigotry is the last bastion of the deeply-rooted tribal consciousness which strives to remain in its territorial past.

Side by side with racism is extremist nationalism which stresses ethnic cohesion at the cost of world-peace: sometimes engineered and orchestrated by political leaders who have the charismatic power of tribal leaders, the nationalism of the terrorist is the last attempt of the native folk-soul to establish itself unequivocally on its own terms. These dual errors can only be corrected and balanced by a study of world-citizenship and universal fellowship. The group-soul will not pass away, nor will distinctive national characters be erased: they can be regenerated by contact with other traditions and made to resonate more strongly by that contact than would have been possible otherwise. The inward spiral of the maze has been walked to its centre and only the threading out will release the true ancient wisdom of the Native Tradition.

The Native Tradition can be used as a tool for progress and integration: the Otherworld insights can help bring into manifestation the evolutionary impulse which will facilitate the process of regeneration. For, of the two methods of easing new ideas into consciousness – that of political persuasion, or that of inner realization – the latter means has the more immediate effect.

In his *Future Shock*, Alvin Toffler posits that:

If the last 50,000 years of man's existence were to be divided into lifetimes of approximately 62 years each, there have been about 800 such lifetimes. Of these 800 fully 650 were spent in caves. Only during the last 70 lifetimes has it been possible to communicate effectively from one life to another – as writing made it possible to do. Only during the last six lifetimes did masses of men ever see a printed word (262).

The advent of education has opened up the whole world to our generation: 'The heritage of any race lies open to another; the best thought of the centuries is available for all; and ancient techniques and modern methods must meet and interchange' (14). While many have progressed to individual consciousness and seek to take the next step to cosmic consciousness, there are still those who exist in tribal consciousness despite access to education; yet mere book-learning is so much rubbish unless it can be applied to life. The progression from tribal to individual consciousness has been, for the most part, effected. People are now aware of themselves as individuals with rights but are as yet unwilling or unable to go further than this. This self-complacency is being challenged on a global scale.

As we approach the year 2000, many prophets of doom arise or are resurrected to prove that the world will end in 1999, as prophesied by Nostradamus; that nuclear war will wipe out humanity; or that the population explosion will exhaust the world's resources. A great deal of false gloom and despondency has overcome many as a result of these prognostications. Those for whom this lifetime is seen to be the only one fear deeply for themselves and their families, whereas those who believe in reincarnation wonder whether there will be another opportunity to reincarnate again. These fears are only the latest formalization of a recurrent tendency to despair when faced with change (57).

> Certainly we have any number of doomsday projections which explore the possibilities of apocalypse in detail. But [there is] revealed another possible scenario – that crisis may be an evolutionary catalyst in the push towards a higher level (221).

Is the millennial panic merely a fear of change? The Chinese word for crisis, 'wei-chi', means both 'beware, danger' and 'opportunity for change' (ibid.): which thought may stimulate new hopefulness for those who fear the end of things.

The forecasts of a New Dark Age, the Western resonance of the Hindu *Kali Yuga* – the last age wherein moral decline, lack of devotion and apocalyptic destruction takes place – can be seen as projections of the inner and outer turmoil now taking place (97). *These forecasts are not inevitabilities*, although neither should their message be ignored, but treated rather as salutary warnings. As when an inlet of water is injected into a pool of still water so that a complex of opposing spirals is created with ripples and opposing vortices, so do we find ourselves in the present age – either retreating into the ancestral past or projecting into an unknown future. The turning of the age is upon us and we will need the tools of the Hermetic Tradition to help us thread out of the maze again and enable us to assess our present situation.

If the arc of the Native Tradition can be traced starting in the Foretime and extending to just beyond the Renaissance, so can the Hermetic Tradition be traced in an arc starting in the Classical period and leading to the present time. Of course, both traditions extend further in both space and effect than these approximate historical eras, contactable through the agency of the Otherworld. Both traditions are harmonics of each other, as well as being echoes of a larger cosmic scale. The Hermetic Tradition harmonizes around the basal chord of the Native Tradition.

We have already mentioned the reviving shamanic traditions of the American Indians and Australian Aborigines: the Western shamanic revival is looked on with less favour by those who fail to comprehend the underlying reasons for revival.

> The revival of modern western magic and the renewed interest in 'native' cosmologies and shamanism as found among the Amer-Indian cultures, for example, show that a 'mythic backlash' has taken place. It has proved to be unsatisfactory, and indeed, possibly pathological, to attempt to repress the vestiges of mythological thought in modern man in the vain hope of eliminating 'superstitition' with the advance of science. Clearly we humans require domains of mystery; we need to know where the sacred aspects of life may be found and how to understand the intuitive, infinite and profoundly meaningful visionary moments which arise in all of us at different times (69).

The present resonances with the Foretime's traditions are clearly being made available at this time for good reasons. Rather like the storm which in 1850 exposed the Stone Age village of Skara Brae in the Orkney Islands (133), complete and perfect as the day it was evacuated so many centuries previous, so are we being permitted a rare and unparalleled glimpse into our ancestors' inner life. There is a rising sensibility that our sophistication and civilization are perhaps gauche, that our computer technology is not the best preparation for the coming millenium, and that we have lost something both precious and vitally useful for survival somewhere along the road to progress: that premonition haunts us.

Yet, as Dion Fortune writes in her *Avalon of the Heart*, these resonances of the Native Tradition are stepping stones on the path of the Western Way:

> things come home to our hearts, and we feel the unbroken line of our national life stretching back into the remote past, and know that it will reach into the far future and that we ourselves are a part of it (79).

EXERCISES

EXERCISE 9   SELF-CLARIFICATION

Over the door to the temple of Apollo at Delphi was the inscription *'Gnothi seauton'* – *know thyself*. This dictum has been at the heart of the mysteries of all nations and it is one which the follower of the Western Way would do well to take seriously. The work of the mysteries is to bring through light to dark places; each participant in this work stands in relation to that light as a lantern does to the sun, so that if the lantern is obscured the light cannot shine. But to 'know oneself' and clear these obscurities is no easy task: it is the work of a lifetime. Access to a format in which we may begin the work of self-clarification is even harder, especially for those outside an organized system of belief and practice. This exercise is an attempt to bridge that gap in a way which is adaptable according to personal circumstance.

It may be argued that so much self-pondering is unhealthy and that the best answer is a trip to the psychoanalyst. Yet self-clarification is not undertaken with any selfish motive. As any initiate of the mysteries knows, in order to be of service each has to be aware of both individual potentialities and limitations. There is also another danger if this work is avoided. There is a famous picture by the pre-Raphaelite painter, Dante Gabriel Rossetti, entitled *How They Met Themselves*. It depicts a medieval couple walking through a wood and encountering their doubles 'who glow supernaturally and appear to assert a stronger right to existence'. It was probably painted to illustrate the concept in Elizabeth Barrett's poem, 'Willowwood':

> And I was made aware of a dumb throng
> That stood aloof, one form by every tree.
> All mournful forms, for each was I or she.
> The shades of those our days that had no tongue (257)

It is a fair illustration of what may befall the traveller in the Otherworld if he or she has neglected the work of self-clarification: to meet oneself coming on the inner levels can be a considerable shock, but one which is nullified if the unassimilated and forgotten aspects of the personality have already been recognized and accepted. Indeed such a meeting in the Otherworld would only occur in the case of someone who was attempting to run before they could walk.

The ability to master outer circumstance before attempting inner work is often a prerequisite of the mystery schools today, as imbalances quickly show up in magical work and render the operation useless. Indeed many people are in such a rush to get to the next life that they ignore this one entirely and launch themselves upon the astral only to end like Icarus. It is important to realize that this exercise is concerned only with your present incarnation, not with past lives. It may be that certain past-life problems will be resolved thereby, but it is not important to know anything about them. Everything that you need to know about yourself is near to hand.

By a closer look at ourselves, our motives, limitations and potentialities the clear thread of our destiny is revealed, allowing us to find our way through the self-made maze, like Theseus through the labyrinth. Some unwind their threads quicker than others. Some have tangled their thread so thoroughly that it will be some time before the turning point is reached. While we must be conformable to the pattern of our present incarnation, our fate is not fixed or predestined. To some extent we each make our own circumstances and while self-clarification may highlight and partially explain them, it does not justify them. Whatever responsibilities we have taken on cannot be off-loaded because we suddenly discover a 'spiritual' destiny. It may be that the path of the hearth-fire, which is parallel to the Hindu concept of the way of the householder, must be undertaken first.

Self-clarification requires that we ask ourselves certain questions: the ones listed below are merely guidelines and can easily be adapted or expanded according to your needs. Rather as the shaman goes aside to wrestle with him or herself, so must we. Some of the questions will be exceedingly painful to answer honestly, and because the mind avoids pain by sliding round it like water round a rock, it will be necessary to have a notebook and pen to hand to note down your realizations so that there is no escaping the issue. You need not show this to anyone; indeed, you can destroy it. The important thing is that you have thought about the painful areas without hiding from yourself.

In this way self-clarification becomes an initiation of fire.

Sit in meditation and visualize a door before you. Pass through it and go down the corridor beyond, at the end of which is another door. This opens into a library. No one else is here, only you. Although there are countless books on the shelves around you, there is only one which you seek. It is before you on a lectern. On the cover is inscribed *The Book of (your name)*. This is the book of your present life, from your birth up until today. Go through it as objectively as possible and see what is written there. Certain episodes will leap out at you, but keep turning the pages to acquire an overall impression of its shapes and patterns.

What experiences have you had? What did they teach you? How far have you created the circumstances which now govern your life? What relationships have you had with family, friends, colleagues and lovers? How have you behaved within them? In what degree have those you disliked been responsible for revealing aspects of yourself which were obscured? What has been the quality of your life in physical, emotional, mental and spiritual terms? What are your potentialities and talents? What are your limitations? How far have the former been employed usefully? How can your negative aspects be made positive? Are your present circumstances balanced? In what way could you exercise more self-discipline?

Examine your spiritual or inner life from birth to the present. What influences have you experienced? Have your inner promptings fallen into a discernable pattern? What religious affiliations have you had and what has been the quality of your commitment to them? If you have never subscribed to any religious or spiritual movement, where are your spiritual faculties committed? If you are aware of a destiny, in what way does it relate to your spiritual path? Are they the same thing?

You need not answer these all at once, but take a few each time and work through these or any other questions which may occur to you. As soon as you have realized an answer, or a lack of one, return the way you came and write down your findings.

This is very hard work and the first sessions may be emotionally exhausting ones. Once you have been through the book of your life to the present time, you need not keep immersing yourself in the past – unless a specific problem warrants it – but pay attention instead to your daily life. A lifetime's habits cannot be broken overnight, but the very fact of self-awareness will begin the work of letting through the light in your lantern. Controlling or transforming your limit-ations is less about cleaning than about composting. All life's experiences teach us something: nothing is wasted. Experiences, good and bad, are the compost which we spread on the soil of the soul. Even major problems can be turned into strengths in this manner, so that you co-operate with your tendencies rather than working against them.

This exercise is not all gloom and doom, however. Make a list of your aims and correlate them with your potential. We seldom use our potentialities to their fullest extent: by maximizing them and working with them we are doing the work of creation. Creative expression is not about *doing* all the time, but is informed by *being* – listening in to the pulse of creation by contemplative reflection.

The evening review is performed by many initiates of the mysteries and while it is not really an extension of self-clarification, it is related. This is an objective observation of the day's activities which is run through the mind backwards, like a film in reverse. You can do this in bed and, if you fall asleep before you arrive at the beginning of the day, it doesn't matter. The purpose of the evening review is to clear the consciousness of the day's activities, leaving it ready for the refreshment of sleep. Dreams will be correspondingly clearer of daily accumulations. No moral judgment is to be exercised. Just aim at a straight run through of events in reverse.

EXERCISE 10   THE RETREAT

A retreat is associated in many minds with a Christian retreat on which prayer, meditation and a special celebration of the sacraments are practised, interspersed with pious conferences given by a retreat leader, but there is no reason why anyone should not undertake their own retreat as a time away from the world, modifying it to their special needs. Most of us live so tightly packed together that the experience of being alone is seldom had; moments of introspection are rare and prolonged meditation upon our relationship to the Otherworld, the Spiritual Realms and Middle Earth is impossible. A retreat is not an escape from the problems of life but an important breathing space in which those problems may be clarified, a time in which our true potential can be realized. This 'holy hiatus' in the headlong course of life can have lasting effects: our ability to cope with life improves, the psyche is stilled and the deep impulses within us are free to rise unfettered. Those who belong to no tradition will have had no experience of or opportunity for a retreat, yet the Native Tradition gives us examples in plenty: the sweat-lodge or *kiva* of the Red Indian, the vision quest of the shaman, the tribal descent to the ancestor's burial-place, are sealed-off *temenos* in which such a retreat was undertaken from the Foretime onwards. In later times the retreat of Abra Melin urges a six month preparation and withdrawal in order to contact the holy guardian angel; the cell of the medieval anchorite constituted a more permanent retreat, as did the cave of the hermit.

Obviously, considerations of time, location and cost enter into any preparation for retreat: the longer the retreat, the longer the preparations. No more than three days should be attempted at first or you will need a considerable back-up team to support your efforts: any longer is a strain on those unused to long periods of solitary survival. Where is the best place? Ideally an isolated spot which is a known sacred site, preferably a little-used one. (Well-known sites attract some intrepid hermits, however, according to one report recently of a single be-tented individual discovered on top of Silbury Hill, the small earthen mound in populous Wiltshire!) This is fine if you are an experienced camper and have your own transport: you can take off when you please. But, be warned, never go anywhere alone where you are likely to be in danger — mountains, mists, bogs, disused mine-workings or collapsing caves must be taken into consideration. If your retreat is likely to end in exposure, sickness, injury or the services of a mountain rescue team, you had better stay at home. If you decide on a spot then at least inform someone of your whereabouts so that you can be found in an emergency. Keep your equipment to a minimum, keep your body temperature from extremes of heat and cold and you have the beginning of an interesting retreat.

But what of those who aren't hardy enough for such exploits in the open air? Surprising though many might find this, both Christian and Buddhist retreat centres are very sympathetic to individuals who wish to have a quiet time away from the world: you need to pick a time when an organized retreat is not in progress and, so long as you observe the common code of courtesy and do nothing which is strictly contrary to the tenets of the centre, a good retreat can be had. Some centres have a hermitage-like hut which can be used by self-catering pilgrims. The advantages of a retreat-centre or monastery over any holiday hotel or camping village are apparent from the quiet and holy atmosphere (although, unfortunately, many more people are discovering monastic holidays and some places may be as noisy as a seaside village), and the presence of experienced explorers of the spiritual realms whose attitude to guests is coloured by their perception that every guest is sent by God is an advantage. They are often willing to talk to genuine seekers of the spirit and will not press themselves upon you.

While it is better to get totally away from everyday life for a retreat, others cannot leave home so easily, either through commitment, age or handicap. The home retreat is perhaps the hardest: life's problems are all too present and the distracting stimuli of television, radio, books and tape-recorder are temptingly within reach. The home retreat is best accomplished in a day or, if you can manage the time, a long weekend. Telephones are perhaps the worst problem if you wish to be undisturbed.

So, you have decided on the place of your retreat and made your preparations: what will you do on this retreat? We are so well versed in filling our day with activity that the retreat can become a trap at first as we attempt to pack every minute with soul-searching meditation and strenuous inner exertion. The state of contemplation is not busy but very tranquil. The self-clarification exercise could be attempted as a beginning, to enable you to revise your aims, seeking to see how the retreat can be used as a springing-off point for them. But, most of all, you are attempting to get closely in touch with yourself. Get used to the feeling of being alone; sit and breathe quietly and evenly, letting all the tensions out of your body. Set aside mental distractions and nagging worries. This is your special time which you are entitled to: it is not selfish or time-wasteful.

If you are frightened of coming to the end of your resources, take a helpful and thought-provoking book which can help you spark off meditation points. Take a notebook and a couple of biros to record your thoughts and realizations in: this can be the start of a spiritual journal which can be kept up after the retreat is over. If you prefer, take some craft or hobby which occupies the hands, but let it be something which is manually absorbing only and not a time-passing distraction. Russian Orthodox monks make prayer-beads while they meditate, and Cistercians hoe vegetables, just as shamans tap their drums and shamankas work their spindles. All these actions are rhythmic, allowing the body its motion, but by-passing it so that the psychic faculties are free to engage in other matters. There is no reason why, if you are totally alone, you should be still and silent. If you are camping, then you can sing or chant, walk or dance, weave ritual patterns through a maze traced on the earth, or make a small natural shrine out of stones or wood as a focus for your retreat. It is entirely up to you. You may wish to undergo the Otherworld Journey in the form of the Two Trees Meditation, or attempt other exercises outlined in this book. Make this time work for you.

Should you fast? Only if you have previously attempted a fast and know how your body is likely to react. Fasting is bad enough in a busy day at work but, when faced by acres of empty time, the body starts demanding more food at frequent intervals. By all means, reduce your intake so that the retreat doesn't become a cordon bleu holiday. Stick to simple foods: eggs, cheese, bread, soup, fruit and fresh vegetables, with spring water or fruit-juice to drink. Campers may need some hot food but the home-retreatant should not suffer from a simple uncooked diet. Retreat centres inevitably serve quite spartan fare.

If you are interrupted explain politely but firmly that you are a) conducting an experiment in survival technique, or b) on a silent retreat: if at home, you will have to use your ingenuity or arrange for someone to answer your phone for you. The help of a sympathetic partner or friend can be engaged to give you time and space, and provide the necessary support should you need it. While some friends may regard your actions as downright anti-social, you will find that others will be sufficiently intrigued to try a retreat for themselves. A group-retreat is feasible, but it needs organization, a good retreat leader and plenty of self-discipline. A group-retreat can give the necessary support for those who are uncertain of themselves in a solitary condition: the retreat-leader should be experienced and able to supply the right kind of impetus for self-motivating discovery.

It is not necessary to repeat the retreat very often — once a year, or once every five years for an organized, get-away-from-it-all one. At least once a quarter we need a small space of contemplation and that can be undertaken at home. The only equipment required is a blanket or long cloak with a hood which can be wound round you, shutting out all distractions. Like the shaman wrapped in his skin-hide, totally absorbed in the inner workings of his being, we can experience the communion of the Otherworld and keep in touch with ourselves. Those who go within and contact their inner resources are better able to make the outward journey in the world of Middle Earth. Remember, the shaman does not make his or her vision quest for self-glorification, but to be a source of help to others.

Whatever the shape of your retreat you will emerge refreshed and spaced. You will be distanced from the problems of living, so that they seem less threatening and easier to cope with. If the retreat has been less successful, don't despair: it will have taught you many useful things, and shown you which areas of your life need adjustment or rethinking. Take away the home-environment, your favourite food and television programmes, your cigarettes or whiskey, the company of other human beings, and you are reduced to yourself. If you are incomplete without these stimuli then you are not in touch with the real you. The retreat is a revealer under whose challenge even seemingly strong personalities are brought up short. Don't expect the effect of the retreat to last for ever: we are none of us practised in the skills of inner awareness to a very high degree. Without daily meditation, results are slow and, even then, you can never afford to rest on your laurels.

Bibliography and Discography

Items are listed in numerical order and numbers will be found to correspond to those in the text. Those marked with letters after the publication details are to indicate the type of work. Thus: F = Fiction, G = General, J = Journal, P = Poetry, R = Recording, T = Text.

(1) Adler, M., *Drawing Down the Moon*, Boston, Beacon Press, 1979 (G).
(2) Ainsworth, W.H., *Windsor Castle*, London, Collins, 1973 (F).
(3) Anderson, W., *Holy Places in the British Isles*, London, Ebury Press, 1983 (G).
(4) *The Apocryphal New Testament*, trans. M.R. James, Oxford, Oxford University Press, 1924 (T).
(5) Apuleius, trans. Robert Graves, *The Golden Ass*, Harmondsworth, Penguin Books, 1950 (T).
(6) Ashe, G., *The Ancient Wisdom*, London, Macmillan, 1977 (G).
(7) Ashe, G., *Avalonian Quest*, London, Methuen, 1982 (G).
(8) Ashe, G., *Camelot and the Vision of Albion*, London, Heinemann, 1971 (G).
(9) Ashe, G., *Finger and the Moon*, London, Heinemann, 1973 (F).
(10) Assagioli, R., *Psychosynthesis*, Wellingborough, Turnstone Press, 1975 (G).
(11) Aubrey, J., *Monumenta Britannica*, Boston, Little Brown & Co., 1980 (T).
(12) *Avalon to Camelot*, 2126 W. Wilson Ave., Chicago, Il (J).
(13) Bachofen, J.J., *Myth, Religion and Mother Right*, Bollingen, Princetown University Press, 1967 (G).
(14) Bailey, A.A., *From Intellect to Intuition*, London, Lucis Press, 1932 (G).
(15) Bailey, A.A., *Glamour: A World Problem*, London, Lucis Press, 1950 (G).
(16) Barker, B., *Symbols of Sovereignty*, Newton Abbot, Westbridge Books, 1979 (G).
(17) Barber, R., *The Arthurian Legends*, Woodbridge, Boydell Press, 1979 (G).
(18) Bellamy, H.S., *Moons, Myths and Man*, London, Faber & Faber, 1949 (G).

(19) Bentov, I., *Stalking the Wild Pendulum*, London, Wildwood House, 1978 (G).

(20) Berlin, S., *Amergin, an enigma of the Forest*, Devon, David & Charles, 1978 (F).

(21) The Holy Bible (R.S.V.), London, Nelson, 1966 (T).

(22) Blake, William, *Poetry and Prose*, ed. Geoffrey Keynes, London, Nonesuch Press, 1975 (P).

(23) Blavatsky, H.P., *The Secret Doctrine*, Pasadina, Theosophical University Press, 1970 (G).

(24) Blavatsky, H.P., *Studies in Occultism*, Sphere Books, London, 1974 (G).

(25) Bord, J. and C., *Earth Rites*, London, Granada, 1982 (G).

(26) Bradbury, R., *Farenheit 451*, London, Hart-Davis, 1954 (F).

(27) Branston, B., *Gods of the North*, London, Thames & Hudson, 1955 (G).

(28) Branston, B., *Lost Gods of England*, London, Thames & Hudson, 1957 (G).

(29) Brennan, M., *The Stars and the Stones*, London, Thames & Hudson, 1983 (G).

(30) Briggs, K., *A Dictionary of Fairies*, London, Allan Lane, 1976 (G).

(31) Brown, A.C.L., *Origin of the Grail Legend*, Cambridge, Mass., Harvard University Press, 1943 (G).

(32) Brown, T., *The Fate of the Dead*, Woodbridge, Brewer, 1979 (G).

(33) Burl, A., *Rites of the Gods*, London, J.M. Dent, 1981 (G).

(34) Burland, C.A., *Myths of Life and Death*, London, Macmillan, 1974 (G).

(35) Cade, C.M. and Coxhead, N., *The Awakened Mind*, London, Wildwood House, 1979 (G).

(36) *Caerdroia*, the magazine of the Caerdroia Project, 53 Thundersley Grove, Benfleet, Essex SS7 3EB (J).

(37) Caesar, *De Bello Gallico*, Harmondsworth, Penguin Books, 1953 (T).

(38) Campbell, J., *Flight of the Wild Gander*, Indiana, Gateway Editions, n.d. (G).

(39) Campbell, J., *The Masks of God*, London, Souvenir Press, 1968–9 (G).

(40) Campbell, J., *The Mythic Image*, Princetown University Press, 1974 (G).

(41) Campbell, J., *Myths to Live By*, London, Souvenir Press, 1973 (G).

(42) Carmichael, A., *Carmina Gadelica*, Edinburgh, Scottish Academic Press, 1928–1971 (T).

(43) Carter, F., *The Dragon of the Alchemists*, London, Elkin Matthews, 1926 (G).

(44) Carylon, R., *Guide to the Gods*, London, Heinemann/Quixote Press, 1981 (G).

(45) Castledown, R., *The Wilmington Giant*, Wellingborough, Turnstone Press, 1983 (G).

(46) Cavendish, R., *King Arthur and the Grail*, London, Weidenfeld & Nicolson, 1978 (G).

(47) Cavendish, R., *Legends of the World*, London, Orbis, 1982 (G).

(48) Chant, J., *The High Kings*, London, Allen & Unwin, 1983 (G).

(49) Chapman, V., *The Three Damosels*, Methuen, 1978 (F).

(50) *Charlemagne Cycle*: (1) *Huon of Bordeaux*, (2) *Chanson de Roland*, trans. D.L. Sayers, Harmondsworth, Penguin Books, 1957 (T).

(51) Charon, J., *The Unknown Spirit*, London, Coventure, 1983 (G).

(52) Chesterton, G.K., *Collected Poems*, Methuen, 1936 (P).

(53) Child, F.J., *English and Scottish Popular Ballads*, New York, Dover Publications, 1965 (T).

(54) Chretien de Troyes, *Arthurian Romances*, trans. W.W. Comfort, London, J.M. Dent, 1914 (T).

(55) *El Cid* (The Poem of the Cid), trans. L.B. Simpson, University of California Press, 1957 (T).

(56) Claremont de Castillejo, I., *Knowing Woman – A Feminine Psychology*, New York, G.P. Putnam, 1973 (G).

(57) Cohn, N., *The Pursuit of the Millennium*, London, Paladin, 1970 (G).

(58) Cooper, J.C., *An Illustrated Encyclopaedia of Traditional Symbols*, London, Thames & Hudson, 1978 (G).

(59) Craighead, Meinrad, *The Sign of the Tree*, London, Mitchell Beazley, 1979 (G).

(60) Crossley-Holland, K., *The Norse Myths*, Andre Deutsch, London, 1980 (G).

(61) Crowley, J., *Little, Big*, London, Gollancz, 1982 (F).

(62) Currer-Briggs, N. and Gambier, R., *Debrett's Family Historian*, 1981 (G).

(63) Daly, M., *Beyond God the Father*, Boston, Beacon Press, 1973 (G).

(64) de Jubainville, H., *Irish Mythological Cycle and Celtic Mythology*, Dublin, O'Donoghue & Co., 1903 (G).

(65) Deacon, R., *John Dee*, London, Frederick Muller, 1968 (G).

(66) Devereux, P. and Thompson, I., *The Ley Hunter's Companion*, London, Thames & Hudson, 1979 (G).

(67) *Diodorus Siculus*, trans. C.H. Oldfather, William Heinemann/Harvard University Press, 1939 (T).

(68) Drury, N., *Don Juan, Mescalito and Modern Magic*, London, Routledge & Kegan Paul, 1978 (G).

(69) Drury, N., *The Shaman and the Magician*, London, Routledge & Kegan Paul, 1982 (G).

(70) Duggan, A., *The Devil's Brood*, London, Faber & Faber, 1937 (G).

(71) Durdin-Robertson, L., *Goddesses of Chaldea, Syria and Egypt*, Enniscothy, Eire, Cesara Publication, 1973 (G).

(72) Durrell, L., *The Alexandria Quartet*, London, Faber & Faber, 1962 (F).

(73) Eliot, T.S., *Collected Poems*, London, Faber & Faber, 1969 (P).

(74) Ferguson, M., *The Aquarian Conspiracy*, London, Routledge & Kegan Paul, 1981 (G).

(75) Ferrucci, P., *What We May Be*, Wellingborough, Turnstone Press, 1982 (G).

(76) Fontenrose, J., *Python*, Berkeley, University of California Press, 1959 (G).

(77) Fortune, D., *Applied Magic*, Wellingborough, Aquarian Press, 1962 (G).

(78) Fortune, D., *Aspects of Occultism*, Wellingborough, Aquarian Press, 1973 (G).

(79) Fortune, D., *Avalon of the Heart*, Wellingborough, Aquarian Press, 1971 (G).

(80) Fortune, D., *The Mystical Qabalah*, Ernest Benn, 1976 (G).

(81) *Four Ancient Books of Wales*, trans. W.F. Skene, Edinburgh, Edmonston and Douglas, 1968 (T).

(82) Gardner, G., *The Meaning of Witchcraft*, Wellingborough, Aquarian Press, 1959 (G).

(83) Gardner, G., *Witchcraft Today*, London, Rider & Co., 1954 (G).

(84) Garner, A., *The Owl Service*, Collins, London, 1967 (F).

(85) *Geoffrey of Monmouth: Historia Regum Brittania*, trans. L. Thorp, Harmondsworth, Penguin Books, 1966 (T).

(86) Gill, E., *Holy Tradition of Working*, ed. Brian Keeble, Ipswich, Brian Keeble, 1983 (G).

(87) Ginzburg, C., *The Night Battles*, London, Routledge & Kegan Paul, 1983 (G).

(88) *The Gododdin*, trans. D. O'Grady, Dublin, Dolmen Press, 1977 (T).

(89) Golding, W., *The Inheritors*, London, Faber & Faber, 1955 (F).

(90) Gordon, S., *Suibne and the Crow God*, London, New English Library, 1975 (F).

(91) Graves, R., *Greek Myths*, London, Cassell, 1958 (G).

(92) Graves, R., *The White Goddess*, London, Faber & Faber, 1948 (G).

(93) Gray, W.G., *The Ladder of Lights*, Toddington, Helios Books, 1975 (G).

(94) Green, M., *A Harvest of Festivals*, London, Longmans, 1980 (G).

(95) Grimm, J. and W., *Grimms Tales for Young and Old*, trans. R. Mannheim, London, Gollancz, 1979 (T).

(96) Gruffydd, W.J., *Math vab Mathonwy*, Cardiff, University of Wales Press, 1928 (G).

(97) Guenon, R., *Crisis of the Modern World*, London, Luzac, 1975 (G).

(98) Guyot, C., *The Legend of the City of Ys*, Amhurst, University of Massachusets Press, 1979 (G).

(99) Hadingham, E., *Ancient Carvings in Britain: A Mystery*, London, Garnstone Press, 1974 (G).

(100) Halifax, J., *Shaman – the wounded healer*, London, Thames & Hudson, 1982 (G).

(101) Halifax, J., *Shamanic Voices*, London, Penguin Books, 1980 (G).

(102) Harding, M.E., *Women's Mysteries: Ancient and Modern*, London, Rider & Co., 1935 (G).

(103) Harris, R., *The Lotus and the Grail: Legends from East to West*, London, Faber and Faber, 1974 (G).

(104) Harrison, M., *The Roots of Witchcraft*, London, Frederick Muller, 1973 (G).

(105) Hartley, C., *Western Mystery Tradition*, London, Aquarian Press, 1968 (G).

(106) Hayles, B., *The Moon Stallion*, London, Mirror Books, 1978 (F).

(107) Head, J., and Cranston, S.L., *Reincarnation: the Phoenix-Fire Mystery*, New York, Julian Press/Crown Publishing, 1977 (G).

(108) Henderson, J., *The Wisdom of the Serpent*, New York, George Brazillier, 1963 (G).

(109) *Hesiod*, trans. R. Lattimore, University of Michigan Press, 1973 (T).

(110) Hitchins, F., *Earth Magic*, London, Cassell, 1976 (G).

(111) Hoban, R., *Ridley Walker*, London, Cape, 1980 (F).

(112) Holt, J.C., *Robin Hood*, London, Thames & Hudson, 1972 (G).

(113) *Homeric Hymns*, trans. A. Athanassakis, Baltimore, John Hopkins, University Press, 1976 (T).

(114) Howey, M.O., *The Encircled Serpent*, London, Rider, n.d. (G).

(115) Iamblichus, *On the Mysteries of the Egyptians*, trans. T. Taylor, London, Bertram Dobell, 1895 (T).

(116) Jackson Knight, W.F., *Elysion*, London, Rider, 1970 (G).

(117) Jarman, A., *Legend of Merlin*, University of Wales Press, 1976 (G).

(118) Jefferies, R., *Story of My Heart*, Longmans, Green & Co., 1883 (T).

(119) Jones, D., *The Anathemata*, London, Faber & Faber, 1952 (P).

(120) Jones, D., *The Sleeping Lord*, London, Faber & Faber, 1974 (P).

(121) Joyce, P.W., *A Social History of Ancient Ireland*, Longmans, Green & Co., 1903 (G).

(122) Julian of Norwich, *Revelations of Divine Love*, trans. J. Walsh, Wheathamstead, Herts., Anthony Clarke Books, 1973 (T).

(123) Jung, C.G., *The Archetypes of the Collective Unconscious*, London, Routledge & Kegan Paul, 1959 (G).

(124) Jung, C.G. and Kerenyi, C., *Introduction to a Science of Mythology*, London, Routledge & Kegan Paul, 1951 (G).

(125) *Kalevala*, compiled and translated by E. Lonnrot, Cambridge, Mass., Harvard University Press, 1963 (T).

(126) *The Old Kalevala and certain anecdotes*, compiled and translated by E. Lonnrot, Cambridge, Mass., Harvard University Press, 1969 (T).

(127) Kerenyi, C., *Dionysus*, London, Routledge & Kegan Paul, 1976 (G).

(128) Kerenyi, C., *Eleusis*, London, Routledge & Kegan Paul, 1967 (G).

(129) Kerenyi, C., *Gods of the Greeks*, London, Thames & Hudson, 1951 (G).

(130) Kirk, R., *The Secret Commonwealth*, Cambridge, D.S. Brewer, 1976 (T).

(131) Knight, G., *The Rose Cross and the Goddess*, Northants, Aquarian Press, 1985 (G).

(132) Knight, G., *Secret Tradition in Arthurian Romance*, Northants, Aquarian Press, 1983 (G).

(133) Laing, L., *Orkney and Shetland: An Archaeological Guide*, Newton Abbot, Devon, David & Charles, 1974 (G).

(134) Larsen, S., *The Shaman's Doorway*, New York, Harper & Row, 1976 (G).

(135) Layard, J., *The Celtic Quest*, Zurich, Spring Publications, 1975 (G).

(136) *Lebor Gabala Erenn* (Book of Invasions), ed. R.A.S. Macalister, Dublin, Irish Texts Society, 1938–56 (T).

(137) Leland, C., *Aradia, The Gospel of the Witches*, London, C.W. Daniel, 1974 (G).

(138) Léon-Portilla, M., *Native Mesoamerican Spirituality*, London, SPCK, 1980 (T).

(139) Lethbridge, T.C., *Gogmagog*, London, Routledge & Kegan Paul, 1957 (G).

(140) Levy, G.R., *Gate of Horn*, London, Faber & Faber, 1943 (G).

(141) Lewis, C.S., *Abolition of Man*, London, Collins, 1978 (G).

(142) Lewis, C.S., *The Chronicles of Narnia*, London, Geoffrey Bless, 1950–59 (F).

(143) *The Ley-Hunter*, P.O. Box 13, Welshpool, Powys, Wales (J).

(144) Loomis, R.S., ed., *Arthurian Literature in the Middle Ages*, Oxford University Press, 1959 (G).

(145) Luke, H.M., *Woman, Earth and Spirit*, New York, Crossroad, 1981 (G).

(146) *Mabinogion*, ed., Lady C. Guest, Cardiff, John Jones Ltd., 1977 (T).

(147) *Mabinogion* (2), trans. J. Gantz, Harmondsworth, Penguin Books, 1976 (T).

(148) MacCana, P., *Branwen, Daughter of Llyr*, Cardiff, University of Wales Press, 1958 (G).

(149) MacCana, P., *Celtic Mythology*, London, Hamlyn, 1970 (G).

(150) Macdonald, G., *Princess and the Goblin*, Harmondsworth, Puffin Books, Penguin Books, 1964 (F).

(151) MacGregor, G., *Reincarnation as a Christian Hope*, London, Macmillan, 1982 (G).

(152) Mackenzie, D.A., *Scottish Folk-Lore and Folk-Life*, Edinburgh, Blackie, 1935 (G).

(153) Mackie, I., *Megalith Builders*, Oxford, Phaidon, 1977 (G).

(154) McMann, J., *Riddles of the Stone Age*, London, Thames & Hudson, 1980 (G).

(155) Magnusson, M., *Hammer of the North*, London, Orbis Books, 1976 (G).

(156) Malinowski, B., *Magic, Science and Religion and Other Essays*, New York, Fress Press, 1948 (G).

(157) Malory, Sir T., *Le Mort d'Arthur*, Harmondsworth, Penguin Books, 1969 (T).

(158) Maltwood, K., *Enchantments of Britain*, Cambridge, James Clarke, 1982 (G).

(159) Maltwood, K., *Glastonbury's Temple of the Stars*, Cambridge, James Clarke, 1964 (G).

(160) Markale, J., *Celtic Civilization*, London, Gordon & Cremonesi, 1978 (G).

(161) Massingham, H., *Downland Man*, London, Jonathan Cape, 1926 (G).

(162) Matthews, J., ed., *At the Table of The Grail*, London, Routledge & Kegan Paul, 1984 (G).

(163) Mead, G.R.S., *The Vision of Aridaeus*, London, Theosophical Publishing Society, 1907 (G).

(164) Meltzer, D., ed., *Birth: an anthology of ancient texts*, San Francisco, North Point Press, 1981 (T).

(165) Meyer, K. and Nutt, A., *The Voyage of Bran, Son of Febal*, London, David Nutt, 1895 (G).

(166) Meyer, T., *The Umbrella of Aesculapius*, North Carolina, The Jargon Society, 1975 (P).

(167) Michell, J., *Megalithomania*, London, Thames & Hudson, 1982 (G).

(168) Michell, J., *New View over Atlantis*, London, Thames & Hudson, 1983 (G).

(169) Mol, H., *The Firm and the Formless*, London, Wilfrid Press, 1982 (G).

(170) Monaco, R., *Runes*, New York, Ace Fantasy Books, 1984 (F).

(171) Moncreiffe of That Ilk, and Hicks, D., *The Highland Clans*, London, Barrie & Rockliff, 1967 (G).

(172) Morris, J., *The Age of Arthur*, London, Weidenfeld and Nicolson, 1973 (G).

(173) Mottram, E., *The Book of Herne*, Colne, Lancashire, Arrowspire Press, 1982.

(174) Mountford, C.P., *Winbaraku and the Myth of Jarapiri*, Adelaide, Rigby, 1968 (G).

(175) Muir, W., *Living With Ballads*, London, Hogarth Press, 1965 (G).

(176) Murray, M., *The Divine King in England*, London, Faber & Faber, 1954 (G).

(177) Murray, M., *The God of the Witches*, London, Sampson Low, 1931 (G).

(178)   Nash, D.W., *Taliesin, or the Bards and Druids of Britain*, London, John Russel Smith, 1858 (G).

(179)   Needleman, J., *Sense of the Cosmos*, New York, Dutton & Co, 1965 (G).

(180)   Neihardt, J.G., *Black Elk Speaks*, New York, Pocket Books, 1972 (G).

(181)   Neubecker, O., *Guide to Heraldry*, London, Cassell, 1979 (G).

(182)   Neumann, E., *The Great Mother*, New Jersey, Princeton University Press, 1963 (G).

(183)   Neumann, E., *Origins and History of Consciousness*, New Jersey, Princeton University Press, 1954 (G).

(184)   *New Celtic Review*, B.M. Oakgrove, London WC1 N3XX (J).

(185)   Newman, P., *Hill of the Dragon*, London, Kingsmead Press, 1979 (G).

(186)   Newstead, H., *Bran the Blessed in Arthurian Romance*, New York, Columbia University Press, 1939 (G).

(187)   *Nibelungenlied*, trans, A.T. Hatto, Harmondsworth, Penguin, 1965 (T).

(188)   North, F.J., *Sunken Cities*, Cardiff, University of Wales Press, 1957 (G).

(189)   O'Brien, C., *The Megalithic Odyssey*, Wellingborough, Turnstone, 1973 (G).

(190)   O'Rahilly, T.F., *Early Irish History and Mythology*, Dublin, Dublin Institute of Advanced Studies, 1946 (G).

(191)   *Oxford Dictionary of Saints*, ed. D.H. Farmer, Oxford, Oxford University Press, 1978 (G).

(192)   Pausanius, *Guide to Greece*, trans. P. Levi, Harmondsworth, Penguin, 1971 (T).

(193)   Pegg, B., *Folk: A portrait of English Traditional Music, Musicians and Customs*, London, Wildwood House, 1976 (G).

(194)   *Pendragon*, 27 Roslyn Rd, Redland, Bristol BS66 6NJ (J).

(195)   Pennick, N., *The Ancient Science of Geomancy*, London, Thames & Hudson, 1979 (G).

(196)   Perera, S.B., *Descent to the Goddess – a way of Initiation for Women*, Toronto, Inner City Books, 1981 (G).

(197)   Pepper, E. and Willock, J., *Magical and Mystical Sites: Europe and the British Isles*, London, Weidenfeld, 1976 (G).

(198)   Petry, M.J., *Herne the Hunter: A Berkshire Legend*, Reading, William Smith, 1972 (G).

(199)   Phillips, G.R., *Brigantia*, London, Routledge & Kegan Paul, 1976 (G).

(200)   Pindar, *The Odes*, trans. C.M. Bowra, Harmondsworth, Penguin, 1969 (T).

(201)   Plato, *The Collected Dialogues of Plato*, ed. E. Hamilton, New Jersey, Princeton University Press, 1973 (T).

(202) Plumb, J.H., *The Death of the Past*, London, Macmillan, 1969 (G).
(203) Plutarch, *Moralia VI*, trans. F.R. Babbitt, London, Heinemann, 1952 (T).
(204) *Popol Vhu*, trans. R. Nelson, Boston, Houghton Mifflin, 1976 (T).
(205) Powys, J.C., *Morwen*, London, Village Press, 1974 (F).
(206) Progoff, I., *The Practice of Process Meditation*, New York, Dialogue House Library, 1980 (G).
(207) Rainwater, J., *You're in Charge*, Wellingborough, Turnstone, 1979 (G).
(208) Rank, O., *The Myth of the Birth of the Hero*, New York, Knopf, 1959 (G).
(209) Readers' Digest, *Folklore, Myths, and Legends of Britain*, London, Readers' Digest, 1973 (G).
(210) Rees, A. and Rees, B., *Celtic Heritage*, London, Thames and Hudson, 1961 (G).
(211) Reyner, K., *This Holiest Erthe*, London, Perennial Books, 1974 (G).
(212) Rhys, Sir J., *Arthurian Legend*, Oxford, Oxford University Press, 1891 (G).
(213) Rhys, Sir J., *The Hibbert Lectures*, London, Williams and Norgate, 1888 (G).
(214) *Rig Veda*, trans. W.D. O'Flaherty, Harmondsworth, Penguin, 1981 (T).
(215) Ross, A., *Pagan Celtic Britain*, London, Routledge & Kegan Paul, 1967 (G).
(216) Roszak, T., *Person/Planet*, London, Granada, 1981 (G).
(217) Russell, G., 'The Glastonbury Tor Maze' in *Glastonbury: a Study in Patterns*, ed. M. Williams, R.I.L.K.O., 1969.
(218) Russell, G.W. ('A.E.'), *A Candle of Vision*, New York, Theosophical Publishing House, 1974 (G).
(219) Russell, G.W. ('A.E.'), *The Song of its Fountains*, London, Macmillan, 1932 (G).
(220) Russell, J.B., *A History of Witchcraft*, London, Thames and Hudson, 1980 (G).
(221) Russell, P., *The Awakening Earth – our Next Evolutionary Leap*, London, Routledge & Kegan Paul, 1982 (G).
(222) Salinger, J.D., *Franny and Zooey*, London, Heinemann, 1962 (F).
(223) Saurat, D., *Literature and Occult Tradition*, London, Bell and Sons Ltd., 1930 (G).
(224) Sawyer, R., *The Way of the Storyteller*, London, Harrap, 1944 (G).
(225) Schnapper, E., *The Inward Odyssey*, London, Allen & Unwin, 1965 (G).
(226) Scott, M., *Kundalini in the Physical World*, London, Routledge & Kegan Paul, 1983 (G).
(227) Screeton, P., *Quicksilver Heritage*, Wellingborough, Turnstone, 1974 (G).

(228) Senior, M., *Myths of Britain*, London, Orbis, 1979 (G).

(229) Severin, T., *The Brendan Voyage*, London, Hutchinson, 1978 (G).

(230) Seward, J., *Book of British Troy Towns*, Thundersley, Caerdroi Project, 1982 (G).

(231) Shaw, M.F., *Folksongs and Folklore of South Uist*, London, Routledge & Kegan Paul, 1955 (G).

(232) Silverberg, R., *The Mound Builders*, New York, New York Graphic Society, 1970 (G).

(233) *Sir Gawain and the Green Knight*, trans. J.R.R. Tolkien, London, Allen and Unwin, 1975 (T).

(234) Sjoestedt, M-L., *Gods and Heroes of the Celts*, Berkeley, Turtle Island Foundation, 1982 (G).

(235) Skelton, R., *Spellcraft: a Manual of Verbal Magic*, London, Routledge & Kegan Paul, 1978 (G).

(236) *Society of the Inner Light*, Study Course, 38 Steele's Road, London NW3 (G).

(237) Spence, L., *Fairy Tradition in Britain*, London, Rider, 1948 (G).

(238) Spence, L., *The History of Atlantis*, London, Rider, 1930 (G).

(239) Spence, L., *The Magical Arts in Celtic Britain*, Wellingborough, Aquarian Press, 1970 (G).

(240) Spence, L., *The Mysteries of Britain*, Wellingborough, Aquarian Press, 1970 (G).

(241) Spence, L., *Myths of the American Indians*, London, Harrap, 1918 (G).

(242) Spiegleman, J., *The Tree*, Phoenix, Arizona, Falcon Press, 1982 (G).

(243) Starhawk, *Dreaming the Dark*, Boston, Beacon Press, 1982 (G).

(244) Starhawk, *The Spiral Dance: A Rebirth of the Ancient Religion of the Great Goddess*, San Francisco, Harper & Row, 1979 (G).

(245) Steinbeck, J., *Acts of King Arthur and his Noble Knights*, London, Heinemann, 1976 (F).

(246) Steinbrecher, E., *The Inner Guide Meditation*, Santa Fe, Blue Feather Press, 1978 (G).

(247) Steiner, R., *Mystery Knowledge and Mystery Centres*, London, Rudolf Steiner Press, 1973 (G).

(248) Stewart, B., *The Initiation of the Underworld*, Wellingborough, Aquarian Press, 1985 (G).

(249) Stewart, B., *Where is St George?*, Bradford on Avon, Moonraker Press, 1977 (G).

(250) Storms, G., *Anglo-Saxon Magic*, The Hague, Martinus Nyhoff, 1948 (T).

(251) Stukeley, W., *Itinerarium Curiosum*, Hampshire, Greg International, 1969 (G).

(252) Summerfield, H., *That Myriad-Minded Man: a biography of G.W. Russell – 'A.E.'*, Gerrard's Cross, Colin Smythe, 1975 (G).

(253) Sutcliff, R., *High Deeds of Finn MacCool*, London, Bodley Head, 1967 (F).

(254) Sutcliff, R., *The Hound of Ulster*, London, Bodley Head, 1963 (F).

(255) Tacitas, *The Agricola and the Germania*, Harmondsworth, Penguin, 1970 (T).

(256) *Tain Bo Cuailnge (The Cattle Raid of Cooley)* trans. T. Kinsella, Dublin/Oxford, Dolmen Press/Oxford University Press, 1970 (T).

(257) Tate Gallery, *The Pre-Raphaelites*, London, Tate Gallery/Penguin, 1984 (G).

(258) Taylor, A., *Drustan the Wanderer*, London, Longmans, 1971 (F).

(259) Tennyson, A., *Idylls of the King*, Harmondsworth, Penguin Books, 1983 (P).

(260) Thom, A., *Megalithic and Luna Observatories*, Oxford, Oxford University Press, 1971 (G).

(261) Thom, A., *Megalithic Sites in Britain*, Oxford, Oxford University Press, 1967 (G).

(262) Toffler, A., *Future Shock*, London, Bodley Head, 1970 (G).

(263) Tolkien, J.R.R., *The Lord of the Rings*, London, George Allen and Unwin, 1954 (F).

(264) Tolkien, J.R.R., *The Monsters and the Critics & Other Essays*, London, George Allen & Unwin, 1983 (G).

(265) Traherne, T., *Poetical Works*, London, P.J. & A.E. Dobell, 1932 (P).

(266) Treece, H., *The Golden Strangers*, London, Bodley Head, 1956 (F).

(267) Treece, H., *The Green Man*, Bodley Head, 1966 (F).

(268) *Trioedd ynys Prydein* (The Welsh Triads), ed. R. Bromwich, Cardiff, University of Wales Press, 1961.

(269) Underwood, G., *The Patterns of the Past*, London, Abacus, 1972 (G).

(270) Valiente, D., *ABC of Witchcraft*, London, Hale, 1984 (G).

(271) Valiente, D., *Witchcraft for Tomorrow*, London, Hale, 1978 (G).

(272) Vansittart, P., *The Death of Robin Hood*, London, Peter Owen, 1982 (F).

(273) Vansittart, P., *Worlds and Underworlds*, London, Peter Owen, 1974 (G).

(274) Vermaseren, M.J., *Mithras, the Secret God*, London, Chatto & Windus, 1963 (G).

(275) Vigars, D., *Atlantis Rising*, London, Andrew Dakers, 1944 (G).

(276) *Vita Merlini*, ed. J.J. Parry, Illinois, University of Urbana, 1925 (T).

(277) Von Franz, M.L., *C.G. Jung, his myth in our time*, London, Hodder & Stoughton, 1975 (G).

(278) Walker, D.P., *Spiritual and Demonic Magic*, London, University of Notre Dame Press, 1969 (G).

(279) Walton, E., *The Mabinog Quartet*, New York, Ballantine Books, 1970–4 (F).

(280)   Waters, F., *Book of the Hopi*, Harmondsworth, Penguin Books, 1977 (G).
(281)   Watkins, A., *The Old Straight Track*, London, Garnstone Press, 1970 (G).
(282)   Weaver, H., *Dowsing the Primary Sense*, London, Routledge & Kegan Paul, 1978 (G).
(283)   Wentz, W.Y. Evans., *The Fairy Faith in Celtic Countries*, New York, Lemma Pub. Co., 1973 (G).
(284)   Whitman, W., *Complete Poetry, Selected Prose & Letters*, London, Nonesuch Library, 1938 (P).
(285)   Whitmont, E., *Return of the Goddess*, London, Routledge & Kegan Paul, 1983 (G).
(286)   Whitson, R.E., *The Shakers*, London, SPCK, 1983 (G).
(287)   Wilber, K., *Up from Eden*, London, Routledge & Kegan Paul, 1983 (G).
(288)   Wilkins, E., *The Rose Garden Game*, London, Gollancz, 1969 (G).
(289)   Williams, C. and Lewis, C.S., *Arthurian Torso*, Oxford, OUP, 1948 (G).
(290)   Williamson, T., and Bellamy, L., *Ley Lines in Question*, London, Worlds Work, 1983 (G).
(291)   Yeats, W.B., *Collected Plays*, London, Macmillan, 1952 (P).

DISCOGRAPHY

(292)   Albion Country Band, *Battle of the Fields*, Island HELP 25 (R).
(293)   Archer, Robert, *Nature's Dream Harp – Aeolian Harp Music*, R. Archer, RA 01, 17 Sanfield Road, Headington, Oxford OX3 7RN.
(294)   Ashley, Steve, *Stroll On*, Gull GULP 1003.
(295)   Bedford, David, *Star Clusters Nebulae and Places in Devon/Song of the White Horse*, Oldfield Music OM1.
(296)   Bellamy, Peter, *Keep on Kipling*, Fellside FE032.
(297)   Bothy Band, *Out of the Wind into the Sun*, Polydor SUPER 2383 456.
(298)   *The Child Ballads*, vols 1–10, Topic Records.
(299)   Clannad, *Magical Ring*, RCA RCA LP 6072.
(300)   Colins, Shirley, *Amaranth*, Harvest SHSM 2008.
(301)   Davey, Shaun, *The Brendan Voyage*, Tara 3006.
(302)   Davey, Shaun, *The Pilgrim*, Tara 3001.
(303)   Gray, W.G., *The Rollright Ritual*, Sulis Music, B.C.M 3721, London WC1N 3XX.
(304)   Horslips, *The Book of Invasions – a Celtic Symphony*, DJM DJF 20498.
(305)   Horslips, *The Tain*, RCA OATS Moo 5.

(306) Kinnaird, Alison, *The Harp Key: Crann nan Teud*, Temple Records SH001.

(307) Lyonesse, *Tristan de Lyonesse*, PDU PLD A6062.

(308) *Maypoles to Mistletoe*, Trailer LER 2092.

(309) Ossian, Springtime Records, SPR 1004.

(310) Pegg, Bob, *Ancient Maps*, Transatlantic TRA 299.

(311) *Plain Capers – Morris Tunes from the Cotswolds*, Free Reed FRR010.

(312) Stewart, Bob, *The Underworld Journey*, Sulis Music, BCM 3721, London WC1N 3XX.

(313) Stewart, Bob, *Unique Sound of the Psaltery*, ARGO ZDA 207.

(314) Stewart, Bob, and Furey, Finbar, *Tomorrow We Part*, Crescent Records AR 5110.

(315) Stivell, Alan, *Légende*, DISC AZ AZ 475.

(316) Stivell, Alan, *Symphonie Celtique – Tir Nan Og*, CBS 88487.

(317) Strawhead, *Songs from the Book of England*, Tradition TRS 0356.

(318) Watersons, *Frost and Fire – a calendar of Ritual and Magical Songs*, Topic 12T 136.

(319) Williamson, Robin, and his Merry Band, *A Glint at the Kindling*, Criminal Records STEAL 6.

(320) Yates, Tom, *Song of the Shimmering Way*, Satril SATL 4007.

Index

VOLUME 2

The Hermetic Tradition

Frontispiece: The Emblem of the Great Work – the Philosopher's
Stone: 'visit the interior of the earth — seek and rectify the hidden
stone'.

To
Gareth Knight

And all who seek to rectify the Hidden Stone

'You are all one, under the stars'
Merlin in John Boorman's *Excalibur*

Illustrations

Acknowledgments

Thanks for advice, support and cups of tea go to: Dolores and Michael Ashcroft-Nowicki, all the Caldecott clan, Joscelyn Godwin, Marian Green, Deirdre Green, Helene Hess, Adam McLean, Kathleen Raine, Anthony Rooley, Wolf and Johann van Brussel, Roma Wilby, The St Mary Cray Green Circle and, again, to the Company of Hawkwood. The illustration on p. 257 is reproduced with the kind permission of T. & T. Clark Ltd, Edinburgh.

INTRODUCTION
The Outward Spiral

Hear with the understanding of the heart.

Thomas Vaughan: *Anima Magica Absondita*

The soul of each single one of us is sent, that the universe may be complete.

Plotinus: *Enneads, IV, 8,1*

The Roman cult of Mithras has associated with it the figure of Aion: a lion-headed god swathed by a serpent. He represented boundless time, which held sway over the ages and the cyclic divisions of the year. In his hands he carried the keys of the solstices: a silver one which opened the Gate of Cancer, the Way of the Ancestors, and a golden one which opened the Gate of Capricorn, the Way of the Gods, which lead beyond the processes of birth and dying and through which the gods could descend to earth. (104) (fig 1.)

These two ways represent eternal laws, as unchanging as the universe itself, and they can also be seen as akin to the two traditions which are the subject of the present work. On the one hand the Native Tradition, which looks to the Ancestors, now elevated to the status of gods, for guidance. On the other the Hermetic Tradition, which looks outwards to the stars, and to the angelic presences which inhabit them, as mediators between mankind and God.

These are different but complementary approaches to the same end: a fuller understanding of our place in the scheme of things. Both have helped to preserve an ancient wisdom which would otherwise have been lost to the world. In Herman Hesse's novel, *The Glass Bead Game*, a group of esoteric philosophers known as The League of Journeyers to the East were said to have 'contributed new insights into the nature of our culture and the possibility of its continuance, not so much by analytical and scholarly work, as by their capacity, based on ancient spiritual exercises, for mystical identification with remote ages and cultural conditions' (142). The same can be said of the explorers of the Western Esoteric Tradition whom we call Hermeticists, who have helped almost single-handedly to preserve

Figure 1:   The Aion

and transmit the ancient mysteries into our own times. It is the Hermeticist who continues to work of the Native shaman, and who expands our knowledge of the universe through his use of just such 'ancient spiritual exercises' as the philosophers of Hesse's novel.

The path of the esoteric tradition has veered sharply through many centuries in order to preserve its teachings: sometimes it has been paved, at others it has appeared as no more than a dirt track, kept open by the tread of a few solitary walkers. It has at no time been a common highway; yet it has rerouted itself time and again in order to accommodate travellers of many kinds. It has explored new and different traditions so that 'however its continuity may be broken by opposing systems, it will make its appearance at different periods of time, as long as the sun itself shall illumine the world.' (325)

We have spoken of the path of the Native Tradition as the inward spiral of a maze which leads into the heart of ancestral earth-wisdom. The Hermetic Tradition is the outward spiral of the same maze: a path of evolving consciousness which is informed by the inner resources of our ancestral roots. Together the two traditions form a glyph of the Western Way, in which neither tradition is 'better' than the other, but where each can inform and teach the other (figure 2). They are complementary opposites between which the esoteric experience of the individual can be measured and balanced. As the Native Tradition saw a move from primitive, tribal or collective consciousness towards an appreciation of individual, self-aware consciousness, so the Hermetic Tradition takes individual consciousness on the journey towards cosmic consciousness, where-in that first, collective awareness is augmented in a macrocosmic way. Such an evolution is the work of many millennia and can only be judged from our present standpoint. The movement has not always been a progressive one, by any means. Both traditions have a tendency to pull out of true: the Native Tradition, as we noted in volume one, has a tendency to atavistic reversion; the Hermetic Tradition tends to pull in the direction of speculative projection and mystifying obscurantism.

The unit of the Native Tradition was the tribe – forged from people, ruler and shaman – and it was held together by genetic blood

The inner spiral   The outer spiral

Figure 2:   The Spiral Maze

linkage in which shared ideas and concepts took the place of religion. But 'when blood became mixed by exogamy (marriage out of the tribal unit), . . . close connections with his ancestors was [sic] severed and man began to live his own personal life.' (321) This severing of the direct link with the ancestral realms and the introduction of new blood, enabled the transmission of new messages into our consciousness, allowing it to develop away from the purely tribal heritage. The collective consciousness of the tribe was open to new influences. In place of a succession of shamans and shamankas, a 'philosophic clan . . . moved across the face of Europe under such names as "the Illuminati." '(23) Instead of a blood descent, a new relationship was established, not with the ancestors, but with teachers upon Inner Planes. The kinship began to be one of brother and sister initiates – a subtle lifting of the tribal relationship.

This concept is thought by some to have a sinister implication, although this is due to its political application. Bands of hooded Hermeticists are *not* out to rule the world. The truth is much simpler. The fellowship of esotericists is a mystical, not a blood relationship. (Although, at a deep level, this latter understanding is also true.) We must rather, for clarification, look to the Jewish concept of the Just Ones who sustain the world by their hidden lives, or to the company of Grail-hermits who, throughout the Grail-quest, advise the questing knights and live obscurely in the woods and deserts. Such is the role of the esotericist in this age (cf. chapters 1 and 3).

The fear and distrust of the shaman and magician throughout the ages has not been ameliorated by the almost aggressive secrecy with which the Western Way has been surrounded. Periods of persecution have, perforce, been responsible for this reserve, but we have also become estranged from esoteric understandings: 'what is natural in psyche has in our culture become unique, occult, and mysterious.' (273) There is also the fear that the esotericist is dealing with forbidden things, terrible powers which could prove destructive.

The Fall of Atlantis is to the esotericist what the Fall from Eden represents to the Jew or Christian – a precocious striving for knowledge which oversets the natural order. According to tradition, Atlantis fell due to an abuse of priestly power which so disturbed the delicate balance of the environment that the continent was submerged in a mighty cataclysm. In Eden, the Fall was brought about by disobedience to God's commandment not to eat of the Tree of the Knowledge of Good and Evil. It does not matter whether we see Atlantis or Eden as geographically locatable in time and space, or as mythic paradigms of lost knowledge; they remain states which have been withdrawn from us – golden ages which cannot return. We stand now on the higher arc of the Atlantis/Eden experiment, at the mercy of our technology, the knowledge of whose uses can heal or hurt depending on how it is harnessed. The danger of pride – spiritual or otherwise – is before us once again.

Yet while these paradigms are known chiefly because of their sudden destruction, Eden and Atlantis remain hauntingly in the consciousness as states of primal perfection. The inner Atlantis reminds us of potentialities which are lost or lie dormant in us. Before the taking of the apple from the tree in the garden, Eden was a place of joy and innocence.

> If Atlantis had never existed, the student of tradition would have found it necessary to invent such a region, as in none of the lands of Western Europe do we find a nucleus from which the adjacent countries received their earliest ideas of religion, myth and magic. (316)

The Mystery Schools from the time of Plato onwards, have ever looked towards Atlantis as the source of their knowledge. The scattered seeds of Atlantis seem to have been blown by the winds and carried by the tides throughout the world. Rationalists have sought to find the Lost Continent itself, and researchers of more or less scholarly repute have tried to assemble the fragments of languages, pot-shards and ethnographical types to account for the great subsidence. While such treasure-hunting is no doubt engaging, it has little bearing on our story. We deal in metaphysical currency here (cf. fig. 3).

Hope keeps us ever watchful for a new Golden Age – indeed, the New Age movement already shows a bright tomorrow blended of such hopes. On the side of despair are the millennial pessimists who foresee the destruction of the world and everything in it. Neither pattern of behaviour is very balanced. As we have stressed throughout this study, we must be wary of seeking to inhabit a new Golden Age: those who try to set up communities of perfection know this to their cost. Yet neither do we wish to live under the futility of ultimate despair. We are neither saviours of the world nor victims of the gods, but intermediaries who can synthesize and mediate the wisdom of the earth and of the stars. This ability is figured again in the image of the Aion, who holds the keys to enable us to correct the over-emphasis implicit in millennial despair and Golden Age hope.

We may perhaps grasp this concept more easily if we realize the interpenetration of microcosm with macrocosm. The interrelation of these two mighty realities is the key to the Hermetic Tradition. The macrocosm represents the eternal reality of Light, the realm of God: the microcosm is its reflection, a fragmentation of the Light, the realm of humanity in creation. This theme has been at the core of mystery teachings of all traditions, represented as a Body of Light which is scattered throughout the universe. Each created thing bears a spark of the divine light. Some forget their original condition, while others remember and become walkers-between-the-worlds, and make the reassembling of the Body of Light their overriding aim. These latter live by a story – the rending of a god, the apportioning of a goddess – whose sacrifice brings creation into being and whose redemptive virtue, resident within the individual spark of divine light, will bring creation back into the Body of Light once again. Yet the Body of Light, like that of Humpty Dumpty, is so fragmented that it seems impossible to reassemble the pieces. Between inertia and the multiplicity of ways determined to achieve this end, the task looks impossible. For some, the realization that their individual divine spark is trapped in flesh brings about a denial of the body itself.

Yet there remain those who seek to reassemble the Body of Light by religious or esoteric means. In whatever generation there are a number of dedicated people who form a quorum sufficient to form a launch-pad for such an enterprise. These Just Ones, as we have already said, are not necessarily in touch with one another, but their work has a cumulative effect. The task of the Hermetic Tradition reflects this aim: to rectify and unite the microcosmic light with the macrocosmic light, to discover the Hidden Stone, the Holy Grail, to forge the seeds of light into a cube of true gold. This is the Great Work and is the end of esoteric philosophy.

The foregoing may confirm some readers in their opinion that esotericism is an escape from the world – an accusation that is likewise levelled at those who enter contemplative religious orders. As the philosopher Frithjof Schuon, has observed:

> All esotericism appears to be tinged with heresy from the point of view of the corresponding exotericism, but this obviously does not disqualify it if it is intrinsically orthodox, and thus in conformity with truth as such and with the traditional symbolism to which it pertains; it is true that the most authentic

> esotericism can incidentally depart from this framework and refer to foreign symbolisms, but it cannot be syncretistic in its very substance. (294)

Hermetic esotericism is concerned with just such traditional symbologies and the truth of their wisdom. Hermeticism is in the peculiar case of guarding the mystical traditions of those religions and systems which have become mere exoteric carapaces or which have fallen out of history as living systems themselves. Exotericism and esotericism need each other. Without its mystical tradition, an exoteric system is like a rose without its perfume. Without the structures of exotericism, esotericism is an image without a temple. High, mystical knowing must percolate through to everyday life or forever be separate from it – a temptation to spiritual pride and elitism.

The problem which confronts any newcomer to the esoteric is that of motivation. Few people are raised in an environment which is informed by a mystical tradition, fewer have any experience of a living spiritual tradition at all: their ethical values and attitudes are shaped by social modification and the underlying ethical conventions of their individual culture. The exoteric world views the esoteric as evil, pertaining to the devil, morally corrupted and sexually depraved. It is all very well for the experienced esotericist to deny these projections – which is what they are – but for those venturing along this path for the first time there is the underlying suspicion that they are involved in something which might be 'not quite right'. The esoteric hinterland has been firmly closed for so long, except to bold explorers, that any expedition thither is held to be foolhardy. Certainly, without the experienced guide at one's side, this is true. The means towards finding a teacher or inner guide are discussed in chapters 3 and 4 of this volume. What was once familiar territory is now virtually uncharted; attitudes and certainties once widely held are now unknown to the modern explorer who shies at every rock and stranger on the way.

How then is the beginner on the Hermetic path of the Western Way to steer a course? By common sense and sensitive intuition, in the first instance, and by resonating with the wisdom of the tradition, in the second. Those who seek to walk the path alone, without the guidance of their tradition, without the sustenance of spiritual bread, are more likely to stray from their way, never to arrive at their destination.

We are all marvellous microcosms wherein matter and spirit are mixed to form totally individual expressions of humanity. During incarnation we will each meet certain very necessary initiations of a mundane kind: we struggle from stage to stage of our lives, learning the lessons of childhood, adolescence and adulthood. Depending upon our experience within each of these initiations, we will formulate a personal philosophy by which we seek to live. We arrive at an optimum point of experience and maturity at which we may decide to try the esoteric way. How do we know that this is 'white' and not 'black' magic? Will we truly be treading the right or left-hand path, as it often called?

'The left-hand path . . . is the path of progress for substance or matter,' reads Alice Bailey's *Treatise on White Magic*. (21) If our path does not lead us to an evolution of consciousness, to a kindling of spirit within matter, then we are indeed walking the left-hand path which diverges from the Western Way in its intent.

As a rule, the Hermeticist does not talk about 'good' and 'evil' because these terms are qualitative and misleading. What is 'good' to one is another's 'evil.' We must see things in terms of balanced polarities. We are not saying that there is *no* expression of good and evil in life – we know very well that there is – but we must not think of these in terms of absolute realities. We shall be seeing how the ancients polarized two eternally opposed causes of good and evil – a dualism which is still hard to escape from in common speech. God and Devil, angel and demon are still polarized sets of images in our consciousness; we are all aware of how destructive this application of image can be in the ascription of feminine images to matter and masculine ones to spiritual states. Such ready definitions of good and evil should be resisted.

This is not to ignore the very real horror of evil as we all experience it: evil remains a name for something unbalanced; whose origins are obscure, like those of the divine spark within us. In our souls we can perceive the evil or unbalanced forces about us, like a bad smell. The appearances of evil are deceptively smooth and charming: they appear in the forms of what we most wish for, but they are paid for in the currency of our own integrity. They lead us from the work of meshing the microcosmic and macrocosmic worlds, into the 'deepening of the plane' (107) – selling our pearl of great price for ready cash.

Those wishing to read more of these matters – and they are not easy to speak about or understand – would do well to read *The*

Cosmic Doctrine by Dion Fortune (90), which has this to say: 'evil is simply that which is moving in the opposite direction to evolution. (It) is that which . . . tends to revert to the Unmanifest. Evil can be viewed, if this is helpful, as the principle of inertia which binds "the good". Good can be seen as the principle of creative movement,' which resists inertia. We arrive at the expressions 'Negative and Positive' which will perhaps enable us to grasp these principles in a more helpful and less relative way. The way of Chaos, as an expression of the Negative pole, can be cleansing and effective, just as the way of creativity as an expression of the Positive pole can represent an imbalanced fertility. Which of these can be said to be good or evil?

So what does the Hermetic way offer as its contribution to the balanced way of evolution? We all have to face situations and decide whether to grasp the nettle or to flee, like the Fool of the Tarot, or the young man in the gospel who left his garment behind him – leaving everything, if necessary, in order to live and fight another day. All disciplines have their martyrs and their survivors. Those who follow the Western Way are not the elect, they do not offer a dogmatic package to salvation: they are co-workers, mediators between micro- and macrocosm who believe in their tradition as a means of spiritual progression. This essential work is not the sole province of esotericists, but of all religious traditions, crafts and skills. The mystic, poet, artist and every member of that Secret Commonwealth we spoke about in volume I – indeed, anyone who has an impinging of Inner realms upon the Outer world – contributes to this work.

The safest means of travelling the Hermetic Path is by means of a spiritual tradition – whether it be one of the orthodox religions or not.

> For it is the height of evil not to know God: but to be capable of knowing God, and to wish and hope to know him, is the road which leads straight to the Good; and it is an easy road to travel. Everywhere God will come to meet you, everywhere he will appear to you, at places and times at which you look not for it, in your waking hours and in your sleep, when you are journeying by water and by land, in the night-time and in the day-time, when you are speaking and when you are silent: for there is nothing which is not God. And do you say 'God is invisible'? Speak not so. Who is more manifest than God? (302)

This comes, not from a Christian, but from a Hermetic text: its truth is universally applicable for the pathwalker.

In volume one we spoke of three different levels of reality known to the Native Tradition: the Otherworld, Middle Earth and the Spiritual Realm. These terms are inappropriate to describe the levels operative within the Hermetic Tradition, so we have used the words *Inner* and *Outer*, to signify the Inner Plane and the Outer or mundane realm of common existence. Depending on which system one is used to working, the Inner Plane can be divided and subdivided into more and more complex parts: we have chosen to use one word only to define 'inner' things. The Spiritual Realms of the Native Tradition can be glossed, hermetically, as the macrocosmic level. However, there is an increasing trend which perceives Inner influences as having a psychological source in the unconscious. This is misleading in esoteric terms: make your own metaphors for these realms, by all means, but do not mistake their origins or confuse them with the workings of your own psyche.

Where the word 'God' appears in the text, this is to signify the ultimate source of reality, which is neither male nor female but pure spirit – unless otherwise stated. We have used the terms *the God* and *the Goddess*, to signify the divine masculine and feminine principles operational within mythological or other systems. Within the Hermetic Tradition, the Emerald Tablet of Hermes Trismegistos is the Rosetta Stone which interprets many mysteries: as a symbol it is balanced by the Rose of Aphrodite, signifying the esoteric wisdom of the divine feminine – a badge which identifies the fellow pathwalker.

We begin our journey in the temenos of the Mystery Schools, where we see how Native Tradition flows into Hermetic Tradition, and how these traditions have been preserved and fostered from ancient times up to our own day. We consider the spiritual traditions and their seeming divergence from the Mystery Schools, in chapter 2, while in chapter 3 we see how the role of the magician is a continuation of both shaman and mystery-priest. In chapter 4 we consider the cosmologies and symbol systems which have informed the divergent Hermetic traditions, and give a list of Inner guardians or contacts with whom the reader can work in a practical way. Chapter 5 sees the goal of the Great Work through the eyes of the alchemist, while in the afterword, *Tomorrow's Tradition*, we attempt to take the next step upon the Western Way.

As in volume one, the chapters have practical exercises and meditations appended so that the reader who is not an initiate of this tradition can experience for him or herself the realities presented here in a first-hand way. These exercises are based upon Hermetic sources, though they are original to this book. If many New Age movements and techniques have been omitted, this is only because we do not yet stand at a point where they can be seen in perspective. Certainly the Western Way will continue by means of many such channels, but we cannot forecast which will have greatest power to effect change and yet still be continuators of tradition.

We have attempted to view the Western Way in the context of tradition but, in a book of this size, much has been omitted in the interests of cohesion. There many facets which we have not dealt with and which the reader can investigate further, given the loose framework which we have provided.

New readers are directed to start with volume one of *The Western Way* before reading about the Hermetic Tradition in order that they may fully grasp the two halves of its totality. The Western Esoteric Tradition is known chiefly through the Hermetic path which has preserved many facets of the Native path. Yet the Native Tradition should not be ignored or neglected for this reason.

To those who have read the first volume and feel that the Native Tradition is indeed their way, we would say this: there are many treasures within the Hermetic way which you would do well to seek. Neither way is an end in itself. We do not leave anything behind by progressing on the evolutionary way to cosmic consciousness: the loved, familiar landscapes of home, the earthy wisdom of the ancestors accompany us still. Dion Fortune, that forthright walker-between-the-worlds had it right when she wrote:

> Do not let us forget that there is our own native esotericism hidden in the superconscious mind of the race, and that we have our own holy places at our very doors which have been used for initiations from time immemorial. Potent alike for the native contacts of the Celts, the work of the Hermeticist, and the mystical experience of the Church of the Holy Grail. (91)

NOTES ON THE EXERCISES IN THIS BOOK

Before attempting any of the exercises in this book, please read these instructions and those given in volume one of *The Western Way*.

The Hermetic Path is not an easy one to follow, although it is based in the Native Tradition and draws its primal impetus from it. Historically it has been syncretic, full of pied meanings and tangles of imagery, involving complex systems of correspondences. We hope to make some of these things a little plainer without throwing the mysteries to the four winds. There is much to be said for simplicity upon this path and for inner balance in the pathwalker who follows it. The complexities of the Hermetic path can be overwhelming for some, while others may get the impression that they are becoming ever more exalted, when in fact they are walking in circles. The cardinal danger of spiritual pride is to be avoided. It is not a bad idea to perform the Self-Clarification exercise (exercise 9, vol.I) before attempting any practical work on this path.

The material in this volume is more intellectually demanding than that found in volume one, where the Native Tradition can be felt as a gut-response or a yearning in the heart. This being so, it is particularly important that the exercises concerning the Hermetic Path are applied practically. This way has had its share of theoretical pundits and armchair estericists, who sap the vitality of the Western Tradition and give nothing in return.

This volume differs from the first in that we refer to more than one tradition, although all those mentioned fall within the broad boundaries of the Hermetic way. If you work out a scheme of study and practice for yourself, please ensure that you do not mix traditions. Certain systems – like the qabalistic – may correlate well with others, but this practice should be used cautiously. When you have had some experience of both Native and Hermetic traditions you will be aware of the subtle interplay of resonances between them, and be able to utilize this knowledge with good effect.

All meditations should be performed seated in an upright chair unless otherwise specified. Your visualizations are not guided fantasy, as it is often called, so make an effort to be truly present within each meditation. See through your own eyes, not as though you watched yourself appearing on a screen. Lone workers who attempt meditation for the first time get nowhere because they have failed to observe the basic rules: quietness of body and mind; controlled direction of the psyche; and an active, attentive spirit. As with all things, a routine time for daily meditation helps. Set yourself a reasonable régime e.g. entering your own inner landscape and mapping it out over a period of weeks; contacting your guardian and listening to any instructions or teachings which the Inner may mediate to you; meditating around a particular mythology or symbology. A Qabalistic text gives this advice about meditation:

> Make yourself right. Meditate in a special place, where your voice cannot be heard by others. Cleanse your heart and soul of all other thoughts in the world. Imagine that at this time, your soul is separating itself from your body, and that you are leaving the physical world behind you, so that you enter the Future World, which is the source of all life distributed to the living. (168)

Meditation is not an exotic technique derived from some far-out Eastern source, but your contact with *your own inner life*.

The reader will be disappointed if he or she looks within these pages for a complete magical system. There are so many books which deal with the classical methods of ritual magic: if such methods are required then you could do worse than consult the works of Gareth Knight, William Gray, and Melita Denning and Osborne Phillips which are listed in the bibliography. The trend, as we enter the Aquarian Age, is away from rigid systems towards freer methods of working. There are as yet few systems which are suitable for the lone practitioner, although Marian Green's *Magic for the Aquarian Age* (118) offers a practical schema. We have given an initiatory exercise, *The Four-Square Citadel* (exercise 5), which gives the reader a magic circle, hermetic chamber or tower of art to work from, as well as giving a first-hand initiation into the power of the elements. Many of the exercises can be adapted, within the limits stated, to create the bases of further work. The reader is at liberty to follow his or her own path, according to individual preference and requirements. The strength of the Western Way lies in the diversity of its practice, and the unity of its aims.

The prerequisite for all meditation and inner work is intent, preparation, conscientious practice and performance, mediation and service. These practices should be self-explanatory, but mediation may need a few words of clarification. Inner work is never done solely for the benefit of the practitioner. Insights, gifts, realizations received from meditation or ritual work are to be mediated to those who need them in the Outer world. This should always typify the initiate's willingness to serve and can take many forms – a short formula or ritual gesture during which the gifts of realization are mediated with understanding and intention to the world. This formal act is the prayer of the Hermeticist. Even if you have not begun to meditate or work formally, you can share in this meditation. At midday, everyday – when the sun is at its zenith, regardless of what clocks designate as noon – people all over the world, from multitudinous traditions, elevate their thoughts to the Inner spiritual sun. They are tuning into their spiritual source and sharing a brief communion with all others who share the aim of the Great Work, the reassembly of the Body of Light, the redemption of the world – whatever their metaphor is for the Great Work. You can share this moment everyday. You need only shut your eyes and silently affirm, in your own words, your dedication to the work and your willingness to serve. Your thoughts and aspirations join those of others. If you have received an Inner gift or realization, offer this in mediation at midday, that others may share it and tune in to it. So the healing of the world may be accomplished.

This is part of a commitment which Hermeticists call 'the unreserved dedication', which is not a gory sacrifice upon an altar, but an unbloody offering of oneself and all one's resources to the service of God – however that term is understood. The unreserved dedication is not offered and indeed is not acceptable, until the initiate *has* something to offer: he or she must first serve an apprenticeship in patient learning and arduous practice. Our Inner and Outer teachers can help us accomplish much, but they can only train the willing candidate.

The work of creation is the continual mediation of life itself. Our contacts on the Inner are the servants of the mysteries, gatekeepers who allow initiates to pass through and experience Inner worlds. When those initiates are properly trained, they in turn stand at the nexus of the worlds as potential helpers and gatekeepers who teach the mediation of Inner energy to those who come after them.

Those who are drawn to the Hermetic Tradition only in order to wear gaudy robes and wield ritual implements will find that possession of these inflates only the ego and not one's prowess in ceremonial magic. Implements and robes are props which condition the practitioner: they set the mood and can represent the inner correspondence to be worked with. While they are helpful and are far more suitable than a boiler-suit or a string vest, robes are not essential. Clean garments are all that the beginner requires. Expensive swords and pungent incenses are not practical for the suburban magician now that a temple or working area is a luxury that few can afford. More often a bedroom, garden-shed, attic or hastily-converted living-room must suffice. The use of the great outdoors is something which the Hermetic Tradition could learn from its predecessors.

While Hermeticists have traditionally met indoors in secret chambers and hidden temples, a secluded outdoor working space can be quite as effective. In a crowded world, only the space inside our brain seems solely private.

With all your work, remember to keep a written record – even if your impressions seem trivial – they may be real realizations. You will find such a record very useful over the years; it will enable you to see an Inner pattern in your work. Like dreams, realization from meditation fades very speedily.

Do not endanger your health or your sanity by an excess of Inner work. If you feel that any image, system or contact is becoming obsessive to you, then do no more work with it. Our remarks about obsessive contacts made on page 102 of volume one hold good here. We have given a revitalization exercise on page 417, but this should not be a substitute for medical help or wholesome rest.

Many meditation suggestions are scattered throughout the text which the reader can work into exercises if required. A list of training centres and established mystery schools is appended at the end of the book.

CHAPTER 1
Schools of Mystery

There is every reason to believe that the so-called secret societies
of the ancient world were branches of the one philosophical tree
which, with its roots in heaven and its branches on the earth, is
like the spirit of Man – an invisibly but ever-present cause of the
objectified vehicle that gave it expression.

> Manly P. Hall: *Secret Teachings of All Ages*

Happy is he who passed through the mysteries: he knows the
origin and the end of life.

> *Pindar*

FLASHES OF FIRE

The Mystery Schools, ancient and modern, are way-showers; they
possess the maps and compasses with which to explore the inner
realms of creation. Through them, those seeking initiation in the
temples and lodges of the Western Mystery Tradition are offered
training in the use and mastery of these tools: no one is cast adrift in
an open boat to sail uncharted seas, or sent forth on a highway that
has not already been walked by others. The mysteries *are* the inner
life of the people, and to discover them is to read the story of a divine
spark kept burning in the temple of the human spirit.

Once, there was no purely 'Native' or 'Hermetic' tradition; only a
universal response by the Firstborn to the Earth-lore and Star-magic
of their shamanic priests. Later, as the single religious impulse of the
Foretime split into separate cults, these two approaches, which we
may think of as chthonic (earthly) and stellar, grew further apart,
until the beginnings of the Hermetic traditions were seeded in Egypt
and the Hellenic world, while in Europe the Native traditions
remained more or less grounded in the magic earth.

However, we have to be wary of assuming that because much of
the later Hermetic philosophy originated in Greece and Egypt,

these areas possessed no Native tradition of their own, or that the development of religion and magic in the Celtic West was so primitive and slow that it required cross-fertilization with other sources to pull it into more subtle realms of experience. In mankind's development, tribal consciousness and Hermetic philosophy are inextricably linked; it would be a mistake to think that one developed smoothly while the other did not.

Certainly, when Alexander of Macedon died in 323 BC, there was already a high degree of interrelation within the mysteries. Alexander's vast empire extended from the Straits of Gibraltar to the Indus Valley on the one hand, and from Germany to the Russian Steppe, the Sahara and the Indian Ocean on the other. Over this huge area, which included Persia, Egypt and Mesopotamia, the Greek cultic religions were laid down, some on already existing foundations, others springing up from a combination of several cultural sources. As F.C. Grant points out in his excellent survey of the period:

> It is important to realize that only very rarely, if ever, did an ancient cult come to an end, supplanted by the dominant cult of the conquerers. Instead the old cults lived on, some of them extremely primitive, others more advanced. (109)

Some, he adds, were changed, either for better or worse, by the effect of the philosophical bent of the Greek mind; others as a 'result of that mysterious inner source of change and development that affects all our civilizations. . . ' (ibid). Professor Grant is a historian rather than an esotericist, but he makes a point here which can be understood in relation to the inner guidance which helped formulate the mysteries. It is indeed to this mysterious inner force that we must look, rather than to any specific geographic or historic point of origin.

This does not, however, obviate belief in a kind of 'table of descent' within the mysteries. They were, as Manly Hall suggests, 'branches of one philosophical tree' (133) and as figure 3 shows, a complex web of interaction does exist, linking schools far apart in time and space. This is not to suggest that there was ever a literal, historical succession involved, but rather that all drew upon a common, inner source of teaching. Nor should we envisage any one of the schools as superior to another: there should be no hierarchies of this kind in the Western Way, whatever the claims of superiority advanced by various orders in our own time.

It has often been said that the Egyptian mysteries are the true foundation upon which the Western Hermetic systems are built. This

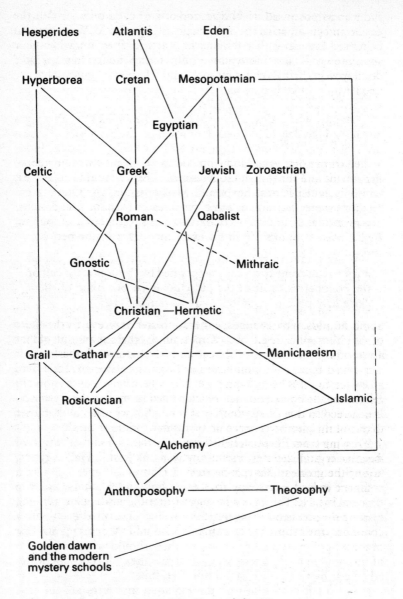

Figure 3: The Tree of the Mysteries

is due in part to an early identification of the Egyptian god Thoth, the scribe and guardian of the mysteries, with Hermes Trismegistos, the supposed founder of Western occult practice. Thus in the Hermetic text known as *Kore Kosmu*, we find Hermes addressing his 'son' Asclepios in the following words:

> Art thou not aware, O Asclepios, that Egypt is the image of heaven, or rather, that it is the projection below of the order of things above? If the truth must be told, this land is indeed the temple of the world. (186)

The truth is less grandiloquent, and by no means easy to reach, so great is the intermingling of sources in the Western tradition. There is certainly evidence of the extreme antiquity of the Egyptian mysteries: persistent traditions relating the Sphinx to a period long before the foundation of religion in Egypt, and the appearance of the four beasts aspected in the Sphinx within later esoteric practice, are an indication of this. (147)

Other traces of Egyptian mystery teaching are to be found in the Western Tradition, however, including the red and white pillars before the temple of Osiris at Memphis, which echo the black and white pillars of justice and mercy in qabalistic teaching; and the symbolic regalia of the God-King Pharaohs – sceptre and ark, sword and mace – which recall both Grail traditions (cf. chapter 5) and the four suits of the Tarot. (Other aspects of Tarot symbolism have been attributed to Egyptian influence or origin, but there is little hard evidence for this (cf. chapter 4). It is also possible to see, in the conical head-dress so often portrayed as worn by Hermes Trismegistos, a recollection of the double crown of Upper and Lower Egypt. None of this, however, adds up to anything more than a systematic borrowing from Egyptian beliefs and practices which has somehow become crystallized into a semi-mythical image of Egypt as originator of the greatest Western mystery teachings.

Egypt indeed had many mysteries, none more important than those of Isis. Her name is said to mean 'throne', 'wisdom' or 'saviour', though she possessed many other titles which testify to the universality of her cult. Above the entrance to her temple at Sais appeared the words:

> I, Isis, am all that has been, that is or shall be: no mortal man has ever seen me unveiled.

The Roman author Apuleius, in a famous passage from his novel *The*

Golden Ass (11), describes her as crowned with the moon and clad in a robe of stars. (cf. Fig 11) In Hermetic lore she became identified as the daughter of Hermes, standing for the innermost secret of the mysteries. Many have sought to obtain a glimpse through her veil, but only she may choose to show herself: like the mysteries, she hides from all but the most steadfast seeker.

The deeper mysteries of Isis, and of her consort Osiris, the god of the sun, revolve around his death at the hands of his brother Set, who cuts Osiris' body into fourteen parts and scatters them through the world. Isis undertakes a terrible journey, suffering great hardship, to seek out the broken body of her lord and to reassemble them. She does so, save for one part, the phallus, which was thrown into the Nile and consumed by a fish. Despite this, such was the creative power of Isis that she was able to conceive by means of an artificial phallus, and bore the child Horus who avenges his father by killing Set.

This is an archetypal mystery-telling, introducing themes found later in the teachings of the Hellenic schools and in the work of modern esoteric orders. It prefigures the death and rising of many gods and shows forth the power of the creative principle. It also establishes Isis as Queen of Heaven, more powerful in the eyes of many of her followers than the great god Ra himself, whose representative-upon-Earth was the Pharoah.

According to one theory the period over which the Egyptian pantheon ruled corresponds to the entire history of the world, so that the Sorrows of Isis, in which she mourns the death of Osiris rather in the manner of Mary mourning the death of Christ, relate to the agonies of our own time. The dawning of the Aquarian Age thus heralds the birth of Horus, who will come as a saviour and introduce a reign of peace and plenty.

The great student of Egyptian esotericism, R.A. Schwaller de Lubicz, described the *magnum opus* of the Egyptian mysteries as 'the reconciliation of Set and Horus', which since it has yet to occur in time could be said to reinforce the idea of the time span of the gods. (298) The reconciliation of opposing forces, and the emergence of a divine principle to bring about the redemption of mankind, are familiar themes which appear regularly in the great mystery cults of the West. From them comes belief in a divine spark in man, a fragment of godhead buried in each of us.

In Egypt this was personified in the person of the Pharoah, the son of the god on earth, whose task it was to perform the rites which would one day restore the world to the perfection of the First Time (*Tep zepi*), a lost Golden Age which existed 'before anger, or noise, or conflict, or disorder made their appearance.' (Eliade) There was no distinction between King and Priest, religious and secular office in Egypt. It was to the 'King in man', the spark of inner fire, that the people addressed themselves in their worship of the Pharoah. He, the King, was a manifestation of higher orders of creation – what de Lubicz calls *anthropocosmos*, cosmic man. In the complex structure of the Egyptian mysteries, every part of the temple, as well as the regalia of the God-King, pointed towards fulfilment, of reaching a god-like state through the enactment of the mysteries. Colours, statues, reliefs, obelisks, were all indicators of the stages of an ongoing process of perfection. Like the steps in the Alchemical Great Work, or the Architecture of the medieval cathedrals, or indeed the standing stones and circles discussed in volume one, these things were concrete externalizations of the highest mysteries.

In the many histories of the ancient world, only one figure is described as being of greater importance than Hermes. This is the Persian mage Zoroaster, who may actually have lived *c.* 1000 BC or even earlier, but who clearly did not predate the foundation of the Egyptian mysteries from which he drew significantly for his own system.

It is from the Persian mysteries, of which Zoroaster is the chief author, that we derive the dualistic spectre which has haunted esoteric philosophy and teaching ever since. In the Zoroastrian pantheon these opposing forces are Ormuzd and Ahriman, who derive ultimately from Ahura Mazda, the divine principle. Known as the Holy Immortals or Amesha Spentas (*spenta* = bounteous, the effulgence of God's goodness) they correspond to the levels of creation, clearly foreshadowing the teaching of later mystery schools such as those of Orpheus and Mithras.

Against the Spentas are arrayed the Devas, the companions of the Evil One, who are seen as ruling over the earth. They are comparable to the Qabalistic qliphoth.

The position of Persian dualism is confused by a Zoroastrian heresy called Zurvanism, which is often mistaken for mainstream Zoroastrianism. In Zoroastrianism proper, Ahura Mazda is supremely god: his Spentas are not on the same footing; Zurvanism, however, made Ahuramazda into a lesser creator or demiurge, hence the cosmic struggle of good against evil which takes place in the world of matter. In Zoroastrian teaching a saviour or *saoshyant* was to be born who would combat evil and bring the struggle to an end once and for all, betokening the *Frasokereti*, the making perfect at the end of time (cf. chapters 2 and 4).

In this we already see both an echo of the Egyptian mysteries, and a prefiguring of the later gnostic position, as well as much that has dogged the feet of recent esoteric practice where the latter has fallen into dualistic thinking. Occasionally, however, there have been moments in which the seemingly endless struggle is balanced by the appearance of a third figure – the Messiah, which as one commentator has already said, becomes a requirement of all dualistic thinking sooner or later. (109)

In Mithraism, which descended from the Persian Mysteries, Mithras stands as a mediator between light and dark, a position adopted by his followers – as, generally, by both the modern magician (see chapter 3) and the follower of Christ (see chapter 2). In humanity, the battle for the soul is fought out in the territory of the flesh. Mithras, entering there, keeps all in balance.

In this he indeed prefigures Christ, with whom he shares a number of other similarities – at times to a startling degree. Mithras is born in a cave on 25 December, watched over by shepherds, and at the end of his earthly life held a last supper with his elect followers before departing mysteriously for heaven. According to some sources he is supposed to have suffered crucifixion and to have risen again three days later: he will come again as a judge at the end of time and lead his followers to heaven. (340)

Joscelyn Godwin, in his authoritative work on the mystery religions, suggests that Mithraism is a clairvoyant prefiguring of Christianity, an idea which sits well with the inner connectedness of the mysteries. Certainly, when one reads the following extract, from a Persian Mithraic text, one is given pause to wonder. Mithras states: 'he who will not eat of my body and drink of my blood, so that he will be made one with me and I with him, the same shall not know salvation.' (104) Beyond this, the similarities are only superficial. Christianity has certainly never been as tolerant of other beliefs as Mithraism, nor has it guarded its secret half so well. On the other hand, it has survived while Mithraism has not, and to this day little is known of the Mithraic mysteries.

Still, the theme is there: the interpenetration of the physical world by the divine: macrocosm entering microcosm, God sending forth an emissary into the world. Certainly Mithraism, which was taken up by the armies of Rome and through them spread to most parts of the world, left its mark on the Native Traditions wherever it went.

While the Mithraic mysteries succeeded those of Zoroaster they followed those of Dionysius, through which the core of Hellenic mystery teaching found its way into the Western Mystery Tradition. Indeed, two streams of consciousness are discernible within the Classical mysteries which we might call, respectively, Dionysian and Apollonian. The mysteries of Dionysius were those of the sacrificed king: they pertained to the underworld side of things, the chthonic and ecstatic cult of maenads and bacchantes. The Apollonian mysteries on the other hand, related to reason, to the heavens and to order; in contradistinction to the chaotic mysteries of Dionysius. Orpheus, whose mysteries grew out of the preceding cults, combines both facets within one. He has the lyre and the gift of music from Apollo, yet ends like Dionysius, torn apart by Thracian bacchantes: the shamanic practices of the Native Tradition overlapping the priestly function of the mystery school.

In the mysteries of Dionysius we again meet the theme of the divine spark trapped in matter. In this case the divinity is literally torn apart by the Titans and eaten by them after being cooked. Zeus, the Demiurge, seeing this destroys the Titans, and from their fragmented substance creates mankind. Thus elements of both Titanic and Dionysiac force are present within man; the Titanic element holds sway, creating the warring nature of mankind. Only when total harmony and balance exist is Dionysius reborn and the perfection of all things brought about. In cosmological terms the Titans are represented by the twelve signs of the Zodiac which rule over our lives: Dionysius is the sun which warms us and causes the fruition of matter.

Dionysius belongs with those gods who descend into the underworld, either in search of enlightenment or of some lost aspect of themselves. Psyche's quest for Cupid, that of Ishtar for Tammuz, of Isis for the scattered members of Osiris or of Orpheus for Euridice, are all synonymous with the search for the absolute by the initiate. In the mysteries this is interpreted as the fragment of divinity within the seeker – through ritual he or she follows the god or goddess on their journey, returning either successful or not, according to their individual merits.

At Eleusis, where the mysteries of Demeter were celebrated every five years, the candidate of the lesser mysteries underwent a symbolic journey in which the quest of Demeter for her lost child Persephone in Hades was re-enacted with the would-be initiate in the role of

Demeter. The journey within was that of the darkened soul: the candidate passed through a door into total darkness: if he survived the experiences met within he passed through a second door into brilliant light – symbolizing rebirth into the heavenly sphere. Here he actually met the gods, experiencing Demeter's journey as his own recovery of lost enlightenment.

In the inner truth of the Elensinian mysteries the birth of the soul into matter is seen as death; only through participation in the mysteries can the initiate rise to a timeless reality where he is utterly free and alive. The soul sleeps in the body for most of the time, awakening only when it has been transformed by ritual and the use of an initiatory drink. To die without this experience is to sleep forever or to wander houseless in the caverns of Hades.

In the broadest sense all such quests and descents represent the theme of the spirit trapped in matter: the lower Ishtar, or Demeter, descend in their search, the greater their suffering; the lower man descends into matter the more he suffers his exile from the blessed realms. The fact that Psyche, Ishtar, Persephone, and Orpheus are able to return from the underworld is a symbol of hope, implying that mankind too will one day escape the prison of the flesh and be assumed again into the glory of the empyrean.

Above all it is in the Orphic mysteries that we first come to terms with this perilous descent into darkness and re-emergence again into primal light. The suffering of Orpheus, who loses Euridice (through fear, first pitfall of all mystery knowledge) and is then dismembered by the Maenads, is a paradigm of the suffering and rebirth of the sleeping soul. As a descendent of Dionysius, Orpheus is the intellectual image of a demi-god raised to deity by his sufferings in the underworld: a perfect symbol for all who follow the path of the mysteries.

The movement from the cult of Dionysius to Orphism, marks a change from a more primitive response towards an ethically-based philosophy and mysticism which included belief in the transmigration of souls, reincarnation and final assumption into godhead. In the Orphic mysteries the first real moment of stillness comes into being: the Dionysian frenzy is stilled; peace reigns. Through the strains of Orpheus' lyre is tamed more than the beasts: the beast in man, the Titanic element, is also at rest for a time.

In some senses the Orphites were 'the first real Christians' (104) – in some senses more Christian than Jesus' own followers. For this reason, perhaps, Christianity borrowed much from Orphism through the agency of the neo-Pythagorean schools of the first century – among whose initiates were Plutarch and Paul of Tarsus: there is considerable borrowing of Orphic matter in the Pauline Epistles.

The Orphic mysteries (or rather the theology built upon them) are complex in the extreme. Those desiring a full account are recommended to consult G.R.S. Mead's *Orpheus*. (226) Here, it must suffice to say that each of the energies ruling creation, the movement and delineation of the cosmos, are tabulated in series of 'Triads', 'Dodecans' and 'Monads'. Descending from the ineffable One, the Godhead, are a number of lesser powers, demigods and deities, who are each related to one another both within their separate triads and cross-related outside these triplicities. The overall rate of movement, of communication, within these correspondences, is so swift and so total as to defeat the grasp of the intellect. Only through the attainment of a super-sensible state of awareness – through initiation – can a proper understanding be arrived at.

Orphic cosmology also suggested that each star or planetary sphere contained aspects of *all* the deities. Thus there were, for example, a lunar Ceres, a saturnine Apollo, a mercurial Hera and so on. And of course there were planetary aspects present within each of the deities, so that an aspect of Dionysius also contained lunar, solar, saturnine declensions within him. The gods themselves thus formed a constantly shifting matrix of planetary influence, which meant that an initiate who invoked a lunar deity was at one and the same time in touch with all the gods and thus all the planetary influences of the heavens.

This complex organization kept the cosmos turning and insured that, however intricate Orphic theology and cosmology became, the most important aspect could be grasped through direct experience. This was that mankind and the gods are related; at a most subtle and sensitive level a blurring of edges occurs, an overlapping of human consciousness and divine awareness. 'Everything that lives is holy' becomes a reality in the interaction of the divine and the mundane. The hierarchy of spiritual creation is supremely complex, but the gods are like a ladder, a system of related possibilities, the potentiality of which is seeded within the whole of creation. We are all, indeed, related – not only in a familial scene (cf. volume one) but also to everything: earth and water, sky and stone; not only because all of creation is made up of different combinations of molecules, but because we are all a part of the divine hierarchy.

This is the true meaning of the mystery teaching concerning the divine spark; the god-like potential of humanity is far better expressed by this means than by any discussion of man as Superman. The divine fragment is that part of us which is always seeking reunion, a reassembly of separated parts into the whole from which they were created; a return to the paradisial state before the Fall. The torn body of the God, scattered through creation, must be restored.

> Man then is of twofold nature, the Titanic and the Dionysiac, the earthly and the divine. The aim of the Orphic life is by purification, asceticism and ritual to purge away the Titanic part of us and prepare ourselves to become fully divine. The body . . . is a tomb from which the soul of the Orphic initiate will finally be released to find the true life. (353)

It sometimes taking as many as a thousand year cycles before the Orphite at last flees the weary wheel of incarnation.

The Orphic school was, above all, syncretic. Orpheus is credited with the dissemination of the mysteries, with passing on rather than inventing, much that became the basis of subsequent Greco-Roman theosophy. Pythagoras followed many of the Orphic teachings and made Orpheus the central deity of his own esoteric system, establishing a canon of Orphic Hymns which were to influence esotericists as far apart in time and persuasion as Pico della Mirandola (351), Athanasius Kircher (102) and Thomas Taylor the Platonist (325).

This is not surprising when one considers that 'the Orphic method aimed at revealing divine things by means of symbols . . . a method common to all writers of divine lore' (270). In later times Orpheus was widely recognized: particularly for the symbolism of the seven stringed lyre and the perfect harmonies he was believed to have produced from it. Combined with Pythagorean knowledge, the Orphic mysteries became central to the Renaissance arts of music and masque, and to the doctrine of the Harmonies and Signatures set forth by writers such as Jacob Boehme (1575–1624) and Marcilio Ficino (1453–99). Orpheus was recognized as a son of Apollo and Calliope, the Muse of harmony and rhythm; Euridice becomes humanity slain by the serpent of knowledge (perhaps an instance of later borrowing from Christian sources) imprisoned in the underworld of ignorance from which only Orpheus could free her. The rending of Orpheus becomes an image of the warring factions of knowledge, nominally pacified by his music. The seven strings of his lyre are the seven keys of the spectrum, or of universal knowledge. (116)

Figure 4:   Hermes Trismegistos

We can see how this wealth of symbolism must have delighted the minds of the Renaissance philosopher-magicians, who sought to reintroduce the mysteries into the world and like Orpheus harmonize them into a single system. That they failed to do so was not for want of effort, as we shall see in chapter 3. They came as near as anyone could to achieving a synthesis of mystery school teaching, magic and philosophy – a goal still sought by many today, though with a good deal less understanding of the common points of balance between one discipline and another.

Between the Orphic mysteries and their partial revival in the Renaissance there is a long gap, not only in time but in understanding. In part this was bridged by the figure of the magician, whose role will be discussed more fully in chapter 3; and the Alchemist, whose work we shall investigate in chapter 5. The magician, in particular, is related to the earlier mystery schools, while the Alchemist draws upon a far wider range of sources, including Arabic metaphysics and Christian mysticism. The single force which unites all these elements is the body of teaching attributed to Hermes Trismegistos, 'Thrice Greatest' Hermes, whose doctrines stand at the very heart of the Western Way.

THE HERMETIC REALITY

Hermes saw the totality of things. Having seen, he understood, he had the power to reveal and show. And indeed what he knew, he wrote down. What he wrote, he mostly hid away, keeping silence rather than speaking out, so that every generation on coming into the world had to seek out these things. (302)

This strikes the keynote of Hermeticism: the coming of the human soul into matter without knowledge, and the search for the hidden mysterious truths seeded throughout the world, through which freedom might be gained. In particular we note that 'every genera-tion' has to 'seek out these things'. The mysteries are not calcified, not frozen in time; they change and grow with the changes that occur in mankind. It is another side to the idea that humanity contains a spark of the divine, seeking always to return to its point of origin. Though the quest here is more one of abstract knowledge, behind it we may detect a deeper goal: 'A desire for the truth, especially about the gods is in reality a yearning for the Deity. For the study and search (for these things) in a reception, as it were, of things sacred. . . ' (270) This is the Hermetic quest: it is reiterated through-out the whole vast spectrum of wisdom, mystery text and inner-directed learning which is the true *Corpus Hermeticum*, the reality behind the texts which have come down to us. These are really only a gathering of fragments, attributed to Thoth Tahuti (later called Hermes) but few of genuine Egyptian origin. They have been copied, recopied, edited, altered and in part destroyed by a succession of Hermetic 'scholars' and exegetes down the ages. As Iamblichus noted, the earliest philosophers and mystics used to ascribe their own writings to Hermes, as god of wisdom and learning, in such a way that one would suppose that he had written them personally! (152) This has given rise to much confusion over the origins of the *Corpus* – added to which Hermes often appears as a character in the texts, making it even harder to discover actual sources for the material. Hermes, we remember, hid much that he had written: enough still remains to be uncovered to make it difficult to write with authority about the existing *Corpus*.

It is, however, safe to say that it was in the melting-pot of Alexandrian mysticism and philosophy during the first three centuries after Christ that the original Egyptian Hermetic writings became cross-fertilized with Judaic and Greek teachings of the Gnostics. The influence of the *Corpus* on Gnosticism was considerable, and it is probably this more than anything which helped preserve the Hermetic tradition, though it cast it permanently into a pseudo-Christian mode (So much so that in the sixteenth century the Humanist philosopher Francesco Patrizi petitioned Pope Gregory XIV to allow Hermes to supplant Aristotle as the arbiter of learning in the universities as he would resonate more harmoniously with Christian doctrine. (107).

In Gnostic literature Thoth became Hermes Trismegistos and Maat his wife was identified with the figure of Sophia or Divine Wisdom. The three grades of initiation recognized by the early Hermeticists – Mortals (probationers), Intelligences (vision seekers), and Sons of Light (perfected ones) – were renamed Hyle, Psyche, and Pneuma (cf. Chapter 2). Hermes became tutor to Isis and Osiris, and was known as one of the sacred ogdoad of the Gnostic cosmology; four pairs of male and female syzygies whose task it was to maintain balance in the cosmos. According to Mead this is the oldest form of the Gnostic structure of deity, and within it Hermes has the supreme task of keeping order amongst the rest.

The title Trismegistos or Thrice Greatest has had several different meanings attributed to it. One of the most interesting is found in the writings of the monk Syncellus, who claimed to be quoting from the writings of Menetho, whose works, though lost, were probably the earliest gathering of Hermetic lore. (147) He, according to Syncellus, refers to certain monuments of the *Seriadic* country, which contained the original teachings of the *first* Hermes. These were later translated and set down in writing by the *second* Hermes ('sometime after the Flood'). From this it is possible to posit the existence of a *third* figure, also called by the name of Hermes, who again worked on the texts, perhaps rendering them into a form of system. All of which indicates three stages of transmission. Hence 'thrice greatest' refers to a *third* avatar bearing the title of the God, to whom came to be attributed the whole lore and writings of the original Hermeticists.

Of what, then, does the *Corpus Hermeticum* consist? Basically it is a series of exchanges, purporting to be between pupil and master, or between Hermes Trismegistos and his 'sons' (i.e. disciples) of various names. They are often repetitive and cover much of the same ground in varying degrees of complexity. The first, and perhaps the best known, is the *Poimandres*, a description of the creation cast in the form of a dream. The (here unnamed) adept falls asleep and is visited by Poimandres (Mind of the Sovereignty) who explains to him all that he has wished to know concerning 'the things that are, (how to) understand their nature, and get knowledge of God' (302):

> When he had thus spoken, forthwith all things changed in aspect before me, and were opened out in a moment. And I beheld a boundless view: all was changed into light, a mild and joyous light; and I marvelled when I saw it. . .

There follows a description of the creation, a mingling of light and dark from which comes forth 'a holy Word . . . and methought this Word was the voice of the Light.' When the seeker desires to understand what he has seen, Poimandres tells him: 'That light . . . is I, even Mind, the first God . . . and the Word which came forth from the Light is the son of God.'
When the dreamer asks how this may be, he is told:

> Learn my meaning . . . by looking at what you yourself have in you; for in you too, the word is son, and the mind is father of the word. They are not separate one from the other; for life is the union of word and mind. (ibid)

Again and again this message is affirmed: there is a god within which gives life to the body and inspiration of all that we do: events in the sphere of incarnation reflect those in the heavenly sphere. It is this emphasis on unity rather than disharmony which marks out the Hermetic mysteries: unity of all things, of God with man, of higher with lower, of divine with mundane. It finds its clearest expression in the *Emerald Tablet of Hermes* with its famous injunction 'as above, so below', so often quoted and so little understood by occultists throughout the ages.

Various legends exist concerning the origin of the Emerald or 'Smagdarine' tablet. According to one source it was found by Apollonius of Tyana (cf. Chapter 3) who entered a hidden cave and took the tablet from between the clasped hands of the corpse of Hermes himself. Another version recounts how it was Alexander the

Great who found the tomb and carried off the tablet to Alexandria – an interesting memory of the transmission of the Hermetic mysteries from its possible place of origin to the city where its truths became disseminated widely. (197)

In reality, the text of the *Emerald Tablet* was for a long time known only in Latin versions dating from the time of the philosopher Albertus Magnus (1193–1280) who was believed to have written the material himself. Subsequently Arabic texts were discovered which dated the *Tablet* to the time of the Alchemist Gebir (722–815) or even earlier, so that the traditional ascription of its composition to Apollonius may in fact be closer to the truth than any of these theories.

Whatever one chooses to believe there is no getting away from the fact that the *Emerald Tablet* is one of the most profound and important documents to have come down to us. It has been said more than once that it contains the sum of all knowledge – for those able to understand it.

The *Tablet* outlines a doctrine of signatures and correspondences which reflect the mind of the Creator. The Greek word from which we derive cosmos means 'order', and we live in an ordered creation through which we are able to move at will yet always find a point of recognition. This is because the cosmos is the product of a single act of generation which has set a signature upon everything. In the finite world in which we attempt to bind ourselves this is scarcely recognized by anyone; yet the youngest mystery school initiate would have known it once, no matter how many different gods he worshipped.

The Smagdarine Tablet describes just such an ordered cosmos: it tells the story of creation, its history and its goal in terms of such blinding simplicity that, in common with other, equally simple statements ('love thy neighbour as thyself', for example) it has been subject to frequent misinterpretation. Our own suggestions as to its meaning will be found in chapter 5, while the text itself has been placed at the end of the chapter, where it forms an exercise in controlled meditation and may be studied free of any commentary.

Initiation, it is said, is always a one-to-one experience: the seeker stands alone (however supported by his or her brethren) before whatever principle he seeks to know. In the Western Way, as we have tried to show, all knowledge and experience thus gained is part of a single initiation we must all undergo. It was for this reason that the Temple of Thoth was called the House of the Net, meaning the enclosing snare of matter. To escape this the captive (the initiate) must learn the parts of the net – its poles, ropes, weights and so forth – in order to turn it to his own use, as a means of catching the food of the spirit. An ancient prayer reads: 'Hail, ye net-inverters, fishers and catchers of the spirit which alone nourishes! By refining your higher selves, ye have produced that which produced you.' (227) Again the familiar theme: discover yourselves and you discover God. It is not strange that the imagery here echoes that of Christ's 'I will make you fishers of men' (Mark, Chap.I,17) which can be read as meaning that those who follow the way will find themselves, and in themselves find God.

This is why Hermetic teaching places such importance on the place of man in the cosmos. He is seen as central in that he touches the boundaries of creation at every level, and because he possesses within him the encoded mysteries of matter, spirit and mind. Plato recognized this in the *Timaeus* (67) which he is believed to have derived from Egyptian sources. Here he defines the cosmos as a living creature, formed after the manner of the most perfect synthesis of creation – the human cosmic being, anthropocosmos, Adam Kadmon. According to Proclus' commentaries on the *Timaeus* (54) this is to be equated with the Orphic Man of Light, who is threefold and contains the essence of all creation. This threefold division of matter into *Phanes* (shining), *Erikepaois* (power, male), and *Metis* (wisdom, female), represents a profound understanding of the breakdown of matter into its component parts, which when reassembled make up the perfection which is the closest we can get to understanding the nature of God.

It is on this doctrine of unity that the foundation of Hermeticism rests. We have grown used to a dualistic tendency in Western philosophy since Zoroaster, but in the Orphic and Hermetic schools the emphasis was on balance, polarity, the coming together of elements into a unique whole. This is why the gnostic Hermes is represented as being the uniting principle in the system of the ogdoads. As one ancient text has it: 'One is the All . . . and if the All did not contain the All, the All would be nothing.' (22) Once again we hear the echo of the divine interaction between God (the One) and creation (Matter, the All). It is not just incidental that Hermes' symbol is a staff with twin serpents of wisdom and understanding coiled about it. As in the Qabala, where the central pillar holds those of left and right in balance, here too the principle is the same.

The mysteries were always intended to be understood in a threefold fashion: with the spirit, the mind and the senses. Such a threefold division has continued to be recognized in Western esoteric practice ever since. Sacred words, uttered in temple or lodge, echo through three worlds: the divine, the intellectual and the physical, bringing all three together in a *rapprochement* which causes them to vibrate harmoniously one with the other.

The universe (or God) is always willing to respond to an harmonious note emitted by those in tune with the infinite Word of creation. To find that note within the self has ever been the most important action of the mystery seeker. Initiation leads towards just this point; study and self-observation, discipline and obedience, self-abdication: all acts of the adept are aimed first at realizing the divine harmonic within himself and then in tuning this to include the whole of the creation in which he stands.

The elements of creation may well be divided and scattered, as the myths of the Titans and the rending of gods like Dionysius and Osiris suggest, but what has been divided can be joined again – in the story of Isis and Osiris even the absence of the phallus did not prevent the creation of the divine child, Horus, the uniting principle which ushered in a new age of peace and harmony.

In this sense the passions of Christ, Baldur, Tammuz, of all the saviour gods, can be seen as a wholly natural process in which matter seeks out its component parts and reunites to form the whole which was the original design of the cosmos. God is lonely for the children that are lost to him, the fragments of himself created so that he could know himself. We should not be surprised, therefore, to find him sending forth his beloved Son – the nearest aspect of himself – into matter to seek out those lost ones.

Christ and Hermes with all of the shepherd gods, are come to gather in their flocks. But they cannot do so unaided. We must be willing to co-operate, to harmonize with them as we do whenever we celebrate the mysteries. Thus the glorious anamnesis of the Eucharist, the love-feast of the Agathadaimon, are aimed at giving us a glimpse outside the walls of our chaotic, fractured universe at the peace and tranquillity which can be ours – if we wish it to be.

This, then, is the Hermetic reality: the maintaining of a divine unity within the mundane sphere, which in turn raises that sphere to divine heights. As above so below, always. God imprints everything at the moment of creation with a divine signature, the DNA of the cosmos, which makes every rose a rose, every man a man, every beast a beast. And this signature contains the very essence of the creator, his message to all that he has caused to have being: like to like, very like to very like, the One and the All contained in each other. As a seventeenth-century Hermeticist put it:

> The Sun and the Moon I see above me influence me neither for good nor bad, but the Sun and Moon and Planets (with) which God's providence has adorned the heaven *in me*, which also is the seat of the Almighty, these have the power to rule and reform me according to their course ordained by God. (84, our italics.)

The methods by which such a point of realization might be attained, the practice behind the theology, are what we must look at next.

THE LANGUAGE OF DESIRE

The Mystery Schools are really containers for certain concepts and images designed to assist in the building of inner worlds where the perfection of humanity and eventually of all material things can take place. A fully functioning and active Mystery School is a power house generating energies from which both the individual seeker and the great teachers of the age can draw strength and sustenance. We must be aware that:

> The highest of our initiations here below is only the dream of that true vision and initiation; and the discourses (on the mysteries) have been carefully devised to awaken the memory of the sublime things above or else are of no purpose. (228)

In other words the 'sublime things' must be reflected by those who attempt to realize them; they must be remembered by the initiate so that he or she can embody the divine truth in themselves. (96)

But entrance to the mysteries is first dependent upon a degree of maturity. In Egypt, it was said that before one can know the spiritual Isis one must first know her terrestrial aspect. This meant that a thorough grounding in knowledge of earthly and mortal existence was necessary before the inner mysteries were opened to the initiate. The same is no less true today, and nothing should be attempted by the serious student until he or she has 'put their house in order', learning to cope with the stresses and strains of the ordinary world. If you cannot survive the daily grind of living you will certainly find it hard to sustain the rigours of a magical working. If, on the other hand, you master both aspects of being, there will gradually begin to be an overlap – your normal life will become permeated with magical understanding, and your magical life with the fruits of human wisdom. In the end, both will be transformed.

> The beginning of wisdom is the most sincere desire for instruction, and concern for instruction is love of wisdom. . . . For she is a reflection of eternal light, a spotless mirror of the working of God, and an image of his goodness.(Wisdom of Solomon 6,17)

Desire is a beginning, but once contact with the invisible hierarchy is made, it is for the initiate alone to keep the flame of his or her intention alive and to learn to be a reflection of 'the working of God, and an image of his goodness. . . '

Without that initial spark of desire, there can be no progress; and even then the journey will seldom be easy or swift. Years of study, discipline and concentration lie before the would-be seeker. He must come to terms with his innermost longings, fears and hopes before he can even begin to reach that state of consciousness where he may expect to walk with gods and converse with angels.

An initiation, by its very nature, is a form of inner pressure designed to 'shock' the initiate into a sense of his or her inner capability. In almost every instance we find that the mysteries contain the dramatic reconstruction of a primary myth, in which the would-be initiate takes his or her part, playing either the central role or the part of an onlooker, but always involved directly or otherwise in the events. At Eleusis human procreation and birth were shown to be the first steps on an initiatory journey: a preparation for the soul's passage through life and the voyage into the Underworld. The little death of initiation prepared the way for the greater life and the greater death. Persephone returns from Hades, but is subject to Pluto thereafter; the initiate survives his ordeals but will never be the same again. Finally, the soul is freed to return to its origin. This world is but a reflection of the Elysian fields, as Plato saw. In its mirror, we see ourselves – but transformed.

Nevertheless, initiation is not a ceremony or set of rituals which automatically ensures enlightenment. It merely marks the ingoing of the candidate; a transition period. The knowledge gained thereafter is of an interior and instinctive kind, purely personal in the way and shape it manifests itself. Though the path is by no means an easy one, certain common practices are as much a part of contemporary training as they were in the great Classical schools.

Apart from preliminary suitability, good health, a sense of integrity, dedication and so forth, the candidate will have to resign him or herself to patient effort during the seemingly tedious period of technical training. Whatever is required by the teacher must be met, in equal measure, by the student. What is important is not the success, but the honest effort at attainment. What took one student six months may take another two or three years, depending upon ability and circumstance. Speed is not important: seemingly brilliant students often spurt ahead in the early stages and then lose interest because they are insufficiently mature to plod through the donkey-work, whereas a seemingly dull and conscientious pupil might take longer to assimilate training but achieve a higher standard of understanding.

Basic to early training is a thorough acquaintance and mastery of the elemental qualities within the student. Fire, Water, Earth and Air is the four-square basis of magical competence, and without a complete understanding of the elements within the self, the student will be as the Sorcerer's Apprentice (who incidentally could not control the element of water in either an Inner or Outer capacity). W.G.Gray gives many excellent exercises in his *Magical Ritual Methods* (115) for familiarizing oneself with one's elemental strengths and shortcomings. Work with the Elemental kings and kingdoms is often scorned and neglected as too basic for the Hermetic student; but like breathing and relaxation it is an essential quality for the esotericist (cf. Exercise 5).

One of the first requirements of a magical school once the initial training is over, is to set the candidate to making a set of ritual implements. These are the mainstay of the occultist – the extension of his personality and the elemental symbols of his or her craft. The Wand, Sword, Chalice and Pentacle or Patten signify the elements of Air, Fire, Water and Earth respectively. The initiate is expected, if not to work the metals himself, at least to work upon the naked blade until it resembles the sword of his will. Likewise, he or she will cut the wood and fashion the wand, engrave or cut the pentacle, paint or scribe the sigils on the cup or chalice. A practical mastery of the elements is basic at this point.

As we shall see, the Gnostics and Mandeans left instructions for their initiates as to how they should leave the earthly sphere and progress through the spheres or levels of the Archons – the rulers of the planets. In the mysteries also, the next step is often a familiarity with planetary powers and influences. The initiate may acquire this by many means, becoming, as we have seen, familiar with the correspondences devised in the Orphic schools. But the method most likely to be used in our own time is the investigation of the planetary attributions on the qabalistic Tree of Life. Each sphere or sephira on the Tree has its ruling planet, its vice and virtue, whereby this power can be usefully or destructively applied. The charity of Tiphareth can easily fall over into selfishness, the dynamic strength of Geburah into destructive violence. The candidate for higher initiations will be expected to progress through these sephiroth one by one as stages along the way, and to equilibrate the positive and negative qualities within him or her self. (See fig. 117)

Gradually the initiate is refining many levels of the self, attuning them to the Inner. This task is never really complete in the lifetime of the initiate, any more than any human being should expect perfection. It is ongoing and repetitious. The basal urgings of our lower nature are never completely rooted out, though they can be kept under control and even used positively as a thrust-block to our attainments. Periods of trial come even to the adept, who is by no means exempt from the trivial or earth-shattering problems of human life. From those who receive, more is required, goes the occult adage. The failings of the humble go unnoticed; those of the famous or infamous are the subject of newspaper headlines.

The responsibility of the adept, the true walker-between-the-worlds, is not just to those students and co-workers on the Outer, but to the forces of the Inner who rely upon their mastery of the Outer, as well as their aptitude in mediating the work of the Inner thence forward. We shall discuss this important aspect of training more fully in the chapter dealing with the Magician and his work.

The Mystery Schools demand firstly 'know thyself'. The Lesser Mysteries are spent in clearing the ground ready for the dawning of this event. The Greater Mysteries come only when this basis is established, when the initiate can stand alone, in command of his inner fortress; when the threshold is swept and made ready for the descent of the Holy Guardian Angel or the Inner Master. The preparation complete, the levels of the self clearly perceived, the initiate is then ready for the identification with the god-forms or archetypes of his or her school.

Identification with an archetype demands a great deal of objectivity and cannot be attempted in early stages of training. Like a dancer or actor who has spent years perfecting the body, the voice, the numerous forms of their art, and who steps upon the stage at last before a live audience, so it is with the initiate. There can be no confusion between theory and practice, no running to the wings to consult a book or a teacher on a point of technique or a personal problem. The initiate is alone with the archetype and the identification one with the other must be a total communication so that the energies of the archetype can be mediated successfully. It is easy to spot an actor who is not really acting: his eyes lack conviction, like a person telling a lie, his movements are not carried through, his voice veers away from the sense of the script, he does not truly interact with the other actors on stage and often hinders their performance. He does not convince the audience either, who sit and shuffle. An initiate's mediation can suffer in just such a way, but he does not just fail his fellow ritualists. The audience, in this instance, is the Outer – for whose benefit a ritual is performed. The producers are the Inner, who are quite justified in taking their work elsewhere and seeking a new cast.

. The first kind of identification required of an initiate comes in an acceptably easy way – he or she is asked to officiate as the officer of a quarter, mediating a particular quality to the lodge or circle. We say easy, but it is often hard work: the qualities of the elemental kings must be present and operative within the quarter-officer. One becomes a doorway or channel through which the quarter-guardians (who may be either god-forms or angels) can come. This requires concentration and alertness, not a passive overpowering by the Inner contact. It is work of a privileged kind, and reveals to the initiate the priestly qualities inherent in his craft. The circle or working area is a division of matter into elements, and those most at home in one quarter with one element will feel drawn there. Nevertheless, an ability to work from *any* quarter is important and should be cultivated; it will anyway follow naturally if the inner elements have been properly balanced. A very good breakdown of this kind of work will be found in Gareth Knight's *The Rose Cross and the Goddess*. (184) and in W.B. Gray's *Inner Traditions of Magic* (114)

Later, the initiate may be asked to participate in ritual dramas which enact the stories of the gods employed by his or her school. Here, just as in the ancient schools, the initiate will represent the Mighty Ones themselves. This is an awesome function which is not assigned to the unready; dangers of over-identification or ego-centric appropriation are present, but may be avoided by a simple procedure prior to the rite in question.

This can be done in two ways. First, the archetype to be assumed is visualized as a mask which the initiate will put on. Just as in the

Greek mystery dramas, the initiate will go apart silently before the ritual and contemplate the mask, possibly holding a dialogue with it in imagination, establishing it as a separate entity from him or herself. The symbolism surrounding the archetype can be rehearsed objectively, the stories and correspondences of this figure compared with those of other pantheons and traditions. Then the mask is assumed, in the wings, as it were, of the working place. The second method takes this a stage further: it may not be suitable in all cases nor be appropriate to certain kinds of individuals. The mask is visualized before one and enshrined: flowers and incense are placed before it, prayers said, invoking the qualities required in the rite – the archetype in question becoming, for a time, one of the 'masks of God'. The assumption of the mask is correspondingly a more awesome thing for the initiate, but there is no danger of over-identification.

Relinquishing the mask at the end of the ritual, the initiate performs the same procedure, only in reverse, returning the mask to the shrine, or visualizing it, face away from him, returning to the Inner. Such an identification is never done for the gratification of the individual – a fact which few appreciate who have not stood in the circle dropping from exhaustion and Inner pressure resultant from the technique. Dion Fortune spoke wisely when she recommended the work of a blacksmith as lighter than that of the ritualist. The pressures and strains are many, not only on the physique but upon the astral and etheric bodies. Depletion of energy is usual at the conclusion of a ritual: energy is built up and mediated properly, not left to slew around in a vacuum. There is nothing abnormal or sinister in this: particularly important pieces of work require more energy than others, and the re-energization of the individual will take correspondingly longer. This will be less so when working with a larger group, where the energies will be shared out and the demands are less great on the individual. In cases where extreme exhaustion is suffered, a good night's sleep and an intake of nourishment will normally suffice to replenish the spent ritualist, otherwise the use of exercise 9 is recommended.

Little enough emphasis is given by modern mystery schools to the training of the body as well as the psyche. A good ritualist should be deft in hand-gestures, have a supple torso, good posture and carriage and be able to operate without falling over his or her feet. Physical clumsiness is often the result of mental unpreparedness or lack of concentration. The demands upon the body are immense and if insufficient training is given to keep the physical instrument in good working condition, then the magical work will suffer also. Sport and dance are obviously helpful here, but they cannot cater for the peculiar requirements of the esotericist, who has to consider *all* his or her bodies! Schools would do well to consider introducing classes of ritual movement and ask their experienced members to speak more openly about the physical side-effects of ritual work. The mature body is, strange to relate, better equipped for the strains of ritual than the young. The ageing body depletes quicker than both but often has greater staying-power. (263)

On the other hand, rewards can be great – provided you do not expect them to be material. Aspirations are high indeed – but then the watchword of most contemporary mystery schools is 'responsibility' – care, that is, for the self and for the divinity within – not in a selfish way but in an effort to bring humankind into line with its infinite potential. It is this end to which the trials, tests, rituals and initiations must lead.

Within each individual is the possibility of becoming, microcosmically, Adam Kadmon. The final outcome of this will be the uniting of all humanity in one being – the Body of Light which Poimandres speaks of as the source of the Word. For this reason many modern schools describe themselves, variously, as 'servants' or 'societies' of light – and the theme has become prominent within New Age movements of recent times. To be a servant of the light is to be, as the initiates of the original schools were, dedicated to the freeing of the divine spark.

This has sometimes led to an ecstatic response, and the ultimate experience of the divine has been sought through both asceticism and an ecstatic sexuality. But if, as the Dionysian mysteries suggest, we are made up in part of the stuff of the Titans, it is little wonder if our response to the infinite arises as much from a sexual as a religious basis.

So often the archetypal presences invoked within the mysteries translate into the basic elements of life itself – sperm and ovum – and we see a sexual polarity problem of the kind we spoke of in volume one (cf. chapter 5 of this volume). Sexuality could be used as an ecstatic method in which union with another human being becomes an expression of the divine union of the Saviour-god with his or her beloved. This was often utilized ritually when a priest or priestess represented the deity in themselves. The abuses of temple prostitution were remarked upon with distaste by several Classical authors who travelled in the Middle East and saw their own mysteries in later ascetic forms which were devoid of the earlier and earthier celebrations which were a part of the Native traditions.

In earlier times, the identification of the priest or priestess with the deity enabled the people or their ruler to have congress with the divine guardian of the tribe. The Classical mysteries still bore this understanding subtextually within their celebrations, yet within the mysteries of Eleusis, for example, the hierophant drank a draught which specifically inhibited his sexual function. He was always chosen from an Eleusinian family and was himself married in the normal way: not, as with many of the Eastern cults, castrated in the service of the Goddess. (356, 339)

Sexuality within ritual is thus a constant reminder of earlier resonances: it should never intervene in the flow of energies in any operation whereby the work becomes earth-bound. The esoteric Judaic and Qabalistic practice of union with one's wife in order to mirror the union of God with the Shekhina, comes nearer to an understanding of how sexuality can be made to express the deepest religious impulse upon earth. The abuse of this in magic occurs when the levels are confused. On the ecstatic or tribal level of consciousness, sexuality is an honest expression of religious fervour translated into human terms.

All of this may well lead one to ask: what does this exalted work have to do with me – surely it is for the highest adepts, dedicated to a greater service than is possible for the ordinary follower of the Western Way. Not so: we are all, if we so desire it, servants of light, and dedication is possible to all – to a greater or lesser degree according to our personal capacity.

All mystery schools and orders, of whatever kind, exist to train the mind and the heart, the intellect and the soul, until they are working together at the highest level of perfection. Such things may take more than one incarnation, depending upon the stage of development already reached by the student. When all have been trained and have fully realized themselves then the work of the Schools, Fraternities and orders will be completed– there will no longer be any need for them since humanity will have reached the point of development intended for it, to aid which those we call Masters have been sent. (91)

The Western Way is one means to that end, one among many, but it is a means only and not an end in itself. Those who think of it in this light will travel no further than the first few steps – they will find themselves traversing the same section of the road again and again, endlessly travelling but never arriving.

Although the emphasis in this book is on the practical, it should not be considered in any way a substitute for proper training or belonging to an order or lodge. There is an increasing tendency towards solitary working, and this is well supported by the habits of the Renaissance, where more often than not a group of people *could not* meet to celebrate the mysteries. So, if you are a lone worker either from choice or circumstance, this book is aimed at giving you a grasp of the essential requirements of the would-be initiate. However, if the opportunity to work with a group comes your way, do not pass it up – providing of course that it appears to be properly organized and governed.

The choice of a school can be fraught with difficulties: there are so many and their approaches are often bewilderingly different. Instinct and inner awareness alone can tell you when you have found one that feels right – though it does not follow that you will feel right to them. If all goes well, however, and you are accepted as a candidate, this should be the beginning of a satisfying and rewarding association, You should have gained at least some idea of what to expect from the foregoing pages; however, we have yet to bring the picture up-to-date, to follow the thread of the mysteries foward in time to the present.

GUARDIANS OF TRADITION

Just as the Medieval and Renaissance mysteries can be traced to a Hermetic impulse, so the schools and fraternities of our own time owe their origin primarily to what may be termed the Rosicrucian impulse. Yet, by one of those paradoxes which seem to govern the transmission of the Western Way, there is no evidence that either the Rosicrucian Brotherhood or its founder Christian Rosenkreutz had any physical existence at all.

The first that anyone in the outside world knew of the Rosicrucians was in 1614, when a curious document entitled *Fama Fraternitatis of the Meritorious Order of the Rose Cross* (6) appeared in Germany and was widely circulated. It purported to be a description of the life of one Christian Rosenkreutz, philosopher, mystic and magician, who had lived to the age of 106 and whose body was then concealed in a secret tomb which was not discovered for another 120 years.

This places the life-time of Rosenkreutz at the end of the fourteenth or the beginning of the fifteenth century, though there are no records from that – or indeed any – time which relate to his actual existence. The description of the finding of the vault containing his uncorrupted remains is written in highly symbolic language which reads like an initiatory text. (Certainly, to follow the steps leading to the discovery of the body, followed by the description of the vault itself, and to mediate upon them, can be a richly rewarding experience.)

The opening of the vault is, in the *Fama*, likened to an event of far-reaching effect: 'for like as our door was after so many years wonderfully discovered, also there shall be opened a door to Europe ... which already doth begin to appear, and with great desire is expected of many.' (6) Judging by the reaction across Europe to the *Fama* and the manifestos which followed it, the desire and expectation must have been considerable. A new hope was seeded thereby which had nothing to do with the effects of the Renaissance – medieval attitudes were still abroad and enlightenment battled uneasily with a mysticism which retained the blinkers of dogma and superstition.

The authorship of the first Rosicrucian manifesto has been traced speculatively to the University of Tubingen and more precisely to one Johann Valentin von Andrae, yet behind the human authors we can detect the beginning of a powerful new stream of inner teaching which found an outlet in this manner. (195) No one knew the whereabouts of the Rosicrucian brotherhood but this did not stop many who read and understood the true value of the manifestos from trying to make physical contact. The fact that there were writings which spoke of a brotherhood of adepts who could be contacted 'through proper channels' was enough to prompt many to advertise in newsheets for more information. Even the philosopher René Descartes went to Germany to seek out the brotherhood and, not surprisingly perhaps, found nothing. Yet on his return to Paris in 1623 he was forced to show himself publicly in order to prove that he had not become invisible– i.e. that he was not a Rosicrucian – for so had the rumours circulated. (365)

When no reply was forthcoming to the various inquiries sent to non-existent addresses or people, enthusiasts were driven to publish their own books and pamphlets to see whether their ideas resonated harmonically with other would-be Rosicrucians similarly situated. Thus the original manifestos spawned a succession of imitators and commentaries, constellating their writers into the formation of a mystery school whose doctrines were set out for all to read who could understand them – an odd reversal of the classical schools who hid their teachings from all but their initiates.

This is surely a prime example of the way a mystery school receives its formatory impulse: it has certainly been a much repeated method since the age of the Rosicrucians. Not that their own writings can be in any way described as clear statements of intent or belief. The language employed is allusive and full of symbolism which must have prevented all but those in the know from understanding what was being said. Ever thus do the mysteries guard themselves from idle curiosity.

Initially we may see von Andrae and his fellow philosophers at Tubingen reacting against the climate of the times, so that when the writer of the *Fama*, who had long since admitted its composition, while denying its importance as a document, included in his will the words: 'Though I now leave the Fraternity itself, I shall never leave the true Christian Fraternity, which, beneath the Cross, smells of the Rose, and is quite apart from the filth of this century.' (207)

At its heart the Rosicrucian impulse was a combination of esoteric Christianity with straight mystery-school teaching as it had been kept alive in the work of the magician and the alchemist. That it transcended both points of origin is an indication of the power of the inner impulse which brought it into being: the symbols of the Rose and the Cross combined to make the first real synthesis of magical and mystical teaching since the original Hermetic impulse.

The idea of an invisible college of adepts is, as we shall see in chapter 4, not so rare as we may think. Rosicrucianism survived because it had no visible foundation, no headquarters, no officers, no dogmas and no rules of membership.

The effect of this on the European world of the seventeenth century was deep and lasting. It paved the way for the French esoteric revival of the next century, which was thus able to draw upon both Native and Hermetic Traditions at a deep level. This was aided in part by the operations of another body of initiates – the Freemasons; for though a conjunction of Rosicrucianism and Freemasonry cannot be ascertained with any surety, Freemasonry became an important vessel of Rosicrucian survival.

Freemasonry itself grew out of the crafts-guilds and friendly burial societies of the pre-Reformation. The Master of his 'mystery' or craft-profession was a powerful man, and together the crafts-guilds exerted a considerable pressure on society. This is still observable today where an ostensibly esoteric movement exerts a high degree of political influence. Masonry's origins, like those of Rosicrucianism, are retrospective in their construction. The supposed 'life' of Christian Rosenkreutz, like the building of Jerusalem's temple and the Murder of Hiram, are all thematically important – yet to claim these resonances as historically traceable is to confuse Inner with Outer realities.

If Rosicrucianism is the Germanic Protestant impulse, as many have seen it to be, then Freemasonry is a British esoteric one: their fusion was not entirely curious. The Protestant ethic had left sad lacunae in the life of medieval confraternities whose esoteric pursuits had probably been no more than an occasional mass celebrated by the guild's priest, or the usual kind of initiatory high-jinks practised upon freshmen at university or apprentices in crafts today. The guilds remained, but their ritual life was severely curtailed. Masonry may well have been formed upon the principles of the crafts-guilds, as an 'inner circle' by masters of their crafts and thence permeated through to learned gentlemen of leisure whose antiquarian and classical background would give them ample scope for the creation of rationalizing legends to accompany these new 'mystery schools'. God was the architect of the macrocosm and Christ, his apprentice, was a carpenter in that microcosm we inhabit. The idea of co-inherence was thus carried forward into a new era of esoteric belief.

There is something fundamentally Protestant in the conception of the Divine Architect which is akin to the more puritan lines of certain Judaic traditions, as well as those of Mithraism, of which Masonry had many echoes. As Mithraism rose through a tangle of syncretic cults to become a unifying principle within the Roman Empire, so Freemasonry today has tended to follow a similar course. Military and Chivalric orders certainly found continuance within Masonry, as did the idea of monarchic restoration and ritual chivalry; and the unfolding translation of Qabalistic texts enabled much Judaic esotericism to be assimilated herein. The theologian and apologist Philo of Alexandria once asked, of the pagan mystery schools:

> Why, O initiates, if these things are good and profitable, do you shut yourselves up in deepest darkness and render service to three or four individuals alone, when you can render it to all by presenting these advantages in the public market? (261)

In our own time, perhaps, this question is being answered. Reliance on authority or tradition is a Piscean trait. The gradual dismantling of the awesome temple scaffolding, the secrecy devolving upon initiates in times of ignorance and persecution, the solitude of the seeker are largely behind us now. Instead of temples, the concert or lecture hall, the spontaneous gathering of seekers; instead of robed occultists, the free dissemination of hidden wisdom, which nonetheless remains intact; instead of isolation, the growing network of those sensitive to cosmic purpose.

There have always been guardians of the mystery traditions, however elusive they may have seemed; teachers have always been on hand to impart the eternal truths. With the gradual relaxing of the inner laws governing the open dissemination of esoteric beliefs in the last two centuries, many schools have come forward, each one claiming the right to train and initiate its followers into the divine mysteries of creation. Some have proved false, having nothing of value to teach; others have grown, flourished, and then faded with the passing of their founders. Still others have passed on their knowledge to those who came after.

When, in the late nineteenth century certain members of the Theosophical Society – then the most prestigious occult organization of the time – began to tire of the emphasis given to Eastern mysteries, they looked elsewhere, finding within the newly translated Egyptian papyri and the wealth of Classical MSS, a fund of Western wisdom to be explored in a practical way. Enthusiastic explorers rather than scholars, they delved deeply into the neglected heritage of the past, and came up with a whole system of magical and theurgic mysteries.

Thus the 'Hermetic Order of the Golden Dawn' was born, admitting Freemasons, poets, clergymen and thinkers to its ranks. It was to outlast many of its own offspring, and became, in the next few generations, the most prestigious organization of its kind since the Renaissance. Most modern esoteric schools trace their descent from the Golden Dawn, and through it, knowingly or not, make contact with both the Rosicrucian impulse and the great Classical and pre-classical foundations.

Behind the often over-elaborate nature of the Golden Dawn rituals lie a multitude of sense-experiences unattainable to those who follow meaning rather than understanding. The incantatory power of these rituals goes far beyond the sum of their elements. It matters not that we can distinguish Chaldean, Egyptian, Geraeco-Roman and Gnostic elements within them; one has only to glance at the 'knowledge-papers' of the Order, edited in a single compendious volume by Israel

Regardie (283, 285) to understand that here is a valid system of working esoterically which has not been exceeded by any other modern-day school.

Theosophy, which indirectly gave birth to the Golden Dawn, had, in the early nineteenth century, already begun to awaken aspects of Western esotericism which had long lain dormant. Its contact with the East brought in a language and conceptualization which helped define areas which had remained indistinct since the Renaissance or had been relegated to the crypt of Christian mysticism. Its leader, Madame Blavatsky, achieved the reputation of a typical shaman with her travels to the East and meetings with Hidden Masters. She bluffed her way through areas of ignorance and contacted the light of the perennial wisdom in ways which now seem haphazard. She believed beyond all else that whatever was true must come from outside her own consciousness. This lead her to fabricate much that was untrue about her sources for *The Secret Doctrine* and *The Veil of Isis*, her two monumental studies of esoteric tradition. (29) Her sources were and still are often traceable, but her studious refusal to admit that they came from elsewhere and were written down but not actually composed by her, led many to doubt her in the end. Sadly, perhaps, because she has much to say that is worth listening to, and had she only admitted her own part in the composition of her writings she would probably have reached a wider audience who would have taken her pioneering more seriously. As it is, and despite the sometimes farcical organization and petty bickering within Theosophy, Blavatsky appeared at the right time to bring a revitalizing influence to bear on the Western Way.

The schools which post-date Theosophy and whose founders were trained therein, are continuators of the work begun by Blavatsky. Anthroposophy, which is still a thriving movement, resulted from Rudolph Steiner's break with Theosophy, which he found too overtly Eastern for his taste. A recent commentator calls Anthroposophy a 'demythologised Theosophy' (75) because it rejects the magical in favour of education and the arts, as well as holistic living.

Steiner emphasized Western elements however, and in his autobiography describes anthroposophy as 'a path of knowledge, leading from the spiritual in man to the spiritual in the universe'. (318) He sees the universe as living and hierarchical, and is thus very much in line with the teachings of the Classical schools. He was also convinced that the ancient mystery knowledge was communicated in picture-dreams, 'pictures which revealed the spirit-world' (ibid). He saw imagination as a door of communication between the worlds, and consciously encouraged the entrance to the ancient mysteries through allowing the subject to experience its spiritual contact directly by means of the senses stimulated by art. His concept of 'Erkraftung des Denkens', or putting force and life into thinkers, through thinking within thinking, and other exercises designed to liberate thought from the bodily instrument, also recalled traditional techniques – although the original mystery teaching was to stimulate the subtle body centres from below upwards, while the Steiner method, in common with other newer schools, is to liberate them from above.

Steiner also, interestingly, developed three forms of higher know-ledge: *Imagination* – a higher seeing of the spiritual world in revealing images; *Inspiration* – a higher hearing of the spiritual world, through which it reveals its creative forces and its creative order: and *Intuition* – the stage at which an intuitive penetration into the sphere of Spiritual beings becomes possible.

This kind of structure, which recalls the grading practised by some Golden Dawn offshoots, is perfectly workable by any group suffi-ciently experienced in working with the mysteries. At the same time it is rather artificial in its formation of levels, which do not always mesh with the intentions of inner impulses behind any contacted school. It is easy to be discouraged when faced with a plethora of complicated hierarchies within any school – though there are ob-viously instances where such structures are valid. (91)

The Golden Dawn worked a system of grades based on the Qabalistic Tree of Life, starting with Zelator (Malkruth) and rising to Ipsissimus (Kether). (183) This is still used by many magical schools today and there are certain initiatory ceremonies connected with each grade. Many are disappointed to find that their teacher is not an Ipsissimus – such a claim should be cautiously questioned in any case. But the grades are symbolic of the initiate's efforts to attain proficiency, just as Bachelor, Master and Doctor are conferred on individuals in the academic world. But just as Doctors of Philosophy do not know everything, neither do those who have had high grades conferred upon them by their schools. There is no end to knowledge, nor to the number of initiations we all take on the Inner.

The division of the mysteries into 'Greater' and 'Lesser' is another form of structuring practised by contemporary Mystery Schools. In any such there is a period of probation followed by the lesser and greater mysteries. These can be seen as three basic levels of work, although about the latter it is difficult to generalize. The lesser mysteries are usually the initial 'outer court' work of the group wherein the images and symbols are embodied in a mythical framework. In the greater mysteries, this earlier work is subsumed in the personality of the initiate – it becomes a living reality about which there can be no question. The initiate enters the 'inner court' of the Temple and finds him or herself in an empty room. Here no deity is enshrined, no great teaching written; here is no symbol to distract or enter the consciousness – only the emptiness of the cosmos: which is, of course, far from empty. Initiation into the Greater Mysteries is indeed a confrontation with the self and with the summation of the divine presence within everything. (cf. afterword) There, macrocosm and microcosm conjoin and are reflected. Even so, there can be no sublime merging with the divine principle yet: the initiate must return to the outer world again, continuing to act as a mirror of·the macrocosm.

Many such *psychotechnologies*, to borrow a term from Marilyn Ferguson, (82) are practised today by the hundreds of modern mystery schools extant in the Western world. All attempt to mediate the inner mysteries of life in some way. We have lost much in the way of methodologies, but tentative New Age experiments are reviving them, in part analeptically, to a standard of efficiency. It is obviously not possible to discuss even a tenth part of the schools offering training today, and even if it were we should feel restrained to do so only of those we had personally experienced. There is no hard and fast rule about joining such a group. Common sense and clear sight will guide you in your first steps and after that the inner guides should be in a position to take over. The Rudolf Steiner School combines elements of Christian esotericism with Rosicrucian, Hermetic and Native mysteries. If you prefer to seek a Qabalistic training, the Servants of the Light organization offers a thorough and effective way into the mysteries of the Tree of Life and the symbolism of the Grail. (12) The Alice Bailey School is strongly Theosophical in origin, subscribing to belief in masters and hierarchical cosmology. It propounds an evolutional development through mundane as well as esoteric means. The vast underpinning literature, dictated by Master D.K. to Alice Bailey, is read by many outside the school, where it has contributed widely to the spread of Aquarian consciousness and cosmic consciousness. The Rosicrucian Fellowship and AMORC are rival schools following the teachings of Christian Rosenkreutz. The former was founded by Max Heindal in 1906. Active in Theosophy, he was contacted by a Rosicrucian Master and took instruction. The school teaches world evolution, reincarnation, inner helpers and masters. AMORC was founded in 1915 by H. Spencer-Lewis and is based on Freemasonic lines with a developed philosophy and practice: it declines the titles of religion or cult. Its glossy literature and vastly public headquarters in San Jose, California, do not lead one to suppose that a mystery school is in operation here. The Builders of the Adytum, founded by Paul Foster Case after he was expelled from the Golden Dawn for publishing their secrets in his Tarot publications, is probably the most Hermetic of those mentioned above. BOTA was founded on Inner contact in 1920 and still uses Tarot and Qabala as its main implements.

Another interesting school which has released its teaching papers is the Aurum Solis or Order of the Sacred Word. Since its reconstitution in 1971 it operates as a private magical group and not a school. It was founded in 1897 by Charles Kingold and George Stanton, two occultists who were in touch with Qabala, as well as Greek and early magical systems. *The Magical Philosophy* (68) which comprises these teachings is, like the Golden Dawn collection, a complete magical system which can be studied and worked by the esotericist who does not belong to any group.

Schools and magical groups are still organized. This normally comes about when one adept is contacted by the Inner and gets his or her 'go ahead' to organize a preliminary meeting with those close to him. A scheme of operation is noted down and the signs and sigils of the company meditated upon. In its early stages the whole project may abort for various reasons: the adept or his company may prove unstable. But if the group fulfils the required dedication the impetus to get organized can be tremendous, sweeping aside daily events or problems as insignificant distractions. Then, having fulfilled its function – which may only be a short-term project – the whole apparatus is disbanded. Thus groups and schools will last only as long as the Inner intends they should, after which the dismantling process begins, often showing itself in the form of personality clashes, changed circumstances, death of leading members and the scattering of those who may be led to found their own organizations and teach others.

The non-initiate may be baffled by such procedures, seeing only half of the picture, and may vow to have nothing to do with such activities. The above statements refer more to magical groups than to training schools which are used by the Inner as a foundation of more important work, and which will not be abandoned in the cursory fashion of the nonce group. The work of Gareth Knight and William G. Gray is of a parallel kind, yet each have different approaches to magic training. Here the beginner can enter in the knowledge that he or she is in the hands of trained and knowledgeable adepts who are able practically to convey much that a training school should impart.

Without a teacher or training school behind one, the work is uphill and cannot be correlated with the student's development. Clearly, medieval magical systems which go in for long and barbarous means and incomprehensible conjurations are not practical. Intent, clear and easy steps which follow logically from each other, careful preparation and self-discipline go a long way. The groundwork of self-training is not book-learned, although it may often be inspired thereby to begin with.

The vexed questions of an Inner teacher will be dealt with in chapter 4. But is an Outer magical teacher necessary? Nothing can replace the guidance of an experienced fellow-worker, but finding one willing to take on students is another matter. Most people proceed without one in the earliest stages of training, keeping their eyes open, reading, studying and correlating their life's experiences with the strong Inner impulse which leads them deeper into the mysteries. Some students join groups unadvisedly and regret it, leaving with their illusions shattered. Others work alone for what seems a lifetime and then suddenly find doors opening for them. There is no rule or set timing for finding a teacher but, once you find one do not expect it to be easier from then on. A teacher will demand regular work and certain results: if you, the student, do not measure up to your teacher's expectations, you will be considered a time-waster, someone who is unworthy to transmit the traditions which are being inculcated within you.

There is certainly no shortage of schools, some better than others, some worse. But as the theologian Don Cupitt expressed it in a recent TV series: 'the truth now is no longer in fixed positions – it is in the quest.' The modern quest for knowledge, whether within the mystery schools or elsewhere, takes many forms. For many the mysteries are now best taught in open court, in small groups or seminars where the mysteries are discussed and practically engaged upon by gatherings of interested people. Both the authors can testify to the remarkably powerful and effective nature of this kind of work, where seemingly random combinations of people are brought together by the Inner to do some specific piece of work and then separate again, sometimes not to meet for long periods.

This way of working is growing in popularity, and many more opportunities exist which combine lectures with practical applications of magic techniques. It has been said that the time of the Mystery Schools is over, and while this may not necessarily be true, the old closed orders of adepts are growing fewer in number. However, as we have tried to show throughout these books, the solitary worker or the small dedicated band of workers can be just as effective as a fully fledged school – especially once Inner contact is established. There is a great need for those willing to put up with occasional discomforts in return for the satisfaction of the work.

All myth, legend and poetry derives from the Mysteries in some sense: they are the potential sparks to ignite a sense of the wonders of creation and the purpose of life. Almost any of the countless themes, characters, fragments of tales – whether from ancient Greek, Egyptian or Welsh Triads (cf. Vol I) can be quarried and utilized for exploration individually or with a group. Once you begin to work with the matter of the mysteries you will find it like controlling a team of eager, high-stepping horses. Feel the reins in your hands and the pull of their heads at the bit. Your chariot will carry you far, across land and sea, both in Inner and Outer realms. The mysteries are not something locked away in dusty tomes on a libraryshelf – they are here and now, living lines of contact with which to enter a wholly different dimension.

> The object of the Hermetic search is that life which is capable of being transmitted to a specific being in order to lead that being *to its own perfection*. . . this available 'life-essence' is called the King, cosmic man; but it must be recognized that attaining the aim of the Hermetic opus is not an end; it is the beginning of the light that illuminates reality . . . the true King, is the living being who has reached the stage of immortal and conscious return to the source of the Soul that animates him. . . (298)

This return to the source is the objective that animates all magical work, fuelling Orphite and Hermeticist, Gnostic and Cathar alike. As we shall see in the next chapter, it is present in esoteric Christianity as well as the Hermetic schools. Divine knowing is all important if we are to find our way further than the first few steps on the road we have elected to travel.

EXERCISES

EXERCISE 1 THE MAZE OF THE GODS

The Roman historian Ammianus Marcellinus gives an interesting account, in his discussion of the mysteries, of 'certain underground galleries and passages full of windings which, it is said, the adepts in the ancient rites (knowing that the Flood was coming, and fearing that the memory of the sacred ceremonies would be obliterated) constructed. . . . These, he says, contained buildings 'which were mined out with great labour. And levelling the walls, they engraved on them numerous kinds of birds and animals . . . which they called hieroglyphic characters.' (147)

This may well be a distant memory of a visit to one of the great pyramids of Egypt, on whose walls were cartouches relating the history of its one-time occupant – or it may again be a fleeting reference to the great labyrinth at Mareotis, mentioned by Herodotus and other ancient historians. Whatever the truth, it conjures up a fascinating image of a vast and secret maze, containing on its walls the knowledge and history of the Egyptian mysteries – perhaps even of an earlier Atlantean mystery centre. The purpose of the exercise which follows is to enter such a place and there to encounter the living forms of the gods who will be our guides and instructors in this particular area of the Western mysteries. As we saw in volume I, the gods are many things: they await the moment when we are sufficiently in tune with ourselves to recognize that we are living vessels of the ancient wisdom – to be filled with as much as lies within our capacity to hold. In this exercise we will make our first contact with some of the powers with which we shall find ourselves working in times to come. In this instance we shall come under the guidance of Hermes, who will conduct us on the first steps of the Hermetic way.

Much of the imagery here comes from Egyptian sources, but this should not be seen as the only way into the Hermetic tradition – there are many other doorways just as valid through which we may gain admittance. As with other exercises in this and in the previous volume, no attempt should be made to embark on an inner journey until you feel sure the time is right. Once you feel ready you should begin by making yourself relaxed, breathing to a regular rhythm, comfortably seated in an upright chair. This done, you are ready to proceed.

Fig 5: An ankh

You are standing at night on softly yielding ground. At first it is quite dark, but as you grow accustomed to the place, the moon comes out from behind a cloud and by its radiance you perceive that you are standing on fine white desert sand, which stretches away on all sides to the horizon in softly sculptured waves. Ahead you see several vast shapes, rooted in the desert and rising towards a sky filled with stars. . . They are strangely familiar, and as your eyes grow accustomed to the subtle light you recognize their shape. You are in Egypt and before you lie the Pyramids of Ghiza. . .

Filled with awe you walk towards these vast and towering monuments, which gleam softly silver in the light of the moon. As you draw near you see that they are not quite as you may have seen them pictured, crumbling and aged by time and weather, but smooth and sharp-edged and faced with white marble upon which you dimly discern hieroglyphs in seemingly endless rows. The whole pyramid before which you stand is covered with writing, but though you may long to pause and examine what is written there, you are drawn onward towards a dark entrance which opens before you. At first you hesitate, for the way ahead is very black and there is no light to show what lies within. Ancient fears of the dark and of becoming lost beneath the great weight of stone stir within you and you feel reluctant to proceed further. Then as you stand uncertainly before the dark entrance, a figure detaches itself from the shadows and comes towards you. You recognize him from his shaven head and white kilt as an Egyptian priest. He holds out his left hand, in which he carries the symbol of his office, an ankh, the ancient Egyptian symbol of life. You see that he is smiling in welcome, and you reach out and take the proffered sign in your own hand. It feels warm and smooth to the touch, and as soon as you have hold of it, begins to glow brightly.

The priest now stands aside and indicates that you should proceed within. You find that your earlier fears have left you with the touch of the ankh and that you are eager to discover what lies within. You enter through a narrow stone door, and as you pass further into the heart of the pyramid the ankh glows brighter, illuminating your path.

With the symbol of life in your hand you go forward unafraid. The passage-way is narrow and twists often to right or left, doubling back upon itself more than once until you have lost all sense of direction. Time, also, seems without meaning here. Is it only a few moments since you entered, or have hours passed? You walk on, holding your glowing ankh before you, until at last you feel a draught of cool air on your face and emerge into a larger, open space.

You are now standing in a long, narrow hall, its roof upheld by an avenue of pillars, those upon the right painted red and those upon the left, black. As you walk forward between them you see that the walls of the hall are painted with brightly coloured figures. Some are in Egyptian dress, but others seem clad in costumes of other lands and times. Though they are only painted scenes they almost seem to move with a life of their own. You do not feel moved to stop and look at them in detail, but much that you glimpse there may return to you later, either in sleep or meditation.

Your feet are drawn onward toward the end of the hall, where you see a door, flanked by two great red and black pillars carved with symbols and hieroglyphs. As you approach, the door opens and a figure comes forth and stands waiting for you, arms folded on his breast. He is manlike, tall and powerful, but from his shoulders rises the head of a jackal, its ear pricked and its eyes gleaming in the light.

You recognize the figure of Anubis, guardian of the mysteries of Egypt and keeper of the threshold of the gods. You stand before him, waiting to hear what he will say. He may ask you your name, or he may wish to know your reason for coming to this place. Think carefully and take time before you answer. You may not lie or speak falsely before Anubis, for he can read the heart as you might read a book. (Pause)

When he is satisfied, Anubis stands aside, welcoming you to the place of the Mysteries, then he steps aside and bids you enter by way of the door through which he came.

Before you do so, Anubis softly speaks the sacred password which will admit you to what lies beyond. Thus prepared, but still not without some trepidation, for it is a great step you now take, pass forward, and find yourself walking down a short corridor connecting the door through which you came with another some little way ahead. Here you pause for a moment to collect your thoughts and to weigh your intention, for behind this door lies the chamber of the Inner Mysteries and you must be certain of your reason for coming before you enter in. You may take your time over this and if you do not feel ready as yet, may turn back at this point and retrace your steps without fear or shame. Many have reached this point before you, and have turned away. If you decide to do so, you may return at another time. (Pause)

Assuming that you decide to go on . . . you step forward and open the door before you. Stepping through, you find yourself in a small, many-sided room. As you hold up the ankh before you, you see by its light that the walls are faced with mirrors of bronze which, as you advance slowly towards the centre, give back a thousand images of yourself. But not all the images are the same. As your vision grows accustomed to the strangeness of the place, you see that there are many different aspects of yourself reflected back from the walls. You may see yourself at different stages in your life to this moment (but never beyond: the future is not for you to read) and perhaps also of other lives. But you must be careful of how you interpret the images you see, for it is easy to become dazzled or glamourized by a particular form or image. If you feel drawn towards one or another you may look closer, but always hold the ankh symbol before you as your sign of life and intention.

Look now towards the centre of the room. There you will see a circular platform with steps leading up to it. Upon it stands a mighty figure holding a book and writing implements. You recognize Thoth, the scribe of the Gods, keeper of the sacred mysteries, teacher of wisdom, known by some as Hermes Trismegistos, founder of the Hermetic mysteries.

As you approach he demands by what right you come there and you respond with the word or phrase given you by Anubis. Thoth then asks your intentions in seeking the mysteries and whether you are drawn to any one aspect. You should answer this as truthfully as possible, but do not be afraid to say that you do not know. Thoth records your name and response in his great book and bids you step up to the platform at his side.

As you do so the walls of the chamber begin to turn slowly, gradually speeding up until they are a blur. Only the platform and the wise head of Thoth, shaped like the sacred Ibis, remain unchanging. As you stand at his side you realize that this is a centre from which all the Mystery teachings are spun forth. All are contained in the great book which lies beneath the hand of Thoth.

Now in the blur of the passing walls, images form, flickering there for a moment and then disappearing again. You see the faces of those with whom you have worked before on the inner planes, and others who are strangers to you. You should try to notice and to remember as much as you can, since these things and people may well become important to you later on. (Pause)

At last the spinning slows and stops. You see yourself again in the mirrors and realize that you are alone. There may be subtle changes now in the way that you behold them, for Thoth has entered your name in the Book of the Mysteries and you are a part of them from now onward.

Slowly you descend from the platform and depart from the chamber by the way you came. In the outer chamber Anubis awaits you, and as you pass before him he places upon your brows a plain circlet of silver or gold. You understand that this is a token of the Mysteries upon which you have now entered. It is plain as yet because your journey has only just begun, but in time it may bear symbols or letters acquired by you on your way.

Taking leave of the jackel-headed god you return to the open air, finding no difficulty in retracing your path through the maze. At the entrance, return the symbol of the ankh to the priestly guardian and go by the way you came, slowly allowing the scene to fade from your consciousness to be replaced by the surroundings in which you began your journey. Wherever you go forth upon an inner journey, or take place in some magical activity, you should imagine the circlet given to you by Anubis, and this will be your sign to others that you have passed through the maze of the gods and returned.

EXERCISE 2   BUILDING THE BODY OF LIGHT

This is a ritual of great potential power, designed to awaken a sense of the cosmic dimension of the Hermetic path. We make no bones about including what is in effect an advanced technique of working. Those who are ready to undertake work at this level will find themselves drawn to approach it; those who are not should still be able to perform the working and obtain from it a sense of well-being and inner fulfilment. It should, however, not be performed more than once when it has proved effective, and it is advisable to eat and rest afterwards.

Begin quietly, seated or standing, in a place prepared. Build the circle of force about you and hallow it with the light of love. Centre yourself and then begin to stretch upward from your psychic centres – further and further until your physical body is far below and a new self, hazy and without substance as yet, stands with head and shoulders in the heavens. Slowly stretch forth with your senses feeling them newly cleansed like windows that have had the grime of centuries wiped from them. Look about you and be aware of the vastness of the heavens, of the mighty beings who guard the cosmos, of those who have responsibility for our own solar system, for each planet that whirls about the star which is our own sun. Take time to hold this new reality and fear nothing. You are, as is each one of us, an immortal soul whose right it is to travel the uttermost reaches of the universe under the protection of the Holy Ones who helped in its formation. Listen and you may hear their voices raised in the music of the spheres.

Now stretch forth your hands and find before you in the uttermost blackness and singing darkness of space a shape which your senses tell you is a vast bowl or Krater. You cannot perceive this with your sight, only feel its outlines beneath your hands. Its surface seems wonderfully worked and you wonder for a moment what scenes are depicted upon it. But it is not yet for you to see such things, and there is another purpose for you now.

Look now into the depths of the bowl, which is perfect blackness and impenetrable dark. Far below, as though you were looking into the uttermost depths of the cosmos, a tiny gleed of light begins to form, impossibly far away and bright. Like a jewel it shines there and as you look it begins to grow gradually larger. Stretch your hand down into the bowl and take forth the glowing thing which is there. It may look like a living flame (which cannot burn you) or like a jewel of surpassing brightness. As you hold it in your hand its light begins to spread through your insubstantial form, filling you with a sense of peace and joyousness.

Look about you now and see that on all sides in the vastness of space are other figures, invisible to you before, but now revealed in a glory of light. They greet you in many different tongues which you have no difficulty in understanding, and you understand that you are now like them, that you share in a common radiance which is both within you and fills the corners of the universe.

Gradually begin to draw in upon yourself and to shrink down towards your body far below. Keep the light within you, for it is a spark of that divine fire from which the cosmos was formed and which has always been a part of you. You are now part of the Body of Light which surrounds and dwells within all of creation. Wherever you go you will take it with you, and you will always be able to recognize it within others. So, too, will you be able to hold converse with the myriad souls who inhabit the vastness of space, and who have welcomed you among them as brother or sister.

Become aware of your surroundings once more, feel the ground beneath your feet and the chair upon which you are seated. Close the circle of power and perform a suitable closing ritual which you have devised. Reaffirm the Light within you by performing a brief ritual of attunement at least once daily.

CHAPTER 2
The Divine Knowing

In their religion they are so unev'n,
That each man goes his own by-way to Heav'n.
Tenacious of mistakes to that degree,
That ev'ry man pursues it sep'rately,
And fancies none can find the way but he,
So shy of one another they are grown
As if they strove to get to Heav'n alone.

Daniel Defoe: *The True-Born Englishman*

Wisdom reaches mightily from one end of the earth to the other,
and she orders all things well. . .
For she is an initiate in the knowledge of God,
and an associate in his works.

Wisdom VIII, 1 and 4

THE GIFTS OF WISDOM

Gnostic, illuminatus, hermeticist, magus, mystic – what a glorious muddle the Western Way must appear to the outsider! The multifarious nature of the Western Tradition has caused many problems of acceptance among those who prefer their concepts in tidy packages. Yet Dr Dee's medium, Edward Kelly, reminds us that what we see as a fragmented and often back-biting set of disciplines is indeed derivative of those great mystery schools we have been considering:

> This Art found its way into Persia, Egypt and Chaldea. The Hebrews called it the Cabbala, the Persians Magia, and the Egyptians Sophia and it was taught in the schools together with Theology: it was known to Moses, Solomon, and the Magi who came to Christ from the East. (121)

He is appealing to a common tradition across a breadth of disciplines, specifically relating his argument to alchemy and to the completion of the Great Work.

But the Great Work can be achieved through many disciplines; through the science of alchemy, through the art of magic or through the philosophy of the mystic. There has been much dispute as to which is the correct means by which to proceed because the disciplines of the Western Way have been fragmented and split off from each other. Science, magic and religion seem to be eternally estranged, yet each of these disciplines corresponds to a cosmic law which everyone must obey: science observes the law of Nature; magic, the law of correspondences; and religion, the law of God. None of these laws is irreconcilable. Science and religion seem to have passed beyond the time where they each held as complementary to the other, while the esotericist is now regarded as a godless creature by one and as a crank by the other.

In order that we may appreciate all sides of this problem we shall be examining the science of alchemy and the art of magic in their proper place, while here we wish to scrutinize the philosophy of religion, the spiritual science. But before we do so, let us first examine the Western Way from the standpoint of the Perennial Wisdom.

The term *Sophia Perennis* or Perennial Wisdom was first coined by the German philosopher, Gottfried Leibnitz (1646–1716) who understood that different religious traditions were not only valid in themselves but that they could inform each other. The syncretism of the Classical mystery schools comprehended something of this understanding, as does the modern Ecumenical movement today, but the Western Way is left out of the reckoning because few class it as a valid tradition at all.

The problem confronting us today is that most religious traditions have become empty structures: exoteric walls and empty esoteric space within them. Yet the Western Way suffers conversely: it is made up of a rich store of esoteric wisdom which has been discarded by religious traditions, yet it has no structure in which to house this treasure. While this is to some extent a generalization, and the state of neither religion nor the Western Way is as parlous as that, we must consider the means by which the ancient wisdom is being preserved and transmitted.

A tradition begins to die when it becomes theoretical: that is the danger not just within the Western Way but in religious traditions the world over. Once they begin to be studied for their own sake rather than being applied directly to everyday life, they lose their impetus to transmit wisdom. More than ever we need skilful mediators who know how to blend traditional wisdom for our own time. The professional defenders of tradition – once the poet and shaman, now the academic and priest – often fail to preserve the essential quality of tradition; they have lost their ability to communicate the wonder and wisdom. Where then are the visionaries of note who can show us the divine truths? We seem to have reached a plateau period when the old metaphors have been overhauled and found wanting, yet new metaphors are harder to find. All things change and evolve, and it is good that they should do so, but when a tradition is confined within narrow, rigid forms, it cannot easily reach those for whom it is intended. As religion takes a nose-dive into the fundamental and popularist, many self-made cults come into being at the request of those who want to see their own visions and dream their own dreams.

It may be asked whether we are not promoting some kind of new religion in these pages. We do not propose anything of the kind: the Western Way includes the whole spectrum of paths from the overtly esoteric to the inherently mystical. We encourage you to find a tradition and inhabit it. (40) Only tradition has the ability to preserve mystical and symbolic teaching in a safe manner, giving transformative realization of the Inner Kingdom. Those who are outside traditional systems are vulnerable in that they seek the Inner Kingdom by means of their own maps and from the the basis of their own efforts: they try to go it alone. Yet the need to explore inner worlds does not decrease with succeeding generations: rather it is on the increase as traditional systems sell themselves short and offer quick and unsatisfying answers to those who come hungry with questions.

The impulse of the Hermetic path of the Western Way derives from this predicament: the need to evolve and the need to preserve. It has produced the natural philosopher, the amateur theologian and the ritualist to counterbalance the stasis of many religious traditions. It has encouraged the skilful adapter, the cunning preserver and the quiet reconciler. Few of these men and women have left the tradition into which they were born; indeed the most successful among them made their way within it and even despite it. Mystics and saints such as Clement of Alexandria, Vladimir Soloviev, Nahman of Bratislav, St Hildegard of Bingen, Blessed John Ruysbrock were not renegades determined to show up their traditions, but explorers and revealers of the way for others. They were not afraid to retain the esoteric riches of their tradition often in the face of exoteric disapproval. Yet it is also true to say that very few have the ability to respond to the esoteric depths of religion while recognizing the necessity for an exoteric structure.

This splitting off of mystical and mundane, esoteric and exoteric has become pronounced in our own day. Many followers of the Western Way would put the blame squarely upon the advent and promulgation of Christianity in the West, which is seen by them as the disturber and destroyer of Native Tradition. This view has blinded many to a true appreciation of the treasures of Western wisdom which took seed within Christianity and grew to maturity there. These lie in profusion about our feet and we cannot see them. We must consider that Hermeticism grew up within the Christian era and that most of its proponents were not Christian due to fear of persecution, but because that was their means of religious expression. We shall be considering more closely the reasons by which the Church became suspicious of its own mystical tradition in the next section. Basically, however, this was due to a division between the ways of faith and knowledge or *gnosis*.

Neither faith nor knowledge can gain us entry into the Inner Kingdom on their own: we need, primarily, the gift of wisdom to guide us, and to bind faith and knowledge together as harmonious travelling companions.

The Lord himself created wisdom:
he saw her and apportioned her,
he poured her out upon all his works.
She dwells with all flesh according to his gift,
and he supplied her to those who love him. (*Sirach I, 9–10*)

Those who yearn after eternal things and wish to know the Inner Kingdom for themselves, speak the language of wisdom which transcends the limitations of human speech. It is the common tongue of mystics and esotericists everywhere, spoken above the snowline where the many-sided mountain of Deity is revealed at the peak. Followers of the Western Way, whether of Native or Hermetic Traditions, know themselves to be of this number and so are the company of *Sophia Perennis*. Included also are followers of the Eastern Way, as a close study of mystical texts both Eastern and Western will confirm.

Some readers will be concerned that the esoteric side of tradition seems exclusive and cliquey. The truth is much simpler. Any *practising* member of a religious discipline is free to enter deeper into the mysteries of his or her tradition at any time. It is a matter of involvement, of identification with and dedication to its inner wisdom. It is often a matter of finding the right key. Frequently one meets sincere religious people who go through the motions prescribed by convention, yet who never touch the inmost heart: they travel by faith alone, in blind hope. Yet if they ever contact this inner heart by means of prayer or meditative awareness, they become knowers as well as believers. They do not migrate from their adherence but are confirmed within it.

On the other hand it is also possible to meet those who steer solely by the means of knowedge, who spurn the way of faith. Some esotericists see themselves as the Children of Light, the race of the new Aeon: such are not the inheritors of the Inner Kingdom. These have succumbed to the sin of spiritual pride which marks them off from the common run of humanity and places them in the same category as those fundamentalists who see themselves as the Chosen Ones, the Elect of God. The true initiates of gnosis are those who have learned by the preliminaries of faith, who have become teachers and nourishers of wisdom wherever it struggles to be made manifest: those who encourage the growth of inner potential in others, not those who boast of their own spiritual achievements.

The companion on the way to the Inner Kingdom is Wisdom, who is the law of knowledge and the mother of faith. She keeps the former within safe boundaries and distributes it to all gnostics; she guides the latter, encouraging it to grasp and realize the true nature of eternal things. A firm Wisdom-contact is essential in esoteric work, especially for those outside a living tradition. To this end we have given exercise 3 which may help the reader focus upon his or her traditional affiliations.

Childhood faith is now threatened, traditional working metaphors are jettisoned, power is syphoned from spiritual to political ends with many fundamentalist cults, and the deep magic of the Inner Story is despoiled. There arises, in response to this fragmentation, a kind of vocational consciousness from among the peoples of the world. The Secret Commonwealth (cf. vol. I) arises again, no longer in a nationalist but in a global response. Whatever aptitudes are available, whatever their traditional or non-traditional provenance, many ordinary people perceive the danger our world is in. Often their response is humanist or ecological, rather than spiritual, yet it is motivated by the earthy ancestral wisdom which is the birthright and gift of every human being who loves the creation.

Together with them, the mystics and esotericists strive to mediate the healing of the Inner world to our world. Awareness of the danger and responsibility for finding a way out of danger, brings humility enough to the children of Wisdom, whether they steer by means of faith or knowledge.

The *Sophia Perennis* is not a religion nor an end in itself, but a bond between riven traditions. It can easily sink to an intellectual appreciation of comparative religion or a collection of woolly New Age aphorisms where one tradition can easily be substituted for another. Each tradition has its essential character: the Western Way is made up of many such. Wisdom is eternally true, however traditions change: if we love the truth, she will ever accompany us, her philo-sophias, (literally 'lovers of wisdom'). Those who have never considered the Western Mystery Tradition in the light of religion, may find it helpful to see it as an esoteric philosophy, along these lines.

Perhaps we may start by admitting that we are wounded: 'The metaphysician (is a) wounded man. A wounded man is not an agnostic – he just has different questions arising out of his wound.' (232) Like the shaman, the wounded healer is one who knows that the true cause of pain is loss of Inner reality – the Inner Kingdom. This realization fired the Gnostics to go upon their own voyage of discovery, just as it later inspired those who went on quest for the Grail and the healing of the Waste Land. Truly, there are many ways of achieving the Great Work.

THE FRUITS OF GNOSIS

'The life of the Gnostics is, in my view, no other than works and words which correspond to the tradition of the Lord,' wrote Clement of Alexandria. (291) This early Christian theologian was a lone voice rising from a sea of discontent and disapproval at the Gnostic experiment. Since Gnosticism, the Western World has never been the same. Its suppression left the Christian tradition poorer, although fragments of its teachings are still to be found in the Hermetic Tradition. Gnosticism still rises periodically to haunt orthodox religion, but its coloured tatters stir painful memories and provoke bigoted reactions. What was Gnosticism that it still has power to awaken the hopes and fears of later generations? The fruits of the Gnostic experiment are often bitter to taste: some have never ripened, others are over-ripe, so it is necessary to be discriminating.

First of all, let us not confuse gnosis (which just means knowledge) with Gnosticism. It is possible to say of St Teresa of Avila that she was gnostic, but not that she was a Gnostic, for instance. Gnosis as divine knowing is the birthright of all spiritual traditions and does not imply their connection in any way with historical Gnosticism.

Gnosticism can be seen as a synthesis of the mystery schools which preceded it. It is 'perhaps the first religion, at least in the West, which is wholly non-tribal and centred upon the discovery of infinity within the (individual) psyche,' (75) and that makes it a vitally important link in the development of the Western Way. It is not without reason that the Gnostics have been claimed as spiritual predecessors by many revival mystery schools in the modern age, rather as the classical mystery schools looked back to Atlantis for their inspiration. Perhaps because Gnosticism did not attempt to explain 'the sacramental rituals . . . as mere magic performed in memory of (historical) events, but as the externalisation of internal psychic alchemy,' and because it regarded the 'Bible not as history but as mythology of the most sublime and valuable kind' (ibid.) that modern Mystery schools have warmed to its teachings. The Gnostic thread runs exotically through the whole Hermetic tradition, as we shall discover.

What we know of Gnosticism today emerges from an incredibly complex welter of traditions: in the melting pot of Gnosis it is possible to find Persian, Egyptian, Hellenic, Platonic, Christian and Jewish elements. These fuse together at the nexus of the Mediterranean culture, at Alexandria in whose environs were to be found the great proliferation of traditions and teachings. Although the great Alexandrian Library was fired in AD 391 and its remaining wisdom subsequently destroyed forever in the early seventh century under Moslem occupation, the accumulated teachings within its rolls had already made good their escape into the living traditions which had made their home in Egypt.

The chief features of Gnosticism were inherited from Zoroastrian sources as well as from the many baptising sects such as those of the Essenes, both of which were functioning before the onset of Christianity. The seeds of Gnosticism took root in the garden of Christianity, where its plants flourished in a riot of colour and spectacular abandon in contrast to the more sober seedlings being trained up. Gnosticism already had the conceptual apparatus of the Mysteries behind it, while Christianity was still finding its feet. Christian

Gnosticism expanded from the middle of the first century AD and had its demise during the sixth century, although its influence post-dated this period. The only true lineal descendant of Classical Gnosticism operative today is the Mandean sect of Iraq which preserves the ritual purity of the early baptising sects: however, it is non-Christian, nearer in type to the Zoroastrian than to the neo-Judaic kind. It is doubtful whether its primitive traditions will outlast this century. (291)

As Gnosticism developed it rejected the Jewish basis of Christianity while yet retaining figures from Jewish scripture – Seth, Melchizedek, Adam and Eve – as forerunners of its traditions. The rewriting of received texts is not of course merely a Gnostic phenomenon; it occurs today in many New Age groups and Christian-based cults which strive to purge mainstream Christianity while retaining some elements from it, especially the figure of Christ himself, about whom new tales are spun, from whom come new sayings and commandments which, in reality, often emanate from that cult's leader rather than from divine sources. It is natural that all religions should seek to promote their antique antecedents, and Gnosticism was no exception.

If Gnosticism has had a bad press, this is because it has been known mainly through its detractors. Such texts as survived were so fragmentary that a full picture of Gnostic belief was impossible. However, the discovery of the *Nag Hammadi* in 1945 and the Qumran texts in 1947 have enabled scholars to begin piecing together the fragments into an astonishing cohesion. The Gnostic codices, like the contents of a time-machine, have survived miraculously to land in our own century. The extraordinary story of their discovery may be read in John Dart's *The Laughing Saviour* (62). Prior to their availability the meagre evidences of Gnosticism could be gleaned mainly from invectives penned by church fathers. Needless to say, such evidence was not from the horse's mouth. Their almost universal detestation by the orthodox wing of the Church ensured the infamy of the Gnostics for all time. Their championship by Clement of Alexandria brought him little reward: this attractively balanced theologian who foresightedly saw the truth within other traditions, especially within Platonism, was demoted from sainthood by Pope Clement VIII in the sixteenth century, because of his doubtful orthodoxy.

The Egyptian alchemist, Zosimus, wrote about a race of wisdom-lovers who live forever at the Inner Door (227). This image applied neatly to the Gnostics whose existence was regulated by communications which came from behind the Inner Door. The Gnostics were Knowers – possessors of an inner wisdom, guardians of a tradition, inheritors of the mystery schools. They envisaged humanity as a set of divine sparks entrapped in matter. The true God was unknown and hidden – he alone was the origin of the light. Creation was the work of a false god, the Demiurge. Every Gnostic lived in the hope of rejoining the true God in the fullness of the Pleroma (heaven). They believed that such a journey was possible, but that the way of return was fraught with difficulty because the divine spark within each individual lived in the forgetfulness of the flesh. It was necessary to combat the King of the World (the Demiurge) by whatever means were possible. He could be denied by means of asceticism, which denies the currency of creation, or by licentiousness which scorns the created order. Some Gnostic sects were so extreme in their practices that they doubtless earned the censure heaped upon them. However, not all sects used either of these means. Similar accusations have been levelled against modern practitioners of the Western Way, but there has been little evidence to support these claims: then, as now, unscrupulous individuals use the cover of esoteric ritual to front their sexual practices, none of which has any bearing on the practice of dedicated initiates.

It is important to bear in mind that though there are common elements within the Gnostic sects, the variations are so numerous that we cannot generalize. Here there is only space to present the barest outline of Gnostic belief and practice, in so far as an understanding of Gnosticism can highlight elements within the Western Way.

The complex apparatus of Gnostic practice was designed to stimulate the divine spark within, to prepare it for the release from flesh and for the hazardous journey of the soul through the kingdoms of the archons, the servants of the Demiurge, who ruled every sphere between earth and that of the Pleroma itself. This journey through the spheres is dealt with in more detail in chapter 4, where we will also unfold something of Gnostic cosmology. (see fig.6)

The descent of the soul into flesh and its eventual return is epitomized in the *Song of the Pearl*, from the apocryphal *Acts of Thomas* (10) in which a prince (the messiah) journeys from his home in the East (the Pleroma) into Egypt (the earth) in order to 'bring back thence the one pearl which is there ... girt about by the devouring serpent.' In order to achieve this, the prince puts on the

Fig 6: The Gnostic Cosmology

garments of Egypt (the flesh) in exchange for his own glorious robe (the divine nature). He forgets who he is, whence he came, or the purpose of his quest. A secret scroll is sent to him by means of an eagle, bidding him awake and remember that he is the son of kings.

He wins the pearl (the divine spark), strips off his filthy garments and takes the way of return, guided by the secret scroll (the hidden gnosis). As he returns, the jewels and robes which he put off at the various stages of his journey thither, are restored to him. (Just as Ishtar had to put off her garments at each of the gates of hell.) 'But suddenly, I saw the garment made like unto me as it had been in a mirror . . . and I knew and saw myself through it.' He remembers totally and is brought before 'the brightness of the Father' fully equipped as a royal prince.

The parallels between this and the parable of the Prodigal Son (St Luke 15, 11–32) are not accidental. Present too are the resonances with the captivity of Joseph in Egypt whose imprisonment and subsequent change in fortunes are all undergone on behalf of his brothers who have forgotten their divine spark. (Genesis 37–45) Christ himself is figured in this Gnostic parable, in his own flight into Egypt, obscure childhood and subsequent return to his Father bringing with him the Pearl of Great Price, the fruits of Redemption. Robert Southwell, the sixteenth-century Jesuit poet, recalls this theme in his poem on *The Nativity of Christ*:

> Despise him not for lying there:
> First what he is enquire.
> An orient pearl is often found
> In depth of dirty mire. (315)

This is a theme to which we will be returning when we examine the inner resonances relating to alchemy and the quest for the Grail (chapter 5). We have presented this mystery story in some detail in order to give a flavour not only of the Gnostic mind, but also of the timeless nature of this theme down the centuries.

The Gnostic was obsessed with the need to know 'Why am I born? What is my purpose? How does evil originate?' These philosophical questions are the forerunners of the kind of scientific enquiry which dictated the shape of the Renaissance and which brought about yet another clash between believers and would-be-gnostics. The Gnostic prefigures the alchemist in his ability to believe in the possibility of transformation, and to use the images and archetypes close at hand to attain this state. The imaginative resources of the Gnostic creation dramas are staggering in their conceptual scope.

Central to the return of the divine spark of the soul were the dual themes of Anthropos and Sophia, both of whom represented that continual obsession of the Western Way – the interpenetration of the microcosm by the macrocosm. The Anthropos is the Adam of Light, otherwise known as Adam Kadmon, within Qabala. He is the first man, the mirror of the macrocosm, but he is deceived by the Demiurge and his archons into forgetting his heritage. Together with the spirit of Sophia (Wisdom), whose daughter he partners – the Eve of Paradise – he is lost in matter. Adam's body is the body of the world: his soul the totality of souls. Likewise the sufferings of Sophia, the exiled wisdom of the true God, were analogous to the sufferings of the created world. Her ultimate union with Christ – her Saviour and that of the world – was the expected portion of Valentinian Gnostics who conceived of their union as the signal for the *apocatastasis*, or the restoration of all things. Adam and Eve, and Christ and Sophia, were seen as types of *syzygy* (partners or consorts) whose reconciliation was important for the balancing of creation. This theme is also of critical importance within the Western Way: we discuss it further in chapters 4 and 5.

It is evident that Gnosticism fostered many levels of dualism which, at the one end, merely reflected the contemporary concern with the fallen nature of humanity, and at the other end polarized an eternally warring good and evil. These were not only the concerns of early Christianity, but are to be understood as deeply ingrained in the Classical world. Saviours, redeemers and messiahs of both sexes were to be found in almost every mystery school and religion at this time: these kept some degree of order in the precipitating superstitions then current. They were the symbols of hope and release from the vagaries of inexorable Fate – the obsession and scourge of the Classical world. The fusion of elements as disparate as Platonic, Orphic, Zoroastrian and Christian models made Gnostic dualism particularly confusing, especially from our modern standpoint which is comparatively naive in its conceptualization of good and evil. The stoic purity of Orphism, the endless battles of Zurvanist gods and demons, the semitic dualities of male and female, all appear in Gnosticism in different forms. The Gnostics may not have had all the pieces of the cosmic jigsaw, but they certainly enjoyed trying to make those pieces fit.

Having established their own idiosyncratic gospels and rich cosmology, they were free to relate to it. They considered themselves to be 'the kingless race' or, conversely, 'the king's children,' the offspring of the true hidden God – a relationship to be prized over that of the evil Demiurge and creator. The neo-Platonist, Plotinus (3rd century AD) was shocked that they should class themselves with the divine: 'brothers and sisters of those above!' (268) The Gnostics had the assurance from the mouth of Christ, no less, who, in conversation with the apostle Andrew, states:

> Know ye not . . . that ye and all angels and all archangels and the gods . . . are out of one and the same paste and the same matter and the same substance, and that ye all are out of the same mixture. (264)

This spiritual elitism rose from the way in which Gnosticism divided humanity. There was the *hylic* or fleshly man, the *psychic* or partially-enlightened man (usually understood as one who was nominally Christian), and the *pneumatic* or spiritual man, who was fully gnostic (one who had heard the secret revelations of Christ and his disciples). This concept is described in *The Origin of the World* (239) as the three Adams. The enlightenment of the Gnostics was of a predestined order – an element which was to appear in the form of Calvinism in later centuries. The pneumatics were variously called 'the elect' or 'the perfected'. As representatives of the then new aeon, the Gnostics strove to utilize the tools provided by Christianity, to work with a system whose catholicity and impact was immense. But, the promotion of knowledge over faith was too unbalanced. Having envisaged a fallen Sophia (wisdom) their gnosis was correspondingly less applicable to daily life. 'The beginning of Perfection is the Gnosis of Man, but the Gnosis of God is perfected Perfection' (227) might stand for the ideal which the Gnostics strove to follow.

Apart from Marcion and possibly Valentinus, there was no attempt to codify the complexities and varieties of expression within Gnosticism itself. Marcion (?–AD 160) was the only one who tried to institute a church after the Christian model, rather than the rather loosely-based cults into which Gnosticism was organized. Gnosticism appealed to the intellectual and cultured section of society – the same section which had been the mainstay of the mystery schools. Christianity appealed to a universal need and even accepted slaves, which had been rare within the mysteries. The Gnostic priesthood was both male and female, after the ancient manner, whereas Christianity maintained a male priesthood. Gnosticism was suppressed for a variety of reasons: its lack of well-distributed literature, its elitism, its reluctance to proselytize and its uncodified nature, are a few contributory factors. Crucially, it did not offer the kind of Imperial cohesion which orthodox Christianity was to give to the empires of Rome and Byzantium. Its suppression was swiftly effected though not finally effective: Gnostic traces, like the tares in the parable, could not be separated from the wheat of orthodox Christ- ianity.

Many of St Paul's letters to the churches in Asia Minor and Greece reflect a manful struggle with the unruly effects of Gnosticism among his proselytes: 'Avoid the godless chatter and contradictions of what is falsely called knowledge, for by professing it some have missed the mark as regards the faith.' (I Tim. 6, 20) Here is the heart of the dichotomy between Gnosis and Christianity.

Christianity has ever afterwards had a love-hate relationship with its own esoteric tradition, as we shall go on to discuss. The effect of the Gnostic experiment was to widen the gap between knowledge and faith to the extent that St Ignatius of Antioch could write:

> It is better if a man knows nothing and does not perceive a single cause of things created but abides in faith in God and in love, rather than that, puffed up by such knowledge, he falls away from the love that makes man alive . . . and rather than that he falls into godlessness through the subtleties of his questioning and hair-splitting. (291)

The way of gnosis is indeed fraught with such dangers, but its dismissal was a prelude to the church's continual distrust of its own saints and mystics. The Gnostic experiment may have been unba- lanced, but then so was the reaction against it.

Christ's words: 'Let your light so shine before men, that they may see your good works' and 'I come not to abolish (the law and the prophets) but to fulfill them' (St Matthew 5, 16–17) was to become the lost Christian legacy. The challenge of Gnosticism reappeared to haunt orthodoxy again and again, in the form of many heresies and the words of the Gnostic Christ still echoed up and down the circles of the archons: 'I am the actual call which causes a call to resound in each one, and thus they recognize (me) through (knowledge), since a seed (of light) is in (them)' (291: lacunae in text.)

What is heresy? It derives from a Greek word meaning 'choice.' We should carefully distinguish esotericism from heresy in our under- standing of the Western Way, because they are not synonymous. Tradition is never a matter of choice. The esotericist is one who explores the levels of a tradition, taking ever deeper soundings and re-emerging enriched. The heretic does not stay long enough to explore, but leaves demanding his entrance money back. Dualism can be pernicious to esoteric tradition, setting up false dichotomies, estranging the seeker from a holistic perspective. The fruits of Gnosis, like that paradisial fruit, bring knowledge of good and evil. The re-membering of the Body of Light, the reassembly of the divine spark, are paradisial longings for a unity which cannot be realized while we are incarnate. We have truly 'eaten of the fruit' of our experience – this is not original sin, but an opening of the inner eyes. God and evil, light and dark, man and woman, matter and spirit – these are the *dualities* which the guardians of tradition everywhere attempt to balance, attempting to resist *dualism* into which these concepts can fall. Rejection of one in favour of the other leads to imbalance and to heresy.

Gnosticism was merely one contender for the orthodox title of Christianity during the early days of the Church when doctrinal matters were still being codified. It failed at about the same time as the barbarian hordes swept across Europe, eclipsing the rich Classical heritage. The Byzantine Empire maintained certain ancient traditions, church and State coalesced to strengthen each other against the onslaughts of armed insurrection and spiritual darkness. It was no time for personal revelation. While Christianity struggled to make its impact upon Europe, using the vehicle of Native traditional practices and customs as a teaching aid, the Gnostic vision was borne eastwards and westwards by Manichaeism and Catharism, respectively.

Manichaeism is not a direct derivative from Gnosticism so much as a parallel development. Its founder, Mani (AD 216–76), was born in Seleucia of mixed Persian and Gnostic-Baptist background. At the age of twelve he had a vision in which his heavenly companion assured help and protection. Further revelations led him to regard himself as 'the Paraclete of the Christians, as the Messianic son of Zarathustra, and as the Maitreya Budda.' (291) – no small claim! He shared the Gnostic belief in the imprisoned particles of light which must be released by spiritual means. Man was a light-bearer, one who must be active in the combat with darkness – a Mithraic concept, as well as a Christian one. All apostles of Light it was believed, saw their culmination in Mani – Noah, Seth, Enoch, Buddha, Zoroaster and Christ. Extreme asceticism marked his followers: vegetarianism, abstinence from wine and sexual intercourse, a general avoidance of harm to all potential vessels of light whether they be human, animal or plant, typified their practices.

The success of Manichaeism was due to Mani's determination that his teachings should be written down and widely circulated. His church spread rapidly, despite persecution, especially in the East. Mani was martyred by being flayed alive and his disciples were banished from Persia. While a few came West, Manichaeism developed mainly in the East where it held its own against the Nestorian church and with Buddhism. It became particularly strong in Central Asia at Turfan, in Chinese Turkestan, where it proselytized and enjoyed a tolerant hearing until its suppression in the wake of the Mongolian invasion. Manichaen scriptures, found in Turfan early this century, are still being investigated. (291)

The legacy of Manichaeism in the West seems small, probably due to the intervention of Islam which drove a wedge between West and East very effectively. Yet Mani's prophecy, 'my hope will go into the West and will also go into the East,' was a true one. Elements of Manichaen dualism can still be discerned within Christianity due to the theology of St Augustine, who, despite his refutation of his early adherence to Manichaeism, nevertheless introduced a flavour of dualism into his writings.

While Manichaeism trecked eastwards, that other remnant of Gnosticism went westwards through Bulgaria and Italy into France and Spain, where it became known as Catharism. (188) It is perhaps significant that their joint journeys came to an abrupt and bloody end during the thirteeth century, almost as though that influence had run its course for that era. But where Manichaeism developed and flourished away from other Christian rivals, Catharism was as much a product of Christian reactionism as a continuation of Gnostic principles.

The roots of dualism are very deep and difficult to eradicate: there remains an unhealthy surplus of its seasoning within the Western Way.

> Dualism carried with it . . . the need for revelation, and the need for redemption. If man cannot while living in the body, truly find god, the God must make himself known. And if the life of the body drags down the aspiring soul to its level and weakened its powers of flight, then the body and its activities can never achieve their destined end without some infusion of divine power from outside, from above. (109)

Within historical perspectives of the Western Mystery Tradition, the Cathars are often promoted as martyrs to a shared esoteric principle. But though their destruction and persecution at the hands of the Inquisition has aroused much sympathy, the full rigour of the

Cathar way of life and their spiritual stance would find little favour almost anywhere today. The way of the Cathar is not the way of the Hermeticist, though its appeal is doubtless not far removed from the kind of 'Aquarian consciousness' prevalent among those who look for the millenium to be accomplished in nuclear holocaust: a truly ultimate dualism of hopelessness wherein matter is utterly dissolved. We shall return to this point in the final chapter.

For both Manichaens and Cathars, the flesh and matter generally were creations of the evil Demiurge. Here an ultimate dualism was postulated wherein evil and good were eternally polarized. The agents of the Light had somehow been imprisoned and uniformed in the colours of Darkness. It is perhaps difficult for us to appreciate this doctrine, living as we do at the latter-end of the twentieth century, mostly ignorant of the spiritual perspectives which underlie our culture, but it is essential to avoid the pitfalls of dualism now as then.

Dualism was a recurrent problem within Christianity. The Incarnation and the Redemption were concepts which were often misunderstood and without the balance of which the extremes of heresy always flourished. The earth and its creations were not cause for joy to a peasant ploughing his feudal lord's fields, nor to his wife burdened with 'boon-work' and many children: for such as these, respite came only on feast-days and at death. The Cathars found creation as a cause of sorrow, since matter was ensnared within the flesh, seen as the prison of the divine spark. Food, sexuality and enjoyment of the world's goods were either rejected as worthless trash, or else subjected to a deep antimonianism which put the body and spirit in two different compartments, having no interaction. Elements of this attitude are still prevalent among those who have a deep distaste for the actions and function of the body: it is rooted in a fear of our humanity. Cathars wanted release from this condition: they yearned for a spiritual condition with all the zeal of the Orphite. Spiritual purity could have no truck with the body and for this reason, the Cathars said that Christ only 'seemed' to be born of a woman, and 'seemed' to die on the cross. Likewise the sacraments, which exalt matter as the gateway of spiritual grace, were rejected totally.

The Church, because it traded in the coin of matter, was seen as the agent of the Demiurge. It is interesting to speculate just what caused the development of Catharism within Provence where the Courts of Love flourished, where troubadours sang ballads of forthright love and where the cultural climate was of the bountiful South. Perhaps, 'the Cathar notion of body-soul division and the need to ascend through a cycle of purification to a dimension of non-material light had some affinities with the more idealist side of courtly love.' (198)

Like the Gnostics and Manichaens, the Cathars had three ranks of adherents: hearers, believers and the perfect. 'There was thus in effect the same division as among the Catholics between the Religious or Monks and other Believers.' (ibid) The perfect ones reached their exalted position by renouncing evil, living continently, in abstinence from flesh-meats and the fruits of sexuality. They alone could reconcile sinners by means of a ritual called the *consolamentum* – a sacramental-like means of purification. Its effect was considered final and was possibly not repeatable: if a perfected one fell into sin after having received the *consolamentum* – whether by eating meat or committing murder (both equally reprehensible acts) – all those who had received purification at his hands were rendered likewise sinful: a chain of evil had been released. Vigilance and a high degree of integrity were key features of Catharism then. Often the *consolamentum* was not received until death, when all sin was remitted. Women were admissible to ranks of the perfect ones; widows kept Cathar communities, educating children and practising the Cathar way of life. It was a form of ideal Christianity, but dualist to the heart.

Their plain life, simple food, laying on of hands, their celibacy and their adherence to the Gospel of St John, make them seem models of the faith: these very points alerted the Church to the dangers of heresy – such cases had occurred across Europe before. The Albigensian Crusade (1208–18) was launched against them: its causes and success are as much dynastic and geographical as religious. (188) By 1242, Catharism had retired to the stronghold-fortress of Montségur whence its inhabitants were led, to be burned and dispossessed of their lands. By the end of the fourteenth century, Catharism was all but dead.

We have dwelt at length with dualist heresy neither to vaunt its attractive qualities, nor to praise the inhumanity of the Church. ('Kill them all – God will know his own,' cried the Abbé of Cîteaux at the siege of Béziers in 1209 when asked how the army was to distinguish heretic from Catholic.) (125). The facts, in so far as they can be established, speak for themselves. The works of the English doctor, Arthur Guirdham who has claimed Cathar incarnations, have done much to popularize the movement. There are various Gnostic churches in America, as well as a neo-Cathar movement in Holland, known as the *Lectorium Rosicrucianum*.

We have followed the threads of Gnosis into heresy, but the trail does not stop there. Gnosis – esoteric knowledge which is gently led by wisdom – reveals itself within the mystical essence of Christianity. Because the impulse of the Western Way has been classed as heretic by the exoteric Church, does not mean that it does not resonate strongly with esoteric Christianity.

ASLAN IS NOT A SAFE LION

In his *The Lion, the Witch and the Wardrobe*, C.S. Lewis presents Aslan – a Lion, King of the Beasts, and son of the Emperor over the Seas – as a type of Christ. Some of the characters in the story expect him to be a tame, domesticated lion, an anthropomorphic, story-book beast, but they are told: 'Aslan is not a safe lion.' Some expect to see Christ in the same guise – a safe, domesticated god, familiar and expected – the reality is different. Indeed, so far from the reality have we come that many adults who read this story as a child and later realize the nature of Lewis's allegory have said, 'Jesus was a bearded man in the Bible, someone I couldn't relate to – but I could have died for Aslan.'

This shows how we have lost touch with the story of Christianity. The dynamic Christ of the Resurrection, the flogger of the temple money-changers, the one who blasted the fig-tree for its barrenness, the one who will come to bring fire and the sword, is at odds with the downtrodden Man of Sorrows in the mode of Attis and Adonis, the saviour god dead in his mother's lap: the one who has latterly become Gentle Jesus, meek and mild. Christ is *not* safe. He is the Anointed One, whose tongue is a sword (Rev. 1,16): the Logos or Word of God. As a yardstick of creativity rather than as a comfortable icon, we must see him.

Commenting on the implicit dualism of Western religion, Dion Fortune says: 'the great weakness of Christianity lies in the fact that it ignores rhythm. It balances God with Devil instead of Vishnu with Shiva,' which are the preserving and destructive aspects of Brahma. More challengingly, Jim Garrison says: 'God as experienced has been shown to possess light and dark dimensions and to be as savage and terrible as God is merciful and forgiving.' (100) What are hermeticists to make of this? Especially one to whom Christianity seems to be the deadest of dead ends?

More words have been written, and more blood spilled over the founder of Christianity and his intentions, than many can bear to contemplate. Christ has become the figurehead and puppet of both saints and sinners, and the measure of his doctrines a tawdry mockery of the gospel. With this gutless and limp effigy we have little to do here. After nearly 2000 years of substitutes, it is time to look hard at the reality.

In this part of the book we shall be looking at the esoteric *not* the exoteric side of Christianity, and we must do so from the basis of tradition. We spoke in volume one of how the Native Tradition was transmitted by means of Christianity. Just as the customs of ancestral importance and national cohesion were upheld by the Church, so, too, the Hermetic Tradition was rescued from oblivion. While it

> designed to obliterate and extinguish the memory of heathen antiquity and authors ... contrariwise it was the Christian Church which ... did preserve in the sacred lap and bosom thereof the precious relics even of heathen learning which otherwise had been extinguished as if no such thing had ever been. (16)

This is not a book of Christian apologetics. We are not concerned with the historical record of the Church as a human institution, but as a preserver of tradition and as a living mystery school. We must be in the singularly unique position, in this century, that those who join a spiritual tradition today rarely bring any spiritual baggage with them unlike the

> Greeks, and Syrians and Egyptians ... (who) came to the Church loaded with packs of their own, crammed with metaphysics and mystical experience, with cosmic lore and traditions ... nor did they dream of dropping all this on the threshold of the Church and forgetting all about it. ... On the contrary they prized these things as heirlooms, as their dowry. (108)

The validation of spiritual life does not come from some projected set of dogmas, but from inner experience resonating to a tradition. In our times, outsiders now come to gaze on the exterior architecture of tradition, and few see the vision in the sanctuary.

The Church has always taught a mystery: that Christ is both fully human and fully divine. Humanly, this is usually translated into

Christ, the man *or* Christ, the god – rarely both together. But the implications of the Incarnation (the taking of flesh) and the Redemption, are of overwhelming importance to the hermeticist if he or she is engaged upon the Great Work.

Neither of these concepts appears to command universal respect even among those nominally Christian, although the Incarnation and the Redemption are the two pillars between which the world is balanced. The central point of balance is the crucifixion and the harrowing of hell – 'this central event is the meeting of many power lines: whatever their provenance before this event in time, whatever their divergence after it – all lines (of tradition) lead through the mystery of the Resurrection.' (217) The mystical content of these concepts cannot have its full effect unless the non-Christian reader is able to dispel the various ideological smokescreens which prevail in this area.

Due to a popularist Theosophical understanding, Christ is now seen as but one among many such saviours of East and West. On the other hand, he is often seen as yet another of the dying and rising vegetation gods of the mystery schools. The answer is not easy. The Hellenic notion of the Logos, together with the Jewish idea of the Messiah, as well as the mystery schools' own saviours are combined in the figure of Christ. (81) The Eastern Orthodox doctrine of *theosis* may be a key: 'God became man that man might become God,' said St Athanasius in his *De Incarnatione*. That alone, among the mysteries of Christianity is unique to its nature, although it is not one which the Church publicizes. Theosis (literally, deification) is nonetheless the key not only to Christ's actions but to Christian belief. (208) Whether one is a believer or not, something changed direction from the point of the Incarnation: not just the birth of a tradition but the opportunity for consciousness to evolve, a necessary bridge between the impacted dualisms of the Classical world and the cosmic hope of the Mysteries. Non-Christian readers are invited to proceed along the mythological consideration, if they so wish.

Saviours had come before, in many guises, but none before made the impact of Christ. 'What is this mystery that touches me? I received the divine image and did not keep it. He received my flesh to save the image and grant immortality to the flesh.' (200) This was the unique promise which has been obscured and remains to be rediscovered within Christianity which is, despite all appearances, a visibly present, though often invisibly operative mystery school. The Hermetic Tradition draws strongly upon the archetypal myths of

Fig 7. The Resurrection – alchemical emblem of the Great Work

Classical, Christian and Native mysteries: each has become part of the other so that they can rarely be distinguished.

The occult enclosure of hermeticism has been a self-protective measure as much as a means of preserving the mysteries from the profane. The Christian mysteries, on the other hand, have become open, though inherently hidden, mysteries. Their traditional wisdom and liturgical symbolism have all but escaped through over-simplification. The *disciplina arcani*, the Christian mystery guardians, once ejected non-initiates from observing the higher mysteries of the consecration, as the medieval rood-screen kept the common faithful from becoming too familiar with the sacramental operation: now anyone can see the act of the Great Work taking place quite openly.

The Great Work is figured forth on altars daily in nearly every country of the world as the *prima materia* of the sacred elements of bread and wine are miraculously changed into the Body and Blood of Christ? How many alchemists achieve the same and show it public-ly? (cf. chapter 5) The transubstantiation of the bread and wine into

*Fig 8. Lady Mary and her Son in the Ship of Faith,
piloted by Wisdom*

the Body and Blood of Christ is something which was not lost upon alchemists in later times who used the Eucharistic symbolism as an emblem for their own work. This central sacrament in which the Incarnation and Redemption are enacted was archetypally representative of the Great Work. Those who received the sacrament were enabled, mysteriously, to become members of the Mystical Body of Christ. (fig. 7)

The hermeticist who is aware of the indwelling divine spark and the attempt which must be made to kindle it and take the evolutionary journey into the heart of the macrocosm, has only to consider the implications of Christ's Incarnation – an involutionary journey into the heart of the microcosm in order to bring Divine Fire to the indwelling spark. The amazingly universal application of this action is not dependent upon production of a baptismal certificate, but applies to all. The story of the divine spark is our story too, as we have already seen. It is the skilful use of this story – whether one uses the Christian model or another – which brings us out of 'the vale of tears' into the Inner kingdom:

Not that one should give up, neglect or forget (one's) inner life for a moment, but (one) must learn to work in it, with it and out of it, so that the unity of (one's) soul may break out into (one's) activities and (one's) activities shall lead (one) back to that unity. (241)

The Resurrection breaks through and overturns the tides of time. As with all mysteries, the Christian one happens outside of time: all that happens *within* time is subject both to the laws of time and nature, which is why the imperfect face of the Church reveals not the tranquillity of the Inner Kingdom but the battered makeshift within the world. (189) The Redemption reconciles the two trees of Eden: the Tree of Life, and the Tree of the Knowledge of Good and Evil. The dualism of matter and spirit is reconciled into the realization that all things created have in them the potentiality of resurrection, of transubstantiation, of the completion of the Great Work itself.

Such are the possibilities of esoteric Christianity but, many will demand, where is it practised? While there have been many specifically occult Christian spin-offs from the time of the Gnostics right up until the Liberal Catholic Church with its Theosophist tenets, we will not find the mystical kernel of which we have been speaking anywhere else except within the traditional folds of the Catholic and Eastern Orthodox churches, who have hosted and preserved their spiritual traditions with rigorous care.

The mystical way of tradition has had to work hard to survive the battle which has been joined between faith and knowledge since the time of Gnosticism. We have only to look at the beginning of Christianity to see how pitiful and unnecessary this battle has been. Two sets of visitants come to the manger in Bethlehem: the shepherds and the kings. The shepherds, impelled by angelic messengers, accept the proclamation of the new-born messiah with uncritical enthusiasm – with faith. The kings, by means of their gnosis, follow a star which is the certainty of their faith until they, too, reach their destination. It is perhaps of note that the shepherds go straight to the manger, while the kings waste time calling upon Herod to suffer unwanted congratulations. (cf. chapter 3)

'The faith of uneducated men is not the less philosophically correct, nor less acceptable to God, because it does not happen to be conceived in . . . precise statements... . . The ears of the common people are holier than are the hearts of the priests,' wrote Cardinal Newman. (244) While faith and knowledge are not exclusive, as we have seen, the Church does not have the apparatus for coping with the mystic who has progressed beyond blind faith into certain faith, which is the gnosis of spiritual illumination.

We have seen how the Gnostic and Manichaen movements catered for the disparate needs of their followers. Modern Christianity seems saddled with a system in which only the 'minimum belief' of the faithful and the highly inflected way of the monk and nun can be accommodated. We need what Jacob Needleman calls 'intermediate Christianity.' (241) The mystical traditions are too circumscribed by experts to be richly and readily available to all; they are not widely taught as a matter of course and those who do stumble upon the esoteric side of Christianity (usually by accident) are without the guidance or assurance of experts in the field, or else are so frightened they mistake their findings for heresy.

As for those psychically gifted or esoterically involved believers – these find themselves out on a limb.

> For centuries the tradition has been to distrust the psychically sensitive people as representing the pagan religions from which the Christian faith has liberated the countries into which it has percolated. . . . But in Europe, the Church has driven the psychic into the underworld. It never disappeared; but it was always threatened, so that it allied itself with pagan rather than with Christian ideas. (259)

The infancy of the Church is over, yet it seems unwilling to push forward to new growth and adulthood; those who seek spiritual maturity find themselves held down in spiritual adolescence. It is little wonder that a mass exodus of Christians is occurring in the direction of other religions or spiritual systems which bother to teach the techniques of prayer and meditation, and which not only treasure but are willing to transmit the traditions which they have inherited to others.

This neglect of the inner life within the Church has led many to speculate as to whether a spiritual renaissance is not due. There are now many spiritual pilgrims abroad and fewer guardians of tradition. If such a renaissance is abroad then it is more likely to arise from the laity rather than the clergy who seem hell-bent on a programme of steady demythologization, liturgical impoverishment and theological inertia: the new chastity, poverty and obedience of the modern age. Few Hermeticists and non-Christians foresee any continuing hope within Christianity as a church-administered religion. The steady devaluation 'in the price of what it is to be a Christian' had so accelerated in the philosopher Kirkegaard's day that he wrote, 'at last it became such an absurdly low price that soon the opposite effect was produced, that men hardly wanted to have anything to do with Christianity.' (176) Some would see the demise of Christianity as an example of poetic justice, in the sense that it has been directly or indirectly the undertaker and executioner of many another tradition.

If the esoteric Christian mysteries are guarded anywhere it is by the unheralded mystic who lives, like a hidden hermit, within his or her tradition. We returned to our concept of 'marginal shamans' who inform the traditional values of the Secret Commonwealth. (cf. volume I) For every mystic whose realizations are written down, there are probably hundreds whose silent practice is unknown. Mysticism is still tarred with the brush of Gnostic and revelatory taint. From past records it would seem that the mystic, like the shamefully-neglected poet, is immediately lauded upon his or her death after a lifetime of being hounded from pillar to post. The incarceration of St John of the Cross and the inquisition of St Teresa of Avila are extreme instances of this practice. Stigmatics and wonder-workers, far from revelling in the reputation enjoyed by pre-Revolutionary Orthodox hermits or *startsi*, have been relegated to obscure monasteries. One feels that a real live St Francis would upset the Church as much now as once he did in thirteenth-century Umbria.

The mystical way is a trackless path on which the pilgrim seeks to encounter God face to face, believing utterly in the promise:

'I will give you the treasures of darkness and the secret places.' (Isaiah 45, 7) Finding one's own inner way is by no means dependent upon how others have travelled, but the length of the journey is considerably diminished if spent in the company of one who is also travelling. In this way, the great mystics of the church have companioned pilgrims from the medieval mystics Julian of Norwich (160), the author of the *Cloud of Unknowing* (50), Thomas à Kempis (179), and St Catherine of Siena (44), to the mystics of our own day: Thomas Merton (233), Caryll Houselander (149) and Ida Gorres. (108) The restoration and preservation of the Christian tradition has been the concern of many mystics and spiritual writers in this century. Two remarkable women, from disparate backgrounds, have contributed much to our understanding: Rosemary Haughton (136) and Lois Lang-Sims (189). Both are aware of the Christian mysteries and the 'lost' esoteric side of their faith. Their books rise solitary from a babel of theological dispute and fundamentalist cant. It is perhaps significant that they are both women within a tradition which, though it has boasted, 'there is neither Jew nor Greek, there is neither slave nor free, there is neither male nor female' (Galatians 3, 28) has held tenaciously onto the very sexual disqualifications that boast was meant to abolish.

When Teilhard de Chardin, writing in the middle of this century said, 'there is the general question of the feminine, and so far it has been left unsolved or imperfectly expressed by the Christian theory of sanctity,' (327) he was hardly underestimating his own traditions's failing in this regard. Though Christ's ministry can be understood by the feminine poles of Mary the Virgin, his mother, who accomplished his Incarnation by her willingness to serve God, and by Mary Magalene who discovered the empty sepulchre on the morning of the Resurrection, the Church has been slow to meditate on this. Much feminist theology has tried to rectify this state of affairs, but has often succeeded in setting matters on their head, substituting female for male symbology, and promoting the ordination of women over more crucial issues. These esoteric matters necessarily upset our esoteric understanding when we see a willing acceptance of a symbol for liturgical purposes: e.g. the representation of and anthems to, the Blessed Virgin, Lady Mary, and an exclusion of her daughters. Mystics have been particularly drawn to Lady Mary: 'Mary is a dimension of Jesus, a dimension which he expressed when he said, "My yoke is easy and my burden light," it is advantageous to address oneself to this dimension in order to reach totality.' (294) (fig. 8)

The Logos and his mother, as the manifest incarnations of God's love, who share in the lot of humanity, are the balances of the spiritual totality. Jung was right to acclaim the doctrine of the Assumption of the Virgin into heaven as of supreme importance for our time, for so does the dualism of male and femaleness stand some chance of being flushed out of Christianity. The spirit – symbolized frequently by Christ – is important, but so is the body – which Christ took through the help of Mary. If the body or soul of a man (i.e. Jesus) had been assumed into heaven, then it was right and fitting that the body and soul of a woman should be also so assumed, says the dogma. 'From this earth, over which we tread as pilgrims, comforted by our faith in future resurrection, we look to you. . . . O Sweet Virgin Mary.' (237) It is interesting to note that though the Protestant churches after the Reformation forsook devotion to or mention of, Lady Mary, hermeticists and alchemists never forsook her. Entrenched within the Protestant enclaves of Rosicrucianism, in the writings of Boehme, Vaughan and others, Our Lady's memory is still sweet. We shall be looking further at the Divine Feminine in chapter 5 where we shall consider the identifications of the Goddess, the World Soul and the Sophianic Lady herself, Our Lady Wisdom.

The hermeticist may often find him or herself at odds with the exoteric or dogmatic nature of the Church, but seldom with its esoteric mysteries. 'What the microcosmic heart does not tell, the macrocosmic heart – the Logos – tells us in a symbolic and partial language.' (294) Christ's parables reveal two levels of understanding – on one level a story, on another, a key to the Inner Kingdom. Jesus speaks about himself in a symbolic way, urging his hearers to squeeze the last drop of meaning out of his parables. His storytelling is aimed to provoke response from among those listeners who have the native wisdom to use the story practically. While he was an enemy of theoretical knowledge, especially when it was imposed upon people who live by simple faith (St Matthew 23), he also encouraged the faith which leads to better knowledge (St John 10). More abundant life, not less, was his saying. Whatever salvific story we live by, first we must believe in it and trust it to show us its treasures. Awareness of the macrocosm, of the Inner Kingdom lies locked within the gospels.

Mystic revelation is not a forbidden, exotic thing: it is merely the skilful understanding and use of spiritual symbolism. In volume one we spoke about the ways in which we can read the landscape, the ancestral stones of our Native Tradition; the same holds true for the Hermetic Tradition. The Gothic cathedrals were known as 'the Bible of the people,' whose architectural mysteries embodied the esoteric story of Christ. To visit one of these today is to step within a forest of stone pillars in whose nemeton are the depictions of saints, angels, and prophets, the yearly round of the seasons, the secret tokens of Christ and Lady Mary. Here, too, at Chartres, one can enter the maze which symbolically represents not only the pilgrimage to Jerusalem, but a return to the heart's home, the Inner Kingdom which is reached by means of life itself. (358, 57, 2) The maze is also our reminder of the interconnecting spirals of the Western Way which is the subject of our present pilgrimage. Within the towering pillars of this Cathedral-forest might we not glimpse the White Hart who has ever been the emblem of spiritual search, in whom the Grail-quest has its quarry? (277)

It is as though Pwyll from the Mabinogion (204) had strayed into the Middle Ages in pursuit of the Otherworldly White Hart, where Arawn's wild hunt rides in a new guise. (cf. volume 1) The quest begun under the aegis of the Native Tradition continues without break into the Hermetic Tradition. From the Gundestrup Cauldron with its depiction of Cernunnos as Guardian of the Sacrificial Hunt to St John of the Cross's 'for the wounded hart appears on the hill' (155) seems a long step, but we should not find any difficulty in reconciling these interrelated images. From within the temenos of a medieval cathedral it is easier to make this important connection. These stones were hewn and erected when spiritual chivalry was abroad – the quest which did not exclude the laity, neither lady nor knight, lord nor peasant. The virile epics of spiritual chivalry, embodied in the Grail legends, combined the Christian mythos with the vigour of native storytelling. Love, both earthly and spiritual, was present in all its complexity: from the urge to protect pilgrims by those monks on horseback, the templars, to the Otherworldly Courts of Love where Celtic paradise and medieval simplicity combined, everyone wanted to be part of the story.

St Francis of Assisi, his head stuffed with such stories, had attempted to be a chivalrous knight before he rode out in defence of Lady Poverty in nothing more than a tattered habit and a handful of ideals, yet he never lost sight of his love for spiritual chivalry and the quest. He founded two orders, one for monks and one for nuns, but, so overwhelming was this troubador of the Lord, that his storytelling set fair to empty the villages of Italy, so he founded an order for lay people, that they might not be left out of the story.

The tribal stories did not retreat, but were reworked and incorporated into that of the White Hart, Christ himself. The Classical remnant which went to found the basis of the Hermetic tradition has for its centre the story of the lost pearl and the finding of the spark of light. Both stories cross-track each other and will doubtless find their meeting in the fullness of time – unless, of course, they meet on the Inner, within the Kingdom itself, outside of time. And while both stories were to be challenged by new metaphors, they still have the power to draw in listeners.

The thirst for knowledge has been overwhelming, often engulfing what the Church saw as the more important concerns of spiritual quest. For, while the academicians and proto-scientists were not satisfied with the sum of medieval knowledge, neither were those on spiritual quest content to remain within the known limits of religion. The earlier splintering of religion from shamanism was to be unhappily mirrored once more between religion and science during the Reformation and Counter-Reformation when faith and knowledge joined battle again, with the help of new combatants – tradition against the word, laws of God and laws of nature set at odds. Too much radical experimentation in the area of physics and metaphysics resulted in an almost total schism within religion. Scientists and magicians were hard-put to reconcile their activities with their beliefs.

The importance of quest is primarily within the exploration of consciousness: however far we go in spiritual quest, we always find what we sought within ourselves. The exploration of the internal workings of man, the microcosm, was still the prime concern of the mystic, scientist and magician. And, although each sought on different levels of experience – each quest was valid. It is our

> God-given task to reconcile and harmonize the poetic and the material realms, to bring them to unity, to spiritualize the material, and to render manifest all the latent capacities of the created order. As the Jewish Hasidim expressed it, man is called 'to advance from rung to rung until, through him, everything is united.' As microcosm, then, man is the one through whom the world is summed up; as mediator, he is the one through whom the world is offered back to God. (355)

This realization is shared by Christianity and by Judaism: it has become the task of the hermeticist also by means of a wonderful ladder of light which joins the traditions of the West in a mysterious manner. We have spoken of tribe and of wandering tradition: within the Jewish spiritual tradition, the two are one.

THE SHATTERED VESSELS

> God arranged the order of creation so that all things are bound to each other. The direction of events in the lower world depends on entities above them, as our sages teach: 'There is no blade of grass in the world below that does not have an angel over it striking it and telling it to grow. (168)

So wrote the Jewish mystical leader, the Hai Gaon (939–1938). This pronouncement will be familiar to the hermeticist who will catch resonances of the Emerald Tablet. It is also a statement about the interrelatedness of the worlds which Qabalism, above all other systems, has understood and given to the world. The development of Qabala within Judaism is extraordinary because of its amazing success and acceptance not only as a mystical tradition within Judaism itself, but as an esoteric system which has been taken over by non-Jews.

Qabala is an instance of a mystical tradition arising organically from its exoteric shell, but one which remained totally integrated within it. It evolved from the oral teachings of the prophets, took on board mystical elements and techniques during the Babylonian exile and the Diaspora whence it developed in significantly localized ways. The exoteric laws of Judaism, rather than militating against its development, have welded it more strongly, keeping the esoteric secrets in the hands of adepts who were also religious leaders.

Two factors above all determine the hardiness of Judaism: tribal cohesion, as exemplified in the family unit, and the adaptability of a nomadic people – as the Jews have been forced to live until this century. The minutiae of Judaic law are often represented as a tiresome burden by non-Jews, but, for those within its folds, they are opportunities for contact with God: the touching of the sacred text of the *Shema* ('Hear O Israel', *Deut.* 6,4.) in the *mezuzah* on leaving and entering a house, the wearing of the *tallit* and *tefillin* – the prayer shawl and phylacteries – the dietary laws and seasonal celebrations, the divine rest of the Sabbath, are the interactions of the faithful people with God. (335) Judaism's mystics are not monks and nuns, but married people living in the world who understand the necessity of reconciling the lives of the body and of the spirit.

No one can date the inception of Qabala. It remained an oral teaching for centuries, the first texts appearing in early medieval Spain. The cross-fertilizations affecting the Mediterranean during the early Christian era are also apparent within the cosmological speculation and formulations of Qabala. Since worship at the Temple in Jerusalem was disrupted first of all in 586 B.C. when the Solomonic Temple was destroyed, and then in AD 70 when the rebuilt Second Temple was burned during the Roman occupation, certain religious obligations and duties could not be fulfilled. Moreover, the dwelling-place of God's Spirit, the *Ruach HaKadosh*, the Shekhina had nowhere to abide but in the souls of the faithful. This is central to an understanding of Judaism's obsession with the preservation of tradition. No matter where the chosen people lived, there also went the Shekhina to share their exile invisibly, as once the tribes had followed Moses through the desert led by a Pillar of Cloud by day and a Pillar of Fire by night – the mystical appearance of the Shekhina which dwelt between the cherubim upon the curtained Ark of the Covenant. In the new exile of the Diaspora, each member of the congregation bore the added duty of retaining a secret tabernacle for the indwelling spirit which could only be wrought by upright life and constant study of the traditions. From such intense study was born the mystical system of the Qabala.

The Qabala is a microchip in which is encoded the whole of Jewish mystical tradition. Because of its unique compression, it is a system which has been borrowed by the Hermetic tradition in order to codify its own complex symbology. But we should not forget that, first and foremost, Qabala is a Jewish spiritual expression, not a Gentile magical system. Qabala is made of many levels of mystical experience, and has had many commentators. We do not have space to list them all: the reader is referred to the bibliography where many titles are listed. (167, 168, 145, 154, 77, 127–30)

What is evident is that the techniques employed by Qabalists included prayer, fasting and the repetition of the holy names of God – the usual religious devices – alongside what we may consider to be more esoteric techniques such as meditation, rhythmic breathing, chanting, the adoption of certain postures in order to perceive the divine vision, and many means of visualization. These techniques have been carefully guarded from the uninitiated because, used without guidance, they cannot only be physically dangerous, but can mislead the practitioner into qliphotic realms – where the shells of creation are inhabited by demons.

One of the main sources of Qabala is the *Zohar* or Book of Splendour, attributed to Moses of Leon (1250–1305), but which doubtless dates before this in oral tradition. Together with the *Sepher Yetzirah* (Book of Creation) it gives us the basis for all subsequent Qabalistic study, establishing a sephirotic system upon the Tree of Life, and the means of undertaking the series of spiritual ascents known as 'merkabah' or ascents in the chariot. The sephiroth are the ten essences or 'sapphires' of God's emanations. (See fig 9) They have tended to become useful filing cabinets within Gentile Qabala, but their original meaning is of jewel-like light through which the different qualities of God's glory are manifest. The *Merkabah* or chariot, was the vehicle by which the mystic contemplated the heavenly halls of God. This form of mysticism derives from the Vision of Ezekiel whose account of the wheeled chariot and

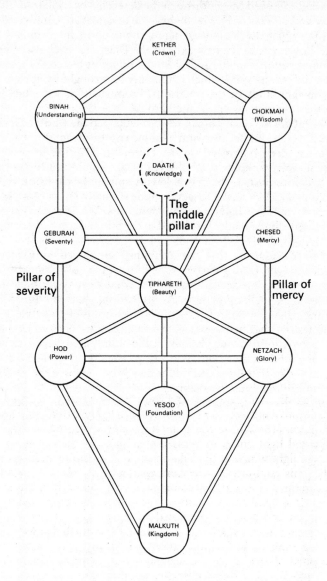

Figure 9: The Tree of Life

the living creatures surrounding it became the object of much meditative study. This vision was considered to be the highest in the canon of Jewish mysticism. (154)

Other Qabalists followed their own intense meditations, notably Abraham Abulafia (1240–92) whose permutations of the Hebrew alphabet brought him fiery visions. (1) His techniques were considered to be very dangerous: it is possible that there was some link between him and the Christian esotericist, Ramon Lull – their systems were very similar. (cf. chapter 3) The Spanish school of Qabala did not long continue after the expulsion of the Jews from Spain in 1492. Exiled again, some returned home to found a centre for Qabalistic studies in Palestine, at Safed where Joseph Karo (1488–1575), Moses Cordevero (1522–70) and others had the opportunity to codify the disparate disciplines which had sprung up during the Diaspora. At this centre the course of Qabala changed, maturing in the work of Isaac Luria (1534–72)

Luria's system was exceedingly complex: he developed the notion of the ten sephiroth as existing within four universes concurrently. In order that God might permeate the whole of creation and that everything might have its god-like response, the vessels (or sephiroth) which held his light were shattered so that they spilled into a lower universe. This shattering of the vessels is analogous to the idea of the divine spark's fragmentation into a scattered body of light. From their primal, but unrelated origin, fragments of the vessels fell into successively lower universes, or levels of existence, until the light was so fragmented that imbalances began to enter in (in much the same way that physical elements like uranium can be degraded through increasing diversification of their constituents). Luria preached the rectification of the light of a state called the Universe of Rectification, the *Tikkun*. (16) Within the many levels and sephirotic vessels, the fragmented light could be reassembled as archetypes – miniature bodies of light which at the Tikkun would constitute an integrated whole. This complex system combines not only the Hermeticists' theory of the divine sparks becoming united into a Body of Light, but also the union and reconciliation of the syzygies, which is a feature of Gnosticism and which preoccupied alchemy.

The final state to which mystic, alchemist and Qabalist work may seem an exalted one which cannot be in any way hastened or anticipated. Truly, these are cosmic matters, yet as Chaim Vital (1543–1620), Luria's chief disciple, wrote:

> In his ascent the mystic is irradiated by the light of the tree and in his descent the light finds a medium through which to flow back into the daily world. . . . In the descent a magic is worked and all the pretended way of ascent (through imaginative meditation) is rendered 'greater than reality' (121)

The meditative techniques whereby an appreciation of the Tree of Life's secrets might be understood became the means by which the Qabalist made the ascent and descent, so that the higher universes and lights of the sephiroth might be experienced with the help of the imaginative faculty. But this experience was not for individual retention, but to hasten the return of the Shekhina and her people out of exile.

Luria's teachings spread throughout the Jewish world, particularly into Russia and Eastern Europe where it influenced the Hasid movement. The Hasidim (the devout) were subject to frequent persecution but in them the living Qabala took root. They brought it firmly back from the mystical flights of medieval Spanish fantasy into the realms of everyday life. Most famous of the Hasidim was the Baal Shem Tov (1698–1760) who founded a tradition of Qabalistic wonder-working. The sufferings of the people were so great at that time, that it is no wonder that the Hasidic masters were looked upon as magicians and saviours. It is interesting to note that this same ability to work wonders was a feature of the Russian Orthodox wandering hermits, the *startsi*: their continual repetition of the Jesus Prayer, 'Lord Jesus Christ, Son of God, have mercy on me, a sinner', was in many ways similar to the recitation and permutation of the Holy Names of God performed by Qabalists. Perhaps Qabalism and remnants of northern European shamanism touched at this point? Certainly the complex systems of Qabala were brought to the people by the means of a storytelling tradition which had its roots in the Native Traditions. Rabbi Nahman of Bratislav (1772–1810) told of the Tikkun, of the creation dramas and the qualities of the sephiroth in the format of simple folk-stories. (240)

As Kaplan remarks, 'the closer one gets to the present, the less dangerous and more universal the methods of Qabalistic meditation become.' (168) The Hasid dances and sings in ecstatic oneness with God, the Lurianic Qabalist performs the mystic unifications which bring male and female aspects of God together in divine embrace, the Spanish Qabalist sits enthroned within the radiance of the Holy Names. Few aspire, in these latter days, to return to the beginnings of

Qabala, to attempt the last ascent in the Chariot of Fire to the Seventh Holy Hall where God himself sits in glory.

Jewish cabals still meet today, drawn from Orthodox or observant Jews, not Gentiles. Their work is part of the Western Way's rich heritage, presenting its face to the Inner world in order that the light of the Divine Countenance might shine more clearly upon the outer world. Their task is not unlike that of other mystics from other traditions:

> A man is born into this world with only a tiny spark of goodness in him. The spark is God, it is the soul; the rest is ugliness and evil, a shell. The spark must be guarded like a treasure, it must be nurtured, it must be fanned into flame. It must learn to seek out the other sparks, it must dominate the shell. (274)

Many Jewish Qabalists cannot comprehend Gentile or even Christian Qabalism, as it often called. (cf. chapter 3) For them, Qabala is the ultimate expression of their religion not, as for Western occultists, merely a technique. We shall be looking closer at the ways in which Qabala has passed from spiritual tradition into psycho-spiritual technique in the next chapter. Occultism has done for Qabala what psychology has done for religion. One person's mythology is another's religion, after all. Unless the reader has direct experience of a living spiritual tradition at first hand, he or she is unlikely to ever understand or even recognize the images, symbols and states which its practice entails. Those hermeticists who employ Qabalistic techniques should have more than a passing acquaintance with the tradition from which it sprang. The books of Z'ev ben Shimon Halevi (see bibliography) will give the general reader a firm background in this area, as well as providing a system of training in authentic Qabalistic method.

We wonder how often this Hebrew children's prayer has been used in other, esoteric, contexts:

> In the name of the Lord God of Israel, may Michael, the protection of God, be at my right hand; and Gabriel, the power of God, at my left; before me Uriel, the light of God; behind me Raphael, the healing of God; and above my head Shekhinat El, the presence of God. (88)

EXERCISE 3   THE TEMPLE OF INNER WISDOM

This exercise is designed to establish a temple of Inner Wisdom, a common meeting place where those of disparate traditions, or from no tradition, may meet. If 'religious loyalty is nothing else than the sincerity of our human relations with God, on the basis of the means which he puts at our disposal,' (294) then we must find and use the most skilful means. Although an accident of birth determines our cultural background, and though we may find our own tradition only after having come to maturity, there exists a companionship of the Sophia Perennis which we all partake of.

The Temple of Inner Wisdom is circular. About it are set many antechambers which give access to the central area. You will enter through one of these. The inner temple is approached through the antechamber which represents your own tradition. This will be furnished according to the appropriate symbology and correspond-ences of that tradition. It should be a place where you feel at home.

If you have no tradition, consider the many paths which have led you to where you stand today. These paths may not necessarily be traditions in themselves, but fragments or derivatives of one. Perhaps you have used a meditation technique which has been helpful, or read a book whose philosophy resonates with yours so that you have adopted it. You may have explored a symbol-system such as the Tarot or Tree of Life; you may have used techniques derived from Eastern religions, such as yoga or I-Ching. If you wish, you may make these the antechambers about the temple, but make sure you are at home there: do not attempt to work from a tradition which alienates you. Before entering the temple, make sure you compre-hend the tradition you have chosen on more than a surface level. Each of these chambers will have a guardian who is at liberty to admit you to the temple: each is a master or mistress of that tradition, so listen to their advice.

If you are still travelling towards wisdom (and when do any of us finally possess it?) or if you are totally bewildered by the multiplicity of traditions available to you, do not hesitate to enter the antecham-ber of the Amethyst Sanctuary. This is a bare, holy room in which hangs an ornate silver lamp with an eternal flame burning in a glass of amethyst-colour. Anyone may enter this place. Its only furnishing is a chair where you may meditate on the Eternal Flame. If you truly wish to enter the Temple of Inner Wisdom, you must bring something of your spiritual experience with you. One will come to you from within the temenos to talk with you and instruct you. This guardian will invite you to enter the temple from the Amethyst Sanctuary when you are fully prepared, and not before.

There are as many antechambers to the temple as there are traditions in the world. To prepare to enter the Temple from your chosen room, sit in meditation and build the antechamber about you, evoking its essential qualities, using the tools of the senses. You should, in effect, be *inhabiting* your tradition before you are allowed to draw aside the curtain which separates you from the temple. The chamber's guardian – who can appear as a religious leader, prophet, mystic or established guide along that path – you will indicate if you are fully prepared.

You draw aside the curtain. The circular hall is of vast proportions. Around it, supporting a golden central dome, are seven pillars. There are no symbols of any tradition here – these all remain in the antechambers for they are the outer semblances of an inner tradition. The sanctuary of the mysteries was an empty room, representing the imageless truth of wisdom.

In the centre of the Temple is a round table on which is a dish of bread and salt, and a cup of red wine. All who enter here must partake of this meal, or they have no place here. This bread and salt of hospitality and the wine of fellowship is served by Sophia herself. She may appear as a beautiful, crowned queen of mysterious aspect, or in other guises. It is possible that the meal will be served by invisible hands, that the meditator will see no figure at all. Yet the presence of Sophia pervades this temple, making it the meeting place of all who are engaged on the search for her gifts.

You may come here to meditate and to meet with all aspects of other traditions. Because you have eaten the bread and drunk of the wine, there is concord between all who come here. You may ask questions about aspects of traditions which trouble you or which you do not understand. Because you represent your tradition in the Temple of Inner Wisdom, do not be surprised if others ask *you* questions.

This exercise may grow in importance over the years: its effect is a cumulative one. The Temple can be used as a place of tranquillity and refreshment. You may meet other pathwalkers here, as well as guardians, saints, and mystics of many traditions. You may even sit at the round table of fellowship and partake of the counsels of Sophia.

Do not despair if you are entering by way of the Amethyst Sanctuary and you cannot seem to get an invitation within. You will enter when you are ready. The Temple is by no means for those who have reached the end of their search for Wisdom. She leads us by winding roads and those who have entered by way of one tradition may find the door temporarily closed to them if the road should lead away from it. Another door will open in time, and meanwhile there is the Amethyst Sanctuary which is always open to one who thirsts and hungers after Wisdom and her gifts.

CHAPTER 3
The Magus and his Magic

Let my lamp at midnight hour
Be seen in some high lonely tower,
Where I may oft outwatch the Bear
With thrice great Hermes.

Milton: *Il Penseroso*

The magician strives to know God's mind as it is externalized in
the Cosmic patterns.

Godwin: *Mystery Religions*

THE RETURN OF THE SHAMAN

Three magicians were attendant at the nascence of Christ. As the
Gospel of Matthew tells it:

Now when Jesus was born in Bethlehem of Judea in the days of
Herod the King, behold, wise men from the East came to
Jerusalem, saying, 'Where is he who has been born King of the
Jews? For we have seen his star in the East, and have come to
worship him . . . (St Matthew II, 1–2)

The New Testament Greek calls them 'sages' but tradition has called
them Magi almost from the start. Early Christian iconography
depicts them visiting the infant Jesus in a cave, their Phrygian caps
identifying them as Persian or possibly Mithraic priests. As we saw in
chapter 6, there are at times startling similarities between the lives of
Christ and Mithras, so that it seems appropriate that the servants of
one sacrificed god should come to the nativity of another.

Who were these first visitors to the incarnate god who recognized
his kingly and divine character in a way which the Jewish people
themselves did not? We may presume little about them, save that
they came from the east, were probably Zoroastrian or Mazdian
priests, and that they followed the courses of the stars. Traditionally,

their names were Balthazar, Melchior, and Caspar: Balthazar was of the white race of Shem, and brought the gold of incarnation; Melchior, of the black race of Ham, brought the frankincense of crucifixion; Caspar, of the yellow race of Japheth, brought the myrrh of embalming and resurrection. Each stood for a race and an art; each was an aspect of ancient wisdom, coming to pay homage to its newest manifestation. They are in at the beginning of Christianity but accorded no place in its subsequent development. Yet 'they saw the child with Mary his mother', presumably in much the same way as they would have identified statues of Isis and Horus, Cybele and Attis, and other such prefiguring archetypes, and presented with the living icon of mother and child, they fell on their knees and worshipped:

> The children of the Chaldeans saw the Virgin holding in her hands Him who with His hands fashioned mankind. Though He has taken the form of a servant, yet they knew Him as their Master. In haste they knelt before Him with their gifts and cried out to the Blessed Virgin; Hail, Mother of the Star that never sets. (191)

Who then were these men, who acknowledged Christ as their master before the start of his earthly ministry? One writer describes them as men who were 'able to understand god' and who knew 'how to minister to the divinity' (270). Both of these descriptions could be applied without alteration to the role of the shaman, with which we dealt in volume one. The magi are still priests, close enough to the gods to recognize a new avatar and to wish to act as intermediaries between divinity and mankind. They are the precursors of the magician, or perhaps we should say his ancestors, and they bear within them the seeds of his craft.

Although there is a great distance in time between the shaman and the magician, there is almost no essential difference in their respective functions. Both stand as mediators of an inner impulse to the outer world: the shaman as a public figure, the centre of his tribe's relationship to the gods; the magician as a private figure, working often in obscurity, but continuing to mediate cosmic forces to his fellow men. No longer the priest of the tribe, he is constrained into a position of isolation; he lives a hidden life which touches that of the man in the street only tangentially. He is 'neither a saint, nor a saviour, nor a prophet, nor a seer. He is a shaman-in-civilization.' (75) (fig.10)

Fig. 10   The Magus

As such the magician operates in a manner wholly different from that of his precursor: where the one had a direct line to the god or gods of his tribe, the other works with different techniques, different contacts, yet is always seeking to break through into the inner realm itself, to speak directly to God, as his ancestors had once been able to do. Thus his magic is the practical extension of a philosophical/ mystical underpinning, and without that foundation it would not exist. To look at the magician without taking into account his dream of unity, however partial or superficial, with deity, is to mistake his whole purpose.

We make the same mistake if we look at magic, or ritual, simply as an exercise in power-seeking – like examining the bodywork of a new car without bothering to look at the engine.

Magic and ritual are microcosmic expressions of the macrocosm: man's tiny torch of desire uplifted to the fire of the stars. We plug into the universe through the enactment of ritual – beginning, as we saw in volume one, with the propitiation of the elements and a desire to enter the womb of the world-mother. The Hermetic approach, as adopted by the magician, is more intellectually motivated, celestial rather than chthonic. The astrological calculations of 'star-led wizards' of Milton's *Ode on the Morning of Christ's Nativity* are a far cry from the instinctive actions of the tribal shaman – yet each in his way is motivated by the same needs and desires, only their methods have changed with the movement from tribal to individual consciousness.

There is no such thing as an archetypal magician, in any age, and to speak of his role with any certainty we are forced to generalize. If we look at some of the major figures who are classified as Magus or Wizard, we will see why this is so. We may also begin to notice certain points in common.

Let us look, for example, at Apollonius of Tyana, who flourished in the first century AD and was by some considered a god rather than a man. He was said to have been begotten by Proteus, god of the winds and patron of shape-shifters – an appropriate choice one might think, for the father of a magician – and to have possessed miraculous powers which enabled him, amongst other things to prophecy accurately the death of the Roman Emperor Domitian. He travelled extensively, performing feats which defied rational explanation, and vanished mysteriously after a long life. He frequently escaped death at the hands of the angry priesthoods of various cults with whom he came into conflict. He is also said to have visited Hades, to inquire of the god of the Underworld what was the purest philosophy then available to mankind. He emerged, five days later, with a bound copy of the precepts of Pythagoras, whose follower he afterwards became, observing a five-year vow of silence until his initiation was complete. Many of his contemporaries compared him with Christ and found him superior while others have regarded him as a figure of evil. (37) His *Letters*, which are all that remain of his once voluminous writings, are redolent with sound advice and mystical perception. To one neophyte he wrote:

> Listen well to me, my son, and I will reveal to you the mystery of wisdom, a mystery unintelligible, unknown and hidden for many, concerning the seasons and the times, the hours of day and of night, concerning their denomination and their influence and concerning the true wisdom hidden therein . . . (298)

He goes on to cite four books of his own 'more precious than golden jewelry and stones of great value' the fourth of which,

> noblest of all, contains powerful and terrible signs . . . that teach the first elements of the visible things created by God, so that he who reads this book may, if he chooses, be successful in realizing such wonders. (ibid.)

He speaks of methods of 'tying' and 'untying' the elements, through the pronouncement of the secret names of God – a method of magical practice which is fascinatingly like that of the Qabalistic magicians of a later age.

Here, then, is a magician who is able to exercise control over the different aspects of nature, and who has evolved or acquired a system with which he can relate magical activity to any hour, day, month or year. All of which, he claims, was taught him by God – an important point to which we shall return shortly.

Meanwhile, let us look at another magician-figure, somewhat more notorious than Apollonius, Simon the Magician, or as he is better known, Simon Magus.

Unlike Apollonius, whose claims he out-vaunted, Simon has come down to us as a picture of the failed magician. His famous contest with St Peter, in which he offered to take to the air like a bird to prove that Christianity was a false religion, ended in a plunge to the unyielding earth. Yet during his life Simon attracted a large following and showed himself by no means bereft of wisdom.

Having learned magic in Egypt he became the leader of a Gnostic cult after a spectacular magical battle with its former head. (37) His followers elevated him to the status of godhead, yet when his miracles were bettered by those of the disciple Philip he renounced his former beliefs for a time and was baptized a Christian. Later, however, he reneged on his conversion, when he unsuccessfully tried to purchase the power of the Holy Spirit with money. After this he became a deadly enemy of all Christians, contesting the miracles of the disciples at every turn until his fatal contest with Peter.

His innate Gnosticism can be recognized in the following passage from his writings:

> I say what I say, and I write what I write. And the writing is this. In the universal Aeons there are two schools, without beginning or end, springing from one root, which is the power of invisible, inapprehensible silence. Of those shoots one is manifest above all, which is the Great Power, the Universal Mind ordering all things, male, and the other (is manifested) from below, the Great Thought, female, producing all things. Hence pairing with each other they unite and manifest the Middle Distance, incomprehensible Air, without beginning or end. In this is the Father who sustains all things, and nourishes those things which have a beginning and an end. (133)

We can see here the basis for a whole esoteric philosophy, a schema and structure of the cosmos which spans from before time and beyond it. Invisible, inapprehensible silence is the very stuff from which all things are generated: one feels that modern philosophers like Wittgenstein and Nietzsche would have approved of the nakedness of this idea.

But does it add to our conception of the magician? Simon Magus has come down to us as at best a victim of spiritual pride, and at worst a monster of depravity and a servant of evil – and the magician has taken colour from this ever since. Yet in his works (or whoever wrote the words attributed to him) are the seeds of a philosophical vision which still informs the work of the magician. Simon's 'universal mind' placed side by side with the 'I am Mind' of the *Poimandres*, parallels the evolution of consciousness argument advanced in volume one of the present work, and shows the magician becoming aware of the primal Light.

By comparison, the magicians of the Middle Ages seem positively backward in both their spiritual and philosophical motivations. This may be due to the influence of medieval Scholasticism, which could be described as the intellectual arm of the Church in Europe, since it governed the physical extent of knowledge – in the form of books, manuscripts and documents – under its scrutiny, and impressed upon them a wholly Christian view. In this the magician had no place, although it is ironic that the conventional stereotype of the magus as a celestially cloaked individual conjuring demons into a triangle from a safe distance, really originates from this time. We must consider that these demons were, in reality, *daemons*, spiritual helpers, esoterically akin to angels, who communicated the wisdom of higher worlds. Psychologically, we might observe that magicians who resorted to such methods of conjuration, were actually recognizing and integrating those aspects of their inner selves which communed with an Otherworld reality. To teat the helpful daemon as demon was to tussle with those inner aspects of the self which were as yet unbalanced or unintegrated. Bad individual aspects were demonic, whereas good aspects polarized as angelic; the unintegrated aspects remained so, bound in the triangle of conjuration forever.

But a far greater degree of curiosity existed during the medieval era than is generally understood. Alchemy flourished, admittedly under difficult conditions, as we shall see, and scientific investigation was a powerful force to be reckoned with, despite being curtailed severely by the control of Rome. Roger Bacon (c. 1214 – c. 1292) whom many consider the archetypal magician of the age, was in reality a proto-scientist, although he by no means excluded magic from his studies, allowing it to contain at least 'some truth.' 'Yet in regard those very truths are enveloped with a number of deceits, as it's not very easie to judge betwixt the truth and the falsehood.' (37) Yet Bacon certainly studied magic from the grimoires which were then available, and wrote a treatise called *The Mirror of Alchemy*, which contains much that is still valuable. (ibid.) Indeed he seems to have taken to heart words attributed to St Jerome by another medieval writer, Gerald of Wales: 'You will find many things quite incredible and beyond the bounds of probability which are true for all that. Nature never exceeds the limits set by God who created it.' (101) In his own cautious way Bacon was more of a magician than many of his more notorious fellows. He shares with the poet Virgil the doubtful honour of being called a worker of marvels after his death, being attributed with a magic mirror which enabled him to see what was happening anywhere in the world, and with the construction of a 'Brazen Head' which would answer faithfully any question put to it. In all probability, given Bacon's far-sighted genius, this is more likely to have been the world's first computer than a magical implement, although this is not to say that we should dismiss its creator from our list of magicians. There has always been a practical, inquisitive side to magic, which Bacon's lively mind represents as well as any.

Perhaps the most famous magician of all time is himself as much a product of the Middle Ages as any of the figures we have been examining. We refer to Merlin, and in the light of his extraordinary qualities and legendary status it is perhaps not surprising if he is found to embody within him the whole range of role-changes through which the magician has passed.

Beginning life as a shamanistic figure, living in the wilds with animals for company and prophesying the life and destiny of kings, Merlin develops rapidly through a succession of metamorphoses into the mage and wonder-worker of the Arthurian cycle. Cloaked in mystery, appearing and disappearing at will, moving in and out of the stories of Arthur and his fellowship in a completely unpredictable manner, he becomes the possessor of greater and greater powers. He can assume any shape at will, call forth whole pageants of imaginary beings from the air and dismiss them with consummate ease. He is, in fact, the pre-eminent power in the land during Arthur's reign, credited with orchestrating the mysteries of the Grail and of the various quests undertaken by the Round Table knights. (331)

He is thus, first and foremost in the consciousness of many, a literary figure, though he in fact stands for a great deal more. As in inner plane reality Merlin is one of the great masters who guide the steps of those travelling the Western Way. To quote the words of a modern magician, Gareth Knight, 'The importance of Merlin is his role as a way-shower to a new phase, or epoch, of conscious evolution.' (185) More than this,

> He represents a humanized Western form of the ancient gods of learning and civilization, such as the Greek Hermes or the Egyptian Thoth. He is furthermore, one of those, akin to Melchizadek in the Old Testament, 'without father or mother, without descent'. (ibid.)

To find Merlin compared with Hermes or Thoth should not surprise us: what is interesting is that it demonstrates his dual nature as a master of both Native and Hermetic traditions. As we said in the previous volume, he is more of a god than a human being, and as such represents the magician on a higher arc of evolution – as almost a summation of all that the worker with magic seeks to become.

If Merlin is an inner resonator who generated the literature which gathered about his name, then Dr John Dee must be considered almost his outer manifestation in the real world. He is probably the single most influential aspect of the magician ever to have lived and a worthy successor to the Arthurian mage. Though his abilities have often been called into question, his influence has continued to be felt right up to the present time.

Born in 1527 Dee rose from comparative obscurity to a position of power as adviser and court astrologer to Elizabeth I. He is considered to have been the foremost mathematician of his day, travelled widely, and left an abundance of writings, diaries and notebooks which testify to his largeness of spirit, depth of occult understanding and qualities of perception. Born while Henry VIII was still on the throne, he lived on into the age of James I, five reigns and five changes of religious allegiance in that troubled age. He died finally in 1608, all but forgotten by the world which he had subtly influenced for so long. During his long life he had synthesized much that has come to be accepted as an integral part of the Hermetic Tradition: Neo-Platonism and Pythagorianism, Qabala, Alchemical and Hermetic materials were moulded into his intricate system of correspondences – of which lengthy lists of angelic beings are a clear indication. His influence on Sir Philip Sidney and his circle, whom Shakespeare refers to as 'The School of Night', was considerable, and through him may well have come the cult of the Virgin Queen which became attached to Elizabeth.

In 1598 Dee visited Heinrich Khunrath in Germany, and may well have planted the seeds of what was to become Rosicrucianism. (364) Certainly his *Monas Hieroglyphica* (65) seems to have formed a basis for the *Consideratis Brevis* and the *Confessio Fraternitatis*, while the figure of the sleeping Venus in the *Chemical Wedding* (178) reflects the way in which Elizabeth was regarded by her courtiers through Dee's influence.

Dee is, then, a prime example of the magician in the political arena, transmitting Inner impulses to the Outer world – always, as we have said, the foremost task of the magus. But though he still moved in a twilight world of mystery and wonder, his work had begun to assume cosmic dimensions. He no longer worked solely with elementals or demons, but was seen to hold converse with spiritual entities of a higher order. Within the confines of his circle Dee could, like his fellow countryman, Owen Glyndwr, call up spirits from the vast deep, but they were of another order now, and the reasons for calling them had changed as well.

It will be seen from the above preamble that it is almost impossible to categorize the magician in any satisfactory way; as a character he eludes us with continual changes of shape and action, so that a modern day magus would find it hard to model himself on any single archetype. Fortunately for those who follow the way of the magus today, they are not called upon to do so. Their training, like that of any other initiate, comes as often from within – where like as not they will find themselves in direct contact with one of the great magicians of the past in their inner plane guise. It is still possible to be overshadowed by the spiritual form of Dee, or Michael Scott, or Roger Bacon, or Giordano Bruno, each one with their own wisdom to teach, their rich store of knowledge to impart.

Though the guise of the magician may have changed through the long ages since first he stepped upon the stage in the skin robe and antlered head-dress of the shaman, his aims have remained much the same. Contemporary magicians like Gareth Knight (179, 181) and W.G. Gray (114–16), follow the same path as Apollonius or Merlin or Dee, for all that their approach and many of their techniques have changed. Each still uses symbol-laden ritual and visualative techniques to focus their inner-guided intention to a point where it becomes actualized. Like the alchemist, striving to be born into the Inner realms, (cf. chapter 5) the magician, past and present, seeks to bring to birth the Inner impulse in the Outer world, acting as both parent and midwife.

That this role is also, to some degree, shared by the mystic, the saint, and the philosopher, accounts for the difficulty we experience when we try to assign the magician to any single heading. Like the 'shaman-in-civilization' with which we began, his function has become fragmented, held together only by the esoteric philosophy which underlies so much of the Western Way. To understand why this is so, we have to look more closely at that philosophical underpinning, and how it has helped shape the magical life.

EXPANDING THE UNIVERSE

The great traditionalist philosopher René Guénon first pointed out in his book *Crisis of the Modern World* (123) that with the dawn of philosophy in the Hellenic world, there came about a division within the mysteries between exoteric and esoteric. The former came to denote a radically realistic view of nature, argued from a purely logical point of view; the latter suggested an inner spirituality which was wholly transcendent. For philosophy as an abstract discipline to survive, it became necessary to concentrate on the exoteric to the exclusion of all else – and this the first philosophers did, creating in virtually a decade a wholly different way of looking at the universe.

Of course this was not the end of the mysteries, but it did cause a shift away from their open celebration towards a protective secrecy which has cloaked the magician and his magical activities ever since. It was secrecy of a new kind from that of the Mystery School – because, although the mysteries were kept secret by their initiates, they were still accessible to all. Those who followed the road of the magician had to move in a twilight world in order to survive.

This resulted in a curious state of things in which, despite the belief that the Greeks were anti-mystical and determined on a course of pure intellectualism, many openly continued as devoted servants of the gods at the same time as they were seeking to dispute them. Plato was a mystery school initiate who was several times attacked for revealing secret doctrines in public debate. Indeed the Platonic writings are to be read as part of mystery teaching, as is evidenced by their author's continued activity as an Inner plane teacher and initiator.

In fact Plato was a disciple of Pythagoras. Although best known as a philosopher Pythagoras was himself initiated into several schools – in Egypt, Greece and Babylon – where he undoubtedly picked up the basis for his numerical theories, as well as a cosmic attitude towards matters of the spirit. He was recognized in his own life-time as an avatar of Apollo – probably the Hyperborean aspect of the god if we are to credit the significance of his meeting with the Hyperborean priest Abaris (see chapter 4). He untypically initiated Abaris into his doctrines without the customary probation of five years silence and obedience, in all probability because he recognized the similarity between his own beliefs and those of the Druids, of whom Abaris was probably an initiate. Certainly there have been frequent claims ever since that the one system influenced or reflected the other.

Pythagoras' followers lived lives of strenuous abnegation – being both vegetarian and nomadic. Their master was virtually outcast from normal society because of these tendencies – so abhorrent to the Greeks – and it is interesting to note that the eremitical traditions within Christianity can probably be traced from Pythagorean inspiration.

Certainly the Essenes followed the Pythagorean mode in their life-style – with goods in common, sun worship and numerology playing a great part. They in turn influenced the development of the Desert Fathers in Egypt and Syria, elements of which could still be discerned in modern Ethiopia until recently.

But Pythagoras would not permit his disciples to speak about his doctrines, and those who broke their vow of secrecy were publicly mourned as though dead and cenotaphs erected to their memory. Because of this many garbled notions have been attributed to the movement and much of the core of Pythagoras' teaching still remains in darkness.

That these teachings became fused and confused with Platonism is little disputed. Plato drew upon the teachings of his master and reworked their mystical direction into a more general philosophy. Both Porphory (325) and Plotinus (268) were affected, and it is still difficult to know whether they ought to be classed as Neo-Pythagoreans or Neo-Platonists. But Pythagorean beliefs continued to be practised from the sixth century BC to the sixth century AD, when the Eastern Emperor Julian closed the Platonic Academy in Athens. After this the Pythagoreans exiled themselves to Persia, where they found a welcome and the recognition of many of their own doctrines in those of the East.

But by this time Pythagoras' teachings had deeply influenced the direction of both philosophy and magic, and had helped to preserve the mysteries far beyond the point at which they might otherwise have perished.

When the great Renaissance philosopher and magician Marsilio Ficino compiled a line of descent for the masters, he put both Pythagoras and Plato firmly amongst them:

> the first was Zoroaster, the chief of the Magi; the second Hermes Trismegistus, the head of the Egyptian Priesthood; Orpheus suceeded Hermes; Aglaophamus was initiated into the sacred mysteries of Orpheus; Pythagoras was initiated into the theology of Aglaophamus and Plato by Pythagoras. Plato summed up the whole of their wisdom in his letters. (227)

This was, of course, written with hindsight, but there is little reason to quarrel with the list, and it shows clearly the inheritance of the Western magician.

Platonism effectively stood things on their heads. Instead of following the direction of the mystery schools, which made the spirit prisoner of the body, it made *everything* in this world a shadowy copy of an original elsewhere – in a spiritual realm far removed from our own. Thus, while outwardly dealing with philosophical structures, the Platonic schools really fostered an esoteric system of thought which went straight back to mystery school teaching. Thus in Plato's 'Myth of Er' (266), as in Cicero's 'Dream of Scipio' (71) later on, the seeds of the greater mysteries were preserved. When Christianity was in the process of formulating its own doctrines, 'it denounced Platonism even as it confessed doctrines that it could not have formulated . . . without the illumination of Plato, thus speaking the language of Zion but with the unmistakable accents of the Academy'. (257)

Plotinus, Plato's chief disciple, forged the links with the magical teachings of the mystery schools even more solidly.

The primary purpose of his teaching was to lead men (those few who were capable of it) back to awareness of and eventual union with the source from which they and all things came – the 'One or Good, which in giving them being gave also the impulse to return'. (336)

Thus Plotinus came to see matter as a principle of evil because it was an absolute limit, the utter negativity and deficiency of being which marks the end of the descent from the Good through successive levels of reality. Yet he found the material universe good and beautiful as a living structure of forms and the best possible work of the Soul – unlike the Gnostic view of matter which he so utterly detested – and he sought ever more deeply to perceive the true nature of the puzzling world about him.

Thus Plotinus' system of Neo-Platonism connects both with magic and science, as well as philosophy, and relates all three to their most ancient roots. Born of humanity's striving to know about its origins, it parallels Christian theology sufficiently to be acceptable to later generations of thinkers as well as those following the inner way.

As we have already seen in chapter 6, there is little point in seeking the origins of Hermeticism. One can, indeed, look to Egypt for much of the material, and perhaps beyond catch glimpses of Chaldea. One can, as a recent commentator suggests, believe that the whole thing is a cultural projection of the Ptolomaic dynasty! (22). But in reality the nearest one can come to the beginning of the Hermetic impulse, and through it of magic, is the period when Christianity was establishing itself, both politically and sacerdotally, in the Roman world.

Here, in the seed-bed of the Graeco-Roman synthesis, as inheritors of Platonic wisdom and Pythagorean understanding, came into being not only what we now think of as the Hermetic mysteries, but Gnosticism and Alchemy also.

The climate of the times being largely unwelcoming for any such thing, the Hermetic mysteries went underground, assuming a desert burnouse under Islam – a cross-fertilization which was, some thousand years later, to return full circle to the West in the medieval mysteries of Alchemy, the Grail and Natural Magic. In this space of time Hermeticism gathered to itself not only the philosophies of Plato and Plotinus, but also the esoteric teachings of the Sufis, combining in a vast hotch-potch of mystical lore, magical system and esoteric philosophy, a brew of East-West mysteries.

Yet when Hermeticism returned to Europe, the reaction was at first one of shocked surprise, turning fast to hatred, at what was seen as a foreign invasion. Those who sought to oppress the Hermetic revival never realized that what they saw advancing towards them was an old and familiar figure, who had left their part of the world long ago and now returned wearing strange garments.

Magic was continually being redefined: in religious terms, as science, and as philosophy. Each person who took up the fragments of the magically-oriented past, impressed their own synthesis upon it, so that during the period referred to above magic went from a religious discipline to a philosophy, both of which approaches it continues to share. The figure of the magician, as we have seen, changed with it, mutating through several guises until what is presently understood by the name bears little or no relation to its origins. Strangely, because it was the age when all magical activity was likely to earn the ultimate penalty for those who were found to be practising it, it is the medieval image which has remained most firmly fixed in the consciousness. This strange figure, shambling through the darker pages of history with his robe of stars (actually a left-over from the Persian magi) his pointed hat and thick lenses (symbol of his proto-scientific attitude) is still a viable image. Yet it is figures like Roger Bacon who typify the medieval magician as he really was: scholar, cleric, seeker, probably in minor orders of the Church (the only way he could obtain the books he needed) and who are the real inheritors of the Classical tradition and the philosophies of Pythagoras and the Platonists.

In fact, the medieval magus would have been able to understand very little of the original matter of the mysteries; few remained in the West who could read the texts, or who, for that matter, even knew of their existence. Yet the 'hidden words' of Hermes did survive: fragments continued to filter through until, at the height of the Renaissance, the trickle became a flood. How this came about is a fascinating story in itself, though one which we can only touch upon here.

It is really due to the scholarship and devotion of one man, Michael Psellus (1018–78/9) who collected and codified many of the Hermetic texts, as well as those of Plato, Plotinus etc, that we still have their legacy today. As it was, the *Corpus Hermeticum* had to wait until 1463 before it found a translator, in the person of the great Renaissance philosopher and natural-magician Marsilio Ficino, who worked on the huge collection of manuscripts at the behest of his patron Cosimo di Medici. Significantly, Ficino was required to translate these before the works of Plato, because it was believed that the Hermetic texts originated in Egypt, which then, as in more recent times among the esoteric fraternities, was considered of far greater interest than Classical and neo-Classical Greece.

With the publication of the *Corpus Hermeticum* the Western world was once more tentatively in touch with the mysteries. We say tentatively, because the Renaissance Hermeticist had only texts, not living traditions, with which to perform his revival. He had to grope painfully towards an understanding of what had once been clearly comprehended and practised by the mystery-initiate, by means of translations of translations, pied scripts and tattered Classical references. It was a task of unimaginable difficulty, yet the Renaissance Hermeticist was equal to the task in enthusiasm if not in a full comprehension of its complexity.

The form of Hermetic gnosticism propounded by Ficino and his like really dates from Hellenic Egypt and not, as was generally held to be the case, from the time of the Pharoahs. But this misunderstanding enabled a kind of reconciliation between post-Christian and pre-Christian lore, giving the Renaissance thinkers an excuse to delve deeper. Thus a mistake in chronology permitted a new renaissance of magic to blossom and provided the foundation upon which the French magical revival of the eighteenth century could build. In this time, once again mistakenly, the literature of the earliest times was related to Biblical sources.

It is easy, with scholarly hindsight and in full possession of good translations, to condemn the medieval magician and the Renaissance investigator with their ragbag of Judaic and Babylonian spells and second-hand grimoires purloined from wandering Arab astrologers. But we forget the length of time and the cultural lacunae which lie between them and the richly syncretic mysteries of Classical Alexandria. In some ways the Renaissance Italy of Ficino and Pico della Mirandola reassembled Alexandria or the Greek Academy with more accuracy than the deeply-dyed ignorance prevailing in the rest of Europe.

In late medieval Europe the end-game of native spirituality and magic was being played out with the pieces of dynastic greed and clerical exactitude. Just as in the Chessboard Castle of Chrétien de Troyes' *Conte du Graal* (47), fantastic pieces were moving of their own volition across a landscape whose interior focus was forever shifting away from the shining turrets and splendid pavilions to a new Hermetic vision. The medieval blindfold was off and other rosy-coloured spectacles were donned in its place. (150)

The Renaissance produced many factors which brought about the death of the spiritual life of the Middle Ages. As Guénon has rightly pointed out, (123) the adoption of neo-Classicism only fostered that part of the Hellenic and Egyptian mysteries which had already been externalized sufficiently to make them acceptable and also less pure than in their original state. The loss was immeasurable and it meant that the Hermetic systems were from the start founded on insecure ground. They had lost touch with their original spark, and every step they took which was away from that point brought about a narrowing which excluded more and more of their old power. Even Renaissance adepts like Ficino, Bruno, Dee, or Francis Bacon, succeeded only partially in reconstructing the sources of their own speculations, and in disseminating some of their realizations into their own blend of Hermeticism. Perhaps they were too cautious; but their efforts became the foundation of modern Western esotericism, just as Hermeticism became, through them, part of the Renaissance as surely as it is a product of medieval and pre-medieval magic and religion.

Pagan, Christian, and Hermetic leftovers bobbed in the same melting pot. It was possible to revision archetypes, long outlawed except as educational paradigms, in the persons of the classical gods. Ficino, who was a Christian priest as well as a natural magician, wrote and sang hymns to Apollo; Bruno couched his philosophical speculations about the origin of the cosmos in dialogues between Jupiter and Mercury (33). Classical subjects began to replace the ubiquitous Christian Nativities and Depositions from the Cross; new passions and new nativities were depicted – The Flaying of Marsyas or the foam-born Aphrodite of Botticelli. Primavera decked in the garb of long-awaited Spring stepped from Attic to Tuscan forests. Everywhere the Classical heritage pervaded like the scent of crushed rosemary.

Here, the mysteries were secularized. The great thinkers and natural magicians were first and foremost Christian: other options were scarcely open to them. Yet here also were the old traditions: of Greece, Egypt, Persia. Their beliefs could not easily be discounted. And so there began slowly to emerge a new form of system *based* on the ancient mysteries, but seen as taking place within the framework of God's law. To be sure these were seen as heretical at the time – but those who practised them saw them differently. To them the deities were spirits of the air, angelic beings created, like humanity, to serve God and creation. Thus, while they became Christianized to a degree they lost none of their energy; they escaped being reduced to the fundamental levels reached, for example, by the 'mythology' of Christianity today. They kept their potency, but under a new guise.

Into this world stepped the figure of the Magician, fully fledged it seemed, escaped like Merlin from his hawthorn tower after a sleep of centuries. The riches of this heritage were as intoxicating as wine.

Hermetic texts, Qabalistic translations, scientific experimentation, the possibility of new interiors. Utopias: the City of the Sun, New Atlantis, ran from the urgent pens of Thomas More, Campanilla, and Francis Bacon, each one the vision of a perfect world, the product of a desire to have the microcosm reflect the macrocosm as perfectly as possible.

The Renaissance magician must often have wondered how really close to perdition he had been during the intervening centuries when esoteric pursuits of any kind had earned their inevitable stigma. Like the court Kapellemeister, whose music was sung at the mass, but who was expected to eat in the kitchen and enter by the back premises, the magician had been in his esoteric hutch ... a tame shaman to be chained in the King's cellars, a coiner of gold pieces, a demonic mascot against divine disfavour – sometimes pandering to the superstitious needs of the people, at others sailing among the stars with gods and angels at his side.

The gift of literacy, imbibed from the great medieval universities, was no longer solely in the hands of clerical academics. Had Roger Bacon still been living, he might have thrown off his Dominican habit and joined the throngs of alchemists and proto-scientists who not only loved God's but nature's mysteries also.

The Hermetic revival broke upon the world and woke it from sleep. Europe's gain was Byzantium's loss. The capture of Constantinople by the Turks in 1453 saw the dispersal of the Eastern Empire's wealth and learning: yet from this disaster the Hermetic texts were able to reappear in Europe, and while the *Corpus Hermeticum* had its effect on the esoteric revival, another tradition was suddenly made available to the West via the expedient of the Jewish expulsion from Spain in 1492 – the Qabala. The Qabala has altered the face of western esotericism and been central to the practice of ritual magic since the Renaissance, providing a fresh angelology, a language of exact macrocosmic correspondence and a ritual framework which has become the norm ever since.

As we have seen, Spain was the cradle of European Qabala. It fostered the great exponents such as Abraham Abulafia and Moses of Leon. It is often thought that Qabala was unknown among Gentiles until the Renaissance, but there is clear evidence that the Catalan philosopher, Ramon Lull (c. 1232–1316), was aware of its teachings to some degree. Lull was born one year before the publication of the *Zohar* – the major source for Spanish Qabala – and was contemporaneous with Abulafia, whose permutations of the Hebrew

alphabet Lull in some measure imitates within his own system.
The *Ars Raymundi*, as it was known to later esotericists, was a
system of astral science, based on the Aristotelian elemental categories; it also combined the divine epithets (as they appear on the Tree of
Life (fig 9) as they could be applied to all aspects of life from the
mineral kingdom, right up the angelic hierarchies and beyond. Lull's
aim was to provide a system which would harmonize all religions.
He himself learned Arabic and saw his system as part of a missionary
effort to convert Jews and Moslems. He was eventually martyred in
Northern Africa.

Yet Lull's influence was considerable. Giovanni Pico della Mirandola (1463–94) who moved in the circle of the Medici court at the
height of the Hermetic revival, recognized Lullism as a proto-
Qabalist system. Pico had some knowledge of Hebrew and was able,
prior to the Jewish expulsion from Spain, to obtain Qabalistic
manuscripts which he translated and used as the foundation for his
Conclusions by which he intended to confirm the Christian religion
by means of Hebrew wisdom. These Conclusions were also drawn
from other esoteric sources, notably Platonic, and neo-platonic
texts, Orphic hymns and Chaldean oracles. Pico's philosophy is in
many ways a restatement of Lull, but instead of going among
Moslems and Jews to prove the truth of Christianity, he went to
Rome in order to show how Christianity is a natural successor to
these concepts. He was forced to make a formal apology in 1487 for
his conclusions, such was the furore that broke out over him. (364)
In his apology, Pico divided Qabala into two parts: the *ars com-
binandi* or the method of permuting Hebrew letters, and 'a way of
capturing the powers of superior things', – the powers of angels and
spirits. This was undoubtedly a magical rather than a theological
conclusion! It is Pico who was responsible for assigning planetary
ascriptions to each of the sephiroth, which leads the aspirant from
the mineral and elemental kingdoms through to the planetary,
angelic and divine realms which form the four worlds of the Jewish
Qabala. In imitation of Lull's ambition to combine and reconcile the
divided faiths, he was the first to make the link which welded Qabala
to Christianity inexorably, sought to prove that by the addition of
one letter, the Tetragrammaton – the Most Holy Name of God
which is always left unpronounced by pious Jews, and is always
substituted by a euphemism such as Adonai, Lord – could be turned
into the Name of Jesus. The Tetragammaton is composed of four
letters: Yod He Vav He or Yahweh. By the addition of a finial Shin,

YHVH becomes YHSHVH or Yeheshuah, Jesus. Such sloppy Christian gematra may seem insignificant in our day, but the effect of this conclusion was to have a widespread effect throughout Europe.

The synthesis began here. In the meantime, the Jewish expulsion from Spain meant the resettlement of Jews throughout Europe; a fresh meeting of minds such as took place in Alexandria occurred. Qabalistic manuscripts were discussed and translated. Johannes Reuchlin (1455–1522), a scholar of the German Renaissance, published his *De Verbo Mirifico* in 1494: following Pico's ideas, Reuchlin gives us a Platonic dialogue in which a Jew, a Greek and a Christian discuss the Qabalistic 'proof' of Jesus as Messiah. Other books followed this. The Franciscan, Francesco Giorgi (1466–1540), working from Venice, fully synthesized Qabala into Christianity, adding the neo-Platonic and Hermetic elements for good measure as part of a gnostic Christian system. (364)

Finally, Henry Cornelius Agrippa (1486–1535) brought Qabala into the form in which it is best known today – as a magical system. His *De Occulta Philosophia* (1533) presents a universe divided into three worlds: the elemental, celestial and intellectual worlds. This division naturally falls into a discussion of natural magic, celestial magic (following Ficino's model) and ceremonial magic which aims to influence the angelic world by means of Qabalistic magic.

Thus a Judaic mystical system became at one stroke the basis of a Christian gnosis and of a magical system. Qabala remains the lingua-franca of Western esotericism, although one which inevitably has its dialects of dissension. Thus Lull's vision of a reconciled and harmonized microcosm is partially fulfilled, in the way in which Gentile Qabala has evolved. It is ironic that Christianity, having rejected its own esoteric tradition, should have taken over and developed the esoteric system of a religion to which it owed its own existence! Yet, though the fathers of Jewish Qabala might quail at the thought of Christian Qabala, we see once more the subtle spread of esoteric concepts whose mysteries live to seed new traditions with old wisdom. The words of Isaac Luria still hold good for those who study Qabala, Jewish or Gentile.

for every handsbreadth (of the mysteries) I reveal, I will hide a mile. With great difficulty, I will open the gates of holiness, making an opening like the eye of a needle, and let him who is worthy pass through it to enter the innermost chamber. (167)

The esoteric way is still a narrow one. Those who find their way easily and their passage unobstructed are likely to be travelling away from, not towards, the mysteries.

Unfortunately, there are no ethical standards approved by occult examining boards to which the aspirant can appeal. Those who dismiss the whole esoteric world as evil and misguided are fearful because of this very lack: nor should the esotericist be complacent on this score. If you have no teacher, no tradition behind you how can you be sure that your work is truly aligned with the Will of God, however you understand that term? As we have seen, such mystery and training schools as still exist often have extremely rigid standards to which students must adhere or leave. The same problems are now facing the medical world with the many practitioners of alternative therapies setting up in business. Some therapies as yet have no authorized body to ensure standards. The field is wide open to charlatans as well as to bone-fide practitioners who genuinely heal their patients.

While there is no 'Hippocratic oath' for esotericists, there is a tacit agreement upon standards between genuine practitioners of the magical arts. This may appear to outsiders as a kind of 'honour among thieves' arrangement. But the problem stands: the Western Way has become so fragmented, so distrustful of itself, that unless a more open and trustful exchange is arrived at soon, many important traditions will founder. We do not suggest that a central agency *should* be set up to arbitrate on such matters, but that we should always have recourse to the Inner, which is our only common ground, should we stand in need of verification.

THE DIVINE CHARIOT

Magic in the West has a long and sometimes ignoble history. This is partly due to the development of Christianity in the West which has excluded many practices fundamental to all religions in its simplification of local customs. All religion is a formalization of disparate beliefs: so is prayer the formalization of magic.

In his role as mediator the magician embodies the answer to this problem by becoming a co-worker in the progressive state of the cosmos – which should never be thought of as static or complete. Through ritual the inner impulse becomes externalized; the magician becomes the representative both of humanity and the orders of creation: his magic a visualized prayer technique. When it works, we can presume that dedication and commitment to the world's good bears it up. But magic is not foolproof – not the answer to every ill or want – as some think who rush into its practice without knowledge or understanding. It will not work on request, any more than prayer for a million pounds or miraculous healing necessarily works for a Christian. It will not turn aside the tide of events any more than lighting a candle will stop an earthquake.

Magicians, like believers, are not saints nor do they have super-human resources: they fail of their high purpose as do other human beings. Yet, while it is allowable for an ordinary mortal to fail, this is not allowed, it would seem, of the magician. If mediation is seriously considered, if either the ritual which bodies it forth or the mediation falls short of its purpose, then the consequences are serious. If this is due to some personal imbalance or pride, then the life of the operator will suffer.

In fact it is an occult truism that if the magic performed is not in accordance with God's will then the work will rebound on the sender; some say, threefold. Similarly we may pray God to send us a thousand pounds, and it may be that we get the money in terms of insurance after a seriously debilitating accident. We should be careful what we wish for, in all instances, for we will surely get it.

But the ethics of magic are nowhere clearly drawn: like other social understandings and rule-of-thumb moralities, magic has its own rules which need to be discovered by each individual experientially. The principle of operation is that no one is harmed – that nothing is unbalanced by the activity of the magician. Ahead is the beacon of the Great Work, the completion of a creative microcosm which perfectly mirrors the macrocosm of the Almighty.

> No magician could progress very far in his search for knowledge without coming to the point in which he realizes, at least tacitly, the unity of all things, and that realization nurtures compassion. Even the use of an effigy is a tacit recognition that the one is connected intimately with the other regardless of the vastness of time and space. (341)

The signature recognizable in everything, makes all matter interactive, in turn promoting the understanding that whatever is done has repercussions for the rest of creation. (ibid.) Compassion must inform the magician's work or it will be as naught. As St Paul says:

> If I speak in the tongues of men and angels, but

have not love, I am a noisy gong or a clanging cymbal.
And if I have prophetic powers, and understand all
mysteries and all knowledge, and if I have all faith,
so as to move mountains, but have not love, I am nothing.
(Corinthians I: 13)

Magic is not an exact science. The effects of working magically are subjective, like any art – clay holds within it many shapes, and words have a way of putting themselves together quite differently to the writer's original intention. Yet magic, like the science of engineering, can be used to build bridges and convey loads which would be impossible in terms of physical laws. The magician is himself a bridge between upper and lower realms. When he stands within the circle of the lodge or temple he steps outside time, to become a mote of dust in the light emanating from God. A mote which, nevertheless, has a causal effect vastly beyond his normal, human ability. Here, ritual becomes an enactment of inner reality in symbolic form. However the symbolism is transmitted, a direct link is formed with the Inner realms. How this happens we may see from the following paradigm:

When a sudden outrush of power from the Inner is experienced in the Outer, this may be picked up and interpreted differently by different people.

a) a magician will perceive this particular inrush as an Inner purgation which will have its effect on the Outer. He creates a ritual which will help syphon through the energy, in co-operation with God's will. His life will be made intolerable until this action is performed.

b) a seer/medium will receive the power and imagise it. A purgation of this type will often appear to the seer with disturbing clarity (cf. Jung's dream of the 1st World War).

c) a mystic will perceive God's Will – the forces of creation working to fulfil a divine purpose. Prayers for harmony within the universe will result, a greater unity with the will of God be sought for.

d) a poet will pick up the energy and transform it into verse, an artist will capture it on canvas or in a bronze cast, composers will introduce new harmonies into their instrumentation: all will seek ultimately to trace the energy to its source.

e) in countries and social groups the response will be less cohesive; if the force is purgative, as in this instance, civil unrest may be felt, wars or disturbances break out, until the inner force loses its cyclonic energy.

f) People may instinctively register the force which is communicating itself in ordinary Outer ways. Peace-movements will be strengthened or criminal activity increase; police vigilance will be prominent.

This is, of course, only a projected paradigm. The Inner forces can and do manifest in many other ways and are received and interpreted differently according to their strength and origin as well as those who feel their effect. When Inner forces of this kind are at work, all one can do is co-operate, help them pass, perhaps even feel their beneficent qualities.

Purgation is a mighty and terrible thing – but it is not evil in itself. The Inner activity is more often than not of a creative nature which will contribute a fresh impulse and vitality, helpful to all. Those who look for the Will of God in such cases, need not passively resign themselves to do nothing but rather actively take up their appointed tasks as they best can.

'For each of those who is allotted a place in the Divine Order finds his perfection in being uplifted, according to his capacity, towards the Divine Likeness; and what is still more divine, he becomes, as the Scriptures say, *a fellow-worker with God* and shows forth the Divine Activity revealed as far as possible in himself.' (70, our italics)

We are, in this, doing what all followers of the Western Way must do in the end – putting our interests aside to become workers in the great force of creation.

It is a theme we should be familiar with by now: the divine spark seeing its identity within the greater whole, the mystic seeking union with God.

The magician, then, places himself as close to the heart of creation as he can in order to work from and with it. He seeks to realize his potential within the framework of matter – becoming a priest in order to carry forward the work of the Inner realms, the Will of God. To be a magician is to be artificer, artist and priest in one. It is a noble art.

However, lest the foregoing picture should seem too attractive, let it also be said that the life of a magician is neither easy nor soft.

William G. Gray once remarked that there are no handouts in magic, only earnings collected when they fall due. This is as true today as it ever was, and is one of the first things we ought to remember before embarking on any esoteric work. It was the first precept of the magicians of the past, and to the degree which they either accepted or denied it were their work and lives full or empty, beneficial or harmful.

Magicians, are people too, and have ordinary lives, jobs and families. While they may be aware of other laws operative within these ordinary lives, they seldom or never engage in the kind of role-playing games described in occult pulp-fiction. Certain adepts who specialize in the kind of psychic first-aid work described by Dion Fortune in her Doctor Taverner stories (95) seem to bear out this fantastic image of the magician, yet there are few who regularly engage in this kind of work. It is specialist and responsible work dealing with the genuine disorders brought about through psychic imbalance, and is best dealt with by the adept who is experienced on multi-levels of reality, who is big enough to take the knocks which inevitably occur.

While on the subject of psychic attack it should be noted that the student is rarely aware of or troubled by such phenomena. It is a form of egoism to imagine that those responsible for sending out negative energies would be bothered with a mere minnow when the intended catch is a salmon. The worst a neophyte is likely to encounter are his or her own imbalances and their equilibration. Certain common-sense measures are always to be observed in esoteric work: seal off your aura, demark your psychic activities by clear opening and closing signs, keep alert on whatever level you operate, use your clan totem (see Vol I) as a shield. Murray Hope's excellent book on psychic self-defence (148) gives many practical means of coping with life in this seemingly unmapped area, while Dion Fortune's *Psychic Self Defence* has seldom been bettered.

The magical life is lived through the seasonal rituals which govern the tides of the year: the spring tide which runs from the Spring equinox and governs the tide of growth and inception of new projects or ideas; the summer tide, which runs from the Summer solstice and is concerned with consolidation and active working; the autumn tide of harvest, running from the Autumn equinox, when projects are brought into fruition and or maturity; and the winter tide of dissolution which runs from the Winter solstice wherein stale ideas and projects are cleared out.

Also to be taken into account are the monthly cycle of the moon, the weekly progression of the days, and the hourly microcosm of the day from dawn to noon, twilight to midnight. These minor cycles have the planetary and zodiacal patterns superimposed upon them, and all are recognized by the magician, who makes them a part of his inner and outer life. (182) He will take into account also, looking over periods of cosmic time, the greater pattern of the aeons – as in the Piscean and Aquarian ages which meet and change the flow of activity during our own lifetimes. Of course, it is by no means easy to correlate all these factors – hence the need for stringent training beforehand. Even the adept will find it difficult at times to adjust to these many combinations, but all ritual magic is at base a method of relating higher to lower, celestial to chthnoic, divine to temporal. The complex systems of inter-related powers taught by the mystery schools, the detailed tables of correspondences to be found in the grimoires of the Middle Ages and the Renaissance, and the techniques of Qabalistic training, all aim at the same target.

Thus the work of the magician is organized around great cyclic events which occur outside space and time: the recurring patterns which are the balancing act of the cosmos. They nova in his year, just as they feature in the dreams of the sensitive, and are reflected mundanely in the outer world. The magician may formulate these events into rituals in which the seasons and elements and the positions of the stars become an expression in the outer world of an inner reality, a sacramental encounter between the desires of humanity and the power and might of God.

Yet we must be careful of seeing the powers of creation as merely symbolic tools to work with but which have no ultimate reality. It is possible to evolve a theory of archetypes every bit as complex as anything to be found in the *Corpus Hermeticum*, but these are useless unless informed with practical application and realization. A grimoire is useless to someone who fails to understand its correspondences as keys to a larger reality. The would-be magician must learn to draw down the elemental powers into his own sphere of working, just as he must also elevate his human understanding to the point where he can appreciate the mysteries of creation and the presence of the divine principle within it.

Magic is the higher understanding of nature, a true vision of the universe as it whirls and roars around us. From ritual to Renaissance to the modern occult revival this has been the heart and centre of magical work. From the tribal shaman to the present day magus their work has arisen out of a fundamental belief in an ordered cosmos, that we are not simply born into the world for the sole purpose of providing amusement for some distant god or gods, nourishment for the soil, or blind animal existence. Rather, we should become part of the universal process of becoming.

> You must understand that this is the first path to felicity . . . the . . . theurgic gift . . . is called indeed the gate to the Demiurge of Wholes. . . . It possesses a power of purifying the soul and . . . produces a union with the gods . . . givers of every good. (152)

Magic as a branch of Hermeticism does not seem to concern itself with saving the soul. To the outsider it seems merely a way, a technique, a methodology. But to participate in magic is to be wound into the fabric of creation as a co-worker, to be purged and purified and made whole. This is to do the will of God in one's own life: it means living close to the wind, ready at all times to veer where it lists.

The qualifications of magical work such as we have discussed here should be written up large over the temple door of every individual who thinks they are ready to follow the life of the magician. Such a prescription might read: A sense of ritual, a sense of humour and common sense. With these three there is not far that you can go wrong.

Brethren should meet in harmony and depart in peace and silence, but this is not always the case. It is not often understood that the magical life imposes subtle pressures which can turn reasonable and pleasant people into aggressive and nit-picking individuals. Under pressure, human nature will out, and ritual work is highly pressured. It is the duty of the magister of the lodge to ensure this is understood and, if necessary, point this out to those concerned. Some ritual work can be quite disturbing, even to the experienced magician: if the quarter officers are mediating their roles properly, the risk of emotional aberration is substantially reduced among those participating. Minor irritations with fellow ritualists can grow from molehills into mountains very quickly, especially when the ritual has exaggerated any personal imbalance. These emotional re-actions are usually quick to pass: if everyone remains objective about it, seeing it as a concomitant of the ritual, then there is no harm.

In a magical order each candidate is scrutinized and required to complete a questionnaire concerning their intentions and present mode of life. The imbalanced, the discontent, the ego-maniac, the depressed, the unhealthy, are all excluded for their own good. In magic, only the best is good enough – anything less than total commitment is a waste of energy and time. The dilettante approach to magic, instanced by many would-be Aleister Crowleys, is no better than Sabbath Christianity.

This may read strangely to those who consider magic as only black. Surely all this talk of 'world service' (20) and 'dedication' is merely a screen covering some ultimately evil intention? Despite what the papers say, this is not so. We have tried to show how throughout this book. But, just as there are unbalanced individuals in all walks of life, so there are in magical areas. These people are news, bad news. We must bear in mind that:

> Theurgy, or high magic, is the raising of consciousness to the appreciation of the powers and forces behind the external world in a pious intention of developing spiritual awareness and subsequently helping to bring to birth the divine plan of a restored earth. Thaumaturgy, or low magic . . . is the production of wonders by the use of little known powers of the mind. (180)

It was all summed up, long ago, by the Roman historian Dio Chrysostom, when he wrote that 'the magi . . . hold that the universe is steadily being drawn along a single road by a charioteer who is gifted with the greatest skill and power.' (227). The Magician does not seek to *become* the charioteer, only to prevent the chariot from running away with him and those of his fellows who journey at his side. The magical life is not usually commenced under the age of thirty, since the twenties are a time when the mundane life is being established as regards education and the beginning of a family. Responsibility is primarily to the family life – the path of the hearth-fire. When children are grown or sufficiently fledged to fend for themselves, the magical life can begin in earnest.

Such strictures do not normally apply within the Native Tradition, since its ways can be upheld and studied within the family unit very easily since they derive from tribal consciousness. The Hermetic Tradition imposes rather more rigorous standards on its followers. The way of involution must be followed until the candidate stands at the initiatory gates of life and starts the way of return on the evolutionary path. (184)

Yet magic is returning on all fronts in our own time – not always purely Hermetic or Native in its approach, but a mixture of old and new. The return of the magician is also the return of the shaman, and

Fig 11. Isis, as described in Apuleius' Golden Ass *from Athan
Sius Kircher's* Oedipus Aegyptiacus *c1652*

'shamanism is being reinvented in the West precisely because it is
needed' (135). Its techniques, as well as those of the Hermetically-
trained magus, point the way to the inner worlds, from where the
long climb begins to the highest expression of both traditions: the
mysteries and techniques of alchemy.

EXERCISE 4 THE HERMETIC WAY

The two texts which follow have been set aside from the main body
of the book both to emphasize their importance and to enable them
to be used as subjects for meditation. As a form of exercise which will
illuminate much that has been discussed in earlier chapters, and
which will prepare the way for succeeding exercises and techniques,
it is suggested that they be read with attention over a period of two

weeks, taking sections or sentences from each in turn and meditating upon them. Write down whatever realization comes to you. This should enable you to build up your own commentary on the Emerald Tablet and the extract from the *Corpus Hermeticum*. At the end of this period you might wish to engage upon a longer meditation (generally periods of from twenty to thirty minutes are sufficient) incorporating material from both texts and from your own notes. This should be seen as the beginning of a prolonged study and extended working with the Hermetic texts in general, which may become the framework for a lifetime's activity as well as deepening the awareness of the mysteries set forth in the remainder of this book.

The Emerald Tablet of Hermes Trismegistos

1   IN TRUTH CERTAINLY AND WITHOUT DOUBT, WHATEVER IS BELOW IS LIKE THAT WHICH IS ABOVE, AND WHATEVER IS ABOVE IS LIKE THAT WHICH IS BELOW, TO ACCOMPLISH THE MIRACLES OF ONE THING.

2   JUST AS ALL THINGS PROCEED FROM ONE ALONE BY MEDITATION ON ONE ALONE, SO ALSO THEY ARE BORN FROM THIS ONE THING BY ADAPTATION.

3   ITS FATHER IS THE SUN AND ITS MOTHER IS THE MOON. THE WIND HAS BORN IT IN ITS BODY. ITS NURSE IS THE EARTH.

4   IT IS THE FATHER OF EVERY MIRACULOUS WORK IN THE WHOLE WORLD.

5   ITS POWER IS PERFECT IF IT IS CONVERTED INTO EARTH.

6   SEPARATE THE EARTH FROM THE FIRE AND THE SUBTLE FROM THE GROSS, SOFTLY AND WITH GREAT PRUDENCE.

7   IT RISES FROM EARTH TO HEAVEN AND COMES DOWN AGAIN FROM HEAVEN TO EARTH, AND THUS ACQUIRES THE POWER OF THE REALITIES BELOW. IN THIS WAY YOU WILL ACQUIRE THE GLORY OF THE WHOLE WORLD, AND ALL DARKNESS WILL LEAVE YOU.

8   THIS IS THE POWER OF ALL POWERS, FOR IT CONQUERS EVERYTHING SUBTLE AND PENETRATES EVERYTHING SOLID.

9   THUS THE LITTLE WORLD IS CREATED ACCORDING TO THE PROTOTYPE OF THE GREAT WORLD.

10   FROM THIS AND IN THIS WAY, MARVELLOUS AP-
PLICATIONS ARE MADE.
11   FOR THIS REASON I AM CALLED HERMES TRISME-
GISTOS, FOR I POSSESS THE THREE PARTS OF WISDOM OF
THE WHOLE WORLD.
12   PERFECT IS WHAT I HAVE SAID OF THE WORK OF
THE SUN.

The Teaching of Hermes

IF THEN YOU DO NOT MAKE YOURSELF EQUAL TO
GOD, YOU CANNOT APPREHEND GOD; FOR LIKE IS
KNOWN BY LIKE. LEAP CLEAR OF ALL THAT IS COR-
POREAL, AND MAKE YOURSELF GROW TO A LIKE EX-
PANSE WITH THAT GREATNESS WHICH IS BEYOND
ALL MEASURE; RISE UP ABOVE ALL TIME, AND BE-
COME ETERNAL; THEN YOU WILL APPREHEND GOD.
THINK THAT FOR YOU TOO NOTHING IS IMPOSSIBLE;
DEEM THAT YOU TOO ARE IMMORTAL, AND THAT
YOU ARE ABLE TO GRASP ALL THINGS IN YOUR
THOUGHT, TO KNOW EVERY CRAFT AND EVERY SCI-
ENCE; FIND YOURSELF HOME IN THE HAUNTS OF
EVERY LIVING CREATURE; MAKE YOURSELF HIGHER
THAN ALL HEIGHTS, AND LOWER THAN ALL DEPTHS;
BRING TOGETHER IN YOURSELF ALL OPPOSITES OF
QUALITY, HEAT AND COLD, DRYNESS AND FLUIDITY;
THINK THAT YOU ARE EVERYWHERE AT ONCE, ON
LAND, AT SEA, IN HEAVEN; THINK THAT YOU ARE NOT
YET BEGOTTEN, THAT YOU ARE IN THE WOMB, THAT
YOU ARE YOUNG, THAT YOU ARE OLD, THAT YOU
HAVE DIED, THAT YOU ARE IN THE WORLD BEYOND
THE GRAVE: GRASP IN YOUR THOUGHT ALL THIS AT
ONCE, ALL TIMES AND PLACES, ALL SUBSTANCES AND
QUALITIES AND MAGNITUDES TOGETHER; THEN YOU
CAN APPREHEND GOD. BUT IF YOU SHUT UP YOUR
SOUL IN YOUR BODY, AND ABASE YOURSELF, AND
SAY, 'I KNOW NOTHING, I CAN DO NOTHING, I AM
AFRAID OF EARTH AND SEA, I CANNOT MOUNT TO
HEAVEN; I DO NOT KNOW WHAT I WAS, NOR WHAT I
SHALL BE'; THEN, WHAT HAVE YOU TO DO WITH
GOD? YOUR THOUGHT CAN GRASP NOTHING

BEAUTIFUL AND GOOD, IF YOU CLEAVE TO THE BODY,
AND ARE EVIL. FOR IT IS THE HEIGHT OF EVIL NOT TO
KNOW GOD; BUT TO BE CAPABLE OF KNOWING GOD,
AND TO WISH AND HOPE TO KNOW HIM, IS THE ROAD
WHICH LEADS STRAIGHT TO THE GOOD; AND IT IS AN
EASY ROAD TO TRAVEL.
                    CORPUS HERMETICUM : XI.ii. (302)

EXERCISE 5   THE FOUR-SQUARE CITADEL

The following exercise is worked in five parts and is a complete
initiatory system suitable for readers of any tradition. There is a
built-in fail-safe in that the four-square citadel can only be built from
your personal meditation: no one else can help you work this
exercise, nor will you find the answers in any books. The exercise is
based on a thorough knowledge of the elements and will only
succeed if you put in sufficient meditation upon each energy. In the
final, fifth part, you will be able to construct the four-square citadel
which forever afterwards will be your own personal temenos from
which you may meditate or work. It is ideal for those who have no
working-area specially designated in their home. Work each part
successfully before going on to the next; you may need several
sessions for each part. On no account attempt to work the whole
exercise in one go. At the beginning of each section state your
intention in these or your own words, thus:

> e.g. I seek for the citadel with no foundations
> Which lies within myself.

Adding for each quarter:

> I seek the power of the East (or South/West/North):
> The seed of power which lies within.

If you have difficulty realizing the Elemental qualities, *Magical
Ritual Methods* by William Gray (115), or *The Practice of Ritual
Magic* by Gareth Knight (182), give excellent pointers on how you
may come to experience them.

A) Sit in meditation with your chair in the middle of the floor, if you
have space: if you do not, then it does not matter. Visualize a circle
about you. If you have room, you may demark this circle on the floor
with wool or string. Face East and visualize the following scene

about you. The circle about you expands until it becomes the utmost limit of the earth from horizon to horizon, the edges of the world tilt away into infinity. You stand at the centre of the circled world: at the four quarters stand four figures of mighty power. They stand at the furthest point of four paths which start where you are standing, and where they have their crossroads. Each of the quarters is a different colour: the Eastern one is white, like crystal; the Southern one is red of transparent hue; the Western one is green as emerald; the Northern one is of opaque blackness. Each Power holds back the elemental forces from rushing into the centre of the circled world. Turn to face each power and sense the nature of the elemental energy which is being controlled.

In order to build your four-square citadel you have to enter into relationship with each Element by means of an initiatory meditation. Face East and meditate upon the Power of Air which is white as crystal. Consider the elemental quality of air from every level of your understanding. As you meditate, the whole Eastern quarter of the circled world is flooded with white light, as the power of the Eastern One builds up: the ground becomes white also, so that the white path disappears. You must journey along the invisible path towards the Eastern edge of the world and bring back the gift of the Eastern power. You journey blind across the whitened world. The snow is deep and cold, but you must travel on without stopping, Despite your uncertainty, tune into the Eastern power and feel it magnetically calling you. A white hare crosses your track and you understand that you are to follow it deeper into the snowscape. Wherever the hare runs, there a path opens up, and the ground is easy to travel. Elsewhere the ground is covered by such deep drifts that you cannot continue, so follow it onwards. You struggle onwards.

Suddenly the Hare stops and turns. It asks you:

'Where do you journey and what do you seek? You reply:
'I seek for the citadel with no foundations which lies within the East.' It asks:
'What are the powers of the Eastern One?'

You answer in your own words, drawing upon your own meditative realizations. If the Hare is satisfied with your answer you may proceed. If it is not, then the Hare vanishes and you must return to your starting place at the centre of the circled world. You may not continue for the path ends here, the winds blow and the snow deepens. If your answer is satisfactory the Hare will leap forward into the middle of the whiteness ahead, drawing you behind it until you stand at your journey's end. Before you is the Archon of the East, arrayed as a mighty power, in the mantle of the snows. In his right hand is a sword of adamant, and on his head burns a crystalline crown. His force and presence are overwhelmingly strong. Pay your respects to him and accept whatever gift he gives you as a token of your regency of the Eastern element. The gift will be an object which is easily held in the hand – only you know what it is: take the first thing that you see, however inappropriate your rational mind considers it – first impressions are generally correct. This is the first gift with which you will build the four-square citadel. Take your leave of the Archon of the East and depart. Swift as thought, you return to the centre of the circled world down the path which is now visible to you and easy to travel. Stand at the centre, face East once more, seeing the path before you and the Archon with his crown of white crystal standing at the furthest East of the world. Raise your gift in salutation and thanks, and set it down in the Eastern quarter of the circle.

As you work each quarter, lay each gift in its appropriate elemental quarter until you have worked all four. It is effective to draw the mandala of the circled world with coloured quarters on a sheet of card, placing each gift upon it, or, if you have a working-area, making a symbolic representation of each gift in the appropriate quarter of your room. However, these are your personal symbols and are not for display to others, because they are the keys to unlock your four-square citadel, so keep them safely.

B) Now face the South and establish the path to the furthest South of the circled world. At the end of it stands the mighty power of the South to whom you must journey. As before, meditate upon the Power of Fire which is transparently red like ruby. As the power builds up, the whole Southern quarter is flooded with light, obliterating the path before you. Again, proceed by instinct across the landscape which opens before you. The earth is red sand through which you trudge under the heat of an invisible sun. The sand is hot and hard to your feet, your throat and mouth are filled with its grittiness. Feel the power and orient yourself once more. Before you appears a sand-lizard, the same colour as the ground. Follow it and your path will be easier. Wherever it goes you can walk safely. It turns and asks you:

'Where do you journey and what do you seek?' You reply:

'I seek for the citadel with no foundations, which lies within the South.' It asks:
'What are the powers of the Southern One?'

You answer in your own words. If the Lizard is unsatisfied with your reply, you must return to the centre and travel this way another time. If your answer is satisfactory, the Lizard will shoot swiftly forward, taking you with it until you stand before the mighty Archon of the South. He is arrayed as mighty power, in a mantle of red glittering sand. In his right hand is a spear of adamant, and on his head burns a crown of ruby. His force and presence are overwhelming. Pay your respects to him and accept whatever gift can only be seen and known by you. Take your leave and depart. Swift as thought, you return to the centre of the circled world down the path which opens before you. Stand at the centre, facing South, and raise your gift in thanks to the Archon standing the farthest South of the path. Salute him and set down your gift in the Southern quarter.

C) Now face West and establish the path to the Westernmost quarter of the circled world. At the end of its stands the mighty power of Water, which is transparently green as emerald. Meditate upon the power of water. As the power builds up, the whole Western quarter is flooded with green light, obliterating the path before you. Again, proceed by instinct across the landscape which opens before you. Everything is green and damp. A jungle of plant-life and creeper surrounds you. The ground beneath your feet is moist and swampy, the atmosphere is hot and clammy. The way is difficult and winding, but ever seek the furthest West. As you struggle to break through the tangle of thick green growth about you, avoiding the swampy patches, a water-snake slithers across your path. Follow it and the way is instantly easier. It turns and asks you:

'Where do you journey and what do you seek? You reply:
'I seek the citadel with no foundations, which lies within the West.' It asks;
'What are the powers of the Western One?'

You answer in your own words. If your answer is unsatisfactory, the Snake will vanish and you must return to the centre of the circled world to attempt this journey again. If your answer is satisfactory, the Snake glides forward swiftly, drawing you with it, until you stand before the Archon of the West. He is arrayed as a mighty power, in a mantle of glimmering greenery. His force and presence are overwhelmingly strong. Pay your respects to him and accept whatever gift he gives you as a token of your regency over the powers of water. This is the third gift with which to build the four-square citadel. Take your leave and return, swift as thought along the path which is now open for you, to the centre of the circled world. Stand at the centre, facing West, and salute the Archon of the West, raising your gift in thanks. Set it down in the Western quarter.

D) Now face North and establish the path to the Northernmost quarter of the circled world. At the end of it stands the mighty Power of Earth, which is black as obsidian. Meditate upon the powers of earth. As the power builds the path is obliterated and flooded with blackness. Again, proceed instinctively through the landscape before you. This time, there is barely light to see by, only a thick gloaming in which you proceed mainly by touch. The ground beneath your feet is alternately hard as rock and shifting as sand: the loose earth has the consistency of gunpowder. Your way is hindered by the shifting ground and the darkness. But feel for true North. The air is cold and the wind is dry. Beneath your feet there is a scrabbling sound and a small furry creature brushes your feet. It is a mole with night-seeing eyes. It asks you:

'Where do your journey and what do you seek?' You reply:
'I seek the citadel with no foundations, which lies within the North.' It asks,
'What are the powers of the Northern One?'

Answer in your own words. If your answer is unsatisfactory, the Mole will disappear and you must return to the centre and travel this path again. If it is satisfactory, the Mole will scrabble into the darkness drawing you with it until you stand before the Archon of the North. He is arrayed as a mighty power, in a mantle of glittering blackness, outlined by silver light. In his right hand is a book of adamant, and on his head glints a crown of black diamonds. His force and presence are overwhelmingly strong. Pay your respects to him and accept whatever gift he gives you as a token of your regency over the powers of earth. This is the final gift with which to build the four-square tower. Take your leave and return, swift as thought to the centre of the circled world, along the path which is now open to you, with light enough to see by. Stand at the centre facing North and salute the Archon, raising your gift in thanks, and lay it down in the quarter before you.

E) It may have taken you many sessions and months of meditation to reach this point, but you have persevered. This last section may also take longer than one session. We will now proceed to build the four-square citadel.

Set your four gifts in their appropriate quarters around your feet, in meditation, where you stand at the centre of the circled world. Slowly circle, regarding each of the paths in turn: East, South, West, North. All paths lead to your feet. The gifts at your feet are your instruments with which to build the four-square citadel – these and no other. Meditate upon their meanings, which are applicable only to yourself and your own theory of correspondences. Here there are no right answers. If you have trouble realizing their meanings, then look along the path of the quarter from which they came and ask the creature of that quarter questions until you are clear. When each gift is activated by your understanding, power will rise from them in a clockwise spiralling movement from the ground upwards. The walls of your citadel rise around you: do not fear that you will be trapped inside, for each side has a door. There are five levels to it altogether, with a connecting staircase which spirals up the centre of the structure. In each level are set four windows which look out on each of the quarters. Each level corresponds from the ground upwards to the room of earth, the room of water, the room of fire and the room of air, respectively. There is a topmost level which has another function. See below.

This is your four-square citadel where you can observe the motions of the inner world. Go to the topmost level and look out over each quarter in turn. As you circle the horizon you can see that where the Archons stood is a tower in each quarter – these are the Watch-towers of the circled world: they are in communication with your own tower. You will come to this level when you wish to communicate with the four watch-towers and their guardians.

Now look over the land through which you travelled so laboriously through the initiations of the elements. In the East, the snow is beginning to melt: the thaw of early Spring breaks over the land and the ground is covered with young plants and green shoots. Only the Eastern Tower is still white. In the South, the endless sandy desert gives way to a land where the Summer's heat is tempered by lakes and rivers, and where trees give shelter from the noonday sun. Only the Southern Tower is still red. To the West, the rain-forests and swampy terrain are tempered by the gentle coolness of Autumn. There are red and brown leaves upon some of the trees, relieving the endless greenness. The ground settles into the splendour of Autumn.

The Western Tower is still green. To the North, the black rocks and barren soil give way to fallow wakefulness and Winter. There are evergreens growing and though the earth looks bleak, it harbours the hope of Spring. The light is the clear brightness of the North. Only the Northern Tower remains deepest black.

There is much work which you can effect in this your citadel. In the rooms of earth, water, fire and air you can work rituals and meditations proper to these elements, furnishing each room according to your preference, but observing the conventions of each element. But you can also balance the elements: for instance, the room of earth has four windows each looking over the four quarters, giving you the following combinations – air of earth, fire of earth, water of earth and earth of earth. These can give you months of meditative activity.

Normally you work with the creatures of the quarters, rather than the Archons of the Elements themselves. The creatures are messengers and intermediaries and are easier to work with than the raw powers themselves. However, if you find it difficult to work with animal forms, you may request each of the beasts to transform into anthropomorphic forms. If you wish to work with the Archons themselves, this is best done by means of the symbols of adamant.

Their symbols are:

East – Sword of Adamant
South – Spear of Adamant
West – Cup of Adamant
North – Book or Tablet of Adamant

(Adamant is a legendary substance of great durability: you may visualize each symbol as made of diamond-like stone, in the appropriate quarter colour.) The topmost level of the citadel can become the Chamber of Adamant where the symbols can be displayed on the appropriate wall of their quarter. To acquire the symbols, work a ritual appropriate to the quarter and request the Archons, by means of their messengers, that you may obtain the symbol you require. You may find that the structure of obtaining the four gifts may be used in a slightly adapted form. The original symbol always remains with the Archon – you are given an authorized copy which is the same in all respects. The Archons and their servants are at liberty to refuse you, until you are worthy of obtaining each symbol. These are powerful tools which should be considered archetypes of any actual weapon or object which you may make in the future.

To enter and leave the citadel, you need only envisage your four gifts again. To form it, set them down and meditate on their qualities and feel the tower rising round you in a clockwise spiral. To leave it, go to the lowest level room and dissolve the citadel in an anti-clockwise spiral until all you are left with are your gifts. Evidently, no one else can have access to your citadel, because everyone's gifts are different. They are your keys and can be personalized symbols of the elements which you can meditate upon when you need the help of a particular elemental energy.

Always close carefully after each session and beware of any imbalances which may arise from working with the Elemental energies: work the Self-Clarification exercise (vol. I) if necessary.

Figure 12:   Four Square Citadel

The Archons of the Elements are the Elemental kings. Some readers will recognize Enochian undertones in this initiatory system. To those who can read the clues, a very interesting game of Enochian chess can be played in a three-dimensional meditation. (Cf. Regardie (283) and Casaubon (43).)

CHAPTER 4
Through the Inner Door

Understand that you are a second world in miniature, and the
sun and moon are within you, as are the stars.

Origen: *Homiliae Leviticium*

All have their keys, and set ascents: but man
Though he knows these, and hath more of his own,
Sleeps at the ladder's foot.

Henry Vaughan: *The Tempest*

CELESTIAL MEMORIES

If the inner resonance of the Native Tradition is the Under or
Other-world, then the inner resonance of the Hermetic Tradition is a
Celestial one. We speak not, of course, of an outer location but of a
working-metaphor, a world-model. These antiphonal inner realities
polarize the two streams of the Western Way in a distinct manner,
but we must beware of ascribing all the devils to a Native underworld and all the angels to a Hermetic heaven, for such is the way in
which symbologies and world-models have been wielded as sticks
with which to beat ideological antagonists in the past. In this chapter
you will find no dogmatic presentations of the cosmos: there are
many maps, drawn from different perspectives, that is all. Each
initiate proceeds according to his or her own lights. The macrocosm,
like the microcosm, is an evolving entity, not a static phenomenon
(90) so we should not try to confine it within half-guessed definitions.

The medieval world inherited the Hellenic cosmos consisting of
the earth, the seven planets, the fixed stars, the zodiac, extending in
spherical progression, beyond which lay the Empyrean. Through
these spheres filtered the power of God by means of the angelic
hierarchies as defined by Dionysius the Areopagite, about whom
more later. This hypostasis of the cosmos is now lost to us – the

Fig. 13   The Hierarchy of Creation

moon is a dead piece of rock, the planets do not behave as Ptolemy believed, the earth is not the centre of the Universe any more than it is the centre of our solar system. Yet, 'those who travel externally to these heavenly bodies will only find empty planets. The real cosmic universe is an interior one.' (304) Our concern is to establish how the celestial world-model has faded from scientific importance yet remained central to hermeticism.

Up until the Renaissance humanity believed itself to be, not at the top of a Darwinian evolutionary ladder, but at the bottom of a vast celestial hierarchy and cosmology – this resulted in a very proper humility. The revision of the Ptolemaic world-model in favour of the Copernican system at the Renaissance resulted in a radical disassociation with the macrocosm, producing an existentialist or, as the medievals would say, a melancholic state of consciousness, in which humanity was prey to being morose and solitary. This disconnectedness with the macrocosm has been partially remedied in our own times where the interdependence of man and animal, tree and river, rock and star are being realized (fig. 13). This lack of a central world-model is reflected by a fearful attitude, expressed in mockery, towards the metaphysical or the spiritual in general. Those who mock have grown up in an era where many current world-models are outmoded or eroded, yet they have nothing with which to replace them.

C.S. Lewis suggests (193) that 'you must go out on a starry night and walk about for half an hour trying to see the sky in terms of the old cosmology' – a sky which was closer than is now scientifically understood, one in which the moon represented an unpassable boundary, the sublunary realm in which Nature alone held sway, beyond which the stars rotated in their fixed courses, represented by a treasury of corresponding imagery.

The Ptolemaic system of cosmology – whereby the earth was the centre of the universe – has remained the *metaphysical* inner world-model of the macrocosm among hermeticists. This is not to say that they reject the Copernican and post-Copernican heliocentric cosmology of the physical cosmos. Adam McLean instances the way in which Robert Fludd was alert to the importance of the Ptolemaic system in the way that it underpinned the hermetic concept of *inner* space, yet he was scientifically aware of the Copernican system at the same time. (211) His work, *Utriusque Cosmi Historia* (The History of Both Worlds, 1617–1621) was a defence of the old world-model. He retained it because he understood how, if the Copernican system was once established in the Hermetic realm of thought, it 'would give rise to a non-spiritual picture of the Cosmos' (ibid). Our sense of cosmic unity was on the line.

The Ptolemaic cosmology saw the world in relationship to humanity: a system of steps up the ladder of the cosmos by which micro- and macrocosm were reflected and interrelated. Fludd's book presents us with the old cosmology, not in terms of astronomical understanding, but as a valid spiritual philosophy for the hermeticist. He follows the emanatory movement of spirit into matter in much the same way that Qabalists saw the prismation of God's glory through the sephirotic vessels. McLean points out that Fludd's system of spiritual evolution was established three centuries before either Steiner or Blavatsky presented their theory deriving from Eastern sources. Fludd's emblems, which illustrate his work, are still the clearest expressions of this cosmic understanding, and reward meditation upon their principles. (105) They are the Western mandalas of the inner spaces, emblems of the soul.

Another factor which contributed to the medieval world-model was Plato's *Timaeus*. (267) This alone of Plato's works was known to the medieval world through a Latin translation by Chalcidius, so that Plato was not known so much as the founder of a philosophy but seen as 'next to Moses, the great monotheistic cosmogonist, the philosopher of creation.' (193) The *Timaeus* presents a benevolent Demiurge (unlike the Gnostic Demiurge who enslaves the spirit in matter). The celestial hierarchies of such cosmologies and their inhabitants are very much the concern of the hermeticist who uses their archetypes in his or her work, often unknowingly. Dionysius the Areopagite (*c*. AD 500), the mystical theologian, supplied both the Christian and esoteric corpus with the authoritative work on angels in his *Mystical Theology and the Celestial Hierarchies* (70). This book deals with the interrelatedness of the divine intelligences who stand, each according to his sphere, receiving power from the order of beings above and passing it to the order below. This lyrical study stresses that only by poetic and symbolic means are such high mysteries to be understood, not in mundane language. Dionysius' angels perhaps originate from the Iranian *spentas* (cf. chapter 1) or from Babylonian guardians where they filter through Judaism into Christian teaching. Yet the divine intelligences who govern the celestial hierarchies have not always been seen as beneficent beings. The Gnostics held that the rulers or archons of each successive level of their complex cosmology were the servants of the evil Demiurge. Each archon governed one of planetary spheres. (cf. Fig 6) Yet, short of worshipping these, the Gnostics believed that after death they would have to encounter and overcome these dread instruments of Fate. A number of interior journeys through the spheres of the archons was necessary to reach the point of no further incarnation: a notion also held by the Orphites. Certain of the Elect (the pneumatics) were believed to have reached this goal, such as Enoch (31), Baruch and Ezra. To this end a series of psalms and invocations were conned so that the Gnostic, after death, might overcome the power of the archons. The Mandaens had the largest literature on this subject, with detailed instructions on how to render up the body to the elements, and the vices assigned to each of the planetary archons who ruled each zone. They form, in effect, a Gnostic 'Book of the Dead' similar to both the Egyptian and Tibetan kind. Says the Naasene Psalm: 'all the worlds shall I journey through, all the mysteries unlock.' (350, 291)

We have only to consider Dante's *Divine Comedy* (61) as a 'Book of the Dead' in the same manner as these Gnostic narratives to see how widely held and practically understood were these complex world-views. Dante travels through 'all the worlds,' through many levels, through Hell, Purgatory and Heaven to gain his initiatory experience. Of course, as for Dante, there are guardians upon the way who guide the traveller through the worlds: we shall be considering these later in this chapter. Enoch (31) travels through the halls of heaven, as well as through the realms of earth and of the Hebraic underworld, Sheol, accompanied by similar visions of apocalyptic terror, as does the Qabalist who explores the interlinking worlds of the Tree of Life.

The shattering of the vessels is yet another statement of inner cosmology whereby each of the sephiroth experiences the emanations of God as a progressive prismation of white light into colour. Here the initiate can follow the path of the great ones who prayed appropriately at each gate linking the Four Worlds of the Tree, reciting the unifications through which the light of God was restored. (168)

The esoteric world is not without its own cosmologies written in our own times. Blavatsky presented an Eastern-influenced world-model which has subtly invaded many levels of consciousness. Rudolph Steiner, rejecting her Theosophical outline, visioned an Anthroposophist cosmology whose complexity and detail is positively Gnostic. (317) Dion Fortune's received text, *The Cosmic Doctrine*, is favoured as a cosmological paradigm by many followers of the Western Way, although its style is dry and its concepts, though concisely logical, lack sufficient illustration. (90) Truly there is no lack of world-models with which to experiment and explore.

These celestial memories are attempts to comprehend the macrocosm, to order it according to human understanding. In the works of Plato and Pythagoras we see an attempt to order the inner world-model by means of music. In *The Myth of Er* (266) we meet the Spindle of Necessity which stands for the cosmic system of stars and planets rotating about the axis of the universe. (cf. fig. 14) On each whorl of the Spindle sits a siren singing a single note. Pythagoras' cosmic ship of music (107) is a similar theme: it sails through the heavens emitting *rhoizimata* or rushing sounds. The Music of the Spheres gives us an insight into the cosmic order which is far more than mere planetary correspondence. If we skilfully strike the seven-stringed lyre of our beings, we resonate with the Music of the Spheres so that microcosm and macrocosm sound in harmony.

'Were it not for the orders of music hidden we should be claimed by the preponderant void', writes Ronald Duncan (121). The seven strings of the lyre correspond indeed to the seven planets known to the Classical world, and gave order to it. A hypothetical 'eighth sphere' was envisaged to correspond to the octave whereby the scale of creation is closed. Robert Fludd invented an instrument which would express this very theory: the monochord's strings could be divided and subdivided, in the manner of a musical abacus, to produce intervals or fractions of the original note. (105) Thus the original note sounded at the creation could be refracted, like sephirotic divisions upon the Tree of Life.

> From harmony, from heavenly harmony
> This universal frame began:
> From harmony to harmony
> Through all the compass the notes it ran,
> The diapason closing full in man.

wrote John Dryden, in his poem 'A Song for St Cecilia's Day'. As alchemy deals with the nature of matter and its transmutation, so music deals with the correspondence of note and planetary archetypes. 'There is another music of the soul and of the spheres which gives to actual music that is sung by voices and played on instruments its reason for existence.' (103) Combinations of notes such as major and minor thirds can be heard as syzygies of harmony, while other, discordant, intervals sound like the warring and irreconcilable archons. Sophia falls from the higher to the lower octave and, with humanity, strives towards union with her syzygy-octave through the scale until they are joined in the apocatastasis of music, through natural harmonic progression.

Music justly deserves its primacy among the arts. Its immediacy transcends the necessity of language or translation of idiom. Music is aural light, pouring inspiration through the prism of the ear, informing us of archetypal natures, of Platonic forms. From the aulos and lyre celebrating the mysteries of Apollo, to the hymns to Orpheus sung by Ficino, music has been one of the hermetic arts. Ficino hymned not just the deity but also its planetary ascriptions and correspondences in a talismanic way. Even the birth of opera can be seen as a development of the Renaissance preoccupation with mythology. Masques enabled monarchs to participate in 'mystery dramas' attired as gods. Modern stagings of operas are the nearest many of us come to experiencing the mysteries which were once staged in the amphitheatres of Greece: in them the archetypal forms are presented by means of light, music, colour and highly choreographed movement. At the end of this book we have appended a discography of evocative music. Through its appreciation we come to understand what Plotinus meant when he wrote:

> We are like a company of singing dancers who may turn their gaze outward and away notwithstanding they have the choirmaster for centre; but when they are turned towards him then they sing true and are truly centred upon him. Even so we encircle the Supreme always; but our eyes are not at all times fixed upon the centre. Yet in the vision thereof lie our attainment and our repose and the end of all discord: God in his dancers and God the true centre of the dance. (269)

If music is a remembrancer of interior states of being, then what of the correspondences and richly freighted lodes of symbolism with which hermeticism is associated? Symbolism is the language of the Inner and its laws are those of the Emerald Tablet. Though the exoteric world is no longer symbolically literate, the vestigial traces of planetary correspondences remain in its fascination with astrology and divination. Yet these half-understood sciences are but two strands in the fabric of correspondences and signatures. In a world which is closely linked by television, radio and telex through the physical means of satellite, we should be prepared to consider the communication network of the Inner which is linked, in an incredibly sensitive manner, by means of symbolism. 'The lower must symbolise the higher, but the opposite is impossible,' writes the philosopher, René Guénon. (124) Yet from the standpoint of a material world, it is hard to realize this fully. The archetypal forms of the macrocosm are no longer potent realities from which the formation of our own microcosm stems: they are remnants of a rejected world-model, archaic ghosts echoing in the windy streets of common man. If the hermeticist clings somewhat superstitiously to the resonant correspondences of ancient worlds, it is in order to have some equipment by which to steer. Just as the archetypes of the Native Tradition have faded, only to appear afresh in our own times, so the Hermetic Tradition needs to revision its own symbologies and estimate their value. Not every word in a dictionary is consistently used in everyday speech, for instance, yet obstruse words remain exact indicators for what is meant: they cannot be discarded because they are used less often.

In volume one we spoke about the pied language of the Celtic poets in whose riddling dialogues and boasting pronouncements were hidden the mystery teachings of the tribe. Such teachings have been hidden not only in language but in number, colour, music, sign, symbol, smell, dress and god-form. These correspondences, like the sum of the notes upon the Spindle of Necessity, harmonized by the aid of one faculty – the gift of the muse, Mnemosyne – memory. The oral traditions of earlier times were upheld under the Hermetic dispensation by means of memory-systems. Memory is part and parcel of the law of correspondences, provoking, as it were, a Pavlovian response to the macrocosmic transmission. Analogous signs, symbols and mnenomics encapsulate certain meanings. Memory is the nervous system of Adam Kadmon, connecting microcosm with macrocosm.

'Individual souls,' said Henry More, the neo-Platonist, echoing Plotinus, 'proceed from the universal soul; hence that ability to reason, remember and initiate action'. Francis Yates in her exhaustive work upon the Theatre of Memory has shown that memory-systems were obsessively employed from earliest Classical times right up until the Renaissance and beyond as a feature of basic education. After widespread literacy prevailed, such systems became the preserve of Hermeticists. (362) The Theatre of Memory was an imaginative device whereby sets of facts were associated with locations. One could, for example, 'store' the titles of the Biblical books by associating them visually with the rooms of one's house. It is a clumsy system, but it gives an insight into the methods of imaginative visualization employed by Renaissance Hermeticists.

The emblematic conceits of alchemical and Rosicrucian books were pictorial initiations which used images to trigger Inner remembrance. All mediums and psychics who are in touch with the Inner use the screen of their Inner vision to receive impressions in this way. Contrary to popular expectation, Inner visions do not physically manifest three-dimensionally in one's living room, but are of an *interior* order. 'Reading the akasha', as it called in esoteric parlance, is merely a method of cosmic picture-reception; not everyone has the skill to pick up these transmissions. Those who can are the prophets of our age. Divination is really of this order, or should be. The scryer sees – not what will be – but a 'Platonic' hologram of past, present and future resonances which form a totality never to be manifest in one particular time-scale. Such work needs the dedicated exactitude of only the most patient esotericist, one who is unlikely to take credit

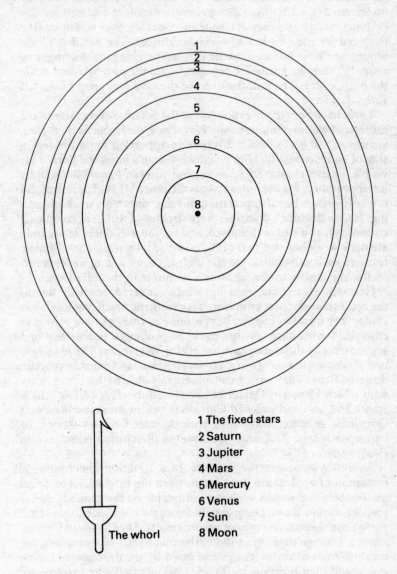

1 The fixed stars
2 Saturn
3 Jupiter
4 Mars
5 Mercury
6 Venus
7 Sun
8 Moon

The whorl

Figure 14:   The Spindle of Necessity

for what he or she visions and who will guide the seeker to self-understanding rather than arid prognostication of events. Memory of Inner things requires a trance of concentration which can be triggered by use of suitable correspondences. The prophet Elisha required to have music, in order that his psychic faculties might be roused: ' "Let the harper be brought," said the prophet. And while the harper played behold the hand of the God was upon Elisha' (II Kings 3, 15).

There have been many exponents of the doctrine of signatures, the greatest of whom is undoubtedly Paracelsus, the hermetic physician, alchemist and philosopher. Everything appearing in nature was a sign of an inner reality: 'you can discern man's immortal part of his visible, innate, characteristic signs, and you can know him even by his appearance; for the outer reveals the inner.' (134) Paracelsus did not only preach but also practised this doctrine in his work of healing. Hacob Boehme's doctrines were structured within as complex a cosmology, as we have discussed, and his theories underlie not only Steiner's work but also that of Blavatsky. Along with many Gnostic features such as Sophia, and the androgynous Adam, he strove to realize the macrocosmic signatures within man the microcosm.

Hermetic correspondences have been rendered unwieldy due to the accumulations of symbolism. It is axiomatic to cite Venus' day as Friday, her metal as copper, her perfume as rose, and her colour as emerald, for instance: the list could be prolonged indefinitely and argued over by different practitioners for an eternity. The planetary and other significances of archetypes stretch from Sumerian practice down to Ficino's day with great consistency. Add to this the imagery with which Christian Qabalists have laden the Tree of Life which stands like an overburdened Christmas tree in some textbooks on Qabalistic practice, and finish with Aleister Crowley's book of correspondences, 777, and you have an ill-assorted relish-tray to choose from. (58)

Symbol-systems are the memory of a tradition and require a minimum of application if we are to learn the language. The ritual use of some god-names is now questionable on the grounds that if you don't know the meaning and therefore the correspondence of the name pronounced, you cannot ensure results. The Chaldean Oracles advise, 'Change nothing in the barbarous names of evocation, for they are titles of divine things energized by the devotion of multitudes, and their power is ineffable.' (367) At the other extreme we must also beware of the shifting metaphors which contemporary society provides us with in these matters. The use by certain psychological schools of hermetic and other symbolisms may lead to a degradation of the traditions represented by these images and archetypes, as well as being a dangerous practice in that it involves the non-integrated use of great Inner energies. The current semantic gap in psychic matters is often bridged by the use of psychological language – again, a misleading and inexact terminology. Modern physics has also sought to employ the language of spiritual disciplines to physical phenomena which cannot be scientifically encapsulated: here there is a venerable tradition in that the medieval and Classical proto-scientists, who were often also philosophers – metaphysicians as well as physicians – used a common spiritual semantic for describing phenomena in either world. We are driven to make our own correspondences, our own metaphors and models and if, for convenience's sake, we seize upon earlier esoteric models, let us be aware that these are metaphors, *not the thing itself*.

It is always important to bear in mind that there are levels of meaning in symbolism: we may not perceive all of them concurrently, and we should always be prepared to explore deep before discarding an image. We should beware of allowing the symbol to *usurp* the Inner reality. For instance, it was a symbolic convention to symbolize God the Father in the Middle Ages as a hoary, bearded patriarch. This symbolism eventually took over until God is now almost totally identified with this imagery in most people's minds. Yet God is neither father nor mother, male nor female, but pure spirit. Despite this, God still lurks in the consciousness of many as a retributive patriarch, ready to strike the sinful dead with his thunderbolts. If such symbolism evokes fear and suspicion, it is void, and other possibilities should be investigated. Levels of meaning are easily muddled by those unused to thinking metaphysically. This is why we need the poet, the lucid mystic and the pragmatic esotericist who can operate objectively in the worlds of symbolism and interpret them to the metaphysically confused.

Yet it remains that correspondences are the essence of the magical art and no hard and fast rules can be applied. The individual practitioner must make his or her own lists: too often Crowley's 777 is referred to by students in search of a quick way into a magical system. (58) Create your own correspondences and then experiment cautiously with their working possibilities – if they don't work, then change them.

How should one go about selecting a list of correspondences? It will of course be dictated by the spiritual system or mythology which you work with. The normal seven planet system is a useful coat-hanger on which to drape your magical garments. The normal ascriptions of the Greek and Roman pantheon need not necessarily be employed: any set of archetypes drawn from either Native or Hermetic sources can be used. Celtic, American Indian, Egyptian, Platonic, Christian or Qabalistic archetypes and their correspondences can be selected. The only criterion is that they should be personally sought, selected and worked with. We give below a few suggestions merely as examples.

PLANETS	ANGELS	SAINTS	EGYPTIAN
Sun	Metatron	St John the Baptist	Re
Moon	Gabriel	St Joseph	Khonsu
Mars	Michael	St Barbara	Sekmet
Mercury	Raphael	St Christopher	Thoth
Jupiter	Tzadkiel	St Gregory	Ptah
Venus	Haniel	St Mary Magdalene	Isis
Saturn	Uriel	St Jerome	Osiris

If the planetary system does not appeal to you, then use another symbol system such as the tarot or the Qabala. Fig. 17 gives further suggestions on working with the Tree of Life. But such schemes cannot be pursued without the help of the inhabitants of the Inner realms. Plotinus says:

> 'Even the Celestials, the Daimones, are not on their unreasoning side immune; there is nothing against ascribing acts of memory and experiences of sense to them, in supposing them to accept the traction of methods laid up in the natural order, and to give hearing to petitioners: this is especially true of those of them that are closest to this sphere, and in the degree of their concern about it.' (268)

These 'celestials' are those very Lordly Ones we encountered in volume one of *Western Way* who stand midway between our world and the spiritual realms whose cosmologies we have read of. It is important to know who they are and how they function upon the Inner. This we can know only through the great scriptures of mystical traditions and the subjective experience of those who have journeyed in these worlds. Before we set foot through the inner door ourselves, let us meet the guardians who will guide our way.

HIDDEN MASTERS: SECRET SIBYLS

In volume one we spoke extensively about the Otherworld and its inhabitants. Both are based on the ancestral Underworld and the wisdom of tribal progenitors: the archetypes are localized expressions of principles which transcend merely Native experience. The Hermetic Tradition, as might be expected, has its own inner correlatives some of which transpose directly, with little or no change, from the Native Tradition, while others originate solely in the Hermetic reality. Some appear from the ranks of the great dead, the ancestors, like Elijah, or from the realms of the gods, like Osiris and Isis. Some arise from hero-saga or other literary sources, Christian Rosenkreutz or Perceval. The tribe sees its ancestors and is comforted: the shaman sees greater beings, but is not disquieted. Likewise the Hermeticist visions the inhabitants of the Inner, who may appear not only in local dress but in the guise of different cultural traditions. It is possible to 'pick up' contacts from the Inner as though they were transmissions of radio channels: the adept can 'tune in' to the appropriate 'station' when necessary. On p. 352 we give a brief list of 'tuning-frequencies' which can be contacted. But we must establish two vitally important principles straight away: the Inner inhabitants, which we can call *contacts*, have many means of appearing to our consciousness and although they are co-workers on the spiritual plane, they are not God.

Yet the question will be asked: where do contacts come from, do they exist and what are they good for? Hidden Masters, Lost Continents, and Otherworldly Visitants – it does not matter whether they ever really existed: what matters is that people behave *as though* they were real. This suspension of belief is not self-delusive, despite appearances, or the lack of them. (Contacts, like God, are not capable of ontological proof.) As any novelist will attest, the creation of archetypes is practically impossible: whatever is thought about has already existed in the timeless dimensions of the infinite. That expression 'as though' is an important one: if it is one which offends anyone's reality then consider the use of the *x* within algebra. If our knowledge of Inner Worlds is sketchy, we are reduced to this kind of algebraic formula in order to proceed with our researches. We take a lot on trust, but we always refer to our known experience in these matters. And this is something which everyone can do.

The implantation of heroic and other archetypes can be traced to childhood and young adulthood; these remain with the individual long after earth-shattering intellectual realizations have ceased to matter. The human psyche is a plastic substance, allowing itself to be moulded, wrapping itself willingly around a desired image. But there is no abiding in this realm: the images fade, leaving only their effect behind. The Prospero in us conjures up inner archetypes with whom to play in imagination, only to banish them when a more exciting newcomer arrives on the scene. We manipulate our inner lives and are manipulated by them too. As to the existence of contacts: there are more existences than the merely physical one. As to the work of contacts, such as the Masters, we will discuss this shortly. But our contacts, and everyone has his or her own, act as way-showers and companions on our way to inner understanding.

The multiplicity of forms and images is perhaps at the root of the differences within the Western Way. There has been little or no attempt to codify levels, methods and messages of the Inner on a purely esoteric basis. If a Martian landed in Piccadilly Circus or Times Square, the first man and woman met would perhaps be representative of the human species, but not of its infinite variety. Likewise, the teeming variety of hierarchical entities, angels, saints, prophets, masters, Indian chiefs and Tibetan doctors which are 'transmitted' to many levels of esotericists make it difficult to generalize about the Inner. So often a medium is contacted by or contacts one entity and then bases a 'world-message' on the results without 'testing the spirits to see if they be of God': the result is a worthless stream of loquacious aphorisms – analogous to the willing babble which might be recorded on our hypothetical Martian's tape-recorder if you or I were asked to 'say a few words' as a representative of earth to the entire Martian race. Discrimination is vital. On the Inner, every level of disincarnate entity may be encountered from atavistic demons to archangels: it is necessary then, to work through approved channels and with tested contacts. Just as we judge what is appropriate to our lives in this world, so we must realize that not everything on the Inner is for us – as those who run thither in an access of psychic enthusiasm find to their cost. The work of the Inner is not to mislead or endanger people and this is why certain high-powered contacts are hard both to establish and maintain.

The concept of Hidden Masters is one which is closer to the Middle East than to the Western Tradition, but the West has not been without its Inner guardians. In modern esotericism the term first appears within the German order known as The Golden and Rosy Cross Brotherhood which was operational in the eighteenth century. This had a line of 'secret chiefs' – a term which was to be bandied about a good deal in both Theosophy and the Golden Dawn. This is the theme of Edward Bulwer-Lytton's novel, *Zanoni* (1862) which had considerable effect upon many esoteric innovators. (207) The vexed question of the Masters continued into our own time. Madame Blavatsky's statements about her Tibetan masters seemed to clarify the situation, but the pale oleographs of turbaned divines which peer from theosophical walls are far from the reality: they are merely the clothing of deeper archetypes which lie beyond expression. Each age pictures them differently, each individual clothes their archetypal forces in suitably arcane robes so that Dr Dee, Merlin and scores of reverend gentlemen appear to fit the bill. Personality cults of the Masters are misleading and unnecessary as we can understand if we refer to Dion Fortune's *The Cosmic Doctrine* (90):

> The Masters as you picture them are all 'imagination'. Note well that I did not say that the Masters *were* imagination . . . (they are contacted) through your imagination, and although your mental picture is not real or actual, the *results* of it are real and actual.

This book, together with Gareth Knight's essay 'The Work of the Inner Plane Adepti', cuts through the swathe of 'bunkum and informed superstition' which surrounds those known as the Masters. (9)

So, what are the Masters? 'Human beings like yourselves, but older. They are not Gods, nor Angels, nor Elementals but are those individuals who have achieved and completed the same task as you have set yourselves.' (90) The Masters are to be understood as those adepts who are not presently incarnate, but who mediate from the Inner those energies with which the earth meshes its microcosm with the macrocosm.

Mystery schools and esoteric movements have been quick to claim as past-masters of their orders those famous in history for their cultural and philosophical achievements: comparison of a handful of such schools yields a remarkably similar list of personages – Socrates, Francis Bacon and Hypatia, for instance. The inner understanding has led to an exoteric confusion when such lists are produced. For, although the mystical hierarchies of ancient streams

of wisdom establish an inner chain of initiates, this does not necessarily imply an apostolic succession of famous incarnate initiates. As
we indicated in volume one, knowledge is not necessarily handed on
from person to person unbroken through the generations, but is
fragmented, hidden and rediscovered in other ways. Julius Sperber, a
German Rosicrucian, writes of the wisdom of Christian Rosenkreutz
as an inheritance from Adam, who retained some knowledge of
paradise after the Fall – this passed into many traditions, including
Zoroastrianism, Chaldean, Persian, Egyptian and Qabalistic
streams and was fulfilled in Christ, passing in turn to the Christian
theurgists of the Renaissance and thence to Sperber's own tradition.
(207) Thus do many mystery schools speak of their own tradition,
but this should not be confused with a blood-lineage.

The generations of humanity are usually reckoned from Cain, yet
the mystical remnant are the descendants of Seth. This tradition of
'inner family' permeates the whole of Judaic and Islamic mysticism,
and was once present in Gnosticism as a Christian understanding.
The inheritance of Adam's wisdom passes to Seth and this is symbolized mystically as 'the seed of Seth' which passes, by means of *inner*
generation to successive initiates. Bound up with this concept is the
understanding of the encoding of life, the spiritual DNA or spark,
which is transmitted via the seed or pearl. (72) This mystical symbol
has often been applied in an exoteric and literal way. Recent
suggestions that Jesus' bloodline succeeded via his offspring begotten of Mary Magdalene are but modern proof of this idea's survival.
(18) The bloodline of Christ is indeed extant, but it is the mystical
body of Christ made up of communicants, not the royal family of the
Hapsburgs that we must look to. Similarly, the Magdalene may be
viewed as a spiritual Mother: one who announced the Resurrection
and who, in Gnostic tradition, was privy to Christ's most secret
teachings. (239)

These extensive examples reveal just how carefully we must mark
our levels in Inner matters. Language, which is based in material
expression fumbles at metaphysical concepts. Even symbolism and
imaginative use of image can go part of the way when it comes to
explaining inner dimensions, and even this can fall foul of fundamental acceptance at face value. The language of the Inner is that
spoken by the prophets and sibyls: Elijah, Isaiah, St Hildegard of
Bingen, (143) Joachim de Fiore (9), St John – these all speak with the
fiery tongue of revelation, from the standpoint outside of time,
breathing apocalpyse and new hope. Like poetry, prophecy is eclec-

tic: certain images are programmed to trigger response in the heart of the initiate which will remain enigmatic to those who would only be fearful if they understood the inner language. The Masters speak in this manner but, as we shall see, according to the individual understanding and capacity of the pupil.

This brings us to another vexed question. It is often argued that the guardians of tradition, whether incarnate or disincarnate, are male. Truly, there seems to be a superabundance of Masters. One might enquire, where are the Mistresses of tradition?

'Why is it that women do not manifest themselves as Masters and Adepti on the inner planes, or indeed on the outer? In the very early days they did so manifest but the dividing line between positive and negative was then very subtle. In the future they will again and even now there are certain adepti in female bodies who have definite inner plane missions and who are genuine adepts.' (91)

This script, emanating from the Master who stands behind the Society of Inner Light, is frustratingly elusive on the subject. In the Western Way there is a tradition that the prophet and sibyl sustain a joint guardianship: they are the Hermetic equivalent of the Native Tradition's shaman and shamanka, and are roles which can be found on both Inner and Outer planes. Theirs are the voices of the Underworld and of the Stars, sending out the antiphonal song, weaving the mediations of the microcosm and macrocosm. If contact is made with this ancient tradition, then the initiate is privileged to be a part of their work. In many ways, the archetype of the sibyl comes from deeper or earlier levels of cognisance than that of the prophet. But, though we can polarize sibyl with the Native and prophet with the Hermetic tradition, we must not be dogmatic on this point: we speak in symbols. The prophets are nearer to our own consciousness and cultural conditioning and have therefore accumulated personae by which they are known to us. The sibyls back onto a phase of consciousness which is outside modern understanding, although this is beginning to resonate once again. The Muses of Classical mythology, the Mountain-Mothers and Cailleachs of Native Tradition, the sisterhoods of sibyls and priestesses of ancient times are comprised within the sibylline tradition. They come from such deep levels that they often appear as a collective rather than an individual entity.

The sibyls usually work chthonically, from the earth, in antiphonal exchange with the prophets, who work from the heavens. Their inter-polarization can be the subject of intense contemplation. (Lest there should be any confusion of levels, we stress again that this complex concept is an Inner one.) The sibyl receives and synthesizes the impulse mediated by the prophets: the prophet receives and synthesizes the impulse of the sibyls. Thus each informs and is incomplete without, the other. This is not to make any statement about the role of women or men. As we wrote in volume one, the levels between sexual polarity and magical polarity are clearly distinguished. The gender of magical polarities is used powerfully as well as symbolically in this paradigm:

Macrocosmic level   Logos   Sophia

Inner or psychic level   Prophet   Sibyl

Microcosmic level   Man   Woman

Figure 15: Diagram of Polarities

Just as there can be a relationship between man and woman, so there can be a relationship between man and sibyl, or woman with prophet. Each male or female operator stands directly under both the Inner level archetype and the macrocosmic archetype, with whom a relationship may also be established. We have used the terms Logos and Sophia to indicate the Divine Male and Female principles, but god and goddess can be substituted, as could any other suitable image. This system of relationships is, *per se*, supraphysical, but of great importance for an understanding of magical working. The Inner Level on which prophet and sibyl stand, is the creative and inspirational one. Thus various schools of thought have typified this function variously as anima and animus, daimon and muse, or, negatively speaking, as incubus and succubus. To find and inter-relate with the source of one's inner wisdom is of paramount importance to the walker-between-the-worlds. Although no specific exercise is here suggested, the reader is invited to meditate upon these things. If any symbols are required for meditation, the cards of the High Priestess and the Hierophant from the Tarot bring awareness of the sibyl and prophet polarity.

The shuttle of their song interweaves microcosmic and macrocosmic levels. The sibyls and prophets are the Just men and women made perfect, who hear our despair and pain, who understand our dedication to the Great Work, and who inspire us secretly within our souls. One might think of them as a celestial and chthonic system of communication cables who can put us in touch with any part of the cosmos – past, present or to come. Any contact we have with them is tenuous, and cannot be long sustained. Like the Mighty Ones, spoken of in volume one, the sibyls and prophets are impersonal, yet their hearts are set on the will of God. A greater understanding of their role might well help revision the rather out-dated concept of the Master in Western esotericism.

Certain adepts already perform the role of sibyl or prophet while yet incarnate among us. These, like the saints, live in obscurity, rarely teaching openly. They are known, after their death, through the work of their disciples. Such adepts are the real hidden ones who perform the work of mediation on behalf of the microcosm. Some are guardians of the ancestral land, others sing the song of paradise: these marginal shamans are indeed the Just Ones – a quorum of which is traditionally believed to sustain the world from destruction. Positively, their work synthesizes 'whatsoever things are good, acceptable and perfect.' (Romans 12,[2])

The concept of an inner communicator is comprehended within the word *maggid* or inner teacher (130), who accompanied the Qabalistic adept. This could be a past-master or expositor of Qabalistic lore, such as Isaac Luria or Abraham Abulafia, or one of the prophets – Abraham or Elijah. We shall be going on to speak more about such teachers, but let us consider that guide which is nearest to us and with whom we established rapport in exercise 7 of volume one; our inner guardian, our angel. 'When a person keeps a commandment, he earns an Advocate' (angel), (168) we are told. This idea of a heavenly 'other' or guardian angel has become rather thinly strained from Jewish into Christian tradition – the Church seems to have become embarassed about its heavenly hierarchies, and rarely alludes to the positive work of angels, despite Dionysius the Areopagite's codifications of inner inhabitants. The popular view of angels is not much better and even that great angelologist, Dr Dee himself was not immune from the narrow view of his own age when he was confronted by an angel in female shape. This meeting, recorded in Casaubon's *A True and Faithful Relation of What Passed for Many Years Between Dr John Dee and Some Spirits* (43), was Dee's first encounter, through the mediumship of Edward Kelly, of a spirit. He asks, rather indignantly, how she can appear thus. She replies:

> 'Angels (I say) of themselves neither are man nor woman; therefore they do take formes not according to any proportion in imagination, but according to the discreet and appliable will both of (God) and of the thing wherein they are Administrators.'

Both Jacob Boehme and Emmanuel Swedenbourg enjoyed such angelic conversations as Dee's. Inspirational writers of all kinds attest to angelic assistance. To cultivate the knowledge and conversation of one's Holy Guardian Angel was, of course, one of the aims of the medieval magician: but let that not limit your own appreciation of your angel.

Angels, unlike the Masters, are not nor have they ever been human. They are an order apart. There are angels not only of individuals, but of countries. They are the watchers and intelligences of God. G. Davidson's *A Dictionary of Angels* is recommended for those who wish to read further, (63) as well as Peter Lamborn Wilson's *Angels*. (360)

Where and how are the Masters to be found? This is a question which has been asked since the Rosicrucian manifestos first made their impact upon early seventeenth-century Europe. (cf. chapter 1) The invisibility of the Masters, of Lost Worlds and other curious phenomena is frankly inexplicable to some occult enthusiasts: they cover this rather grey area by rationalizations and crank literature. The truth is much simpler, and involves a clear perception of levels once again.

The Mirror of Wisdom by Theophilus Schweighardt (301) surely scotches the question of an earthly location for the Masters. He writes:

> that according to the announcement of the brethren although the incorporated gathering of all Rosicrucians does not take place in one particular place, nevertheless a true-hearted, devout and upright man can easily and without great trouble come to speak with one of the brethren.

He proceeds to give clues as to their location and advises the reader to turn 'towards the sunrise, noon and evening and finally towards midnight,' if they wish to seek the College of Rosicrucian adepts. This reads like a mystery instruction which tells the seeker to look within, not without. The keys of the four-square watch-tower of the day are precisely noted. More openly he says, 'Thou seest that the Collegium hangs in the air, where God wills, he can direct it. It is moveable and immovable, constant and inconstant . . . and thou must undergo . . . examination.' He is telling us that the College of Masters is contactable through the common means at our disposal – meditation, prayer, a good life – the very boring commonplaces which hide the mystery so effectively that few realize their value. Those seekers whose inner sight and senses are roused will find a master:

> I assure thee that a brother will appear in person to thee. It seems wonderfully incredible, but . . . I assure thee, thou shalt find the Art and Collegium, and thus is the only way, for else there is no avail to seek the place, for it is not and yet it is.' (ibid.)

Beginners in the mysteries are often driven to their wits end by this sort of calm assurance, that 'when the seeker is ready, a master will appear.' What does it *mean*, they ask? What are the proper channels for approaching them? So many great promises seem to be made within mystery orders that we may do well to look closely at the kind of answers one of these gives:

> If a man sets out to look for the Path he evinces a desire. That desire is noted by those who watch on the Inner Places and he will be 'assigned to a class' according to his temperament. After he has gone a certain way under that tuition he will be put in the care of what is called a 'guide': . . . (who) will try to impress the teaching he wishes to convey on the soul of his pupil by telepathy, and the pupil must try to catch what is 'said'. Later the pupil will be put into touch with one of the Lesser Masters and be one of a number of pupils for whom that Master is responsible. A guide has only one pupil at a time, but a Master has many. As the pupil advances further he will be passed to Masters of higher grade. His problem will always be to catch what his Master says. (90).

This neat hierarchical system coincides with that of both the Theosophical and Alice Bailey Schools: it is, in fact, from *The Cosmic Doctrine* by Dion Fortune, the founder of the Society of the Inner Light. We would say, from our own experience, that things are not always so neat and tidy, that progression is not assured. There is, in effect, no merit system of an earthly kind. Some esotericists form lasting attachments with their Inner Teachers and progress as described, but most attend different seminars in the College of the Masters and learn a balanced curriculum, specializing only later on in their experience.

Gaining a contact is something which normally occurs consciously only later: it is not something a student will be either aware of or feel the need of – it is enough to learn the basics at the outset. Yet, even in the early stages of training, one should be alert for the contacts which perhaps have already laid their foundations.

The choice of a magical name very often reveals one's secret affiliations with the Inner in this regard. Members of the Golden Dawn took Latin tags as their names, often using the acrostic formed from it, such as W.B. Yeats took: Deus est Demon Inversus or DEDI (dedicated). Dion Fortune (Violet Firth) took as her own name a contraction of Deo Non Fortuna. Not all initiates choose names or affiliations in this way. Very often the candidate places him or herself under the patronage of a past traveller of the Western Way. This may well be a case of an overshadowing teacher, as described above, or it may be a case of 'soul-likeness.'

Soul-likeness is sometimes misunderstood as reincarnational memory but as one modern occultist has remarked, 'Yes, I remember some incarnations, but are they *mine?*' This is a valid question which the reader should ever bear in mind: those who are sensitive to the workings of the Inner have at their disposal a great deal of information. Just because your psyche has keyed into the Egyptian Book of the Dead does not necessarily make you a priest or priestess of Maat in a past incarnation. Soul-likeness is the immediate recognition between the worlds which we sometimes experience with people and places in our everyday life. It is possible that both genetic and inner memory are at play here. In the cycles of occurence it is inevitable that there should be an overlay of worlds when we, as it were, see down a corridor of time. The trainee pathwalker will use these opportunities wisely and not discuss them publicly.

Isaac Luria, the Qabalist of Safed, 'could look at a person and tell him how he was connected to the Supernal Man, and how he was related to Adam'. (168) Not all of us are so discerning, and even those in the position of teacher would be chary of finding such relationships for their students. Such correspondences can be fraught with danger, as a visit to any mental home will reveal. When you are operating between the worlds, never confuse yourself with any Inner role or entity: always seal off one operation from another so that

Merlin or Morgan le Fay is not in the driving seat of John or Ann Smith, when you return to everyday life. Mental homes are full of Napoleons and Mary Queen of Scots – weak personalities submerged in stronger ones.

A real Inner Teacher will not seek to dominate a relationship with a student; indeed he or she will develop the strong and strengthen the weak aspects of the student's personality, nurturing the student's essential self without imposing an exclusive imprint. Of course, great teachers leave their mark upon good students: we have only to listen to some of the most accomplished musicians of our time to hear the unmistakable technique and discipline learned in the master-class of a past virtuoso of that instrument. Learning from one's contacts is like that.

It is often asked, 'how will I know when I've made a contact?' or 'how do I know that my Inner Teacher is reliable?' To the first question we would say that we all make contacts throughout our lives. Whenever our hearts go out to distant friends or when our imaginations are engaged in a gripping book, we are using the same facility to 'contact' something which is not present. These subtle influences shape our lives and are, to all intents and purposes, the contacts which we all experience.

An Inner Teacher is something else. It is unlikely that one will be acquired without a good deal of basic training, usually of a formal mystery school nature. If one follows a tradition, an Inner Teacher will be standing ready on the periphery of that tradition to help those students who seek the esoteric depths. (cf. exercise 3) As to the Inner Teacher's reliability, we refer the reader to volume one of *Western Way* and to Isaac Luria's advice: 'It must certainly speak the truth, motivate one to do good deeds, and not err in a single prediction.' (168) We judge by results, or by our intuitive rightness in this matter. Contacts and one's own wishes are easily confused, unfortunately, and it is hard to tell when one is merely using the rationale of the Inner's influence to smooth one's own way. Wayward mediums have been known to insist that a holiday in the Bahamas is what the Masters have ordered, when they want to get away from things themselves. Inner maturity is a hard thing for anyone to learn: the Inner Teacher will not spare your finer feelings when it comes to showing up your own imbalances: the only way is to be humble and take advice. The preceding remarks assume that the reader is not in receipt of any training but, of course, the dangers of going through the Inner Door are considerably lessened by the tuition of an Outer Teacher.

Such warnings sound dire enough, but there are benefits also. Service to the Inner, to the will of God – as mystics would term it – is rendered with love and there is a reciprocating love which more than balances our service. (cf. chapter 3) This does not mean that money and all good things will necessarily shower upon you, but that spiritual gifts are given to the co-workers with God. Love is the ultimate discrimination in this field of operation: if your work promotes your ego and polishes spiritual pride, ask your angel for clarification of yourself and your motives. You cannot weave microcosm and macrocosm together at the cost of your pearl – the divine spark.

The pressures of inner work are immense. Esotericists have jobs like other people, and have to cope with children, bills and overcrowded housing. Conditions are tough and only the resilient survive the pace. There is no ideal hermetic existence in a country retreat where dedicated disciples do your living for you, while you meditate in blissful quietude. The brief solitude of the study and meditation period must be managed so as to provide a daily temenos and refreshment of the spirit, from which one may emerge to face one's daily life. The increasing 'impatience' of the Inner to bring through certain teachings sets grindingly hard conditions upon sensitives who undertake to mediate these into the outer world. Yet this mediatory work is of such importance that many make the sacrifice of time and effort to ensure its proper grounding. At this point, we can see that the work of prayer and mediation are substantially the same: the mystic and the esotericist, who can work at this level of awareness, have a reciprocal function.

Mediating the impulse of the Inner is a matter of timing and rhythm. Great store is currently set by many ordinary citizens by their biorhythms – calculated charts of emotional, mental and mundane potential for the month: the esotericist already knows his or her biorhythm and aligns the personal pattern with the macrocosmic one. All esoteric work is done according to prevailing Inner currents, tides and influences. These are measured by means of moon phases, astronomical alignment and conjunction, the flow of seasonal tides. Time and time again, synchronistic events prove that rhythm is of the essence on the Inner, especially when it is aligned with purpose, pattern and power. Certain Inner alignments come round, rather like stellar alignments, once in a millennium whereby the resonance of one historical time-scale is available to us centuries later. This, as we have already described, is happening now with the rediscovery of the Native Tradition. Certain aspects of the Hermetic Tradition are not 'in phase' at this time. We have striven in this book to deal with those which underlie many contemporary concerns: resonances which will shortly be making their presence felt in common consciousness.

The resonances of the Inner are mediated to us via the Hidden Masters and Secret Sibyls but that does not make us merely passive receivers. After an apprenticeship serving the Inner, the student is given the means to become a journeyman. Esoteric books often speak of this process as 'the foundation of a magical personality', which sounds grandiose but is no more than the assumption of suitable travelling garments for work on the Inner. The Magical Personality is the *real* robe of the magician. It is acquired by a long process involving a deep knowledge of the self, an integration of one's imbalances, a strengthening of one's potentialities until the working image of the self – the Body of Light – can be constructed. This is not an exalted self-image or egocentric idealization of the self, but a vehicle of the higher self – the *merkabah* or chariot by which one makes the ascents. Rather than being the assumption of a mask-like persona, the magical personality is an identification with the Holy Guardian Angel, the Otherworld guide. This stage is accomplished when the student has served his or her apprenticeship in the Great Work, when the student pays homage to no one under God, but is prepared to get on with the work of his or her destiny as a trusted co-operator of the Inner. The student becomes, at length, a teacher of others.

It is often asked how one goes about this process: by faithful practice of daily meditation, by continual awareness of the tides of one's own life, by observation of the shifting pattern of Inner and Outer tides, by dedication to the Great Work, by working harmoniously with one's contacts. Only so will the work of integration be achieved.

Adepthood is the adulthood of the Inner – the inner maturity to work between the many levels of life effectively and responsibly, without inflicting one's imbalances on others. To be adept means to be skilled, to be master of one's craft. An adept is no more than this.

The Magical Personality sounds an awesome thing but we should be aware it is liable to become as static as the psyche of an analysand who boasts of being 'individuated'. There is no such thing as final enlightenment: the cyclic nature of human life renders us all liable to forgetfulness as well as to awareness. We spend our lives striving to establish the ever-shifting parallels by which the Inner can be perceived and mediated, discovering new possibilities, alert to the dangers of self-deception or self-complacence. Yet once the magical identification of self with teacher occurs, things can never be the same again. The period of overshadowing and then of integration occur at different rates, according to individual experience, but there is a deeper comprehension of both Inner and Outer events because the life-experience of the teacher becomes part of the adept's consciousness. This subtle process does not make the adept into Superman. In fact, the further the adept travels into and co-operates with the Inner, the less noteworthy he or she becomes in Outer matters. Personality is not melted down or dissolved, nor does it become part of a uniform expression: personal identity is, rather, made the spearpoint of Inner mediation. Here, we reach the limits of descriptive language, where personal experience alone can explain.

It may be that you have already started your apprenticeship in the College of Masters, that you have a set of working contacts and that you travel often through the inner door. In the next two sections, those who have not begun their exploration, may find a few indicators of how they might start. There are many ways into the Hermetic Landscape, and many guardians.

GUIDES AND GUARDIANS

'These great ideas (archetypes) are not at all sterile, they multiply their likenesses throughout the universe', (68) so wrote Marcilio Ficino. Some archetypes which appeal to national consciousness rarely cross their localized frontiers, but, mythologically speaking, many do emigrate from their native traditions because their archetypal energies are universally acceptable. Thus, Hermes appears locally in almost every culture, under a different name: Merlin and Thoth are well-known resonances, as we have seen.

We spoke in volume one about the regeneration of forms. It is the task of each generation to localize the formalizations of the forces it intends to work with: if these forms are inappropriate for that time, then they must be regenerated by means of practical work, so that the synthesis of energies can mesh. For instance, one may decide to use a little-known Sumerian deity in one's ritual. If the form, whose energy you require to co-operate with, has been unused for many centuries, then one works up to the ritual by first meditating on every known aspect of that deity in great detail and then earths the principles behind the outer form by mediating them cautiously. If there are any unbalanced results from this method, then the form has not been regenerated. This applies in the Hermetic Tradition as well as in the Native Tradition, where extremes of atavistic reversion are often encountered. If you desire to drive along a motorway, a hansom-cab or a Celtic war-chariot are equally inappropriate vehicles, for instance. There is no point in working with any energy, however it is imaged, if you have no personal rapport with it. The rhythmic Inner alignments we spoke about above, must be carefully scanned for suitable resonances which overlap with one's own inner work.

The following list is made up of archetypes which can be contacted, as well as concepts which permeate the Hermetic Tradition which can be utilized as symbolic meditation subjects. If you intend to work with any of the characters or concepts mentioned, then be sure that you find out as much as possible, if you are unfamiliar with these archetypes: the entries are considerably contracted due to exigencies of space. Most of us are woefully ignorant about the stories which inform our culture. Many of these archetypes are now only known through folk-story, mythological cycles or psychoanalytic commentary, where they can be safely ignored as fit for children and madmen. This objective distancing of ourselves from the living essence of Inner life has done more than anything to erode our spiritual tradition. A religious tradition is, after all, nothing other than a story to live by – and there are as many stories as there are human lives.

> We must learn God's story, our tradition. It is one of our worries today that so many young people do not know elementary concepts and language and even personalities that characterize our tradition. Knowing God's story is a prerequisite for knowing our own. (25)

Many of the archetypes are as the masks of God and have been so used in our own age by the exponents of Jung. The neo-Gnostic nature of Jung's work has enabled us to use and discuss the archetypes which until recently were subsumed in saints, angels and literary figures. However, there arises the question that each archetype is an energy of great power and cannot be used in psychological 'ritual workshops' with impunity. To work with these figures you must *know* them. The archetype which *you* experience as a friendly guardian under the form of Anubis, will not necessarily so appear to someone else of your acquaintance. If you intend to use these, or indeed, any other archetypes as a basis for ritual work with others, make sure that everyone present is experienced in mediating that degree of energy.

Which leads us to the question of respect:

Angels won't be invoked
Ancient folios are not Yellow Pages (229)

is good advice. One does not command the appearance of any energy on the Inner, one *requests*. Further, if you construct a ritual working from the results of your experience, don't mix systems. Celtic and Enochian systems won't necessarily mix, neither will Gnostic and Native systems. Isis and Demeter should not appear in the same ritual – one is an aspect of the other, but from a different mythos. Gentile Qabala has successfully combined both Jewish and Christian aspects; Gnostic and alchemical systems have much in common, but don't push the correspondences too far.

Use this section imaginatively, add your own examples and work with whichever excites you. It may be that one of these archetypes carries the key to your own spiritual heritage. If you find a particular preference for a tradition arising as a result of this experience, you might well combine this with exercise 3.

Abaris. Master of the Hyperborean mysteries which are based in North-West Europe, some say in the region of the British Isles. Abaris was a servant of Hyperborean Apollo. He lived without food and travelled on a golden arrow (which was the symbol of Apollo). He is said to have been initiated into the Pythagorean mysteries. His fragmentary mythos bears a similar ring to that of *Bladdud*, the legendary founder of the pre-Roman city of Bath: he also had the ability to fly, and instituted the temple and worship of the goddess Sulis – later to become Sulis-Minerva, under the Romans. If Bladdud visited Greece as legend credits, and was initiated into the mysteries, it is possible that the two myths have become identified with each other. Abaris links the Celtic Native Tradition with that of the early Hermetic Tradition. The Hyperborean mysteries, of which he is master, are safer to work with than those of Atlantis.

REFERENCES: Stewart (323), Chapman (45), Lievegoed (195).

Adam and Eve. Our primal parents. They can be understood, mythologically, as every man and woman. Sibyl and prophet are their inner resonance, just as Logos and Sophia (q.v) are their cosmic and ultimate reality. Their Fall and expulsion from the garden, however interpreted, is representative of a loss of the perfect state. Their prayer of return to that state can also be ours:

> O precious Paradise, unsurpassed in beauty, Tabernacle built by God, unending gladness and delight . . . with the sound of the leaves pray to the Maker of all: may He open unto me the gates which I closed by my transgression, and may He count me worthy to partake of the Tree of Life and of the joy which was mine when I dwelt in thee before. (191)

The Orthodox icon of the Descent into Hell, shows the glorified Christ extending either hand to Adam and Eve; he stands upon the bridge of the Cross, and the unregenerate ancestral forces, depicted as locks and bolts, are broken asunder.

REFERENCES: Graves (110, 112), Every (78), Apocryphal New Testament (10)

Adam Kadmon/Anthropos. Common to many traditions, the concept of the Hidden Adam or macrocosmic man, finds its fullest expression in the Qabalistic Adam Kadmon whose body is seen as a cosmic glyph of the Tree of Life itself: all ten emanations (sephiroth) of the Tree of Life are superimposed upon Adam Kadmon's Body of Light. The original stature of Adam was that of the cosmos itself but, as in the Orphite belief in the apportioning of the deity into men by Titans, the Body of Light is scattered. However, Adam Kadmon, made in the image of God, *is* the Universe in its totality 'The body of Adam is the body of the world, and the soul of Adam is the totality of the souls.' The concept of Anthropos is a Hermetic resonance of the Qabalistic one: 'but All-Father Mind, being Life and Light, did bring forth Man (Anthropos) co-equal to Himself.' Exercise 6 provides a method for experiencing this energy. Any extensive work with Qabala will put the reader directly in touch with this archetype.

REFERENCES: Halevi (127), Mead (227), Rudolph (291) Drower (72).

Aeon/Aion. The Aeon is seen as the coming age in which a saviour-figure will come to restore all things to their proper order. Many

speak of the Aquarian Age as a fulfilment of their hope. The child of
the Aeon is Horus/Harpocrates (q.v.). Aion, the god of time, was
associated with the cult of Kore at Alexandria. His birth was
celebrated on the night of 5 January, which is now the eve of the
Epiphany of Showing of Christ, which strengthens the connections
of the Aeon with Aion. Latterly, Aion was identified with Mithras as
god of time. A statue from the Mithraeum at Ostia, shows him as a
lion-headed man, a serpent girdling his body six times; in his hands
are a key and sceptre. He has wings with symbols of the seasons on
his back, a thunderbolt on his breast, and at his feet are the hammer
and tongs of Hephaistos (representative of the alchemist), the pine
and tongs of Aesclepios, (representative of the healer) and the
caduceus of Hermes (representing the Hermetic Tradition. (cf. fig. 1)
He is often fused with Agathodaimon (q.v.)

REFERENCES: Guénon (124), Godwin (104), Lindsay (197).

Agathodaimon.   His name means 'Good spirit'. Porphyry tells us
that he was represented among the Egyptians as anthropomorphic,
with blue-black skin, with a girdle about his waist, carrying a
sceptre, and wearing a winged crown. He is the first aspect of
Hermes Trismegistos, identifiable with the Anthropos (q.v.) or
Cosmic Man of Light, 'who has heaven for head, aether for body,
earth for feet and for the water round (him) the ocean's depths.' He is
perhaps identifiable also with Kneph-Kamephis or Lord of the
Perfect Black, who teaches Isis the mysteries of alchemy. Agathodaimon is the shepherd and guardian of all initiates who invoke him
thus:

> O mayest thou come into my mind and heart for all the length of
> my life's days, and bring unto accomplishment all things my
> soul desires . . . come unto me, Good, altogether good . . . thou
> whom no magic can enchant, no magic can control, who givest
> me good health, security, good store, good fame, victory and
> strength, and cheerful countenance.

REFERENCES: Denning and Phillips (68), Lindsay (197), Mead
(227).

Akashic Records.   Although there is no Western name equivalent to
this concept, the concept itself is discernible within the Western Way.
The Akashic Records are a vast computer-bank of the Inner, whose

guardians are the recording gods, Thoth and Hermes. In earlier times, this role was held by Mnemosyne and the Muses (q.v.) who are the guardians of the Well of Memory which the initiate drinks (cf. exercise 2, vol.I). The Hermeticist's task, like that of the shaman, is to tap this memory-system of Hermes and retrieve information not currently available by other means.

Angels. These are the inner protectors of humankind and the helpers of God. They are beings who have never been incarnate, like humanity, and therefore, cannot attain to the perfection of perfected man. They are common to the Middle Eastern mysteries from Sumer onwards. The archangels Raphael, Michael, Gabriel and Uriel are still invoked to protect the ritual temenos of the magician, just as the evangelists, Matthew, Mark, Luke and John are still invoked to guard the beds of sleeping children. The Hebrew version of this protection is given on p. 283. All have their origin in the Babylonian invocation: 'Shamash (sun god) before me, behind me Sin (moon god), Nergal (Underworld god) at my right', Ninil (earth goddess) at my left.' Such invocations are lorica-prayers (breastplates) and are often found in Celtic tradition, notably St Patrick's Breastplate. Dr Dee and Edward Kelly worked out a complex angelic system. Qabala has its own angels and archangels. Exercise 5 will give the beginner a taste of the archangelic qualities as represented by their elements.

REFERENCES: Davidson (63), Dionysius the Areopagite (70), Oxford Dictionary of Nursery Rhymes (252), Wilson (360).

Anima Mundi is the world-soul, the planetary angel or mediator. In Plato's *Timaeus*, she is described as the animating principle of creation. She can be visualized as an angelic figure or as a caring mother who holds her mantle of mercy around the totality of the globe. Christians may wish to visualize her as *Mater Misericordia*, Mother of Mercy, sheltering all human souls under her cloak. Her imagery is closely associated with that of the Shekhina (q.v.) and Sophia (q.v.). Ecologically-minded readers will find that this archetype can be worked with in meditation for the healing of the earth on more than a physical level.

REFERENCES: Plato (265).

Anubis. Son of Nephthys (q.v.) and Osiris (q.v.). He is a form of chthonic Hermes, guardian of the dead, a guide to initiates and to all lonely travellers. He is depicted as a black-skinned man with a jackal's head.

REFERENCES: Hope (147), Lurker (203).

Apocatastasis means the reestablishment or restoration of all things to their primal unity. It was used by the theologian Origen to denote the return of all created things to God, including that which was considered Fallen. The Gnostics saw it as the end of the Aeon when the Logos (q.v.) and Sophia (q.v.) would celebrate their nuptials in the Wedding Chamber of the Pleroma. This concept is found in many traditions within the Western Way. The Zoroastrians call it the *Frasokereti* or 'the making-wonderful' when a saviour would be born of a virgin from the seed of a prophet, and grow up to combat evil and bring an end to the world. Christians understand this as the Day of Judgement when every creature will be judged and either enter heaven or become one with the damned. (Yet 'Christ is risen and there is none dead in the tomb') Qabalists have seen it as the *Tikkun* wherein the breaking of the vessels will be rectified. The final redemption in Judaism is described as the *Tzaftzaf*, or 'breaking-forth', which is referred to as 'spiritual pressure, where one breaks through to a higher level, sensed by the mind.' This concept is closely associated with the partnership of the Syzygies (q.v.)

REFERENCES: Kaplan (167), Origen (246), Rudolph (291) Lossky 200).

Apollo. His name is said to mean 'appleman' or 'destroyer'. He is closely associated with Mabon (cf.vol.I) in his role as Hyperborean Apollo. For his complex mythos, see Graves (111). He is the son of Zeus and Leto, a daughter of the Titans. His symbol of the lyre was invented by Hermes who gave it to him in return for Apollo's caduceus. Apollo, like Zeus (qv.) is closely associated with the Muses (q.v.). Because he is such an old archetype, his mythos reflects the many changes it has undergone. Hermetically, Apollo is seen with his lyre of seven strings – one who has perceived and represented the keynotes of the seven planets.

REFERENCES: Graves (111), Kerenyi (171).

Asclepios. The son of Apollo and Coronis, he is the god of healing. He had sanctuaries or Asclepeia at Tricca, Epidaurus, Cos and Pergamus where the patient slept, either on the skin of a sacrificed animal, or near a statue of the god. He appeared to counsel patients in dreams which were subsequently interpreted by an hereditary priestly family. This form of temple sleep can still be performed under Asclepios' aegis either in a consecrated circle or in bed, after having invoked the healing power of sleep. He is shown as a mature bearded man, leaning upon a staff or tree trunk around which winds a serpent. His symbols are the pine-cone, cock and caduceus of healing. He is sometimes shown accompanied by a child in a hooded cloak known as Telesphoros – 'finisher or healer.' Asclepios heals on all levels.

REFERENCES: Kerenyi (172).

Christian Rosenkreutz is the hero of the *Chymical Wedding* and of the Rosicrucian manifesto the *Fama Fraternitatis*. He is the initiate who has entered the Hermetic chamber of the Rosicrucian vault for this time and who has made a compendium of ancient wisdom which all pathwalkers upon the Western Way can utilize. His life, told in the *Fama* relates a parallel one to that of Christ: he travels in the East and is acclaimed by sages; he returns to contact the wisdom of the West and founds the Fraternity of the Rose Cross. The members of the brotherhood travel into many countries, pursuing their various arts, agreeing to meet yearly. The discovery of the Vault or tomb of Rosenkreutz is told in the *Fama*: it is a text of great implication for the hermeticist. Rosenkreutz appears either as a venerable man, in his guise as Master of the Rosicrucian tradition, or else, in the guise of a candidate to the mysteries, as a young man or youth, in simple clothes with crossed red-bands over his shoulders – a similar figure to that of the Fool in the Tarot.

REFERENCES: Allen (6), Knight (178, 184), McLean (208).

Cundrie is the Grail messenger in *Parzival*. She is analogous to the figure of Sovereignty (cf. vol.I, chapter 1) and appears as the Loathly Lady of Celtic tradition. She is the personification of the Waste Land, yet is closely associated with the Shekhina and Sophia (q.v.). In *Parzival* she admonishes King Arthur, saying that his kingship and the fame of the Round Table have been diminished by the behaviour of Parzival who has neglected to ask the Grail Question by which the Wounded King and the Waste Land would be healed. She laments and demands that a champion ride to right this wrong. In the event, Parzival succeeds in his quest, but only at her urging. Cundrie later brings news of the redemptive hope of the Grail's achieving to the Templeisen, as von Eschenbach calls his Grail company. She appears to them dressed in a white wimple, covered by a black hood which is embroidered with golden Turtle-Doves – the sign of the Holy Spirit, of the Divine Feminine principle and of the Grail itself. Her cloak of black can be visualized as having an emerald silk lining, indicative of the emerald stone itself – the Grail. (q.v.) Cundrie is of hideous aspect – a woman of disfigured beauty, lined by grief, yet she is the guardian of the Grail-quest who will accompany the initiate path-walker, and advise him or her. She is a fund of wisdom. Her beauty is restored when the Grail is achieved – although this is not stated within von Eschenbach's story.

REFERENCES: Matthews C. (219), von Eschenbach (344).

Dante.　As Virgil conducted Dante through two of the three regions of existence by virtue of his shamanic experience as poet and underworld-commentator, so Dante may act for our age. A meditative reading of the *Divine Comedy* will give the reader many insights into these realms of states of being. Dante's historical appearance – a scholar's gown with tightly-buttoned sleeves and black hood – are appropriate for visualization purposes.

REFERENCES: Dante (61), Jackson-Knight (153)

Daimon.　The daimon is the inner entity or guardian who guides our steps or inspires us. (In this volume we have discussed the daimon in a particular sense as pertaining to the inner masculine quality which Jungians call the *animus*, but here we consider it in its general sense.) Much like the angel, the daimon is the psychopompos of the soul and the mouthpiece of the inspiring god. Orpheus may be seen as a type of daimon, or the Agathodaimon (q.v.) who, like the Good Shepherd, leads the soul through the tangled paths of the worlds. Plato's daimon is discussed by Plutarch. In Roman myth every man had his *genius* and every woman her *Juno*: a concept similar to the Jungian anima and animus. The character of the daimon is as the inner helper for the hermeticist. The Tibetan concept of the personal inner deity or *yidam* is the Eastern equivalent of the daimon.

The word daimon is often confused with *demon*, which is, indeed, a diminishment of the archetype by those who make the gods into the demons of succeeding generations. The concept of the medieval magician who conjures demons to do his will is a faint memory of an adept working in close harmony with the daimon.

REFERENCES: St Augustine (14), Plato (265), Plutarch (271).

Demeter/Cybele/Rhea. The name of Demeter means 'mother', and she mediates the initiatory sacrifice of motherhood to the initiate. Her mythos was taken and amalgamated with that of Isis so that there are many resonances between the two stories. She is the bountiful earth. With Kore and Hecate, she forms a powerful triplicity of goddessly energies. Her search and mourning over the lost Kore is at the core of the Eleusinian mysteries which she instigated during her exilic wandering. She strove to make an immortal out of Triptolemus, the child of her host, but initiated him instead into the mysteries of agriculture, by which the barren earth is rendered fruitful by good husbandry. In her sorrowful aspect she appears as the Black Demeter of Phygala, and is thus closely associated with the goddesses Cybele and Rhea. Rhea was the Titaness married to Cronos (cf. vol. I). She alone, with Metis, escaped the banishment of the Titans when Zeus her son contended with them. She, like her Asiatic counterpart, Cybele, is a mountain-mother, a wielder of Titanic force, like the Celtic Cailleach Beare (vol. I). Cybele's mythos deals with an earlier resonance of Demeter's sacrificial motherhood and is not as suitably regenerate as hers. Hecate seems to have taken over the more terrifying aspects of Cybele and Rhea as a goddess of the cross-roads and of wild beasts. Demeter appears as a mother with barley-sheaves, usually accompanied by Kore and Hecate. Rhea is a massive, seated figure of hieratic power. Cybele appears in a chariot drawn by lions. The image of the Tarot Empress is an objective form for beginners to work with.

REFERENCES: Graves (111), Pausanius (256), Vermaseren (339), Lucian (202)

Demiurge. In Plato, the demiurge or creator had none of the malefic overtones associated with the Gnostic demiurge or false god. He was seen as a benign creator in the *Timaeus*. The Christian image

of God the Father has been much devalued because of its association
with a white-bearded patriarch who has become a tetchy demiurge
after the Gnostic model, akin to William Blake's Old Nobodaddy.
However, the reader can initiate a rerouting of this false image by
meditation, if he or she considers the statue from Chartres Cathedral
showing God lovingly creating Adam from the dust: or a reading of
Proverbs 8 will provide the image of God creating the world with the
help of the Shekhina/Sophia (q.v.) who is described as 'master-
workman' delighting in creation. Hermeticists who are non-
Christian might wish to consider working with the Egyptian forms,
Khnum or Ptah.

Khnum created children upon his potter's wheel and implanted
the seed in the mother's belly. He was called 'Father of father and
mother of mothers.' He is depicted as a ram-headed god. Ptah was
the 'master of gold smelters and goldsmiths.' His temple was called
the goldsmithy and his priest had names like, 'the Great Wielder of
the Hammer' or 'he who knows the Secrets of the Goldsmiths.' Ptah
is the craftsman-god who appears as a closely-wrapped figure, with a
tightly-fitting cap, carrying a sceptre with the *djed* or sacred-tree
symbol on it.

The images of God as Creator have received the fearful projections
of many ages and this archetype stands in need of much positive
meditation if the true energy of creation is to flow smoothly. The
Gnostic demiurge is analogous to Satan or the Devil in Christian
terminology: it is terrible that a misapplication of symbolism should
confuse God and God's antagonist. Contrary to popular belief,
pathwalkers of the Western Way do not pray to or invoke the devil.
The dualism of God and Devil has severely hampered the Christian
tradition: the problems of good and evil are best considered within a
reading of the book of Job.

REFERENCES: Blake (27), Lurker (203), Plato (267), Rudolph
(291).

Dionysius.   As Dionysius Sabazius, he is the breaker-in-pieces, the
Western equivalent of Shiva. Yet he is himself rent in pieces by the
Titans. This was a feature of his mysteries where a bull-calf (some say
a child) was torn apart, and eaten raw. His devotees were the
Maenads, frenzied, inspired women whose rites good citizens took
care to avoid. Dionysius has the chaotic power of Cybele (q.v.) and
should be invoked cautiously. His appearance may be as a rather

dark man with long hair and beard, with richly embroided robes, in his Underworld aspect, enthroned with his consort Ariadne, whom he raised to immortality as his bride. He also appears as the young lord of the hunt, his nakedness casually draped with a panther-skin, in his hand a thrysos or pine-cone tipped wand. He is also called the 'child of the double door' signifying his joint birth from the womb of Semele, his mother, and from the thigh of Zeus (q.v.) his father. Yet this title also denotes the two births of the initiate: the physical and initiatory births.

REFERENCES: Danielou (60), Graves (111), Otto (248).

Elijah Enoch Metatron. Elijah is the great wonder-working prophet of Jewish tradition. (I Kings 17ff) He ascends to heaven in a fiery chariot and passes his succession to his disciple, Elisha, who prays for a double share of his master's spirit. Elijah then enters the seventh hall of God and perceives the divine will. From then onwards he is a master or prophetic guardian of tradition. He appears in times of danger to comfort and lead the way to justice. As a co-worker with God, he helps all who call on his name. With Enoch he guards the seventh level of paradise. At the seder table (the Jewish passover supper) Elijah is invited to join the guests: 'Elijah opens up for us the realm of mystery and wonder. Let us now open the door for Elijah.' He anounces the Messianic promise to creation. He can be envisaged as a prophet in desert dress, venerable and bearded, yet not aged. His oracular bird is the raven. His Islamic name, Khidir, means Green One. He is 'the psychopomp whose duty is to stand at the crossways of Paradise and guide the pious to their appointed places.' He has been identified with the archangel Metatron (q.v.)

Enoch, who guards the gates of paradise with Elijah is called Idris in Islam. His name means 'dedicated or initiated'. He never tasted death. He oversees and instructs the world and is identified with the archangel Metatron. His journey through the regions of the inner and outer worlds is found in the apocryphal *Book of Enoch*, which has awesome prophecies regarding the end of the world. Enoch is known among the Mandaens as Anosh.

Metatron is the greatest of the archangels. His stature is 'equal to the breadth of the whole world,' – which was the stature of Adam (q.v.) before the Fall. Clearly, Metatron is identifiable with the Body of Light. He stands at the gate of Kether on the Tree of Life and can be visualized as a shining angelic form with many wings.

REFERENCES: Bronstein (32), Davidson (63), Book of Enoch (31), Halevi (129).

Fisher King/Wounded King.   The wounded king of the Grail cycle. All partake of the Grail mystery but he – his suffering suspends him between the worlds. He is at once identifiable with the wounded land, with the Grail guardian and with Christ. The *Corpus Christi Carol* is sung of him. He usually appears as an ancient, wasted figure, lying on a bed. To offer the cup of healing to him is to work for the mending of all riven things. He is the wound in creation, which only the highest form of self-sacrifice can restore. He cannot relinquish his role as Grail Guardian until the Grail-achiever comes to take his place.

REFERENCES: Matthews (219), Stewart (322).

Four Holy Living Creatures/Elemental Guardians.   These mighty correspondences. are best understood as guardians of the cosmic year. They are applied in many traditions, as below. They appear in Ezekiel's vision, and then are applied to the Four Evangelists in Christian tradition.

Vision of Ezekiel	Evangelist	Qabalistic World	Element	Fixed Zodiacal Sign
Man	St Matthew	Aziluth	Fire	Aquarius
Lion	St Mark	Yetzirah	Water	Leo
Bull	St Luke	Assiah	Earth	Taurus
Eagle	St John	Briah	Air	Scorpio

REFERENCES: Halevi (129), Knight (182)

Grail.   The vessel of redemption, knowledge and fulfilment. It is sought everywhere on quest, but achieved by few. It is not a physical object, although real cups, chalices and cauldrons partake of its virtues as the inner symbol superimposes over them by means of worship or cult focus. It is a powerful resource for meditation and many pathworkings can be made from the texts available. It is important to followers of the Western Way because it unites Native with Hermetic traditions in its forms as cauldron and alchemical stone. It represents a passing forward into other realms and gives direct access to the Higher Mysteries.

REFERENCES: Jung. E. and von Franz (166), Knight (185), Malory (216) Matthews J. (220, 221,) Matthews. J. and Green (222), Quest of the Holy Grail (277), Perlesvaus (258).

Hermaphrodite. The perfected Great Work is symbolized by this figure, sometimes also called the Rebus or Androgyne. Rather than being seen as a blatantly sexual anomaly, the ancients realized the hermaphrodite as the summation of perfection. Exercise 8 gives a meditative use of this figure. The word is a conflation of the god Hermes with the goddess Aphrodite, and can be considered as the symbol of the yin-yang in the West.

REFERENCES: Fabricus (79)

Hermes is the messenger of the gods, the guardian of travellers and imparter of wisdom. He invented the lyre and exchanged it for the caduceus of Apollo, with which he cared for the celestial herds. He can be visualized as Roman Mercury, with winged sandals, cap and caduceus, or as Agathodaimon (q.v.). He lays his staff upon the eyes of the dead and is sometimes called 'the whisperer'. As chthonic Hermes he is the keeper of wisdom and ancient knowledge, coming in dreams and meditation to impart his secrets. As *Thoth-Tehuti*, he is seen as the inventor of the Egyptian system of hieroglyphs and the keeper of the book of initiation. Hermetically, he can be seen as on the famous pavement at Siena; a mature figure in heavy robes, with a high pointed cap.

REFERENCES: Graves (111), Kerenyi (176), Mead (227).

Horus/Harpocrates. Horus is the child of the Aeon (q.v.), the son of Isis and Osiris, from a union effected by Isis after Osiris' death and dismemberment. Horus' symbols are the two eyes of moon and sun, or he is seen as a hawk-headed man. As a child he appears seated in a lotus, with his finger to his lip, signifying silence. He shares the symbolisms of Apollo and Mabon. (vol I)

REFERENCES: Hope (147), Lurker (203).

Isis. Isis is the divine saviour goddess, her power alone brought together the scattered fragments of her brother/husband's body, emblematic of the unification of the Body of Light. Her cult spread throughout the Roman world as far as Britain. Like the Lady Mary, she subsumes all lesser manifestations of the Divine Feminine Principle under her cloak. She is a particularly relevant archetype for the present age, being a comprehensive manifestation of the Goddess. Her influence continues to the present day. The Fellowship of Isis, a world-wide network of all pathwalkers who acknowledge the Divine Feminine, was founded in Ireland in the 1970s. Isis appears dressed in white robes with rainbow-like translucence, with an ankh or systrum in her hand. Her girdle is knotted in a distinctive way, making the shape of an ankh-shaped loop. A beautiful invocation to Isis and her many aspects can be read in Apuleius. (cf. fig. 11)

REFERENCES: Apuleius (11), Hope (147), Plutarch (270), Witt (361).

Joseph of Arimathea.   The wise Jew who gave Christ burial in his own tomb, and who provided the shroud. He also collected the blood and water from the side of Christ at the Deposition from the Cross, in two cruets – the earliest form of the Christian Grail. After the crucifixion, Joseph was imprisoned for many years and kept alive only by the Grail which he had with him. He was instructed secretly by Christ during his captivity, and fled to Europe with his family to found a line of Grail guardians. He is said variously to have landed in France or, more usually, come to Glastonbury where he founded the first Christian church, in honour of the Lady Mary (q.v.). He is the contact for Grail wisdom.

REFERENCES: de Borron (64), Matthews, J. (221) Apocryphal New Testament (10)

Just Ones/Sibyls/Prophets.   The 'Lamed-Vau' or thirty-six hidden saints are those for whom the world exists, according to Jewish tradition. They reveal themselves in times of danger. They keep the world in balance, as mediators between the worlds. Like the angels, the sibyls and prophets can be seen as totally Inner figures, but their role is also a grade of inner-working which those still incarnate may attain to. Like the Just Ones, they are as the hidden inspirers and sustainers of the earth. (cf. 153) They can be visulized as a double choir who sing the song of creation antiphonally. Jan van Eyck's picture of *The Adoration of the Lamb*, may serve as an inspiration for this visualization, or they can be seen after a more Classical Greek mode as a chorus of men and women who chant the mighty themes of the story.

REFERENCES: Schwartz-Bart (300)

Logos. The Logos is the word of God, just as Sophia (q.v.) is the wisdom of God. Gnostics, Platonists and Christians have all used this concept. St John's Gospel (chapter 1) will give much for meditation. For practical purposes, the Logos can be visualized as Christ the King – crowned, robed in glory and standing triumphant upon the cross, or as Christ Pantocrator, Lord of the Earth, with an open book. The Logos comes to ransom the soul in order that he may unite with his syzygy: gnostically, with Sophia; or, in the Christian tradition, with the individual souls of the created faithful in the person of Lady Mary. His energy is that of God the Son and Wayshower. The following chant is his promise:

> Send me, O Father!
> Seals in my hands, I will descend;
> Through Aeons universal will I make a Path;
> Through Mysteries all I'll open up a way!
> And Forms of Gods will I display;
> The secrets of the Holy Paths I will hand on,
> And call them Gnosis.

REFERENCES: Mead (227), Rudolph (291).

Mary, Lady: The Blessed Virgin. Just as Isis subsumes all earlier goddesses under her aegis, so Mary comprehends all the goddessly aspects of the Divine Feminine throughout the world. Wherever a Goddess shrine was located, under the Christian dispensation the shrine's original focus is remembered by Our Lady of (that place). She shows us God as Mother. Although orthodox theology does not admit her a goddess and accords her honours such as are shown to angels and saints, Lady Mary is enshrined in the hearts of the faithful with a special love because she shows them the face of their first homely Mother. She can be visualized in either of three aspects which correspond to the three mysteries of the Rosary: as a young maiden dressed in white with a blue cloak; as the sorrowing mother in black, at the foot of the cross; or as the Woman Clothed with the Sun (Revelations 12).

Mary Magdalene.   One of the female disciples of Jesus who discovered his Resurrection and declared it to the disciples hiding in the Upper Room. The loyalty and special place of Mary Magdalene is of so impressive a character that it has passed into folklore – often to the extent of making her Christ's physical consort. She shares the virtues of Sophia (q.v.) and of Cundrie (q.v.). She knows Christ's inner teachings and is trusted with them by him, although the other disciples complain that she is only a woman. Her reputation of a reformed prostitute is due to her identification with the Penitent woman in St Mark 14. She and Lady Mary, the Virgin, are the female pillars flanking the Incarnation of Christ, just as the two Josephs – Lady Mary's husband and of Arimathea, are the male pillars. Mary can be visualized as a woman of mature beauty, with long unbound hair, and a green cloak.

REFERENCES: Baigent (18), Bible (26), Rudolph (291) Nag Hammadi (239)

Melchizedek was the priest-king who came to welcome Abraham after his victory over the Kings of Edom, with gifts of bread and wine. This is seen as a type of the Eucharist and of the Eternal High priesthood of Christ. Melchizedek is hermetically considered to be an inner master because he had neither 'beginning of days nor end of life.' He is regarded to have come from the planet Venus bringing honey and asbestos. His motif is woven into the Grail legends. His is a strong and high contact which will bring the reader into the presence of eternal things. He can be seen as in the statue outside Chartres Cathedral, bearing a cup in which can be seen a stone or piece of bread, and crowned as a king.

REFERENCES: Bible (26), Matthews (221), Fortune (96)

Merlin.   The archetypal magus of the Western Way, he is the genius of Britain and guide to many inner realms. He can appear as a white-bearded sage, a beautiful youth or as a savage wildman. His contact can be productive of prophetic insight and he is especially important to the Western Way because he stands behind the Native mystery impulse and yet has strong affinities to the Hermetic path. His origins are obscure, but his name means 'from the sea' and he has been identified with an Atlantean master.

Fig. 16 Orpheus and the Nine Muses

REFERENCES: Knight (185), Tolstoy (331).

Mithras.   God of creativity and light, he bears a strong resemblance, in his mythos, to Christ as Divine Child born at the Winter Solstice. As a slain god his symbol is that of the bull, the raven and Sol Invictus (the Triumphant Sun). His cult was very much a male-oriented one which had a series of initiatory grades: the Crow, the Secret, the Soldier, the Lion, the Persian, the Runner-of-the-Sun, the Father and the Father of Fathers. Mithras usually appears as a youth, dressed in Phrygian cap and short tunic: he is an excellent overseer of esoteric training, upon which his followers set great store.

REFERENCES: Godwin (104), Cumont (59), Vermaseren (340), Mead (225)

Mnemosyne and the Muses.   Zeus lay with Mnemosyne for nine nights and she later gave birth to the nine muses (cf. fig. 15). She is 'memory as the cosmic ground of self-recalling.' Her dual role is of memory and of forgetfulness (Lethe). These aspects are combined in exercise 2 of volume I. The Muses do the work of the sibyls. When they all sing, sky, stars, seas and rivers stand still to listen. They can appear in bird-shape or as imaged in the Mantegna tarot. Their names, patronage and symbolic representations are given below. Their energies have been greatly neglected since the Hermetic revival of the Renaissance, but there appear no subsequent forms or symbolic representations which can replace these:

MUSE	PATRON OF	SYMBOLS
Clio (giver of fame)	History	heroic trumpet and waterclock
Euterpe (giver of joy)	Flute-Playing	flute
Thalia (festive)	Comedy	shepherd's crook and comic mask
Melpomene (the singer)	Tragedy	Tragic mask and Hercules' club
Terpsicore (she who dances)	Lyric Poetry and dance	cithara
Erato (awakener of desire)	Love poetry	tambourine
Polyhymnia (she of many hymns)	Storytelling and heroic hymns	lyre or portative organ
Urania (the heavenly)	Astronomy	celestial globe and compasses
Calliope (of the beautiful voice)	Epic poetry	stylus and tablets

References: Kerenyi (173), McLean (209).

Nephthys. the sister of Isis. Her function, like that of St Brigid (vol. I) to the Virgin, is to be the midwife and guardian of the Holy Child. She has the ability to be a revealer of hidden things, according to Hope. She appears as the supporter of Isis, her arms protectively raised: her head-dress has the basket of offering upon it, which is her symbol. She can be seen as an inner guardian of Isis' veiled role as Mistress of the Mysteries.

REFERENCES: Hope (147)

Orpheus. His early beginnings bear traces of the Thracian shaman. Ovid's *Metamorphoses* gives a romantic story of his descent to Hades to reclaim his wife Eurydice. Like Hermes and Thoth, he often appears as a spokesman for the gods. His reappearance in medieval times as Sir or King Orpheo established him in Native Tradition as a harrower of the underworld, a visitant to Faery. The Orpheus of the Renaissance is the spirit of music incarnate, the master of the muses. Tamino, in Mozart's *The Magic Flute* is based on Orpheus: he wins through the tangled webs of the Queen of Night in order to rescue Pamina. Orpheus is an oracular god, after the manner of Bran the Blessed (cf. vol I). His dismemberment and beheading make him one with Osiris and others (q.v.). Ficino restores Orpheus as psychopompos, divine intermediary and celestial musician. He appears very like Apollo, of whom he is a close resonance. Traditionally he is depicted as singing in the wilderness, surrounded by enthralled beasts, or, as in fig. 16, with the muses.

REFERENCES: Warden (353), Ovid (249), Orphic Hymns (247).

Osiris. The brother and consort of Isis, Osiris is one of many verdant gods who is cut down. His mythos is in Plutarch. His appearance as a green-skinned figure in white wrappings reminds us of his nature, as does his symbol of the *djed* or Tree, in which, according to some legends, he is shut. Like John Barleycorn and others, he is 'the grain of wheat' which must fall into the earth in order to bear seed.

REFERENCES: Budge (34), Hope (147), Plutarch (270)

Persephone. is the Underworld name of the Kore (which means maiden). She descends to the Underworld, abducted by Hades, the

King of that realm. She changes her nature rapidly from that of maiden to chthonic hag, and while she is under the earth, Demeter mourns and winter reigns. But she is the merciful maiden and is hospitable to the initiate who takes the Underworld journey. Her appearance can be as a Spring Maiden of hieratic stillness and simplicity, or else as a heavily robed queen with black glittering diadem upon her head; her unbraided hair frozen into lines of icy water. Her Underworld aspect should not be shunned, since the initiate must go the way of the White Cypress to the Well of Memory within Persephone's realm or turn back from the mysteries.

REFERENCES: Graves (111), Matthews, C. (218), Stewart (322), Fortune (93, 94)

Prester John. The mysterious Christian king of the East. He is the son of Parzival's half-brother, Feirfiz and Repanse de Schoye. A description of his kingdom and its strange inhabitants (the phoenix and unicorn) show it to have been a type of Paradise. The Grail is sometimes described as being kept there in a great temple, and Prester John is considered by some to be the Grail-guardian for our own age. Sometimes he appears as a glorious king in rich robes and with a triple crown, but more usually as a young man in a plain white robe whose features have a slight Middle-Eastern cast. He holds the keys to several inner landscapes including that of the Eastern Grail and the paradisal home.

REFERENCES: Matthews. J. (220, 221), Silverberg (308).

Prometheus brought fire from heaven. He is considered to be the Titan who created humanity and who resisted their planned destruction by Zeus (q.v.) The sufferings of the world were visited upon him because of his championship of the earth's inhabitants: he was chained to a pillar where a vulture tore out his liver all day throughout eternity, although every night the liver would grow again. With the exiled Shekhina (q.v.) he represents the pain of incarnation but he is ever hopeful of humanity's potential. He is a mighty man and a rugged wielder of the earth's elements. He stole fire from heaven to give to man in a hollow fennel stalk. This symbol of the upheld stalk has been reversed to become the symbol of nuclear disarmament, whether consciously or not. It might well serve as a useful symbol of meditation.

REFERENCES: Kerenyi (173), Graves (111).

Psyche. The story of Cupid and Psyche is told in Apuleius, where it may be meditated upon. Beautiful Psyche is a type of the soul, which is what her name signifies. She marries the god Cupid, but lies with him in darkness. Her sisters suggest that she is wed to a monster and at their bidding she secretes a lamp to reveal the beautiful god sleeping. She incurs the jealousy of Venus, Cupid's mother and, as in the folkstory the world over, she has to perform impossible tasks. She achieves these with Cupid's help and is made immortal. The story has been retold by C.S. Lewis in a way which points many features concerning the interrelationship of the Goddess's light and dark aspects.

REFERENCES: Apuleius (11), Lewis (194), Knight (184)

Saints. St Paul calls them 'a great cloud of witnesses'. In the early Church, all Christians were saints, but the title was latterly reserved to those who merited honour by their holy lives. All manner of humanity is represented by the saints. Most people in the Christian West are given the names of saints to be their Inner world patrons. Many energies are represented under the patronage of saints which would once have been associated with gods: their patronage can be invoked still by prayer and meditation, and they can serve as guardians for the pathwalker. They can be seen as facets of a mighty crystal which is the Body of Christ.

Seth. As the inheritor of Adam's paradisal experience, Seth has been a figure of redemptive hope to many traditions: his descendants, both earthly and spiritual, partake of the Gnosis of life. Among the Mandaens, Seth is called Shitil and at death, the soul must outweigh his purity if it is to enter into the kingdom of light. He can be envisaged as a tall, strong man whose form is almost angelic. His head is intelligent and between his brow is a flame of light, representing his state of inner illumination. He is one of the guardians of Gnosis.

REFERENCES: Nag Hammadi (239), Quinn (278), Rudolph (291).

Shekhina is the Jewish figure of wisdom. She 'brings the gift of the queen to them that wander with her in exile.' (121) She is God as

Spirit, the co-worker at Creation. (Proverbs 8) She represents the emanatory presence of God among created life, and so is closely associated with both Sophia (q.v.) and Anima Mundi. Her symbolism bears traces of earlier Goddess cults. She is the Pillar of Cloud by day and a Pillar of Fire by night which accompanied the Ark of the Covenant in the desert. She is the cloud on the sanctuary in the temple of Solomon. She is best visualized in these images, or as a mighty pair of wings which are outstretched over one's head. (cf. prayer on p. 283). However she is also seen as a sorrowful widow who walks the road in exile, like Isis or Demeter (q.v.).

REFERENCES: Patai (255)

Sophia. Divine Wisdom herself and syzygy of the Logos (q.v.), Sophia can be found, under many forms, throughout the world. Iconographically she is represented as a winged angelic figure dressed in red and gold, with a diadem on her head, and with the world at her feet. The Temple of Wisdom, Exercise 3, will give the reader a direct contact with her. She 'dwells with all flesh' according to the gift of God and therefore can be the possession and heritage of all living things.

REFERENCES: Nag Hammadi (239), Rudolph (291), Bible (26).

Syzygies are divine partners or consorts, according to the Gnostics. Sophia and Logos are the prime syzygies (q.v.) but Solomon and Sheba can be seen as a type of this concept, representing the union of knowledge with wisdom. William Blake's theory of emanations, which was probably derived ultimately from Eastern sources, represents a Western view of the Shiva/Shakti union in his *Jerusalem* poem which shows a system of deities and their consorts. In alchemy, the union of the syzygies is shown in the image of the *coniunctio* or the *hieros gamos*, the holy wedding.

REFERENCES: Blake (27), Rudolph (291).

Zeus, who subdued his father Uranos by castrating him, seems to have taken on the mantle of the evil demiurge. Yet he is aptly named *Pantomorphos* – of many forms. Like Math and Gwydion (cf. vol. I) Zeus is a shape-shifter. His many amours and unions should not be seen in a fundamental light, but as reflecting the divine union with all life. As a type of the Norse god Odin, Zeus lies with Mnemosyne (q.v.) for nine nights, just as Odin hangs on the windy Tree for nine days and nights: both are initiates of the mystery knowledge. Zeus is married to divine female representations of the three Native levels of existence: the Underworld – Persephone; the earth – Maia; and of heaven – Hera, and so he has knowledge of the three realms like the shamanic Odin who comprehends the three levels of the World Tree, Yggdrasil. Zeus may appear in any form, as stated, but his symbol of the thunderbolt suggests his power. He can be visualized as the Emperor card of the Tarot.

REFERENCES: Graves (111), Kore Kosmou (186), Kerenyi (173).

THE HERMETIC LANDSCAPE

Everyone has an inner landscape: 'the way to this place – and the place itself – have been unknown for a long time, and it is hidden from the greatest part of the world. But notwithstanding that it be difficult and laborious to discover this way and place, yet the place should be sought after,' wrote Thomas Vaughan in his *Lumen de Lumine* (338). If you have already attempted the Two Trees Meditation in volume one you will have begun to see certain facets of the Otherwordly landscape which is the inner reality of the Native Tradition. Such mapping can take many years until real familiarity is achieved. You may perhaps have noticed how certain locations appear over the years in your dreams – these represent the personal landscape which may impinge upon the greater archetypal reality of a tradition.

Just as the Native Tradition has its Otherworld, so the Hermetic Tradition has its own landscape. But whereas the Otherworld is rarely depicted, the Hermetic landscape has frequently made its appearance within the emblematic designs of both magical and alchemical texts. If we return for a short while to the Otherworld, we will remember that one of the aspects of the Native Tradition's inner reality is that of the island-paradise or garden. Aspects of this can be seen within medieval illuminations: angels sporting in paradise, fantastic beasts prancing in the Garden of Earthly Delights as in Bosch's picture. The image of the garden is common to both Native and Hermetic Traditions, and here we can step from one reality into another. The fusion of otherworlds is achieved by the connecting impulse of Rosicrucian and alchemical imagery which used earlier symbologies on which to base their own inner explorations. The result is a compelling mixture of the two.

The key image of this mixture keeps its perfume:

> O no man knows
> Through what wild centuries
> Roves back the rose. (347)

The rose is a signature of the tranquil continuity of the esoteric tradition: wherever it grows, there the tradition flourishes. Esoteric knowledge has been personified as a beautiful veiled maiden who must be sought by the lover of wisdom. This identification has made it possible to address the Virgin as 'rosa mystica', or, in the words of the Song of Songs: 'a garden locked is my sister, my bride.' There is no way into the *hortus conclusus* save by love, by desire to find the hidden rose which grows within. That which is spoken by 'sub rosa' is 'under the rose' – the knowledge which is transmitted only within the hidden garden itself, the wisdom which is freely given by the beloved to the lover. In alchemy the rose symbolizes this wisdom and the *rosarium* – the rose garden – symbolizes the Great Work itself. The symbol of the Rosicrucians is the Rose-Cross: the rose of the spirit blooming upon the cross of the elements – a symbol also of the marriage between pagan and Christian streams. Before the rosa mystica became the symbol of the Ever-Virgin Mother, it was the Lady Venus' sign. (217)

The garden makes its easy transition as an inner landscape for both Native and Hermetic traditions through the medium of not only pictorial representation, but also through the works of poets and mystics. From the medieval allegory of *La Romaunt de la Rose*, where the poet's quest is for the rose itself, down to Edmund Spenser's *Fairy Queen*, the Otherworldly paradise slowly becomes transformed. Enclosed within the intricate knot-gardens of sixteenth- and seventeenth-century Europe the spiritual journey is enacted by Christian in Bunyan's *Pilgrim's Progress* and by Christian Rosenkreutz in *The Chymical Wedding* (178). The esotericist makes his or her way along the ceremonial mazes, planted in mimicry of spiritual progresses. Trees, arbours and herbs are planted according to planetary correspondences, so that the microcosmic *hortus conclusus* mirrors the macrocosmic garden of the heavens.

Within the landscape are the hermit's oratory, the alchemist's laboratory, the astrological tower from which planetary movements are observed and computed. There are lakes, streams and cunning displays of water which fountain from Classical water deities and from creatures of the deep. Sometimes the overtly Hermetic nature of the garden is apparent as at Edzell Castle, Angus, Scotland, where a garden of the planets can still be seen (212), or as in the now desolate gardens devised by Salomon De Caus for the Elector Palatine at Heidelberg. (210)

Beyond the places of habitation, in the wilder and inaccessible regions stands the Mountain of Initiation – sometimes called Mount Abiegnus or the Invisible Magic Mountain, where the initiate stakes his or her adepthood in pilgrimage and discovery. As in the Kingdom of Prester John, here, too, the traveller encounters beasts which seem proper to the pages of heraldic and alchemical scrolls – the green lion, the crow, the unicorn and the phoenix. Here sits the pelican in her piety and there soars the crowned eagle. Each beast symbolizes a secret process to be undergone. The traveller finds the way by means of sigils graven in the rock which indicate some part of the way. The totemic symbols of the Hermetic Tradition are as powerful and elusive as those ancestral totems which we sought in volume one.

These are but some of the aspects of the Hermetic landscape, waiting to be discovered. Just as Books of Hours presented Biblical scenes with glowing intensity for the active participation of the faithful in the Middle Ages, so do the emblem books of Hermetic allegory reveal a rich mine for our own meditation. *The Western Mandala*, by Adam McLean, (213) is a particularly good starting point for the apprentice Hermeticist, but more and more alchemical texts complete with their illustrations are being made available. Imaginative work with some of these will present further opportunities to enter the Hermetic landscape and explore deeper. The means of entry can be the black and white pillars of the Tree of Life, which can be visualized as a gateway before you. Your guide should be a personage appropriate to the scene to be contemplated: Hermes or Christian Rosenkreutz, for instance.

But the emblem books are not the only sources to which we can go for inspiration. The Tarot, which is now interpreted in the light of modern consciousness, is really a book of medieval emblems which embody important aspects of the esoteric world-model: the grim reaper of death, the rota of Fortune's Wheel, the savage, sublunary world of the Moon card. The four suits represent the four elements. In stylized forms they give us a glimpse into another part of the Hermetic landscape. The origins of the Tarot have been a vexed question in esoteric circles. The argument that they derive from Egyptian sources can be traced to the rediscovery of things Egyptian which motivated the French esoteric world at the time of Napoleon's Egyptian campaign, when the Rosetta Stone was deciphered. This, like the translation of the Corpus Hermeticum in the fifteenth century, led to a series of revivalist inventions (cf. chapter 1). Paul Christian (48) gives a splendid pathworking in his *History of Magic* in which the reader is asked to imagine the initiation of a candidate within the Great Pyramid wherein all the images of the Major Trumps are operative. The initiate goes along a route, rather like a man in a Ghost-Train, meeting frightful, fearful and tempting images which he overcomes by means of the Major Trumps – failing only if he cannot comprehend the lesson of each trump. A similar pathworking, along Gypsy-lines appears in Basil Rakoczi's book *Fortune Telling*, wherein the reader goes through the three caverns of initiation. (281)

Adam McLean has suggested an alternative source for the development of European tarot – one which is essentially Western in origin. (209) His study of the Mantegna tarot (c.1465) is persuasive. These cards, which number fifty in total, emanate from the School of Ferrara and are based upon the Platonic academies of the mid-fifteenth century Renaissance. The cards are split into five decades, representing a) the conditions of life from beggar to pope; b) the nine muses and Apollo; c) the seven liberal arts, including philosophy, poetry and theology; d) the seven cardinal virtues, with the spirits of astronomy, chronology and cosmology; and e) the celestial hierarchy of the seven planets together with the eighth sphere, the primum mobile and the First Cause. Despite the different entitling of the cards, their symbology is remarkably similar to traditional packs. The card representing Mars in the fifth decade, for instance, is identical to the Chariot; Jupiter stands in a mandorla, like the World. Obvious qualities like Justice and Strength are almost identical. Whereas the conditions of life decade give us the Fool from the beggar, and the Magician, who is like the artisan with his table and tools of the trade. The squire and knight pass into the minor trumps.

Although there are fragmentary tarot packs dating from before this time which follow the traditional schema, it is interesting to conjecture just what kind of symbolism is common to both. The Mantegna tarot shows the basic virtues, qualities, cosmologies, abilities and conditions of human life which were the unwritten norms of medieval life. These images were familiar to all, even the unlettered. Look through your own tarot pack with new eyes: just what kind of symbolism and culture created this book of wisdom, which its numerous archetypes? With the key of the Mantegna tarot we can unlock many of these mysteries for our own time. Few modern tarots have succeeded in replacing the old symbolism with one which is efficient in our own age. The mighty archetypes behind the major trumps are now commercially mangled in the mouths of latter-day tarot-readers who, in striving to bring the cosmic message to their clients, reduce even the microcosmic message of the tarot to a handful of glib material applications. It is possible to enter each card as though it were a picture, explore the scene and speak with the archetype. In this way, the tarot can become an initiatory system. (120)

As with the Tarot, so with the Qabala. To the uninitiated, the Tree of Life appears like an underground map – a two-dimensional set of blobs connected by lines. But each of the sephiroth is a multi-dimensional place and is as real a destination as Oxford Circus or Île de la Cité. In a book of this size it is imposible to indicate the possibilities of exploring such a complex glyph as the Tree of Life. The reader is referred to *A Practical Guide to Qabalistic Symbolism* by Gareth Knight (183), where the correspondences and inner symbolism may be more readily explored. Here is a vast field of exploration indeed, which has occupied both Hebrew and Gentile Qabalists for centuries. There is no one method of applying corres-pondences – you find some of your own, but here the way-showers have been many and the multiplicity of signposts may prove confus-ing. The Qabala gives a unique method of exploring the Hermetic landscape in that its system is also a way of life, for those who can realize its possibilties.

The Tree of Life is a depiction of the Man of Light, Adam Kadmon, in whom the ten prime attributes of God are manifest. (127) These may also be seen as the emanations for the many archetypes which are used in magical workings (cf. figs 3 and 7). The Middle Pillar of the Tree is the spine of Adam Kadmon upon which the Western equivalent of the chakras are to be found. The side pillars of Mercy and Severity, the white and black pillars, are the right and left sides of Adam Kadmon. The totality of the Tree of Life is a macrocosmic Body of Light. Any exploration which we make within this wondrous universal glyph is a discovery of ourselves also.

There are many more systems and symbolic paradigms in the Hermetic Tradition, which the reader can explore in similar ways.

CHART OF CORRESPONDENCES UPON THE TREE OF LIFE

no of sephira	planetary image	virtue	vice	magical image
1. Kether	Primum Mobile	attainment of the Great Work	none	An ancient bearded king in profile
2. Chokmah	The Zodiac	devotion	none	A bearded man, a father
3. Binah	Saturn	silence	avarice	A mature woman, a mother
X. Daath	Sirius	selfless perception	spiritual pride	A head with a male and female countenance facing in either direction
4. Chesed	Jupiter	obedience	bigotry, tyranny	A strong king, crowned, seated on a throne
5. Geburah	Mars	courage	cruelty	A warrior in a chariot
6. Tiphareth	The Sun	devotion to the Great Work	pride	A child, king or sacrificed god
7. Netzach	Venus	unselfishness	lust	A beautiful naked woman
8. Hod	Mercury	truthfulness	dishonesty	A hermaphrodite
9. Yesod	The Moon	independence	idleness	A beautiful naked man of strength
10. Malkuth	The Earth	discrimination	inertia	A young woman, crowned, seated on a throne

Chart of correspondences upon the Tree of Life

No. of sephira:	Planetary image:	Virtue:	Vice:	Magical image:
1 Kether	Primum mobile	attainment of the great work	none	An ancient bearded king in profile
2 Chokmah	The zodiac	devotion	none	A bearded man, a father
3 Binah	Saturn	silence	avarice	A mature woman, a mother
X Daath	Sirius	selfless perfection	spiritual pride	A head with a male and female countenance facing in either direction
4 Chesed	Jupiter	obedience	bigotry tyranny	A strong king, crowned, seated on a throne
5 Geburah	Mars	courage	cruelty	A warrior in a chariot
6 Tiphareth	The sun	devotion to the great work	pride	A child, king or sacrificed god
7 Netzach	Venus	unselfishness	lust	A beautiful naked woman
8 Hod	Mercury	truthfulness	dishonesty	A hermaphrodite
9 Yesod	The moon	independence	idleness	A beautiful naked man of strength
10 Malkuth	The earth	discrimination	inertia	A young woman, crowned, seated on a throne

Figure 17: Chart of Correspondences upon the Tree of Life

Ultimately, the systems and symbols do not matter – it is what they stand for that we should be concerned with. Symbols are power-houses which should be used with care. The celestial hierarchies, angels, and evolutionary beings are metaphors of our own condition: realizations of what we may be.

> Apart from the constant circulation through his astral body of planetary and solar and cosmic energies, every human being has appropriated, out of the greater Whole, enough of the astral energy wherewith to construct his own individual and separate astral body, responsive to his peculiar note, coloured by his peculiar quality, and limiting him or not according to his point on the ladder of evolution. (21)

We take what we need from these symbol systems, learning our theory of levels, which is the work of a lifetime. Their cumulative effect is to tune us, prepare us for the Great Work itself. We have looked outwards at the heavens, the time has come to look within, to find the balanced point, to fashion the Stone.

> The pupil who receives force from his Master on a higher plane for the purpose of transmission to the physical plane must be prepared to effect the transmutation of the corresponding amount of force in his own nature from a lower place to a higher in order to preserve the necessary balance. (90)

This is the work of the alchemist who, in pursuit of the Great Work of transmutation, does not retain the inner force and impression, but in order to transmit it to the mundane world, transmutes that part of himself in a reciprocal exchange: matter for spirit.

EXERCISE 6 THE CADUCEUS OF HERMES

'It is taught that there is a single Light, in the form of a Man, which radiates through all the four universes, *Atzilut, Beryah, Yetzirah* and *Asiyah*, reaching down to the physical elements. This Light is bound to the Lights of the Supernal Man, which are called the ten *sefirot*. These are clothed in this Light, which is called the "Light of the Quarry of Souls" and in it are included all souls below'. This description of Adam Kadmon is at the same time a description of the Tree of Life which forms the basis for this exercise. Our purpose here is to create an affinity with the macrocosmic body of the universe, to heal those souls who are included within it, and to maintain our unity within the Body of Light. It is not necessary to have any knowledge of the Qabala in order to perform this exercise, although if you are well-read and practised in the subject you will be able to utilize it in more sophisticated ways.

First of all, sit in an upright chair, or stand, weight balanced equally on either foot. Then make a cross of light in the following manner. This action seals the aura and stabilizes the subtle bodies. Say:

Between heights,	(Touch top of forehead with the middle and index fingers of the right hand)
And depths,	(Touch solar plexus)
Between justice,	(Touch right shoulder)
And mercy,	(Touch left shoulder)
I am centred.	(Cross hands over the breast.)

As you perform this, visualize white light which comes from above your head, descending into the earth, beneath your feet. The cross is completed by a bar of white light from shoulder to shoulder, extending beyond your actual body. If you wish to put yourself under the protection of God with your own form of words, do this also. Establish your auric field by a steady circulation of breath: visualize your breathing as a double band of light which outlines your body from left ear to left foot and back over the head, and from forehead to feet, from feet to back of the head. There is no need to maintain this visualization after a while, once the pattern is established.

Your feet are upon the physical earth of this world, but your body is going to stretch through the worlds of inner space. Visualize the earth beneath you as it is seen from space: a planet with land-masses and seas. Here you are firmly established. Your body is stretching up through inner space, until the moon is at the level of your genitals: visualize it as the moon you know in the night sky. Stretching further you travel onwards until the sun is at your heart. Sirius at the level of your throat – a needle-bright star – and above your head is the primum mobile itself – which can be visualized as a whirling white nebula, the centre where creation is endlessly effected. It is very important that you do not equate these positions exactly with the subtle centres of your etheric body. See the planets as aligned vertically in front of you. When you have completed the stretching, visualize the spheres before you. You are now indeed a giant. Your body and that of Adam Kadmon are aligned over each other. For the first time you perform this exercise, do nothing other than this. Quietly establish a steady rhythm of breathing, and very slowly reverse the instructions, coming gently back down to your own size and to your own place. Seal off by the formula given above, write down any realizations and then eat and drink to ensure that you are well-earthed.

Once you have taken this part of the exercise in your stride, it is time to build the next part, which continues from where you have aligned all five positions before you. Your visualization should be aligned to *inner* and not outer space. If you experience any dizziness or disorientation, make sure you reverse the procedure slowly and seal off completely. This time, feel two great forces of polarized intensity – like two great poles of electrical current – rise from the earth beneath your feet, either side of your body. Breathe evenly and slowly. The energies weave and grow – positive and negative forces about each of the spheres, until they stop just below the primum mobile, at the level of your ears (see fig. 18). Remember, the energy interweaves the spheres, *not around your own body*. You have now built the Caduceus of Hermes upon the body of Adam Kadmon. As you meditate, you will notice an exchange of energies between the two currents of the wand. Be aware of the cosmic unity of all life, of your own vocation as an instrument of the Inner. Be especially aware that the wand which you have built is also the symbol of Asclepios, the god of healing, as well as the staff of Hermes. It can bring healing to all who need it: every divine spark within every human body goes to comprise the Body of Light. Do not hold this visualization very long, the first time. Do not attempt it if you are emotionally unbalanced or unstable on any level. If commonsense measures are observed, this exercise is cosmically beneficial, but it is a powerful one and should not be attempted often. NOTE: the positive and negative streams of energy on the caduceus should *not* be taken to denote good and evil influence, but reciprocal flows of energy which each have a necessary function. (179)

EXERCISE 7 OTHERWORLD GATEWAYS AND SYMBOLS

Working with symbol systems is a basic skill which needs to be acquired by all who follow the Western Way. There are, as we saw in

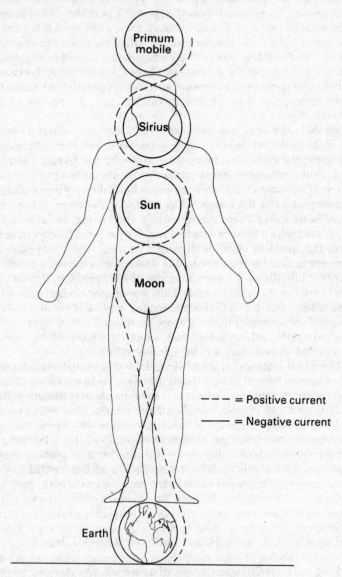

Figure 18:   The Caduceus of Hermes

volume I, many gateways to the otherworld, or to other dimensions of existence. Those who follow the Hermetic path should not necessarily need to visit actual sites – though these can sometimes serve as lenses to magnify and concentrate the will of the operator. For most the skill and building power of the imagination should be enough. A visionary glimpse of the Pylon Gate or the Cave of the Sibyl, to name only two of the many hundreds of entrance glyphs, should enable the proficient operator to project themselves into the realms of the infinite.

Symbols in themselves hold no reality; they are constructs made up of the collective belief of those who work with them. Magically speaking, the esotericist takes these symbols, and having externalized them, makes of them gateways to an inner reality totally different from the outer reality in which he or she may be standing in contemplation of the image. Thus infused with power, the symbol becomes a focal point for the operator's whole being, and as such can be imbued with a kind of external reality which can be experienced. Thus the guardian angel or elemental contact, which may have no *concrete* reality (at least not in our dimension) assumes a *symbolic* reality – initially in the consciousness of the operative, but latterly exterior to that consciousness. Thus the angelic archetypes of the kind often mediated in Qabalistic magic, may build up in pillars of textured colour rather than anthropomorphically, until it is possible to almost taste and feel the colours, which have received the impress of a reality outside our normal understanding.

The whole question of what we actually understand as real comes into question here. It has been said that we spend a great deal of time and energy establishing perimeters of reality and in reaffirming them daily in order to protect ourselves from the madness which would result in the apprehension of *too much* reality. In this instance we may see the work of the esotericist as establishing a bridgehead between two kinds of reality: inner and outer, enabling others to pass from one to the other without fear. It should not be difficult to envisage invisible lines of force in the air about us – even, perhaps, with geometric precision. Most of the time we remain unaware of the existence of these vital links with the infinite, though they are really no different from the shining paths which connect the stone circles and standing hills of the Native tradition. When we draw upon the air a great symbol of power, representing some age-old truth, we are locking our own sigil into the web of invisible force which surrounds us.

Such an understanding requires a radical alteration of our daily consciousness, and for this reason we use symbols and signs as visual keys. To the ancient mind signs were of the greatest importance: they were efficacious representations of things which could not be seen with the naked eye but which could nonetheless be understood by the inner optive: 'all things which the eye can see are mere phantoms and insubstantial outlines; but the things which the eye cannot see are the realities. . .' (22) This is to posit a different order of reality; it harks back to the *synthemata* of Iamblichus (152) or forward to the efficacy of signs discussed by the artist David Jones. (158)

An example of the kind of thing we are speaking of might be the drawing or making of a three-dimensional pyramid. The four faces of this figure can represent a number of things: North, South, East or West; a god form, a colour, name or archetype. These can then be seen as meeting at the apex of the pyramid, which becomes the point where the powers interact and are balanced to produce an effect such as a flash of visionary insight or an opening of an entry-port upon another dimension.

Meditation upon such figures can bring much into focus which before seemed hazy or insubstantial. All traditional figures of this kind are the product of inner teaching. The Grail, drawn as a cup, takes on the form of inverted pyramids, and is particularly effective as a glyph of upward aspiration and downward energizing:

Here the nexus point stands for the position of the operator, in which the initiate (lower pyramid) receives and transmits the downward flowing energy of the gods meeting his own upward mounting aspiration (upper pyramid).

Or take the star, five pointed or otherwise. This may be seen as the endless knot or pentacle with each point representing a different aspect of deity, or a symbol of force (one of the aspects of the Grail for example). Draw this out and try different combinations of symbology until you feel you have arrived at a workable system, then use it for meditation for several days or even weeks depending on the results you receive. This can also relate to the positioning of sacred objects in the temple or working-area, or indeed to the places taken by participants in any ritual performed under the aegis of this system. It can equally well be related to star-alignments or ley-line points, cardinal positions in the ritual temenos, or aspects of deity assumed by the operators.

With these few examples, and others which are readily available in the writings of Regardie, Gray and Knight (see bibliography) it should be possible, in a comparatively short space of time, to build up a thorough working system of 'telesmic' imagery which will be of considerable help in any magical work undertaken either singly or in a group. Do not be concerned, however, if you get little immediate response; some are better equipped to work with symbols than others. If more effort is required, longer periods of study and meditation, it is well worthwhile pursuing the elusive moment when a chosen symbol will 'click' into place in your consciousness. Once this step has been achieved you will find that the rest follows naturally.

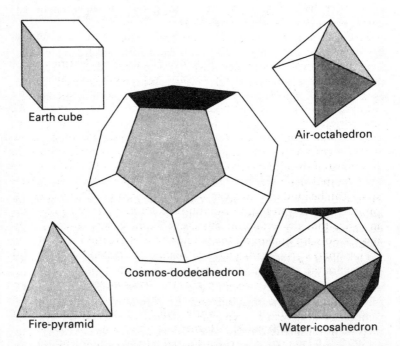

Earth cube

Air-octahedron

Cosmos-dodecahedron

Fire-pyramid

Water-icosahedron

Figure 19: Platonic Solids

CHAPTER 5
Alchemy: The Fire-tried Stone

You should understand that alchemy is nothing but the art which makes the impure into the pure through fire.

Paracelsus

Matter is the last step on the path to God.

Rudolph Hauschka: *The Nature of Substance*

THE HUNTING OF THE GREEN LION

'Matter cannot be created or destroyed,' says the scientific law of conservation: 'But, it can be transformed', replies the alchemist. God's Great Work is the creation itself in which are set the signatures and correspondences by which it may evolve. Everything created has life: not *human* life, but a life according to its proper nature, and an inner corrollative analogous to the Platonic forms. Science scoffs at the idea of matter being alive, as is evident from its disregard of the integral ecology of the natural world. Alchemy has ever treated matter as its *prima materia*, from which the divine spark can be kindled into awareness of its potential. The alchemical process concentrates upon isolating the *prima materia* of creation in order that the evolution of matter might ensue. And, as with matter, so with humanity: the whole chain of creation releasing its divine sparks, rising through the planes of existence in a joyful return to the primal unity – such is the vision of alchemy.

If the search of the philosophers is for Wisdom, then the quest of the alchemists is for the philosopher's stone – the keystone of the earth's structure itself – the *lapsit exillas* which fell from heaven and from which all matter is formed. In this stone is encoded the cipher of life's mysteries – the male and female components, which, in the outer world are divided, but which, on the Inner, are conjoined. In the pied language of alchemy both Wisdom and the Philosopher's stone are described as 'a gift and sacrament of God and a divine matter, which deeply and in diverse manners was veiled in images by the wise.' (15) If such language seems unduly veiled, we must consider that our very existence is due to a genetic process of alchemical complexity. What is hidden under the sign of emblem and glyph with alchemy, is scientifically discernable under the microscope as the genes and chromosomes, the individual DNA of human consistency. The real *prima materia* of humanity is the flesh wherein we are incarnate: the way in which our bodies develop is partly encoded into us already at birth, partly attribut-able to the physical conditions in which we grow up. The potential of every human being resides within the genes, and within the spiral of DNA: a strange alchemy dictates our transmutation from the fusion of ovum and sperm, through the cyclic metabolic renewal of our cell-structure, to our eventual demise when our flesh joins the chain of matter. Physics had sought to comprehend this mystery; medical science is now striving to recreate the conditions in which the mystery of life can be transmitted and genetically altered, with who knows what eugenic possibilities? The fact remains – though science may be able to produce crude DNA spirals and graft one life upon another, it has not discovered the hiding place of the spirit.

> I behold how all things in the
> aether are mixed with pneuma.
> I see in spirit how all things
> are sustained by pneuma:
> Flesh hangs itself upon soul,
> Soul is upborne by air,
> Air hangs itself upon aether.
> Fruits rise up from the depth,
> A child is lifted from the womb. (15)

The spirit is the inner corollative of the flesh, and no life can be reproduced upon earth without a corresponding ensoulment upon the Inner.

The conception of a child is the most mighty alchemy, but while the birth of a child necessitates its taking one or other gender as a requirement for earthly life, so the work of the alchemist, which is an attempt to be born upon the Inner, necessitates the reconciliation o_ opposites within the finding of the Philosopher's Stone. The true secret of alchemy is that the operator *becomes* the Stone.

But what is this Stone and how do we become it? Its beginnings are obscure, black like the rich soil of the Nile Delta which gave its name to alchemy. (Egyptian, *keme* = black earth.) The Greeks, who understood the symbology of colour, knew that the inner tincture of black was really gold (197) so, although Apollo was pictorially depicted with black hair, his hair was symbolically golden. This mystery was also seen in the cult of Isis: the Hermetic document, the *Kore Kosmou* (197 or The Universal Maiden, tells how Isis was given the secrets of alchemy which were to be transmitted only to her son, Horus. She is given 'the gift of the Perfect Black' – who, in the context of the text, we must see as Osiris himself – the consort with whom she is united, in alchemical union. Yet she herself is the black earth, and the pupil of the eye of Osiris: (227) she is the veiled mystery who appears outwardly as Black Isis, but whose inner reality is the Bright Isis of the Stars.

Here is the kernel of the mystery which assigns feminine symbolism to matter and masculine symbolism to spirit, Isis and Osiris, Sophia and Logos, White Queen and Red King, are syzygies whose union can only be achieved by the levels of the alchemical process. Nowhere is it stated or implied that matter = woman, spirit = man – nor should we seek to impose these meanings upon our understanding. This union of complementary opposites: matter and spirit, queen and king is the subject of this chapter.

But surely alchemy is merely the foundation upon which chemistry was established, many object? Indeed, alchemy includes proto-scientists and chemists within its history as well as mystics and magicians. It is not easy to reconcile the application of both physics and meta-physics within one discipline if one sees science from a contemporary standpoint.

This book has been much taken up with the nature of the spirit: for only by understanding things eternal will we begin to perceive the things temporal, and for this reason, we have left a discussion of matter to last. We cannot look upon matter with the fundamentalism of rational science, nor with the disdain of the Manichaen, when we approach it with the compassionate perception of inner awareness and eternal correspondence. 'Aristotle wrote of the *prima materia*, Plato of the *hyle*, Hermes of the *umbra horrenda*, Pythagoras of the "Symbolical Unity", and Hippocrates of the deformed chaos,' says Robert Fludd (307) showing how crucial matter was in relation to esoteric philosophy. The language of metaphysics was applied continuously to the realm of physics throughout the Western world up until the Enlightenment (that much-misapplied term). Now the New Physics has come full circle in its self-understanding of science by its use of Eastern spiritual terminology: that which is inexplicable in mundane scientific language can be encapsulated within cosmic conceptualizations. This ironic turn of fate, whereby the once-despised mythological paradigms have become the new currency of physics, should be cautiously heralded. The spiritual symbolism of mythology, which has become the stock in trade of the psychologist, may become the banner of the New Physics with as little justification and sense of guardianship. When the alchemists spoke in symbolic language they, at least, knew the interior reality of the symbol. This is the difference between the shaman and the psychologist, or between the alchemist and scientist, let us be clear on that score.

Alchemy is spiritual chemistry for, although it is said to have developed from physical experimentation to 'soul-alchemy', it has ever been concerned with the reconciliation of opposites, as described in the Emerald Tablet. We have already seen how planetary correspondences were observed in all the manifestations of nature in chapter 4: the colours, shapes, sounds, smells and tastes by which our senses tell us the story of any created thing became the palette and keyboard of chemistry. These subtle correspondences were the first study of alchemy, beginning with base matter – the metals, minerals and compounds of matter which were the foundation of the hierarchical chain of being itself. If a metal could be transmuted then the chain of existence was affected. The creation of gold from lead can be looked upon as the Hermetic equivalent of bringing back faery gold from the Otherworld: a transference of energy from the Inner to the Outer. Alchemists 'understood that what they were working with was not so much the actual substances as spiritual properties concealed in the metals.' (273) We might say, they attempted to bring out the inner potential, the divine spark within the metal. 'Lead is gold fallen sick' (232): the metal of Saturn/Cronos no longer has the lustre it once had in the Goldern Age.

The alchemist stands in direct succession to the Smith of the Native Tradition – he who forged the first tools from the ores of the earth itself and who was held in superstitious regard as the guardian of a great mystery. The Smith is the weapon-maker of the Gods: Govannon, Wayland, Hephaistos – the blackened, lame one.

The alchemist seems to have shared the almost universal distrust which is meted out to all metal-workers, tinkers, and miners from the time of Prometheus onwards. The miner burrows into the womb of the earth herself, careful to propiate her – as we see from the finds excavated from the Neolithic mine, at Grime's Graves in Norfolk. The metal-worker knows the mystery of fire-transmutation. The tinker and jobbing blacksmith knows the mystery of metal and has the horseman's word – the means of controlling animals, the lingua franca or *shelta* of all smiths. And as such people were anciently under the patronage of the goddess Brigid, so the alchemist pays careful attention to the service of the Anima Mundi of Our Lady Earth.

The Alchemist was the midwife and priest of transmutation: 'metals and minerals were born, grew, married, copulated, gave birth and died. Rocks and stones had bodies, souls, emotions and wants'. (55) Entering into a real relationship with the metals and elements in his or her charge, the alchemist administered alchemical sacraments to these living children of the earth. Like the real midwife and priest, continence, sobriety, watchfulness were necessary in the lying-in chamber – the laboratory – a word in which the Benedictine motto, 'laborare est orare' (to work is to pray) was made manifest.

We can see within alchemy the descent of the Western Way, in microcosm: it arises in the cosmological speculations of Native Tradition, receives the tributaries of philosophy, Gnosticism, Qabala, magic and Rosicrucianism, finally splitting off into a complex meander of chemistry and psychology within our own time – the studies of the physical and psychic constituents of creation, of which we are still amazingly ignorant. The Hermetic texts drew upon knowledge of Egyptian alchemical techniques as well as upon Hellenic scientific thought which subsequently informed both Platonic and Neo-Platonic philosophy. The insights of Gnosticism, themselves derived from multifarious Middle Eastern sources, fructified the symbology of alchemy – as we shall go on to see. By the time Qabalistic magic and Rosicrucian elements fed into this ever-powerful stream, the Western Way had received all the necessary nutrients to help it survive. Alchemy virtually became the equivalent of the Tantric and Varjayana path of the West.

The transmission of this powerful path can be traced historically from many standpoints. Most commentators favour a straight scientific appraisal, ignoring the esoteric adjuncts as an embarrassing and medieval excess. But by using this means, alchemy is robbed of its true meaning – the marriage of macrocosm with microcosm. Science must be seen in context as a holy art, rather than as an unholy interference with creation. Scientists and proto-scientists up until the dawn, or rather, twilight, of rational science, devoutly believed in the interelation of their studies with God; they harnessed their work with the yoke of prayer. This was especially important as the arts of metallurgy, herbal medicine, astronomy, astrology, and so on were considered to have been imparted by the Fallen Angels to humanity, according to Hermetic tradition. (197) This distrust of the scientist lives on today, based firmly upon the fear of knowing what should not be known, except by God.

Aristotle's theory of the four elements – which were seen to be in a state of flux, changing from one into the other – underlies the basic alchemical process. This theory can be demonstrated by fig. 20. A combination of air and fire results in heat, the combination of earth and water results in coldness. This schema gave rise also to the theory of the humours – the presiding elemental genius of the body by which individuals were judged to be phlegmatic, melancholic, sanguine or choleric, according to their makeup. All the elements were seen to derive from the *prima materia* – and indeed were subjected to the process by which they were returned to their prime condition. Yet the sum of the elements was the quintessentia or fifth element, a condition which was sought by alchemical means, by combining the elements in various processes. This can be seen in fig 21 which is a three-dimensional representation of the Great Work. When the elements are in balance, the quintessentia can result: the fifth element is itself a perfected mirror-image of the *prima materia* from which the other four derive. The numerous and lengthy processes to which the elements were subjected have been variously described both chemically and psychologically, as well as in mythological and symbolic terminology. However, since there is little space for a breakdown of the complex chemical processes here we must consider alchemy by means of the Emerald Tablet itself. The many emblem books of the seventeenth century – notably *The Rosarium Philosophorum* (290) and the Mylius Engravings (238) give a clear breakdown of the classical alchemical processes.

The following is a compressed meditation upon the Emerald Tablet.

The *prima materia* was understood to have been 'generated by fire, born of water, brought down from the sky by wind, and nourished by earth' (307) – the formation of matter, balanced by the elements, yet whose essential core – its DNA – remains a secret. All things created derive from its substance, yet its perfection is the achievement of the Great Work. The *prima materia* must be given over to the mother to be shaped or 'fixed'. When the 'child' is growing it must be purged of its separate elements in order that it grows strong: the soul and spirit of the *prima materia* are matured. Next, the correspondences between micro-and macrocosm must be comprehended: the 'youth' is sent to its father for instruction in matters sublime. When this is achieved the 'adult' returns to earth in order to practise this wisdom. The *prima materia* has been united with the quintessentia, which it mirrors, and discovers its adamantine purity and strength. This process is that by which everything is created and, if imitated with wisdom, can effect healing, long-life and illumination of the whole world. The guardian of this work is Hermes Trismegistos himself: the child of the philosophers and inheritor of their accumulated wisdom; the youthful initiate in the mysteries of both mother and father, God and Goddess; and the mature guardian of the mysteries, the Agathodaimon of all who seek to achieve the Great Work.

This meditation upon the text of the Emerald Tablet is offered as a working model for those who wish to go further in this Work. Alternatively, the reader may wish to work with the three unidentified concepts which are termed salt, sulphur and mercury. These are not to be taken only as physical or chemical substances, but apply respectively to the body, soul and spirit. Together with the glyph of fig 21 and the Emerald Tablet, the correspondences of these processes and their interrelation can be explored in meditation. Similarly, the classical terms for the main alchemical processes can be employed in a meditative manner, namely, the nigredo, albedo and rubedo which we shall be investigating later in this chapter.

Mercury, the metal of Hermes himself, is a bridge between the chemical substances employed in alchemy. Of all the metals, quicksilver (mercury) 'did not participate in the last stages of earth's densifying (but) remained a fluid.' (138) Just so, Hermes Trismegistos does not remain anchored in one mythos, but ranges throughout the systems and mythologies of many cultures, as messenger. The mercurial powers of Hermes are best assimilated under his symbolical representation as the Green Lion of the alchemical processes: his

Figure 20:   Aristotelian Table of the Elements

Figure 21:   The Crystalline Structure of the Great Work

continual shape-shifting connects the many levels, systems and processes and produces a wealth of knowledge as set forth in the Emerald Tablet:

> The green lion is extremely agile
> And blows forth the sun's colours
>   So that the reflection
>   May be seen on the plain (6)

Hermes, as the Green Lion, explores the heights and depths: the heavens, the earth and the waters beneath the earth. His example is the pattern which the alchemist follows. (fig. 22)

Figure 22:   The Green Lion

Alchemy is the soul-price of the cosmos: it teaches us to relate the infinite to the mundane, to find the presence of the divine in the daily circle of being. The process is a spiritual code used – as is the Tree of Life – by those who seek the Stone, as a system of correspondences through which to relate everything micro- and macrocosmically. The search for the Stone consists in refining the soul, purging it of elemental influences, until all that remains is a single unit – a perfectly tuned microcosm, reflecting the macrocosm. All matter is a mystery: the processes of alchemy are a ladder wherewith to transcend time and space until one stands at the highest point of creation, which is God.

We have said that all matter is alive, in a mysterious manner. The 'deepening of the plane', whereby matter is despiritualized – a thing detestable to the Pythagoreans – seems an ominous possibility in our own time within the black alchemy of nuclear technology. The heavier radio-active elements, which have been derived from yet other elements, stand in danger of being totally cut off from the spiritual world. 'The descent of the spirit into matter has now reached a turning point in the earth and from now on it is man's task to recognise and release the spirit in matter. The descent of the spirit into matter reached a turning point at the element lead.' (209) The role of science in mitigating the sufferings of humanity has been vast, but when it loses the insight of its primal function within the cosmos, it loses faith with creation. Rudolph Steiner believed that science's role could be crucial:

> The initiate-ruler, the philosopher of personality, the priestly reconciler of knowledge and faith are equally unable to rescue modern humanity from the fruit of its own attainments. Only a man trained in the scientific thinking motivating the technological research and developments of modern civilisation can discover those *new* elements which must enter human consciousness if mankind is not to fall victim of its own achievements. (318)

Steiner obviously has little faith in the various modern fragmentations of the shaman – the esotericist, psychologist and priest – perhaps he looked to new alchemists who stood for planetary evolution, who combined spirit and matter, science and metascience.

This bringing together of all the disciplines of art, science and the spirit was the aim of the Rosicrucian manifestos. Francis Bacon's vision in the *New Atlantis* (1627) and his Great Instauration (1582 et seq.) propounded 'the universal and general reformation of the whole wide world through the renewal of all arts and sciences.' Subsequently the Royal Society was founded in 1660 but, short of it being the 'invisible college made manifest' after the Rosicrucian model, it soon became the cradle for rational science. Such 'externalisations of the hierarchy' rarely result in anything other than a talking-shop unless they are truly contacted. Yet these contacts have been not Inner spiritual beings, but creations of proto-scientists. From Rabbi Judah Leib's creation of the golem in sixteenth-century Prague (310) to Dr Frankenstein's monster is a long step: as far as Roger Bacon's Brazen Head is from the computer. The magician is credited with the creation of homuculi – a geni in a bottle, possibly a wild fundamentalization of the creation of the Child of the

Philosophers – yet what are we to make of conception *in vitro* and the other experimentations to which human flesh, with its divine spark, is subjected? Such creations are to be serviceable machines, obedient to their masters: but can such things ever be friends and counsellors after the fashion of the Inner guardians? Does the ghost in the machine answer back?

If spiritual symbols have been subverted to physical applications, as with the terminologies of God and Goddess, how terribly has the craft of alchemy been inverted that the habitations of the divine spark in matter should become scientific familiars? The ultimate materialism of the Great Work has hounded alchemy from the very beginning: not the inner gold of the spirit, but the outer currency of mundane commerce is demanded on request.

> All clamour aloud: 'We want to be rich!' Rich! Yes, you desire wealth and say with Epicurus: 'let us provide our bodies and leave our souls to take care of themselves. Even as Midas in the fable, we wish to turn all things to gold. 'So there are people who seek this gold in Antimony, but since they do not care for God, and have cast far away from them the love of their neighbour, they will look at the horse's teeth of Antimony forever without knowing a thing of its age and quality. Like the wedding guests at Cana, they may behold, but. . . know nothing.

So writes Basilius Valentinus in his *Triumphal Chariot of Antimony* (341)

Our search for the stone must continue: it promises healing, long life and illumination, not earthly gold. 'The Stone, the Light of the Earth, serves as a guide to all created things and makes hidden things manifest.' (197) Yet, what if it remains hidden itself? How are we to proceed? The only method is to take the path of the walkers-between-the-worlds, the way of the Master-Men who, by the uses of imagination, pass between the worlds in search of this precious thing, with wisdom as our guide.

THE WANDERING VIATICUM

Those who follow the alchemical path of the Western Way travel by signs and stories, as all good travellers from the Canterbury Pilgrims up to the benighted travellers in Italo Calvino's *Castle of Crossed Destinies* have done. (41) Those who want to make an alchemical excursion will perhaps first read accounts of such journeys for informative tips on how they are to proceed, only to find that they can make no sense of alchemical texts because they can only be read by means of symbolic keys. It take patience and determination to learn the symbolic language of the wise: the *disciplina arcani* of the mysteries kept no better guard from intrusion by the profane than this method of writing does. Yet, as Paracelsus says, 'resolute imagination can accomplish all things'. (134)

The problem arises: to whom should we go for guidance? Faced with the numerous commentaries on this and that text, the student of alchemy may well falter. While a more hardy traveller in these realms will assure the beginner that he or she knows as much about alchemy from individual resources and experience as the greatest commentator alive, this statement is hard to accept. Yet, we are all alchemists to some degree, transmuting our bodies and natures into something other by the ingestion of both food and ideas. Just as metabolism replaces all our cells so that we are physically reconstituted within seven years, so with our consciousness: our motivation shifts tack from necessity to necessity, all the time guided into new channels of experience as year succeeds year. Our progress in alchemical exploration depends very much upon input of ideas and experiences. Therefore it is doubly important that we study original texts, where possible, and carefully monitor what modern commentators tell us.

Where once we would have studied under physical guardians we must now learn to listen for the teachings of the inner guardians who ensure that the mysteries are transmitted. This may come about by virtue of our interest or study, but inner contacts or teachers have a way of arriving without announcement within our consciousness, as we have already seen in the previous chapter. Jung himself had many inner contacts, including one whom he called Philemon, of whom he wrote:

> Psychologically, Philemon represented superior insight. At times he seems to me quite real, as if he were a living personality. To me he was what the Indians call a guru. (He) and other figures of my fantasies brought home to me the crucial insight that there are things in the psyche which I do not produce, but which produce themselves and have their own life. Philemon represented a force which was not myself. (165)

Clearly, Jung has been pathwalking in a state of solitary discovery; he is unwilling to acknowledge rationally that his inner teacher could be real – he only 'seems' real. Nevertheless, this did not stop Jung from listening and recording, nor from writing up his own experiences for the benefit of other would-be travellers. It is a pity that later Jungians have rarely chosen to follow his example, got out of their armchairs and travelled thither themselves. The temptation to intellectualize about inner experience is great. Because Jung has opened up for the modern world the reality of archetypes, *as he experienced them*, many are now content to sit back and work from his findings rather than their own.

Jung wrote: 'only an unparalled impoverishment of symbolism could enable us to rediscover the gods as psychic factors, that is, as archetypes of the unconscious.' We have already spoken of how symbolism must be grounded in first-hand understanding: so it is with the archetypes of the inner worlds – we cannot presume to work with them at second-hand, nor relegate them to the unconscious. Such an understanding will help our reading of alchemical texts. The complex processes and strange symbolic beasts, kings and androgynes of alchemy are the signature of those inner energies we call the gods; they are not abstractions or productions of our psyches, working in some objective sense from a projected theatre of memory. Their effect is real, not illusory. Hidden under many guises these inner energies, called by psychology the archetypes, come through us – they do not originate within us, as Jung himself acknowledged. The poet W.B.Yeats corroborates this understanding:

> There are, indeed, personifying spirits that we had best call but Gates and Gatekeepers, because through their dramatic power they bring our souls to crisis, to Mask and Image. . . They have but one purpose, to bring their chosen man to the greatest obstacle he may confront without despair. (366)

Without such encounters, our alchemical quest cannot be maintained because, without these Gates and Gatekeepers, we cannot find our way onwards. The alchemical archetypes are, at base, our *neter* – the Egyptian term for archetype or salt – the *prima materia* of our search, the basis upon which the other elements work. We still say of certain characters about us whose daily intercourse leavens the lumpishness of life, that they are 'the salt of the earth:' so with our archetypes. Yet the *archai* – Greek for principles or beginnings – are 'something more universal than the elements.' (197) We need careful preparation in order to work with them in full co-operation. This is where the ground-work of correspondences comes in and where the reader can prepare the way for him or herself by the means we have suggested in chapter 4.

One means of preparation is the making of a talisman which must be seen, not as a good-luck charm method of fine-tuning. A talisman is 'a magical figure charged with the Force which it is intended to represent (286).' Israel Regardie's book *How to Make and Use Talismans* gives practical advice on their construction. However, whether they are made of paper, virgin parchment or precious metals, it is not the quality of the material which matters, but the quality of the meditation and concentration by which they are consecrated which counts. The Egyptian sculptor imbued each statue in a similarly talismanic way, by concentrating the divine energy of the god portrayed with its appropriate correspondences; the hieroglyph for sculptor was 'he-who-keeps-alive.' (55)

Another method of preparation is by means of music, whose subtle correspondences do indeed activate the *archai* in a universal manner, once the right harmonic permutations are discovered. Orpheus with his lyre was able to change the nature of beasts and men by the permutation of but seven strings. If you choose to work by means of music's alchemy, then he is the one to contact. The Head of Orpheus, like the Head of Bran the Blessed, is still singing for those who have ears to hear. In the book will be found a discography of suitable music, but at no time should recorded music, however beautiful, replace that which you make yourself:

> Remember that song is the most powerful imitator of all things. For it imitates the intentions and affections of the soul, and speech, and also reproduces bodily gestures, human movements, and moral characters, and imitates and acts everything so powerfully that it immediately provokes both the singer and hearer to imitate and perform the same things. (351)

Ficino sought to reproduce planetary correspondences by means of his Hermetic hymns. Fabio Paolini, a professor of Greek at Venice in 1589, wrote about the talismanic alchemy of music also, noting that although musicians in his own time were masterly skilful, 'none has produced effects superior to Orpheus.' (ibid).

For most people, the most immediate means of preparation will be the reading of the alchemical texts and the contemplation of alchemical emblems. These have a deep inner effect, as Jung himself recorded in his psychological study of alchemy (164). Just as the architectural language of medieval symbolism presented books in stone in every cathedral, so the alchemical archetypes were portrayed as emblems, conveying initiatory clues. How shall we go about working with these? Gerhard Dorn (floriat 1565-78), a disciple of Paracelsus, advises on the means to approach the Great Work thus:

> Through study one acquires knowledge; through knowledge, love, which creates devotion; devotion creates repetition and by fixing repetition one creates in oneself experience, virtue and power, through which the miraculous work is done and the work in nature is of this quality. (345)

Marie-Louise von Franz speculates that the 'study' spoken of above means the actual reading of the alchemical texts – that exposure to them can itself have an effect. Although the processes described, verbally and pictorially, within the texts correspond to the chemical admixture of various substances, they are also emblematic of the inner human condition – which is what the psychological schools have made their study.

Such intelligent reading and contemplation is the start of the initiatory journey. In *The Chymical Wedding of Christian Rosenkreutz* (178) the hero, Rosenkreutz himself, describes his own initiation in such a way that only those who had themselves experienced it could understand. Yet, if we meditate upon the hidden words and images – 'fixing by repetition', as Dorn has it – we will find some of the keys which we seek. In default of operational Mystery Schools and mystery guardians, we are driven to seek for nourishment in the mystery stories which remain to us. Did the world but know it, the mysteries are scattered at our feet – whole initiatory systems which wait for someone to exposit them after having travelled with the archetypes which are their inner guardians. They are explored only by meditating, by entering the story – just as the Classical Mystery schools initiated their candidates, by making them live the mystery in identification with the cult deity (cf. chapter 1).

The expositors, guardians and paradigms of the Great Work have been the subject of these two volumes. Alchemy is the most total expression of the Western Way, concerned as it is with the transmutation and perfection of consciousness. The Native Tradition's guardians sought to effect the change from tribal to individual consciousness, just as the Hermetic Tradition's guardians have sought to transmute individual into cosmic consciousness. Both shaman and magician have tried to interrelate the microcosm to the macrocosm, in their different ways. Their roles have fragmented in diverse ways; their symbologies have varied with bewildering complexity, but we can trace the similarities and choose how we would wish to align our own inner journey towards the Great Work. The Foretime was motivated by a chthonic identification; its alchemy was effected by means of earth, wood and stone. Later ages looked to the celestial hierarchies for their integration in the Body of God, yet they still recognized the chthonic signatures of metals, the talismanic properties of all created things. The cauldron and alembic were both transformative vessels which met in the universal image of the Grail. Shaman and alchemist are connected by the same story involving the difficult inner-world journey of the initiate, his quest for otherworldly guides and for the drink which will bring healing, long-life and illumination to his tribe.

When esotericism is under attack, often the only survivor is the central story of the mystery which can masquerade merely as a folk-tale or be reinstated as an initiatory key, as necessary. In such a way is the esoteric wisdom of the Tarot said to have survived: what better place to hide the mystery than in a pack of cards, which can be found in the hands of any wandering rogue whose greasepaint hides the true nobility of a master? The marginal shamans of both Native and Hermetic traditions have survived as storytellers, troubadours and playwrights in order to transmit their inherited wisdom. So has the ancient role of the poet-shaman been instrumental in keeping alive the old traditions of transformation. And what matter if the mysteries become the stuff of a story by which to beguile the long winter nights, as long as they are still told and live in our hearts? It is to these faithful guardians – *the makars*, as the medieval Scottish poet, William Dunbar called his fellow-poets – that we must be grateful that we possess a traditional mystery system within the West, springing directly from our Native roots to flow into the Hermetic stream of alchemy.

Just as the Hermetic inner landscape harks back to the natural perfection of the Native Otherworld, so do the transformative images find their root in Paradise itself. The scenario in which the transformative symbol is sought, varies little from story to story. In the apocryphal text *The Apocalypse of Moses*, dated to about the early Christian era, we read how Seth, the inheritor of Adam's wisdom in Hermetic tradition, is sent by his father to obtain the oil of mercy from Eden. He is refused by the archangel Michael, but is promised that it shall be forthcoming 'to the holy people at the end of time.' (278) This oil of mercy is a healing oil which will restore Adam to his former wholeness but, although Seth does not obtain it for the healing of his father, he is promised that his line shall indeed produce a saviour who will administer healing to Seth's descendants. We have already seen how the Story of the Pearl is similarly associated with Seth's lineage (chapter 4): to possess the Pearl is to obtain paradise. These stories and the discovery of the Emerald Tablet (chapter 1), point to a quest to be undertaken, a challenge to be answered. They are the archetypal myths of the Hermetic quest for the divine spark's reunion with God in Paradise, whereby the world shall be healed and where there shall be no more death or ignorance.

From the Native Tradition sprang yet another such story – that of the Grail. There is no one source for this legend, although we can look to numerous references to the healing waters, springs or fountains of the Otherworld which brought wisdom and healing. We notice, too, the cauldron of transformation which variously produced the food of one's desire, brought the dead to life and healed the sick. It is always in the possession of a Goddess of Sovereignty, maiden of the well or woman or otherworldly power. (219) Underlying the theme of the Waste Land – a paradigm of the earth's condition of disharmony in the cosmos – is that of the ravaged earth-mother who cannot give her bountiful gifts to the sovereign who is likewise a Wounded King. The Wounded King's champion is the untried hero who must somehow find the healing draught which will make his sovereign whole once more: he must seek to free the waters which are

Figure 23: Alchemical King and Queen

chained by evil custom so that the Waste Land of the earth-mother may blossom once more. Then and only then can the Sovereign and his Sovereignty be united in alchemical union. (fig. 23)

Who can tell how many times this mystery has been expounded and in how many different ways? The healing draught which unites Sophia and Logos within Gnosis, Wounded Kings and Waste Land within the Grail corpus and Red King and White Queen within alchemy can only be caught in the vessel which the adept fashions for this purpose. It is krater, cup and stone. Those who achieve this height of the Great Work – the union of the Great Above and the Great Below – are granted to drink from the wandering viaticum by which the initiate is sustained upon the journey towards the apocatastasis when all things will have their healing. The draught that he or she drinks is for the healing of the world, not a magical potion which benefits only the seeker. This wandering viaticum – the way-bread and drink of the world – is like the alchemical Stone in that it is found in unlikely places, after great searching and cannot be retained for personal use. Like the kernel of the mystery-story which cannot be grasped by the ignorant, the Grail cannot be used for evil purposes – its healing cannot be mediated by the unworthy. Yet neither is it achieved by the pedant. Its healing comes only to the simple, to the holy-fool, the initiate who to gain eternal life, stands on the brink of the abyss and leaps lightly over with all the trust of his ancestor, the shaman.

The dimension of the inner quest for the transformative symbol is further deepened by the admixture of Native and Hermetic traditions at the nexus of Christianity when the Native stories of the poet-singer become fused with the Hermetic craft of the alchemist-magician. Makar and artificer, troubadour and guildsman, master-man and Qabalist, Grail-knight and Rosicrucian sage are caught up together in a marvellous exchange of material. The exponents of the Mystery Schools had been subsumed into Christianity, or else followed their own unorthodox ways of transmission and the Hermetic tide had not returned when the Grail legends were eventually written down. Celtic champion had become medieval knight in the quest for the transformative vessel. The Dux Bellorum, Artos, had become King Arthur, that most Christian king who 'carried the image of the holy Mary, the ever-lasting Virgin, on his shoulder' at the Battle of Guinnion. (248) The Grail legends became the healing lance of spiritual chivalry. The Grail itself became identified with the cup of the Last Supper, or with the cruets in which Joseph of Arimathea caught the blood and water from the side of the Crucified Lord. Seth's mighty descendant had returned to redeem his people and give them, at long last, the oil of mercy. The people's native story entered the lists of the Christian story, cross-fertilizing with the hero-myths of all lands.

If the Grail legends are the epitome of Catholic Europe's inner-mysteries, then those of Christian Rosenkreutz are the underlying mysteries of Protestant Europe after the Reformation. They may seem to be a totally Hermetic invention, but their roots are deeper. In the tradition of the Master Men of Celtic tradition, Rosenkreutz enters the mountain of the goddess and lifts her veil – just as Thomas the Rhymer and Tannhauser do. (217) He has elements of Spenser's Red Cross Knight but, instead of vanquishing dragons and freeing maidens, he goes on a quest for inner wisdom and vouchsafes himself the champion of the ignorant, the sick and the tormented. In the *Chymical Wedding*, he both unites King and Queen, and is himself united with Lady Venus, who represents the inner wisdom. He can be identified with both Hermes, Christ and Perceval at the moment of accomplishment – whether of the Philosopher's Stone, the Redemption or the Grail, is for the reader to say.

Both sets of legends – those of the Grail and of Christian Rosenkreutz – show a remarkable similarity in dedication to the Great Work. The company of Arthur's Round Table and the Congregation of the Rosicrucians each meet once a year, respectively at Camelot during Pentecost, and in the House of the Holy Spirit at Christmas. Both swear to do good service to all who ask of it, freely and without favour. While Arthur's knights subdue dragons, quelling atavistic, evil customs in the land, Rosicrucians strive to heal the sick and counsel the ignorant. Evidently spiritual chivalry did not die at the Reformation and Renaissance. (6, 185)

The storytellers, the makars, who had once enjoyed an honourable place in society and lost it again, were able to return with the letters of learning after their names, having vindicated the mysteries and brought them to a new generation. It was time to return to the physical participation in the mysteries, within the boundaries of alchemy, magic and science. The fragmented shaman – smith, magician, astrologer, priest, poet, philosopher – was united in the person of the alchemist, once more under royal patronage to pursue the Great Work. It was a brief return of an ancient way of life which was to dissipate under the ignorance of the 'new learning', which despised the emblematic processes of the alchemical story and looked upon them as childish allegories which prefigured the glories of science. The transformative wisdom of the Grail was ignored in favour of a material end to all ills. The Stone of the Philosophers became so much rubbish again – unless, of course, it was capable of generating real gold or eternal life. The demise of alchemy's classical age was brought about by disbelief in its internalized mythological sequences. Neither Hermes, Christ nor Arthur were of interest, except as curious literary remains. The earth could return to Waste Land and the soul to perdition. Surely the makars were dead, and the wandering viaticum appeared not at all during this period – none were worthy to drink, because none were able to transform. Both Native and Hermetic traditions died back, to seed from the Inner in a later century, in our own time.

If the Foretime's wisdom is the natural resonance of the Native Tradition in our own time, so then is Alchemy the current resonance of the Hermetic Tradition for today. There is still much work of recovery to be done among those who are committed to the survival of the Western Way. Some of the fragments of tradition are so scattered as to be like the pieces of Osiris' corpse, to be gathered with much toil and sorrow. Yet, whatever has been lost in the physical world is still recoverable by means of meditation and analeptic memory. (cf. exercise 2, vol. I).

The Rosicrucian heritage connects the Grail and the Elixir of Life, spiritual chivalry and hermetic quest, physical and soul alchemy. The Rosicrucian and alchemical texts of the early seventeenth century unconsciously drew upon the Gnostic usages of early Christian Alexandria, via the medium of Islamically preserved alchemical wisdom. Thus, at a time when Christianity was further fragmented at the period of the Reformation into Catholic and Protestant, an old esoteric Christian impulse was able to permeate Europe. Up until the middle of the seventeenth century the patterns laid down at this period were virtually upheld throughout the Western world. Cut off from each other by cultural and religious boundaries, as though by the corridor of time, Catholic and Protestant Europe developed in totally different ways. The speculative Rosicrucianism of Northern Europe countered the much symbolically-curtailed Christianity which Protestantism presented: robbed of the sacramental liturgy, the esoterically unfulfilled turned to the transmutations of alchemy; deprived of the Virgin Mother, alchemists invoked Pan Sophia, the World Soul, the White Queen of the alchemical union. Meanwhile, in the Catholic South, where liturgical business went on as usual, philosophy and physics took on the pallor associated with Northern skies: the ascetic thinking of Descartes and Pascal countered the over-blown superstitions of a world-order with which science had no accord. Esoteric development seems to have progressed only in the north. The centre of esoteric attention moved from Italy to Germany where, from the time of Boehme and the Rosicrucians, until the time of Goethe and Steiner it continued unabated. The French estoeric revival only took place after the French Revolution. Greece never experienced a Renaissance due to its occupation by the Turks but, with pre-Revolutionary Russia, maintained the esoteric Christianity of the mystical Orthodox rite. Spain expelled its esoteric cabals in the fifteenth century. Britain, along with America, is currently undergoing a rediscovery of both Native and Hermetic traditions. Migrations of people and of ideas have shaped the esoteric development of the West: what one part of the world has rejected, another takes up as its saving idea and motivating force. In the cycles of recurrence and Inner resonance, the synthesis of one tradition with another brings us a closely-interlocking pattern in which to operate according to our ability and inclination.

We each have the potential to approach alchemy as our own study, according to our individual talents whether as poet, singer, magician, scientist or craftsman. Alchemy is crucially important to the future development of the West, which is still unable to adjust to either physical sexuality or inner polarity, let alone the interpenetration of microcosm and macrocosm. We have yet to plumb the deepest mysteries of reconciliation: it is a path walked in darkness, illumined only by the lantern of love.

THE CHYMICAL WEDDING

In an age which is concerned with revamping the old symbologies and archetypes, there is much dispute about the rightful position of divine masculine and feminine symbols, just as there has been a corresponding debate about the respective roles of men and women. In the esoteric world such disputes are rarer: the symbolisms of Lord and Lady, God and Goddess are the everyday currency of the Inner Planes. Let us proceed intuitively upon this ground and not attempt to use symbols as weapons. The Divine Masculine and Feminine are the two-sided door – Janus/Janua. In terms of developing consciousness, we come through the door which portrays the Goddess, for she is the primal image of our birth into the mysteries. If we refuse to pass through her mysteries we may not proceed upon our way: she stands at the entrance of the inward spiral of the Native Tradition. Our way out of the labyrinth is by means of her wisdom. On the reverse, inside the door is the God who stands at the end of the outward spiral of the Hermetic Tradition. We cannot emerge without the assistance of his knowledge. Just as these dual influences affect whole ages and cultures at different times, so too do we encounter the God and Goddess at the appointed time in our own life-cycle. Our own parents tell us of Mother and Father, our own relationships, of wife and husband; our own children, of son and daughter. As we age physically, so our inner understanding appreciates the ever-youthening aspects of masculine and feminine, but this is merely one expression – the physical realization – of a complex set of polarities: the Inner world polarities are yet different again.

We spoke in volume one of the problems which can occur when the inner companion is projected upon a physical person. To avoid confusion, let us refer to figure 15 (p. 342) where the polarities and their levels are set our clearly. Each man stands under the macrocosmic archetype of the Logos or God, and is capable of mediating that force; each woman stands under the macrocosmic archetype of the Goddess or Sophia, and is capable of mediating that force. As man is able to experience the love of a woman, the inspiration of his inner companion – the muse or sibyl – and behold the macrocosmic beauty of the Goddess, so, too, is woman able to experience the love of a man, the inspiration of her inner companion – the daimon or prophet – and behold the macrocosmic beauty of the God. Further, each polarity is able to mate on its own plane i.e. man with woman, prophet with sibyl, God with Goddess: each of these levels, which are mysteriously within us, are also capable of mating, but each partner must be aware of these levels in the first place, which is not the case in most modern relationships. The mating, in such cases, occurs only in the conjoining of flesh during sexual union – the other levels are not polarized and so cannot mate.

The alchemical understanding of the *coniunctio* is this very mating on every plane which produces the rebus or hermaphrodite of the Great Work – a reconciliation which prefigures the union of microcosm with macrocosm. This is at the heart of that lost tantra of the West, the secret of which is the highest working of alchemy.

To assume the roles of the White Queen and Red King is only

possible if both partners are initiates within the Great Work: this is the reason for the alchemist's working with his *soror mystica*, who was invariably his wife. Those who see the woman's role within the work merely as a conjuror's assistant – all tulle and tights – do not understand it at all. Yet neither is the *soror mystica* a passive agent in the operation. Indeed, if the operator is female, she will require the assistance of a *frater mysticus*.

But where does this leave the non-initiate who has married a partner who is not only ignorant of inner realities but positively refuses to believe in their existence? How does one come to a re-evaluation of one's relationship without tearing at the delicate webs of love which already bind one human being to another? The radical revisioning of male and female roles has had the same effect that science has had on a metaphysical perception of the world – it has sundered the work wrought on the looms of light, shattered the mirror of the mysteries, left us dissatisfied. Those who long to mate on higher levels with their partner and are unable, remain in a state of frustration which is not physical. They lack true sacramental union. 'Only those who are rightly married can go to the higher degrees,' writes Dion Fortune, in her study of laws of sexuality and polarity. (92) By 'right marriage', she does not mean legally-sanctioned but divinely-sanctioned partnership. This does not mean to say that partnerships should be abandoned when esoteric duty calls. The esoteric laws on this point are clear enough: whatever contracts are entered into must be abided by, especially when children are involved. The law regarding marriage is often mocked, but it reflects the understanding that marriage is a sacrament which one human being gives to another in the token of flesh. Who knows but if we go on quest for the Grail, which is the vessel of this polar-alchemy between the sexes, that it may be bestowed by the lover upon the beloved, that the wounds of Wounded Lord and Waste Land may be healed at last?

The royal way of alchemy is by no means easy to achieve. Opposites are difficult to reconcile. The Great Work is only achieved by intense effort and delicate preparation. No alchemist would casually throw his elements into the prepared bath with the abandon with which some people jump into bed with each other: the result of either operation would be negligible.

The seemingly irreconcilable division of opposites has been the subject of many myths and legends. The traditional story about the incestuous love of the sun for the moon, his sister, is one which finds its home within the alchemical and hermetic symbology. God sets sun and moon in the sky so that they follow each other around the heavens, never meeting, except at the moment of eclipse when they are seen to embrace. Yet the unsatisfied yearning of the sun and moon gives us light by day and night. 'Life is poured into all things through the moon and sun, and therefore they are called by Orpheus the vivifying eyes of Heaven.' (84) In an early Hermetic text, Hermes is addressed as one 'whose tireless eyes are sun and moon – that shine in the pupils of the eyes of men.' Hermes, the child of Sun and Moon, mediates the imagery of God and Goddess within the symbology of all myths, and so we perceive all things as partaking of these dual natures on many levels. Yet, in the *Revelations of St John* (chapter 22) we are told that there shall be no need for sun or moon in the Holy City, because the light of God will be shining in and through us: the need to steer by the celestial influences of either divine masculine or feminine will be over because we shall *be* the light itself.

We are yet earth-bound and not spiritual beings, however, and the neo-Pythagorean invocation to the Eternal Feminine is still appropriate to our needs:

> Honour be to woman on earth, as in Heaven, and may she be sanctified, and help us mount to the Great Soul of the world who gives birth, preserves, and renews – the Divine Goddess who bears along all souls in her mantle of light. (295)

Those who wish to work with these archetypes of reconciliation can employ many different scenarios drawn from whatever tradition they find appropriate. One such is the Gnostic *apocatastasis* when the Bride, Sophia, is raised up to her Bridegroom, the Logos. They form the gateway of the bridal chamber where they are to conjoin and, each holding out a curved hand, form an O through which the created hierarchies pass – mineral, vegetable, animal, human, angelic etc. When everything has passed within, their union takes place. Similarly, the reconciliation of the Shekinah with God can be visualized, after the Qabalistic Sabbath meditation of *yichudim*. The Assumption and Coronation of the Virgin is another image of this reconciliation: although her body and soul have been assumed to heaven, she is, with her Son, a bridge over which the whole creation may enter into the final unity of Paradise. (fig. 24)

Alchemy ultimately answers the challenge of dualism by not passing up the challenge of duality. The 'evil' nature of the flesh – a fear which lay at the very heart of many of the Classical mystery

*Figure 24: Alpha and Omega: Logos and Sophia – emblems of
eternal hope*

schools, was not resolved until alchemy became a working system.
Here it was realized that the task of transmuting the fleshly envelope
towards a higher spiritual plane of existence, could begin while one
was yet still living, and that the effect of this transmutation could
become a means of uniting the scattered Body of Light for the benefit
of all creation. The unification of the alchemist and the *soror mystica*
in the bridal-chamber and of the elements within the furnace were
paradigms of this gathering-in.

The alchemical processes vary considerably from text to text:
some relate the integration of two opposites – as in the *Rosary of the
Philosophers* (290) – where Sun and Moon go through two sets of
processes. Others represent the elements as being subjected to seven
stages, corresponding to the seven-fold planetary system, rather as
the Gnostic sects who were taught to traverse the seven spheres of the
archons in order to arrive at the pleroma, purged of all the vices
attributable to the guardians of each sphere. Some tell of the birth of
the perfect Mercurius who emerges only at the end of this seven-fold
cycle of transmutations through the nigredo, albedo and rubedo
stages of the alchemical process – Hermes Trismegistos goes through
the seven days of creation in reverse, to appear triumphant.

The black, the white and the red stages are the archetypal pattern,
not only of alchemy, but also of the Native folk-story. Perfection is
seen to reside in a combination of these three colours: the lan-
guishing prince or princess of the story can only marry one whose
cheek is pale as the snow, whose lips are red as blood, whose hair as
black as the raven's wing. This ancient motif is a feature of the
Grail-knight's awakening from the unreal dream: he sees the blood
in the snow as a black raven stoops upon its prey and remembers his

quest. This symbolic key is far more complexly employed within alchemy where each stage has its own mythos. Some systems give further colours – the peacock's tail and the yellowing – but we shall only be considering these basic three.

In the *Nigredo*, the Wounded King encounters the Waste Land, Christ enters the tomb, Osiris is scattered by Set. The King of the alchemical process is sundered of his flesh and putrefaction sets in. In the *Albedo, a* sevenfold bath is prepared. The bones of the scattered one are restored by Isis, the White Mass of the Holy Mother is celebrated where the Virgin offers up her child, the Wounded King drinks of the Grail: the heavenly dew of the planets is bestowed. In the *Rubedo*, the glorified body is resurrected, Isis joins with Osiris to produce Horus, the Grail Knight succeeds his Wounded King and marries his master's daughter. The Stone of the Philosophers is achieved. (79)

Just as the alchemical elements were separated, purified, changed and reunited, so have the divine sparks of creation been separated from their source, changed by earthly experience; purified by the trials they encountered, they shall, likewise, return to the primal unity. The figures of Adam Kadmon in Qabala, of the Gnostic anthropos, and of elusive Mercurius in alchemy are paradigms of the same esoteric truth. Our touchstone is the symbol of the scattered Body of Light: be it Pearl, Grail, Philosopher's Stone.

Alchemy is the philosophy which enables us to transcend the limitations of mortality: our divine spark is transmuted into the elixir of life so that the physical vehicle becomes a temple in truth. To find and isolate the quintessentia – the undying part of ourselves – is the quest: like the oyster that forms a pearl, we must learn to live with irritation, toil and an inglorious life in order to achieve this quest. The transmutation of the earthly into the heavenly is, however, not only the concern of alchemy. In the daily transubstantiation of the mass, bread is offered at the altar and mysteriously becomes the Body of Christ. The moment of Redemption, whereby matter is given the potentiality of spiritual regeneration, is offered for all by one who is the high priest of these mysteries – a priest forever after the order of Melchizedek (Hebrews 5,6). Alchemy was able to claim 'the earthly philosopher's stone is the true image of the spiritual and heavenly stone, Jesus Christ.' (55) This was neither blasphemous nor alien to the Hermetic tradition; all who follow the way to cosmic consciousness and regeneration of matter use the bridges which tradition provides for us. Christ, partaking of both earthly and divine natures, was seen as such a bridge: his resurrection and the Assumption of his Mother figure frequently in alchemical emblems as symbolic of the achieved work. Significantly, the term *Corpus Christi* – the Body of Christ – has three meanings: the glorified body of Christ, the consecrated bread upon the altar, and the community of believers who form the macrocosmic body of Christ.

In the mythos of Christ is seen the meeting of two traditions. As Dionysius is torn to pieces by the Titans, or Orpheus by the Maenads, within the Native Tradition – itself a later paradigm of the ritual sacrifice in which the tribe partakes of the tortured body of John Barleycorn – so the ritual mythos of the Hermetic Tradition shows us the dissolving of the Red King in the alchemical bath of natron which turns to pure gold. There are many vegetation gods who bear names meaning verdancy: from the Mesopotamian Tammuz, to Osiris, who is the Green One, the drama unfolds. Gold-leaf hammered out thinly and held to the light will glow green and gold, like the green and gold lion, the Mercurius, in whom are hidden all the philosopher's secrets: the chlorophyll of the *prima materia*.

The foundation mysteries of the Native Tradition speak of the apportioning of the body of the Goddess to form the world: so the foundation mysteries of the Hermetic Tradition are those of the scattered God. Their reunion has been celebrated from Sumeria to Ireland: from ritual mating of the Goddess's representative with the King, the homage of the King to Sovereignty, to the Gnostic Bridal-Chamber. (217) Red King and White Queen are God and Nature, Christ and Sophia, Mercury and Venus – a chess encounter which is mate, death and remaking of creation in one.

> Syria has Adonis, Greece has Dionysius, Egypt has Osiris but these are merely the Sun of Wisdom. Isis is the sister, wife and mother of Osiris; Typhon cuts his limbs into pieces, but she binds them together. (307)

The stone which fell from heaven – the proto-Grail – is matter, personified by its guardian, the Anima Mundi or Sophia. Only when the quintessentia embraces the *prima materia* can the stone which is rejected become the keystone of creation. The Rosicrucian alchemists were correct in their appaisal of Christ as the philosopher's stone because he, of all created humanity, has achieved not only birth and death, but also resurrection in his created body.

The mysterious encounter of Christ in the depths of the Underworld which brought about the Resurrection can only be guessed at:

he brought his heavenly light, like that Star of Bethlehem at the place of his birth, into the darkness of the tomb. As one in human flesh, he embraced the human condition of death and dissolution, making it his sister and bride. Thus the laws of nature were altered in an inapprehensible way. The Shroud of Turin bears the imprint of this mysterious encounter – of which the initiate should be loath to speak to the unwise. Flesh was offered voluntarily for the redemption of all flesh: a sacrifice which could not be unacceptable. What Christ has done changes the laws of the created world for ever afterwards. (217) Word and Wisdom, Logos and Sophia have embraced – this side of the apocatastasis – but our Anima Mundi cannot rest from mantling 'the guilty globe' until the whole creation is returned to the primal unity: only then can she enter the eternal embrace of the Bridegroom.

The Golden Age Restored, an alchemical treatise, speaks of matter personified as the 'pure and chaste virgin of whom Adam was formed and created': the alchemist, like Christ, must choose her and say, 'her garments are old, defiled, and foul, but I will purge them, and love her with all my heart.' (307) The alchemical work is therefore one of planetary service for, only by dedication to the lot of the earth and those living on it, can the Great Work be achieved at last.

We have heard how the Emerald Tablet was found in the hands of Hermes Trismegistos, how the Oil of Mercy was eventually given to Adam's successors, how Adam passed to Seth the precious Pearl of gnosis: these are ultimately stories of the inheritance of an unworldly wisdom. Genetically we are part of the Body of Light: the two serpents upon Hermes' caduceus rule our every cell with their encoded spirals of DNA. The cup of gnosis waits to be held to our lips at the end of the quest. These are the esoteric paradigms of the hermeticist – the stories which our ancestral shamans once told and which have been reshaped by successive generations of travellers on the Western Way. This is the story which will be told until the sigh of the last blade of grass, when creation will run backwards as a succession of brilliant sparks in the darkness, into the abode of Light.

The sign of the Aeon is the Hermaphrodite – the rebus of alchemy. This being is the product of a union between Hermes and Aphrodite, the Sun and Moon, God and Goddess of Hermetic and Native Traditions. The totality of the two traditions is comprised of the Emerald Tablet of Hermes and the rose of Aphrodite. As the Native Tradition has come down to us via the shaman as poet/mystic/

quester, so has it been preserved within the wisdom of the Rosicrucian-alchemist, whose symbol is the rose of the Goddess upon the cross of the elements' regeneration. The Hermetic Tradition has been transmitted by the shaman as magician/philosopher, who follows the laws of the Emerald Tablet of the God, Hermes Trismegistos. The union of these disparate functions of the shaman is happening in our own time, where the two traditions meet in the New Aeon – the Aquarian Age.

There is much speculation about this phenomenon: will it be yet another projection of the Golden Age or merely the imagining of mystics at the fag-end of an esoteric era? The Aeon comes as a child: and, like the child Harpocrates, its finger is to its lip. It is a new creation, with the knowledge of both parents – Isis and Osiris – remembering both the nemetons of the Goddess and the temples of the God. It has been – and will be – many things. It is coming to birth while you read this page: the song is already woven between the chthonic sibyl and the celestial prophet.

Figure 25:   Sun and Moon shine upon the Rose-Cross of the Great Work

EXERCISE 8 THE SHEPHERD OF STARS

'The ultimate ideal is for every human being to be psychically androgynous' (68) – *not*, we note, physically so. The meaning of this dictum can be realized within the following exercise. In exercise 6, you experienced the elements and learned to integrate them: in this exercise you learn to balance the male and female halves of your inner nature. Seated in meditation, visualize this scene before you.

You are standing, as it were, at the edge of the world. Before you are the two equilibrated pillars: to your left the white pillar – the merciful pillar of the Tree of Life, denoting the Divine Masculine energy which is positive and outer in its effect. To your right is the black pillar, the Pillar of Justice on the Tree of Life, denoting the power of the divine Feminine which is inner and negative in its effect. (Though not in any malign sense: *negative* here means restrictive – the polarized opposite of positive outflowing energy.) Behind the pillars is a vast night sky of deep indigo in which are the stars and planets; the heavenly bodies appear to have eternal stillness and yet to spin on their axes at the same time.

Begin by concentrating upon the individual force of the pillars: if it helps, rehearse the symbolism of a mythos you feel at home with and transfer its energy to the pillars, in order to focus on their effect. Do not hurry; allow the polarized forces to rise. Without touching either pillar, feel their interlocking energies as a magnetic field which is almost tangible. When the power is stabilized and firmly established, visualize the power of each pillar emanating as a ray, like the beam of a spotlight, into the heavens beyond you. At the point where the rays intersect a naked figure stands in an oval of polarized light. It is an adrogyne, formed of the dual energies – one half female, the other half male – either side of the body is composed of a completely perfect man and a completely perfect woman. The figure is beautiful with the power and purity of an angel, yet it is the sum of the pillar's energies in human form. A rainbow scarf swathes the body lightly.

It is sufficient to visualize the scene above, as you stand before the pillars, allowing any realizations to rise from within. But you may wish to go a stage further. The initiate of the mysteries has to 'pass between the pillars', or die to the world, in the mystical sense. The uninitiated can only read this mystery at its face value, perceiving the loss and sacrifice implied in this symbolic action. Yet the initiate gains more than is sacrificed at the dedicatory altar. The androgyne which stands behind the pillars is your potential self, perfected and balanced. When the time is ripe, and you feel prepared, step between the pillars, take the step forward into space, and stand in the twin rays. You are identifying with the potential and essential nature of the whole earth, representing its place in the cosmos as a balanced and thriving unit. As you stand in the starry vault, receiving the power of both pillars, before you appears the Shepherd of Stars, the guardian of flocks. He says, 'I am Alpha and Omega, the Guardian of the Gates, the Keeper of the Keys of Time.' Meditate upon his words: listen to any other words he may have to tell you. Beyond this point you may not go. Visualize yourself back before the pillars, feel the power return to the pillars and their force shutting down for this time. Seal off, in your usual way, making sure you are well earthed.

If you have a tarot pack of the more traditional kind you may find it helpful to contemplate trump twenty-one, the World, on which the androgyne appears, The Shepherd of Stars will appear in whatever shape is appropriate to your needs.

EXERCISE 9 REVITALIZING YOUR ROOTS

We are near the end of the book. If you have read both volumes and worked the exercises consistently you will have begun to walk the Western Way. Perhaps you will have set yourself a regular routine of meditation or practical work. You will then have discovered how much time and energy are diverted from other areas of your life. If this is the first time you have worked with or on the Inner planes you may be disturbed at the depletion of your energy: this is to be expected in the early stages, but everyone, from neophyte to adept experiences this depletion at some time or another, especially after prolonged periods of work. Your physical frame may be ill-suited to take the kind of battering that living on more than one level involves, and you may need to plan your work with care. Any period of prolonged exhaustion is dangerous and leaves the subject open to illness: if your energy is seriously depleted, a long holiday from Inner work is indicated. And that means a *complete* break.

This exercise is designed to help generate vitality and should be regarded as the psychic equivalent of glucose tablets – use it occasionally, but don't expect to survive for a long period on it. It is *not* to be regarded as a substitute for normal rest and refreshment.

Do you remember the great Tree of Tradition on which you found your clan totem? (ex.1, vol.I) This Tree is the axile tree of the Western Way, the central landmark which cross-intersects all levels of the tradition. It is an image which can be fruitfully meditated upon and worked with in many ways, but for this exercise we are going to draw on its vitality. There is no need to travel down the central bole of the trunk: if you have already worked the Clan Totem exercise, you should be able to visualize the Tree and be instantly there. Take your personal totem with you on this exercise, as your passport and strength.

Sit, relax and establish an easy rhythm of breathing. If you are tired and tense this is particularly important, so don't skim it. Five minutes of regular breathing will start to vitalize you in any case. Visualize the Tree before you. It is a beautiful day – just the kind of weather you like best. The earth is springy under your feet. Lay your hand on the trunk of the Tree and feel the green strength running beneath the warm bark. Acknowledge your belonging to the Tree of Tradition.

Turn and look about you. If you have travelled extensively in the Otherworld you may recognize certain features of the landscape. Beside the Tree, sitting on a low mound is the Guardian of Tradition. You may not have met him before: you will see him according to your ancestral alignment – there is no one way of seeing him. He is Guardian both of the Tree and of a natural spring which rises next to a slab of greenish stone. In his hands is a drinking horn.

Greet the Guardian and request to drink from the spring. He may challenge you and ask by what right you come to drink of the spring. In this case, show your totem of belonging. If it is acceptable – and he has the right to refuse you if he feels you are not true to the tradition – he will dip the horn into the spring and hand it to you. Drink and be deeply refreshed. The waters of the spring rise under the roots of the Tree itself, coming from the very depths of the Underworld realm of the ancestors. Return the horn with thanks and go back to the Tree itself. Sit with your back against its trunk, leaning back to share its pulsing vitality. Feel the strength seeping back into you. Enjoy this feeling of well-being and then return to your own time and place.

Certain kinds of devitalization occur because of the kind of inner tide which is running. The waning phases of the moon, the autumn and winter tides as well as personal bodily rhythms need to be taken into account – especially at the onset of menstruation or the menopause. Inner work, other than very general meditation work, should not be attempted if one is pregnant when all the physical and psychic energies should be engaged in nourishing the growing child. While male bodily rhythms are not so marked as female ones, men should likewise record and plot their own inner patterns of response.

Figure 26:   The Virgin Wisdom

AFTERWORD
Tomorrow's Tradition

Ultima Cumaei venit iam carminis aetas;
Magnus ab integro saeclorum pascitiur ordo.
Iam redit et virgo, redeunt Saturnia regna,
Iam nova progenies caelo demittitur alto.

Now comes the last age according to the oracle at Cumae:
the great series of lifetimes is renewed. Now comes the Virgin
goddess once again, the golden days of Saturn's
reign return and a new race descends from heaven.

Virgil: Eclogues

The sleeping place of the Age of Gold is in the depths of every
human heart.

J.C. Powys: Morwyn

We have come a long way, in space and time, since we set out on an
imaginary journey with a helpful guide at the beginning of volume
one. We have explored the inward spiral of the Native Tradition,
visited ancient places, either in person or in the imagination, performed meditations and visualizations, found an inner guide and
teacher, faced the guardians of the road and passed beyond them
through doors into inner worlds. There perhaps we have begun to
map out our own inner landscape, to seek the answers to questions
which have disturbed or fascinated us in our daily lives. Now, in
following the outward spiral of the Hermetic Tradition, we have
perhaps discovered, as was suggested in volume one, that the place
arrived at is no longer the same as that from which we began.

We stand on the verge of a new beginning which is neither a
millennial dream nor the desire for a lost Age of Gold, but rather a
nexus of traditions. The Native path has been walked almost to its
end: in places it is worn thin. The Hermetic way has been explored in
greater and greater depths. What, then, is the next likely step on this
road we have been following from Foretime to Futuretime?

There can, of course, be no single answer, nor any 'right' answer: each individual must decide for himself. Some suggestions have already been made within these pages. One which overrides all these is the step towards some new kind of magical discipline – one which is also, paradoxically, the oldest kind: a dimensionless, cosmic awareness which transcends all boundaries, all paths and all other disciplines. The mind has no limits: it can reach out beyond any boundaries of time and space we care to set. And it can communicate with others of the like disposition. Telepathy is no figment of the imagination, as many who read this will know already; a universal development of the power to communicate over vast distances may not be so far off. Above all we must recognise that there are no limits to what we can achieve other than those we set ourselves, no bolts and bars between the worlds except those we have personally hammered home. The soul is not a bird trapped in a cage: it can and does fly free – returning to its home after long voyaging. All the exercises and techniques in this book will be as nothing to this realization, nor will they work properly without its consent.

The ancients were right to attach so much importance to the idea of the vital spark that sought to rise above earthly confines, and as we have seen repeatedly it is a mistake to believe that this teaching meant that we should despise the body. Through its windows we can catch glimpses of the infinite, which to look upon otherwise would be like looking directly at the sun without protective glasses for our eyes. We see heaven through a darkened glass indeed, but as much for our own good as for any other reason.

This may come as a surprise to those who think that practitioners of esoteric disciplines seek only to transcend the physical. In truth if we are wise we will realize that our physical selves are of the utmost value. From their safe harbourage we depart on voyages of discovery and to them we return, as from any journey, to the welcome of home. Microcosmically, there is an echo here of the soul's longing for the place of its origin, wherever we may personally believe this to be. In our long search for the promised land, the paradisial home of our exiled states, we learn that there must always remain a point of contact with the roots of being. While we yet remain in incarnation the body is that point of contact for us.

So before flying forth towards whatever infinite realm you seek or are drawn, remember to be in tune with yourself as well as with the infinite. Make friends with your human chariot before you leave it behind; and be sure to return to its welcome embrace at your journey's end.

This two-volume book is by no means a complete course. If the Western Way is sufficiently appealing for you to work within its many traditions, then you will no doubt find that you have been walking it for some time already. You may wish to regularize your practice of its wisdom by joining a mystery school or magical group, or you may want to continue mapping your own way or participate in one of the living spiritual traditions. Whatever you decide, the most important thing is to *use* your acquired wisdom. All that we have tried to teach within the confines of these pages is worth nothing unless it is applied to your own lives on a daily basis. If the Western Way remains an abstract study in your hands, then it is likely to become an extinct tradition before long. Only when it is applied directly does it become real, multi-dimensional, a *path* rather than a concept. Our hope is that you will find useful ways of improving your perceptions and deepening your inner experience of the Western Way: indeed, we hope that you find better and more skilful ways of signposting it for others. It is said that the teacher and the taught comprise the teaching between them. The teaching is different for everyone: it is the individual reaction to it that reflects the ancient traditions from one generation to the next.

You should create your own programme of study, meditation and practice: these three disciplines form the basic components of an esoteric way of life. Study gives us the material to work with, meditation shows us new approaches to the work and helps fix our individual response in a symbolic way, practice grounds our inner experiences in outer reality. It is often the last of these which students of the Western mysteries find most difficult: to some extent ritual working fulfils a part of our practice, but the major part is inevitably going to fall within the bounds of our mundane life – the home, the office, in relationships. 'Solitary occult practice is fine – it's people who wreck everything' is a cry often heard on the lips of the beginner: try to prevent this by adopting a clear-headed approach to your fellows.

Everyday life is the best training ground of all. If you need to run to your inner teacher, tarot pack, or table of correspondences for a solution to every mundane problem, then you are not facing up to life's realities. To test this out, try to live one whole day in accordance with esoteric principles: eat and drink with total attention to the items being consumed, their taste, the goodness being derived from their digestion. See everyone you meet as possessed of the divine spark: each being is as much deserving as yourself. Even those who irritate you may possess qualities you never guessed at and which you might do well to imitate. Perform your daily tasks with total attention to the principle involved: cleaning the house is but an extension of self-clarification, and is itself a reflection of macrocosmic order. When faced with sudden decisions try to see the principles and choices before you as they a) affect you, b) affect others, c) affect the cosmos. Be as attentive to your moments of relaxation: rest hard as well as working hard: feel the cessation of work as the commencement of creative stillness which will in turn be the thrustblock of your work. At the end of one day so spent note down your responses: you may begin to understand just what is involved in the word *practice*.

Whatever material you choose to work with, let it be an expression of your own perception, not a revival which has to be learned like a part. If you have already started practical pathwalking, you will have discovered that the way feels right when you use your own compass and not some complicated device which has been patented by someone else. No one can make you an adept: that rank – which is really no more than a title given to one who has reached a stage of development within the scheme of creation – can only be awarded by you yourself, either in colloquy with an inner teacher or with the inner spark of divinity.

> God said to man: I have placed you in the world that you may more readily see what you are. I have made you neither earthly nor heavenly, neither a mortal nor a immortal being, in order that you, as your own sculptor, may carve features for yourself. You may degenerate into an animal, but by using your free will you may also be reborn as a god-like being. (67)

We have taken many things for granted in this book. The belief in other states of being and other worlds, other orders of creation above and beyond what we recognize in our normal functioning state. We have stated that mankind has a future; that it is not necessarily doomed to extinction – that it may in fact be on the verge of a wholly new development. That this is no mere speculation can be seen clearly enough if we look at the discoveries being made daily in quantum physics and other areas of scientific research which are the outer manifestation of Alchemy and are bringing creation in a full circle towards its beginnings.

But science is not enough: it fails to satisfy because it cannot answer the really important questions; its theories and laws, when added up, do not make up the sum total of creation – not even a tenth part of it. As esotericists we have ourselves to use as indexes of creation, alchemically perfecting the elements within us until they fit exactly into the puzzle of the cosmos.

It is not enough simply to be aware of these things, to enquire into them for the sake of curiosity alone. We have to be a living part of the process which transforms the scattered particles of the Body of Light into a wholly new and original being. Adam Kadmon must be built up, piece by piece; Osiris, Dionysius – all the wounded saviour gods – made whole; the Fisher King restored. But to do this, to help bring it about, we have to be functioning parts of the process. This underlines the importance of 'being in touch,' of being connected to the heart of the cosmos, knowing that there we will feel an answering touch, a note with which to resonate.

> None of the gods of heaven will ever quit heaven, and pass its boundary, and come down to earth; but man ascends even to heaven, and measures it; and what is more than all beside, he mounts to heaven without quitting the earth; so vast a distance can he put forth his power. We must not shrink then from saying that a man on earth is a mortal god, and that god in heaven is a mortal man. (302)

Towards this end we have given exercises and techniques aimed at connecting us to the infinite worlds around us, of bringing back the wisdom of the otherworld to our own dimension and making it a lasting part of our own eternal becoming. The techniques on their own mean nothing, without the commitment to the truths that stand behind them. To this end we have given much that is in the nature of an esoteric philosophy – a framework on which to hang the stuff of wonder. It is to these truths that we each dedicate ourselves as followers of the Western Way, whether in the end we call them gods or states of mind; and it is these fundamental axioms we have tried to bring before you through the intricate web of belief, practice and teaching which is the backbone of all traditions.

For choosing to believe in a universe with purpose we make no apology, assuming that those who read these pages share our belief. As the Zoroastrian magi believed, the universe is indeed a great chariot: it need not matter that we know little or nothing of the driver (who may well be ourselves collectively), only that it is proceeding towards a point of completion rather than destruction, and that we, as passengers, should be present when it arrives.

The image of the esotericist as black magician or harmless crank has been slow to fade. The shaman and shamanka, the magician and pathwalker – however we tend to see ourselves – are all subjected to this image. Friends, family, even your employer, may look severely on your efforts and brand you godless, cracked, perhaps even evil. Confronted with the esoteric many people react in an orthodox and fundamentally, exoteric way. You will have to weigh these disadvantages of following the Western Way; for even though a spirit of tolerance exists towards esotericism at present this does not mean that this will always be so. Fundamentalism is on the march again, witch-hunts and brainwashing have happened in this century: they are not just the record of an ancient past. Discretion and silence have kept the esoteric traditions from the uninitiated during such times of persecution; now that times are kind to us it is the responsibility of anyone walking the Western Way to ensure that the teaching is carefully practised and sensibly taught; that traditions are disseminated wisely and practically demonstrated to a world which may think them unnatural.

You may be doing nothing more than meditating in a small group or meeting at an ancient site for the festivals; or you may be teaching at open seminars or giving lectures and pathwalkings to beginners. Whatever you practise, *you* are the public image of the Western Way: people look to you to practise what you preach. You owe respect to the teachers – whether inner or outer – who have instructed you, and you certainly bear responsibility to those you seek to teach. We must all imitate the instructions contained in the Rosicrucian Manifesto: dress and behave in the manner of the country you live in, do not draw attention to yourselves, do not accept money for your services (which are of the Inner and not yours to sell), meet with your contemporary pathwalkers periodically, find one worthy person (at least) to whom you can transmit your tradition and what you have learned. Above all, always be true to your inner principles. The Tree of Tradition is rooted in the ancestral past; be true to that past and ensure that its branches grow strong in our own time and that fruit grows upon it for tomorrow's tradition.

This being said, what of that future? Where does esotericism go next? Can the Hermetic and Native traditions fuse to keep the former from hierarchical stasis and the latter from atavistic reversion to type? We believe that this fusion is now becoming manifest in many imperceptible ways; just as there will soon no longer be any clear boundary between East and West, so it will become harder and harder to see the join between Hermetic and Native traditions.

> Each race maintains its cultural traditions, and each cult survives until the faculties which it was designed to initiate have become the normal inheritance of the species. Then it ceases to be esoteric and becomes exoteric. . . As long as there are souls that require the discipline the cult lives on. (90)

This is exactly the case of the Native Tradition – elements of its wisdom may now be atavistic but until its lessons are assimilated it cannot be abandoned like a worked-out quarry. The Native Tradition's resonance is particularly strong at this time because much that has been esoteric is now becoming exoteric and thus available to all. The resonance of the Hermetic tradition is both for this time and for future ages: much remains which will be the work of competent pathwalkers to synthesize into forms more exoteric.

The barriers between East and West are melting also, though it will be generations before they are finally down. For those walking the Western Way initial contact with the roots of the western mysteries is recommended. A pull to the East may well be experienced: Eastern spiritual schools appear tempting and there may be incarnational links – but birth has placed us in the West. At a certain point the mysteries reach a plateau where all traditions are in accord. Already, with the fore-shortening of Eastern and Western margins, many new factors are coming into play. The seizure of Tibet by the Chinese in 1958 has had the unprecedented effect of sending forth a body of secret Tibetan teaching in the persons of fleeing lamas who are the living exponents of what will be a migrating native system into the West. The parallels between this exodus and that of the fabled Atlantean escape routes to the West are not inconsiderable. Then too a culture about to be overwhelmed sent forth emissaries into the world who may well have seeded the teachings of the Western mysteries. Such migrations have ever done their work of cross-fertilizing, and energizing dying traditions, providing a vast influx of new energy.

The fact that to gain esoteric training people have had to journey to the East, as in the story by Hermann Hesse with which we began has meant that Eastern teaching has not always been properly assimilated into Western life. The Tibetans who will now live their lives in the West bring their knowledge at first hand and are adapting it as usefully as they know, using their skilful means. (Anderson)

The ultimate solution of our world problem lies in ... a knowledge that is neither Eastern nor Western, but which is known to both. When we have joined hands with the Orient and when we have united the best thoughts of the East with those of the West, we shall have a synthetic and balanced teaching which will liberate the coming generations. (19)

Meanwhile our task as the guardians of the Western Way is to work towards a synthesis of Native and Hermetic traditions, taking the 'best thoughts' of each to form a new whole. Cosmic consciousness is the goal of tomorrow's tradition, built firmly upon the realizations of both Native and Hermetic ways: into cosmic consciousness, threading in and out of the maze to discover a new collective awareness.

The re-emergence of the Divine Feminine and the mingling of masculine and feminine energies, are elements which mark the birth of the Aquarian Age. At last the division of the paths is being ended; people are beginning to realize that there has only ever been one goal, even though there were many ways to reach it. The Western Way is not exclusive, it is just our most familiar path. Those who walk it must learn to think differently to the rest of warring humanity, must indeed relearn all we have forgotten since the Beginning, the Foretime, when living *was* life, was creation, was nature, was God. There is no great synthesis at this level, no simple answer. Finally, no philosopher's stone – unless it be ourselves. Only a new way of being, a possibility of realizing the truth of our place in the cosmos.

In looking to the future we have much to keep in mind, much to consider and meditate upon before we can be freed to explore the endless dimensions we have sought so long. As we look back along the winding maze of the Western Way we see many signposts. All are pointing the same way: *at us*. A long line of teachers stand behind us: another line stretches out into the future. We all stand as links in a chain of transmission which must not be allowed to fail. We ourselves are like solar systems, whole cosmologies, with fixed stars and wandering planets. There are no known limits to where we may go or how far we may travel. We stand with map and compasses in hand, ready to begin a new journey and we are, in some senses, our own guides, for that country is very familiar. All we have to do is step forth. That experience awaits you, in your own time and in your own way. May your journey be as happy and joyful as ours has been, and may you always return safely.

Hermes, offspring of Dionysos who revels
    in the dance
and of Aphrodite, the Paphian maiden of the
    fluttering eyelids,
you frequent the sacred house of Persephone
as guide through the earth of ill-fated souls
which you bring to their haven when their time
    has come,
charming them with your sacred wand and giving
    them sleep
from which you rose them again. To you indeed
Persephone gave the office, throughout wide
    Tartaros,
to lead the way for the eternal souls of men.
But, blessed one, grant a good end for the
    initiate's work. (13)

BIBLIOGRAPHY AND DISCOGRAPHY

Items are listed in numerical order and numbers will be found to correspond to those in the text. Those marked with letters after the publication details are to indicate the type of work. Thus: F = Fiction, G = General, J = Journal, P = Poetry, R = Recording, T = Text, M = Music, I = Instructional or Meditation tape.

(1) Abulafia, A., *The Path of the Names*, Berkley, Trigram, 1976 (T)

(2) Adams, H., *Mont St-Michel and Chartres*, London, Hamlyn, 1980 (G)

(3) Agrippa, C., *Occult Philosophy*, Wellingborough, Aquarian Press, 1975 (T)

(4) Ahern, G., *Sun at Midnight*, Wellingborough, Aquarian Press, 1984 (G)

(5) Albertus, Frater, *Alchemist's Handbook*, Routledge & Kegan Paul, 1976 (G)

(6) Allen, P.M., ed., *A Christian Rosenkreutz Anthology*, New York, Rudolf Steiner Publication, 1968 (G)

(7) Allen, R.H., *Star Names: their lore and meaning*, New York, Dover Books, 1963 (G)

(8) Anderson, W., *Open Secrets, a Western Guide to Tibetan Buddhism*, Harmondsworth, Penguin, 1980 (G)

(9) *Apocalyptic Spirituality*, ed. and trans., B. McGuinn, London, SPCK, 1979 (T)

(10) *Apocryphal New Testament*, ed. and trans., M.R. James, London, Oxford University Press, 1924 (T)

(11) Apuleius, *The Golden Ass*, trans., Robert Graves, Harmondsworth, Penguin Books, 1950 (T)

(12) Ashcroft-Nowicki, D., *The Shining Paths*, Wellingborough, Aquarian Press, 1983 (G)

(13) Athanassakis, A.N., trans., *The Orphic Hymns*, Missoula, Mont., Scholars Press, 1977 (T)

(14) St Augustine, *The City of God*, Harmondsworth, Penguin Books, 1972 (T)

(15) *Aurora Consurgens*, ed., M.-L. von Franz, New York, Pantheon Books, 1966 (T)

(16) Bacon, F., *Advancement of Learning and New Atlantis*, London, Oxford University Press, 1906 (T)

(17) *The Bahir*, trans. A. Kaplan, New York, Weiser, 1979 (T)

(18) Baigent, M., Lincoln, H., and Leigh, R., *Holy Blood, Holy Grail*, London, Cape, 1982 (G)

(19) Bailey, A.A., *The Externalization of the Hierarchy*, London, Lucis Press, 1957. (G)

(20) Bailey, A.A., *The Rays and the Initiations*, Lucis Press, 1960. (G)

(21) Bailey, A.A., *A Treatise on White Magic*, London, Lucis Press, 1934 (G)

(22) Bamford, C., 'Natureword, the Hermetic Tradition and Today' in *Natureworld* by R.A. Schwaller de Lubicz, Mass., Lindisfarne Press, 1982 (G)

(23) Banks, N.N., *The Golden Thread*, London, Lucis Press, 1963 (G)

(24) Barbault, A., *Gold of a Thousand Mornings*, London, Neville Spearman, 1975 (G)

(25) Bausch, W.J., *Storytelling: imagination and faith*, Twenty-Third Publishers, Mystic, Conn., 1984 (G)

(26) *The Holy Bible*, (R.S.V.), London, Nelson, 1966 (T)

(27) Blake, W., *Poetry and Prose*, ed. G. Keynes, London, Nonsuch Library, 1975 (P)

(28) Blakeley, J.D., *Mystical Tower of the Tarot*, London, Watkins, 1974 (G)

(29) Blavatsky, H.P., *The Secret Doctrine*, London, Theosophical Publishing House, 1970 (G)

(30) Bolton, J.D.P., *Aristaeus of Proconnesus*, London, Oxford University Press, 1962 (G)

(31) *Book of Enoch*, trans. R.H. Charles, London, SPCK, 1982 (T)

(32) Bronstein, H., *A Passover Haggadah*, Harmondsworth, Penguin, 1974 (G)

(33) Bruno, G., *The Expulsion of the Triumphant Beast*, trans. A.D. Imerti, New Brunswick, Rutgers University Press, 1964 (T)

(34) Budge, E.A.W., *Osiris: The Egyptian Religion of Resurrection*, New York, University Books, 1961 (G)

(35) Burckhardt, T., *Alchemy: Science of the Comos, Science of the Soul*, trans. W. Stoddart, London, Stuart & Watkins, 1967 (G)

(36) Burton, U. and Dolley, J., *Christian Evolution: Moving Towards a Global Spirituality*. Wellingborough, Turnstone, 1984 (G)

(37) Butler, E.M., *The Myth of the Magus*, Cambridge, Cambridge University Press, 1979 (G)

(38) Butler, E.M., *Ritual Magic*, Cambridge, Cambridge University Press, 1979 (G)

(39) Butler, W.E., *Apprenticed to Magic*, Wellingborough, Aquarian, 1962 (G)

(40) Caldecott, S., *The Treasures of Tradition*: in *Resurgence* no. 102, January-February 1984 (J)

(41) Calvino, I., *The Castle of Crossed Destinies*, London, Secker, 1977 (F)

(42) *Cambridge History of Judaism volume I: The Persian Period*, ed. W.D. Davies and L. Finkelstein, Cambridge, Cambridge University Press, 1984 (G)

(43) Casaubon, M., *A True and Faithful Relation Of What Passed For Many Years Between Dr. John Dee and Some Spirits*. Glasgow and Portmeirion, Antonine Publishing Company Ltd. with Golden Dragon Press, 1974 (T)

(44) St Catherine of Siena, *The Dialogues*, London, SPCK, 1980 (T)

(45) Chapman, V., *Bladdud the Birdman*, London, Rex Collings, 1978 (F)

(46) Chevalier, G., *The Sacred Magician – a Ceremonial Diary*, Frogmore, Paladin, 1976 (G)

(47) Chretien de Troyes, *Conte du Graal*, trans. R.W. Linker, Chapel Hill, University of North Carolina, 1952 (T)

(48) Christian, P., *The History and Practice of Magic*, London, Forge Press, 1952 (G)

(49) Christie-Murray, D., *A History of Heresy*, London, New English Library, 1976 (G)

(50) *Cloud of Unknowing*, ed. E. Underhill, London, Stuart and Watkins, 1970 (T)

(51) Colquhoun, I., *The Sword of Wisdom – MacGregor Mathers and the Golden Dawn*, London, Neville Spearman, 1975 (G)

(52) Coomaraswamy, R.P., *The Destruction of the Christian Tradition*, London, Perennial Books, 1981 (G)

(53) Cooper, J.C. *The Illustrated Encyclopedia of Traditional Symbols*, London, Tha.nes & Hudson, 1978 (G)

(54) Corbin, H., *The Man of Light in Iranian Sufism*, Shambhala, Boulder, Colarado and London, 1978 (G)

(55) Coudert, A., *Alchemy: The Philosophers' Stone*, London, Wildwood, 1980 (G)

(56) Court, S., *The Meditators' Manual*, Wellingborough, Aquarian, 1984 (G)

(57) Critchlow, K. *Temenos and Temple*, in *Temenos*, I, 1981 (J)

(58) Crowley, A. 777, privately printed by Ordo Templi Orientis, n.d. (T)

(59) Cumont, F., *The Mysteries of Mithras*, New York, Dover Publications 1956 (G)

(60) Danielou, A., *Shiva and Dionysius*, New York, Inner Traditions Int., 1984 (G)

(61) Dante, *The Divine Comedy*, trans. L. Binyon, London, Agenda, 1979 (T)

(62) Dart, J., *The Laughing Saviour*, New York, Harper & Row, 1976 (G)

(63) Davidson, G., *A Dictionary of Angels*, New York, Free Press with Collier-Macmillan, 1967 (G)

(64) De Borron. R., *Joseph d'Arimathie*, ed. W.A. Nitze, in Roman de L'estoire dou Graal, Paris, Classiques Français du Moyen Age, 1927 (T)

(65) Dee, J., *The Hieroglyphic Monarch*, New York, Samuel Weiser Inc., 1975 (T)

(66) De Jong. H.M.E., *Michael Maier's Atalanta Fugiens: Sources of an Alchemical Book of Emblems*, Leiden, E.J.Brill, 1969 (G)

(67) Della Mirandola, P., *On the Dignity of Man, On Being and the One, Heptaplus*, Indianapolis, Bobbs-Merrill, 1965 (T)

(68) Denning, M. and Phillips. O., *The Magical Philosophy* (5 Volumes) St Paul. Llewellyn Pubs, 1974–1981 (G)

(69) Dionysius the Areopagite, *The Divine Names and the Mystical Theology*, trans C.E. Rolt, London, SPCK, 1940 (T)

(70) Dionysius the Areopagite, *The Mystical Theology and the Celestial Hierarchies*, trans. and ed. The Shrine of Wisdom, Fintry, Shrine of Wisdom, 1949 (T)

(71) *Dream of Scipio*, trans. R. Bullock. Wellingborough, Aquarian, 1983 (T)

(72) Drower, E.S., *The Secret Adam: A Study of Nasoraean Gnosis*. Oxford, Oxford University Press, 1960 (G)

(73) Eliade, M., *History of Religious Ideas vol. I: From the Stone Age to the Eleusian Mysteries*, London, Collins, 1979 (T)

(74) Eliade, M., *History of Religious Ideas vol II: From Gautama Buddha to the Triumph of Christianity*, Chicago, University of Chicago Press, 1982 (T)

(75) Ellwood, R.S., *Religious and Spiritual Groups in Modern America*. New Jersey, Prentice Hall Inc., 1975 (G)

(76) Ellwood Post, W., *Saints, Signs and Symbols*, London, SPCK 1962 (G)

(77) Epstein, P., *Kabbalah: the way of the Jewish Mystic*, New York, Weiser, 1978 (G)

(78) Every, G., *Christian Mythology*, London, Hamlyn, 1970 (G)

(79) Fabricius, J., *Alchemy*, Copenhagen, Rosenkilde and Bagger, 1976 (G)

(80) Ferguson, J. *Illustrated Encyclopedia of Mysticism and the Mystery Religions*, London, Thames & Hudson, 1976 (G)

(81) Ferguson, J. *Jesus in the Tide of Time*, London, Routledge & Kegan Paul, 1980 (G)

(82) Ferguson, M., *The Aquarian Conspiracy*, London, Routledge & Kegan Paul, 1981 (G)

(83) Ficino, M., *The Letters of Marsilio Ficino vols I – 3*, London, Shepheard Walwyn, 1975–1981 (T)

(84) Figulus, B., *A Golden and Blessed Casket of Nature's Marvels*, London, Vincent Stuart Ltd., 1963 (T)

(85) Fleming, D.L., *Contemporary Reading of the Spiritual Exercises*, St Louis, Institute of Jesuit Sources, 1980 (G)

(86) Fludd, R., *The Origin and Structure of the Cosmos*. Edinburgh, Hermetic Source Works, 1982 (T)

(87) Fontenrose, J., *Python*, Berkeley, University of California Press, 1959 (G)

(88) *Forms of Prayer for Jewish Worship*, ed. Assembly of Rabbis of the Reform Synagogues of Great Britain, 1977 (T)

(89) Fortune, D., *Applied Magic*, Wellingborough, Aquarian, 1962 (G)

(90) Fortune, D., *The Cosmic Doctrine*, Wellingborough, Aquarian, 1976, (G)

(91) Fortune, D, *Esoteric Orders and their Work*, St Paul, Llewellyn Press, 1978 (G)

(92) Fortune, D., *Esoteric Philosophy of Love and Marriage*, Wellingborough, Aquarian Press, 1970 (G)

(93) Fortune, D., *Moon Magic*, Wellingborough, Aquarian, 1956 (F)

(94) Fortune, D., *The Sea Priestess*, Wellingborough, Aquarian, 1957 (F)

(95) Fortune, D., *The Secrets of Dr. Taverner*, St Paul, Llewellyn Press, 1979 (F)

(96) Fortune, D., *The Training and Work of an Initiate*, Wellingborough, Aquarian 1930 (G)

(97) Fouquet, J., *The Hours of Etienne Chevalier*, London, Thames & Hudson, 1972 (T)

(98) French, R.M., *The Way of the Pilgrim*. London, SPCK 1930 (G)

(99) Gadal, A. *Sur Le Chemin du Saint-Graal*, Haarlem, Rozekruis Pers, 1960 (G)

(100) Garrison, J., *The Darkness of God: Theology after Hiroshima*, London, SCM Press, 1982 (G)

(101) Giraldus Cambrensis, *The Journey through Wales*, trans. L. Thorpe, Harmondsworth, Penguin, 1978 (T)

(102) Godwin, J., *Athanasius Kircher*, London, Thames & Hudson, 1979 (G)

(103) Godwin, J., *The Golden Chain of Orpheus*, in *Temenos* 4 and 5, 1984 (J)

(104) Godwin, J., *Mystery Religions and the Ancient World*, London, Thames & Hudson, 1981 (G)

(105) Godwin, J., *Robert Fludd*, London, Thames & Hudson, 1979 (G)

(106) *Golden Verses of the Pythagoreans*, trans. Editors of the Shrine of Wisdom, Fintry, Shrine of Wisdom, n.d. (T)

(107) Gorman, P., *Pythagoras*, London, Routledge & Kegan Paul, 1979 (G)

(108) Gorres, I.F., *Broken Lights*, London, Burns & Oates, 1964 (G)

(109) Grant, F.C., *Hellenistic Religions – The Age of Syncretism*, New York, Bobbs-Merrill, 1953 (G)

(110) Graves, R., *Adam's Rib*, London, Trianon Press, 1955 (G)

(111) Graves, R., *Greek Myths*, London, Cassell, 1958 (G)

(112) Graves, R. and Patai, R., *Hebrew Myths*, London, Cassell, 1963 (G)

(113) Graves, R., *Seven Days in New Crete*, London, Cassell, 1949 (F)

(114) Gray, W.G., *Inner Traditions of Magic*, London, Aquarian, 1970 (G)

(115) Gray. W.G., *Magical Ritual Methods*, Toddington, Helios, 1971 (G)

(116) Gray, W.G., *Western Inner Workings*, New York, Weiser, 1983 (G)

(117) Green, M., *Experiments in Aquarian Magic*, Wellingborough, Aquarian, 1985, (G)

(118) Green, M., *Magic in the Aquarian Age*, Wellingborough, Aquarian, 1983 (G)

(119) Greene, B and Gollancz, V., *God of a Hundred Names*, London, Gollancz, 1962 (G)

(120) Greer, M.K., *Tarot For Your Self: a Workbook for Personal Transformation*, North Hollywood, Newcastle Publications Company Inc., 1984 (G)

(121) Grossinger, R., *The Alchemical Tradition*, Berkeley, North Atlantic Books, 1983 (G)

(122) Grossinger, R., *The Night Sky*, San Francisco, Sierra Club Books, 1981 (G)

(123) Guénon, R., *Crisis of the Modern World*, London, Luzac, 1975 (G)

(124) Guénon, R., *Symboles Fondamentaux de la Science Sacrée*, Paris, Gallimard, 1962 (G)

(125) Guirdham, A., *The Great Heresy*, Jersey, Neville Spearman, 1977 (G)

(126) Guthrie, W.K.C., *Orpheus and Greek Religion*, New York, W.W. Norton, 1966 (G)

(127) Halevi, Z., *Adam and the Kabbalistic Tree*, London, Rider, 1974 (G)

(128) Halevi, Z., *Kabbalah: Tradition of Hidden Knowledge*, London, Thames & Hudson, 1979 (G)

(129) Halevi, Z., *A Kabbalistic Universe*, London, Rider, 1977 (G)

(130) Halevi, Z., *The Work of the Kabbalist*, London, Gateway Books, 1985 (G)

(131) Hall, M.P., *The Adepts in the Western Esoteric Tradition*, Los Angeles, Philosophical Research Society, 1949 (G)

(132) Hall, M.P., *Magic*, Los Angeles, Philosophical Research Society, 1978 (G)

(133) Hall, M.P., *The Secret Teachings of All Ages*, Los Angeles, Philosophical Research Society, 1975 (G)

(134) Hargrave, J., *The Life and Soul of Paracelsus*, London, Gollancz, 1951 (G)

(135) Harner, M., *The Way of the Shaman*, New York, Harper & Row, 1980 (G)

(136) Haughton, R., *The Catholic Thing*, Dublin, Villa Books, 1979 (G)

(137) Haughton, R., *Tales from Eternity: The World of Faeries and the Spiritual Search*, London, Allen & Unwin, 1973 (G)

(138) Hauschka, R., *The Nature of substance*, London, Rudolph Steiner Press, 1983 (G)

(139) Hawkridge, R., *The Wisdom Tree*. New York, Houghton Mifflin Co., 1945 (G)

(140) Heller, A., *Renaissance Man*, London, Routledge & Kegan Paul, 1978 (G)

(141) *Hermetic Journal* ed. A. McLean. issn. 0141 6391, Edinburgh, 1978 (J)

(142) Hesse, H. *The Glass Bead Game*, London, Cape, 1970 (F)

(143) Hildegard of Bingen, *Meditations*, trans, G., Uhlein, Santa Fe, Bear & Co 1983 (T)

(144) Hoeller, S.A., *The Gnostic Jung and the Seven Sermons to the Dead*, Wheaton, Theosophical Publishing House, 1982 (G)

(145) Hoffman, E., *The Way of Splendour: Jewish Mysticism and Modern Psychology*, Boulder, Shambhala, 1981 (G)

(146) *Homage to Pythagoras*, Lindisfarne Newsletter 1981, West Stockbridge (J)

(147) Hope, M., *Practical Egyptian Magic*, Wellingborough, Aquarian, 1984 (G)

(148) Hope, M., *Practical Techniques of Psychic Self-Defence*, Wellingborough, Aquarian, 1983 (G)

(149)   Houselander, C., *Letters*, London, Sheed & Ward, 1965 (G)

(150)   Huizinga, J., *The Waning of the Middle Ages*, Harmondsworth, Penguin, 1955 (G)

(151)   Huxley, A., *The Perennial Philosophy*, London, Chatto & Windus, 1946 (G)

(152)   Iamblicus., *On the Mysteries*, trans. T. Taylor, San Diego, Wizard's Bookshelf, 1984 (T)

(153)   Jackson-Knight, W.F., *Vergil: Epic and Anthropology*. London, Allen & Unwin, 1967, (G)

(154)   Jacobs, L., *Jewish Mystical Testimonies*, New York, Schoken Books, 1976 (T)

(155)   St John of the Cross, *Four Poems*, trans. Y. Orta, Oxford, Carmelite Priory, Boar's Hill, 1984 (T)

(156)   Johnston, W., *Christian Mysticism Today*, London, Collins, 1984 (G)

(157)   Jonas, H., *The Gnostic Religion: The Message of the Alien God and the Beginnings of Christianity*, Boston, Beacon Press, 1963 (G)

(158)   Jones, D., *Epoch and Artist*, London, Faber, 1959 (G)

(159)   Jones, P., *Physics as Metaphor*, London, Wildwood, 1983 (G)

(160)   Julian of Norwich, *Revelations of Divine Love*, Wheathampstead, Anthony Clarke, 1973 (T)

(161)   Jung, C.G., *Answer to Job*, London, Routledge & Kegan Paul, 1954 (G)

(162)   Jung, C.G., *Archetypes and the Collective Unconscious*, London, Routledge & Kegan Paul, 1968 (G)

(163)   Jung, C.G., *Memories, Dreams and Reflections*, London, Collins and Routledge & Kegan Paul, 1963 (G)

(164)   Jung, C.G., *Psychology and Alchemy*, London, Routledge & Kegan Paul, 1968 (G)

(165)   Jung, C.G., *Word and Image*, ed. A. Jaffe, New Jersey, Princeton University Press, 1979 (G)

(166)   Jung, E. and Von Franz, M., *The Grail Legends*, London, Hodder, 1956 (G)

(167)   Kaplan, A., *Meditation and the Bible*, Maine, Weiser, 1978 (G)

(168)   Kaplan, A., *Meditation and Kabbalah*, York Beach, Weiser, 1982 (G)

(169)   Keen, M., *Chivalry*, New Harlem, Yale University Press, 1984 (G)

(170)   Kempis, T., *The Imitation of Christ*, trans. R., Dudley, Wheathampstead, Anthony Clarke, 1980 (T)

(171)   Kerenyi, K., *Apollo*, Dallas, Spring Publications, 1983 (G)

(172)   Kerenyi, K., *Asklepios*, New York, Pantheon Books, 1959 (G)

(173) Kerenyi, K., *Gods of the Greeks*, London, Thames & Hudson, 1951, (G)

(174) Kerenyi, K., *Hermes, Guide of Souls*, Zurich, Spring Books, 1976, (G)

(175) Kerenyi, K., *The Heroes of the Greeks*, London, Thames & Hudson, 1959 (G)

(176) Kierkegaard, S., *For Self-Examination and Judge for Yourselves*, trans. W. Lowrie, Oxford, Oxford University Press, 1941, (G)

(177) Klibansky, R., *Continuity of the Platonic Tradition*, London, Warburg Institute, 1939, (G)

(178) Knight, G. and McLean, A., *Commentary on the Chymical Wedding of Christian Rosenkreutz*, Edinburgh, Magnum Opus Hermetic Sourceworks, 1984 (T)

(179) Knight, G., *Experience of Inner Worlds*, Toddington, Helios, 1975 (G)

(180) Knight, G., *A History of White Magic*, London, Mowbrays, 1978 (G)

(181) Knight, G., *Occult Exercises and Practices*, Wellingborough, Aquarian, 1982 (G)

(182) Knight, G., *The Practice of Ritual Magic*, Wellingborough, Aquarian, 1979 (G)

(183) Knight, G., *A Practical guide to Qabalistic Symbolism*, Toddington, Helios, 1965 (G)

(184) Knight, G., *The Rose-Cross and the Goddess*, Wellingborough, Aquarian, 1985 (G)

(185) Knight, G., *The Secret Tradition in Arthurian Legend*, Wellingborough, Aquarian, 1984 (G)

(186) *Kore Kosmou*, trans. A. Kingsford and E. Maitland, Minneapolis, Wizard's Bookshelf, 1977 (T)

(187) Lacarriere, J., *The Gnostics*, London, Peter Owen, 1977 (G)

(188) Lambert, M.D., *Medieval Heresy*, London, Edward Arnold, 1977 (G)

(189) Lang-Sims, L., *The Christian Mystery*, London, Allen & Unwin, 1980 (G)

(190) Le Roy Ladurie, E., *Montaillou*, London, Scolar Press, 1978 (G)

(191) *Lenten Triodion*, trans. Mother Mary and Archimandrite K. Ware, London, Faber, 1977 (T)

(192) Lewis, C.S., *The Business of Heaven*, London, Fount, 1984 (G)

(193) Lewis, C.S., *The Discarded Image*, Cambridge University Press, 1964 (G)

(194) Lewis, C.S., *Til we Have Faces*, London, Fount, 1978 (F)

(195)   Lievegoed, B.C.J., *Mystery Streams in Europe and the New Mysteries*, New York, Anthroposophic Press, 1982 (G)

(196)   Lindisfarne Letter no 9. *Poetry and Prophecy*, West Stockbridge, 1979 (J)

(197)   Lindsay, J., *The Origins of Alchemy in Graeco-Roman Egypt*, London, Frederick Muller, 1970 (G)

(198)   Lindsay, J., *The Troubadours*, London, Frederick Muller, 1976 (G)

(199)   Lionel, F., *The Seduction of the Occult Path*, Wellingborough, Turnstone, 1983 (G)

(200)   Lossky, V., *The Mystical Theology of the Eastern Church*, Cambridge, James Clarke & Co. Ltd., 1957 (G)

(201)   Love, J., *The Quantum Gods*, Compton Russell Element, Tisbury, Wilts., 1976 (G)

(202)   Lucian, *The Syrian Goddess*, Constable, 1913, (T)

(203)   Lurker, M., *Gods and Symbols of Ancient Egypt*, Thames & Hudson, 1974 (G)

(204)   *Mabinogion*, ed. and trans. Lady Charlotte Guest, John Jones, Cardiff, 1977 (T)

(205)   McClain, E.G., *The Pythagorean Plato*, Nicholas Hays, 1978 (G)

(206)   McGregor-Mathers, S.L., *The Book of the Sacred Magic of Abra-Melin the Mage*, Wellingborough, Thorsons, 1976 (G)

(207)   McIntosh, C., *Rosy Cross Unveiled*, Wellingborough, Aquarian Press, 1980 (G)

(208)   McLean, A., *A Compendium on the Rosicrucian Vault*, Hermetic Research Series, 12 Antigua Street, Edinburgh, 1985 (G)

(209)   McLean, A., 'A Hermetic Origin of the Tarot Cards?' in *Hermetic Journal*, vol. 21, Autumn 1983 (G)

(210)   McLean, A., *Journal of Rosicrucian Studies I*, Autumn 1983, 12 Antigua Street, Edinburgh (G)

(211)   McLean, A., 'Robert Flood's Great Treatise of Rosicrucian Science' in *Hermetic Journal* No. 17, Autumn 1982 (G)

(212)   McLean, A., 'A Rosicrucian Alchemical Mystery Centre in Scotland' in *Hermetic Journal* No.4, Summer 1979 (G)

(213)   McLean, A., *The Western Mandala*, Hermetic Research Series, 12 Antigua Street, Edinburgh, 1983 (G)

(214)   McWaters, B., *Conscious Evolution*, Wellingborough, Turnstone Press, 1983 (G)

(215)   Macrobius, *Commentary on the Dream of Scipio*, Columbia University Press, New York and London, 1952 (T)

(216)   Malory, Sir Thomas, *Le Mort d'Arthur*, Harmondsworth, Penguin Books, 1969 (T)

(217) Matthews, C., 'The Rosicrucian Vault as Sepulchre and Wedding Chamber' in Stewart, B. *The Initiation of the Underworld*. Wellingborough, Aquarian Press, 1985 (G)

(218) Matthews, C., *The Search for Rhiannon*, Frome, Brans Head, 1981 (P)

(219) Matthews, C., 'Sophia as Companion on the Quest' in *At the Table of the Grail*, ed. J. Matthews, Routledge & Kegan Paul, 1983 (G)

(220) Matthews, J., *At The Table of the Grail*, Routledge & Kegan Paul, 1983 (G)

(221) Matthews, J., *The Grail, Quest for the Eternal*, Thames & Hudson, 1981 (G)

(222) Matthews, J. and Green, M., *The Grail Seekers Handbook*, Wellingborough, Aquarian Press, 1986 (G)

(223) Mead, G.R.S., *Apollonius of Tyana*, University Books, New York, 1966 (G)

(224) Mead, G.R.S., *Fragments of a Faith Forgotten*, New York, University Books, 1960 (T)

(225) Mead, G.R.S., *Mysteries of Mithras*, Theosophical Publishing Society, 1907 (G)

(226) Mead, G.R.S., *Orpheus*, J.M. Watkins, 1965 (G)

(227) Mead, G.R.S., *Thrice Greatest Hermes*, J.M.Watkins, 1964 (G)

(228) Mead, G.R.S., *Vision of Aridaeus*, Theosophical Publishing Society, 1907 (G)

(229) Meltzer, D., *Six*, Santa Barbara, Black Sparrow Press, 1976 (P)

(230) Menahem Nahum of Chernobyl, *Upright Practices*, New York, Paulist Press, 1982 (T)

(231) Merry, E., *I Am: the Ascent of Mankind*, Rider, 1944 (G)

(232) Merton, T., *Asian Journals*, Sheldon Press, 1944 (G)

(233) Merton, T., *Seven Story Mountain*, Sheldon Press, 1975 (G)

(234) Miller, R., *Continents in Collision*, Amsterdam, Time-Life, 1983. (G)

(235) Milton, J., *Complete Poetry*, New York, Anchor Books, 1971 (P)

(236) Moore, V., *The Unicorn: William Butler Yeats' Search for Reality*, New York, Macmillan, 1954 (G)

(237) *Munificentissimus Deus (Pope Pius XII)*, Daughters of St Paul, Derby, New York, 1950 (T)

(238) Mylius, J.D., trans. P. Tahta, *Alchemical Engravings*, Magnum Opus Hermetic Sourcebooks, Edinburgh, 1984 (T)

(239) *Nag Hammadi Library*, trans. J.M.Robinson, Leiden, Brill, 1977 (T)

(240) Nahman of Bratislav, *The Tales*, Paulist Press, New York, 1978 (T)

(241) Needleman, J., *Lost Christianity*, New York, Doubleday, 1980 (G)
(242) Needleman, J. ed., *Sword of Gnosis*, Baltimore, Penguin Books, 1974 (G)
(243) Nennius, *British History and the Welsh Annals*, London and Chichester, Phillimore, 1980 (T)
(244) Newman, J.H., *The Arians of the 4th Century*, E.Lumley, 1871 (G)
(245) Nicholas of Cusa, *The Vision of God*, New York, 1960 (T)
(246) Origen, trans. Gasser, M., *An Exhortation to Martyrdom and Other Writings*, London, SPCK 1979 (T)
(247) *Orphic Hymns*, Text, trans., and Notes by A.M. Athanassakis, Missoula, Montana, Scholars Press, 1977 (T)
(248) Otto, W.F., *Dionysius, Myth and Cult*, Bloomington, Indiana University Press, 1965 (G)
(249) Ovid, *Metamorphoses*, trans. M.M.Innes, Harmondsworth, Penguin Books, 1955 (T)
(250) *Oxford Classical Dictionary*, ed. N.G.K. Hammond, and H.H. Scullard, London, Oxford University Press, 1970 (G)
(251) *Oxford Dictionary of the Christian Church* ed. F.L. Cross and E.A. Livingston, London, Oxford University Press, 1957 (G)
(252) *Oxford Dictionary of Nursery Rhymes*, ed. I. and P. Opie, London, Oxford University Press, 1951 (G)
(253) Paracelsus, *The Archidoxes of Magic*, Askin Publishers, 1975 (T)
(254) Paracelsus, *Selected Writings*, ed, J. Jacobi, New Jersey, Princeton University Press, 1951 (T)
(255) Patai, R., *The Hebrew Goddess*, New York, Avon Books, 1978 (G)
(256) Pausanius, *Guide to Greece*, trans. P. Levi., Harmondsworth, Penguin Books, 1971 (T)
(257) Pelikan, J., *Vindication of Tradition*, New Haven and London, Yale University Press, 1984 (G)
(258) *Perlesvaus: The High History of the Holy Grail*, trans. S. Evans, J.M.Dent, 1911 (T
(259) Perry, M., *Psychic Studies*, Wellingborough, Aquarian Press, 1984 (G)
(260) Perry, W.N., *A Treasury of Traditional Wisdom*, Allen & Unwin, 1971 (G)
(261) Philo of Alexandria, *The Contemplative Life*, Paulist Press, 1981 (T)
(262) Pindar, *The Odes*, C.M. Bowra, Harmondsworth, Penguin Books, 1969 (T)
(263) Piske, L., *The Actor and His Body*, Harrap, 1975 (G)
(264) *Pistis Sophia*, ed. G.R.S. Mead, New Jersey, University Books, 1974 (T)

(265) Plato, *The Collected Dialogues* ed., E. Hamilton, New Jersey, Princeton University Press, 1973 (T)

(266) Plato, *The Republic*, trans. D. Lee, Harmondsworth, Penguin Books, 1955 (T)

(267) Plato, *Timaeus and Critias*, trans. D. Lee, Harmondsworth, Penguin Books, 1965 (T)

(268) Plotinus, *The Enneads*, trans. S. Mackenna, Faber, 1956 (T)

(269) Plotinus, *Enneads*, trans. Stanbrook Abbey, Callow End, Worcester, n.d. (T)

(270) Plutarch, *Moralia V*, 'Isis and Osiris' trans. F.C. Babbitt, London, Heinemann, Cambridge, Mass., Harvard University Press, 1957 (T)

(271) Plutarch, *Moralia VI* 'On the Sign of Plato' trans. P.H. De Lacy and B. Einarson, London, Heinemann, Cambridge Mass., Harvard University Press., 1968 (T)

(272) Ponce, C., *The Game of Wizards*, New York, Penguin Books, 1975 (G)

(273) Ponce, C., *Papers Towards a Radical Metaphysics – Alchemy*, Berkeley, California, North Atlantic Books, 1983 (G)

(274) Potok, C., *The Book of Lights*, Heinemann, 1982 (F)

(275) Potok, C., *The Chosen*, Harmondsworth, Penguin Books, 1970 (F)

(276) Powys, J.C. *Morwyn or the Vengeance of God*, Village Press, 1974 (F)

(277) *Quest of the Holy Grail*, trans. P. Metarasso, Harmondsworth, Penguin Books, 1969 (T)

(278) Quinn, E.C., *The Quest of Seth*, University of Chicago, 1962 (G)

(279) Quispel, G., *Secret Book of Revelation*, Collins, 1979 (G)

(280) Raine, K., *Defending Ancient Springs*, Oxford University Press, 1967 (G)

(281) Rakoczi, B.I., *Fortune Telling*, MacDonald, 1970 (G)

(282) Reeves, M., *Joachim of Fiore and the Prophetic Future*, SPCK, 1976, (G)

(283) Regardie, I., *The Complete Golden Dawn System of Magic*, Phoenix, Falcon Press, 1984 (G)

(284) Regardie, I., *Foundation and Practice of Magic*, Wellingborough, Aquarian Press, 1979 (G)

(285) Regardie, I., *The Golden Dawn*, Saint Paul, Llewellyn Publishers, 1971 (G)

(286) Regardie, I., *How to make and use Talismans*. Wellingborough, Aquarian Press, 1981 (G)

(287) *Rider Book of Mystical Verse*, ed. J.M. Cohen, Rider Books, 1983 (G)

(288) Roberts, R., *Tarot Revelation*, Privately Printed, L.C. 80–50329. n.d. (G)

(289) Robertson, S.M., *Rosegarden and Labyrinth*, London, Routledge & Kegan Paul, 1963 (G)

(290) *The Rosary of the Philosophers*, ed. Adam McLean, Edinburgh, Hermetic Sourceworks, 1980 (T)

(291) Rudolph, K., *Gnosis*, Edinburgh, T. and T. Clark Ltd., 1983 (G)

(292) Schaya, L., *Universal Meaning of the Kabbalah*, London, Allen & Unwin, 1971 (G)

(293) Scholem, G.G., *Major Trends in Jewish Mysticism*, New York, Schoken Books, 1961 (G)

(294) Schuon, F., *Esotericism as Principle and as Way*, Bedford, Perennial Books, 1981 (G)

(295) Schure, E., *The Great Initiates*, New York, Mackay, 1913 (G)

(296) Schwaller de Lubicz, R.A.S., *Nature Word*, West Stockbridge, Lindisfarne Press, 1982 (G)

(297) Schwaller de Lubicz, R.A.S., *The Opening of the Way*, New York, Inner Traditions Int., 1981 (G)

(298) Schwaller de Lubicz, R.A.S., *Sacred Science*, New York, Inner Traditions Int., 1982 (G)

(299) Schwaller de Lubicz, R.A.S., *Symbol and the Symbolic*, New York, Inner Traditions Int., 1978 (G)

(300) Schwartz-Bart, A., *The Last of the Just*, Harmondsworth, Penguin, 1984 (N)

(301) Schweighardt, T., *The Mirror of Wisdom*, trans. D. McLean in *Hermetic Journal* no. 25 (T)

(302) Scott, W., *Hermetica* vol. I. Boulder, Hermes House, 1982 (T)

(303) Scruton, R., *From Descartes to Wittgenstein*. London, Routledge & Kegan Paul, 1981 (G)

(304) Serrano, M., *El/Ella: Book of Magical Love*, London, Routledge& Kegan Paul, 1973 (G)

(305) Serrano, M., *Nos: Book of the Resurrection*, London, Routledge & Kegan Paul, 1984 (G)

(306) Serrano, M., *The visits of the Queen of Sheba*, London, Routledge & Kegan Paul, 1960 (G)

(307) Shumaker, W., *The Occult Sciences in the Renaissance*, Berkeley, University of California Press, 1972 (G)

(308) Silverberg, R., *The Realm of Prester John*, New York, Doubleday & Co., 1972 (G)

(309) Sinclair, J.R. *The Alice Bailey Inheritance*, Wellingborough, Turnstone Press, 1984 (G)

(310) Singer, I.P., *The Golem*, London, Deutsch, 1983 (N)

(311) Slade, H., *Contemplative Meditation*, London, Darton Longman & Todd, 1977 (G)

(312) Smith, M., *Jesus the Magician*, London, Gollancz, 1978 (G)

(313) Solomon, J., *The Structure of Matter*, Newton Abbot, David & Charles, 1973 (G)

(314) Sorabji, R., *Time, Creation and the Continuum*, London, Duckworth, 1983 (G)

(315) Southwell, R., *Poetical Works*, London, John Russell Smith, 1856 (P)

(316) Spence, L., *Occult Sciences in Atlantis*, London, Aquarian Press, 1970 (G)

(317) Steiner, R., *Atlantis and Lemuria*, New York, Anthroposophical Publications Co., 1923 (G)

(318) Steiner, R., *The Course of My Life*, New York, Steiner Books, 1977 (G)

(319) Steiner, R., *Evolution and Consciousness*, London, Rudolph Steiner Press, 1979 (G)

(320) Steiner, R., *Occult Science, an Outline*, London, Rudolph Steiner Press, 1979 (G)

(321) Steiner, R., *The Occult Significance of Blood*, London, Rudolph Steiner Press, 1967 (G)

(322) Stewart, R.J., *The Underworld Initiation*, Wellingborough, Aquarian Press, 1985 (G)

(323) Stewart, R.J., *The Waters of the Gap*, Bath, Bath City Council, 1981 (G)

(324) Szekeley, E.B., *The Gospel of the Essenes*, London, C.W. Daniel, 1976 (G)

(325) Taylor, T., *Selected Writings*, ed. K. Raine, Princeton, Princeton University Press, 1969 (T)

(326) Teilhard de Chardin, *Hymn of the Universe*, London, Collins, 1965 (G)

(327) Teilhard de Chardin, *Towards the Future*, London, Collins, 1975 (G)

(328) *Temenos*, ed. K. Raine, 47 Paultons Square, London SW3 5DT. issn 0262 4524, 1981 et seq. (J)

(329) Temple, R., *Conversations With Eternity*, London, Rider, 1984 (G)

(330) Tillyard, E.M.W., *The Elizabethan World Picture*, London, Chatto & Windus, 1943 (G)

(331) Tolstoy, N., *The Quest for Merlin*, London, Hamish Hamilton, 1985 (G)

(332) Trinick, J., *The Fire-Tried Stone*, London, Stuart & Watkins, 1967
       G)

(333) Underhill, E., *Mysticism*, New York, Dutton and Colne, 1961 (G)

(334) Underkircher, F., *Le Livre du Cueur d'Amours Espris*, London,
       Thames & Hudson, 1975 (T)

(335) Unterman, A. *The Jews: Their Religious Beliefs and Practices*,
       London, Routledge & Kegan Paul, 1981 (G)

(336) Urmson, J.O., *Concise Encyclopedia of Western Philosophy and
       Philosophers*, London, Hutchinson, 1960 (G)

(337) Vaughan, H., *The Complete Poems*, ed. Alan Rudrum. Harmonds-
       worth, Penguin, 1976 (P)

(338) Vaughan, T., *The Works of Thomas Vaughan*, New York, Univer-
       sity Books, 1968 (T)

(339) Vermaseren, M.J., *Cybele and Attis*, London, Thames & Hudson,
       1977 (G)

(340) Vermaseren, M.J., *Mithras, the Secret God*, London, Chatto &
       Windus, 1963 (G)

(341) Versluis, A., *The Philosophy of Magic*, London, Routledge & Kegan
       Paul, n.d. (G)

(342) Vidal, G., *Julian*, London, Heinemann 1964, (N)

(343) Virgil, *The Eclogues*, Harmondsworth, Penguin, 1980 (P)

(344) Von Eschenbach, W., *Parzival*, trans. A.T. Hatto, Harmondsworth,
       Penguin, 1980 (T)

(345) Von Franz, M.L., *Alchemical Active Imagination*, Irving, Spring
       Books, 1979 (G)

(346) Von Franz, M.L., *Alchemy*, Toronto, Inner City Books, 1980 (G)

(347) Waddell, H., *Songs of the Wandering Scholars*, London, Folio
       Society, 1982 (P)

(348) Waite, A.E., *The Brotherhood of the Rosy Cross*, New York,
       University Books, 1961 (G)

(349) Waite, A.E., *The New Encyclopedia of Freemasonry*, New York,
       Weathervane Books, 1970 (G)

(350) Walker, B. *Gnosticism*, Wellingborough, Aquarian Press, 1983 (G)

(351) Walker, D.P., *Spiritual and Demonic Magic*, London, University of
       Notre Dame, 1969 (G)

(352) Wang, R., *The Qabalistic Tarot*, Maine, Weiser, 1983 (G)

(353) Warden, J., *Orpheus: the Metamorphosis of a Myth*, Toronto,
       University of Toronto Press, 1982 (G)

(354) Ware, T., *The Orthodox Church*, Harmondsworth, Penguin, 1963
       (G)

(355) Ware, K., *The Orthodox Way*, London and Oxford, Mowbrays,
       1979 (G)

(356) Wasson, R.G., *The Road to Eleusis*, New York, Harcourt Brace Jovanovitch Inc., 1978 (G)

(357) West, M.L., *The Orphic Poems*, Oxford, The Clarendon Press, 1984 (G)

(358) Whone, H., *Church, Monastery, Cathedral*, Tisbury, Compton Russell Element, 1977 (G)

(359) Wilby, B., *New Dimensions Red Book*, Toddington, Helios Books, 1968 (G)

(360) Wilson, P.L., *Angels*, London, Thames & Hudson, 1980 (G)

(361) Watt, R.E., *Isis in the Graeco-Roman World*, London, Thames & Hudson, 1971 (G)

(362) Yates, F., *The Art of Memory*, London, Routledge & Kegan Paul, 1966 (G)

(363) Yates, F., *Giordano Bruno and the Hermetic Tradition*, London, Routledge & Kegan Paul, 1971 (G)

(364) Yates, F., *Occult Philosophy in the Elizabethan Age*, London, Routledge & Kegan Paul, 1979 (G)

(365) Yates, F., *The Rosicrucian Enlightenment*, London, Routledge & Kegan Paul, 1972 (G)

(366) Yeats, W.B., *Autobiography*, New York, Collier-Macmillan, 1974 (G)

(367) Zoroaster, *The Chaldean Oracles*, Wellingborough, Aquarian, 1983 (T)

DISCOGRAPHY

(368) Abelard, P., *Planctus Jephtha*, Studio der Fruhen Musick, Reflexe 1C 063–30–123 (M)

(369) *L'Agonie du Languedoc*, Studio der Fruhen Musick with Claude Marti, Reflexe 1c 063–30–132 (M)

(370) *The Art of the Psaltery*, Les Musiciens de Provence with Maurice Guis, Arion ARN 36613 (M)

(371) Ashcroft-Nowicki, D., *The Halls of Osiris*, Sulis Music, BCM 3721, London WC1N 3XX (I)

(372) Ashcroft-Nowicki, D., *The Journey of the Fool*, Sulis Music, BCM 3721, London WC1N 3XX (I)

(373) Bearns, R and Dexter, R., *The Golden Voyages tapes 1—4*, Awakening Productions Inc.

(374) Chants d'Exil, Boston Camerata, Erato Stu 71429 (M)

(375) Dowland, J., *Songs, Books III*, Consort of Musicke, Oiseau-Lyre I DSLO 508–9, 528–1 & 531–2 (M)

(376) Dunstable, J., *Motets*, Hilliard Ensemble, HMV ASD 1467 031 (M)

(377) Gesualdo, *First Book of Madrigals*, Consort of Musicke, Oiseau-Lyre HO 128–1 (M)

(378) Hildegard of Bingen, Abbess, *A Feather on the Breath of God*, Gothic Voices, Hyperion A66039 (M)

(379) Hovhaness, I., *Fra Angelico* op.220, Unicorn Records UNS 243 (M)

(380) Hovhaness, I., *St Varten Symphony* op.80, Unicorn RHS 317 (M)

(381) Kindler, S and Warner, P.L., *Lemurian Sunrise*, Waterfall Music 105 (M)

(382) Knight, G., *The Calling of King Arthur*, 8 Acorn Avenue, Braintree, Essex (I)

(383) Knight, G., *Contacting the Western Masters*, 8 Acorn Avenue, Braintree, Essex (I)

(384) Knight, G., *Dion Fortune's Magical Battle of Britain*, 8 Acorn Avenue, Braintree, Essex (I)

(385) Knight, G., *Dion Fortune's War Letters*, (2 tapes), 8 Acorn Avenue, Braintree, Essex (I)

(386) Knight, G., *The Phaidon Scripts*, (2 tapes), 8 Acorn Avenue, Braintree, Essex (I)

(387) Knight, G., *Visions of Lost Atlantis*, 8 Acorn Avenue, Braintree, Essex (I)

(388) Lassus, O., *Lagrimi di San Pietro*, Consort of Musicke, Oiseau-Lyre DSDL 706 (M)

(389) Lawes, W., *Dialogues, Psalms and Elegies*, Consort of Musicke, Oiseau-Lyre DSLO 574 (M)

(390) Matthews, C. and J., *Walking the Western Way*, Sulis Music, BCM 3721, London WCIN 3XX (I)

(391) Mozart, W.A., *The Magic Flute*. (Zauberfloëte) Berlin Philharmonic (Boehme) DG 138 981–3

(392) *Music from the Time of the Popes at Avignon*, Jean-Claude Malgoire and the Florigeum Musicium de Paris, CBS 76534 (M)

(393) *Music in Christian and Jewish Spain*, Hesperion XX, Reflexe lC 163–30–125/26 (M)

(394) *Music of Ancient Greece*, Atrium Musical de Madrid HM 1015 (M)

(395) Orff, G., *Trionfi*, BASF 59–21346–3 (M)

(396) Pinter, J., *Secrets from the Stone*, Sona Gaia Productions C123 (M)

(397) Scriabin, A., *Symphonies 1–3*, Melodiya 80030 XHK (M)

(398) Upper Astral, *Crystal Cave: Back to Atlantis*, New World Cassettes AM109 (M)

(399)   Vaughan-Williams, R., *Job: a Masque for Dancing*, HMV 2673 (M)
(400)   Vaughan-Williams, R., *The Sons of Light*, Lyrita SRCS 125 (M)

Index

PENGUIN

ARKANA

NEW AGE BOOKS FOR MIND, BODY & SPIRIT

With over 200 titles currently in print, Arkana is the leading name in quality books for mind, body and spirit. Arkana encompasses the spirituality of both East and West, ancient and new. A vast range of interests is covered, including Psychology and Transformation, Health, Science and Mysticism, Women's Spirituality, Zen, Western Traditions and Astrology.

If you would like a catalogue of Arkana books, please write to:

Sales Dept. – Arkana
Penguin Books USA Inc.
375 Hudson Street
New York, NY 10014

Arkana Marketing Department
Penguin Books Ltd
27 Wrights Lane
London W8 5TZ

PENGUIN

ARKANA

NEW AGE BOOKS FOR MIND, BODY & SPIRIT

By Caitlín Matthews

Mabon and the Mysteries of Britain
An Exploration of the *Mabinogion*

The *Mabinogion* exemplifies the great folk traditions and mystery lore of Britain: the archetypes and mythological themes of the proto-Celtic oral tradition. Yet the stories – part fiction, part mythology, part folk legend and part history – are often impenetrable to the general reader. In *Mabon and the Mysteries of Britain*, Caitlín Matthews provides a literary guide to the patterns of this great text. Further explorations guide the reader to the Western Mysteries as they emerge from the tales of Culhwch, Olwen, Taliesin and the Four Branches. And here two major figures of the native tradition are revealed – Mabon, the Wondrous Youth, and Modron, his mother, the Great Goddess herself.

Arthur and the Sovereignty of Britain
King and Goddess in the *Mabinogion*

The stories of the *Mabinogion*, rich in legend and the primitive magic of the Celtic Otherworld, heralded the first flowering of European literature and became the source of Arthurian legend as we know it today. Caitlín Matthews here provides full commentary on these stories, exploring parallel texts and sources and shedding light on Sovereignty, the Goddess of the Land and the spiritual principle of the Feminine.